Woman in Red

Woman in Red

By

Eileen Goudge

Hardcover edition first published in 2007 by Vanguard Press, A Member of the Perseus Books Group
Paperback edition first published in 2008 by Vanguard Press

Vanguard books are available at special discounts for bulk purchases in the United States by corporations, institutions, and other organizations. For more information, please contact the Special Markets Department at the Perseus Books Group, 2300 Chestnut Street, Philadelphia, PA 19103, call (800) 810-4145, ext. 5000, or e-mail special.markets@perseusbooks.com.

The Library of Congress has catalogued the hardcover as follows:
Goudge, Eileen.
Woman in red / by Eileen Goudge.
p. cm.
ISBN-13: 978-1-59315-441-8 (hardcover : alk. paper)
ISBN-10: 1-59315-444-5 (hardcover : alk. paper)
I. Title.

PS3557.O838W66 2007
813'.54—dc22
2007003747
PB ISBN: 978-1-59315-500-1

10 9 8 7 6 5 4 3 2 1

To Sandy.
All my love always.

All are but parts of one stupendous whole,

Whose body nature is, and God the soul.

From "An Essay on Man," by Alexander Pope

ACKNOWLEDGMENTS

First and foremost, I would like to thank my publisher, Roger Cooper, at Vanguard Press, for having the vision, not just in striking out into new territory, but in asking me along for the ride. I am forever indebted to you, Roger, for helping me realize my own dream and in encouraging me along the way with your unflagging energy and enthusiasm.

I would also like to thank, as always, my friend and agent, Susan Ginsburg, without whom no book would be possible. Susan, you are the glue that holds it all together.

This book wouldn't have been as authentic without the people who assisted me in researching it. Thanks to Robin Schwartz, for her invaluable help in the legal department. And to Char Bawden, of Judd Cove Oysters, who in addition to giving me the ins and outs of oyster farming took the time to hand deliver three dozen of the most succulent oysters I've ever tasted. Thanks also to Holly King, of the public library on Orcas Island, for picking up the slack, thus allowing me unfettered time to devote to my writing. And, last but not least, a special thanks to Bill and Valerie Anders, for giving me my own moon shot.

PROLOGUE

Nine years ago

"All rise!"

A rustle of movement around her, the scrape of chairs and feet. Alice was slower to react, her senses dulled, as if by blunt instrument, by two days of testimony: dry, reasoned discourses on skid patterns, blood-alcohol levels, and degree of vehicular damage in relation to bodily injury, all of which seemed to have as much to do with her son, with David, as a chalk outline on pavement with the living, breathing person brought to such a cruel end.

With her palms flat against its surface as leverage, she pushed herself up from the table at which she sat. Her lawyer, Warren Brockman, shot her a look, his gray eyes kind and concerned, and she nodded almost imperceptibly to let him know she was okay. In fact, she was anything but. The blood was draining from her head, and she felt unsteady, a faint, persistent buzzing in her ears, the muscles in her legs quivering like after a mile run.

Lies! she had screamed silently as her son's killer sat up there on the stand, visibly remorseful, as only an innocent man would be—or one who was going out of his way to appear so—giving his distorted version of events. She'd listened and she'd screamed in her head, biting down on the inside of her cheek until it bled to keep her mouth from flying open, her outrage from spewing out into the courtroom.

Now the jury was back with a verdict.

She glanced to her right. Owen White's attorney, a boxy, graceless woman in an unflattering chartreuse dress, stood beside her client, a hand resting lightly against the small of his back. Her strategy had been to paint *him* as the victim, an innocent man relentlessly hounded by a mother unhinged by grief. He even looked the part: soft and harmless, with his pale, forgettable face and blameless blue eyes, his thinning hair the same flesh tone as his skin, and off-the-rack suit that belied his wealth. He might have been any of the nameless, faceless, middle-aged men you came into contact with out in the world, in banks and insurance offices and rental agencies, the ones who smiled at you and chatted easily as they pushed a form across their desk for you to sign.

On the witness stand, he'd answered her lawyer's questions in a quiet, respectful tone. She'd detected no gleam of sweat on his brow, and his eyes behind the wire-rim glasses he wore had been clear as a baby's conscience, only turning sorrowful as they'd come to rest briefly on Alice from time to time, as if he weren't unsympathetic to her plight.

But she knew the real story. Which was why she'd spent the past eighteen months and nearly all of her and Randy's savings trying to bring the man responsible for their son's death to justice.

If only Randy were here now! Her husband had scarcely left her side through the dark tunnel of days following David's death. But once the criminal investigation had been put to rest, he'd grown increasingly impatient with her as the months had dragged on and her pursuit of justice showed no sign of flagging. When she'd insisted on filing a wrongful death suit, he'd gone along merely to appease her and had attended the subsequent court proceedings only sporadically, using the excuse of not being able to miss any more days of work.

In a way she didn't blame him. All he had wanted was to mourn their son in peace. Randy wasn't even convinced they had a case. Wasn't it possible she'd been mistaken? he'd asked, challenging her. The light would have been fading at that time of day and David was all the way down the block, a distance of at least a hundred yards. A little boy they both knew had been prone to taking risks, he could easily have darted out into the road on his bike, just the way Owen had told it.

But she knew she wasn't mistaken. And now, suddenly, she found herself despising Randy almost as much as she did the man responsible for all this. Why wasn't he as outraged as she? What kind of a father would allow his son's murderer to walk free? Randy's glaring absence might even have swayed some of the jurors in Owen's favor. How must it look to them? A crazy lady who couldn't convince her own husband.

Do I look crazy? Alice wondered. *No*, she thought, taking a mental inventory of herself. She'd chosen her dark gray suit with the navy piping and a pair of low-heeled navy pumps for today's court appearance. Her brown hair was pulled back, fastened at the neck with a tortoise-shell barrette, her only jewelry a simple pearl necklace and the tiny diamond studs in her ears.

Throughout the proceedings she'd been a model of restraint as well, someone of whom her parents could be proud. She hadn't indulged in any outbursts, and except for the one time she'd wept silently into her hands at the coroner's description of David's injuries, she hadn't given in to tears. It was as if she'd been training all her life for this; it was what she did, what she was good at. Even at the funeral, she had felt it was her job to provide solace to others. Grieving was something you did in private, with a minimum of fuss.

She looked over her shoulder at her parents. Her mother wore a bright, expectant look as she gazed up at the bench, as if confident that the judge, a large, fleshy-faced man now settling into his seat, would make sure the jury did the right thing. Lucy Gordon believed that anything could be overcome with the right attitude. Like when Alice had been little and prone to car sickness; her mother, convinced it was a case of mind over matter, would press her to join in on sing-alongs and play games like I Spy on long trips to distract her until the nausea passed. (Though, if Alice had managed to keep from throwing up those times, it had had less to do with positive thinking than with a deep-seated terror of making a mess.) Now, with her perpetual schoolgirl's face, framed by a ruffle of graying auburn hair, tipped up in a firm, fixed smile, Lucy was once again refusing to let pessimism get the upper hand.

In contrast, Alice's father stood rigidly at Lucy's side, his austere face frozen in a kind of grimace. Was he angry at her, for putting the family through so much grief? Alice wondered. It was hard to know with her dad. He was a man of few words, an architect whose language was that of line and space. The only time she'd ever seen him cry was as his grandson's coffin was being lowered into the ground, and even then she wouldn't have known if she hadn't seen the tears leaking from under the dark glasses he'd worn.

Denise, six months pregnant with her second child, stood beside them, a hand resting on the dark head of Alice's younger son, Jeremy. There were those who might have questioned Alice's judgment in having her seven-year-old here for the reading of the verdict, she knew, but Alice had felt it was important for Jeremy to be a part of this moment, one that, either way, would define the rest of their lives.

She turned around, focusing now on the ornately framed painting on the wall to the left of the bench to keep her stomach from going into free fall, as the judge banged his gavel and court was called back into session. Ironically, it was a portrait of Owen's father, Lowell White, who'd donated the land upon which the courthouse sat—a bit of history she hoped hadn't factored into the jurors' decision. A handsome, florid-faced man, with thick black brows and dark, wavy hair gone gray at the temples, he bore little resemblance to his son. His eyes seemed to meet hers, dancing with bemusement as if he knew something Alice didn't, and she was reminded of the unsolved mystery surrounding his disappearance when Owen was a small boy, a mystery, passed from one generation to the next, which had become a part of Grays Island lore.

"Has the jury reached a verdict?" asked the judge.

The foreman, a big man with military-issue hair and a once-muscular physique now going to seed, rose to his feet. "We have, Your Honor." Like most of the jury, his was a familiar face to Alice, a manager at the bank where she and Randy had an account, someone she might have smiled at pleasantly in passing and never given a second thought to before this.

The judge instructed the bailiff to bring him the verdict. The foreman handed the folded piece of paper on which it was written to the short, heavy-set man in uniform, who carried it over to the judge. The judge glanced at it, his expression unchanging, before reading it aloud. "We, the jury, find in favor of the respondent."

The words fell like a blow to some soft, unprotected part of Alice's body. She felt all the breath go out of her. Black specks swarmed at the periphery of her vision, and for a frightening moment she thought she was going to pass out. Yet she showed no emotion; her face was as smooth as a pane of glass. Her mind, too, was glass, the full impact of those words sliding away like so many raindrops off a windowpane. She thought, *If I stay very, very still, it will be as if none of this ever happened.*

Warren put his arm around her shoulders and said in a low voice, "I'm so sorry, Alice. We did our best." But she was unable to respond. It was like when she'd given birth, a great, heaving pressure beneath the numbness from the epidural.

Then her sister Denise was at her side, a large, moist presence, looking like a very pregnant Holly Hobbie in her smocked maternity dress. Her brown eyes, pooled with tears, seemed to fill up her whole face, a face as incapable of concealing emotion as a child's. Denise only shook her head, wise enough to know that there was nothing she could say or do right now that would help the situation.

It was their mother who rushed in to embrace Alice, while their father hung back, still wearing that stern look, though Alice could see now that his anger wasn't directed at her—he was staring hard at Owen's back as if he'd like to plant a dagger in it. "Oh, honey." Lucy's voice was choked with emotion. "Don't take it too hard. Look at the bright side. Now you and Randy can get on with your lives."

As if such a thing were possible.

It wasn't until Alice's gaze fell on Jeremy, standing next to his grandfather, looking up at her with a pinched, worried expression, that she roused herself and spoke.

"I'm fine," she said in a calm voice that seemed to be coming from outside her, that of a doctor assuring them that the patient was recovering nicely. "I just need to get home."

"Let me drive you," said Denise.

"No, really, I'm fine," she assured her. In Denise's present, distraught state, she appeared more at risk than Alice of getting into an accident.

For a moment Denise looked as if she were about to insist, but she let it go. Younger by four years, she'd always been the one Alice looked out for, from the time they were children. When the other kids in school had made fun of Denise for being fat, Alice had made sure the bullies knew who they were dealing with. And with her sister's first baby, it had been Alice, not Denise's husband, in bed with a herniated disc at the time, who'd seen her through a difficult labor. Now that the roles were reversed, they were both somewhat at a loss as to how to handle it.

Alice managed a small, bitterly resigned smile, as if to say that yes, it was a blow, but not entirely unexpected. And in a way, she wasn't surprised. Owen White was a respected member of the community, the heir to one of the island's great fortunes, and she . . . well, she'd become the resident crazy lady. Even those of her neighbors who'd gone out of their way to show support in the days after David's death now looked at her askance. Yes, it was tragic, their eyes seemed to say, but she'd gone too far. Was it fair to punish a man whose only crime was that he'd been in the wrong place at the wrong time?

Walking to her car, holding tightly to Jeremy's hand, she thought that if there truly were a hell, she was in it now. The events of that terrible day ran like a film on a continuous loop inside her head, one she always hoped would have a different ending but never did.

It had been early evening and Randy had phoned to say he'd be working late, that they shouldn't wait for him. But when she'd gone outside to call David in to supper, he wasn't in the driveway shooting hoops, where he'd been the last time she'd checked, and there was no sign of him anywhere. Darkness had been closing in, the sidewalk in front of their house swallowed up by the shadows of the gingko trees that lined their street. Yet she hadn't felt worried, not then. She remembered being annoyed at him instead. At eight and a half, David was far too independent for his own good. While Jeremy was content to play in his room for hours, David had been on the move ever since he'd learned to walk; it seemed she spent as much time looking for him as looking after him.

She'd walked out onto the sidewalk still calling his name. She was halfway down the block before she spotted him, a small, fair-haired boy in a white T-shirt and jeans pedaling furiously toward her on his bike. He'd lifted a hand to wave to her, and almost at the same instant a car had rounded the corner onto their street, a silver Mercedes moving at a speed well beyond the posted limit. Alice had opened her mouth to shout to the driver to slow down, but the words caught in her throat, swallowed by the shriek of brakes and the sickening thud that followed, one that had slammed through her as if she herself had experienced the impact.

David, she'd thought, breaking into a run.

She'd found him sprawled facedown on the pavement, not moving. His bicycle, an old Raleigh that had belonged to Randy and that David loved above all things, had been flung into the middle of the road by the impact, twisted into something resembling bent coat hangers. Later, Owen would claim the boy had darted out into the middle of the road and that he'd been unable to brake in time. But that wasn't what Alice had witnessed. David had been in the bike lane that she herself, along with those of her neighbors with young children, had campaigned for; she'd had a clear view of him from where she'd stood.

But it had been her word against Owen's; by the time the neighbors had stepped outside to see what the commotion was about, it was all over. When Alice reported that the driver had been drunk, no one believed that, either. Owen White had a reputation as a churchgoing man, nothing like his flamboyant father, who'd been known to tip back a few in his day. Yet Alice had smelled alcohol on him even from where she'd knelt, clutching her son's broken body to her chest. She'd screamed at Owen to get help, but he'd just stood there wearing a stupefied look, as if not quite grasping what any of this had to do with him, before he'd finally stumbled to his car and driven off.

It was several hours before the police finally caught up to him, by which time Owen had sobered up and gotten his story straight. If his behavior had seemed erratic at the time, he'd explained, it was only because he'd been in shock. As to why he'd left the scene of the accident, it was only to find a phone to call for help. After a cursory investigation that was more a formality than anything, the official cause of death was ruled accidental. Another tragic case of a little boy riding his bike where he shouldn't.

"Mommy, why aren't we going?"

Alice roused from her thoughts to find herself sitting behind the wheel of her car, Jeremy buckled in beside her. He was solemn-faced little boy with her dark hair and fair complexion, dressed in the suit she'd bought him for his brother's funeral, which he was already outgrowing. He was eyeing her quizzically, wearing the deeply worried look she'd seen too often of late. Jeremy had always been the more thoughtful and sensitive of her two boys, but since David's death he'd been so withdrawn that at times it was almost as if she'd lost both her sons.

She forced a smile. "We are, honey. I just needed a minute is all."

"Are we going home?" he asked, when she'd started the engine.

"Yes, honey. Straight home." Where else would she go? To the grocery store for a quart of milk? To pick up her mail at the post office? Mundane chores she couldn't imagine ever doing again much less tackling now.

"Will Daddy be there?" There was a querulous note in his voice that sounded almost panicky.

Alice realized now that it had been a mistake bringing him with her today. But she'd wanted so much to believe the jury would see things her way, she hadn't been thinking straight. Now she was a bad mother on top of everything else. The thought pierced her like a shot through the heart.

She did her best to maintain an even tone as she replied, "Daddy's at work, you know that. But we'll call him as soon as we get home." Even as she spoke, anger was rising up in her again. Where had Randy been when she needed him most? Where was he *now*?

Alice backed out of her slot and was heading toward the exit when she saw Owen at the other end of the lot. She slowed at once, braking to a stop. He was walking with his wife, who had accompanied him every day to court. Elizabeth White, a tall, rail-thin woman, reminded Alice of a greyhound, with her narrow face and long, arched neck, her wide-set protruding eyes. They looked relaxed, smiling at their victory as they strolled along, arm in arm. They would go home to a celebratory supper and a good night's rest, while Alice was left to pick up the pieces on her own. She watched Mrs. White step around to the passenger side when they reached their car, the same silver Mercedes that had mowed David down, while Owen paused to reach into his pocket for his keys.

Later, Alice would remember almost nothing of what came next. In that moment, though, every detail was magnified: a puddle of grease gleaming dully on the pavement near where Owen stood; the reflection of trees swimming across the windshield of a Chevy Malibu pulling out behind him; the innocent sounds of children playing in the small park adjacent the courthouse. The last signposts of the known world before it tilted on its axis, sending her spinning off into space.

Alice had no awareness of her foot pressing down on the gas pedal; it was as if the car were being propelled by a force beyond her control. Then there was only the startled face of her son's killer as she closed in on him, and Jeremy's high-pitched scream.

CHAPTER ONE

Present day

The dog was waiting on the landing when the ferry pulled into the berth. Black, with white paws and a white blaze on its chest, it made Colin think of an English butler in bib and morning coat, standing in readiness to greet guests arriving at the lord's manor for a weekend of grouse hunting. A border collie, from the looks of it, a breed more common to sheep farms than the wilds of the Pacific Northwest. Yet it looked perfectly at home, sitting there on its haunches in the late afternoon sunlight that slanted over the sun-bleached asphalt.

"Old McGinty's dog," volunteered the man at Colin's elbow.

Colin turned toward him. The man was no youngster himself, with his rheumy eyes and thin white hair luffing in the stiff breeze. "McGinty, the artist?" he inquired.

The man gave a somber nod. "Sad about his passing. It was all over the news. Around here, though, we knew him just as Old McGinty. Him and his dog, you never saw one without t'other." He shook his head, eyeing the collie. "Poor thing. Ever' day, rain or shine, he's here to meet the four-forty from Anacortes." Colin must have looked puzzled, for he explained, "The old man went to the mainland once a month or so, and he always took the same ferry back. Except this last time. When he didn't show, that's how we knew something must've happened to him. Weren't nothing would've kept him from that dog, not as long as he had breath in him."

Poor Dickie, Colin almost muttered aloud before realizing that it couldn't be the same dog he recalled from childhood. Besides, it would have sparked his fellow passenger's interest, and Colin recognized a town crier when he saw one. He wasn't ready for the whole island to know his business just yet. If people remembered him at all it would be as the boy who used to visit his grandfather every summer. They wouldn't recognize the tall, solemn-faced man, his dark hair prematurely flecked with gray, as that eager, fleet-footed boy all grown up, except perhaps for the faint resemblance he bore to his grandfather—around the eyes and mouth mostly, which carried the same sadness as had the man they'd known as Old McGinty. "So who's looking after him now?"

"Neighbor up the road took him in." The old man wore a prideful look, as if to say, *Around here we look after our own.* "But feedin' an animal and ownin' it ain't the same thing. That there's a one-man dog." He pointed a bent twig of a finger at the border collie now rising from its haunches, ears pricked and nose held high in anticipation of his master's arrival.

The man said good-bye and joined the flow of passengers making their way toward the exit ramp, but Colin, lost in thought, gave no reply other than to nod. He remained where he was on the upper deck, in no particular hurry to disembark, as the flow slowed to a trickle of stragglers. The chill of autumn was in the air, but it was memories of summers past that crowded his mind as he leaned into the railing, squinting toward shore, the sharp wind off the sound prying at the upturned collar of his jacket.

It had been more than a decade since his last visit, but not much appeared to have changed. Bell Harbor was just as he remembered it, with its picture-postcard marina and quaint, century-old buildings lining the waterfront—shops and eateries, like the Rusty Anchor, with its namesake anchor out front, where his grandfather would take him for fish and chips on Sundays; and the souvenir shop filled with items to fascinate a young boy. Higher up, on the hill, the commercial buildings gave way to houses and farms, then to unbroken tracts of evergreens as the island climbed toward its highest point, Mount Independence. Already, in mid-October, there was a sugar-dusting of snow on its peak. He was reminded of the time his grandfather had driven him up to the summit in his old Willys, the one year Colin had visited at Christmastime, how wondrous those virgin white tracts had seemed to a city boy used to snow plows and dirty slush clumped along the sidewalk.

"I used to take your dad up here," William had remarked. "He ever tell you about it?"

"He doesn't talk about those days too much." Colin had felt keenly the awkwardness of the moment. He'd been fourteen at the time, his voice reedy with all the changes in his body, which had sprouted a foot seemingly overnight.

"I don't suppose he would." William had squinted off into the distance, wearing a look of sad resignation. There had been only the creak of snow settling under their boots and the whiffling of wings as a cardinal swooped from the branches of a nearby hemlock.

His grandfather was often given to such silences; they'd been as much a part of him as his shock of white hair and the old leg injury that had caused him to limp. And yet they were seldom uncomfortable, even when Colin sensed an underlying sorrow; it was like the sound of the wind in the trees on the cold mountaintop, lonely and peaceful at the same time.

The years melted away, Colin's memories of those boyhood summers sharper than of recent events. He pictured his grandfather bent over his easel, Dickie curled asleep at his feet, and saw the boy he'd been racing down to the cove with his binoculars at the sighting of a whale. Another boy might have been homesick or lonely for the company of other kids his age, but for Colin, those summers had been a welcome respite. He'd experienced a kind of freedom he hadn't known before or since. If his grandfather had spent long hours holed up in his studio, leaving Colin to his own devices, it was just what a young boy sprung from the confines of a row house in Queens, where the great outdoors had consisted of a scrubby patch of grass out back, had needed. Grays Island, with all its nooks and crannies to explore, had been like a magic carpet at his feet, and those endless days of summer had rarely seen him indoors.

But that was Before. Before the world, quite literally in his case, had come tumbling down around his ears.

Colin's mind closed like a fist around the thought, the chill in the air seeping into his bones. The hope that he could escape the more recent past by coming here seemed foolish all of a sudden. It would never be any further away than the nearest bottle in which to drown his sorrows.

A final call from the loudspeaker roused him from his reverie, and he made his way back inside and down the stairs. He was among the last to disembark, and as he exited onto the walkway that ran parallel to the loading ramp, where a caravan of vehicles was crawling its way toward the street, his gaze was drawn to the woman just ahead of him. Slim, dark-haired, around his age—late thirties—and wearing an expression of such intense preoccupation as she trudged along pulling her wheeled suitcase, she seemed scarcely aware of her surroundings. She looked vaguely familiar, but he couldn't place her. Someone he'd met on the island? Or maybe it was just that she reminded him of someone he knew. These days, every woman who bore even the slightest resemblance to Nadine brought a tug of painful recognition, of yearning.

The thought that earlier had attempted to surface—the part of his past he'd just as soon forget—thrust its way into his consciousness with such startling suddenness he had to pause to catch his breath, reeling with more than the swaying motion of the ramp. He was gripped by a deep terror. What if he were to discover that he'd traveled all this way only to find he couldn't escape his demons?

When he finally caught up to her, the woman appeared to be bracing herself against some unseen force as well. She stood poised on the landing, scanning the passenger waiting area, wearing the anxious, hyperalert look of someone not quite sure of her bearings. Her full-length wool coat that might have been purchased at Goodwill and cheap imitation leather suitcase were at odds with her refined, if somewhat worn, appearance. To the eye of an attorney practiced at spotting such telling details, it suggested someone of privilege who'd fallen on hard times.

He paused beside her, inquiring pleasantly, "First visit?" Normally, Colin wasn't in the habit of making conversation with strangers, but something about her drew him to her. Even with her light brown hair pulled back in a ponytail, and no makeup other than a touch of lipstick, he could see that she'd once been beautiful. She still was in a stark kind of way, as if whittled down by hard circumstances, like a granite peak by the elements. Her wide-set eyes, an indeterminate shade that shifted from gray to green, held the shadow of some deep sadness, and her delicate features didn't match the look of determination on her face—not that of some grand ambition, but of a woman reaching into herself for the simple courage to take the next step.

She cast him a startled, almost frightened, glance, then her expression smoothed over. "No. It's just that it's been a while. I can't get over how little it's changed," she replied, gesturing around her. Her tone seemed that of someone whose own life had altered so drastically, it hardly seemed possible that time had more or less stood still here on the island.

That was something he understood all too well. Hers could have been any one of the faces he'd looked upon in countless AA meetings, those for whom despair had become a way of life and the effort it took to simply go through the motions was almost more than they could manage. Yet they kept going somehow, just as he had, one day, one step, at a time.

"I used to come here as a kid," he remarked. "It's been a while for me, too."

She glanced up at the sky, where a thick, gray cloud cover had moved in, bringing the threat of rain. "Not exactly tourist season."

As if on cue, a sudden chill blast of wind sent a loosely tied tarpaulin nearby rattling. She pulled up her collar, holding it tightly about her neck as she hunched inside her coat, shivering. "Actually, I'm here on business," he informed her. "Family business."

"That makes two of us." Her lips curled in a smile that didn't reach her eyes. She obviously hadn't had much practice at it lately.

"Colin McGinty." He put out his hand.

She hesitated before taking it. "Alice," she said, not giving her last name. Her hand, narrow and long-fingered, might have seemed elegant, that of a pianist or a ballerina, if not roughened in a way that told of hard manual labor.

"Someone coming to meet you?" If she had family on the island, it was more than likely, he thought.

"No," she said simply, not offering an explanation.

"I'd offer you a ride, but mine doesn't look to be here yet," said Colin, scanning the cars along the curb for the white Chevy Suburban Clark Findlay, his grandfather's lawyer, had told him to look out for.

"Thanks anyway, but I don't have far to go." After a moment, in which she appeared to have forgotten he was there, she straightened her shoulders and tipped her suitcase onto its wheels. "Well, I guess I should be off. It was nice meeting you. Enjoy your stay."

As he watched her walk away, he continued to wonder about her. Had she taken a wrong turn somewhere? Hooked up with the wrong guy? Or merely gotten hooked, like him? Before Colin could ponder it further, she'd turned the corner and was out of sight.

He hoisted his backpack onto his shoulder. That was when he noticed the border collie he'd spotted earlier. It was standing half a dozen feet away, its intelligent brown eyes fixed on him with a mixture of curiosity and wariness. Colin sank into a crouch and extended a hand. "Here, boy. It's okay. I won't bite."

The collie—a male, he saw—edged closer. Despite looking well-cared-for, he was skittish in the way of pets left to fend for themselves. It was a good minute or so before he'd crept close enough to take a tentative sniff. "Good dog," Colin murmured encouragingly. "See? Nothing to be afraid of." He patted Dickie's head—for he couldn't stop thinking of him as Dickie—which was black except for the softly folded tips of his ears and the patches of white around his eyes and on either side of his nose. The dog allowed it, but it was clear he was only tolerating it out of politeness. Either that, or he thought Colin might know something about his master's whereabouts. When it became clear that Colin wasn't going to be of much help in that department, he retreated, sinking onto his haunches to regard Colin with a look almost of reproach.

Colin drew himself up. "I'd take you with me, but I'm guessing you know the way." The dog cocked his head, eyes fixed on Colin as if in comprehension. How much longer would he go on waiting for his dead master? The thought wrenched at Colin. But was it any better knowing there was no hope? When he dreamed of Nadine, with her smile as wide as the world in which she'd lived—a world in which everyone had a good side and every bad thing its shades of gray—he would invariably awake with a fresh sense of loss, knowing that was all he would ever have of her from now on: memories.

When several more minutes had passed with no sign of Findlay's SUV, Colin fished from his pocket the scrap of paper with the lawyer's number on it. But he was unable to get a signal on his cell phone, and when he went off in search of a pay phone, there were none to be found. On Grays Island, the lack of modern conveniences seemed a conspiracy of sorts, a gentle reminder to slow down, not be in such a rush. Here, people moved at their own pace, not by your timetable, and if you couldn't reach someone by phone you'd run into him or her eventually.

His grandfather's lawyer proved no exception. Moments later a mud-spattered Suburban that might once have been white pulled up to the curb. The driver, a very un-lawyerly looking man in a fisherman's hat, stuck his head out the window. "You must be Colin," he said, with a grin. "Hop in."

Colin climbed into the passenger seat. "Thanks for coming to meet me." He stuck out his hand, which was seized in a firm, dry grip. Clark Findlay looked to be in his late forties, early fifties, gangly as a late-summer plant that's bolted, and freckled all over.

"No problem. Sorry I'm late." The lawyer spoke casually, as if it were the norm. "I got tied up at the office. Missus Brunelli. Her husband, Frank, passed on a few months back. She's lonely and likes to talk. I didn't have the heart to cut her off. How was your trip?"

"Long," Colin replied, with a weary smile. The flight from JFK had been delayed, and he'd had to stay the night in Seattle, followed by the four-hour ferry ride.

"That all you brought?" Findlay jerked a thumb at the backpack Colin was tossing into the backseat.

"I travel light," he said.

"Smart man. Anyway, you won't need much. Couple changes of clothing, warm jacket, boots, that's about it." As if Colin needed to be reminded of the island's dress code, or lack thereof. "'Course, it depends on how long you plan on sticking around." Findlay darted a curious look in his direction as he edged his way back into traffic.

Colin offered no response. He didn't know any more than Findlay what his plans were.

They turned off Harbor and began the climb up Crestview. At the summit stood the Queen Anne–style mansion that had once been the home of shipping magnate Henry White, since converted into a bed-and-breakfast. However many times it had exchanged hands throughout the years, it would always be known to the townsfolk as the White House, a place as firmly fixed in the local firmament as the lore surrounding its original owners, Henry's son, Lowell, in particular. Now, seeing its windows lit up and its gingerbread strung with fairy lights, casting a welcoming light in the gathering dusk, Colin wondered briefly if he wouldn't have been better off getting a room there rather than facing the cold, shuttered cottage where his grandfather's presence would be so keenly felt.

Findlay turned left at the top of the hill, headed in the direction of Ship's Bay. "I had Edna give the place a thorough cleaning. It's in pretty decent shape, all things considered. There was some damage with the last storm—some off the roof, a couple of trees down—but Orin took care of that." Orin Rayburn and his wife, Edna, Colin recalled, had worked for his grandfather. "That reminds me, he wants to know if you plan on keeping him on once everything's settled." Findlay was referring to the fact that the probate period was almost up. "You didn't say whether or not you were planning to sell."

"I haven't decided yet," Colin replied.

"For whatever it's worth, property values have gone way up in the past few years. Fifteen acres of prime waterfront could set up a man for life," the lawyer went on.

Or save his life, Colin voiced silently.

The idea that had been growing in his mind ever since he'd learned of his inheritance. The bulk of the estate had gone to his father, never mind that Daniel hadn't even attended the funeral. (Nor had Colin, for that matter, but that was a whole other story.) The house and land on which it stood had been left to Colin, with a small bequest for his brother, Patrick. Colin was free to dispose of it however he wished, but he suspected the reason the old man had left it to him was because he, of all the family, would benefit from it the most—in ways that had little to do with financial gain.

Colin might have fallen out of touch these past few years, not just with William but with the world, so lost in the corridors of his despair he'd been a stranger to himself, but it seemed his grandfather had known what he needed. Just as years ago William had understood when Colin, his life consumed at the time by college and girls and the self-centered concerns of young men, had stopped visiting on a regular basis. Not once had William made him feel guilty. Instead, he'd encouraged Colin to go out in the world, to find himself. When Colin had graduated from Haverford, William's gift to him had been a roundtrip ticket to Greece. The note attached had read: *You're only young once. Enjoy it while you can.* Almost as if he'd had a sixth sense of what was to come.

"I wasn't thinking about the money," Colin replied now. Though in all honesty he could use it. He hadn't held a steady job in more than five years. The former rising star of the Manhattan D.A.'s office, frontrunner for the top spot when his boss retired, had exactly three hundred dollars to his name at the moment. *Make that two hundred and fifty*, he amended, subtracting the amount he'd withdrawn from his checking account to pay for the ferry ride and last night's hotel.

Anyway, there was no point in discussing his future when it was all he could do right now to put one foot in front of the other. He gazed out the window at the twilit landscape skimming past. Houses and barns and pastures had given way to the deep, fathomless green of firs and hemlocks, amid which pale-skinned alders glowed ghostlike and the occasional flash of a white tail signaled a deer. Then they rounded a bend, coming suddenly upon the stretch of pebbled shoreline that curved around the bay, where the last fiery rays of the setting sun had broken through the clouds to cast a shimmering path over the water. If this were a movie, Colin thought, he might have dismissed it as cheap theatrics, but now it brought tears to his eyes. He'd forgotten how beautiful it was.

Within minutes they were turning onto a dirt road that led up a steep, wooded incline before dipping down into a clearing, in the middle of which stood his grandfather's house, facing out on the cove below. Colin climbed out of the SUV when it came to a stop and for a long moment just stood there, taking it all in. The shingled Craftsman cottage, with its square porch columns festooned in vines, and quarter-sawn oak door set with a beveled pane, was almost exactly as he remembered, if slightly more weathered. Out back was the artist's studio where his grandfather had spent so many hours at his easel, and the raised beds, fenced in to keep out the deer, where a kitchen garden had once flourished. His grandfather, when he wasn't painting, had enjoyed gardening, he recalled. He smiled, remembering William telling him once that a seed planted was the simplest way to get results in life as well as a reminder that the best things are often the least complicated.

Below, a path sloped downhill through wind-flattened grass and scrub to the cove. Protected by tall bluffs on either side it was inaccessible by any other approach except boat, the only creatures populating its driftwood-strewn beach the seabirds presently foraging for supper.

Colin pointed out the glistening flat where the tide had receded. "When I was a kid, a man from up the road used to farm oysters there," he recalled. His grandfather had leased the use of the land in exchange for a small share of each harvest.

The memory provoked another, sensory one, so keen he could almost see Mr. Deets crouched there on the beach, shucking an oyster still dripping with seawater for Colin to sample. He'd eaten it more out of bravado than anything, thinking it would be something to brag about to Patrick when he got home. But as it slid over his tongue he'd been pleasantly surprised. It was like nothing else he'd ever tasted, the essence of the sea itself.

"That would have been Frank Deets," Findlay commented. "He passed away a few years back. Lung cancer." He tapped his chest. "I handled the estate for his niece."

"I'm sorry to hear that," Colin told him. The few times in recent years that they'd spoken over the phone, his grandfather hadn't mentioned it and now Colin felt a genuine sense of loss. Mr. Deets had been an eccentric old guy, but Colin had liked him.

Now he stood gazing reflectively out at the view, as it dissolved into darkness, until Findlay at last prompted, "Would you like to see the inside?" As if Colin didn't know his own way around.

What he would have liked was to be left alone, but not wanting to appear rude, he shrugged and fell into step with Findlay as he led the way up the path to the house.

Inside, the place was tidy, but a distinct air of disuse hung over it. Wandering from room to room, Colin was struck by the silence; every creak of the floorboards seemed amplified. The hearth where a fire would blaze in the cool of summer evenings was swept clean, newspapers yellow with age stacked on the hearth beside a basket of kindling. The kitchen, too, was bare except for the handful of provisions stocked in anticipation of his arrival.

Elsewhere in the house, bleached oblongs stood out on the walls where paintings had hung. The only one of his grandfather's works that hadn't been sold off was the portrait over the fireplace. *Woman in Red* was perhaps his grandfather's best-known piece and the most sought after, yet though he'd occasionally loan it out to museums, William had rejected all offers that had come his way over the years.

Colin could understand why it had been so difficult to part with. The nameless woman in the portrait, seated on a sofa wearing a red print dress, shoeless with her legs tucked under her, was beautiful in a way that had captured his imagination as a boy and stirred him even now. There was something both innocent and sensual in those bare feet, that dress pulled demurely down over her knees and the glossy chestnut hair, rolled up in back and pinned into loose curls on top of her head, tendrils spilling down her neck. The light from the window at her back made her flesh appear to glow and her eyes—deep green and shot full of gold, the color of turning leaves—translucent in a way that was almost unearthly. Even her expression, contemplative, with a hint of a smile on her lips, suggested hidden depths.

Once, a long time ago, Colin had asked his grandfather about her. The old man's gaze had turned inward, and after a long pause he'd answered cryptically, "That's a story for another day, son. Why don't we save it for when you're old enough to have me tell it to you over a bottle of that good cognac your folks send for Christmas every year."

Sadly, that day never came.

He'd have asked his father, but Daniel's mood always darkened whenever the subject of his old man came up, so Colin had learned early on that it was best not mentioned. He'd never understood why his father had felt so much animosity toward William, only that it had something to do with his grandparents' divorce. Colin was nine before he'd even met the grandfather he'd known until then only from the cards his grandfather sent on his and Patrick's birthdays and at Christmas, always with a twenty dollar bill tucked inside. His mom, who believed that family was family no matter what, had finally persuaded Daniel to let Colin and Patrick fly out for a week-long visit. In the end, though, it had been just Colin. His brother, who'd been thirteen at the time and the star of his Little League team, had refused to go. From then on, it became the pattern, Colin going off every summer for longer and longer visits, while Patrick stayed behind to indulge in his favorite activities: sports, girls, and later on, cars.

Now, as Colin studied the portrait, he thought about the story William had never gotten around to telling him . . . and the one Colin had never gotten around to telling his grandfather: The story of how he'd lost everything and come undone.

His eyes shifted to the mirror on the wall to the right of the fireplace, where a somber face looked back at him—a face that, at first glance, didn't appear much altered from the one in the framed photo on the mantel from his college graduation. The same ink-blue eyes and the Roman nose he'd inherited from his grandfather on his mom's side. It was only upon closer examination that he saw the lines that hadn't been there before. His smile that had once been one of expectation was rueful now. He knew what to expect: Not a life filled with promise, but one in which the only thing standing between him and the proverbial abyss was a folding chair in some church rec room or VA hall filled with other people in similar straits.

He turned to find Findlay eyeing him curiously. In this small community, there had to have been a fair amount of speculation concerning the return of Old McGinty's grandson. Not that Colin cared. It was a welcome change from being talked about for other, less benign reasons, like the gossip that had circulated around the D.A.'s office during his drinking days.

"I've always wondered about her," he said, bringing his gaze back to the portrait. "Was she from around here, do you know?"

Findlay nodded. "Her name was Eleanor Styles."

Colin flicked him a glance. "You knew her?"

"I wouldn't go so far as to say that. I saw her around, sure, but she didn't get out much, not with her husband so sick. And then she got sick herself." He shook his head pityingly, the same look on his face that he'd worn when speaking of Deets' passing. "My dad, though, he remembers when she was a sight to behold—hands down the prettiest girl on the island."

"She *was* beautiful," Colin agreed.

"The way Dad tells it, half the men in San Juan County were in love with her," Findlay went on. "No one could believe it when she married Joe Styles. Not that he wasn't a nice enough fellow, but a little out of her league, if you know what I mean. Then the war broke out . . ." His voice trailed off. "Joe made it home, but he was never the same after that. Some sort of head injury. I'm sure it couldn't have been easy for her, either, but she stuck with him, right up till the end."

"How did she and my grandfather know each other?"

"She bred dogs to bring in extra cash. border collies. Your grandpa bought one of the puppies. I guess they became friendly after that." Color rose in the lawyer's pale, freckled cheeks. "Not that I'm suggesting there was anything between them," he was quick to add. "It was just . . . you know . . . the war. And people looked out for each other in those days."

From the way Findlay spoke, as if those long ago events had occurred just yesterday, Colin almost expected to see a younger and more vibrant William, from the days when he'd sported a full head of coal-black hair, stride into the room, Dickie at his heels. But, of course, it wouldn't have been Dickie back then. There had been a succession of dogs through the years, all of them border collies. Each had lived to a ripe old age and was buried out back behind the woodshed.

Colin turned now to Findlay. "I'd offer you a drink, but I'm not sure what's on hand." He eyed the cherry breakfront where William, not a drinking man himself, had kept a small supply of liquor for when company came.

Just as he'd hoped, the lawyer took the offer as his cue to leave. "Thanks, but I should be heading off. My wife'll have supper on the table before too long, and if I let it get cold I'll have some explaining to do. You know how they get." Findlay winked, one husband to another, before he caught himself and his comradely expression gave way to an embarrassed look.

Colin felt stripped of his defenses, his whole, sad history laid bare. But, of course, everyone must know. In the stunned days after 9/11, it was all people had talked about, who among their circle of friends and acquaintances had been touched by the tragedy—a friend of a friend, the cousin of an old college roommate, the uncle of a former employee. On Grays Island, it would have passed from one person to the next like a found penny. *You know Old McGinty? Terrible about his grandson, isn't it? He lost his wife. They're saying she was in the first tower when it was hit. Never had a prayer.*

The old pain stirred to life once more, but he put on a smile, saying, as he saw Findlay out the door, "Thanks again for coming to meet me. I really appreciate all your help."

"My pleasure." At the door, Findlay handed Colin the keys to his grandfather's old Volvo. "It's been mostly sitting in the garage these past few years, what with his eyesight so bad and all. But the engine still runs, and I had Orin gas it up. Anything else you need, just give a shout. I'll have those papers ready for you to sign, if you want to stop by my office later in the week."

When he was gone, Colin breathed a sigh of relief. Not that he wasn't grateful to Findlay, just that the need to be alone had become as persistent as a dog whining at the door to be let out. Which reminded him . . . Had the border collie at the ferry landing made it home all right? It was a long walk and with night falling he'd have to make his way in the dark over unlit roads where he'd be in danger of being hit by a passing car. But Colin had more pressing problems at the moment than worrying about a dog that had appeared better equipped to care for itself than he was. Like what he was going to do with himself now that he was actually here. Up until this moment, he hadn't dared think that far ahead.

Well, there was one thing he could do. It wouldn't solve everything, but it would be a start. He pulled the phone book from the drawer in the old stereo cabinet, on which the phone sat. It had been a while since he'd seen one this thin—it wouldn't even hold the "A's" in the Manhattan directory—and it reminded him of just how small a place the island was. In the yellow pages, under the listings for health services, he found what he was looking for and dialed the number for Alcoholics Anonymous.

There were two meetings a week, every Tuesday and Thursday evening at seven, he was informed. If he left now, he could grab a bite to eat in town and still make tonight's, at the Lutheran Church. As he hung up, he found himself thinking of the woman he'd met earlier. Alice. Suddenly he remembered where he knew her from. It had been in all the papers, and now he did the mental arithmetic. Yes, the timing would be about right.

God help her, he thought, pausing as he reached for his jacket. She'd have a tough go of it. For if his every movement was going to be scrutinized, he wouldn't be the only one.

CHAPTER TWO

Standing over the sink in the ladies' room of Svenigan's, Alice stared at the faucet. There was no handle. How were you supposed to turn it on? After several frustrating moments, the toilet flushed in the other stall and an older woman emerged, sidling up to the sink. Alice, making a show of touching up her lipstick, watched out of the corner of her eye as the woman waved a hand under the faucet and water came gushing forth. Then she remembered about motion sensors: They'd just been coming into vogue back when she'd been in the habit of frequenting public restrooms.

These days, she felt like a foreigner in her own country, everything rushing at her faster than she could take it all in: billboards displaying unfamiliar brand names, computerized kiosks where there had once been smiling tellers and ticket takers, the maze of automated messages and prompts that greeted her when she called a place of business. Any little thing might confound her, even something as simple as a faucet.

The woman seemed to shoot her a curious glance, as if trying to place her. Alice wondered if she was being paranoid; even so, she kept her face averted as she washed and dried her hands. She'd arrived a day early in the hope of speaking with Jeremy before the rest of the family descended on her. It would be less awkward this way, without everyone else around. For Jeremy especially. Being a teenager was difficult enough, and she wanted to be a part of her son's life, not just another complication.

Sixteen. He's sixteen. She struggled to absorb that unbelievable fact. She'd kept track of every birthday and watched him grow through the snapshots Randy and her sister had sent—each new spurt in height, each new sign of maturity, both a source of wonder and of pain—but it still felt unreal. She couldn't stop picturing him as the little boy he'd been, frozen in time like in the photo she wore in the locket around her neck. She hadn't seen him since. Randy had stopped bringing him to visit her in prison. He'd written her a letter explaining that it was for the best; Jeremy had grown so withdrawn he barely communicated, and the visits only made it worse. Both he and Dr. Turner, the psychologist Jeremy had been seeing at the time, were concerned about Jeremy's mental state.

It had nearly killed Alice to be cut off from her son, but in the end she'd gone along. What choice had she had? Now she wished she'd fought harder. Her judgment had been clouded by the guilt she'd felt and she hadn't seen that she'd only been making it easier for Randy, who hadn't wanted to face her for reasons of his own, reasons that had soon become apparent when she was served with divorce papers. Now, as a result, she was a virtual stranger to her son. Worse, Jeremy seemed to have no interest in getting to know her. Her letters had for the most part gone unanswered. When he did write, it was only a few cursory lines. *How are you? I'm fine.* He always signed those letters, *Your son, Jeremy.* As if she didn't know her own child. The thought caused something to twist in her gut, and she took a deep breath to quiet her anxiety at seeing him again.

Ain't no sense trying to undo what's done. Might as well try stuffing an egg back into a chicken once it's laid, drawled a voice in her head, that of Calpernia King. Big, black Calpernia, tough as the tire iron she'd used to beat her abusive boyfriend near to death and about the last person Alice, in her old life, would ever have thought to call a friend. Yet in the nine years she'd spent at Pine River, she'd come to know and love Calpernia, who, for all her tough talk, had always had Alice's back. She wished Calpernia were here now. She could use all the reinforcement she could get.

Alice made her way back to the entrance of the cafe, to retrieve the suitcase she'd left behind the coat rack. Thankfully, Svenigan's was nearly deserted at this hour. The dinner crowd wouldn't begin showing up until the shops downtown had closed for the day and thoughts turned to Ina Svenigan's short rib lasagna chased by a slice of her homemade marionberry pie. The plump, middle-aged woman working the register paused to glance at Alice for perhaps a beat too long, and Alice could only hope the years had done their work in making her less recognizable.

As she made her way up Harbor Street tugging her suitcase behind her, her thoughts turned once more to Jeremy. He ought to be home from school by now; she'd call him as soon as she checked in at the bed- and-breakfast. The thought caused her to quicken her step as she headed up the hill, her heart tumbling over in her chest like an eager child dashing ahead of her. Then she remembered about his after-school job—Denise had written to her about it—and her excitement waned. The call would have to wait.

The wind picked up, bringing rain that lashed at her already raw cheeks. She'd booked a room at the Harbor Inn, known locally as the White House—a small act of defiance on her part, though it hadn't been under White family ownership for decades. It stood at the top of the hill, a lit beacon, its round turret and gables making it look like something out of a fairy tale. *One in which a princess gets spirited away, then returns to her kingdom and lives happily ever after*, Alice thought, smiling grimly.

It was where she and Randy had spent their wedding night—a fairy tale gone awry in the end. Not much had changed since then, she saw as soon as she walked in. A spacious entryway wainscoted in oak and lit by antique brass sconces opened onto the reception area in what had once been the parlor, a large cozy room hung with paintings of sailing ships. A log fire burned in the fireplace and a tray of cheese and crackers had been set out along with a decanter of red wine.

No one was about, so Alice rang the brass bell on the desk. Moments later, a smiling white-haired woman in a dark green cardigan embroidered with jack-o'-lanterns came bustling through the side entrance. Her smile faded as soon as Alice gave her name.

"Alice Kessler?" She peered at the reservation book, frowning. "I'm afraid there's been some sort of mistake. We don't have a reservation under that name. Are you sure it wasn't one of the other inns?" Even when she looked up, her eyes seemed to avoid Alice.

"Quite sure." Alice put on a perplexed look, though she had a pretty good idea of what was going on here. It was just the first of what would be many such rebuffs, she thought, with a sinking in her gut. "The gentleman I spoke with over the phone said you had plenty of vacancies," she went on, maintaining a bright, pleasant tone. "Is there a problem?"

"I'm afraid so. We're full up at the moment," she was informed.

"I see." Alice spoke quietly but in a way that made her displeasure known. She should have been prepared for this. It was a small community and people had long memories, many of whom had ties to the Whites.

Heat rising in her cheeks, she said in an overly polite voice, "In that case, may I use your phone? If it's not too much to ask."

None too graciously, the woman pushed the phone toward her. Alice punched in Denise's number, which she knew by heart, praying that her sister was home. Otherwise, she'd be out of luck, no money for a taxi—what little she had on her was in traveler's checks—and the nearest accommodations a long walk away. She couldn't call her mother, either; Lucy met with her book club on Thursdays. Besides, Lucy wasn't expecting to hear from her until tomorrow and, knowing her, she'd gone to some lengths to prepare a homecoming that would only be spoiled by Alice's early arrival.

Luckily, Denise picked up on the second ring. "God! Why didn't you tell me you were coming in early?" her sister chided, sounding delighted to hear from her nonetheless.

"I was hoping I'd get a chance to talk with Jeremy, you know, before having to face everyone else," Alice said.

"Well, your timing sucks." Denise gave a good-natured if frustrated laugh. "I've got a houseful of nine-year-olds at the moment—Taylor's Brownie troop, in case you're wondering what all that noise is about," she added, raising her voice to be heard above the shrill chorus in the background. Gary's still at work and Ryan's at football practice, so I have no one to watch them. I hate to make you wait, but. . . . "

Alice was quick to assure her, "It's fine. Get here when you can." She'd waited nine years, she could wait another half hour or so.

It was fully dark and raining heavily by the time Denise pulled up in front of the inn in her ancient Honda Prelude. Emerging from the driver's seat with a yellow rain slicker tented over her head, she rushed forward to envelop Alice in a damp embrace that smelled faintly of chocolate-chip cookies, reminding Alice of everything warm and good she'd missed.

"You're cold as ice!" Denise cried. "Why didn't you wait inside?"

"Let's just say the temperature in there wasn't much warmer." Shivering inside her coat, Alice glanced over her shoulder at the inn's brightly glowing windows.

Her sister didn't question her further, but Alice hadn't missed the flicker of uneasiness in her eyes—this was no ordinary homecoming, they both knew. "Well, even blue with cold, you look good," observed Denise, pushing a hand self-consciously through her own unkempt hair.

"You mean, for someone who just got out of prison," Alice said.

"Hush now," Denise scolded, in the same tone their mother would have used. Briskly, she took hold of Alice's suitcase, dragging it over to the Honda and heaving it into the trunk, which was plastered with bumper stickers like the ones that read, *Well-behaved women rarely make history* and *One people, one planet, one future*.

Her sister's constancy was reassuring in this new, jarring world Alice had entered into. Denise was still the same girl who'd cried over every mangled, furry heap by the side of the road and who'd marched in every demonstration, only older now and the mother of two. It had been a bit of a shock, the last time Denise had visited, to see that her baby sister was going prematurely gray.

"Remember that old VW bug you used to drive?" Alice remarked when they were on their way.

"God, yes. Dad used to threaten to dress up Grampa in his old World War II uniform to shame me into getting rid of it." Denise gave a laugh that seemed somehow forced. Hunched over the wheel, she looked as though she were navigating her way through a heavy snowstorm instead of the rain that was a fact of life in this part of the world. "I used to wonder if that's part of why he and Mom fell in love, because they both had fathers who'd been wounded in the war. God knows they didn't have much else in common, unless you count the fact that they were the only two people on the planet who liked rutabaga."

"They had us, too," Alice reminded her. She was thinking about how strange it would be to walk into her parents' house, the house she and her sister had grown up in, and not find her father there. That had been one of her worst moments in prison, when she'd learned of his death. Now she recalled the words he'd murmured in her ear just before they'd taken her away in handcuffs. *Don't worry about Jeremy. We'll look after him.*

She'd clung to him for a long moment, as if she were being sucked out to sea by a strong tide and he was a stanchion. *I'm sorry, Daddy,* she'd choked. *I know I let you down.*

He'd pulled back to look at her, the stern lines in his face giving way to an expression of infinite sadness. *You'll always be my girl. Don't ever forget that.*

And she hadn't. But now he was gone and she would never have the chance to make it up to him. Sitting in the car, staring out at the darkness and listening to the hiss of water under the tires, she felt a renewed sense of loss.

After a bit, she ventured, "How's Mom doing?"

"Better. You know her, she never stays down for long. Besides, with all her activities, she barely has a moment to herself. She belongs to so many clubs I can't keep them all straight. Did she tell you she also signed up for a cooking class? Who knows, maybe she'll be the next Julia Child. Oh, that reminds me. She's planning a supper for the whole family. You're not doing anything on Sunday, are you?"

"Gee, I don't know. I'll have to check my calendar," Alice answered dryly.

Denise didn't respond, and a heavy silence fell, weighted with all that was left unsaid. Her sister had to be thinking about the changes that lay ahead, not just the good ones but the fact that the status quo that had existed for the past nine years would be disrupted. For one thing, Denise's husband, Gary, was deputy chief of police; however much he might like Alice, her presence would put him in an awkward position. And the children Denise taught in school all had parents who might take a dim view of her harboring a paroled convict.

"Thank you, by the way. For coming to get me," Alice said at last, in a tone that conveyed gratitude for more than the ride. *Thank you for not abandoning me. For coming to see me all those years. For giving me a reason to live.* "Gary won't mind my staying the night?"

"Please. You're my sister." Denise waved aside any such concerns, but Alice noticed she hadn't given a direct answer. Now, she chattered on, "Wait'll you see how big the kids have gotten. Ryan's as tall as Gary. He just made the varsity team, did I tell you? We're all thrilled about it. Of course, we told him he can't put football over his schoolwork, not if he wants to go to a decent college." With them barely scraping by on her and Gary's combined income, it was a scholarship or community college, Alice knew.

"Speaking of school, is Taylor still planning to boycott fourth grade?" she asked. Her sister had told her that Taylor was getting teased a lot and often came home from school in tears.

"Oh. Well. You know how kids are. She'll get over it," Denise said with a lightness that belied her concern. "Ryan had me for a teacher, too, and it certainly hasn't affected his social life. In fact, if the girls don't stop calling, we'll have to put in another phone line."

Denise herself had been the butt of every fat joke in grade school, the girl who'd sat on the sidelines at dances and gotten picked last for every team. Alice thought that was what made her such a good teacher; she could empathize with the kids who had trouble fitting in.

Alice wondered what it had been like for Jeremy. She'd missed practically his whole childhood. Oh, what she would have given to have been there even for the tough times! The tears and tirades, the awkward prepubescent years. Instead, she'd had only his infrequent letters that she'd scrutinized like tea leaves, struggling to read some meaning in them. Now, she ventured cautiously, "Have you spoken with Jeremy? About me, I mean."

Denise shot her a guarded look. "We don't see him as much as we used to. He's been pretty busy with his after-school job."

"How does he seem to you?" All day the question had been beating like a moth's wings against the window in her heart where Alice had kept a light burning all these years.

"Okay. Really, Alice, he's *okay*. He's a great kid. And so smart! I really think he has a shot at the Ivy Leagues."

"I know he's smart," Alice replied sharply. "I'm his mother, remember?"

"I didn't mean . . ." her sister started to say, but it was too late: the old pain surfaced, punching through the wall Alice had carefully constructed around her emotions. Suddenly it was all too much. She felt dizzy and disoriented, like when waking from a deep sleep, her head still clouded with fragments of a dream. Only this was no dream.

"I know you didn't mean anything by it," she said, realizing she'd been unfair to take it out on Denise.

Her sister cast her a woeful look. "I'm sorry. I know this is hard for you. And I'm not making it any easier, am I? It's just that I don't know how much to tell."

Alice's response was immediate and unequivocal. "I want to know about my son."

Denise sighed. "Well, as far as I can tell, he's coping pretty well. But it hasn't been easy for him, either. He hears things at school. You know how it is. Kids can be so mean. My advice is to take it slow. He'll need time to get used to you being back in his life."

Denise turned onto Fox Valley Road, which hadn't been resurfaced since Alice had last traveled it, judging from all the potholes. They splashed through one after another, each new, bone-jarring lurch seeming to echo Alice's thoughts.

The only thing that had gotten her through all those years in prison was knowing she'd be coming home to Jeremy one day. Now apparently she was considered an intrusion. How was she supposed to deal with that? How did you take it slow when you only know one speed? "I'm not here to make things harder for him," she said quietly, gripping tightly to the door handle as they bounced through yet another pothole, mud flying up to spatter the windshield.

"I know, hon. And I'm sure it'll all work out. It's just that it's not going to happen overnight." Denise reached over to pat her on the knee.

It was strange seeing Denise cast in the role of big sister. Growing up, she had been the one who could never get it together. Forever on a diet in the hope of being able to fit into smaller clothes, and in a perpetual state of disarray that extended from her flyaway hair to the mess on her side of the closet they'd shared. Now, glancing down at the trash littering the floor at her feet—torn receipts and crumpled straw wrappers, an empty coffee container and something that might have been a Barbie doll poking out from under a T-shirt—Alice saw that not much had changed. Yet Denise had become the stable one. The one with all the answers. While she, Alice, had none.

The rain had tapered off by the time they pulled up in front of Denise's rambling farmhouse. It was a good half-hour's drive from town, but, as Denise liked to say, where else could they have gotten such a spread? Ten acres with its own pond and a barn that housed a horse, chickens, and a pet pig named Mirabelle—a 4-H project that Taylor hadn't been able to part with.

As she climbed out, Alice took note of Gary's cruiser, parked next to one of those seventies' gas-guzzlers, full of dents, which had to be Ryan's. Her anxiety mounted. She and Gary had in the past always gotten along well but she hadn't seen him since she'd last been to this house and she didn't know quite what to expect. Would he be standoffish or welcome her with open arms? There was another concern as well: He wasn't just her brother-in-law; he was the law. And in prison, it was the law you answered to. Some of the COs had abused that power, seeming to take pleasure in harassing the inmates: writing up bogus charge sheets, giving out work orders when they knew you had a class or were expecting a visitor; making you wait for hours, sometimes days, for your meds. Even now, the thought of someone in uniform caused Alice to break into a sweat.

She was climbing the steps to the porch when the front door swung open and a figure emerged: a big man in jeans and a flannel shirt, square and solid as an appliance built to last. "Alice. Good to have you back." Gary stepped forward to give her an awkward hug. He smelled of aftershave, his close-cropped sandy curls still damp from the shower. The receding hairline was the only concession to the years. That, and the few extra inches around his middle.

The wary look in his cop's eyes didn't match his words of welcome. He obviously had mixed feelings about her reemergence into their lives; Alice understood, and she didn't blame him. It was awkward, given his line of work and who he ultimately answered to. "Good to *be* back," she said, with forced cheer. "How have you been, Gary?"

"Oh, you know me. Just chugging along. Your sister keeps me busy when I'm not on patrol. If it were up to her, I wouldn't have a moment to myself," he teased, slinging an arm around Denise's shoulders and grinning as though they were posing for a family photo.

"Listen to you," said Denise, giving him an affectionate jab with her elbow. Turning to Alice, she explained, "I've been trying to convince him to run for county commissioner. We'll need him on our side when they vote on the Spring Hill project."

Alice didn't know much about the project, except that Denise and her fellow activists had been campaigning against it for weeks. Some big housing development slated for Spring Hill that they were trying to block. She was familiar with the area, though; it was the virgin tract that bordered on their grandmother's old property. Nana used to take her and Denise on hikes there when they were young, pointing out all the different birds and flowers and insects along the way. Now it seemed Denise was determined that it remain untouched for future generations to enjoy.

"I keep telling her if she's so worked up about it, she ought to run for office herself," Gary said.

"She'd have my vote," replied Alice with a laugh, before remembering that as a convicted felon she'd lost that right. Her smile fell away, and she could see from Gary's expression, an odd mixture of pity and disdain, that the same thought had occurred to him.

As she followed them into the house, Alice recalled what a wreck it had been when they'd first bought it. Their every spare hour had been spent scraping and sanding and painting, restoring the old floors and woodwork until they gleamed. They'd made it into a real showpiece, though at the moment it looked like a tornado had hit it: The living room floor was strewn with construction paper cutouts, discarded socks and shoes, and random items of clothing, while dirty plates and glasses lined the coffee table, along with an empty milk jug and a half eaten plate of chocolate chip cookies.

"Guys! Look who's here!" Denise called to the two children at the center of the chaos. "Sorry it's such a mess," she apologized, "but you didn't give us much notice." A teenage boy with his father's sandy curls and athletic build looked up from the computer screen that was occupying his attention. On the sofa, a slight, dark-haired girl dressed in a rumpled Brownie uniform looked away from the TV to stare at Alice.

Alice scarcely recognized her niece and nephew. Ryan had been the same age as Jeremy when she'd last seen him—Alice and Denise used to jokingly refer to Ryan and Jeremy as the twins—and Taylor an infant in Denise's arms. It was a shock when Ryan rose to greet her, easily as tall as his father, sporting a small diamond stud in one ear. She remembered him as a sweet-natured little boy, and it was a relief to see that he hadn't changed when he stepped forward to hug her: a fleeting impression of body heat, musky boy's scent, limbs bumping up against hers. His face was red when he stepped back.

"This must seem weird to you," Alice said, to put him at ease.

"Kind of." He shuffled from one foot to the other, smiling shyly.

"Well, it's pretty weird for me, too," she confided. "You probably don't even remember me."

"I remember playing over at your house when I was little," her nephew said.

"You and Jeremy were always building forts." Alice smiled at the memory. Made of cardboard and stuff scavenged from the garage, those forts usually collapsed with the first rainfall or heavy gust of wind.

"I'm still at it," he said, with a grin. "Only now it's called Shop."

"Well," she said. "I see I have some catching up to do."

"It's cool that you're here. You can have my room, if you like," he said, making Alice fall in love with him all over again. Ryan was the kid who made you smile even when he was getting into mischief.

"Thanks, I appreciate the offer, but the sofa will do just fine," she said. She turned to her niece, now peering out from behind her brother. "You must be Taylor. You were just a baby the last time I last saw you. And just look at you now." She was blossoming into a real beauty, with Denise's clear blue eyes and porcelain skin.

Taylor gazed at her with an intentness that bordered on rudeness. Alice could only imagine what she must be thinking. The aunt that she'd heard so much about must seem a legendary figure sprung to life: the incarnation of much dark discussion between adults when it was presumed little ears weren't listening.

"You look just like your mom," Alice continued when she got no response. Except that her niece was slim as an arrow. Taylor lowered her eyes, wearing an embarrassed look. "But you must get that all the time. You're probably sick of hearing it."

Taylor's thin shoulders lifted and fell in an elaborate shrug.

Alice tried a different tack. "Did you know I went to the same school as you?"

"Uh-huh." The girl gave her a long, considering look, as if wondering how anyone who had gone to Woodrow Wilson Elementary could have ended up in prison.

"I didn't have my mother as a teacher, though," Alice forged on. "Which, I'm sure, is kind of weird. But at least you get plenty of help with your homework."

Denise cut in before Taylor's silence became even more uncomfortable. "Speaking of homework, if that TV isn't off in about three seconds, you'll be spending the weekend cracking books, young lady." She swooped in like a commando, seizing the remote control when Taylor didn't act quickly enough and generally creating a distraction that smoothed over the awkwardness of the moment.

At dinner, it was Denise's lively chatter that carried them through. Gary, too, made a game attempt at conversation and Ryan brought Alice up to date on all his activities. It wasn't much different from the family meals Alice had shared with them in the past, if you didn't count the fact that no mention was made of the reason for her long absence—she might have been back from an extended trip, from the way everyone was acting. Listening to Denise jabber on about family doings and the latest gossip from the teacher's lounge at school, Alice had the strangest feeling she was in a play from which lines of dialogue had been deleted.

"I ran into Aileen Findlay today at the market, and she told me that McGinty's grandson's in town," Denise remarked, as she was passing out bowls of ice cream for dessert. "He came in on this afternoon's ferry. Clark took him over to the house."

"I wonder what he's up to," Gary muttered.

"You cops, you're all alike. You think everyone has some hidden agenda," Denise mock-scolded, giving him a swat on the arm. "Who knows? Maybe he's planning to move here, now that he's inherited the old man's place. Apparently, he used to spend summers here as a kid."

"More likely, he's looking to sell," Gary speculated darkly. Like many of the island's long-time residents, he was innately suspicious of mainlanders. "I know the type. Some fancy lawyer from New York thinking he can swoop in and make a quick profit."

"I don't think that's it," said Denise, sitting down to eat her ice cream. "He appears to be at loose ends, from what Clark could see. Apparently he lost his wife on 9/11. God, can you imagine? The poor man, he probably still hasn't recovered." She cast a fond look at Gary, as if, for all his grumbling, she couldn't fathom life without him. "And then to lose his grandfather on top of that . . . "

Alice was thinking that it had to be the grandfather of the man she'd met at the ferry landing. That was why his name had sounded so familiar. "Are we talking about the same McGinty who painted Nana's portrait?" she interjected. No one in the family had seen the actual painting, only reproductions of it, but it was a part of the family lore. There was also a bit of a mystery surrounding it. All Nana would say, if pressed, was that she and Mr. McGinty had been friendly at one time. But from the quickness with which she'd always dismissed the subject, Alice had always suspected there was more to the story.

Denise nodded. "He passed away about six months ago. You should've seen the crowd at the funeral! There were reporters and everything." She paused, frowning in thought. "The odd thing was that none of his family came." She shook her head. "Must have been some bad blood."

"You're right about that," Gary put in, as he spooned ice cream into his mouth. "I remember my dad telling me it was the talk of the town when McGinty's wife divorced him. She took the kid and moved to New York. That was the last anyone ever saw of them."

"That's so sad. Imagine not being able to see your own child!" Denise blurted before catching herself. Her cheeks reddened.

An awkward silence settled over the table, all eyes carefully avoiding Alice's. It was the eight-hundred-pound gorilla in the room, and suddenly Alice had had enough. Putting her spoon down, she turned Ryan, asking in as casual a tone as she could manage, "Do you know when Jeremy gets off work? I thought I'd give him a call after supper."

Ryan shrugged. "He's working for some landscaper, I think. That's all I know."

"You two don't hang out together?" she asked, surprised. There was a time they'd been practically joined at the hip.

"Not really." Her nephew kept his gaze on the pool of melting ice cream he was slowly stirring in his bowl. "I see him around, sure, but the guys he hangs with . . ." He caught himself, as if to keep from saying something that might worry her. "I don't have much in common with them."

"When you do see him, does he . . ." Alice paused, not wanting to appear any more pathetic than she already did; someone who, like Old Man McGinty, didn't know her own child. But in the end, desperation won out over pride. "Does he ever talk about me?"

The silence that ensued burned its way into her flesh. Then Ryan lifted his head and his eyes met hers. In them, she read the answer she'd been both seeking and dreading, one as bleak as the gray walls behind which she'd spent the past nine years.

"What was it like being in jail?" Taylor piped just then, as if she'd read Alice's mind. She'd been mostly silent throughout the meal, as if taking Alice's measure, or perhaps wondering what it would do to her social status having a jailbird for an aunt in addition to having her mother as her teacher. Now, her voicing what had to be on everyone else's mind came as a rude shock, immediately plunging the table into silence.

Denise was the first to speak. She shot Taylor an admonishing look. "Honey, I don't think—"

"It was hard." Alice cut her sister off, meeting her niece's intent, clear-eyed gaze. "The worst part was being away from my family. Jeremy and . . ." Her throat tightened, and she took a small sip of breath. "Your mom and dad, and grandma. And you guys." She darted a glance at Gary, whose lips were pressed together in a disapproving line. "I've missed so much, but I'm hoping you'll give me a chance to make up for it."

"Courtney Quist says you tried to run over Mister White, and that's why he's in a wheelchair." Taylor's big blue eyes were merely curious, not accusatory.

"Taylor! That's enough." Gary spoke sharply. He looked angry, though Alice suspected it was more at her than his daughter.

"No, it's okay," Alice told him. She turned back to her niece. "I didn't mean to hurt anyone, Taylor. I was just . . . after Jeremy's brother died . . . " *Killed . . . he was killed*, corrected an angry voice in her head. "I was so sad. I wasn't in my right mind. Honestly, I don't remember much of what happened. When I think about it now, it's mostly a blur."

Only it did happen. Not just to you. To us, said the ravaged look on her sister's face.

"Taylor, honey, why don't you clear the table while your brother does his homework," Denise said, abruptly pushing her chair back and standing up. "I'll help you with yours after we get this cleaned up, then you can watch TV." Suddenly she was back in action, bustling about the kitchen, dumping leftovers into plastic containers, and running plates under the faucet.

"Let me help with that," said Alice, carrying her bowl over to the sink.

Denise shooed her away. "No, you must be tired from your trip. Go put your feet up. I'll have Gary make up the sofa bed in the den." She shot him a meaningful glance: the age-old language between husband and wife that communicated more than any words. She was asking him to go along with the pretense that Alice was just an ordinary visitor.

"No, please. Let me do it," Alice said, heading for the doorway. "Sheets and blankets still in the hall closet?"

Denise, elbow deep in suds, called over her shoulder, "Laundry room."

Alice came to an abrupt halt. "Since when do you have a laundry room?"

"Since we added on a couple of years ago. Didn't I tell you? I guess I forgot to mention it," Denise said distractedly. "Anyway, no more running up and down the stairs to do the wash. Plus, we doubled the size of our bathroom. Remember how tiny it used to be? You could crack a kneecap just sitting down on the john. Go take a look. Make yourself at home."

Home. Alice wondered where that was. Right now she didn't feel as if she belonged anywhere, least of all in her sister's house, where the strain of keeping up with Denise's efforts to maintain a kind of normalcy was already beginning to show. She felt exhausted, as if she'd traveled, not just halfway across the state, but back in time. Right now, she longed to stretch out someplace quiet where she wouldn't have to put on a brave face. But there was something she needed to do first. Something that couldn't wait until tomorrow.

After she'd made up the sofa bed in the den, she reached for the phone on the desk and punched in her old number, a number she'd dialed so many times while at Pine River, she could almost hear the jingle of change tumbling into the pay phone on her cell block. It rang and rang at the other end, each trilling burst causing an invisible band about her chest to tighten. Finally, just as she was about to hang up, it was picked up.

"Hello?" Jeremy's voice, deep as a man's. The rare occasions he'd deigned to come to the phone when she'd called all those other times, their conversations had been brief and mostly one-sided. It came as a shock now to hear how much older he sounded.

Alice felt herself go perfectly still. It was as if she were encased in a brittle membrane that would shatter if she moved so much as an inch. Her lungs had stopped drawing in air and her blood had ceased to flow. The only part of her still functioning was her heart, its rhythmic beat like a clock keeping time in a house where no one was home. Her voice, when it emerged, was queer and high-pitched. "Jeremy? It's me. Mom."

CHAPTER THREE

"Dude, you miss the bus or what?" Rud peered at Jeremy as though he knew exactly why he was still hanging around on campus when school had let out nearly an hour ago.

Rud, of course, needed no reason to be kicking around after hours—he and his buddies moved in their own orbit, like planets around a fickle sun. Normally Jeremy would have welcomed the chance to hang with them, but right now all he could think about was getting rid of Rud and Chuckie, so they wouldn't see when his mother pulled up.

He'd asked her to meet him here rather than at the house. He hadn't wanted to get into it with his dad, who'd been acting so weird since she'd come back, all itchy, like when he'd been trying to quit smoking. Now Jeremy wondered what to expect. Whatever she was offering, he wasn't interested. He'd gotten along just fine without her all these years, what did he need her for now? At the same time, he was curious. He wanted to hear it from her own mouth: To have her explain to him *why*.

Only it might be a case of being careful what you ask for. He'd read in one of those how-to-fix-what's-wrong-with-your-life-in-thirty-days-or-less books that the only way to deal with a situation like this was to meet it head on, to dig deep where it hurt the most. What if he dug all the way down and never got to the bottom? All he'd end up with was a giant hole.

And now here was Rud, the coolest guy he knew, grinning at Jeremy like he was a fly whose wings he'd plucked. "Me and Chuckie here," Rud jerked a thumb toward his sidekick, Chuckie Dimmock, a large, pimple-faced boy who never made a move without Rud's approval, "are heading over to Mike's to watch the drag races. Wanna come along?"

"Nah. I got stuff to do," Jeremy said. Any other time he would have leapt at the offer, but not now.

A slow, knowing smile spread across Rud's face. "Oh, I get it. You waiting on some chick."

Jeremy must have looked startled, for Rud let out a hoot, slapping him on the back. Kurt Rudnicki might be the whitest white boy who ever spoke ghetto-speak, with his pale skin and white-blond hair, gelled into spikes that glistened in the late afternoon sun, but he wasn't dumb. He just didn't have all the details straight. "Yeah, that's it," Jeremy said, in a lighthearted tone, hoping to deflect Rud's interest by making a joke of it. "She should be here any minute."

"Anyone we know?" Rud asked.

"Nah. She's no one," Jeremy muttered, wishing desperately that they would just *leave*.

"You doing her?" Chuckie leered at him.

"No!" Heat flared in Jeremy's cheeks.

"Yo, we got to educate this boy." Rud slung his arm around Jeremy's shoulders, leaning in close, his brown eyes dark holes drilled into the pale, sharp ridges of his face. "Now the thing to do is keep her guessing. Have her think you are doing *her* a favor. You listen to your Uncle Rud now, you hear. He knows what he's talking about. It's all about power, my man, and if you ain't got the power, you ain't got shit."

Jeremy's cheeks burned. "Yeah, well, I'll try to remember that." He injected as much sarcasm into his voice as he could without pissing Rud off.

Rud and Chuckie hung around a bit longer, jiving with him, while Jeremy sneaked surreptitious glances at his watch every now and then, growing increasingly desperate. When they finally took off, the relief he felt momentarily took his mind off the business ahead. It wasn't until he was alone again that the anxiety crept in once more.

The only other signs of life on campus were a group of kids in costume chatting animatedly outside the auditorium, where they were rehearsing for a play, and the varsity team on the football field below doing relays. Jeremy, who just minutes before had wanted only to be alone, felt a sudden sense of isolation that deepened with each shrill blast of Coach Sullivan's whistle and chorus of laughter from the drama club. He wasn't on a team and he didn't belong to any clubs. Socially, he wasn't even in the same universe as his cousin Ryan. Ryan charged the ions in the air just walking down the halls, while Jeremy moved about invisible as a mote of dust, torn between praying he wouldn't be noticed and feeling vaguely let down that he'd succeeded so spectacularly on that score.

Now all that was changing. Over the past few days, people had begun to eye him in a new and unwelcome way. Just this afternoon he'd walked into a classroom only to have the conversation abruptly cease. Even his teachers seemed to regard him differently, as if he were a rare specimen that required special handling. And that wasn't all. Everyone knew that Mr. White more or less ran the town. It wasn't just that he was mayor; he had the power that came with money, and according to Uncle Gary he didn't hesitate to use it. Which made Jeremy uneasy about how things would shake down now that his mother was back on the scene. Life, he suspected, was about to get very difficult for all of them.

He was distracted from his thoughts by a car now making its way toward him between the rows of parked cars, an older model Toyota Celica, metallic green, with a cracked windshield and a sticker on the front end that read *Rehab is for Quitters*. He smiled to himself. It was like something you'd expect to see on Rud's bumper.

The Toyota pulled to a stop, and a woman climbed out, dressed in jeans and a blue North Face parka like the one his aunt Denise wore. Lean like a runner, with dark brown hair pulled back in a ponytail and skin so pale he might have been looking at her underwater. She paused, glancing about uncertainly. Jeremy felt a tug of recognition. When her gaze fell on him, he froze.

"Jeremy?" She began walking toward him.

He pushed himself off the chain-link fence he was slouched against. "Hey," he said, lifting his hand in a lackluster wave. His mouth was dry, and his heart was beating high and quick in his chest. Suddenly he didn't know what to do with the muscles in his face.

She stopped a few feet shy of him, as if afraid he might bolt, staring at him as though she could fix him in place with her gaze. "You're taller than in your pictures."

He shrugged. "You look different, too."

"I suppose I must." She brought a hand self-consciously to her cheek. Her gaze was hot and searching; he could feel it on his skin like a sunburn. "Shall we go for a ride? We can talk in the car." She noticed him looking at the Toyota. "I bought it from a friend of your aunt Denise," she explained. "It was her son's. He's in jail on a DUI and she needed the money to bail him out." Her mouth slanted in an ironic little smile. "It was the best I could do on short notice."

He shrugged and started toward the car, glancing about to make sure no one was watching before he climbed in. When they were both buckled in, he waited for her to start the engine, but she just sat there, looking at him, as if he were the one in the driver's seat. Jeremy felt a ripple of unease, remembering what had happened the last time he'd been in a car with her. He didn't think she would do anything like that again, but it was an ugly reminder nonetheless.

"We could go for a bite to eat," she suggested.

"I'm not that hungry," he said. Usually by the time school let out he was starving, but at the moment his stomach was in knots. Besides, in a public place they'd draw too much attention.

"Why don't we take a little drive then." She turned the key in the ignition and shifted into gear, maneuvering the Toyota out of the parking lot as carefully as someone learning to drive. Exiting the school grounds, she sneaked a glance at him as she made a right turn onto Church Street. "It's good to see you. You have no idea how much I've been looking forward to this." Her tone was casual, but he hadn't missed the little catch in her voice.

Jeremy felt the pressure to respond in kind, but he couldn't bring himself to do it. She wanted something—he could feel it radiating off her like heat—something he didn't have to give.

"Where are we going?" he asked after a bit, as he stared out the window, slouched down in his seat.

"I don't know. You tell me."

Jeremy cast about in his mind, trying to think of a place where they were unlikely to be spotted by anyone he knew. "Dad and I saw this bald eagle's nest when we were hiking in the park last summer." He said the first thing that popped into his head. "I could show you, if you like."

"Sounds good." He had the feeling she would've said the same thing had he suggested a trip to the moon. "I've heard that in parts of Alaska bald eagles have made such a comeback, they've actually become pests. I saw a show about it on TV," she remarked, as she made the turn at the intersection.

He wondered if it was a show she'd watched in prison, and that made him realize how little he knew about her life at Pine River. He had only sketchy memories of going to visit her there as a kid—a room with tables bolted to the floor and gray, cinderblock walls; guards in uniform buzzing him through a series of doors. There was so much he was dying to ask, all the things she hadn't told him in her letters. But he didn't dare. She might get the wrong idea, and think he gave a shit, and the last thing Jeremy wanted was for this to turn into some tearful mother and son reunion. The truth was she was a stranger to him.

They drove in near silence until they reached the turnoff for the state park, where they began the steep climb up the hill, through a tunnel of evergreens thick with ferns the size of small trees. The road ended in a parking area near the summit, and they got out and hiked the rest of the way along a marked trail. The eagle's nest was right where he remembered it, at the top of an old-growth Douglas fir that had lost most of its foliage. "Looks like no one's home at the moment," Alice said, shading her eyes as she peered upward.

"They're probably out hunting for food," Jeremy said.

"They?"

"It's a pair. There were babies in the nest the last time I was here."

She gazed out at the sound below, where small islands wreathed in mist were strewn like so many scattered stones, some scarcely more than a knuckle of rock with one or two trees clinging to them. "I haven't been up here in years. I'd forgotten how peaceful it is," she said. She turned to him, her eyes bright with unshed tears. "Thank you. You don't know how much this means to me."

He dropped his gaze, feeling embarrassed, knowing she wasn't talking about the scenery. "Yeah. No problem."

"I hope we can do this again."

Jeremy went on staring at the ground. With the autumn rains had come the moss that blanketed everything around him in a thick green fuzz. Right now he wanted nothing more than to sink down onto all that furry softness and close his eyes. "I don't know," he hedged. "I'm pretty busy these days. You know, what with school and my job."

"I see."

"My boss wasn't too happy when I told him I needed the afternoon off."

"Well, maybe we could have dinner one evening then."

"Maybe." Jeremy spoke dubiously. "But that's usually the only time Dad and I get to hang out."

He glanced up and saw the hurt on her face. But she did her best to cover it, asking, "How is your dad, by the way?"

"Good. They made him district manager."

"I'm not surprised. He's worked hard for it."

"The only bad thing is that it means more time on the road." Randy's territory covered most of western Washington, many of the doctor's offices and clinics he regularly called on separated by hundreds of miles. "What about you? What'll you do?" Jeremy asked.

"For work, you mean?" She smiled. "I don't know yet. First, I have to find a place to live."

"So you, like, plan on sticking around?"

She seemed surprised by the question. "Of course. Why wouldn't I?"

He shrugged. Part of him wanted her here; another part of him wished she'd stayed the hell away. Mostly, he just felt confused.

"The only reason I'm here is because of you. I want us to spend some time together," she went on, the raw need in her voice making him cringe. "You'll be in college before long, and I've missed so much already."

Yeah? Well, whose fault is that? he felt like saying. He frowned, struggling to keep from giving in to the tears pressing behind his eyes. "I don't know about college. I might take a year off, do some traveling."

She gave him a quizzical look. "Aunt Denise tells me you have a shot at the Ivy Leagues."

He snorted in derision, pretending it was no big deal, though he'd sent for all the catalogues and had been thinking of little else for months. "Let's see how I score on the SATs."

"Maybe I could help with that. I was sort of the unofficial tutor at Pine River. They nicknamed me Teach." She smiled, which shocked him a bit—he wouldn't have imagined she'd have any fond memories of that place. "It wouldn't be the same with you, I know. The ladies I worked with were just studying for their GEDs, and you . . ." She paused. "You could probably teach me. But I could quiz you on the stuff you've learned."

"I don't need your help." He spoke more harshly than he'd intended.

Alice fell silent. All around him the woods crackled as if with static in the stiff breeze blowing in off the water. Violent slashes of yellow stood out amid the deep green—the laurels and poplars his boss, Mr. Barbour, called weed trees—marking the passage of Indian summer into autumn. Overhead, bands of cirrus clouds stippled the sky, and on the ground below boulders and fallen tree limbs lay like the ruins of an ancient civilization.

"I'd be doing it as much for me as for you," she said at last, her voice so soft he almost didn't catch the tremor in it.

"Thanks, but I've gotten along just fine without you all these years."

She shook her head, her eyes filling with tears. "I'm still your mother."

"Yeah? I had a mother once," he shot back. "She used to bake me cookies and tuck me in at night. You? I don't even *know* you."

She looked so bereft, Jeremy almost felt sorry for her. "I never stopped loving you, not for one minute," she said.

"All I know is that you weren't around! I used to cry myself to sleep every night, I missed you so much." His own tears came now, hot and fierce, betraying him. He gave his runny nose a furious backhanded swipe. "I was just a kid. Shouldn't you have thought of that before you . . . you . . ." His throat closed up before he could finish the sentence.

Her own face contorted, as if in pain. "I'm sorry, Jeremy. I never meant for it to turn out this way."

"You make it sound like an accident. I was there, remember? You weren't thinking of me when you ran down Mister White. You were thinking of David. You chose *him* over me. A dead boy." The memory he'd done his best to bury reached up now like some hideous, decayed thing rising out the grave.

"It wasn't like that," she said, the tears in her eyes spilling down her cheeks. "I wasn't in my right mind at the time. I know that sounds like an excuse, but it's the truth."

"If you really cared about me, you'd go away and leave me alone!"

"Jeremy, please . . . "

She placed a hand on his arm, and he shook it off, abruptly turning around and stalking back toward the car. He hadn't gone more than a few dozen feet when he slipped on some wet leaves and lost his balance, pitching backward to land on his rear end. Alice cried out in dismay and came rushing over, but Jeremy only glared up at her from his sprawled position on the ground, as if it were her fault that he'd fallen. Ignoring her proffered hand, he scrambled to his feet, slapping at the dirt and leaves that clung to his jeans.

By the time he straightened, his face was wiped clean of any emotion. "Are we done now? I'd like to go home," he said in a queer, dead voice he scarcely recognized as his own.

After she'd dropped her son off at his house, Alice drove slowly back toward the motel where she was staying. She replayed the meeting with Jeremy in her mind. Could she have handled it better? Been more up front with him instead of following Denise's advice to take it slowly? Somehow she didn't think it would have made a difference.

Jeremy was hurt and angry, and no amount of explaining was going to change that. It would take time for those wounds to heal. Meanwhile, she would just have to be patient, let him know by her mere presence alone that if she hadn't been there for him before, she was now.

Still, the rejection hurt. In a way, Jeremy seemed further away than when she'd been in prison. Back then, she'd at least had the hope of a happy reunion.

He was so different from his brother. David had been a happy-go-lucky kid, hurtling through life as if he'd somehow known he needed to cram everything into those few short years. Jeremy, in contrast, had been watchful and sensitive. She recalled one time, when he was around three, she'd walked into the living room and found him crying as though his heart would break, where moments before he'd been playing happily with his toys.

"Oh, sweetie, what is it? What's the matter?" she'd asked, scooping him into her arms.

"It got hurts," he'd finally managed to choke, pointing a chubby finger at the sliding glass door to the patio, where a sparrow that had flown into the glass lay stunned.

After his brother's death, Jeremy had retreated into his own world, holing up in his room for hours on end with his comic books and action figures. So ghostlike she used to worry that he would one day simply fade away. She hadn't been equipped to deal with it, though. She hadn't realized it at the time, but both her marriage and her sanity had been gradually coming undone. Randy and she, though they were sleeping in the same bed, might have been in separate universes. Even in their shared concern for Jeremy they'd been at odds, disagreeing on everything from which psychologist would be best for him to whether or not Jeremy should be forced to finish what was on his plate when he said he wasn't hungry.

The motel was situated on Whale Watch Lane, a short walk from the outlook known for its frequent whale sightings. It catered mostly to the summer crowd, so it was fairly deserted this late in the season. But Alice didn't mind that her cabin smelled musty or that the wind, when it was blowing in off the bay, filtered in through the cracks around the door and window frame. For the time being it was home. Best of all, the manager, a middle-aged man who'd reeked of nicotine, hadn't looked askance at her when she'd checked in; as long as her money was good, she could be Jack the Ripper for all he cared. The hot shower she yearned for would have to wait, though; there was something she needed to do first.

She turned onto Bellmore Road instead, headed in the direction of the church where she and her family used to attend services when she was growing up. Pulling up in front, she saw that it was exactly as she remembered, a century-old white clapboard structure with a modest spire sitting in the middle of what had once been an apple orchard. Alice recalled wandering through the orchard with her sister after services, hunting for apples amid the stunted trees that remained, while their parents had lingered on the front steps of the church, chatting with fellow congregants. Now she scarcely noticed the trees as she made her way along the narrow path that led to the small churchyard in back. It was where her father and grandparents, Nana and Grandpa Joe, were buried. And her son.

David's grave, tucked all the way in back, under an old maple tree, would have been difficult to locate if she hadn't known the way by heart. There was only a simple bronze marker engraved with his name and the dates of his birth and death. She'd wanted a proper headstone, but Randy had insisted on something simpler.

"You think advertising it to the world is going to change the fact that our son's dead?" he'd shouted at her, when their disagreement had flared into an argument. "I don't need some fancy inscription to remind me. He's *gone*, Alice. That's the only thing that matters."

Looking into his grief-stricken face she had seen that he blamed her. For not being more vigilant, perhaps—if she'd been a better mother, David would still be alive. And she'd given in to Randy then because she'd known he was right: She *was* responsible for their son's death. If not directly, then through her negligence. Reflecting on it now, Alice saw that moment as the turning point. In the immediate aftermath of their son's death, she and Randy had clung to each other like survivors of a shipwreck, but in mourning they'd gone their separate ways. Randy wanting to move on, Alice unable to.

Yet however many times she played it back in her mind, she could never see a different outcome. It was as if she had been heading down a steep slope, picking up speed along the way, until she'd finally lost control.

Luckily, neither she nor Jeremy had been hurt when her car plowed into Owen White. Owen wasn't so fortunate. Emerging from a coma after two days, he'd learned that he would never walk again. Alice had been out on bail when the news reached her, and it had been clear from the cold shoulders and pitiless looks she'd gotten as she'd walked the streets of Bell Harbor that she'd already been tried and found guilty. If it hadn't been for her family, she didn't know how she would have coped. The only one who'd been less than supportive was Randy; he'd seen that final act of insanity as a betrayal of sorts, proof she had already left him, if only in her mind.

Four months later she was led off in handcuffs, bound for the Pine River Correctional Facility in Olympia.

Alice blinked away the tears obscuring her vision as she gazed down at David's grave. It felt as if she'd lost two sons. But how could she expect Jeremy to forgive her when she couldn't forgive herself? She wouldn't shed any tears for Owen White; he'd only gotten what he deserved. But her family had paid a steep price for what she'd done, and for that she was deeply sorry.

She caught a flash of movement out of the corner of her eye and turned to see a dog streaking down the path that led to the outlook: black with a blaze of white on its chest—the border collie from the ferry landing the other day. Alice briefly considered going after it—maybe it was lost and its owner was looking for it—but the dog quickly vanished from sight. Anyway, didn't she have enough problems of her own? No job, nowhere to live. Without her modest savings—her share of the inheritance when Nana's house was sold—she, too, would be roaming about without a roof over her head.

With a deep sigh, she started back toward her car.

CHAPTER FOUR

Colin found the dog curled asleep on the porch. It was the morning of his third day on the island and he'd just poured himself a mug of coffee and stepped outside to enjoy the sunrise. The furry bundle materialized into a dog on all fours: the border collie from the ferry landing. It scooted out of reach, then sat back to eye him warily.

"Good morning to you, too." Colin placed his mug on the porch railing and squatted down on his haunches so that he was eye level with the dog. "Hungry?" he asked. The dog cocked its head, fixing its liquid, dark eyes on him with keen interest. "I'll take that as a yes." Colin went back inside, returning several minutes later with a bowl containing Rice Krispies mixed with a little bit of hamburger meat left over from last night's supper. He set it down, saying, "I'm sorry if it's not what you're used to. I wasn't expecting company."

The dog took an exploratory sniff. Apparently it met with his satisfaction for he wolfed it down. It wasn't until Colin tried to grab hold of his collar that he retreated, looking faintly offended that Colin had presumed he could be bought off so cheaply. "All right, fair enough," Colin conceded. He backed off, his hand held out in a conciliatory gesture. "You call the shots from now on."

The dog was looking past him toward the house, ears pricked and eyes alert—eyes that seemed to hold an almost human intelligence—as if at any moment he expected to see his master step out the door onto the porch. "You're welcome to have a look around if you like," Colin told him, "but I guarantee you won't find what you're looking for. I'm afraid I'm it." He regarded the animal ruefully. "A pretty poor substitute, I agree, but if you're game, I could use the company."

He'd forgotten how remote a landscape this was, a place where nature held sway and civilization seemed a distant rumor. On the plus side, he hadn't slept this well in years. In the absence of modern-day distractions like TV and the computer, he went to bed when it was dark and rose with the sun. He ate when he was hungry, regardless of mealtimes, and found himself perfectly capable of sitting for hours on end doing nothing but gazing out at the water or watching the deer graze. His grandfather had left a sizeable library, art books mostly as well as biographies of notable artists, and Colin had been perusing them, regretting that he hadn't inherited so much as a thimbleful of the old man's talent. If he were an artist, he'd have been able to capture on canvas what remained locked inside him, just as William had in the portrait over the fireplace. He'd always heard that great art was born of great suffering, and if that was true, then he would have created a masterpiece.

After a shower and a breakfast of hot cereal and a boiled egg, he headed back outside. The sun had disappeared behind the storm clouds that had piled up along the ridge and a cutting wind was blowing in off the ocean. In his old life, Colin would have opted for an indoor activity on a day like this. But he'd already adopted the islanders' habit of ignoring bad weather. A long walk would clear his head, he thought, throwing on his parka and a pair of old Wellingtons that he'd found in the mud room.

The border collie was right where he had left it, holding vigil on the porch. Colin whistled for him, mildly surprised when the dog fell in behind him as he stepped off the porch. He started down the path to the cove, the dog following at a wary distance. Worn to a groove by decades of foot traffic, the path traversed the grassy slope like a frown line in a Brobdingnagian brow before disappearing into the rocks that lined the pebbled beach below. There, driftwood lay piled in heaps, like massive free-form sculptures. Farther out, the tide had retreated to leave a great flat of silt that glistened in the gray light, stubs of rebar bearded with algae protruding here and there like broken teeth: what was left of the old oyster beds. Useless now, growing nothing but barnacles.

Colin remembered when he was a boy looking out his window at night and seeing the distant glow of Mr. Deets's lantern bobbing along the shoreline. Deets always did his harvesting after the tide had gone out, which at certain times of the year meant getting up at an hour when most people were still in bed, often making more than a dozen trips back and forth to his truck before his work was done, work that over the years had left him with calluses on his hands as thick and ridged as the shells of the oysters themselves.

In the daylight hours, Colin would often tag after him, helping to pound in stakes and tighten lines, digging out the oysters that had broken loose and become buried in the silt.

Deets, a crusty old loner, hadn't been much of a conversationalist, but Colin had found him oddly companionable. At home in Queens, with his family, there had been nothing but talk, with very little of substance to say. His mom whiling away her free hours gossiping with the neighbors, and his dad and brother endlessly rehashing sports plays. At an age before Patrick could even add and subtract he could recite the batting average of every player on the Yankees team.

Colin lowered himself onto his haunches, scooping up water as clear as gin from one of the tide pools. He recalled Deets's telling him that there was no better place on earth for growing oysters, and now it seemed a shame to see it lying fallow. But Colin had far bigger concerns at the moment. Like deciding what to do with this place. The sensible thing would be to sell it. As Clark Findlay had pointed out, the land alone was worth quite a bit, and Colin could certainly use the money. When the small account he'd inherited along with the house was depleted he'd be broke, with no prospects. Then what? He'd be just another recovering drunk standing amid the smoking ruins of his burned bridges.

Nonetheless, something kept getting in the way of common sense. For one thing, this place was the only thing keeping him anchored. Without it, he'd be truly lost. More so than in the days and weeks after 9/11, when, in a city plastered with grainy Xeroxes of missing loved ones, he'd at least had a role to play: that of Family Member. For in losing his wife on that day he'd been thrust into the ranks of the similarly bereaved, their collective grief a kind of national emblem. Like the war heroes of previous generations, they'd been sought after by the press and trotted out at official ceremonies. Politicians had courted them and charitable institutions had raised money on their behalf. And if the outpouring of public sympathy had seemed overwhelming at times, it had provided him both with a dark purpose and a reason to go on . . . and to drink.

Two years later, he'd come to the realization that the statute of limitations on his mourning had run out. He'd watched the compassion in other people's eyes turn to pity, then disgust. Yes, you lost a loved one, they seemed to say, but so did a lot of other people, and look how they're moving on. His excuses for not showing up for work on time had worn equally thin, and his frequent hangovers hadn't gone unnoticed. His boss had begun assigning him the bottom of the barrel cases: petty offenders and prostitutes, low-level drug dealers and, in one nastily ironic instance, a drunk driver charged with reckless endangerment. Outside of work, friends who'd helped him through the early days of his bereavement had stopped calling. In the end, there had only been his best friend, Billy Munroe, whom he'd known since the second grade, and even Billy had finally checked out on him after one too many drunken late night calls. "Christ, man, get it together!" Billy had exploded before hanging up for the last time. "This is getting old."

But by then Colin had been past the point of being able to pull himself together. He'd realized on that day, to his horror, horror that had gradually hardened into a kind of grim acceptance, that his dead wife was no longer the reason he drank. While the keenness of his loss remained undiminished, except when dulled by booze—a Ground Zero-size hole in his gut that no amount of public sympathy could fill—it wasn't why he'd been pretty much shit-faced all day, every day. Colin had drunk because he couldn't not drink.

It hadn't always been that way. In college, and later on in law school, at Columbia, he'd done his share of partying, sure, but he'd known when to stop after the party had gone on a little too long. And maybe Nadine had had something to do with it as well. He'd met her during his first year of law school. Even after all this time, he could still recall every detail of that meeting. He'd stopped for a bite to eat at his favorite diner, on Broadway and One Hundred and First, where the food was cheap and the portions enormous, enough to last him all day and still leave money for subway fare, when he'd looked up from the menu to find, in place of his regular waitress, a black-haired beauty with buttermilk skin and the most kissable lips he'd ever laid eyes on.

"You're staring at me," she'd said, with a self-conscious laugh, as he'd sat there gaping at her in speechless wonderment. "Do I have something in my teeth?"

"No, I'm sorry . . . I just . . . you're not Sally," he'd stammered in reply.

"No, I'm not Sally." The girl had given him a saucy little smile, as if they were in on some private little joke. "Did you want to order, or would you rather come back when she's here?"

He'd smiled back. "I'll have the BLT, light on the mayo." She was scribbling the order on her pad, when he'd remarked, "I haven't seen you around before. You new here?"

"It's my first day." She'd leaned in to confide, with a whiff of some subtle scent that had gone through him in a heady rush. "Don't tell anyone, but I'm not really a waitress. This is just what I do to pay the rent." She'd explained that she was an actress, injecting a note of irony into her voice, to let him know she was aware that she was a walking cliché.

"Have you been in any plays I might have seen?" he'd asked.

"Not unless you were one of the six people who caught the off-off-Broadway production of *Cry in the Wilderness*," she'd said, with a twinkle in her eye.

He'd found her attitude refreshing. The other actresses he'd known all took themselves so goddamn seriously. When his sandwich came, he'd found himself eating more slowly than usual, stealing glances at her as she'd bustled about. When she wasn't taking care of other customers, he'd chatted her up over endless refills of coffee.

Her name was Nadine and she'd lived in the city all her life, he'd learned. She was a fan of Woody Allen movies and her favorite music was jazz; until two years ago she'd lived with her parents, in a co-op on the Upper West Side, but now she shared a fifth-floor walk-up in Chelsea with three of her friends. When the check came, Colin had asked if they could meet for coffee later on. Nadine had grinned at that—he was already so wired on caffeine it would take him the rest of the day to come down—but she'd taken him up on the offer nonetheless.

Six months later, they were married. He'd been in his second year of law school and she'd still been making the rounds of auditions, waitressing on the side. They were living in an Alphabet City tenement, barely able to make ends meet, yet he had never been happier. With Nadine, every day was an adventure. She had friends from all walks of life, and the parties she was fond of throwing were a mix of young professionals and out-of-work actors, hard hats and transvestites, university students and professors. Colin grew used to coming home from a day of classes to find his wife out on the stoop chatting with one of the homeless people from the neighborhood.

Nadine herself had been a study in contrasts. She'd hated to cook but was a connoisseur of every ethnic eatery on the Lower East Side. She was allergic to dogs and cats but loved nothing better than to spend an afternoon at the zoo. Her only real flaw had been that she was maddeningly late for everything. Yet whenever she finally did breeze in, amid a storm of windblown hair and effusive apologies, after having kept him waiting for half an hour or more, it would always be as if his day hadn't truly started until just then.

The irony was that the day she'd died was one of the few he could remember her leaving for work on time. By then, she'd given up acting in lieu of a full-time position as assistant manager at Windows on the World. He remembered her last words to him as she'd been dashing out the door. She'd paused, turning to him with that grin of hers that could melt a polar ice cap, "Hey, you, in the white boxers. Anyone ever tell you how sexy you are?"

Two hours later she was dead.

Now, five years later, Colin stared at his reflection in the shallow water rippling at his feet. He didn't know how long he'd been hunkered there, caught up in his memories, but it must have been a while for his muscles registered a complaint as he straightened. I should get to the gym more often, he thought, wincing. His main focus, in the six months since he'd gotten out of rehab, had been staying sober. That was where he'd been, in fact, at a halfway house in Arizona, when he'd learned of his grandfather's death. The news had devastated him, largely because he hadn't had a chance to say good-bye; he'd been so caught up in his own problems, which, fueled by alcohol, had become all-consuming, that he'd kept in only sporadic touch. He hadn't even been in any kind of shape to attend the funeral.

Now it was time to figure out what to do with the part of his life that didn't revolve around AA.

He looked around to find the dog eyeing him as if it were wondering the same thing. A bleak smile surfaced on Colin's face. "Come on, boy, let's get you home," he said, starting up the path.

His neighbors up the road turned out to be a couple around his age named the Henleys. They had two young children, a boy and a girl who expressed delight at the return of their missing pet. The little boy threw his arms around the dog's neck, burying his face in its fur, to which it submitted with a dignified tolerance.

"We were wondering where he'd gotten to this time. Thanks for bringing him back," said Nora Henley, a brisk little woman with thick, reddish-blond hair cut in a wedge. She eyed the dog with a mixture of pity and exasperation. "We took him in because we were afraid he'd be put down otherwise, but now I'm not so sure we did him any favors. I think he'd gladly have followed the old man. The poor thing hasn't been the same since he went." She brought her gaze back to Colin. "I'm sorry about your grandfather. We've only been here a year, so we didn't know him all that well. But he was a good neighbor. Tommy"—she glanced toward the little boy now fetching the dog a bowl of water— "really took a shine to him. We all felt he'd have wanted us to look after Shep."

Shep. Colin turned the name over in his mind. Yes, it fit. What was he but a shepherd who'd lost his purpose in life? "I was around your son's age when I first started coming here," he told the Henleys. "My grandfather had a different dog then, a border collie like Shep. His name was Dickie. I wonder if they're from the same bloodline."

"Mr. Deets would have been the one to ask," said Doug Henley, a rangy, bespectacled man with thinning brown hair, a good foot taller than his diminutive wife. "He lived in this house for over forty years, did you know that? That's what his niece told us."

Colin recalled now the lawyer, Findlay, having mentioned something about a niece. As a kid, Colin hadn't been aware of Deets having any family; a lifelong bachelor, he might have sprung from sea, like the creatures from which he'd made his meager living.

"She lives in Seattle," Doug went on. "That's why she sold the place; she didn't want to be bothered with the upkeep. Frankly, I don't blame her. It was pretty rundown when we bought it." He put an arm around Nora's shoulders. "My poor wife got stuck with most of the work. I was busy wrapping up things on the mainland at the time." He explained that he'd sold his partnership in a group dental practice to open a private practice here on the island.

Colin could see all the work that had gone into refurbishing the old fisherman's cottage. Cedar shingles replaced the original batten-board siding, and a new metal roof gleamed where the old moss-grown one had been. The garden, too, had been transformed, flowerbeds and tidy borders reinforced with railroad ties where there'd been only a wild green tangle. There was even a man-made brook that spilled into a pond stocked with koi.

"The only thing we haven't gotten to yet is the shed," said Nora, gesturing toward the ramshackle structure out back. "It's so crammed full of old stuff, I couldn't even tell you what most of it is."

Colin's pulse quickened. "Mind if I take a look?"

"Be our guest," said Doug, looking as if he'd be only too happy to have Colin take any or all of that junk off his hands.

"Thanks." Colin headed around back under the watchful eye of Shep.

As he pushed open the door to the shed, its rusty hinges gave with a loud squeal of protest. Inside, he batted blindly about overhead until his hand met with a pull chain. He yanked on it and the light came on, throwing into shadowy relief a stack of old crates pushed up against one wall. It took his eyes a little while longer to assemble into individual shapes the jumble around him: coiled ropes, a leaning tower of buckets stacked one atop the other, a pile of burlap sacks covered in mold that gave off a dank odor. Inside a box containing various pieces of equipment, he found an assortment of rusted shucking knives and a pair of leather gloves stiff with age. All that was left of a small yet once-thriving oyster farm.

By the time Colin emerged from the shed, streaked with grime, a vague plan had begun taking shape in his mind. Why couldn't he start an oyster farm of his own? He had the land and nothing but time on his hands, and there was enough equipment here to cobble together a basic operation. He could always buy whatever else he needed. A fine plan . . . except it would mean staying on Grays Island, not selling his grandfather's place. Could he afford to do that?

Can you afford not to? countered a voice in his head. What was waiting for him back in New York except more excuses to drink? It wasn't as if he had a job to go back to, or friends urging him to return. And this way he'd at least have a purpose, even if it made sense to no one but him.

He shook off the excitement growing in him. He'd have to do his homework before he made any final decisions. For now, he merely informed the Henleys that he'd be happy to haul off any of the junk they wanted to get rid of. They told him he could have it all, and he jotted down their number, promising to return as soon as he'd lined up a truck.

He was walking away, with a new spring in his step, when he happened to glance back over his shoulder. The dog, Shep, had gone back inside, but Colin could see him in the window, peering out at Colin, ears pricked as if in expectation. It seemed a good omen somehow.

Two hours later, Colin was standing in line at the public library with several books on oyster farming to check out. The librarian, a pretty young woman with long blond hair held back with a headband, was taking her time with the elderly man in front of Colin, suggesting some books he might like in place of the one he had on reserve that wasn't in yet. No one seemed to be in any hurry, even those in line behind Colin. No clearing of throats or rolling of eyes; no one muttering loudly, *Is this going to take all day?* A reminder that he wasn't in New York; that was why people moved here, to get away from just that sort of thing. His impatience must have shown on his face, though, for he caught the eye of a woman walking past, who smiled knowingly. A woman he recognized at once as Alice Kessler.

As soon as he'd gotten his books stamped, he went in search of her. He found her at one of the tables in the periodicals section. "Hello again. Colin McGinty, we met at the ferry landing," he said to refresh her memory.

But it was clear from the way she was looking at him that she'd needed no introduction. "Yes, hi. How are you?" She kept her voice low, as if not wanting to draw attention to herself.

"Not bad." He realized, to his surprise, that he meant it. For the first time in months he didn't feel an oppressive pall hanging over him. He eyed the newspaper spread open in front of her to the real estate section. "Find what you're looking for?"

"Not in my price range. But I'm not exactly in a position to be picky. As long as it's four walls and a roof over my head, it'll do. What about you? Looks like you've decided to stick around awhile." She gestured toward the books under his arm.

"For the time being, at least. Until I get things sorted out." Colin felt reluctant to discuss his plans. They seemed wildly impractical even to him at this point.

"Family business?" She reminded him of his stated reason for being here.

This wasn't the time or place to get into it, so he merely said, "It's complicated."

"With family, it's always complicated." She smiled. "Just when you think it's safe to go back into the water . . . "

"You sound as though you've had some experience with that." She shrugged, as if to say, Who hasn't? "So what are your plans? Beyond finding a place to live, that is," he asked.

Her expression clouded over briefly. "I've been job hunting, but so far no luck. Seems good-paying positions are hard to come by on this island."

"Keep looking. Something will turn up eventually." Easier said than done when you're a convicted felon, he knew.

A flush rose in her cheeks, as if she'd read his mind.

An older woman seated at the other end of the table made a shushing motion, and Colin leaned in to whisper, "What do you say we grab a cup of coffee? I wouldn't want to run afoul of the library police." She hesitated long enough for him to wonder if he'd overstepped the bounds, then she nodded and rose to her feet.

Outside, they strolled along the sidewalk in companionable silence. She was wearing her brown hair loose today; it was blowing around her face in the wind. She looked prettier than he remembered, not so pale and pinched. Only her eyes were the same—those of someone cold and hungry peering in through a window at a happy family seated around the dinner table.

The weather had warmed up a bit, so they got their coffees to go and headed for the town green. Across the street stood the museum, housed in a log cabin from the days when Grays Island was a remote trading post, but with tourist season winding down there was no one else about, except a teenage boy tossing a Frisbee to his dog and a maintenance worker pruning one of the trees. They sat down at a picnic table, steam rising from their cups to mingle with their breath.

"This is nice," she said, looking around her at the grass carpeted in gold and crimson leaves, the sturdy maples, the creek that wound along the north end of the green. "I've been so busy since I got back, I haven't had a chance to sit back and enjoy the scenery."

"Seems like I've been doing nothing but that," replied Colin.

She turned to him. "I heard your grandfather left you his place." At the startled look he gave her, she added, in a rueful tone, perhaps thinking of her own notoriety, "Word travels fast in small towns."

"Well, you heard right."

"There's talk that you're planning to sell."

"That so? Well, they must know something I don't," he said. "Actually, I'm thinking I may hang on to it."

"So you'd live here full-time?"

"Looks that way."

"Don't you have a job to go back to?"

"Let's just say I'm between jobs at the moment."

"I understand you're a lawyer."

"Was," he corrected. "In my previous life, I was a prosecutor for the Manhattan D.A.'s office."

"I see. Well." She blew on her coffee before taking a careful sip. She appeared unsettled by what he'd just told her. It was easy to see why. What must it have been like for her, all those years in prison? Put away by a hard-hitting prosecutor not so different from himself.

"I'm sorry if I've made you uncomfortable," he said, touching her arm.

"Ah, so you've heard. The infamous Alice Kessler." Her mouth twisted in a pained smile.

"Only what I've read in the papers," he said.

"Don't believe everything you read."

"I don't. Anyway, it was a long time ago."

"Not to people around here. To them, it's like it happened yesterday."

"Like you said, it's a small town."

"You're probably wondering why I came back."

"Why did you?" He sipped his coffee, eyeing her thoughtfully over the rim of his cup.

"My son. His name is Jeremy. He's sixteen." He saw something flare in her gray-green eyes. "He's living with his father right now, but I'm hoping . . ." She bit her lip, and fell silent. After a moment, she said, "What about you? There must be a reason for moving here besides the fact that you inherited a house."

"I'm not sure I have one, unless it's that this just happens to be the last stop on the line." Colin zipped up his jacket against a sudden gust of chill, and sat gazing out vacantly over the green. "If you know so much about me, you probably also know that I lost my wife. Things kind of went downhill after that."

"I'm sorry." He could tell from the way she said it that she was no stranger to that kind of loss.

"She died on 9/11. She was in the North Tower when it went down," he went on, finding it strangely cathartic to be talking about it with someone who wouldn't wrinkle her brow in an attempt to understand the unfathomable, who wouldn't be looking for a graceful way of segueing to a less painful topic. "After that, I started hitting the bottle, until it dawned on me one day that the problem wasn't what was eating me, it was *me*." He gave in to a bleak smile. "You'd think that's when I would have known it was time to quit, but it actually took a little longer than that before I finally decided to get sober. I had to lose my job first, and pretty much every friend I ever had. That was six months ago. I haven't touched a drop since."

They exchanged a look that communicated more than any words. She wasn't like most people he met outside of AA meetings, those for whom a life crisis meant getting laid off from their jobs or having their mother-in-law move in with them. Alice Kessler knew what real suffering was.

Now her mouth hooked up in a mirthless little smile. "We're a fine pair, aren't we? They say misery loves company, but right now I wouldn't wish either of us on anyone."

"It must be some comfort, at least, to know you're not the only one being talked about," he said, with a laugh.

"Fortunately that's not the only thing we have in common," she replied, her expression sobering. "I don't know if you were aware of this or not, but apparently your grandfather was a friend of grandmother's. In fact, he painted her portrait. The famous one, of the woman in the red dress. I was wondering if you knew what became of it."

Colin jerked upright, nearly spilling his coffee. "You're Eleanor's granddaughter?" He could see the resemblance now, and he wondered if perhaps that was why he'd been drawn to her from the beginning. Alice's coloring was darker than Eleanor's, her eyes more gray than green, but it was the same face: fine boned yet strong as tempered steel. The face of someone who didn't tread lightly through life. "What an amazing coincidence. Now I know why you looked familiar. You're the spitting image of her."

Alice looked pleased. "So you're familiar with the portrait."

"I ought to be. I own it."

Now it was her turn to look surprised. "Really? Would you mind . . . I mean, I'd love to see it sometime." She seemed hesitant to impose.

"Anytime you like," he told her. "I'm usually home. Just give me a call whenever you feel like stopping by. Here's my number." He scribbled it on the back of his napkin.

She carefully folded the napkin and tucked it into her pocket. "Are you sure it wouldn't be a bother?"

"Are you kidding? You'd be doing me a favor," he told her. "It's so quiet out there, I can hear myself think. Which in my case tends to be dangerous."

She broke into a smile, a genuine one that for a dazzling instant lit up her whole face, like when the sun made one of its rare appearances from behind the clouds. In the parking area at the other end of the green, music drifted from a car radio, some seventies ballad, and closer by the boy tossing the Frisbee sent it sailing skyward once more, a spinning blue circle that hung aloft for a long moment, seeming to defy gravity. In that brief moment Colin felt his spirits lift as well.

"All right then. I'll take you up on it," she said. "But first I have to find a job and a place to live, in that order."

"What kind of job are you looking for?" he asked.

"You mean what am I good at besides making license plates?" She shook her head. "Not much, I'm afraid. I used to be a pretty good cook, but I'm a little out of practice."

"There are lots of restaurants on the island," he said.

"None that are interested in hiring a convicted felon. Believe me, I know. I've applied to all the ones advertising for help."

"Something will turn up, I'm sure," he said. "In the meantime, don't give up hope. In AA, we have a saying: 'Fake it 'till you make it.' I've been doing a lot of that myself lately."

"Thanks. I'll keep that in mind." This time her smile seemed forced. She stood up, tossing her empty cup into the trash. "Well, I should get going. It was nice talking to you. I'll give you a call when I know what my plans are."

"Good luck with the search," he said, shaking hands with her as they parted.

"Thanks. See you soon, I hope."

He felt a quickening inside at the thought. It wasn't just that he wanted to get to know her better, it was the sense of connection he felt with her. They were kindred spirits, no matter the different circumstances which had landed them both in the same place. Like him, Alice Kessler knew that the world was full of dark corners and jagged edges.

CHAPTER FIVE

May 1942

Eleanor Styles awoke to the sound of the dogs barking in the kennel outside. Even in her groggy, half-aware state, she could tell from the high pitch of the barking that it wasn't a deer or raccoon that had gotten them so worked up, more likely a visitor of the two-legged variety. Immediately she was out from under the covers and on her feet. A glance at the clock by the bed told it was half past eight. So late! Usually, she was up while it was still dark, but she'd had trouble sleeping the night before and hadn't dropped off until well after midnight.

She reached for the chenille robe draped over one of the bed's four squat posts. Normally it would have been hanging in the closet, but with her husband Joe off fighting in the Pacific, she'd allowed some things to slide. It was enough just keeping the rest of the house tidy and looking after her daughter—not to mention the dogs and chickens and victory garden to tend to. It was only in the bedroom she'd shared with her husband of over ten years that her presence had gradually begun to assert itself, like the blackberry vines that had swallowed up the fence along the drive in Joe's absence. Shoes were tucked willy-nilly under the bed and her work overalls, still damp from bathing the dogs yesterday, slung over the padded rocker. Various tubes of ointment and bottles of worming tablets littered the dressing table where powder and perfumes had once stood, and on the nightstand, in place of Joe's *Reader's Digest*, sat a war bond pledge booklet leftover from last week's drive, a book on canine diseases, and an article clipped from the newspaper listing the new blackout rules.

She padded barefoot over to the window, peering out through the fog of her breath on the pane at a car pulling to a stop in the yard, a dark green Packard she didn't recognize. She was unaccustomed to visitors, especially at this hour, and with the new war restrictions, fewer automobiles were out on the road these days. Was it some sort of official business? She grew cold at the thought. But, no, the man getting out of the car—youngish, dark haired, wearing khakis and a shirt rolled up at the sleeves—didn't look like a messenger. And if it was bad news, he'd have been an odd sort to deliver it, smiling like he was, as if in pleasant thought, his face tilted up to catch the sun. As he made his way up the front path, she noticed that he walked with a limp. From the practiced way he hitched the leg along with scarcely a break in stride, it appeared to be an old injury.

She let out the breath she'd been holding and forked a hand through her hair, which only made it crinkle into a halo about her head, hair the reddish brown of the madrona tree under which the man was now pausing to look around. Then a new thought occurred to her: If it wasn't bad news about Joe, it might be official business of a different sort. In a panic, her eyes flew to the barn, which had been converted into a kennel with an outdoor run enclosed in chicken wire, where at the moment all six dogs were barking madly at the stranger's approach. Catching a movement in the window of the small, furnished room off the dogs' quarters, she wondered if her visitor had noticed it, too. Was that why he was taking his sweet time? Her heart lurched at the thought as a knock sounded.

Putting on her slippers and tightening the belt on her robe, she went to answer the door.

"I'm sorry. I hope I didn't wake you," the man apologized, noting her attire. "I saw the smoke from your chimney and thought . . ." He craned his neck to look upward.

"I keep a fire burning at night," she said. With the wartime ban on oil, even coal was scarce, and the old house Joe's father had built was so poorly insulated that even in the spring months she had to maintain the fire 'round the clock.

"William McGinty," he introduced himself, touching his brow in a jaunty two-fingered salute. "And you must be Missus Styles." She nodded, thinking the name sounded familiar—had they met before? No, she would have remembered that face. He was around her age, thirty or so, tall and whippet-lean, with startlingly blue eyes and a shock of black hair that didn't seem to want to stay put. He looked harmless enough, but that did nothing to put her mind at ease. He could be one of Sheriff LaPorte's henchmen, for all she knew. As captain of the home guard, LaPorte had made it his business to mercilessly hound anyone suspected of being an enemy agent. Like poor Otto Haller, the town's elderly German druggist, who'd been forced to sell his pharmacy and move off the island, his life had become so intolerable. *What would LaPorte do if he were to ever get his hands on a real fugitive?* she wondered, feeling an icy chill pass over her.

"What can I do for you?" she asked. Her tone was pleasant, but she kept a hand on the doorknob and an eye on the shotgun propped just inside.

"I was driving past and happened to notice your sign. I was wondering if you had any puppies for sale." The man named William gave her a wide smile that engaged his whole face, a face that might otherwise have seemed austere in its stark angularity.

Some of the tension went out of her shoulders. "Not at the moment, but I have a litter due any day. Was it a male or a female you were looking for?"

"Either one will do. I don't really have a preference." He shifted from one foot to the other, favoring his good leg. Glancing past him, she could see the clothesline hung with yesterday's wash, which she hadn't gotten around to taking down: a sheet billowing in the breeze, a red-checked tablecloth with a burn mark where she'd gotten a bit too assiduous with the iron one time, a corduroy pinafore of Lucy's, a flannel nightgown, several slips, a blouse.

And a pair of men's skivvies.

A jolt went through her. Oh God. How could she have been so careless?

Had he noticed it, too? He might not have thought anything of it, but if he were to learn later on that her husband was off fighting overseas, he'd wonder what she'd been doing with men's underthings on the line. And if he should happen to make mention of it, and word got around . . .

Her gut clenched at the thought. In an attempt to keep him from noticing anything was amiss, she asked, "What made you decide on a border collie?"

"No particular reason." He made a vague gesture with his hand. Like I said, I saw your sign and . . . well . . . I just thought . . ." He seemed suddenly unsure of himself, as if it had only been an impulse.

"They're working dogs," she informed him, speaking more sharply than she'd intended. "If all you want is a pet, I'd suggest another breed." She had no patience for people who acquired puppies the way they did toys, often discarding them when they ceased to be amusing or proved difficult to housebreak.

But he took no offense. His smile only broadened, deepening the creases that bracketed his wide, expressive mouth like parentheses. She was struck once more by how blue his eyes were; a shade so deep it was almost purple, the color of the crocuses that had recently begun pushing their way up out of the spring-thawed ground. "If you don't mind me saying so, Missus Styles, you sure have a funny way of doing business," he said, in that tone of easy familiarity that made it seem as if he were taking liberties somehow. "If you've got something against me buying one of your puppies, just say so, and I'll be on my way."

She relented a bit, saying in a less frosty tone, "My dogs aren't boxes of soap powder for sale. I want to be sure they go to good homes."

"In that case, why don't you come have a look at mine. I'll introduce you to my wife and son. We live out on Cove Road." So he was married, which surprised her for some reason. "Actually, I wanted the puppy for my son. He has a birthday coming up in a few weeks. He'll be nine."

Eleanor gave in to a small smile. "I have a daughter the same age. They must be in the same class at school. I'm surprised we haven't met before."

"Usually it's my wife who picks Danny up from school," he explained. "Most afternoons, I'm holed up in my studio."

She knew then why his name had struck a chord. "Wait. I know you. You're *that* William McGinty. The artist." There was usually a mention of him in travel articles about the island, and recently there had been a show of his paintings at Darvill's bookstore downtown. "I've seen some of your work," she told him.

"What did you think?" he asked, as if honestly interested in her opinion.

She thought back to that day. She'd been out shopping, with a half hour or so to kill before she had to pick up Lucy from school. She'd ducked into Darvill's, where she'd become captivated by the display of paintings on the walls, landscapes mostly, scenes from around the island, rendered in such detail it was almost as though she were looking at them through a window. "There was one in particular, of a deer standing at the edge of a clearing, with snow falling. It was so . . . I can't explain it . . . It made me feel so peaceful." She felt herself warming. "But what do I know about art? I only know what I like."

"When you get right down to it, that's all that really matters," he said.

She sensed he was being sincere. Before she knew it, she was saying, "Would you like to come inside? I was just about to put on some coffee."

"If you're sure it's no trouble," he said.

"No trouble at all." Eleanor had an ulterior motive. She was hoping to distract him long enough for Lucy to wake up. A whispered word to her daughter to take the wash down, and he'd be none the wiser about the skivvies. "You take yours black, I hope," she asked as she ushered him inside. "I'm fresh out of milk. It's such a long way into town, I usually wait until I have a whole list of things to get."

"Black is fine," he said. They were passing through the hallway on their way to the kitchen when he paused to take a closer look at one of the family photos lining the wall, of Joe in uniform. "Your husband?"

"Yes." She felt a little flutter of panic. Suppose he put two and two together and realized men's clothing didn't belong on the line with her husband away at war.

"A navy man, I see. Where's he stationed?"

"Last I heard, the Philippines. It's hard to keep track. Sometimes weeks go by without a single letter, then we'll get a whole bundle all at once." Even then, the letters would be riddled with holes where the censors had snipped out any mention that might be considered classified information.

"He's fighting for his country. I guess that's all anyone needs to know." William's expression hardened all of a sudden. "I tried to enlist, but they wouldn't take me on account of this." He rubbed a hand over his bum leg, grimacing a bit as if it pained him, though she sensed whatever pain he felt was more mental than physical. With nearly every able-bodied man his age off fighting in the war, he had to feel the frustration of being sidelined.

"How did you injure it?" she asked, looking down at his leg.

"I broke it skiing when I was in college. Shattered near every bone. Damn thing never healed right."

"Consider yourself lucky." The words flew out of her mouth, and she saw a flicker of surprise cross his face. It was an unpopular view in these times, to say the least, but hadn't there been enough death and destruction due to war? Myra Brookbank had lost her son Ernest in the battle of

Tobruk, and just last week Nellie Gerard had gotten word that her husband's plane went down at Bataan. Eleanor herself prayed nightly for Joe's safe return.

"I'm not sure my wife would agree. These days, having your husband around can be a bit of a liability." He spoke lightly, but she caught a trace of bitterness in his voice. Eleanor was appalled. What kind of wife would prefer a dead hero to a live husband?

They exchanged a meaningful look; then they were in the kitchen and she was lighting the stove, the moment past. "Have you had breakfast?" she asked, as she was filling the coffee pot at the sink. "I could fix you something to eat."

"Thank you kindly, but I've already put you to enough trouble," he replied, looking ill at ease, as if he weren't used to being fussed over. But she didn't miss the look of longing on his face as he eyed the fresh-baked loaf of bread on the counter.

She insisted, "It's no trouble at all. I may be short on supplies, but the one thing I have plenty of is eggs." She explained that she'd invested in laying hens, intending to sell the eggs to earn extra cash, but that due to rationing, she and Lucy ended up eating most of what the chickens laid.

She went to the icebox and took out a bowl of eggs, some still dotted with feathers. At the kitchen counter, with its cracked porcelain tiles that Joe hadn't gotten around to replacing, she took out half a dozen of the largest ones, wrapping each one in newspaper before placing them in a paper sack. She handed the sack to William. "These are for you take home. No charge," she said, when he offered to pay. He started to protest, but she held firm. "It won't do you any good. I always get my way."

"Always?" One of his brows quirked up in bemusement.

"Most of the time, anyway." Eleanor smiled, almost forgetting her purpose in inviting him in. It felt good, having him in her kitchen—another adult with whom to observe the morning rituals. It made her feel less lonely. "It's easier when the only one around to talk back is less than half your size." Though Lucy could be as stubborn as she at times.

They talked while she sliced bread and set strips of bacon in the pan to fry. William told her a story about his son, when Danny, at age five, had been learning to ride a bike, falling off it more times than he'd stayed on but not quitting until he'd gotten the hang of it. Listening to him speak, the tender look on his face making it appealing in a way that had nothing to do with good looks, Eleanor felt suddenly self-conscious of her own appearance as she moved about the kitchen in her robe and slippers, setting out plates and napkins, pouring coffee.

She was about to go wake Lucy, who was showing no signs of rousing on her own, when the back door swung open unexpectedly. Eleanor froze at the sight of Yoshi. The boy looked equally startled. Seeing the strange man seated at the table, he came to an abrupt halt in the doorway, the empty bucket he was carrying, to collect the scraps he mixed with the dogs' food, slipping from his hand and clattering to the floor. Eleanor, jolted into action, clapped a hand over her mouth, letting out a muffled cry.

William leapt to his feet, planting himself in front of her, as if to shield her. But she was quick to clear up any misunderstanding. "It's not what you think. He's . . . he's a friend. It's all right, Yoshi," she reassured the boy. "You're safe." She swung around to fix William with a hot gaze, as if challenging him to dispute it. The moment hung there like something swollen about to burst, William staring at Yoshi as comprehension slowly sank in, Eleanor praying that he wouldn't do anything rash. At last, the silence was broken by William.

"What's your name?" he asked the boy, not unkindly.

Yoshi, his head hung low, didn't reply. At eighteen, he was a boy still, with a boy's slight build and unevenly cut bangs that hung in a ragged fringe over his forehead.

"His English isn't very good. But he's harmless, I promise," Eleanor explained, tripping over her words in her haste to get them out. Yoshi had worked for Joe on his fishing boat before the war, an orphan who'd become almost like a son to them. After Joe had gone off to battle she'd allowed Yoshi to continue sleeping on the boat, paying him to do odd jobs for her. Then, last month, word had come that Japanese Americans were being shipped off to internment camps, and she'd taken the bold move of hiding him in her barn. When Sheriff LaPorte had come looking for Yoshi, she concocted a story about his having run off. She knew the risk she was taking—she could be charged with treason—but she couldn't bear the idea of Yoshi being locked up when he'd done nothing wrong.

She cast William a beseeching look. "You won't tell anyone, will you?"

Until now she'd entrusted the secret only to Lucy. Could she honestly expect this man whom she'd only just met to keep it as well? A man not fit to wear a uniform who, for all she knew, might wish to snatch some glory for himself, if only to become a hero to his wife.

Her heart sank as William slowly shook his head, wearing a look of disgust. *We're done for*, she thought. *This is where he'll tell me I'm a disgrace to my husband and my country*. She felt herself growing angry in anticipation of his words. What right did he have to judge her, or Yoshi? He hadn't seen how hard the boy had worked for little pay, hauling in nets that would have bowed the backs of men twice his size. Even now, he remained grateful for every scrap, uncomplaining in the face of what most people in his shoes would consider an outrage. And what was so patriotic, anyway, about locking up innocent people. *American citizens*, for God's sake. Everyone who went along with it ought to be ashamed. And if she were to be punished for it herself, then at least she'd go down with a clear conscience.

When William spoke, it was a moment before his words filtered through the storm of recriminations gathering in her head. "What kind of a person do you take me for?" he asked.

"I wouldn't know," she replied, thrusting her chin out.

"You know I like dogs." He retrieved the bucket Yoshi had dropped and handed it to him. When William straightened, she saw that he was smiling.

Eleanor remained distrustful nonetheless; she wasn't a woman to be won over by a charming Irishman with a quick wit and a ready smile. "So does Hitler, from what I've heard."

"You really think I'd turn him in?" He flicked a glance at Yoshi.

"You might see it as your patriotic duty."

"Patriotic?" He snorted in contempt, and turned to address Yoshi. "You can relax. I won't breathe a word of this to anyone." The boy eyed him in confusion as William went on, more sternly, "But you're going to have to be a lot more careful from now on. If it had been someone else who'd spotted you, it would have been a different story." Yoshi nodded slowly in comprehension, looking very pale. Eleanor could imagine how it must have happened, the boy not quite awake yet, stumbling around back, not paying attention to William's Packard parked in the drive.

He's right, she thought: They'd grown lax, and had nearly paid a steep price for it.

"I . . . am most grateful to you, sir," Yoshi managed in his halting English.

"You can drop the 'sir.' My friends call me William. Or just plain Will. Now," he turned toward Eleanor, his stern look melting, "why don't you set an extra place for Yoshi here? Seems to me we ought to get to know each other if I'm going to be in on this."

"In on what?" she asked warily.

"You don't expect me to just walk away and pretend I never saw anything?" he said in disbelief.

She tensed. "What are you suggesting?"

"Well, for starters, you don't want people asking questions, so I'll be bringing your supplies from now on," William went on, as if he'd had it all figured out in the time it had taken her to catch her breath. "All it would take is one nosy Parker wanting to know why you're buying enough to feed three people for the home guard to come sniffing around."

"Wouldn't they be suspicious of you?" she asked.

He shrugged. "Maybe, but I have nothing to hide."

She tipped her head back to look up at him, this tall, austere-faced man with his great head of black hair in need of combing. She felt a curious mixture of gratitude and lingering mistrust. Why was he doing this? He barely knew her, and Yoshi was a complete stranger.

"Even so, if you were to get caught, you could get into a lot of trouble," she cautioned. "Why stick your neck out?"

"Maybe it's to make sure there's a pup in that litter with my name on it," he said, breaking into a grin. "Or maybe I'm just plain crazy. Who knows? But you're hardly in a position to refuse."

"So much for winning every argument." She threw up her hands in surrender.

Without further ado, William sat down at the table, unfolded his napkin, and smoothed it over his lap. "I take mine over easy," he said, as she cracked eggs into the skillet.

A minister's daughter, Eleanor had been nineteen and pregnant with another man's child when she married Joe Styles. He was ten years older than her and nobody's idea of a catch. A working man, a fisherman by trade, with hard, callused hands and a face as creased and weather-beaten as an old tarp. But he had one shining attribute: He'd gladly taken her when no one else would. In fact, Joe acted as though she were the one bestowing this great favor on him, not the other way around, never once making her feel dirty or ashamed, as her parents had. And when Lucy was born, he'd loved her, too, as if she were his own. So Eleanor told herself it didn't matter that she felt no passion for him. Passion was what had gotten her into trouble. Joe had given her something far better: unconditional love.

But there was no denying that her life with Joe wasn't what she'd imagined for herself when she'd graduated from secretarial school at the age of eighteen. Her first and only job had been with the firm of White and Conner and though a whiz at typing and shorthand, she'd been utterly ignorant about the ways of the world. Her new boss, on the other hand, was a man of the world. Lowell White was handsome in the louche way girls found so thrilling, with an air of late nights and cocktails and ruby-lipped women that swirled about him like smoke from the cigarettes that were forever dangling from the corner of his mouth. He was also an astute businessman. Most of his family's fortune had been lost in the Great Depression, but Lowell had used that very slump to his advantage, little by little buying up real estate while it was dirt cheap and selling at a profit when prices went up. By the time Eleanor had come to work for him, he already owned vast tracts and was rich beyond imagining, with the grandest house on the island and a fifty-foot yacht.

Lowell may have been known to have a weakness for pretty girls, but he never showed Eleanor any special favoritism. In fact, her first few weeks on the job he seemed oblivious to her charms: the small waist and high, full bosom; the long, shapely legs that had driven the boys in school to distraction. She might have been a filing cabinet or the blotting paper on his desk, for all the attention he paid her. That he found her unattractive didn't bother her at first, but as the weeks wore on, she began taking special care with her appearance, choosing her most flattering outfits, using a shade of lipstick darker than the one she normally wore, and arranging her tumble of russet hair atop her head like Betty Grable's. Male clients began to take notice—a few even asked her out on dates, which she, of course, refused—but her boss remained oblivious.

So when one morning he stopped at her desk and told her he had some business on the mainland and needed her to come along, she thought nothing of it. She was pleasantly surprised when, on the ferry ride, he chatted amiably with her the whole way. He was different away from the office, warm and personable, asking about her family and her interests. Before long he knew her entire history, brief and uninteresting though it was: that she lived with her parents in the rectory behind the Episcopal Church, and that she had an older sister named Lillian, who'd gotten married last year, a wedding at which Eleanor had been maid of honor.

By the time the business was wrapped up, the ferry they'd planned to take back was long gone. With several hours to kill until the next one, Lowell offered to buy Eleanor dinner. She readily accepted, imagining it would be just a quick bite at a local tavern, but the restaurant he took her to was fancy, the kind her parents couldn't have afforded. Seeing the red-jacketed waiters gliding past, the damask tablecloths set with silver and crystal that gleamed in the candlelight, she felt as if she'd walked onto a Hollywood set. If it hadn't been for Lowell, steering her lightly by the elbow as they were escorted to their table by the captain, an intimidating-looking man in a starched shirtfront who'd greeted Lowell by name, she'd have turned right around and left. Instead, she found herself sinking into the chair Lowell pulled out for her and nodding mutely when he asked if she'd like some champagne.

After her second glass, she began to feel more relaxed. Never mind that the other girls in the office might get the wrong idea. She knew this wasn't what it looked like; Lowell was being the perfect gentleman. So it came as a shock when, halfway through the meal, he leaned across the table and said, quite matter-of-factly, "You're very beautiful, you know."

Eleanor was speechless. "Thank you. That's nice of you to say," she replied primly when she'd recovered her wits. She lowered her head so that her hair, worn loose that day, fell forward to cover her cheeks that were flushed with more than the champagne.

"I'm sure you hear it all the time," he went on in the same matter-of-fact tone, "but I have a feeling you don't believe it. I just wanted you to know it's true. You are. Breathtaking, in fact."

She peeked from behind the curtain of hair to find him eyeing her with an almost fatherly bemusement. Usually when men said such things, they wanted something in return. But Lowell White seemed content merely to have her bask in the glow of the compliment.

"I . . . I don't know what to say," she stammered.

He smiled, and lit a cigarette. His eyes that in daylight could sometimes appear world-weary were seductively heavy-lidded in the candlelight. "When you're a little older, my dear, you'll know that it's a beautiful woman's prerogative to say nothing at all."

"I'm eighteen!" she protested, which only made him smile all the more.

"Eighteen," he echoed, as if marveling that he himself had ever been that young, though he couldn't have been more than forty. "Well, that calls for another glass of champagne."

It might have been crushed diamonds he was pouring, the way it sparkled as it swirled up from the bottom of her glass. And why was it she'd never noticed before how perfectly shaped his hands were? Square and manly as his physique, which was muscular from sailing. Not like her father's pale, narrow ones that, splayed against the nubby black cover of his bible, resembled dove's wings. Lowell's thick brown hair, combed back in brilliantined waves that to a less discerning eye might have given him the appearance of a slick salesman, had sprung several curls that looped down over his forehead. She found herself wanting to brush them back, thread her fingers through his hair. *What's come over me?* she wondered, aghast at the direction her thoughts had taken.

On the ferry ride home, she imagined it was all her doing when he slipped an arm around her shoulders and, later on, when he gently kissed her good night. She must have led him on in some way, though in her tipsy state she wasn't exactly sure how. At the same time, she felt excited by his attentions, even knowing that her parents would disapprove. She hadn't felt this way with any of the men she'd gone out with before: the deep thrill that had shot down through her belly when Lowell's gaze had lingered a beat too long or his fingers had brushed hers. Each precious moment of the evening she tucked away to be savored later on; she was reluctant even to wash away the smell of cigarette smoke that lingered in her hair when she woke the next morning.

But amazingly, at work, it was as if nothing had happened. Lowell barely glanced at her when he walked in, greeting her only with a curt, "Good morning, Miss Miner," as he breezed past on the way to his office. All morning she was close to tears, wondering what she could have done or said that had put him off. It wasn't until she was leaving work at the end of the day, after having stayed late to type a letter, that everything fell into place.

She was making her way down the stairwell when she looked behind her and saw her boss, hurrying to catch up with her. They were alone, and when he reached her he grabbed her by the shoulders, roughly almost, pushing her back against the wall and kissing her. Not a gentle kiss this time, but a deep and passionate one that involved his tongue.

"God. I've been going out of my mind all day," he breathed. "It's been torture."

Eleanor trembled, wanting for him to go on kissing her and at the same time feeling she was in over her head. He was her boss, after all. And suppose the stories whispered about him were true? "I . . . I thought I'd done something to make you angry," she said in an unsteady voice.

"Angry?" He gave a short, guttural laugh, as if at the absurdity of such an idea. "My God, I could barely concentrate. You've been driving me crazy, looking like that. Even your perfume . . ." He snatched up a handful of her hair, burying his face in it with a groan. "It was all I could do not to walk over there and kiss you in front of everyone." She shivered, both thrilled and scandalized at the thought.

After that, they began slipping away together after hours. She'd lie to her parents about working late or going to the movies with friends and she and Lowell would go on long drives, or he'd take her out on his boat. It was exciting at first, but after a while she began to grow impatient. Why did they have to sneak around? It wasn't as if they had anything to hide. If it became a problem at work, why, she'd just find another job.

But when she timidly broached the subject, he claimed he was only being cautious for her sake. "I could set you up with another job just like that," he said, with a snap of his fingers. "But that wouldn't solve the problem."

"What problem is that?" she asked, half dreading his reply.

"Your parents. Think how it would look to your father, him being a minister and all. His innocent young daughter under the spell of some middle-aged rogue. Believe me, it's best we take it slow."

"Maybe if he got to know you a bit first, it'd be easier when I told him," she suggested.

"What exactly did you have in mind?" asked Lowell, with a sardonic arch of his brow.

"I don't know." Flustered, she cast about in her mind. "You could start attending services on Sunday, for one thing. If they knew you were a churchgoing man . . . "

Lowell cut her off with a laugh. "Darling, you're forgetting one thing. I'm hardly the God-fearing type."

Eleanor kept her mouth shut after that, fooling herself into believing he would eventually do the right thing.

The night she lost her virginity they were out on his yacht, anchored off one of the uninhabited islands that dotted the sound, where there was only the moon to bear witness. He took his time, plucking away at her inhibitions stitch by stitch until at last they came unraveled. He stroked her as she shivered with pleasure, parting her legs as gently as if they were petals on a rose. When he finally entered her, she scarcely felt the pain. Even then he took his time, making love to her the way she'd always dreamed, not giving in to his own pleasure until he'd brought her to climax. As Eleanor fell back against the cushions and tilted her head up to the sky, the stars spilling across it seemingly within reach, she knew at last what it was to desire and be desirable. The fact that she hadn't waited until they were married seemed inconsequential. He would make an honest woman of her before long, as soon he got around to popping the question.

Worry didn't begin to creep in until several more months had gone by without his making a single move in that direction. She began to notice things, too—how he would sometimes seem distracted when they were together, staring off into space while she chattered on. Then there were the personal calls he'd take in his office with the door shut, when she'd steal glimpses through the glass and feel a flutter of uneasiness noting the expression on his face: the same one he'd worn when romancing her. She told herself she was imagining things—he loved *her*!—but it grew harder to dismiss her fears. When her nineteenth birthday came and went without so much as a card from Lowell, she was crushed.

The hurt and worry made her physically ill. She was tired all the time and sick to her stomach. The fact that she'd missed a period didn't overly concern her—she'd always been irregular—but when another month passed with no sign of it, she could no longer deny what she'd known deep down: She was pregnant. A week later, a doctor in Anacortes confirmed it.

It should have put her into a panic, but Eleanor felt a strange sense of peace come over her instead. Now there would be no more putting off the wedding. Her parents would be upset when she told them, of course, but once they calmed down and saw how good it could be, they'd come around. Lowell, too, once he got over the shock, would be happy about the baby. How could he not be? Hadn't he told her a thousand times that he loved her?

And when she broke the news to him, she thought at first that's how it was going to go. They were at the office after hours. Everyone else had gone home, so they were alone. Lowell took her in his arms, soothing her. "My poor darling. Don't you worry. I know a doctor who'll take care of it, no questions asked."

Horrified, she jerked free of his arms. "You want me to *kill* our baby? How could you even suggest such a thing?"

He smiled, as he had countless times before, at her provincial ways, but this time it wasn't out of affection. "That's being overly dramatic, don't you think. Really, Ellie, this sort of thing happens all the time. If every woman felt as you do, there would be far more unwanted children in the world."

"But . . . I . . . I want this baby." She hadn't fully realized it until the words were out, and now she faced him in defiance.

"Unfortunately, it takes two, and I have no intention of becoming a father just yet," he said, lighting a cigarette, and peering at her through the smoke that swirled lazily up around his head.

She began to weep, still believing it was the shock making him act this way. "You can't mean that. I caught you by surprise, is all. But don't you see? Maybe it's all for the best. And it's not as if we weren't going to be married anyway."

"You thought I was going to marry you?" Perched on the edge of his desk, he laughed in disdain, stubbing out his cigarette. "I'm sorry if I ever gave you that impression, but frankly, my dear, it never occurred to me. And if you insist on having this child, I'll deny it's mine."

"But everyone knows—" She caught herself, realizing that no one knew about them, in fact. That had been part of his game plan all along, the reason he'd kept their relationship a secret, in the event of something like this. But if anyone had been in the dark, it was her.

Lowell scribbled a number on a slip of paper and handed it to her. "When you're willing to see reason, call this number. Don't worry about the expense, I'll take care of it."

But she didn't have to think about it, not for one second. Furiously, she crumpled the piece of paper and tossed it onto the floor.

Lowell pushed himself off his desk, saying, "You're a fool then. If you want to do it the hard way, you'll be doing it without me. We're through, Eleanor. Now why don't you pack up your desk and go." Cruel words that pelted her like icy raindrops.

Eleanor couldn't believe the man she loved, whose child she was carrying, was the same one standing before her, eyeing her so coldly. She covered her face with her hands and wept softly into her fingers, blocking out his hurtful presence. At the sound of his footsteps fading into the hallway, she sank slowly onto her knees, as if in prayer. She didn't know how long she knelt there—minutes, hours?

When she finally dragged herself to her feet, she felt stiff and achy all over, as if from a beating. In a kind of trance, she gathered up the personal items off her desk. As she walked out the door for the last time, she felt not only stupid but dirty, knowing *she* would be the one whispered about around the office in the days to come. Lowell's latest conquest. Discarded like all the others when she'd ceased to amuse him.

Her parents, when she told them, were more devastated than angry. Her father became an old man overnight, stooped and gray, while her mother drifted about, wan and red-eyed, avoiding Eleanor whenever possible. They wore their daughter's shame as if it were their own, telling no one, fearful of being judged.

One day Eleanor's father took her aside. "I've been praying long and hard on this, Ellie, and I think God has an answer for us." As though her pregnancy were as much his dilemma as hers. "Do you remember Joe Styles?" She nodded, vaguely recalling him from Sunday services, a square-set man with a weather-beaten face who sang the hymns in a deep baritone that carried above everyone else's voices. "Well, I spoke to him about you," her father went on, a grim set to his jaw, as if determined to get through this before he could weaken and change his mind. "I told him about your, uh, circumstances, and he thinks he can help. He's a good man, Eleanor. You could do a lot worse."

It had dawned on her then what her father was getting at: He expected her to marry this Joe Styles, a man she only knew to say hello to. Eleanor would have been mortified, if she hadn't been so numb. Instead, she only sat there in silence, listening to her father go on about Joe's attributes: He didn't smoke or drink, and he owned his own fishing boat and a house to boot. She had such a sense of disconnect, she even found herself agreeing to meet with the man. A quick and painless death would have been equally welcome, but that wasn't an option.

The meeting took place the very next day, in the rectory parlor, with her parents no doubt hovering on the other side of the closed door. If Joe Styles had said one wrong thing, it never would have gone beyond that. If, for instance, he had told her he was willing to overlook the fact that she was pregnant with another man's child, in essence spoiled goods. Instead, Joe said only that he would be honored to have her as his wife, and that his home would be hers if she wanted it.

"It's not much. But it's solid and there's an extra room, for when the baby comes," he said of the house his father had built with his own hands. "As for that, you should know I'd treat it no different than if it was my own."

Seeing Joe perched on her mother's Hunzinger chair, surrounded by the porcelain figurines Verna collected, the old expression, bull in a china shop, came to mind. Joe wasn't so much a big man as one who gave the impression of brute strength, with those great meat hooks of hands and a thick, veined neck that thrust from his shirt collar like that of a straining ox. Even the suit he was wearing was all wrong, shiny in spots, the jacket too tight, as if it had been purchased years before the daily effort of hauling in his catch had added twenty or thirty pounds of extra muscle to his frame.

Even so, Eleanor, recalling her father's words, had thought, *I could do worse*. Joe was a man of simple means and education, and not much to look at, but he was kind-hearted, and what more could she ask? It wasn't as if she were in a position to be choosy. The fact that she didn't love him and couldn't imagine ever feeling for him what she had for Lowell, didn't greatly concern her. This was a decision based not on want but on need.

"And if I were to agree to this, what would you be getting out of it?" she asked bluntly.

His face reddened at the implication, and he seemed at a momentary loss for words as he stared down at his thickly callused hands, curled loosely on his knees: a man clearly unaccustomed to expressing such intimate thoughts. "I'd want only what's freely given," he said at last, shyly bringing his head up to meet her gaze. "If you don't see fit to share my bed, I'll respect that." Looking into his eyes, she saw that he was sincere.

"I can't make any promises," she told him. "Why don't we see how it goes?"

"Does that mean . . . ?" Something flared in his eyes making her wonder if he'd had ideas about her long before her father had approved him.

"Yes, I'll marry you." She rose to her feet and extended her hand—as if it were a business deal they were concluding. Pride prevented her from showing any gratitude. She couldn't bear having him think that he was doing her any favors. "Would the Sunday after next be convenient?"

Over the years she had come to love Joe, in her own way. He was a good husband, better than she deserved, and a considerate, if uninspired, lover. More than that, he was utterly devoted both to her and to Lucy, who couldn't have been any dearer to his heart if she'd been his own flesh and blood. And as far as Lucy was concerned, the sun rose and set by her papa. After Joe shipped out, Lucy had moped about for days. Since then, she'd written to him religiously, at least once a week, often tucking into the envelope some remembrance of home—a pressed flower or a bird feather, a pretty picture cut out of a magazine. While Eleanor's letters were filled with the minutiae of daily life—the chimney she'd had to have patched and the rain that was wreaking havoc with her garden, the new pastor who'd taken over when her father retired—Lucy wrote about how heartbroken she'd been when her best friend moved away and the boy in school she secretly had a crush on. Each letter ended with her telling him she was counting the days until he came home and that she prayed every night for God and President Roosevelt to look over him.

On the morning of William McGinty's serendipitous visit, Eleanor woke her daughter after he had gone, singing out, "Rise and shine, sleepyhead, breakfast is getting cold."

Lucy sat up in bed, rubbing her eyes. She lifted her head to sniff the air, smelling bacon, which was odd. Usually they only had bacon on Sundays. "Do we have company?" she asked.

Eleanor grew warm, thinking of William and the surprising turn of events brought about by Yoshi's ill-timed appearance. "Now what makes you think that?" she replied briskly.

"I thought I heard voices." Lucy yawned, stretching her arms over her head. In her flowered nightgown she looked small and defenseless, her bare feet scratched from running shoeless about the yard. Eleanor saw that her silky auburn hair was clumped in back where a rat's nest had formed.

She used her fingers to work out the knots, ignoring Lucy's attempts to squirm out from under her. "A man was asking about puppies," she said.

Lucy grew still at once. "Is he going to buy one?" she asked hopefully. Already, at nine, she was aware of how thinly stretched their finances were. She turned her face up to Eleanor, small and heart-shaped, with Eleanor's green eyes and Lowell's olive complexion.

"We'll see. I told him to come back when Belle has her litter," Eleanor replied. "Now come on, get dressed. We have lots to do today." She shooed her daughter out of bed, then before Lucy had gone two steps she impulsively pulled her close, hugging her tightly. "That's for being so good. And for keeping our secret." She drew back to look her daughter gravely in the eye. "You know what would happen if you ever told?"

Lucy nodded, her expression solemn. "Yoshi would have to go away to a bad place, where they keep people locked up."

"That's right," Eleanor said.

"But why? He didn't do anything wrong." Lucy had been wrestling with this for some time, ever since Eleanor had explained about the internment camps to which Japanese Americans like Yoshi had been sent, in the wake of Pearl Harbor. To Lucy, it had been like finding out there was no Santa Claus, learning that the president she revered could do something so unjust.

"It's because of the war," Eleanor gently explained once more, stroking her daughter's head. "People are afraid of anyone who looks like the enemy. They think if they lock up all the Japanese we'll be safe. But they're wrong. The reason men like your papa are fighting this war is so the world will be free of just that sort of thing."

Lucy nodded slowly, her eyes welling with tears. "I wish Papa could come home."

"I know, baby. Me, too," said Eleanor.

But at the moment she wasn't thinking about Joe. Her thoughts were with the tall stranger who'd appeared on her doorstep earlier that morning. William McGinty. The compassion he'd shown went deeper than mere chivalry. Maybe he felt a need to prove his worth. Whatever the reason, fate had thrown them together, and after these long months of struggling to hold it together, with money tight and the ever-present worry of her secret getting out, it was a relief knowing she had someone to share the burden.

William McGinty was no stranger to hardship himself. During the Great Depression his parents had lost everything they owned. His father's prosperous dry goods business went under and the bank foreclosed on their two-story brick house in Omaha. With little more than the clothes on their backs, the family had had no choice but to go to live with his mother's sister and her husband, in McCredie Springs, Oregon, where the population numbered in the hundreds and moonshine was the main source of income. They were good, hardworking people, his aunt Lillian a nurse in a doctor's office and his uncle Ripley, Uncle Rip for short, the owner of a small plumbing supply business, but they weren't much better off financially. Uncle Rip's business was barely staying afloat and Aunt Lillian's salary only covered the rent on their two-bedroom house. William's mother and father and three sisters had all slept together in one room, while William and his brother shared the sofa-bed in the living room.

The two boys had always been close, but the tight quarters, coupled with the fact that their parents were so preoccupied with finding work that William and Stu were left to their own devices for the most part, made them inseparable. William, at nearly fourteen, had taken it upon himself to instruct his eleven-year-old brother in the art of manly pursuits, such as throwing a curve ball and shooting at tin cans with his BB gun.

It wasn't long before William graduated to Uncle Rip's old squirrel rifle. When his uncle took him hunting, William turned out to be as good at hitting small animals as tin cans. The difference was that he took no pleasure in the kill; it was only to put food on the table. And with so many hungry mouths to feed he couldn't afford to be what his uncle referred to, usually accompanied by a well-aimed wad of spit, as "soft."

One day when William was showing off to his brother, shooting at Coke bottles lined up along the fence, a shot went astray, catching Stu in the arm, near his shoulder. Stu crumpled to the ground, blood bubbling up from the wound and quickly soaking his shirtsleeve. For a terrible moment William thought he was dead.

In a panic, he sank to his knees before his brother, ripping off his own shirt and pressing it to the wound. "Oh, God, Stu. Please. Say something."

Stu's eyelids fluttered open and his mouth twisted in a pained smile. "Nice shot," he'd managed.

By the time William had half dragged, half carried Stu back to the house, his brother had lost consciousness again. The doctor Aunt Lillian worked for was summoned and, after an examination showed it was only a flesh wound, the bullet was removed. Everyone breathed a sigh of relief when the doctor pronounced that Stu would survive, none the worse for the wear.

Two days later an infection set in. This was before penicillin was readily available, especially in remote areas such as theirs. All they could do was apply poultices and hope for the best. But Stu only got sicker, developing a raging fever, his arm swelling to the size of an Easter ham. Throughout the ordeal, William, certain that it was all his fault, seldom left his brother's side, praying for the Lord to take him instead, should it come to that.

But either God hadn't heard his prayers or He'd had other plans for William. On the fourth morning of Stu's delirium, William woke from the doze he'd fallen into, as he'd sat slumped in the chair at his brother's bedside, to find that Stu was dead. His parents and sisters, aunt and uncle, were all gathered round, his mother weeping inconsolably, lost in her grief, while his sisters clutched to her with their faces buried in her skirt.

But William refused to believe it. "*No!*" He'd reared up and grabbed his brother's lifeless body, shaking Stu as he did on mornings when his brother pretended to still be asleep. "Stu!" he'd cried, half out of his mind. "Come on, this isn't funny. You're scaring everybody. Quit it now. I'm serious. If you don't get up off this bed right now, I'm going to . . . to . . . "

"That's enough, son." A heavy hand had fallen on his shoulder, and William had twisted his head up to find his father gazing down at him, a bleak, unforgiving look on his face that remained with William to this day, burned into his memory. His father hadn't spoken a word of blame, not then or in the days that followed, yet there was no question in William's mind as to whose fault it was. Even if his parents could have forgiven him, he knew he could never forgive himself.

He'd vowed then and there never again to pick up a gun, and all these years he'd kept that vow. It hadn't been a sacrifice until just recently, but with the war on, he had mixed feelings, memories of Stu mingling uneasily with his guilt at not being able to fight for his country.

And it wasn't just his guilt he had to contend with. Martha had lost her beloved younger brother at Pearl Harbor, and now her patriotic fervor knew no bounds. It wasn't easy for her, with every other man in uniform, to have her husband enjoying the relative comforts of the home front. She fought against those feelings, he knew, conscious of the fact that he wasn't to blame, but deep down she was ashamed of him. As a result he found it equally hard to be around her, and these days was quick to seize upon any excuse to get out of the house, like this morning when he'd volunteered to drive Danny to the meeting place for his Scout campout this weekend.

Now, as William guided his Packard over the rutted dirt road leading to the cove, he wondered how Martha would feel about his aiding in the concealment of a Japanese boy who in her eyes might well be an enemy agent. He didn't regret his impulse—how could he? It was the only decent thing to do—but there was no getting around the fact that it wasn't just himself he was putting at risk.

She deserves to know. But somehow he couldn't imagine telling Martha about Eleanor Styles and the strange scene at her house. Martha wouldn't understand why he hadn't immediately reported it to the authorities. And if he couldn't confide in his own wife, what did that say about their marriage?

Not that Martha wasn't a good wife in other ways. She was lively and intelligent, and seldom refused him in bed. Only lately he could tell her heart wasn't in it. She was so involved in the war effort, selling bonds and organizing drives, it occupied her thoughts to the exclusion of all else, except Danny, as if with each fresh display of patriotism she was compensating for the very visible presence of her husband in wartime. In this new, khaki-colored world, the only uniform William wore was his paint-spattered shirts, and his only contribution to the war effort so far was the posters he'd done for the State Department, advertising war bonds.

For several minutes after he'd pulled into his yard and shut off the engine, he remained in his car, gazing out at the cove below. The tide had gone out, leaving a glistening gray flat marked with pylons where Deets had staked out his oyster beds. They'd lain fallow for some months now, a reminder that his neighbor, like so many others, was off fighting overseas. Other than that, in this peaceful spot, the war might have been a distant rumor. Farther out at sea, a fishing boat was pulling in its net, gulls swooping overhead, diving for scraps. If the weather held, he thought, he'd set up his easel outdoors. In winter, when the sun's path was low, their house lay almost perpetually in the shadow of the neighboring hills, but this time of year, on nice days, the morning sun poured over the landscape, allowing him to capture its richly varied hues.

He got out of the car and started toward the house. He could see Martha through the front window, polishing the breakfront where the good china was kept. Her pale yellow hair was pinned up in back, the curls on her forehead bobbing with each vigorous circular swipe of her arm. She was frowning, as she often did when intent on some task, as if no amount of elbow grease would amount to an end result that would meet with her satisfaction.

But something else was on her mind at the moment, he could see as soon as he walked in. "Sorry I'm late," he said. She smelled of lemon oil and the perfume she wore, something flowery that made him think of the sachets she tucked into drawers. "I stopped to ask about a puppy."

She seemed too preoccupied to comment, though earlier they'd argued about whether or not Danny was old enough for the responsibility of owning a dog. "Have you seen the paper?" she asked, straightening, using the back of her wrist to push a wisp of hair from her forehead.

"No, why?" he asked.

She snatched up that morning's edition of the Bell Harbor *Sentinel*, which must have been delivered while he was out, and brandished it at him. "General Wainwright surrendered!"

"God help us." He stared morosely at the headlines announcing the fall of Corregidor.

"Do you know what this *means*?"

"It means that thousands more of our boys are now prisoners of war," William said, with a sinking heart, as he scanned the fine print.

"Well, yes, of course," she said, with an impatient sweep of her hand. "But it also means the Japs could *win* this thing. There'll be no stopping them now. We're barely hanging on in Midway as it is. Honestly, anyone would think MacArthur was asleep at the wheel!"

"I'm sure he's doing all he can."

She glared at him, as though he and MacArthur were in cahoots somehow, before conceding with a sigh, "I suppose you're right. It's just that I feel so helpless sometimes." She looked anything but. She was fully made up, wearing a dress that showed off her neat curves. No housecoat and slippers for Martha McGinty. If she were all alone in the house, she would be as perfectly turned out as if expecting company. He had to admire her for it. At the same time, he found himself thinking of Eleanor Styles, the silken brush of her slippered feet as they'd moved over the worn linoleum in her kitchen and the way her sleep-scrambled hair that was the color of autumn leaves had caught the sunlight slanting in through the window.

"You're doing your part," he reminded her.

"What good does it do to peddle war bonds and organize scrap metal drives when the whole world is going up in flames?" she demanded, her pretty face flushed with indignation. "I swear, if I were a man . . ." She caught herself before she could complete the sentence. "Never mind, you must be hungry. You've been gone for *hours*. Let me fix you some breakfast."

"I've eaten, thanks," he told her.

"I thought you were only dropping Danny off," she said, frowning in puzzlement.

William wrestled once more with his conscience, wondering if he dared trust her with Eleanor's, and now his, secret. Once upon a time they'd talked about everything.

But all he said was, "I told you, I stopped to ask about a dog. You know the house down the road from the old

Pritchard place, the one with the sign out front? The woman invited me in for coffee and ended up feeding me. She sent me home with these." He held up the sack of eggs. "Anyway, she said she'd let us know in a couple of weeks."

"Know what?" Martha asked distractedly, bent once more to her polishing.

"About the puppy." A note of impatience crept into his voice. "I told her we were hoping to have it in time for Danny's birthday."

Martha shook her head, her lips pursed. "I swear, Will, you and that boy will be the death of me one day. As if I don't have enough to do as it is without a puppy to clean up after. No, don't give me that look. You know perfectly well whose shoulders it will fall on."

"I'll make sure Danny knows it's his responsibility," William said.

"All right. I'll think about it," she said, in the tone that meant she'd already made up her mind.

"He's a good boy. He doesn't ask for much." William remained firm. Usually he let her have her way, it was easier than getting into a fight, but this time he wasn't going to give in.

She relented with a sigh. "I suppose I don't have a choice, do I? It's two against one."

"The beauty of democracy." He smiled, giving her apron strings a playful tug.

Her scowl melted, and in that instant he caught a hint of the woman he'd married, following a whirlwind courtship in Paris, where at the time he'd been taking classes at the Sorbonne and she was the au pair for the children of a wealthy Parisian couple.

He was heading off to his studio out back when she called after him, "I'm going into town in a little while to pick up those pamphlets for the blood drive. Do you need anything?"

He paused, frowning in thought, then shook his head.

What he needed couldn't be found in any store. He didn't even have a name for it, this new restlessness of his. Like when he was a boy and he'd known it was time to leave home. Except he had no desire to leave this place. As he was stepping out the back door, he paused to look around. The snug cottage, with its exposed timbers and wainscoted walls, its stained-glass transom that cast a mosaic of light over the freshly waxed floorboards, was smaller than Martha would've liked, but on winter nights with the wind howling in off the bay and rain lashing at the windows, there was no cozier place.

It wasn't until he was letting himself into his studio that he realized the moment had passed for him to confide in Martha about the Japanese boy holed up at the Styles place.

CHAPTER SIX

Present day

"I made your favorite—pork roast and scalloped potatoes," Lucy said as she led the way into the kitchen. "We've got to fatten you up. You're much too thin." She paused, turning to Alice with a look of consternation. "Are you getting enough to eat?"

"You mean, can I afford a decent meal?" Alice replied. She'd arrived on Sunday ahead of the others, so she and her mother were alone for the moment; they could speak frankly. "Don't worry, Mom. I'm not destitute yet." She still had almost ten thousand dollars of her grandmother's money left, though even with her watching every cent it wouldn't last long at this rate.

"Just remember, Rome wasn't built in a day." Lucy reached for Alice's hand and gave it a little squeeze. Ever the optimist. She would have given pep talks to a prisoner on death row.

"Don't worry," Alice assured her. "I'm not giving up. I can't afford to."

"Well, the important thing is, you're home. That's all that really matters." Lucy ran a thumb under one moist eye, saying with an apologetic laugh. "I'm sorry. I promised myself I wasn't going to do this. It's just that it's so good to have you back. I just wish your father . . ." She let the sentence trail off, her look of bright optimism momentarily fading. In the living room that had been done over in Alice's absence, with lots of ruffled chintz and pickled pine, devoid now of any masculine touches, she looked small and lost.

"I know, Mom. I miss him, too." Alice blinked back tears of her own. "It seems so strange not having him here." She looked around, as if half expecting to see her father.

"Don't you start, too!" Lucy scolded, shaking a finger at her. "This is supposed to be a celebration. Goodness, I can't remember the last time we all sat down around the dinner table." Though of course she knew how long it had been: exactly nine years. "Now why don't you finish setting the table while I check on the roast. Your sister should be here any minute."

She didn't mention Jeremy. When Lucy had called to invite him, he'd said he'd try to make it but that he didn't think he could; he had a test to study for. Alice hadn't given up hope, though. Maybe he would decide to come at the last minute. She set an extra place at the table just in case.

When she was done setting the table, she went into the kitchen to see what else she could do to help. She found her mother on her knees, wrestling a casserole dish from the jumble of pots and pans in one of the lower cupboards.

"Need a hand with that?" Alice asked, smiling at the picture her mother made.

"No . . . I've got it . . . it's just that it's wedged in with all this other—" With a clatter of pots, Lucy straightened, rocking back on her heels, the casserole dish triumphantly in hand.

Lucy set her to work dicing onions for the ratatouille she was making to go with the pork roast and potatoes. Alice, watching her move about the kitchen, was relieved to see her mother looking so well. The last time Lucy had visited her at Pine River, she'd been little more than a bundle of bones loosely wrapped in skin. She couldn't even be bothered with her hair, which she'd worn short, in a wash and wear cut that made her look less like a perennial schoolgirl than a very old elf. But last year's hip replacement had made it easier for her to get around. She'd also regained most of the weight she'd lost after Alice's father died. Now, with her face filled out and her hair in a shining silver bell, she was her old self again.

"I've taken up water aerobics. Doctor's orders," Lucy informed her, when Alice commented on her appearance. She paused to shake her head in wonderment. "A year ago if you'd told me that three afternoons a week I'd be paddling around in a pool with a bunch of old ladies, I'd have laughed at the idea. But I should have done this years ago. It's done me a world of good." She scooped up the onions and dumped them into the oil sizzling in the frying pan, adding cut up peppers and eggplant. She handed Alice a spatula, saying, "You stir that while I finish making the gravy."

"Smells good," Alice said, when her mother pulled the roast, crackling, from the oven. "Do you know, this is the first meal I've looked forward to since I got back. At Pine River, the closest thing we had to gourmet was creamed chicken on toast."

Lucy didn't respond, except to shoot her a pained look.

Alice, reminded of the scene at Denise's, felt her back go up. "What? I'm supposed to pretend I was away on a long trip? Mom, I did time. I ate my meals off plastic trays and worked in the prison laundry." She held up hands that were still chapped and raw. "I had to ask permission for every little thing, to get my hair cut, to have a reading lamp in my cell, even for the luxury of being able to step outside for some fresh air." After days of having doors slammed in her face, every one a reminder of where she'd been, she wasn't in the mood to play this game of pretending that chapter in her life was closed. Prison was a fact of her existence; it had changed her in ways that were unalterable. Her family was going to have to accept that if they wanted her back in the fold.

"Well, dear, that's all behind you now. Why dwell on it?" Lucy spoke with forced cheer, becoming suddenly animated, bustling to and fro, rattling pans and running the tap, exactly as Denise had done when ducking the subject. Alice suppressed a sigh. Some things never changed. Whatever had happened to make her mother so fearful of any unpleasantness—the privations she'd suffered as a child during the war or the trauma of her beloved Papa coming home a changed man—it was as irreversible as the experiences that had shaped Alice.

Alice remembered a time when she'd been that way, too. Wasn't that what had led to her nervous breakdown? She'd kept up a brave front after David's death, until finally the effort had caused her to come apart and scatter like so many Pick-Up sticks. But prison had cured her of faking it. There, if you lived in a dream world or put on airs, the other inmates would beat it out of you, literally in some cases. Honesty, even when raw and hurtful, had been the only means for survival.

Suddenly she found herself missing her friend Calpernia. Calpernia King had a nose for bullshit as finely tuned as a Geiger counter, and would regularly bust Alice's chops when she tried to paint a pretty picture or give someone the benefit of the doubt. Like the time Alice had defended her cell mate, Sonia, after Sonia was accused of stealing. "You can talk all you like, don't mean shit. You just blowing smoke out yo' ass," Calpernia had sniffed, her cornrowed head thrown back, her hands planted on her ample hips. A week later, Alice had found a book and pen she'd been missing under Sonia's mattress.

Lucy glanced at the clock. "I don't know what's keeping your sister." She lowered her voice to add confidentially, "Between you and me, I think she's stretched too thin. This Spring Hill business has her in a such a tizzy, she doesn't know whether she's coming or going. With all those rallies and whatnot, I'm surprised she has any time at all for her family."

"What about Gary? Where does he stand in all this?" Alice asked. She'd gotten the feeling he was only paying lip service to the cause in the interests of family harmony. Also, that all was not as it seemed when it came to her brother-in-law.

"Between a rock and a hard place, that's where," Lucy said, casting her eldest daughter a dark look. "He has certain responsibilities. It's not just his wife he has to please." A reminder that Gary, as deputy chief of police, wasn't exactly a free agent.

Meanwhile, the debate over Spring Hill raged on. The environmental group Denise was active in had filed a lawsuit, temporarily blocking the planned development, in what was shaping up to be a bloody battle. At the center of it all stood the mayor. Owen White had been the one to champion the development early on and put pressure on the planning commission, claiming it would create new jobs and pump much-needed money into the local economy. But there were those, like Denise, who weren't seduced by his promise to set aside a portion of the land for a wildlife preserve. What kind of wilderness would it be, she'd wanted to know, with condos and tennis courts a stone's throw away?

Alice's thoughts turned to Jeremy and the day they'd hiked up the ridge at Moran State Park. She hadn't seen him since then. He hadn't returned any of her calls, and when she'd spoken to Randy about it, her ex-husband had cautioned her not to expect too much right off the bat. It hurt knowing Jeremy was so close yet so far from reach, but she told herself this couldn't go on forever. Eventually something would have to give.

Meanwhile, she would continue on. Just as her grandmother had before her. Nana had been a survivor, too, taking care of her sick husband while single-handedly raising a child and putting food on the table. If it hadn't been for her resourcefulness, the property would have been sold off years before land on the island became so valuable. Alice's only regret was that Nana hadn't seen any of that money in her lifetime. It was only after her death, when the house was sold, that its value was realized.

"By the way, you know who I ran into the other day? Colin McGinty," Alice remarked, as she sprinkled herbs over the ratatouille now simmering on the stove. She warmed at the memory of their chance meeting at the library, recalling how at ease she'd felt in his company. She turned to her mother. "You knew his grandfather, didn't you?"

"A long time ago," Lucy answered, stirring flour into the pan drippings. "When I was a little girl, he used to come by the house to visit Mama. They were quite friendly at one time, as I recall."

Friendly enough for him to have painted her portrait, thought Alice. "I'm surprised Nana never mentioned him. Did they have a falling out at some point?"

"Oh, I don't think it was anything like that. It was just . . . well, you know it was the war and, after Papa came home, she had her hands full." Lucy paused in the midst of her stirring, her expression softening. "Poor Papa. I wish you could have known him before. He was the most wonderful man. Always smiling, and never too busy to make time for me and Mama."

"I could see that," Alice said, gently laying a hand on her mother's arm. The grandfather she'd known had been out of it most of the time, but he'd had his good days when glimmers of the old Joe would surface.

Nana had been devoted to him, too, but Alice had sensed that her grandmother had a hidden side to her heart. Could she have been in love with William? It was easy to imagine how it might have happened, the handsome artist and the young wife with her husband overseas. Theirs wouldn't have been the only such wartime romance. But if Lucy knew anything about an affair, she wasn't letting on. Either that, or she refused to believe her parents' marriage had been anything but storybook. Knowing her mother, Alice thought it was probably the latter. Lucy would deny the *Titanic* was going down as it was sinking.

Lucy shook her head slowly, staring sightlessly ahead. "Hard to believe they're all dead now. The years go by so quickly."

"Speaking of which, you know the portrait Mister McGinty did of Nana? Well, it seems he left it to Colin," Alice informed her.

Lucy brought her gaze back to Alice. "Is that so? I'd heard something to that effect, but you never know what to believe, with all the talk that's been going around."

"Anyway, I told Colin I'd never seen the actual painting, and he said I was welcome to stop by anytime I liked." On the spur of the moment, she suggested, "Why don't you come with me?"

Lucy appeared hesitant, and before she could reply Denise blew in, with Gary and the kids, apologizing for being late. Still no sign of Jeremy, though. When it became clear that he wasn't going to show, Alice quietly removed the extra place from the table, trying not to feel too disappointed.

Dinner was more relaxed than the other night at Denise's. Now that Alice's niece and nephew had gotten used to her, Taylor didn't stare at her as if she had two heads, and Ryan no longer acted as if she were company for whom he had to put on a polite show. Tonight, he might have been any teenager, teasing his sister and cracking jokes at the table. Alice, for the first time since she'd gotten back, felt like she was a member of the family once more.

Gary was the one false note. He was his usual jovial self, but it seemed forced somehow, as if he were only going through the motions. Alice sensed that he was uneasy around her, and she wished there was a way of reassuring him that she wasn't going to do anything to embarrass him. She had no intention of violating her parole and, if any of the townsfolk gave her a hard time, she wouldn't pick a fight. She didn't want any trouble; she only wanted to get on with her life.

"I heard you applied for the position at Svenigan's," he remarked at one point. Alice must have looked surprised that he knew, for he explained, "Ina mentioned it to me the other day when I stopped in for a bite to eat."

"Unfortunately, I didn't get the job." Alice kept her voice light, not wanting to spoil the meal with a lot of negative talk. Anyway, the opening had been for a waitress, and she was hoping to get closer to the kitchen, where she might actually get to do some cooking.

"Too bad. They could have used you," Gary went on, in that falsely hearty tone, as he helped himself to another slice of the roast. "In fact, I told Ina if she doesn't find someone soon, she's going to have to start giving customer discounts for the wait time."

Alice put her fork down, eyeing him across the table. "She told me the position had been filled."

Silence fell. Gary looked embarrassed. Even Denise was quiet for a change, the kids taking her cue and ceasing their chatter as well. There was only the clink of forks as Taylor and Ryan became suddenly fixated on what was on their plates.

"Would anyone like more potatoes?" piped Lucy brightly, at last.

For once, Alice was grateful for her mother's ability to act as if everything were normal in the face of even the most awkward situations. She smiled and held out her plate, though she'd lost her appetite. "Thanks," she said. "Everything's delicious, Mom. You really outdid yourself this time."

They were cleaning up in the kitchen afterward when Denise took Alice aside, saying, "I'm sorry about what happened—with Svenigan's, I mean. Gary didn't mean anything by what he said."

"I know he didn't," Alice replied lightly. "Anyway, it's no big deal."

"It *is* a big deal." Denise's cheeks reddened. She looked as if she were about to cry . . . or tear someone a new one. "They should have hired you. It's unfair. It might even be illegal." Her expression darkened. "In fact, I have half a mind to tell Ina Svenigan where she can put her marionberry pie."

"It's all right," Alice said, more firmly this time. "I can take care of myself."

"I know you can. It's just . . . people can be so petty sometimes. I hate to see you go on being punished for something that happened so long ago," she said.

"Relax, okay? I'm not one of your charity cases." Alice had meant it jokingly, but it came out sounding hard.

Denise drew back, hurt. "I wasn't implying . . . "

Alice laid a hand on her arm. "I know you weren't."

A corner of her sister's mouth turned up in a rueful smile. "Okay. I'll back off. But you have to promise to let me know if you need anything. Even us tree huggers need a warm body to rescue once in a while."

"I promise. But no hovering, okay?" Alice handed her a dish towel. "I'll wash. You dry."

Two weeks into her job search Alice was more discouraged than ever. She couldn't even get hired to do temp work. It all boiled down to one thing: she was unemployable. A convicted felon who also had a reputation for being mentally unstable.

It had been another long and frustrating day when she dragged herself to the eatery near her motel where she often took her meals, one rainy day in November, a hole-in-the-wall seafood shack that specialized in fish-and-chips, appropriately named Fisherman's Catch. She'd gotten to know the owners, Captain and Baby, who were a couple of real characters. Baby, so nicknamed because of her tiny stature—she couldn't have been but five feet tall—was perpetually bellowing out orders to her huge, shambling ox of a husband, a retired merchant marine turned short-order cook, in a voice loud enough to bring the whole fifth division running. Yet for all her hollering, he was devoted to Baby, and she to him. "Ain't she something?" he'd say with a chuckle, gazing in worshipful adoration at his red-headed scrap of a wife, as she bustled about, issuing orders, like the world's smallest commando.

With her customers, Baby liked to take charge as well and she saw to it that they got what they needed, even if it wasn't what they'd ordered: a kind word when someone was down, a piece of advice for those in need of counsel, a kick in the ass when called for. What Alice liked most about coming here was that Baby and Captain treated her no differently than they would anyone else. They had to know her history—who on this island didn't?—but from the way they acted it was obvious they couldn't have cared less.

"What'll it be, hon, same as usual?" Baby rasped today.

"Soup of the day and the toasted cheese sandwich," Alice said, like always.

Baby's response never varied either. "Sure you wouldn't like a piece of pie to go with that? On the house."

Alice summoned a smile as she handed back the menu. "Thanks, not today. Any more freebies and I'll be putting you out of business."

"That wouldn't be hard to do." Baby leaned in to confide, "Between you and me, we're not exactly getting rich off this place. Fact is, we're barely staying afloat. Some retirement, huh? Me and the Captain, we had it all planned out. Sell when the time was right and move someplace warm, where it don't rain eight frigging months out of the year." She cast a doleful glance out the window, where the rain was pouring down in sheets, her brown nugget of a face crinkled in irony. "So much for that pipe dream."

"You'd really sell this place?" Alice was surprised. Baby and Captain seemed as much a fixture as the cloudy marine-varnished tables and fishing net that drooped from the ceiling, studded with dusty sand dollars and starfish so ancient they looked as if they'd turn to dust if you so much as touched them. "In a heartbeat," Baby replied without hesitation. "If some poor sucker was fool enough to make us an offer, we'd be out of here so fast you wouldn't see us going."

"I'd buy it, if I had the money," Alice said, indulging in a little wishful thinking.

She'd always fantasized about opening a restaurant. Randy used to joke that she was a frustrated chef, with all the dinner parties she'd thrown. Even when she wasn't entertaining, she'd loved experimenting in the kitchen, dabbling in herbs and spices and condiments the way a painter would with his palette, creating new recipes and coming up with fresh takes on old standbys.

The years at Pine River had been especially hard in that respect, because she'd missed all those flavors, missed having her senses come alive at the scent of a roast chicken pulled crackling from the oven or a simmering pot of fish chowder filled with meaty chunks of wild salmon and halibut. Prison food all looked and tasted the same: dull, pasty, gray. The first thing she'd done upon her release was to head straight for the nearest market, where she'd bought a hunk of aged Cheddar and a bag of sweet, juicy, Washington apples.

Baby's bright blue eyes narrowed speculatively. "You would, would you? Well, in that case you're as crazy as they say. No offense," she said, holding up a hand to silence the protest forming on Alice's lips. "You and I both know there's plenty of folks in this town got nothing better to do than wag their tongues. I don't pay them no mind. But ain't no getting around the fact that even if you had the cash, you'd need the customers. And, hon, you're about as popular as Typhoid Mary right now."

"Well, there's no point in discussing it." Alice felt embarrassed to have even brought it up. "It was just wishful thinking."

"Tell me about it. That's how me and the captain ended up in this leaky boat." Baby gave a rueful grin, showing a row of teeth that looked too big for her mouth, and too perfect, to be anything but dentures. "Now look at us. Too old and broke to swim for shore."

"But you love it!" Alice protested.

"I'll tell you something," Baby said, with a sigh. "You leave work every night smelling of fry oil, the bloom kind of wears off after awhile. Sure, I love it, but I hate it, too. And damn if my feet ain't begging me to quit. They're like a couple of old mules tired of pulling."

"Why *don't* you just sell it then?"

"Simple. No takers." The old woman gave a sanguine shrug. "Last time we put it on the market, half the folks who looked at it passed on account of its being too close to the highway for them to tear it down and build one of those fancy new McMansions in its place. The other half were smart enough to know what it took us ten years to figure out: You can't make money on a restaurant this far out of town when the tourist season's only four months out of the year."

"People will make a special trip, if it's worth their while," Alice reasoned.

Baby shot a look toward the kitchen, where Captain was pulling a batch of sizzling fries from the deep fryer. "Don't get me wrong, I love the old coot, but he ain't exactly Paul Prudhomme."

"I didn't mean . . ." Alice started to say.

"I know you didn't, hon." Baby gave her a motherly pat on the shoulder. "But let's be honest. You're not here for the food. You come 'cause it's cheap and there's lots of it. That, and ain't nobody gonna give you a hard time, not as long as I have anything to say about it."

Alice smiled. "I'll take that over oysters Rockefeller any day."

Baby eyed her thoughtfully for a moment. "Look, if you're serious about this, maybe there *is* a way." With a quick survey of the room first to make sure no one needed a refill or change for their bill, she sat down opposite Alice. It was between lunch and dinner hours, so the place was pretty empty, just an old man sipping coffee at the counter and a couple at one of the other tables getting ready to leave. "Course, I'd have to take it up with the Captain, but suppose, just for the sake of argument, that you were to make us an offer. Say, whatever you could afford right now, and so much a month once things get rolling."

"I don't know. I hadn't really thought it through," said Alice, her pulse quickening nonetheless. *This is crazy*, she thought. *Why are we even discussing it?* Even so, she found herself asking, "What sort of money are we talking about?"

"Just enough to tide me and the Captain over. We have our eye on a condo in one of those Sun City retirement villages. With our social security and a little extra thrown in, we ought to be able to swing it. There's just one thing . . ." Baby leaned in, her eyes narrowing. "How good a cook are you?"

Alice smiled. About that at least she had no doubts. "It's been a while, but I don't think I've lost my touch."

Baby nodded, seemingly satisfied. "Then I take back what I said before. If the food's great, they won't care who's in the kitchen, even if it's Typhoid Mary."

"You're serious about this?" Alice eyed her in disbelief.

"Serious as a heart attack."

"I couldn't offer you much as a down payment. Four or five thousand at the most." Even that would be stretching it.

Baby frowned. "That's less than I was counting on. But we might be able to work something out."

Suddenly it hit Alice: This could really happen. And was it really so crazy? With all she'd been through, it seemed fitting in a way, as bizarre as the circumstances that had brought her to this point. As she and Baby talked, a plan began to take shape. They settled on five thousand down, with the rest of the money to be paid in monthly installments once revenue was coming in. All of it subject to Captain's approval, of course, which they both knew was just a formality. Baby wore the pants in the family; Captain merely did as he was told.

The more they discussed it, the less crazy it began to seem. Alice calculated that she'd have just enough left over to upgrade the place a bit and purchase supplies. Money would be tight, but she might, just might, be able to swing it. And at least she wouldn't have to worry about finding a place to live. The restaurant came with a small one-bedroom apartment upstairs, which currently Baby and Captain shared with their three cats. There was just one catch . . .

"I'll need to apply for permits and there are people who could make it tough for me," she said, thinking of Owen. She wasn't being paranoid in imagining that he was behind a number of the doors that had been slammed in her face. At one place where she'd applied for an office job and been turned away, she'd learned later on that the building was owned by none other than Owen White. And at another, a souvenir shop on Harbor Street, a sympathetic young clerk had murmured to her as she was leaving, *A word of advice: Watch your back.*

Baby knew at once who Alice was referring to, and she sniffed in contempt. "You mean Mister Big Shot?" Clearly she had her own thoughts about the mayor. "I wouldn't let him worry you. You look like a woman who can take care of herself."

Hearing her own words to Denise coming out of Baby's mouth, Alice smiled. Even so, she knew she'd be making herself vulnerable. And even if she managed to get the permits and pass all the inspections, there were other ways of putting a restaurant out of business. One bad review or rumored report of food poisoning, and she might as well pack it in. At the thought, she felt some of the wind go out of her sails. But what was the alternative? If she were to walk away from this, she might as well admit defeat altogether.

No, she thought, something in her rising up in rebellion. *If prison didn't kill me, this won't.* Those first few days at Pine River, she'd been certain she wouldn't make it through the week. But she had. And the week after that, and all the ones that followed. She'd endured the numbing sameness of each day that began with the rude alarm clock of their automated cell doors clanging open and shut, the thousand and one indignities, the indifference and sometimes cruelty of the COs, the human tide of flotsam and jetsam that washed in and out over the years, and, hardest of all, being separated from her family. And nine years later she'd emerged with her sanity and her dignity intact. A survivor. If she could survive that, she could survive anything.

It all came together with stunning swiftness. Their lawyer drew up the papers and before the ink was dry, Baby and Captain were on their way to the airport, headed for Arizona. It wasn't until the dust settled and reality set in that Alice realized what a daunting task she faced. The kitchen, in keeping with the décor, hadn't been updated since the Nixon administration. The ancient Garland stove needed work as did the old Hobart mixer, and on the captain's last day, as if it too had decided to throw in the towel, the temperature control on the deep fryer had given out, nearly causing the grease to catch fire. As for the overall structure itself, according to the engineer's report, the plumbing was touch-and-go, the roof leaked in spots, and there were areas of dry rot.

How was she going to pay for all this? And even if by some miracle she managed to whip the place into shape, there was still no guarantee she'd be able to make a go of it. She'd have to generate business somehow. And how could she do that when she couldn't even afford to hire help?

That particular prayer was answered in the form she least expected. Several days into her new career as restaurateur she was in the kitchen scraping an archeological dig's worth of grease off the stovetop grill when the phone rang. A familiar voice greeted her at the other end.

"Hey, girlfriend."

"Calpernia!" Alice broke into a grin. She hadn't spoken to her friend since she'd left Pine River. "How did you find me?"

"Your sister."

Alice recalled now giving her Denise's number. She remembered too that Calpernia was supposed to have met with the parole board and was eager to find out how it had gone—a little apprehensive as well, knowing her friend's propensity for shooting off her mouth. "God, it's good to hear your voice. In fact, I was going to call you. You beat me to it."

"You'll never guess where I am."

"I give up. Where are you?"

"Bus station. They must've decided I wasn't a threat to society no more, cause, girl, you is talking to a free woman." Calpernia gave her signature laugh, low and rich and just a tad dangerous, like a cool ride on a hot day in a stolen car.

"Oh, Cal. That's great news. I'm so happy for you." Alice had been keeping her fingers crossed. "So what now?"

"I'm on my way to my daughter's. My baby, Shaniqua, she got her own place now, down in L.A. Still can't believe she all grown up and all, with a family of her own."

"You must be excited to see her." Alice recalled when Calpernia's daughter, eighteen at the time, had been pregnant. Shaniqua had visited regularly up until then, but after the baby came the visits had tapered off. Calpernia had yet to meet her nine-month-old grandson.

"Girl, you don't know." Her friend heaved a sigh, one that held years worth of pent-up longing. But, of course,

Alice did know. She'd felt the same way herself, about Jeremy. Now, weeks later, what had she accomplished other than to drive him even further away? "But I ain't staying," Calpernia went on. "Week or two, and they'll be ready to throw me out. Shaniqua say the place so small you can hear the neighbors fart."

"Where will you go after that?"

"Hell if I know. But I'll work something out. How bout you? How you doing, girl?"

"Okay, I guess." Alice spoke in a measured tone, not wanting to burden Calpernia with her worries. "It's good to be back, but it's tougher than I thought it would be."

"Those white folks giving you a hard time?" It was an old joke between them.

Alice smiled. "Let's just say it's been interesting."

"What's happening with your boy?" Calpernia asked more gently.

"Not much." Alice gave her a quick rundown, feeling the old guilt wash in. Jeremy was right about one thing. Whatever her reasons, the fact was she hadn't been there for him all those years.

Calpernia listened without comment, then said, "He'll come around. He just hurtin,' is all."

"I hope you're right." Shaking herself loose from those thoughts, Alice said in a more upbeat tone, "Sorry, I don't mean to sound so gloomy. It's just that I'm a little overwhelmed right now. Did my sister happen to mention that I bought a restaurant?"

Calpernia let out a gasp. "No way. For real?"

"I'm afraid so. There's just one problem. Well, two actually. I'm up to my eyeballs in debt and I don't have the faintest idea what I'm doing." A crazy idea popped into her head and before she knew it the words were out. "Hey, how would you like to go into business with me?"

Calpernia laughed so long and hard, Alice thought she must be attracting attention at the other end: a two-hundred-pound black woman who looked mean enough to wrestle you to the ground and steal your purse while she was at it, busting her gut at some bus station pay phone. Finally, she stopped laughing and blew out a breath. "Damn. You one crazy white girl, you know that?"

"I'm serious," said Alice, realizing as she spoke that she meant it.

"Yeah, and how you gonna pay me? You said yourself, you broke."

"All right, I can't pay you much. But as soon as the money starts coming in, I can give you a share of the take."

"I ain't too good at arithmetic, but even I knows what zero out of zero come to."

"Look at it this way, we have nowhere to go but up."

There was a long silence at the other end. Just as Alice was beginning to think they'd been disconnected, Calpernia cut loose with another one of her hot-wired laughs. "Oh, hell. What do I got to lose?"

For a moment Alice wasn't sure she'd heard right. "You mean you'll do it?"

"I didn't say that." Calpernia was at once her old prickly, imperious self. "It ain't like I got no prospects of my own. Only one reason to do this that I can think of, and that's to save yo' skinny white ass. You don't know squat 'bout running no restaurant."

"Neither do you," Alice pointed out.

"That ain't the point. I been around. I know shit."

Alice laughed. "Well, I won't argue that."

"Long as you know you ain't my boss," Calpernia grumbled.

"Agreed."

"All right then. Now that we got that straight, when do I start?"

They talked for a few more minutes, making tentative plans, until Calpernia's bus pulled into the station. As she hung up, Alice recalled her first introduction to the force of nature known as Calpernia King. It was in her first week at Pine River and Calpernia had approached her in the yard, tailed by her posse, a huge, hulking presence, as black as the asphalt over which her broad shadow was cast. Her head a swirling mass of braided hair extensions, the tiny beads woven into them rattling like dice as she'd leaned into Alice's face, the whites of her eyes amid all that blackness seeming to jump out at Alice.

"Yo, white girl," she'd drawled. "What you in for, holding up a Mister Softee truck?" She'd eyed Alice with a disdain reserved for someone so far beneath her, it was a wonder she was even speaking to her. One of the women in her posse, a skinny black girl with bad teeth and tracks on her arms, had snorted in derision, as if trying to curry favor, and Calpernia had swung around to glare at her, demanding, "What you laughing at, bitch?"

Alice had said nothing; she'd just walked away.

That had set the tone for the next few months. Calpernia in her face, Alice doing her best to ignore it whenever she could. Until one day, after they'd been working alongside each other in the laundry for several weeks, somebody had said something that had struck Alice as funny and she'd started to laugh. She'd laughed herself silly, doubled over, tears streaming down her cheeks, until the CO on duty that day, a tough old lesbian named Rusty, had given her a look that meant she'd better get down to business or else. The trouble was, Alice couldn't seem to stop. Rusty had been on her way over, wearing a menacing look that spelled trouble, when all at once Calpernia had walloped Alice on the back, then grabbed her arm and squeezed it hard until the laughter died. She'd called over to Rusty, "Don't you worry bout her. She a'ight now."

After that, according to the unspoken code of prison relations, she and Calpernia were friends. As they got to know each other, Alice learned that the 'tude, as it was referred to among the black inmates, was merely a front and Calpernia's reputation largely the product of her own invention, a means to ensure respect and a minimum of harassment. If she was in for attempted murder, it had only come after years of abuse at her live-in boyfriend's hands, the final straw being when she'd found him messing with her then fourteen-year-old daughter. She'd waited until he was passed out drunk, then beaten him bloody with a tire iron, breaking nearly every bone in his body and leaving him blind in one eye. The boyfriend had pressed charges, denying all her allegations of abuse, and she'd had the further bad luck of being tried by an eager beaver young prosecutor looking to make his bones. Her court-appointed lawyer had attempted to persuade him to go with the lesser charge of aggravated assault, but Calpernia had stubbornly refused. In the end, she'd gotten eight to ten, same as Alice.

Now it occurred to Alice that not everyone would see Calpernia as she'd come to: a person you could count on to always have your back, who for all her rough edges had a kind of nobility to her. In this mostly white, middle-class community, she would blend in about as well as a pimped-out Cadillac in a parking lot full of SUVs. But if anyone could handle it, Calpernia could. And at least Alice would have company if she went down in flames.

Denise came over later in the week to help out. Together they spackled the holes in the walls and ceiling where Alice had taken down the nautical prints and fishing net with its hundred-year-old catch, after which they spent the day painting the kitchen and dining area. When they were finally done, they stood back to admire their handiwork. "I think we've earned ourselves a cold beer, don't you?" said Denise, idly scratching at a spot of dried paint on her nose. "Man, I don't know when I've worked this hard."

Alice fetched a Coors from the fridge for Denise and a Diet Coke for herself. Denise commented when Alice returned, "I forgot. You can't drink." She grimaced in sympathy. But Alice found her sister's making mention of the fact that she was a parolee encouraging. It meant the stigma had worn off somewhat, in Denise's mind.

Denise pulled chairs out from under the plastic tarp covering them. They were sipping their drinks, gossiping about old times, Denise with her feet propped on the rungs of Alice's chair, when the bell over the door jingled and Gary walked in. "Hey, ladies." He stopped to look around, giving a low whistle. "Wow. That's some job you did. I don't know when I've seen this place look so good."

"Yeah, you can hardly smell the grease," Denise said. "I swear I used to break out just walking into this place. You could practically see the fat globules in the air."

"Old Cap'n, though, he made a mean fish-and-chips," Gary recalled fondly. He gave Alice a long, considering look. "You sure you know what you're doing? No disrespect, but you haven't exactly had much experience running a restaurant. It takes more than a fresh coat of paint."

Alice wondered if his concern was that of a caring brother-in-law . . . or if he was hoping she'd fail. Gary was a hard one to read. He smiled a lot and said all the right things, but his eyes didn't always back them up: they were the eyes of someone looking out at you through a Polarized window. And there was no doubt his life would be easier if she were to slink away in defeat, forced to look for work on the mainland, thus removing a source of embarrassment from his otherwise orderly existence.

"I guess I'll just have to figure it out as I go along," she said, with a shrug. "You want a beer?"

"I'll have to take a rain check on that. I'm still on duty." He was wearing his khaki uniform, gun in its holster on his hip and his two-way clipped to his shirtfront. He turned his attention to Denise. "By the way, Taylor wanted me to remind you she has that thing at Scout hall tonight."

"What thing?"

"Beats me. I figured you'd know."

"Omigod." Denise abruptly sat up, clapping a hand over her mouth. "I completely forgot. I was supposed to bake cupcakes." She sighed, wearing the guilty, harassed look that seemed the sole province of motherhood. "I suppose I could pick some up at the store." She spoke as though it would be a sacrilege somehow.

"Why don't I whip up a batch?" Alice volunteered. "It won't take long, and it's the least I can do after all your hard work."

"You're sure it's not too much trouble?" Denise eyed her with naked gratitude.

"No trouble at all," Alice assured her. "Anyway, it's time I took this baby for a test drive." She gestured toward the newly rebuilt Hobart. "If I can't manage cupcakes, I'm *really* in trouble."

"All right then. I'll leave you girls to it," said Gary, with a tip of his hat. "You need anything, let me know. I have a meeting in town, but I'd be happy to stop at the store afterward."

"What meeting is that?" Denise wanted to know.

Gary turned away, as if to inspect the paint job, but not before Alice had seen the furtive look that crossed his face. "Just routine stuff," he replied with what seemed studied nonchalance. "I shouldn't be too long."

"Thanks, but I think I have everything I need," Alice told him, wondering what he was keeping from his wife.

"Okay then, I'm off." He dropped a kiss on Denise's cheek and headed for the door, his leather holster creaking and his boots leaving tracks in the film of plaster dust that covered the floor.

Denise sat there, shaking her head. "I can't believe I forgot."

"You mean you're not Supermom?" Alice teased.

Denise refused to be jollied out of her conviction that she was the world's worst mother. "What's happening to me? I used to be so organized," she groaned.

Alice suggested gently, "Maybe you're taking on too much."

"It's not just that. It's this damned development." Denise abruptly stood up, pacing back and forth in agitation. "I get the feeling that no matter what we do, they're always one step ahead of us. That's how it works around here. It's all about who you know and which strings to pull. I can't prove it, but I just know they have the whole thing wired."

"So why fight it?" Alice asked.

Denise whirled around, her face flushed and errant wisps of hair sticking out from under the bandana knotted around over her head. "I'll tell you why. It's not just because it's the last truly wild place on the island. It's because to give in would be like giving up. Look at you. What happened with you was awful, sure, but at least you took a stand. You didn't just roll over and die."

"It would have been better if I had. Look at what it cost me," Alice turned toward the window. The sun had come out, sparkling on grass that was still wet from the rain that had fallen earlier in the day. It was little things like that, the things other people took for granted—a view out a window not covered in steel mesh, a slice of blue sky, a leaf trembling on a branch—that stood as reminders of how much that single, irretrievable act had cost her.

"I'm sorry. That came out wrong. I didn't mean—" Denise broke off, and Alice turned to find her wearing a woebegone look.

"I know you didn't mean anything by it." Alice got up and went over to put her arms around her sister. "And it's not wrong to fight for what you believe in. I'd be right there beside you if I didn't have my own battles." She drew back to look at Denise. "So where does it stand now?"

"The court ruling should come down any day."

"And if it doesn't go your way?"

"I can promise you this much, we won't take it lying down," vowed Denise, with fire in her eye. "We'll chain ourselves to the trees if we have to."

"That could get uncomfortable, especially this time of year. Unless you plan on wearing a slicker and thermal underwear," Alice said, hoping to lighten the mood a bit. Her sister's concern was warranted, but she tended toward the extreme. There was only one right way, as far as Denise was concerned: *her* way.

Denise got the message and, with a sigh, she plopped back into her chair. "Let's talk about something else, okay? This is only going to depress me."

"All right then," Alice said. "On a more mundane subject, which will it be? White or chocolate?"

Her sister stared at her blankly for a moment before it sank in that Alice was talking about the cupcakes. "White. That way I won't be tempted to eat as many." Denise had always had a weakness for chocolate. "Just remember to save some for Gary, for when he gets home. Poor guy." She shook her head. "It's not enough he's on patrol all day, he has to contend with all that stupid bureaucracy. You think teachers have it bad, try being a cop."

CHAPTER SEVEN

The mayor's office, situated on the second floor of the municipal building, had a view of the more gracious prewar courthouse across the street, where at the moment a storm was brewing. From where he sat, at his desk facing the window, Owen White saw no immediate cause for concern. The sidewalk in front of the courthouse, still damp from the rain that had fallen earlier in the day, was clotted with more fallen leaves than people. But already a small crowd of activists had gathered and soon there would be swarms of them: tree huggers like Gary Elkin's wife, all shaking their fists and railing against the court ruling of which Owen, privy to certain inside information, already knew would go his way. Small-minded people who lacked the vision to see past their own noses and who sought to turn this island into some sort of time capsule. Why, if they'd been running the show in his father's day, Owen thought, there would *be* no Grays Island as they knew it. The quaint waterfront downtown that drew in flocks of tourists each summer would still be a mucky tidal flat and the properties that fetched such handsome sums today a useless sprawl of farms and orchards.

Thankfully cooler heads would prevail in this current debate as well. With a few well-placed phone calls, the mayor had made certain of that. The court would rule in favor of the Lighthouse Foundation, the charitable institution to which the late Elroy Cuthbert had bequeathed eleven hundred acres of pristine woodland, with views of the sound that stretched from Moran State Park to Mount Independence. No matter that Cuthbert had left the land to the foundation intending that it never be built on or that Cuthbert's daughter, Eunice, was contesting the proposed development. The language of the trust was such that nothing specifically prohibited the sale of the property, which Owen interpreted to mean that the old man had been of two minds. The Spring Hill development—a hundred and eighty residences, as well as a golf course and a man-made lake stocked with trout—would go forward as planned and the money Owen had discreetly invested in it would yield a hefty return.

He glanced at his watch now and saw that it was close to four. In exactly two minutes the deputy chief of police would come knocking on his door. Owen insisted on punctuality; he believed it to be a sign of respect, respect for oneself as well as the person whose valuable time you were taking up. And he had little use for slackers and fools. Gary Elkins was neither. His problem was merely one of unfortunate circumstance: He had the bad fortune to be related, if only by marriage, to the woman responsible for ruining Owen's life.

Oh, he knew he was viewed as a success story, someone who'd triumphed over adversity, but Owen wasn't thinking about that or the prestige he enjoyed as mayor. He glanced down at his atrophied legs with a small, crooked smile. It was the first thing people saw when they looked at him: the wheelchair. Thirty-five pounds of steel and polyurethane that in a perverse way had proved to be the making of him. Because of it, people saw him differently, as noble, saintly even. Which was why Owen seldom referred to the tragic incident that had left him partially paralyzed; there was no need to: He made a statement simply by entering a room. Both times he'd run for office, first as county commissioner then six years later as mayor, it was what had been chief on voters' minds, how admirable it was that he hadn't allowed his handicap to limit him in any way.

He'd proved himself in other ways as well. Chiefly, in emerging from the shadow of his father, long gone but far from forgotten in the minds of the townspeople. A triumph, given that Lowell's mysterious disappearance had been the defining fact of Owen's existence from boyhood on. He'd grown up hearing the stories whispered about his father, endured the cruel rhymes chanted by the other children in the schoolyard.

Lowell, Lowell, where's the money you stole?

For it was discovered after Lowell's disappearance that there were certain discrepancies in his books. Large sums of money were missing from his corporate account, money slated for shareholders of the limited partnerships he controlled. Rumor had it that the money was tucked away in a Swiss account, and that Lowell had gone off to start a new life in some foreign country with some mistress—for wasn't it a known fact he was a womanizer? Others put forth a more innocent explanation, that he'd been out on his boat that night and fallen overboard (which would have been hard to do with the yacht moored in its berth at the time).

Whatever the explanation, he was gone, leaving his family to a lifetime of uncertain status: his mother a widow for all intents and purposes without a grave to lay flowers on, his children not knowing whether to revere their father or revile him.

It hadn't helped that Owen was a sensitive, sickly child. His mother, without her husband to focus on, had fussed over her only son, her obvious favoritism putting a wedge between him and his sister Caroline. It wasn't until Owen went off to college that he was finally able to carve out an identity separate from his parents. Eventually he returned to take over the family business. He married and became active with his church and various charitable institutions. Under his careful management, the business became more profitable than ever. If it hadn't been for Fate casting Alice Kessler into his path, like a bad throw of the dice, he might have gone on that way indefinitely, quietly living out his life, doing only good works.

No one, not even his wife, had been aware of the extent of his drinking. He'd never embarrassed her in public and his conduct at work was never once called into question. And if, during his rare blackouts, he'd come to his senses on more than one occasion to find himself behind the wheel of his car, luckily no one had been the wiser.

Until the night he'd run over David Kessler. Drunk as a lord and taking a turn too fast in his Mercedes, he'd been unaware of the little boy riding his bike along the shoulder of the road until he felt the sickening thud and heard the horrid crunch of metal beneath his wheels.

After that, he'd quit cold turkey and hadn't picked up another drink since. Time might even have softened his memory of that terrible event, or at least allowed him some measure of peace, except for one thing: the boy's mother. Each time he'd looked into Alice Kessler's face, those unforgiving eyes, it had been as if he were peering through a window into his own soul. Even if he were to beg for her forgiveness, she wouldn't give it to him. And when she'd run him down that day, she'd done more than make a cripple of him, she'd sentenced him to a purgatory in which his failings were compounded by every sympathetic look, every show of compassion he received, in the very pedestal he'd been placed on. Each time he hoisted himself into his wheelchair a small part of him knew it was because of a little boy who was dead because of him.

And now, just when he'd begun to put the past behind him, Alice was back to torment him again. And this time she wouldn't rest until she'd finished what she'd started. Not that he was worried she'd do something rash. All those years in prison, he didn't doubt she'd had ample time to regret her actions, if only for the toll it had taken on her. No, it was her mere presence that he feared; it was like a cancer eating away at him. Ever since she'd come back he'd had trouble sleeping at night, and the nightmares had returned—terrible nightmares of screeching brakes and wheeling headlights, of a small crumpled body lying in the middle of the road, that had him lurching upright in bed, in a cold panic. And with the nightmares had come the headaches that used to plague him; not the ordinary kind, easily remedied with a couple of aspirin, but ones like some medieval torture device clamped to his skull, growing more excruciating with each turn of the screw.

Owen knew that if he didn't find a way to get rid of her, permanently this time, there would be no peace for him, ever. No escape from those eyes that saw him as he really was, the mind that knew the truth and the heart that wouldn't forgive.

Not that she would be so easily gotten rid of. Not as long as her son was on the island.

From a distance, Owen had watched the boy, Jeremy, grow to manhood, knowing it was only a matter of time before Alice returned to reclaim him. He knew that Jeremy was a good student but that he'd had fallen in with the wrong crowd at school, a thuggish bunch led by a sterling character named Kurt Rudnicki. While Jeremy was busy polishing his college resume, Rudnicki was working on his rap sheet; at sixteen he had already been busted twice for shoplifting and once for minor drug possession.

Owen didn't think Jeremy was in any real danger of following in his buddy's footsteps—he was too smart for that—but he knew that bad things tended to come from keeping bad company, so who knew what might happen?

Which was why he was keeping his eye on the boy. On the rest of the family, too. It was like a game of chess: You always had to think several moves ahead. All he had to do was get his pieces in alignment while eliminating hers one by one, until she had no choice but to call it quits.

A knock on the door roused him from his reverie. With a hint of annoyance he called, "Yes, what is it?"

The door eased open and Gary Elkins poked his head in. "Sir? Is this a bad time? I could come back later on, if you'd like."

"No, no. Come in, Gary. Sit down." Owen waved a hand toward the leather sofa in the seating area at one end of his large office and wheeled himself out from behind his desk. "I was so caught up, I hadn't realized what time it was," he said with a smile. "This business with the parking meters—it took an hour just to weed through the memos." And if the tree huggers thought putting in a few extra parking meters downtown was a call to arms, what would they do when they learned of the court ruling on Spring Hill? Owen felt a grim pleasure at the thought. "What can I get you? Coffee, tea?"

Gary shook his head, his polite smile vanishing almost as quickly as it appeared. "I'm good, thanks." Owen watched him lower himself onto the sofa, looking as uncomfortable as a child called into the principal's office. "I don't want to take up too much of your time."

"Nonsense. I'm never too busy for my deputy chief of police," Owen said. He propelled himself over to the sofa, the mag wheels of his Invacare Tracer EX2 cutting twin tracks in the dense pile of the carpet. "I don't mind telling you, it's a comfort knowing I can count on you, with all that's been going on." He gestured vaguely toward the window, through which drifted the chants of the crowd gathering on the street below. "We may not always see eye to eye, but we both know how to get the job done, even if it means ruffling a few feathers along the way."

He chuckled softly, catching a glimpse of himself in the mirrored cabinet against the wall just then: a pale, balding man dressed in chinos and a navy sports coat over a pale blue Izod shirt, his upper body disproportionately bulky against his atrophied lower half. Despite the confident look he wore the strain he'd been under was apparent, if only to him, in the deepening of the lines around his eyes and mouth and in the pallor underlying his tan, which gave him a faintly jaundiced look. Disturbed, he averted his eyes, focusing on Gary instead.

Gary shifted on the sofa, his eyes darting around the room as though he feared that if he looked directly at Owen's they would betray him. Finally, when it became clear to him that the mayor wasn't in any hurry to state his business, he cleared his throat and asked, "Was there something in particular you wanted to see me about?"

"As a matter of fact, there is." Owen waited a beat, his expression hardening before he got down to business. "I want to know everything there is to know about your sister-in-law. Keep close tabs and report back to me. She doesn't make a move without us knowing about it. Do I make myself clear?"

Gary's face, with its broad Nordic cheekbones and deep-set eyes, a rough draft of the more handsome one it might have been had it not been so crudely drawn, flushed a mottled crimson. "I've already told you everything I know." A surly note crept into his voice. "It's not like there's a law against opening a restaurant."

"No. But may I remind you that she's on parole. All it would take is one little slip." He leaned forward in his wheelchair, fixing Gary with his ineluctable gaze. "You're an officer of the law. It's your business to stay on top of such things. Do you have a problem with that?"

Gary flashed him a look of pure hatred, then quickly dropped his gaze, mumbling, "I'll see what I can do."

"I'm not asking you to *see* what you can do. I'm asking you to do it." Owen's tone hardened.

Gary brought his head up to look at Owen. His eyes glinted and the mottled red in his cheeks had deepened to the color of old bricks. "It's just . . . if my wife ever found out I was spying on her sister—" He broke off, swallowing hard.

"Spying? I think you've seen too many James Bond pictures." Owen's face relaxed into a smile, and he lifted his arms off the padded leather rests of his wheelchair to show he meant no harm. "Let's not make more of this than there is. All I'm asking, Gary, is for you to do your job. And to keep me informed, so that there are no . . . surprises. Under the circumstances, I don't think that's unreasonable, do you?"

Gary met his gaze with surprising defiance. "Sir, I have to tell you I'm not comfortable with this. I'm not saying I don't think you have a right to feel the way you do." His gaze involuntarily shifted downward, taking in the wheelchair. "But, hell, she's family. And she's paid her debt. All she wants is the chance to start over, make a new life for herself."

"Do you see me preventing her from doing that?" Owen spoke in a soft, unthreatening tone. "If I wanted to put her out of business, all it would take is a single phone call."

"I don't see what you need me for then," Gary said sulkily.

Owen looked at him as if he were a dim-witted student slow in getting it. "You're a team player, aren't you, Gary?"

"I'm not sure I follow you." Gary eyed him warily.

"I don't believe I need to remind you of a certain matter that would be very embarrassing to you and your family if it should get out." Owen paused to let the message sink in. "Your son's on the football team, isn't he? And your daughter's, what, in the fourth grade? This is a time for them to enjoy being kids. It'd be a shame to spoil it for them," he went on in the same unthreatening tone. "Now, don't get me wrong, Gary. I like you. I like what you're doing for the community, and I'd hate to lose a good man over something like this."

Gary's whole body went rigid. Owen felt a strange sympathy for him in that moment. It wasn't as if Gary had accepted a bribe to turn a blind eye to some sleaze ball dealing in meth or child porn. It had only been to look the other way should one of the customers get a little too friendly with one of the girls at the gentleman's club out on Route 6. But a bribe was a bribe, and Owen had it all on videotape. He and the owner of the Kittycat Club, a lowlife by the name of Buck Duggan, had an understanding: Buck tipped Owen off to any dirty cops, in exchange for which he was allowed to remain in business. Owen had found it helped having members of the law enforcement in his pocket. Gary didn't know it, but he wasn't the only one. He merely happened to be most useful at the moment.

Gary nodded slowly in understanding, his eyes fixed on Owen with a mixture of keen hatred and grudging respect. "I copy you on that, sir," he said, with just enough irony to make his point. He rose to his feet, holding himself stiffly at attention. "Anything else I can do for you while I'm at it?" *Shine your shoes, wash your car, cut off my balls and hand them to you on a silver platter*, said the expression on his face.

Owen regarded the big man in the khaki uniform as if he hadn't noticed Gary towering over him. "Thank you, that will be all," he said crisply. He gripped the handrims on his wheels, giving his chair a neat turn, and was heading back to his desk when the rising chants from outside made him pause. Slowly, he wheeled around to face Gary. "Oh, just a friendly bit of advice. I'd keep my wife on a shorter leash, if I were you. This Spring Hill business isn't over yet, and it looks as if things could get ugly. You wouldn't want to see her get hurt."

"Go for it, dog," Rud urged thickly, his eyelids at half mast as he peered at Jeremy through his tequila-and-beer-induced fog. "Wha'choo waitin' for, an invitation to the *prom*?" The girl sprawled on the mattress, clad only in bra and panties, was in a similar state of inebriation. She looked up at them, giggling as if Rud had said something wildly amusing.

Jeremy hung back, unsure but not wanting to appear uncool. "Fuck you, man. Look at her, she's wasted."

"Don't mean she don't want it." The mattress was on the bedroom floor, its bedding consisting of a single dirty sheet that was presently crumpled at the girl's feet. Rud nudged her with the scuffed toe of his motorcycle boot. "You want it, don't'cha, babe?" She mumbled something unintelligible, and he returned his bleary-eyed gaze to Jeremy. "See? What'd I tell ya?"

Jeremy wanted to say the party was over as far as he was concerned, he was out of here, only he thought it might piss Rud off. He was never quite sure of his footing with Rud, who, like a capricious king, could be all smiles and high-fives one minute and making you feel like a piece of shit the next. Jeremy settled instead for a contemptuous snort, adopting the pose of someone who was above such sophomoric stunts.

The evening had started out fun. Chuckie Dimmick's older brother, Mike, had given them the keys to his apartment, and Rud and Chuckie had invited some people over to party. But the fun had started to sour after Rud proposed a game of strip poker, the penalty a shooter for each item of clothing lost in the match. Rud and Chuckie and Kenny Lambert had merely gotten drunk while keeping most of their clothes on, while Rud's girlfriend, Crystal, had ended up passed out half naked on the living room floor, her friends having drifted off one by one. All except this one.

What was her name—Karen? Carolyn? Jeremy, who'd consumed his share of alcohol, stood swaying on his feet, bare-chested, wearing only his jeans, as he contemplated how best to extricate himself from this sticky situation. He gazed down at the girl, who peeked up at him kittenishly through the tawny hair tangled about her face. He felt a sudden tug of desire that left him sickened.

"What, you a faggot or something?" sneered Chuckie Dimmick, whom Jeremy had mentally dubbed Chuckie Dimwit, a real mouth-breather who wasn't capable of an original thought. Jeremy didn't know why Rud hung out with him—Rud was way smarter than that—unless it was because every king needed his sycophonts. Chuckie was looking at Rud now, seeking his approval. "Yeah, I bet he likes it up the ass. Don'cha, Jizz?" He nudged Rud with his elbow and cackled drunkenly at his own joke.

"Shut the fuck up, moron," Rud snapped at him. Chuckie's pimpled face went slack with a hurt expression that was almost comical, exaggerated as it was by a combination of stupidity and alcohol. Rud turned his attention back to Jeremy, slinging an arm around his shoulder and leaning in to mutter, "Dude, you don't want people thinkin' you some kinda pussy. That wouldn't be cool, would it? Now do your uncle Rud proud. I'm countin' on you." He drew back to wink slyly at Jeremy, as if they were in on some private joke.

"Fuck you," growled Jeremy, only he was grinning as he said it, so as not to confirm his own growing suspicion that he was, indeed, a pussy.

Rud leaned in close once more, advising in a low and noticeably less warm voice, "Yo, don't be trippin' on me, man. You makin' me look bad here, being as I'm the one who set you up and all."

"You guys are so full of shit," Jeremy said with a laugh, not wanting to jeopardize his already tenuous standing with them. He shook his head in mock disgust, and tried to push his way past Rud and Chuckie. Before he knew it, Rud had him by the arm and was shoving him onto the mattress, accompanied by hoots of laughter from Chuckie and Kenny. By the time Jeremy managed to scramble to his feet, the other boys were tumbling out into the hallway.

The door slammed shut and the room was plunged into darkness. Jeremy could hear his friends' muffled guffaws and the sound of a heavy piece of furniture being dragged across the floor on the other side. He staggered over to the door. Finding it wedged shut, he banged on it with his fist. "Come on, guys! Open up! This isn't funny!"

Behind him the girl—Carolyn? Carrie Ann?—said, with a drunken laugh, "What, you scared of the dark? Big boy like you?"

Jeremy's hand, which had been hovering over the light switch, dropped to his side. "I didn't say that."

"Come over here," she called. After a moment's hesitation, Jeremy crossed the room and sat down on the mattress, pulling his knees to his chest. "Sorry, what's your name again? I'm a little fucked up at the moment, in case you hadn't noticed." She gave a soft giggle that turned into a hiccough.

"Jeremy," he said.

She squinted at him with one eye shut. "Jeremy. That's cute. You like girls, Jeremy?"

"Yeah, I like girls," he shot back defensively. Now that his eyes had adjusted to the dark, he could see that she wasn't half bad-looking.

"So you're not gay?"

"Don't listen to them. They're full of shit." Jeremy jerked a thumb in the direction of the door, behind which the cackles and guffaws were fading as his friends moved into the next room. "Look, this wasn't exactly my idea," he said coldly, "so if I'm not in the mood to party, you'll have to excuse me."

"Whatever." She let out a soft burp and flopped onto her back, peering up at him through a web of tangled hair. "You know what? You remind me of someone. That guy in the movie, I can't think of his name. You know the one about the geeky kid who gets the girl in the end? I think Jeff Bridges was in it. He plays the dad."

"I don't think I know that one," said Jeremy, with as much sarcasm as he could muster.

"Too bad. It rocked." She skimmed a bare foot along his blue-jeaned thigh, and he instantly felt himself go hard, which only made him more pissed. He pushed her foot away. "Don't do that."

"What?" She resumed her rubbing.

"What you're doing." He scooted over a few inches.

"What's the matter? You don't like me?" She put on a mock offended face.

"Sure, I do. It's just . . ." Suddenly Jeremy couldn't think why he was being this way. Maybe Rud was right; maybe there *was* something the matter with him. He wasn't gay, or anything; that much he knew. The throbbing in his groin testified to that. But there had to be something seriously fucked up with a guy who just sat there like lump while a nearly naked girl played footsie with him, his dick about to pop the zipper on his jeans.

"What?" she prompted.

She ran her nails down his arm, nails polished a metallic blue that glittered in the moonlight slanting in through the blinds, making him break out in goose bumps. This time, when he didn't pull away, she looped her arms around his neck and drew him down beside her. The next he knew they were kissing. She tasted of stale beer and cigarettes, but for some reason that only excited him further. He opened his mouth and let his tongue play over hers.

He wondered if she could tell that he was a virgin. Was it possible to know a thing like that just from kissing someone? Would it make any difference to her if she did? Concerns that, sober, would have left him paralyzed with anxiety, but that in his present drunken and aroused state seemed as harmless as the IM chatter popping up on his computer screen at home.

They kissed a while longer before Jeremy was sufficiently emboldened to work a finger past the elastic band of her panties. Timidly at first, stopping when he felt the electric brush of her pubic hair against his fingertips. But she didn't push his hand away, so he kept on going.

She was wet. Oh God. He felt as if he could come just from touching her down there.

She unsnapped her bra and wriggled out of her panties. He brought his hand up, and he could smell her on him and it was like he was tripping on some drug, like the time he took Ecstasy, his blood fizzing in his veins and his skin so sensitive to the touch it was as if the whole world was being absorbed through his pores, the thoughts that had been troubling him all week—thoughts of his mother—tucked off in some remote region of his brain, where they drifted like smoke from a distant fire.

He cupped her breast, running his thumb over the nipple, which stiffened at once, sending a new jolt of pleasure through him. He'd done that. Him. It would have been the most perfect moment in his thus far pathetic life if just then she hadn't murmured thickly, "Jimmy. Oh, yeah, baby. Do it."

Jimmy? Who the fuck was Jimmy? Had she meant to say Jeremy? He froze for an instant, the part of him that was whispering that this might not be such a good idea nearly getting the better of the other, fired-up Jeremy who had only one thing on his mind. *Fuck it*, he thought. She wanted it, she'd said so herself. If it wasn't him, she'd be doing one of the other guys. And did he want to die a virgin? Not just a virgin, but a *pussy*, who'd messed up the one chance he'd had to do something with his dick other than jerk off.

With the speed of someone scrambling for the last seat on a lifeboat he shed his jeans, kicking them off with such force they hit the floor and kept right on going, skating with a soft slithering sound over the floorboards before pooling against the wall. Naked, he stretched out alongside her, the room spinning, as if the mattress were a raft slowly rotating along the eddies of a stream. They kissed some more, and then her hand was on his dick, fingers curled about the shaft moving in slow, delicious strokes . . . *oh God, oh Christ . . . if she doesn't stop I'll come. . .*

But he didn't want her to stop. He wanted this feeling to go on forever.

Once again, more feebly now, the voice of reason asserted itself. *She's drunk. She doesn't know what she's doing. She thinks you're some guy named Jimmy. Better quit before this gets out of hand.*

But it was just static in his head, and he tuned it out. Who cared if she thought he was someone else? If she was too wasted to know the difference, that was her problem. And if he didn't happen to have a condom on him it was probably all right. She hadn't said anything about it, which meant she'd most likely done whatever it was girls did to take care of such matters. She clearly wasn't inexperienced.

As he entered her, she cried out. *Yeah, like that, don't stop.* It was all the encouragement he needed. Then he was coming, in a blinding rush. He rolled away moments later to find her passed out cold. The dizzying high he'd been on gave way to shame. Carrie Ann, her name was Carrie Ann, he remembered it now. She was lying on her back with her eyes closed and her jaw slack, her legs splayed limply apart, snoring lightly. He kissed her gently on the lips, and she stirred, muttering something in her sleep.

"Carrie Ann?" he whispered. But she didn't rouse; she was dead to the world. And what would he have said, anyway, that he was sorry? For what? For fucking her when he knew it was wrong, or for not being this Jimmy guy? No, it was better this way. With any luck, by morning she wouldn't remember a thing. It would be like it never happened.

When he was called into the principal's office the following day, one look at Mr. Givens's face told him that he hadn't been summoned to discuss helping another kid who may have been struggling in math, the usual reason Mr. Givens wanted to see him. The expression on the principal's face was grim. As he sank into the chair opposite Mr. Givens's desk, Jeremy sensed he was in trouble, the kind of trouble that had last night's activities written all over it. A cold wave of panic went through him, and he felt his hangover drain away like so much dirty water from a stopped-up rain gutter, leaving him clear-headed, every circuit in his brain buzzing.

"I just got off the phone with Missus Flagler," said Mr. Givens. Jeremy must have looked blank, for he added, more pointedly, "Carrie Ann's mother."

Jeremy's spine stiffened, and he nodded slowly in mute acknowledgment that he did indeed know Carrie Ann.

"She's extremely upset," the principal went on, his normally jolly face—with its polished-looking pink cheeks and clipped white beard that made him look like a modern-day Santa Claus—flat and expressionless. "It seems Carrie Ann ran into some trouble last night. Would you know anything about that, son?" He stared hard at Jeremy across the cluttered surface of his desk.

Jeremy rearranged his features in what he hoped was an innocent expression. "Uh, well, yeah we were at a party last night. Me and her and some other people. Okay, we had a little too much to drink, but . . ." He shrugged, as if to say, *you know how it is*. But even as he spoke, images from last night flashed through his head: Carrie Ann passed out drunk on the mattress, her thighs sticky with his come; then later, he and Rud and Chuckie carrying her outside while Kenny, the only one sober enough to drive, brought the car around. Shame welled up in him when he thought about how they'd dumped her in front of her house, like so much garbage.

"I'm afraid it's not as simple as that."

"She's all right, isn't she?" A new fear crept in. Jeremy had heard about people dying of alcohol poisoning. Suppose something like that had happened to Carrie Ann?

"She's fine," said the principal, in a tone that conveyed that, while she wasn't in any mortal danger, something was seriously wrong nonetheless. "But the police have been called in, so if there's anything you need to get off your chest, I think now's the time."

"The police?" Jeremy's voice went up an octave.

"She claims she was raped."

After several moments of silence, in which every noise seemed amplified—the distant shrilling of the third period bell, the humming of the fax machine and tapping of a keyboard in the outer office—Mr. Givens prompted him once more. "Well, do you have anything to say for yourself?"

Jeremy shook his head, which wobbled as if too heavy for his neck. "No, sir."

The principal's eyes narrowed. He seemed to be trying to assess whether Jeremy was holding back or if it was the shock making him so uncommunicative. He must have decided that Jeremy was innocent, at least until proven guilty, for he said, not unkindly, "In any case, I don't think you should say anything to the police, not until we've spoken with your dad. I have a call in to him. I've left several messages, in fact. Do you know where I might be able reach him?"

Jeremy searched his mind, which was running in crazed circles, trying to think where his dad might be. Randy always kept his cell phone on, so Jeremy could reach him in case of an emergency, but parts of his territory were in areas that had spotty service.

Some impulse made him reach into the back pocket of his jeans and pull out a folded piece of binder paper with a phone number written on it. He'd been carrying it around for weeks, with no thought of ever needing it. Not until now.

He handed it to Mr. Givens. "Try my mom."

CHAPTER EIGHT

It took Colin several days just to weed through the junk in the Henleys' shed. With only a vague idea of what to do with the equipment now piled in his grandfather's old studio, he located, with the help of the Internet, a small-scale oyster farmer down on the Kitsap Peninsula, by the name of Len Jarvis. Colin was on a plane the next day, and hours later he was standing ankle deep, in rubber boots, in the shallow water off Hood Canal, listening as Len Jarvis took him through the process of stake and line oyster culturing.

Len dipped a hand horned with calluses into the water and pulled up a half shell to which clung a dozen or more baby oysters no bigger than the nail on his pinkie. "Now that there's your mother shell," he said, explaining how the discarded shells of shucked oysters were mixed with oyster larvae. Once the larvae had adhered and were sufficiently grown, the mother shells with their "babies" attached were fixed to lengths of rope with a stringing machine, like so many bulbs on strands of Christmas tree lights. The lines were then strung out in evenly spaced rows along the tidal flat, fixed at either end with lengths of PVC pipe embedded in the silt. It took several years for an oyster to fully mature, so it wasn't for those seeking quick results, Len warned.

"You have your predators, too," he went on. There was a tiny snail called an oyster drill, and something known as Denman Island disease. Starfish could be a problem, too. There were also the herons, seagulls, and otters that patrolled these waters in search of food. "We don't mind 'em taking their fair share, but they can be greedy little bastards, if you let 'em." He squinted off into the distance at the lines strung out in rows, held by barnacle-crusted stakes at either end. "Course the *real* culprits are our own kind."

Colin gave a solemn nod.

"Back in my father's day, the pulp mills had killed off most of the shellfish around here," Len said. "We've come a long way in bringing 'em back, but with pollution it's an ongoing battle." He turned to Colin. "You planning on doing this as a hobby, or are you looking to go into business?"

"I'm not in it for the money," Colin said.

"Good. Because you won't get rich." He regarded Colin for a moment, sizing him up. "Funny sort of work for a man like you. I'd have pegged you more as a city boy. Just out of curiosity, what got you interested?"

Colin told him about Mr. Deets, and the summers he'd spent on Grays Island, smiling to himself as he reflected on happier times.

They spoke a bit longer, Len refreshing Colin's memory as to the different varieties of oysters cultivated in these parts: the Pacific, which could grow to the size of a man's fist; the Olympia, which was the only native to these shores; the small, sweet Kumumoto, which had been brought over from Japan. As they walked back toward shore, Len dipped a hand into the water once more, this time extracting a fully grown specimen. Using the shucking knife he pulled from his back pocket, he pried it open, severing the abductor muscle and running the knife along the crevice between the two halves of the shell, all in one expert motion. He offered it to Colin, who tipped it into his mouth, briefly savoring the salty-sweet taste of it on his tongue before it slid down his throat. If the best memories of his childhood could be distilled into an essence, it would be this, he thought.

Two hours later, after a tour of the hatchery, during which Len introduced him to the astounding fact that a single oyster could produce up to five million eggs, Colin was on a plane headed home. He didn't know if he'd be as productive, but he felt the glimmerings of excitement, a sense of what the future might hold, a feeling he hadn't had in very long time.

In the days that followed he set about fashioning the rudiments of an operation. With the table saw he'd salvaged from the Henleys' shed, he cut PVC pipe into even two-foot lengths, into which he drilled holes with which to secure the ropes. The work was repetitive and time-consuming, but it didn't bother him. It eased his mind and kept his hands occupied. And at night, for the first time in years, he had no trouble falling asleep.

He wasn't without company, either. The dog, Shep, seemed to have more or less taken up residence at his place. He'd sit on his haunches, at a dignified distance, following Colin's every move. Occasionally Colin would find himself talking to the dog, explaining what he was doing or simply shooting the breeze. There was a queer kind of formality to the proceedings, Colin hard at work, with the border collie standing in silent attendance, like a butler in his morning coat.

After a long day at his workbench or down on the cove pounding in stakes when the tide was out, Colin would return to the bungalow, which he still thought of as his grandfather's, and light a fire to take off the chill. Often, as he did so, he would find himself gazing at the portrait over the mantel. It haunted him. Something about the expression on Eleanor Styles's face was both playful and melancholic, as if she'd known the contentment she was feeling in that moment wouldn't last.

His thoughts would turn then to Alice Kessler. Something about her had stayed with him as well. Maybe it was that he felt a kinship with her. She too was struggling to build a new life amid the rubble of her old one. He'd heard from his grandfather's caretaker, Orin, whom Colin had kept on to do odd jobs on an as-needed basis, about the café she'd bought and was in the process of renovating. He admired her courage in taking on such a risky enterprise; not only was she refusing to be beaten down, she was flying in the face of her detractors.

He was disappointed that he had yet to hear from her, but supposed he would eventually. The portrait would still be here, whenever she had the time to stop by. For much to the regret of the dealers who'd called with offers, he'd decided to keep it. If his grandfather had wanted it in some stranger's possession, he would have sold it years before.

One day in late November, Colin happened to glance out the window and noticed an old green Toyota coming up the drive. He watched as it pulled to a stop and a slender brown-haired woman climbed out, a woman he recognized at once as Alice Kessler. As he hurried off to meet her, he felt his pulse quicken.

"Alice. What a nice surprise," he greeted her.

"I'm sorry, I should have called first." Her eyes dropped to his jeans and work shirt, streaked with dirt and PVC dust. "Is this a bad time?

"Not at all. I was just about to take a break," he fibbed. "Why don't we go inside. I'll make some tea."

Her gaze fell on the border collie, who sat looking up at her, his head cocked and ears pricked. "Hello, boy. Don't I know you from somewhere?" She bent down, holding out a hand. Shep took a tentative sniff, his plumed tail sweeping slowly from side to side. She straightened, observing to Colin, "Looks as if you've found yourself a pet."

"More like he's found me." Colin smiled down at Shep. "He's a very discerning fellow. He doesn't give his affections easily. I'm still not sure if I've made the final cut."

"Well, at least you have each other for company. It must get lonely out here." Her gaze took in the wind-scoured bluff and cove sparkling below, and to the east the high brow of the ridge, with its line of trees like bristles on a comb.

"It does at times," he conceded.

She looked better than when he'd last seen her. Healthier. The jeans that had hung on her before were filled out nicely in all the right places and the hollows in her cheeks not so pronounced. But her eyes hadn't lost their look of melancholy. And he sensed a certain tension in her as well, as if this were more than a social call.

In the kitchen, he put the kettle on to boil. He'd given up coffee; it reminded him too much of AA meetings, the ever-present smell of it in the air and seeing those new in sobriety, like him, clinging to their Styrofoam cups as if to a lifeline.

"So, I hear you bought a restaurant," Colin remarked, as he put the kettle on to boil.

"Word travels fast." Alice smiled ruefully, removing a stack of newspapers from one of the chairs before taking a seat at the table. "Yes, I'm now the proud owner of a former fish-and-chips joint. It was pretty much on its last leg, but it's amazing what a few cans of paint and a liberal application of elbow grease can do. The grand opening is next week. Nothing fancy, just family and friends. I hope you can make it."

Colin warmed. "I wouldn't miss it for the world."

He turned to find her eyeing him curiously. "What about you? From the looks of it, you've been doing more than catching up on your reading."

"As it so happens, I'm thinking of going into business myself." More than thinking, but he didn't want to commit himself to anything just yet.

"Would it have anything to do with oyster farming?"

He broke into a grin. "Don't tell me you're a mind reader on top of everything else?"

"No. Just observant." She gestured toward the brochures he'd left sitting out on the table, picking up a pamphlet titled *Small Scale Oyster Farming in the Pacific Northwest*. "I'll say one thing, if you were looking for a change, this is about as extreme as it gets."

"That it is." Extreme as a dive into an icy-cold lake—just the wake-up call he needed. "Maybe that's why I like the idea."

"Does this mean you're giving up on lawyering?" He caught a flicker of consternation in her eyes, and wondered why it should matter to her one way or the other.

He shrugged. "Looks that way. For now, at least."

She lapsed into silence, and he caught that preoccupied look on her face again. Then she roused herself and put on a smile, saying, "Well, good luck with it. I guess we're sort of in the same boat. I just hope the gamble pays off for both of us. If the road to hell is paved with good intentions, I'm sure that's true of failed enterprises."

"Look at the bright side," he said. "You'll have at least one customer you can count on. If your cooking is any better than mine, which is a pretty sure bet, you'll be seeing a lot more of me."

She smiled then, a slow-breaking smile that lit up her whole face. All at once he felt absurdly happy to have her here. It was the first time since Nadine's death that he'd felt that way about another woman. With Alice, he knew he didn't have to fake being okay. He could just be himself, wounds, warts, and all.

"What a lovely place," she said, as he led the way into the living room carrying the tea tray. "I can see why you and your grandfather were so close." He shot her an inquiring look, and she explained, "You can tell a lot about a person from their house, and it's obvious what kind of person he was. Very unpretentious, I'd say. Someone who didn't put style over comfort and who probably didn't give a hoot what anyone thought. The kind of man," her eyes, dancing with bemusement, dropped to the tray Colin was lowering onto the coffee table, "who'd serve tea in chipped mugs and sugar out of a box."

Colin smiled somewhat sheepishly. "I'm sorry it's not fancier, but it's the best I can do on such short notice. As for my grandfather, that's him in a nutshell."

While he poured the tea, she moved in to get a closer look at the portrait. For the longest while she didn't speak. She appeared dumbstruck.

He stepped up alongside her. "Nothing prepares you for it, does it?" The reproductions he'd seen were a classic case of something being lost in the translation. "Do you think it looks like her?"

Alice studied it, frowning. "In a way, yes. But she looks . . . more at ease than I remember her. My grandmother was always running around doing six things at once. She didn't have a lot of time to sit and relax." She sounded sad, for some reason.

"As for whether or not she meant something to your grandfather, I asked my mother about it," she went on. "Unfortunately, she couldn't tell me much. Either she doesn't know, or she didn't want to tarnish Nana's memory. I have a feeling they might have been lovers, though, and seeing this . . ." she gestured toward the portrait, "I'm almost sure of it." She turned to face Colin. "I know this is going to sound strange, but I can't say I disapprove. She deserved to be happy, even if it was with someone other than my grandfather. Not that she didn't love Grandpa Joe, but it wasn't a marriage in the typical sense. He wasn't . . . all there."

"I guess we'll never know the real story," Colin said.

"No, but thank you for this. I'm glad I finally got to see it," she said, her gaze returning to the painting. "I would have come sooner, but—" She broke off, turning to him with a contrite look. "Look, I have a confession to make. I had an ulterior motive in coming here." She retreated, sinking down on the sofa. "It's my son. He's in trouble."

"What kind of trouble?" Colin asked, thinking it was the kind of trouble that needed a male perspective, or maybe someone to counsel the boy. Her next words took him completely by surprise.

"He needs a lawyer."

"I see." Colin blinked in surprise, and sat down.

"He didn't do anything wrong," she rushed to qualify. "He's being falsely accused."

"Of what?"

Some of the color went out of her cheeks. "Rape."

"That's pretty serious."

"If you knew Jeremy, you'd know he isn't remotely capable of doing such a thing. It's all a big mistake. Or . . ." Her expression darkened. "He's being set up."

"Where is he now?" Colin asked.

"At home, with his dad. They booked him down at the station, but his uncle—my sister's husband—arranged it so he could get out on bail before the arraignment."

"His uncle's a lawyer?"

"A cop, actually. Deputy chief of police." She paused. "Which is where you come in. We need a good criminal attorney, and the lawyers around here . . ." She spread her hands in a helpless gesture. "Let's just say they haven't had a lot of experience with this kind of thing."

Colin, feeling something akin to panic at the thought of climbing back into the saddle, hastened to set her straight. "I wish I could help, but the thing is, I'm not practicing anymore. Of course, I'll do whatever I can, to help you find someone else to represent him, if you'd like."

Her face fell, but she quickly rallied, saying, "I don't want just anyone. I need someone I can trust."

But Colin was already shaking his head. No, he'd left all that behind. The mere thought of entering a courtroom . . . "I understand, and believe me, if it were anything else—"

She didn't let him finish. "When you said you weren't practicing, does that mean you can't or you won't?"

"I'm still licensed, if that's what you mean. But that's not the point. I haven't been inside a courtroom since . . . " *I lost my job for being drunk twenty-four seven.* He sat back. "Well, you know the story. Trust me, I'm not just saying this for my own sake. Your son deserves better than someone on as shaky legs as me."

Alice went on eyeing him with a directness he found unnerving. "Tell me something," she said, her eyes piercing through his defenses. "Were you good at it?"

"Yes, I was good at it," he replied wearily. So good, in fact, that his boss had continued to cut him slack long after he would have fired anyone else.

"That's all I need to know."

"It's not as simple as that," he started to say, but she cut him off again.

"Look, I realize it's a lot to ask. We barely know one another. But this is my *son.* If anything happens to him—" She broke off with a small, choked sound. He could see that she was struggling not to give in to tears. "I already lost one son," she said, when she'd regained some of her composure. "I can't lose another one."

Colin wavered, torn between the strong desire to come to her rescue and the equally strong desire to rescue himself. At last, he came to a decision. Letting out a breath he hadn't realized he'd been holding, he told her, "All right. I'll see what I can do."

She looked so relieved that for a moment he thought she was going to burst into tears. "Thank you. You don't know what this means to me."

Colin, feeling as if he were digging himself in deeper with each passing minute, said only, "You can thank me when I've actually accomplished something."

"So what happens now?"

"If we're lucky, the judge will let him off with probation. He's young and he's had a clean record up until now. That counts for a lot." Colin paused, asking, "He *hasn't* been in trouble before, has he?"

"No, of course not. At least, not as far as I know," she added, more hesitantly. Color rose in her cheeks. It had to pain her that she'd been so out of the loop. Then her expression hardened. "But one thing I *do* know: He didn't rape anyone."

Colin felt obligated to caution her, "That may be the case, but if he pleads not guilty, it'll mean a trial, and believe me you don't want that." This was his standard rap in situations like this. In his role as assistant D.A., his job had been to put criminals away, even if it meant having them cop to a lesser plea. "Don't look so worried," he said, more gently. "If what you're saying is true, the case could be dismissed due to lack of evidence. We'll know more after I've spoken with the D.A. I'll also need to have a word with Jeremy."

She perked up. "We could drive over there now."

Colin pondered it a moment, a grayness settling over him like the thick fog that had engulfed him in the months after Nadine's death. Was he only giving her false hope? And putting himself at risk of drinking again? It wasn't too late to back out, he told himself. He hadn't committed to anything yet.

At last, he rose heavily to his feet. "Let me get my coat."

She was quiet on the drive to her ex-husband's. Colin didn't doubt the situation would be complicated by some residual tension there. She hadn't spoken a word against her ex, but he sensed there was some history. How could there not be? In any event, it was bound to make a bad situation that much worse, which made Colin wonder again if he was doing the right thing.

But then he'd look at Alice, and think about all she'd been through, what she was still going through, and his reservations would fade. She needed him, and it had been a long time since Colin had felt needed.

After a series of winding roads they finally pulled up in front of a split-level ranch house on a street lined with other, similar looking houses. He was getting out of the car when she placed a hand on his arm. "I'm not asking you to go easy on him, but he's had a pretty rough time of it," she said, in a voice soft with appeal. "Just . . . keep that in mind, okay?"

"And if he's not telling me everything I need to know?" said Colin, testing her to see if she was capable of dealing with the fact that her son might not be as innocent as she believed.

"Then you'll do what you have to," she said. Her face was pale but her tone firm. She clearly wanted the truth, at whatever cost.

Jeremy Kessler was nothing like the punks Colin was used to dealing with. The boy who rose from the living room sofa to offer him a limp handshake was slightly built, with curly dark hair and his mother's watchful gray-green eyes. He looked younger than his age and utterly defenseless. The kind of kid who'd probably been picked on in school. He didn't strike Colin as sexually experienced, much less someone who would force unwanted attentions on a girl. On the other hand, Colin knew that looks could be deceiving. One of the most difficult cases he'd ever tried had been a baby-faced fourteen-year-old from the Bronx, who with several fellow gang members had robbed a bodega at gunpoint, pistol-whipping the owner to within an inch of his life. At his sentencing, the boy had cried for his mommy.

Jeremy's father—tall, fair-haired, with the look of an aging high school athlete—stepped forward to introduce himself. "Hi, I'm Randy. Thanks for coming on such short notice." He had a salesman's ready smile and firm handshake, but beneath Randy's manufactured grin, Colin sensed the man was just as worried as his ex-wife.

"No problem," Colin said. He cast a quick glance at Alice, who wore a carefully neutral expression, before he turned his attention to the boy. In a mild, conversational tone, he observed, "I understand you're in a bit of trouble, Jeremy." Jeremy gave an almost imperceptible nod, and Colin went on, "First time?"

"Yeah," Jeremy replied, in a voice that was barely above a squeak.

"How about school-related? Detention, suspension, that kind of thing."

"I'm not sure what you're getting at," interjected Randy, the bonhomie of a moment ago giving way to an impatient scowl. "But let's be clear on one thing: *He's* the injured party here."

Colin turned to Randy, saying, "I can't help him unless I know all the facts."

"The only thing you need to know is that he's being railroaded." Randy rushed once more to his son's defense.

Colin ignored him to address Jeremy. "Is there someplace we can talk in private?"

Jeremy looked to his dad for approval, but before Randy could weigh in, Alice spoke up. "Jeremy, why don't you take Mister McGinty to your room?" Jeremy shot her a veiled look, but he didn't offer any protest.

Colin still wasn't sure he would take the case; some of it depended on how cooperative Jeremy was going to be. So it was with surprise and no small degree of concern that he found himself slipping easily into that role, the gears meshing as smoothly as if the machinery hadn't stood idle for the past five years.

When Colin and Jeremy left the room, Alice cautiously lowered herself into the wing-backed chair by the fireplace. The living room that had been eclectically furnished and cluttered with toys when she'd lived here had been done over in her long absence. It was now an almost exact replica of her former mother-in-law's, down to the ginger jar lamps and framed Audubon prints on the walls. Which suggested that the only woman currently in Randy's life was Mrs. Kessler senior. Alice wondered why he hadn't remarried. Randy was still a handsome man. He could have almost any woman he wanted. But it wasn't any of her business, so there was no point in speculating.

Randy sank down on the sofa that still bore the faint imprint of their son's lanky frame. "This feels a little like déjà vu, doesn't it?" she said to break the ice.

Ignoring the reference to her own past legal woes, Randy asked point blank, "What do you know about this guy, other than the fact that he was some hot shot prosecutor back in New York?"

"I know that he's good. And that there's no one else on the island even remotely qualified." Alice didn't need to remind him that most of the crime around here was on the level of petty theft and DUIs. Warren Brockman, who'd represented Alice during her trial, had primarily handled civil cases before that.

Randy sighed, dropping his head to push his hands through his hair, which was longer than he used to wear it and styled in a way that flattered his square, defense linebacker's face. He looked as if he'd been up all night, which he probably had. "Point taken. Sorry, I didn't mean to go off on the guy like that. It's just that . . . hell, Alice, I don't have to tell you, of all people, how this could end up. I don't want to see the same thing happen to Jeremy."

"I don't want that either," she said quietly.

"Look, I don't mean to open old wounds. It's just that I've been worried sick." Randy eyed her morosely across the expanse of thick-pile carpet that no doubt had been selected by his mother, a shade of Arctic blue that Alice would never in a million years have chosen. At last, he let out an audible breath. "Would you like a drink? I could use one myself."

"Thanks, no," she said.

He rose and went into the next room, returning a few minutes later with a tumbler containing his usual whiskey and soda. He sank back down on the sofa, where he sipped his drink in silence, absorbed in his thoughts, separated from her by more than the four or five feet of space that stood between them. After a minute or so, he roused himself to ask, "So, how have you been? Things going okay?"

"As well as can be expected," she said, with a shrug.

"There's a rumor going around that you're opening a restaurant."

She smiled. "I've heard the same rumor myself."

"So is it true?"

"The grand opening is a week from tomorrow. I hope you and Jeremy can make it."

Randy looked surprised but pleased to be invited. "I'll try, if I'm not on the road."

"Jeremy tells me you were promoted. Congratulations."

Randy gave a snort. "Yeah, for what it's worth. All it means is more territory to cover. If I didn't need the money, I'd be cutting back on my hours instead. This thing with Jeremy . . . I can't help thinking that if I'd been around more . . ." He shook his head, a distraught look on his face.

"You can't blame yourself," Alice said. She knew all about blame. Hadn't she blamed herself, for everything from David's death to the fact that Jeremy wanted nothing to do with her?

"Who else should I blame?" he threw back at her.

"Maybe no one's to blame. Things don't always happen for a reason."

There was a pause before Randy said softly, "You mean David." They exchanged a look more expressive than any words. "I still think about him. A lot."

"Me, too." Her throat tightened.

"I should have been there that night. If it weren't for these crazy hours . . ." His hands balled into fists, and she could see a muscle working in his jaw.

Alice felt something give way in her chest, an anger against Randy she hadn't realized she'd been holding on to. The years had taken their toll on him as well. He appeared humbled in a way that was obvious only to someone who knew him as well as she did. In her long absence, he'd clearly had a lot of time to think. She wondered now if he regretted more than not being there the night David was killed. "It's funny," she said. "I always thought you blamed *me*. I was there. I should have kept a closer eye on him." *Why hadn't they talked about this before? It might have changed everything.*

"Listen to us. Ten years, and it's like it happened yesterday," Randy observed with a dry little croak of a laugh. He contemplated this for a moment, sipping his drink as he stared sightlessly ahead. When he brought his gaze back to her, she saw that his eyes were bloodshot. "Maybe I did hold you responsible in a way, but it wasn't because of that. I didn't understand why you couldn't let go. Why you wouldn't stop hounding the guy."

Our son's killer, you mean, she silently amended. Alice sat back, the flicker of a connection she'd felt with him fading. "I guess there are some things we'll never agree on. Why don't we just leave it at that?"

Just then, the door to Jeremy's room cracked open. Jeremy stepped out into the hallway looking shaken. Colin emerged behind him wearing a flat, unreadable expression. Alice felt herself go cold. What had they talked about in there? Had Jeremy told him things he wasn't comfortable sharing with her or Randy?

Randy put his drink down on the coffee table and jumped to his feet, closing the distance between him and Jeremy in several long strides. "You all right, son?" he asked, putting an arm around Jeremy's shoulders.

Jeremy nodded, but Alice could see how pale and shaken he was. She wondered if this was indeed history repeating itself.

CHAPTER NINE

November 1942

In the summer of that year the Allied forces under the command of General MacArthur began waging an all-out assault on Guadalcanal. The letters Eleanor had been receiving from her husband started coming less frequently. Each night, she and her daughter would gather around the old Philco, straining toward its amber glow as toward a feeble flame by which to warm themselves, listening to the latest broadcasts out of Washington. When the news wasn't good, they would trudge off to bed burdened by the weight of their fears. Eleanor knew that even the victories weren't without casualties, and she and Lucy lived in dread of a telegraph from the War Department.

Lucy had stopped asking when her papa was coming home; several of the children in her school had lost fathers to the war and she knew there was a chance she might also lose hers. Eleanor worried, too. The difference was that, while Joe remained Lucy's chief preoccupation, Eleanor's thoughts had been straying to other things. Whenever she was reminded of the reason for that distraction, a slow heat would unfurl up her neck to flood her cheeks, and at night, as she knelt beside her bed, she would pray all the more fervently for her husband's safe return.

The man responsible for this new and unwelcome tide of emotion was William McGinty. In the months since they'd met he'd been coming by the house once or twice a week, sometimes more often. He never showed up empty-handed. Usually it was basic supplies he brought, food and items of clothing he thought Yoshi might need. But always there would be at least one luxury item tucked in with the staples: a small sack of coffee or sugar, a pound of butter, a bar of soap. If he wasn't in a hurry to get back, he would stay and chat.

Eleanor had come to treasure those stolen hours, hoard them like the rationed sugar he brought. Conversations with friends and neighbors usually centered around the war, but William talked about things that took her mind off such weighty concerns, stories about his student travels abroad and all the fascinating people he'd met along the way. He brought her a Europe untouched by war, one of ancient canals and labyrinthian streets so narrow they could barely accommodate a car and a bicycle at the same time; outdoor markets where you could buy any kind of foodstuff or household item imaginable; rural villages where humble thatched-roof cottages stood side by side with soaring cathedrals.

In her mind, she could see the moon reflected in the waters of the Seine off the Pont du Change, the pigeons that flocked Venice's San Marco Plaza, and the special way the light fell over the rooftops of Florence, a phenomenon known as *chiaroscuro*, she was informed. She learned about the artist named Gaudi and his famous palace in Spain, ugly and beautiful at the same time, from which the word gaudy had come; and the wonders of the Louvre where William had studied the techniques of the Old Masters. There were fondly recollected meals, in which she could almost taste the wine, made by vintners who'd been doing it exactly as had their ancestors for hundreds of years, and the bread baked in great, crusty loaves in wood-fired ovens. It was as if he'd handed her the keys to a hidden door, though which she could escape, for brief intervals, to a better world.

One day in early November they were sitting at the kitchen table, chatting while they sipped coffee and nibbled on freshly baked gingerbread, Eleanor telling him about a wedding she'd attended the weekend before, when William asked with his usual forthrightness, "What about you and Joe? How did you two meet?"

Eleanor's eyes darted to the doorway, through which she could see Lucy, seated cross-legged on the living room floor with Yoshi, who was teaching her how to tie a sailor's knot. She lived in dread of Lucy's finding out that Joe wasn't her real father, so it was a subject she normally sidestepped. Now she turned her gaze to the window, staring out at the rain pouring down, wondering how best to reply.

She looked back at William to find him eyeing her intently. She searched his face for some hint that he'd gotten wind of the old rumors that must have circulated around the time Lucy was born, but his blue eyes were clear and guileless. "We met at church," she told him, settling on a partial truth.

"So was it love at first sight?"

Eleanor felt warmth steal into her cheeks. "I don't know about that. I thought he was nice. And apparently he liked me well enough. Beyond that, we didn't really know each other all that well when we got married. I suppose you could call it a whirlwind courtship."

"And if you had it to do all over again?"

"Goodness, what a question!" She dropped her gaze, feeling self-conscious all of a sudden. "Why, yes, of course. Why do you ask?" Time and again she'd asked herself the same question, and it always came back to the same thing: Lucy. For Lucy's sake, yes, she would do it over again.

"I'm sorry, I don't mean to pry. It's just that the war has got me thinking. Every day we're reminded of how fragile life is, how it can be snuffed out at any moment. You can't help wondering if you're making the most of it, if you wouldn't be happier doing something else . . . or with someone else."

He bent to run his hand absently over the thick ruff of the dog curled at his feet. He never went anywhere without Laird, named after William's Scottish forbears and every inch the aristocrat, with his sleek lines and perfectly shaped head, his thick glossy coat black as midnight, except for his snow-white paws and the patches of white around his eyes and on his chest. For it seemed the now-grown puppy intended for his son preferred William's company. Laird lifted his head to give William a questioning look, and when it was clear nothing was required of him, he settled back down with a contented sigh.

"Would *you* do it differently?" she asked, wondering once more about his wife. He rarely mentioned her except in passing, but from what little Eleanor had been able to glean, their marriage clearly wasn't what it ought to be.

"Honestly? No." His reply brought a jab to her midsection that caught her unawares, a blow she hadn't thought to protect herself against. One that was softened by his next words. "I wouldn't have my son if I hadn't married Martha."

"So no regrets?"

He shrugged. "We all have regrets. It's human nature, I suppose."

Eleanor ventured hesitantly, "Your wife. Does she know about these visits of yours?"

William fell silent, peering out at the rain-soaked yard. Beyond it lay the field that bordered on her property, where the grass that had stood high in summer was broken and stubbly and the blackberry vines reddish-brown with autumn's rust. The far end of the field was marked by a nearly impenetrable wall of green, Douglas firs and hemlocks mostly, through which she could make out only faintly the path that wound its way up Spring Hill, where she enjoyed hiking in the warm weather months. When he spoke at last, his voice was quiet, troubled almost. "No, she doesn't know. I couldn't think of a way of telling her without putting you and Yoshi at risk."

"I suppose it's for the best," Eleanor said dubiously. "It's just . . . I can't help wondering what she would make of your spending so much time in the company of a lady whose husband is overseas." It was the closest she had come to voicing what she'd long suspected: that these visits were spurred by more than mere generosity on his part.

She saw in his eyes the answer she'd been seeking, and felt all at once giddy with the knowledge, like at her friend's daughter's wedding, when the champagne she'd drunk had gone to her head. When he spoke, though, his voice was flat. "Martha's pretty preoccupied with the war efforts. I doubt she even notices when I'm not around," he said.

"Besides, she's used to my wandering off in search of things to paint." He paused to sip his coffee. "Speaking of which, I have a favor to ask."

"Anything," she replied without hesitation. "Whatever it is, I'm sure it won't come close to repaying you for all you've done."

His expression turned shy. "I'd like to paint your portrait."

It wasn't at all what she'd been expecting, and she said the first thing that popped into her head. "Why ever would you want to do that?" She self-consciously brought a hand to her cheek, toying with a curly tendril that had slipped out from under the scarf she'd tied around her head that morning when she could do nothing with her hair.

"You'll have to take that up with my muse," he said, with a laugh.

"Your muse?"

"She decides what I'm going to paint. She can be bossy about it, too. I have very little say in the matter."

"I see." Eleanor got into the spirit of it. "And this muse of yours has decided you should paint me?"

"Apparently so."

"I suppose I should be flattered. On the other hand, it could just as easily be a rock or a tree. Or the ocean on a stormy day," she added, with a glance out the window, at the patch of slate-colored ocean off in the distance, pressed under the heel of an ominous sky.

"True, but the ocean never sits still for long, and I'm hoping you will, for this."

"What exactly is involved?" A little flutter of unease worked its way up from the pit of her stomach.

"I'll do a few preliminary sketches first, but all in all it shouldn't take more than three or four sittings."

"It would have to be mornings, when Lucy's at school." She spoke slowly, hesitant to commit herself. It wasn't that her daughter required her full-time attention these days. When Lucy was around, she spent almost as much time with Yoshi as with her. Right now, for instance, she'd abandoned her knot-tying to follow him outside. Eleanor watched through the window as they sloshed across the muddy yard on their way to the kennel, Lucy in her slicker and boots and Yoshi with his head ducked low and the collar of his jacket pulled up around his ears. No, it wasn't so much the shirking of her parental duties that concerned Eleanor as her reluctance to have Lucy witness the spectacle of her mother posing for a portrait, like some society lady or . . . or indolent mistress. She blushed, too, at the thought of all those hours alone with William, him studying every nuance of her face and form. Would he be able to read in her face the feelings she did her best to hide? Would her eyes tell him what her heart could not?

And what would people think, if they knew? Something like this, however innocent, could resurrect the old rumors about her hasty wedding and the baby that some had speculated wasn't Joe's. Those who had whispered about her before would find her current behavior even more shocking, she a married woman with her husband off fighting overseas.

And Joe, what would *he* think?

"Would tomorrow be convenient?" William's voice broke into her thoughts.

"Tomorrow?" She turned toward him, her fears subsiding at the sight of his open, smiling face. "Tomorrow will be just fine."

Minutes later he was pushing back his chair, saying, "I should be off. I promised Danny I'd take him to see the new Gary Cooper picture. Have you seen it yet?"

She shook her head. "I don't get to the pictures much." In fact, she hadn't seen a movie since the war broke out.

A wistful look flitted across his face, as if he were thinking about all the places he'd like to take her. Then he turned to go, Laird at his heels, only lightly touching her shoulder in passing. At the door, he paused to ask, "You're sure you're all right with this? I wouldn't want to impose."

"It's not that." She hesitated before going on, fearful that he would think she was making too much of this. It wasn't as if he'd asked her to pose nude, for heaven's sake. "It's just . . . Are you sure it's wise? People might get the wrong idea. Not just Martha."

"Ah. I see." He nodded slowly, wearing a thoughtful look. "Well, in that case, it'll be our little secret." He broke into a grin, and she thought, *Isn't that just like a man? Problem solved, case closed.* Even so, she gave into a small smile of her own.

"We seem to be in the habit of keeping secrets," she observed dryly.

"Loose lips sink ships." He quoted the slogan on the poster displayed in every other shop window in town, along with the more lurid one depicting a caricature of the enemy, with exaggerated slant eyes and a protruding front teeth, that read simply *Jap Beast.*

What ships were in danger of being sunk here? she wondered.

Outside the dogs began to bark with the high yipping noises they made when let out to romp in the yard. All of last season's pups had found homes and the only dogs remaining were the two males, Panda and Cab (named after

Cab Calloway), and her three bitches, Suki, Niobe, and Jasmine. Laird was Jasmine's son, the only male in that litter, and now his ears pricked at the sounds in the yard and he whined softly at the door, glancing up at William in mute appeal. William's eyes, though, were on Eleanor as he turned the knob, the hint of wistfulness she'd caught earlier now nakedly apparent. A look passed between them, in which Eleanor saw mirrored in his face all of her inchoate yearning.

Then he was out the door, and she was left trembling on the threshold of something she dared not name, wanting it and fearing it at the same time.

William was well aware of the risk involved, but whatever trepidation he might feel had nothing to do with the threat to his or Eleanor's reputations. It was his own heart he feared. In painting her portrait he would be expressing with his brush what he couldn't in words. And what if, once unleashed, those feelings could no longer be contained? Would Eleanor be scandalized? Would she put a stop to any further visits? He would rather go on this way, in a perpetual state of longing, than risk being cut off from her.

For there was no denying it any longer: William was in love.

It was a feeling he hadn't known in such a long time, it was a revelation for him. Everywhere he looked colors seemed brighter and even the bleakest landscapes were washed in light. He felt more kindly disposed toward the world in general, even those people he didn't particularly like. Alone in his studio, he'd catch himself staring idly at the half-finished canvas propped on his easel, a seascape commissioned by a retired boat builder in Oregon, seeing only Eleanor's face. He would imagine how he'd paint her, what pigments would best bring out the red and gold highlights in her hair and capture the luminous quality of her skin.

He sensed that she shared those feelings, and thought it would have been easy to seduce her. The notion didn't strike him as morally reprehensible, not in any general sense. While living in Europe he'd abandoned the hidebound morals inculcated in him as a child. But it wasn't just the quick pleasures of the bed he desired. He wanted more than that; he wanted a life with Eleanor. And how was it possible? He had his family to think of; hers, too. The thought of Eleanor's husband off fighting for his country, while he, William, fulfilled his lust in their marital bed, left him feeling slightly queasy. It would eat at Eleanor most of all, he knew. He'd have to stand by helplessly and watch the woman he loved be consumed by guilt, knowing he was the cause of it.

Martha deserved better, too. He had loved her once, and if that love had grown fractured with time, she was still his wife, the mother of his son. He owed it to her, and to Danny, not to let his small lie grow into an even bigger one.

And yet . . .

He dreamed of Eleanor with his eyes open. He imagined what it would be like to lie next to her in bed, her bare flesh gliding over his, his face buried in her hair that was twelve different shades of brown and red, her soft mouth parting at the touch of his lips. He saw her face framed by the white of her pillow, her green eyes beckoning to him. He saw the smooth plane of her belly and her long legs opening to him, taking him in.

If he couldn't make love to her, painting her portrait would be the next best thing. For the first time in months he itched to pick up his brushes and palette. Already he was plotting how best to capture her on canvas. He wanted to depict her as he saw her: a woman gloriously in her prime who mistakenly believed the best years of her life were behind her.

"Don't look at me. I'm a wreck," she said, with a breathless laugh as she let him through the door. "Are you sure about this? You'll be wasting a perfectly good canvas." She was wearing a faded housecoat, her hair haphazardly pinned up, the dogs roiling at her feet. Yet to him, she had never looked more beautiful. She bent to grab hold of a dog collar, scolding, "Now, look, you, it's back to the kennel if you don't behave yourself." The offending creature instantly sank onto its haunches, looking up at her shame-faced until she stroked its head and let it loose.

She straightened, tucking a stray tendril of hair behind one ear, her face flushed with exertion. "I'm a little behind schedule," she apologized. "Lucy was late getting off to school. And the dogs—" she pointed toward Niobe, now romping on the braided rug in front of the fireplace with Laird "—must have known you were coming. The only way I could get them to stop barking was to let them into the house."

He smiled. In one hand, he carried the battered wooden case containing his paints and brushes and in the other his folded easel and a blank canvas wrapped in brown paper. "The more, the merrier," he said. "They can keep Laird company while I paint."

"Wait here while I change. I won't be a minute." She spun on her heel, disappearing down the hall. Only then did he notice she was barefoot. Minutes later, in less time than it would have taken Martha to change hats, she was back, wearing a red print dress belted at the waist, her hair arranged in loose curls on top of her head. Dangling from one hand was a pair of high-heeled pumps.

"No, leave them off," ordered William, when she bent to put them on. "I'd like you barefoot." He hadn't planned to paint her that way. But seeing her all dressed up in her Sunday best without her shoes, he realized it captured her, the two sides of Eleanor that were often at war with each other: the part that wanted to be respectable and the part that wanted to run wild, like a child through high grass on a summer day.

She shot him a quizzical look, tossing the pumps aside. "If you insist. But I won't look very elegant."

"You're perfect just as you are." It was a moment before he could tear his eyes away.

"I'm afraid my last pair of stockings has a hole in it," she said, glancing down at her legs in dismay, which, like her feet, were bare. "They're so hard to come by these days, I might as well wish for the Eiffel Tower. So where do you want me?" Her eyes darted around the neat, if somewhat shabby room, with its threadbare furnishings and woodwork polished to a shine.

Naked in bed, came his silent, unbidden reply. But all he said was, "Why don't we try the sofa. You'll be more comfortable and the light's good." He waited until she'd positioned herself on worn, plush cushions, her legs tucked under her, her toes peeking from the folds of her skirt. "There, like that. Don't move an inch." He got out his pad and a stick of charcoal and began sketching her. Midway through his third failed attempt at capturing her on paper, he paused, frowning. "You look tense. If you're uncomfortable, we could try another position."

"It's not that," she said. "I was just wondering what you plan on doing with the portrait once it's finished. I mean, if it's going to be on display . . . "

"I haven't given it much thought," he answered truthfully. "I may decide to keep it."

Her eyes widened in consternation. "Won't your wife . . . I mean, she'd have to wonder . . . "

"She might," he agreed, "if I were to show it to her, which I have no intention of doing."

Silence rose up to fill the room, eddying with all the implications of his words. William saw the troubled look on Eleanor's face, and for a panicked moment he thought she might decide to call the whole thing off.

But the silence held and the moment passed.

"What do you look for in a subject?" she asked, after a bit.

He paused to consider it, absently scratching his chin. "I'm not sure I can explain it. It's different with each one. Like, for instance . . . Have you seen the portrait I did of Mister Humphrey that's hanging in his store?" Wizened old Humphrey, who had to be at least ninety years old, owned the stationery shop downtown where William bought a lot of his supplies. "What made me decide to paint him were his hands. They're all twisted and knobby, but beautiful in their own way, like tree roots pushing up out of the ground."

"And what do you see in me?" Her green eyes looked directly into his, and a silent communication passed between them. William felt the tiny hairs on the back of his arms and neck stand up.

"I see a lady in waiting."

She arched a brow. "Because of Joe, you mean?"

"Well, no, not exactly." He searched for the right words. "It's just . . . there's so much out there you haven't seen. A whole world. And here you are . . . " *Trapped with a man you don't love*. "Living out in the middle of nowhere." He held up a hand before she could voice the protest forming on her lips. "I don't mean that you're not here out of your own free will, but I'll bet you can count on one hand the number of times you've been off the island."

He could see from the way her face was reddening that he'd hit a nerve, but she only laughed and said, "You're wrong. I'd need both hands." She held them up, fingers splayed apart, the tiny diamond in her wedding ring winking in the pale light filtering through the window. "Still, it doesn't mean I'm not adventurous. Just poor."

"I'm sorry, I didn't mean to offend you," he was quick to reply. "All I'm saying is that you're different from most of the people around here. You have a curiosity about the world. I never would have suggested to Mister Humphrey, for instance, that he ought to get out more. He's perfectly happy right where he is."

She stiffened a bit. "And I'm not?"

"I'm not the one to answer that," he said gently.

"I have a child to think of. I can't just waltz off whenever I feel like it." Frowning, she said, "Anyway, how did we get on this subject? I thought you wanted to paint me, not dissect me."

"Point taken," he said with a smile, bending once more to his work.

When William was finally satisfied with what he'd drawn, he set up his easel and unpacked his paints, unrolling the felt cloth smelling of linseed oil in which his brushes were wrapped. Before long he was so absorbed in his work he scarcely noticed the minutes slipping by. It wasn't until Eleanor stirred and stretched that he glanced at his watch and saw that more than an hour had passed. He called a break, and Eleanor went into the kitchen to fetch them something to drink. William, alone in the room with nothing to occupy him, became aware of the sounds drifting in from outside: the rusty caw of a crow; a hammer banging in the yard; the more distant drone of an airplane.

Not bad, he thought, contemplating the progress he'd made so far. He'd captured something in her expression, a combination of youthfulness and womanly experience. And her eyes . . . they seemed to be gazing out at those far flung places she dreamed of visiting one day. He decided he would title it simply *Woman in Red*. The image would speak for itself.

Over the next few days they fell into a routine, William coming over every morning after Lucy had been packed off to school. Now, when he dreamed, it was of Eleanor in the red dress. Barefoot. And after a while what was in his mind's eye became blurred with what he saw in reality, like watercolors running together, lending a vibrancy to her image that he couldn't have created on his own. He became obsessed with the portrait, working in a kind of fever, as if guided by some unseen force.

The irony wasn't lost on him, either. What was perhaps his best work might never see the light of day. Yet surprisingly the thought didn't trouble him. He wasn't doing this for money or fame; he was doing it out of love.

It was well into the morning of the fourth day that he realized the bulk of his work was done. The details he could take care of back in his studio. He felt a strange sense of loss as he put down his brush and said, "Want to come have a look?"

He hadn't allowed her to see it before this, not wanting to grow self-conscious. Now she peered over his shoulder, asking with a kind of wonder, "Is that really how you see me?"

He tilted his head to look up at her. "You don't think it looks like you?"

"I didn't say that. It's just . . . it reminds me of someone I used to know."

"Who?"

"Me, when I was young." A wistful smile played at her lips, as she stood there studying the canvas, her hand resting absently on his shoulder.

Something made him reach up and touch her face. "You're still young."

Color rode up on her cheekbones and her eyes shone with what might have been tears. Slowly, she shook her head, saying, "It's been a long time since I felt that way."

Something made him ask, "There was someone before Joe, wasn't there?"

She nodded, her gaze fixed on a point just past his ear. "I thought I loved him at the time. Now I realize it was just infatuation. I didn't know any better, you see. The proverbial minister's daughter." She gave an ironic laugh. "And he . . . well, he turned out to be the proverbial rake." She paused before continuing on. "If it had been just a broken heart, it would have been all right. Broken hearts mend. But there was a . . . complication."

At once, he guessed what she was getting at. "You were pregnant."

"Yes," she said in a small voice.

Eleanor did something then that took him completely by surprise. She slowly sank to her knees and placed her head in his lap, almost as though in supplication. For a moment William scarcely dared to breathe, as if with some shy woodland creature he feared he would startle into bolting. A hush fell over the room, in which the ticking of the clock over the mantel seemed unnaturally loud. One by one, he removed the pins from her hair, freeing it to tumble down her neck and shoulders. It slipped through his fingers like heavy silk, parting to reveal the soft indentation at the nape of her neck, with its little tuft fine as a baby's. He might have been making love to her for how alive he felt, how keenly in the moment.

Her voice floated up from the cradle of his lap. "You asked me once why I married Joe. I wish I could say it was because I loved him, because I do now . . . in my own way. He's a good man. He married me when no one else would have. And Lucy . . . she's his heart. The way he dotes on her, you'd never know she wasn't his." Eleanor lifted her head to look up at him, her eyes searching his for any hint of the judgment she'd so liberally heaped on herself. "Promise you won't tell anyone. You're the only one who knows besides Joe and my parents. I haven't even told Lucy. She worships Joe. If she found out . . ." Eleanor grew pale at the thought.

"I promise." William smoothed back the hair that lay in a delicate web over her cheek, holding her chin cupped as he looked into her eyes. "There's just one thing I want you to promise me in return."

"What?" she asked, with obvious trepidation.

"That you'll stop thinking of yourself as a scarlet woman. You did nothing wrong. As for me, I could never think less of you, no matter what."

"Thank you." The look of gratitude she wore was almost more than he could bear. He was only saying what any decent human being would say. Why should that make him a saint?

The moment stretched on, moving from mere silence into a realm where nothing else seemed to exist. They were on a plane far removed from this shabby little room, poised as still as the image on the canvas before them, a tableaux in real life: William with his hand cradling her chin as Eleanor kneeled before him, seeming to rise like some beautiful flower from the silken puddle of her dress spilling across the floor at his feet.

Then in some distant part of his brain William became aware of the sound of a car approaching along the drive. Eleanor quickly rose to her feet, patting her hair and smoothing her skirt as she hurried over to the window to peer out at the shiny, dark Buick pulling to a stop in front of the house.

A man in uniform wearing a somber look got out, and she clapped a hand over her mouth, letting out a muffled cry. "No," she pleaded in a voice barely above a whisper. "No, please."

She froze at the knock on the door, and William could see that she was trembling. She appeared to age a dozen years in the time it took her to trudge across the living room and down the hall.

From where William stood, just out of the line of sight of the man poised in the doorway, he could see only a burly khaki shoulder and the crisp brim of a military cap. He heard a deep voice intone with regret, "Missus Styles? I'm afraid I have some bad news . . ."

CHAPTER TEN

When Alice was little her favorite thing in the world had been helping her grandmother in the kitchen: Nana, cupping her hand over Alice's smaller one, guiding it as she cut floury circles of dough with the biscuit cutter, or teaching Alice the proper way to frost a cake, applying a thin layer first to catch the crumbs. So it seemed appropriate that Alice christen her newly refurbished restaurant the Pantry, in honor of her grandmother's, which had been so well-stocked the family used to joke that she could have survived off it the rest of her days without another trip to the store. Besides, none of it would have been possible without Nana's money. Her grandmother, she thought, would have been pleased to see it so well spent.

The only cloud over the occasion of the grand opening was the thought of what lay ahead for Jeremy. At the arraignment, the judge hadn't cut him any slack. Despite Colin's efforts to have the case remanded to juvenile court, Jeremy was to be tried as an adult, on the full count of rape. It was almost more than Alice could contemplate much less cope with, but she was doing her best. And if there was a silver lining to the cloud, it was that her son no longer avoided her like the plague. He couldn't afford to. Small comfort, but at this point she'd take what she could get.

The night of the party Jeremy came in, accompanied by his dad, a half hour or so after everyone else had arrived. He approached her cautiously, submitting limply to a hug.

"Sorry we're late," Randy apologized. "I didn't get in until just a little while ago."

"You're here now, that's all that matters." She gave her ex-husband a peck on the cheek. His hair was still damp from the shower and he smelled of Brut, the scent of which evoked memories of when they used to date in high school.

"Nice turnout," he said, glancing about the crowded room.

"Amazing, isn't it? It seems I still have a few friends left." Alice spoke lightly, but she'd been deeply touched by the show of support, proof that not everyone was against her. In fact, over the past weeks, friends and acquaintances from the past had been quietly making their allegiance known. Like Patsy Rowland, who'd been on the cheerleading squad with her in high school. It was Patsy who'd donated the tables and chairs for the restaurant, from the hotel she and her husband used to own.

"More than a few, I'd say." Randy seemed genuinely pleased for her. "From the looks of it, you shouldn't have too much trouble drumming up business," he said. "I like what you've done with the place, too. Very cozy."

Alice, seeing it through his eyes, was struck with new appreciation for all she'd accomplished, in a relatively short amount of time with very little money. The old walls that had been gray with grime were painted now in soft peach and apple-green hues, and the windows hung with the gingham curtains her mother had stitched. An antique butter churn stood by the front door, alongside a crate of apples from Denise's trees. The old pine floorboards had been stripped and refinished and she'd had wainscoting put in. Above it were shelves that displayed homemade preserves and pickles, along with various items scavenged from the flea market: souvenir plates, an old pewter coffee service, a splatter-ware pitcher and matching bowl, vintage bottles and tins from companies long defunct. "Thanks. I wish I could take all the credit, but I couldn't have done it without Denise's help," she said.

He smiled. "I remember when you two used to sit out in the hot sun all day selling lemonade."

A reminder of just how long they'd known each other.

She laughed and shook her head. "God, I can't believe you remember that far back."

"I remember a lot of things." He held her gaze a beat longer than necessary, giving Alice a funny feeling in the pit of her stomach.

Eager to get off this subject, she grabbed his elbow, saying, "Come on, let's get you something to eat." She showed him to the buffet table, where Jeremy was already helping himself to a plate of food.

"It doesn't seem to have affected his appetite, at least," Randy murmured. He and Alice exchanged a smile, that of parents enjoying a small reprieve from their shared worry over their son. If she'd harbored any bitterness toward her ex-husband, it was gone. Randy had been a rock throughout this latest ordeal, calling often to strategize about Jeremy's case, his solid presence the other day in court keeping her on an even keel. She didn't know how she'd have managed without him.

Jeremy, on the other hand, seemed to be coping well enough. He'd lost that pale, shell-shocked look, she noted, watching him with his cousin Ryan, the two of them chatting as they shoveled food into their mouths. She couldn't tell whether or not he was having fun, but at least he wasn't hiding in a corner.

A short while later, as she was wandering over to the buffet table to have a word with Patsy Rowland, she ran into Jeremy, on his way back for seconds. For a moment he just stood there, looking ill at ease, holding his plate awkwardly in one hand. Finally, summoning his manners, he said, "Food's good. Especially that crab thing, with the mushrooms."

"Thanks. I'm glad you like it."

"You do all the cooking?"

"Your grandma did some." Alice had made the curried chicken salad and mushroom-crab strata, the garlic roasted string beans and creamed escarole; Lucy had supplied her signature Coca-Cola ham and candied sweet potatoes. She leaned in to confide, "Though between you and me I'm not quite sure how I'm going to manage when I'm on my own." She'd hired the daughter of one of Denise's teacher friends to wait tables and a kid from down the road to wash dishes, but other than that it looked as if she'd be flying solo, at least until Calpernia arrived. "If you know of anyone who's looking for something part-time, I could use an extra hand in the kitchen. The pay isn't much, but meals are included."

"I might know of someone," he said.

"Great. Tell whoever it is to give me a call."

"Actually, I was thinking I could use the extra hours myself." He was regarding her in a way that made her think of Colin McGinty's skittish dog: shy and hopeful at the same time.

Alice was so astonished, it was a moment before she could respond. "What about Mister Barbour?"

Jeremy shrugged, and looked away. "He cut back on my hours. The season's kind of winding down, so he doesn't need me as much anymore."

"Well, in that case, of course I'd love to have you work for me." She tried to keep the enthusiasm from her voice, not wanting to overwhelm him. "How soon can you start?"

"I have this thing tomorrow after school, but I'm free the rest of the week."

"How about Tuesday then?" He nodded, and she said with more feeling, "Thanks, Jeremy. This will be a real help."

"Yeah, well, I just thought . . ." Color bloomed in his pale cheeks. "You know, since you're helping out with Mister McGinty and all, that I should do my part. I'll even work for free, if you don't have the money to pay me."

Alice's throat grew tight. "If anyone deserves to be thanked, it's him." Colin had refused any payment, saying he would agree to handle the case only on a strictly *pro bono* basis. "As for your working for free, I wouldn't dream of it." She placed a hand lightly on his arm. "You don't owe me a thing."

She scanned the crowd in search of Colin and spotted him talking to Gary. He'd donned a sports coat and tie for the occasion, which made him stand out amid the other, more dressed-down guests. But he would have stood out regardless. There was something about him that drew the eye, an intensity that showed, not in the restless energy of someone like Denise, but in the quiet assuredness he brought to everything he did.

She'd seen it the other day in the courtroom, when he'd stood up to address the bench. "Your Honor, my client is a sixteen-year-old boy, with no history of juvenile delinquency or school misconduct," he'd argued, after the judge had refused his request to have the case remanded to juvenile court. "He's an ordinary teenager engaging in age-appropriate activities. He went to a party, he met a girl, they engaged in consensual sex. I see no reason this should even go to trial, much less that he be tried as an adult."

The district attorney, a wiry man with brushy, graying hair who couldn't sit for long without twitching in his seat like someone with a bad case of hemorrhoids, had sprung to his feet to interject sarcastically, "Where you come from, Mister McGinty, a rape charge might be commonplace, but around here we take such things pretty seriously." Earlier, Alice had seen him dart a nervous look at one of his colleagues when the judge had granted Colin permission to practice in this jurisdiction on a *pro hac vice* basis. Clearly, he hadn't been expecting a heavyweight from out of state to be handling Jeremy's case.

Ignoring him, Colin had steadfastly kept his eyes on the bench. "Your Honor, with all due respect, no one is disputing the seriousness of the charge, but we would like to make sure this young man is not being made an example of beyond what justice is called for."

The prosecutor had jumped in once more. "If this young man is old enough to engage in sexual activities, consensual or otherwise, he's old enough to be tried as an adult!"

"Mister Cantwell has a point," Judge Voakes had weighed in.

Finally, Colin had turned to the prosecutor, observing coolly, "I take it Mister Cantwell never engaged in sexual activity himself as a teenager." The prosecutor's rabbity face reddened, as Colin continued, "As for the rest of us, if it were a crime, we'd all be on trial."

A ripple of laughter had gone through the courtroom, and Alice had thought, *Score one for Colin.* She'd believed in him, in the face of his own doubts, and her faith had been validated. He clearly hadn't lost his touch. For the first time since the start of the ordeal she'd felt hopeful.

"So you guys are like, what, friends or something?" Jeremy was asking now.

Her cheeks warmed. What Jeremy wanted to know was if there was something going on between her and Colin. She chose her words carefully. "I haven't known him very long, but, yes, I'd say we're friends."

"So you like him?" Jeremy wasn't letting her off the hook so easily.

"The main thing is, do *you* like him?" She was quick to turn the tables.

"Yeah. He's cool."

"That's all that matters then," she said. "But he can only help you if you're willing. Just remember, he's on your side. We all are."

Jeremy looked down at his feet. When he raised his head at last, that strained look was back and he had trouble meeting her gaze. "Look, I wasn't being completely honest with you before . . . about Mister Barbour. The truth is, I was fired."

"Fired?" she echoed, in disbelief. "Why?"

"Because of what happened."

"With the girl, you mean." It wasn't a question.

Carrie Ann Flagler. Alice couldn't even bring herself to speak the name aloud. In court, she'd tried to catch the girl's eye, to force her to look over at them and see what her lie was costing them, but they might have been invisible as far as Carrie Ann was concerned. She'd sat flanked by her parents, a thin, nervous-looking woman and her bulldog of a husband, who at one point had shot Alice an evil look, as if the fault could be traced back to her. Carrie Ann herself had struck Alice as plain and unremarkable, a moon-faced girl with close-set eyes and brown, professionally streaked hair, who'd docilely answered the questions posed to her in a barely audible voice, every now and then flicking glances at her father, as if to be sure her responses met with his approval.

"He didn't say that was the reason," Jeremy replied with disgust, "but I know it was. I heard it from one of the other guys."

"I guess Mister Barbour has never heard of innocent until proven guilty," she said, indignant.

"It's no big deal," Jeremy said, with a shrug. "I probably would've quit anyway. He was always riding me about something."

They were interrupted just then by Denise, swooping down on Jeremy as if she hadn't seen him in ages. "Hey, you! Where have you been keeping yourself? You forget about your old aunt, or what?" She grabbed hold of him and gave him a squeeze, rocking him from side to side for a moment before releasing him. Her sister had had too much to drink, Alice noted. Not that Denise wasn't entitled. She was a one-woman mule team, always looking after everyone else while putting herself last. It was nice to see her cut loose for a change. "How have you been? I mean, really." She dropped her voice, looking deeply into Jeremy's eyes as she stood there swaying slightly on her feet. "You're not going to let this get in the way of your studies, are you? This other thing," she went on, dismissing the court case with an airy wave, "will get sorted out in no time. But college . . . sweetie, that's your future."

"Yeah, I know, I'm the Great White Hope of Grays Island," Jeremy replied, in a voice thick with irony. "Can't let anything screw that up."

But the irony must have been lost on Denise; either that, or she was choosing to ignore it. "That's my boy." She patted him on the cheek. "It'll all work out. You'll see. In the meantime, we're rooting for you, kiddo. You know that, don't you?"

"Yeah, I do. Thanks, Aunt Denise." He eyed her affectionately.

Seeing the bond between them, Alice felt a quick, hard thrust of envy. At the same time, she knew that if it hadn't been for Denise all those years, Jeremy would have been the worse for it.

Jeremy wandered off, and Denise leaned in to Alice. "Am I imagining it," she whispered urgently, with a gust of boozy breath, "or is Susie Quinn hitting on my husband?"

Alice glanced over to where Gary was having what looked to be a perfectly innocent conversation with an old school chum. She peered at them nonetheless, as if to assess the situation, saying in a theatrically hushed voice, "I couldn't say for sure, but they *do* look awfully cozy." When Denise got like this, the only way to handle it was with humor. Usually her sister ended up laughing at herself. But this time she seemed determined to milk it for all it was worth.

"I always knew Susie was a slut," she said, as if her suspicions had been confirmed. "Ramona Saucedo told me that, in high school, she slept with half the football team."

"Not half. A third maybe," Alice acknowledged. Never mind that Susie was now a happily married mother of two.

"Well, she'd better keep her hands to herself," Denise growled, sotto voce. "If I ever found out Gary was cheating on me, he'd be one sorry son of a gun, by the time I got through with him. Divorce would be the least of it."

Alice knew that Denise didn't really believe that Gary would ever be unfaithful to her; Alice was less certain. He had been acting so secretive lately. Suppose he *was* having an affair?

They were interrupted just then by their mother, on her way to the kitchen carrying a stack of dirty plates—never mind Alice's having told her to leave the clean-up for Eduardo to take care of in the morning. "You girls, always whispering about something," Lucy clucked, shaking her head in mock exasperation. "What are you two plotting now?"

Alice and Denise exchanged a look, and Denise answered with a giggle, "Nothing you want to know about." Lucy, without meaning to, had succeeded where Alice had failed in reducing Denise's fears to the stuff of meaningless girl talk.

"Having a good time, Mom?" Alice asked, turning to her mother. She couldn't recall when she'd last seen her look this elegant. Lucy was wearing a stylish print dress and low-heeled pumps, her silver hair clipped back on one side with a marquisette barrette. She'd even had her nails done.

"Oh, yes. It's a wonderful party!" Lucy's eyes shone and her color was high, no doubt due to the half-drunk glass of champagne in her hand. It didn't take much to get her tipsy. "And whatever anyone says, I just know the restaurant will be a huge success."

"Just what *have* people been saying?" Alice wanted to know.

Lucy looked uncertain, as if wishing she'd kept her mouth shut. "Oh, honey, it's nothing. Just a few mean-spirited busybodies who think you don't deserve to get ahead." She spoke airily, in an attempt to make light of it. "But if they imagine some silly boycott is going to put you out of business—" She broke off, color flooding her cheeks.

"Boycott?" Alice stared at her in shock.

Her mother's brow creased in consternation. "I'm sorry, dear, I shouldn't have mentioned it. Please don't let it worry you. It's just a handful of cranks with nothing better to do than stir up trouble. I'm sure it'll all blow over in no time."

"Did you know anything about this?" Alice swung about to face Denise.

From the sheepish expression her sister wore, it was clear that she'd known all along. Even now, she attempted to minimize it, saying, "Mom's right. You shouldn't pay any attention to those idiots. Anyway, they're the ones who'll suffer, not you. Think of all the great meals they'll be missing out on."

Alice didn't doubt that it would blow over, but the mere thought that there were people plotting behind her back had drained all the fun out of the evening. She didn't want to spoil it for her mother and sister, though, so she only said, "You're right. To hell with them. Here, Mom, why don't you let me take those? I was just on my way into the kitchen." She relieved her mother of the plates and headed off, feeling a sudden, urgent need to be alone.

She bumped into Colin along the way. "Need a hand?" he asked. "Or maybe someone to vent to?" he added in a lowered voice, taking in the grim set of her jaw.

"You're supposed to be enjoying yourself, not listening to a tale of woes," she told him.

"Okay, I confess, I have an ulterior motive. You see, parties aren't really my thing. If you put me to work, you'd be doing me a favor. Cook, bottle-washer, lawyer, advisor, whatever . . . I'm at your service." He gave a little bow, flashing her a lopsided grin.

Alice didn't know quite how to respond. Lately, she'd found herself growing increasingly dependent on him, and that bothered her. Still, it would be rude to reject his offer outright.

"All right, you can keep me company. But that's all. You're not allowed to lift a finger." She continued on her way, Colin falling into step beside her. "So have you always hated parties, or is this a recent thing?" she quizzed him, as she pushed her way through the swinging doors into the kitchen.

"I used to love them. But that was in the days when parties were just an excuse to drink. I don't remember what went on at half of them. Now that I'm sober, it's a little like being thirteen again, trying to get up the nerve to ask the pretty girl to dance." He flashed her a smile that made her blush, and disregarding her command took the dishes from her, scraping them and stacking them in the sink.

"I know what you mean," she said. "I tend to get a little maxed out on socializing. A function of prison life. You get so little privacy, you end up craving it after a while." He showed no sign of discomfort at the direction the conversation had taken, and now she abruptly turned to face him. "You know, I just figured out what it is I like about you."

"What's that?" he asked.

"I don't have to tiptoe around you," she said. "Most people act as if my having done time is a disease that might be catching. My own family, for instance. They look pained if I so much as mention it."

He shrugged. "It can be a pretty sensitive subject."

"But you're not like that."

"I come at it from a different perspective. Besides," he went on, "We're not related."

"Meaning?"

"Maybe your family feels they let you down."

"That's crazy. Why should they think that?"

He shrugged. "No reason. But that doesn't always stop people from feeling guilty."

"There was nothing anyone could have done," Alice insisted.

"I'm not sure I buy that, at least not where your lawyer was concerned."

"What do you know about it?" she asked, eyeing him suspiciously. The years at Pine River had left her deeply wary of people nosing around behind her back. Usually when they did, it wasn't because they were planning a surprise party for you.

"I looked it up," he told her. "They have all the old newspapers on microfiche down at the library. I also got hold of the transcripts from your trial, over at county records."

"Why go to all that trouble? I could have told you what you wanted to know."

"I thought it might help with Jeremy's case. And from what I could see, he's not the only one who got a bum rap. If you don't mind my saying so, your lawyer didn't do such a good job defending you."

"What makes you say that?" she asked, though privately she'd come to the same conclusion.

"For one thing, he should have moved for a change of venue."

"Maybe, but unless you know of a way to turn back the clock, what good does it do to second-guess him now?" she asked in frustration.

He shrugged, leaning back against the counter. "My point is that lawyers make mistakes. Even good ones."

"What are you saying?"

"It's not too late to find another lawyer for Jeremy."

"I don't want another lawyer." Alice had seen him in action; she knew what he was capable of. "What I *want* is for my son's name to be cleared. Tell me honestly, what are his chances?"

He eyed her thoughtfully for a moment, as if gauging how much information she could handle. "I spoke with the D.A. on Friday, and he's not prepared to offer any kind of plea deal. From our conversation, it was pretty clear that he thinks he can win this one."

"Based on what evidence?" She wrapped her arms around her middle, shivering in the warmth of the kitchen.

"The rape kit, for one thing. So far the test results are inconclusive, which doesn't exactly put Jeremy in the clear. But they're still waiting on the results of the DNA sample, which could add another wrinkle."

Alice seized upon that. "You mean Jeremy might not have been the only one who was with Carrie Ann that night?"

"There's always that possibility. And the eyewitnesses all testified that the three other boys had been drinking heavily." Colin spoke guardedly, as if not wanting to get her hopes up.

"And if it turns out she *was* with one of those other boys?"

"It wouldn't let Jeremy off the hook, but it would shoot some pretty big holes in the prosecution's case. They'd have to show probable cause, and that's a lot harder to do when there's more than one suspect." Nonetheless, Colin was quick to warn, "I don't want you to pin too much on this, though. Chances are it'll turn out to be a dead end."

Alice felt her spirits, briefly buoyed, sag once more.

Slowly she let out a breath, looking around her. The kitchen that had been so chaotic earlier in the day was quiet. There was only the low hum of the refrigerator and the muted din of voices from the next room. Suddenly she was sure she had bitten off more than she could chew. The hulking old Garland, the scarred butcher block counters, the Hobart mixer under its plastic shroud, all seemed to mock her in some way, as if daring her to make a go of this possibly doomed enterprise. And how would she be able to save Jeremy if she couldn't save herself?

She felt Colin's touch against her arm, and she turned her head to find him eyeing her as if he knew exactly what was going through her mind, because in a sense weren't they in the same boat, both struggling to stay afloat? "I just wanted you to know what's at stake here," he told her. "You should think it through carefully before we move ahead. I might be good at what I do—or at least I was at one time—but I've only been sober a little over seven months. And as we say in the program, however long it took you to screw up your life, that's how long it'll take, and then some, to get it straightened out."

"We all have our baggage," she said.

"I'm not trying to compare it to what you went through . . ." He paused, as if searching for the right words, before continuing, "I'm not sure if anyone who hasn't been through it themselves could possibly know what that's like. But there are other kinds of prisons, and the kind people like me end up in, believe me, they can be just as hard to get out of." His gaze turned inward, and she saw the pain on his face, coupled with some deep yearning.

"But you got out," she said gently.

"For now, yes. But most days I feel like I'm barely hanging on." He pointed toward the shelf over the counter, which held an array of bottles, various oils as well as the wine she used in cooking. "That bottle of Bordeaux there. I'll bet you wouldn't even have noticed it, if you didn't know it was there. Me? It was the first thing I saw when I walked in. Not so long ago I'd have headed straight for it and, after I'd drunk every drop, gone in search of the wine cellar. And the next day I'd have woken with a wicked hangover and done the same thing all over again. So you see? I'm not exactly the Rock of Gibraltar."

She shook her head. "I don't expect you to be. That's not why I asked you to take Jeremy's case. I did it because you know what it's like to be knocked off your feet. And you picked yourself up and moved on. I see that as a strength, not a weakness."

His eyes searched her face, and she felt some powerful current pass between them. Mutual attraction . . . even lust . . . wouldn't have explained it. It was more than that. She had the sense that they were the only two people in the world, a man and a woman who were barely hanging on and who saw in each other a kind of lifeline. Colin seemed to feel it too. He reached up, lightly brushing her cheek with the backs of his knuckles as if to remind her, or perhaps himself, that they were still in the land of the living. She shivered, feeling tiny sparks ignite under her skin where he'd grazed it. "Well, here we are. We survived, didn't we?" he said, wearing an expression that was both sad and ironic. "I guess that's something in itself."

She took a step back, as from a high place from which she might tumble. "So are we okay? You're not bailing out on me?"

He shrugged once more. "I'm game, if you are. Now all we have to do is get Jeremy on board."

She eyed him in confusion, feeling a small pulse of alarm. "What makes you think he isn't?"

"For one thing, he's not entirely convinced that he's innocent."

"What do you mean? Of course, he's innocent!" she said, taken aback. Had Jeremy told him something in confidence that she and Randy weren't privy to?

"I think the line is blurred in his mind," Colin went on to explain. "He doesn't seem to understand that taking advantage of a girl when they'd both had too much to drink doesn't necessarily make him a rapist. Just a teenager who exercised some bad judgment."

"Should I talk to him?" she asked.

"No, why don't you let me handle it. I think I'm making some headway."

"There's something else, isn't there?" she said, taking note of the troubled look on his face. "What is it? What's wrong?"

"I'm not sure," he said, his frown deepening. "But I'm getting a funny feeling about all this. I haven't been around long enough to know all the politics at play here, but I agreed with Randy—I think Jeremy's being railroaded.

Alice felt the blood leave her face. Colin was merely confirming her own suspicions. "You're not imagining it. In fact, I'm pretty sure that's what's going on." She shared her concerns about Owen White. "I would have said something to you sooner, but I didn't want you to think I was being paranoid."

Colin nodded thoughtfully. "I'll nose around a bit, see what I can find out. You think your brother-in-law might be able to give us some insight?"

"Gary?" She hadn't thought of it before, but now it occurred to her that if anyone was privy to what went on behind the scenes, it was him. As deputy chief of police, he knew where all the bodies were buried, so to speak. "I'll talk to him," she said. "He can keep an ear to the ground, if nothing else." Another thought occurred to her, and she frowned, saying, "There's just one problem. Say we get wind of something fishy. How are we going to prove it? It's not like we'd have evidence."

"You never know when a piece of information will come in handy. Even something that might not have seemed relevant at first," Colin said, with the same air of authority he'd shown in the courtroom. "One way or another, we'll get to the bottom of it. And if what we suspect is true, we'll find a way to nail the bastard."

Alice was far less certain. "Sometimes I think Randy's right—I should have left well enough alone," she said, thinking about her own situation. "If I hadn't known the truth about David's death, if I hadn't witnessed it with my own eyes, I probably would have believed Owen's lies, and we'd all have been better off in the end."

"It's different this time."

"Why is that?"

"You have me." He gave her a crooked smile, as if to say, *for whatever it's worth.*

Alice didn't know how to respond. It was almost more than she could take in, that this man who until a short while ago had been a complete stranger, linked to her only through some remote connection involving their grandparents, would be sticking his neck out for her. In prison, when someone did something for you, there was almost always a price tag attached. Even Randy, who'd vowed to stick with her through good times and bad, had let her down. If her own husband, David's father, couldn't stay the course why should she believe that Colin would?

And yet . . . somehow she did. It wasn't so much a matter of friendship as of fellowship. In helping her, maybe he was helping himself in some way. Either way, his words were like balm, calming her fears and soothing some ache deep within her. It had been a long time since she'd allowed herself to grow close to another human being, with the exception of Calpernia. And here was this man offering the one thing she wanted most: the chance to save her younger son that she'd been denied with her firstborn.

"I don't know how I can ever repay you," she said.

"You don't have to." He was standing directly underneath the overhead light fixture, its harsh glow throwing his face into stark relief. His eyes glinted darkly from shadowed sockets and his jaw line and cheekbones were as sharply defined as if honed by a blade.

Their eyes met and held, and for a moment she could have sworn he was about to kiss her. She could feel it almost as surely as the pulse throbbing at the base of her throat. She had a sudden wild urge to twine her arms around him, to kiss him all over and taste the salt of his skin on her lips. Tension gathered as the moment stretched out, and a fiery bolt shot down through her belly, spreading through her lower regions: a heat so intense it bordered on discomfort. She hadn't slept with a man in nine years—or a woman for that matter, despite the commonly held belief about prison life—and however starved she was, the thought was terrifying. And from the look on Colin's face it was obvious he was equally fearful.

Alice was the first to speak, "Well, I hope you'll at least allow me to treat you to some free meals," she said with a shaky laugh. "While I'm open, that is, which might not be for long. I hear there's talk of a boycott. It seems the scarlet A stands for Alice, in my case."

Colin didn't look too concerned. "I don't see you letting the local witch-hunters stop you, not after all you've overcome so far."

"They don't worry me as much as Owen does." Having expressed her fears aloud, they seemed more real than ever. And now the scope of what she faced unfurled before her, frightening in its dimension. "He could shut this place down in a heartbeat. I have a feeling the only reason he hasn't so far is because he has something bigger in mind. Something that'll take me down along with Jeremy."

Alice was cleaning up after the last guest had gone when the front door swung open and a familiar voice called out, "Damn, girl, don't tell me the party's over? And here I done got all dressed up for nothing."

Alice looked up to find Calpernia King filling the doorway like a total eclipse of the sun. Suitcase in hand, decked out in tight white jeans and a white rabbit chubby over a hot pink jersey top with the word *Diva* spelled out in shiny metal rivets across the mighty prow of her chest. When they used to talk about the first thing they'd do when they got out, Calpernia's plan had been to head straight for the nearest beauty salon, which was just what she'd done, judging by her three-inch nails painted in a mosaic of iridescent colors and the multitude of braided hair extensions coiled atop her head like some elaborate tribal headdress. Now she spread her arms wide to take in the flying missile of Alice hurtling toward her.

Alice hugged her long and hard before pulling back with a grin. "God, it's great to see you. Why didn't you tell me you were coming?" She'd sent an invitation but hadn't heard back.

"Thought I'd surprise you. I'd a got here sooner but the damn car broke down. And ain't like you got ferries running every hour." Calpernia broke into a wide smile that showed the gap between her front teeth and instantly transformed her from bad-ass street to soul sister.

"You should have at least phoned," Alice chided. "I would've picked you up at the ferry landing.

"And spoil the surprise? Girl, you know me better than that."

Alice did indeed. At Pine River, Calpernia King had more or less ruled the roost, defining her own order as she saw fit. In the yard and gen pop she'd always had a little knot of other inmates around her, like a large tree providing shade, or, in her case, protection from rival inmates. Calpernia had a natural air of superiority about her that said *don't mess with me if you know what's good for you* and, for the most part, no one had, including the COs. To the best of Alice's knowledge there had never been a clash between Calpernia and another inmate that resulted in bodily harm.

"Well, you're here now, so as far as I'm concerned the party's just begun," Alice said, finding a couple of clean glasses and popping the tab on a can of leftover Mountain Dew she'd pulled from the cooler. It might not be champagne, but it was cold and bubbly and would do the trick. She lifted her glass in a toast. "Here's to our release. May we live long and prosper."

"I don't know 'bout that," said Calpernia, tipping back her glass, "but I sure do plan on getting me some peace and quiet. I ain't hardly slept a wink since I got out. Shaniqua's place, I might as well been back inside, with the baby and all that ruckus next door."

"Speaking of which, I found you a place," Alice informed her. Calpernia would have been welcome to stay with her, but the terms of their parole prohibited them from living together. "It's not much, just a one-room studio over a garage, but it's free."

At once, Calpernia's back went up. "I ain't no charity case. I can pay my own way."

"You will, just not out of your pocket." Alice explained the circumstances. The house was for sale, and the owner, a friend of her mom's, had agreed to let Calpernia stay on as caretaker until it was sold. All she had to do was water the plants and keep an eye on the place.

Some of the fire went out of Calpernia's eyes. "Okay. Long as I don't owe nobody nothing," she allowed grudgingly.

Alice chuckled, feeling a surge of wicked pleasure. "One thing's for sure. This island won't know what hit it."

"Yeah. This ol' milk bucket 'bout to catch itself a fly," said Calpernia in her most exaggerated Southern drawl. "They see me coming, they gon' run for cover." She threw her head back in a rich, deep laugh that rippled through her in waves, like heat off sun-baked asphalt.

"Most people around here are happy to leave you alone as long as you mind your own business," Alice assured her. "It's just a handful who go out of their way to make things difficult." She thought once more of Owen White. "Normally I'd tell them to take a flying you know what, but I can't afford to right now. I need all the customers I can get." She recalled what her mother had let slip, and felt the small stitch of anxiety in her belly tighten.

"Girl, you got this place looking so fine, if the cooking's half as good, y'all have folks lining up at the door." Alice would have hugged her again if Calpernia hadn't been strutting around, surveying the room. She paused to finger an embroidered tea towel, eyeing it as she would an artifact from a lost civilization. "Just take me some time for me to get used to all this white-bread shit, is all. I feel like I'm in one of those shows on Nick at Night. *Fresh Prince of Bel-Air* or the one about the old guy moves his family uptown."

"*The Jeffersons*," Alice supplied, smiling at the image of Calpernia in the role of George Jefferson.

Calpernia swung around to face her, hands on hips. "See. That's what I'm talking about. You know shit like that." But she was grinning, so Alice knew not to take her seriously.

"Sit," Alice ordered, pulling out a chair. "I'll get you something to eat."

"Good. 'Cause I ain't eaten all day." Calpernia plunked down in the chair without further ado. "I'm so hungry ol' Lorena's cooking would taste good," she said, referring to the head cook at Pine River, a three-hundred-pound former school dietician with the humorless countenance of a sumo wrestler, who'd managed to make everything taste like wet cardboard.

In the kitchen, Alice put together a plate of leftovers and made hot cocoa for them both—the kind with real milk, which still seemed an impossible luxury after having been in a place where everything came out of packet. Being reunited with Calpernia was reminding her of all she had to be grateful for: her family and friends, and the fresh start she'd been given. Colin came to mind as well, the thought warming her as she stood in the kitchen stirring the cocoa, recalling the scene that had taken place earlier in the evening in that very spot.

By the time Calpernia had cleaned her plate and they'd finished their cocoa, Alice's eyelids were drooping. She'd been up since four-thirty that morning and the next day's wake-up call would be the same. "Better get used to it," she told Calpernia, as they were turning in. "We're open for lunch and dinner, which means by noon you've already put in a full day."

Calpernia eyed Alice incredulously, as if she thought she'd arrived in the nick of time to keep her from burning up upon reentry. "And you was figuring on doing it all yourself?"

"Just the cooking. I hired a girl to wait tables, and someone to wash dishes. My son offered to help out, too." Calpernia paused on the staircase, giving her a probing look. "So you and him is a'ight?"

"Let's just say I've been making progress." Alice let them into the small apartment at the top of the stairs, which still held remnants of its former occupants, such as the spectacularly ugly floral drapes and Windex-blue shag carpet stained with cat pee. "At least we're communicating," she said, bending to pull the cushions from the foldout sofa. "It's a start. Though it's partly because he can't afford to shut me out of his life right now. You see, he's in a bit of trouble . . . "

"Girl trouble?" Calpernia guessed, no doubt thinking of her daughter's getting knocked up.

"In a way." Alice told her about the false charges against Jeremy, and they exchanged a look that could be shared only by those with firsthand knowledge of where something like that could lead. "Pretty ironic, isn't it? I can't seem to escape the past, no matter where I turn." She shook herself free from those thoughts, and straightened, turning to smile at Calpernia. "Which is why I'm glad you're here. You're the only one who knows exactly what I'm going through."

"Mmmmhmmm. Yeah. Ain't that right," said Calpernia, in the singsong call-and-response of the Baptist church, whose rhythms were almost as familiar to Alice after nine years.

"It's funny when you think about it," she mused aloud. "Way back when, who'd have thought that one day we'd be in business together? I can remember when I'd have been dead meat if I'd so much as asked you for the time of day."

Calpernia let loose with another of her deep, throaty laughs. "Never thought I'd be sleeping on some white chick's sofa, neither," she said, shaking her head. "But, girl, you a'ight, you know that?"

As Alice went to fetch sheets and blankets, the worries that had been crowding her head all day drifted away. For the moment, it was enough to know that she wasn't alone. Whatever lay ahead, Calpernia King would have her back, just as she had at Pine River.

When the Pantry opened for business the following day, Alice was satisfied that she'd done everything she could to ensure its success. She'd placed a sign along the main road leading to the turnoff for Fisherman's Lane. She'd taken out an ad in the *Courier* and gotten her niece and nephew to pass out flyers around town. The rest was in God's hands.

And it seemed God was smiling on her for a change, because at lunch and dinner nearly every table was filled, friends and family for the most part, some of the same loyal souls who'd attended last night's party. Alice didn't let it worry her too much when business slowed to a trickle in the days to come. She recalled her mother's cautioning that Rome wasn't built in a day, and thought to herself that Rome wouldn't be fed in a day, either. But by the end of the week she was close to despair. It wasn't just the out of the way location, she knew. Nor was it the food—the word of mouth reviews, even from those without a vested interest in boosting her confidence, had been mainly positive. Which meant the boycott she'd gotten wind of from her mother was more than just a handful of Owen White loyalists out for blood, as Lucy had naively chosen to believe. Either that, or people believed the rumors about Alice and were steering clear of her because they thought she was crazy. Hadn't she already shown what she was capable of? How did they know that she wouldn't poison them?

The only customer she could count on, rain or shine, was Colin McGinty. She found herself looking forward to the familiar sound of his voice greeting Katie out front, and to the moment when he would stick his head into the kitchen to compliment her and Calpernia on the meal. If she refused to let him pay, he always left a generous tip, sometimes more than the cost of the meal.

The new routine seemed to be having a positive effect on him, too, for the faint air of melancholy that had clung to him had dissipated. His step was lighter these days, his tone more buoyant. She could almost forget at times that he was her son's lawyer, that they were bound by something other than friendship and an appreciation for good food. Until one day he made a special appointment to see her during off hours. It was during the lull between lunch and dinner, when the restaurant closed. Alice took off her chef's whites and poured them each a glass of Perrier.

"This is about Jeremy, isn't it?" she said, as they sat down at one of the tables in back.

He nodded, his expression growing somber. "I would've phoned, but I figured you'd want to hear it in person." He paused, before continuing. "The D.A.'s office just faxed over the results of the DNA test on the semen. Apparently Jeremy was the only one Carrie Ann Flagler was with that night."

Alice had known that the chances were slim of a less damning result, but she'd continued to hope nonetheless. Now she could see that there was no easy way out, not unless the girl decided to come clean. Still, she postulated, "Unless one of the other boys used a condom."

"Possible, but hard to prove. All three boys deny having sex with her."

She drew in a breath, trying to steady her nerves. "So, okay, Jeremy was the only one. That doesn't make him a rapist."

"No, of course not, but it's not just his word against hers. Of course, we'll get our own experts to run tests, but in the meantime . . ." Colin's voice trailed off, his expression telling her all she needed to know.

Alice, holding her hands clasped in her lap to keep them from trembling, asked, "So what are we looking at?"

"Most likely, it'll go to trial.

"When?"

"I can probably buy us another six months. We still have the evidentiary hearing, and there are pre-trial motions I can file. Meanwhile, drum up as many witnesses as you can who'll testify to Jeremy's good character."

"What about *her* character? There must be people who could testify that she's not exactly the Virgin Mary."

"I'm sure that's true, but it won't do us any good. The D.A. will file a motion *in limini* to block any testimony on her sexual history. At least, that's what I would do in his place."

It hit Alice then, with the full force of a blow. "So there's a real possibility Jeremy could go to prison?"

"There's always that chance, yes." His eyes met hers and she saw the compassion in his face, mixed with a hard dose of reality—he knew better than to pull punches with her. But Alice needed no reminding of what was at stake. *It's happening all over again*, she thought, *only this time with Jeremy*. Colin's voice seemed to come from very far away as he went on, "But I'm still optimistic. And don't forget, a lot can happen between now and then." He dropped his voice. "What did you find out from your brother-in-law?"

"Nothing so far," she told him. When she'd floated the idea of foul play, Gary had looked at her as if she were insane. But it wasn't so much what he'd said as what he *hadn't* said. Gary hadn't asked what she was basing her suspicions on. There had been something evasive about his manner, too. He'd seemed jumpy and he'd had trouble meeting her gaze. Had he been hiding something, or was it just that she'd placed him in an awkward position?

Colin echoed her thoughts, asking, "Do you think he knows something?"

"I can't be certain, but I got the impression he wasn't being a hundred percent straight with me." She chose her words carefully, not wanting to portray her brother-in-law unfairly.

"Maybe your sister can get it out of him."

Alice frowned, reluctant to drag Denise into this. "I wouldn't want her to think I was accusing him of withholding information."

"I'm sorry," Colin said, putting his hand over hers. "I know this puts you in an awkward position."

"I'm sorry, too," she said. "But when it comes to my son, I'll do whatever I have to." Even if it meant putting her beloved sister on the spot.

Colin drained his glass, then pushed his chair back and rose to his feet. "I should get going. I have a biologist from Western Washington coming out to the house. He's supposed to be one of the country's foremost experts on bivalves."

"How's that going?" she asked, walking him to the door.

"So far so good, but I'm still a long way from being fully operational. It keeps me occupied, though, and that's sort of the point." His eyes were clear as he spoke, his expression that of someone looking to the future, not mired in the past. Clearly this fledgling enterprise of his, however unlikely an undertaking for a big city lawyer, was just what the doctor had ordered. "For such a simple creature, oysters can be pretty complicated. You'd be surprised how many things can go wrong."

"I never thought running a restaurant would be this hard, either," she said "If it gets any slower, we won't even have to bother opening up."

"I hope it doesn't come to that. I sure would miss your cooking."

"You and about five other people," she said, with an ironic laugh.

He made a sympathetic face. "I wish I knew what to tell you. You seem to be doing everything right."

"The trouble is, it's not enough. We need some sort of gimmick to get people in the door."

Calpernia, busy setting the tables for dinner, must have overhead, for she appeared before them just then. Dressed in a flowing skirt and scoop-necked jersey top that swagged like bunting from her breasts, her hair coiled atop her head in elaborate whorls and sporting earrings the size of chandeliers, she might have been the deposed queen of some newly democratized African nation. "Long as it don't involve no black folks putting on costumes," she muttered seditiously, folding her arms over her chest.

"The thought hadn't occurred to me. But if you have any other bright ideas, I'd love to hear them," Alice remarked dryly.

Calpernia pondered it a moment, frowning in thought. Then all at once she erupted into motion, smacking her forehead with the heel of her hand. "Damn! Don't know why I didn't think of it before. My old grandpa down in Mississippi would've come up with it in about two seconds flat and he never made it past the second grade."

Then she told them her idea.

CHAPTER ELEVEN

Jeremy was enjoying a newfound popularity. Other boys who'd barely acknowledged him in the past were giving him knowing leers or thumbs-up signs when they passed him in the halls. And the other day Jimmy DeLorenzi, a jock who'd only spoken to him once before, to ask if he could borrow Jeremy's notes for a class he'd missed, had taken him aside during study hall to murmur, with a brotherly clap on the back, "Hang in there, buddy. Everyone knows Carrie Ann's a slut. We got your back, okay?" Even the girls were nicer to him. He was no longer a nameless, faceless neuter. In their eyes, he carried about him now a hint of danger, a suggestion of non-parental approved activities. With one regrettable drunken episode, he'd gone from invisible man to cool dude, while Carrie Ann Flagler was shunned, a social pariah.

Jeremy should have been happy about it, but he was miserable. He knew he should hate Carrie Ann for what she'd done, but more and more, it had come to seem as if they were in this together, like in movies where two people are trapped in a collapsed mine shaft or clinging to a liferaft in the wake of a shipwreck. Maybe in her mind she wasn't lying; maybe she truly believed what she'd told the police. Things had a way of getting distorted when you were drunk—who knew that better than him? And she'd been so wasted that night. They both were. If Jeremy's memory of that seminal event weren't so clear—however crappy it ended up, you didn't forget your first time—he might have wondered if it had, in fact, happened just the way she'd said.

Most of the time, when he didn't have to meet with his lawyer or appear in court, he didn't think about it. Whole hours would go by, and then out of the blue it would hit him: He'd been accused of rape. Him. Jeremy Kessler. Who'd never so much as grazed a girl's breasts before this. It was so surreal, he could almost believe it was happening to someone else.

One blustery day in early December he was hurrying along the corridor at school, trying to make it to his science class before the final bell, when something he spotted out of the corner of his eye brought him to a sudden halt. Carrie Ann. She was crying, scrubbing furiously with a wad of wet paper towels at graffiti that had been scrawled on her locker with what looked to have been a Magic Marker: the single, crudely drawn word SLUT. He watched her for a moment, feeling vaguely responsible somehow, though anywhere but in this upended universe, where all normal rules were suspended, her humiliation would have been cause for celebration.

She didn't appear to notice him, she was so caught up in her frenzied scrubbing. He was about to sidle past when she whipped around suddenly. "*What are you looking at?*" she hissed, her face screwed into an angry red knot.

Heat flared in his cheeks. "N-nothing," he stammered. He'd been warned by his parents and Mr. McGinty to steer clear of her. Until now, that hadn't been a problem. She wasn't in any of his classes. But Jeremy should have known he'd run into her eventually. He should have been prepared.

"It's all your fault. *This whole thing*." She flung her arm out in a gesture that seemed to take in, not just the defaced locker, but the whole school. She was quivering, her voice choked with tears. "You've been shit-talking me. Telling everyone I made the whole thing up. Haven't you? Go on, admit it." She advanced on him, the wad of paper towels in her hand, now reduced to a blackened clump, thrust at him accusingly.

"I haven't said a word to anyone, I swear," Jeremy blurted in knee-jerk defense. At the same time he was thinking, *This is all wrong. Shouldn't* I *be the one accusing her*?

"Yeah, right," she said in a sarcastic tone. "I saw you talking to Jimmy. Now suddenly you're his best friend? He didn't even fucking know you *existed* before this." She swiped angrily with the back of her wrist at the tears running down her slapped-red cheeks. It came back to him now, Carrie Ann calling out Jimmy's name while they were having sex. He recalled, too, that she and Jimmy DeLorenzi used to be a couple, before Jimmy dumped her for supposedly cheating on him. "In fact, I'll bet you put him up to this," she gestured toward her locker

"Why would I want to do that?" Jeremy spoke with such surprised innocence that Carrie Ann halted in her tracks, her angry expression switching to one of narrow-eyed disbelief.

"You're kidding me, right?"

"I don't think you're a slut," he said, his face growing even hotter at the hazy memory of them tangled together naked on the mattress in Mike Dimmock's apartment.

"You hate me, though." She spoke as though it were a fact.

He shrugged. "Yeah, I probably should."

Her eyes widened. "You mean you don't?"

He thought for a moment, probing the recesses of his mind the way he might have probed an infected tooth with the tip of his tongue. Finally, in a tone of near-wonderment, as if he were having difficulty believing it himself, he replied, "No. I guess I don't."

"Wow." She stared at him incredulously.

Now that they were actually having a conversation, if that's what this was, Jeremy felt emboldened to continue. "Look. I'm sure I *would* be pissed if I thought you were doing this just to mess with me. But I'm guessing you really believe that stuff you told the police. Why else put yourself through all this?"

He expected her to erupt in anger again. After all, wasn't he all but accusing her of making the whole thing up? But Carrie Ann just stared at him with a thoughtful, assessing look, as if she were seeing him for the first time. When at last she spoke, her voice was surprisingly calm. "I'm not supposed to be talking to you, you know. My parents would kill me if they knew."

"Yeah. Mine, too." A corner of his mouth hooked up in a tentative smile. He didn't see Carrie Ann as his tormenter, but more as a kid who'd been playing with matches and who'd accidentally started a fire, one that had quickly spread out of control. "Want some help with that?" He indicated her locker, where the first two of the letters scrawled on the front had been rubbed into a indecipherable gray smear, leaving only the U and the T.

She frowned. "What if someone sees you? It'd look pretty weird, wouldn't it?"

He glanced around. "Yeah, well, there's no one to see."

Jeremy fetched more paper towels from the boys' bathroom and helped her scrub off the rest of the graffiti, neither of them speaking another word. They were just finishing up when the third period bell rang. That was when the full realization hit him: He'd blown off biology to help a girl who could send him to jail.

Reflecting on it as he hurried off to his next class, he thought that as bizarre as it might have seemed to others, it had felt like the right thing to do. There was no reason his parents or Mr. McGinty had to know. They wouldn't understand. Jeremy wasn't sure he understood it, either. All he knew was that after weeks of feeling like shit, he felt a little better about himself. Not so much better as *different*, more in charge.

He imagined how it had gone down with Carrie Ann: her parents confronting her that night when she'd stumbled into the house, and Carrie Ann blurting out some tearful, drunken version of what had happened. And once adults got involved, things had a way of snowballing. Look at his own parents. A month ago they hadn't even been speaking and now they were on the phone with each other practically every other day. Jeremy didn't know how he felt about that. Part of him was glad that his parents were getting along, but another part of him was fearful. He and his dad had been managing just fine without his mom all these years. Wasn't it better for things to stay as they were than to risk getting hurt again if down the line she decided to take off?

Luckily, his fourth period class was gym, for Jeremy doubted he'd have been able to concentrate right now on anything more mentally taxing than kicking a ball around the soccer field. He was so preoccupied with the thoughts tumbling in his head—Carrie Ann, his mom, the Bio class he'd blown—that he didn't see Rud until he'd practically bumped into him.

"Yo, dude. Just the man I wanted to see." Rud greeted him as if they were the best of friends, as if he and his buddies hadn't left Jeremy swinging in the wind. "Me and Chuckie are heading over to Mike's after school, to check out the bro's new hog. Wanna come along?"

Jeremy ducked his head, mumbling, "I don't know. I've got some stuff to do." He felt confused by this sudden onslaught of attention. Lately, Rud had been seeking him out more and more, where before Jeremy would have been invited along only if he happened to be standing there when they were all piling into the car. Either Rud felt guilty for not sticking up for him or Jeremy, in his new notoriety, had suddenly become worthy of his friendship.

"Dude. This is a brand-new Harley we're talking about. A *Harley*, man." An unlit cigarette dangled from the corner of his mouth, and now, as Rud leaned in, Jeremy caught a whiff of stale smoke and a trace of some flowery scent that had to be his girlfriend's perfume. "Now let's you and me take that sucker for a spin and you can forget about all this other crap. Do you good, dude."

Jeremy kept his eyes averted. He knew that if he were to look into Rud's face and see the warm affection with which Rud was no doubt regarding him, he'd be sucked in. For what few outside Rud's inner circle would have guessed was that, for all his bad rep, Rud could be extremely charming when he chose to be. And if it was just an illusion, it was a seductive one. In that moment Jeremy wanted nothing more than to bask in that warmth, to believe that Rud really gave a shit about him. It seemed like the hardest thing he'd ever had to do to say, "I'm sorry. I wish I could. You . . . you guys have fun without me."

"Whoa. Dude. You're the one missing out, not me."

Rud took a step back, his eyes dismissing Jeremy with a cool glance that let him know he'd committed a major social blunder in even suggesting that his going or not going would in any way affect Rud's ability to have a good time. Jeremy was at once filled with an almost crushing regret. Only the thought of how much he'd hate himself for doing so kept him from belatedly accepting Rud's invitation, if it was even still open. As he trudged off to gym, any sense of empowerment he'd felt in helping Carrie Ann dissipated, leaving him feeling lonely and depressed.

He ran into his cousin a few minutes later in the locker room.

"Hey, Germ. What's up?" said Ryan with a grin, greeting him by his childhood nickname.

His cousin was just out of the shower, naked except for the towel wrapped around his waist, his hair standing up in wet spikes. Under any other circumstances, when faced with his cousin's blatant physical superiority, Jeremy would have indulged in the usual comparisons. He'd have keyed in on the cut of Ryan's biceps, his six-pack abs, the mat of hair on his chest (Jeremy's sported only a few feeble outcroppings), not to mention the sheer confidence with which Ryan strode naked through a locker room filled with other boys making similar comparisons. But right now he was so preoccupied, he scarcely noticed.

"Nothing much," he lied. "What's up with you?"

"We just got slaughtered. Four and O, and Resnick fumbles a pass in the final quarter. Shit, we'd have had it, if it weren't for that," Ryan reported cheerfully enough, even as he shook his head in disgust. If it had been a playoff instead of a practice game, it would have rolled off him just the same. Nothing much got in the way of Ryan's naturally optimistic approach to life, a trait Jeremy used to envy but which right now irritated him.

Growing up, they had been close, more like brothers than cousins. Then, the summer between the eighth and ninth grades, Ryan had morphed overnight into the man-sized individual standing before him now, while Jeremy, still a skinny, scab-kneed kid, was left to fumble his way through adolescence. He'd still been playing with action figures when Ryan became interested in girls—an interest that was returned in spades. Every other girl in school, it seemed, had a crush on Ryan. Not only that, he succeeded at everything he set out to do, whether it was sports or trying out for the lead in a school play. In short, Ryan was everything Jeremy wasn't.

"That sucks," he said now, in a lackluster tone.

His cousin gave him a funny look. "You okay?"

Jeremy shrugged, saying sarcastically, "Sure. Why wouldn't I be? I just blew off Mr. G's class, and I'm sure he'll expect a damn good explanation, which unfortunately I don't seem to have. Not to mention I may get my ass thrown into jail for something I didn't do."

Ryan nodded slowly, as if in appreciation of the gravity of the situation, but his innate good cheer remained intact. "I wouldn't sweat it too much, if I were you. My dad says the worst that could happen is you'll get probation, maybe community service."

Jeremy felt a flash of anger toward his cousin. What did Ryan know? His whole life, he'd had everything handed to him on a silver platter. "On the other hand, I could end up doing time," he said. "Like mother like son, right?"

"Cool it, Germ. You're starting to creep me out." Ryan was still smiling, but a small crease had appeared between his brows. "Anyway, what happened with your mom . . . that was different."

"Yeah, I suppose rape must seem pretty tame next to attempted manslaughter. Especially since I'm not into knives or duct tape."

Without warning, his cousin grabbed him by the arm and steered him over to a deserted row of lockers, where he shoved Jeremy onto the bench. "You shouldn't talk that way, not in public," he warned in a low voice. "*I* know you're only joking, but some of these other guys . . ." He cast a glance over his shoulder. "You don't want to get in even worse trouble."

Suddenly the events of the past few weeks descended on Jeremy in an avalanche. "Since when do you give a shit?" he shot back. He knew it was unfair to take it out on Ryan, but at the moment he was too pissed off to care.

"I'm your cousin, dumb ass. Of course I give a shit." Ryan seemed more surprised than offended that his loyalty was in question.

"Really? I hadn't noticed."

Even as he heaped scorn on his cousin, part of Jeremy wanted nothing more than for it to be like it was when he and Ryan used to ride around on their skateboards and hang out after school in Mr. Kim's store, leafing through comic books and sneaking peeks at *Playboy* when Mr. Kim wasn't looking. But he knew that wasn't possible. They'd both gone their separate ways. If this were a race, Ryan would be up near the finish line and Jeremy would be lagging far behind.

Now Ryan was giving him a pitying look. Somehow that was what hurt Jeremy most of all. He was so insignificant, he couldn't even get a rise out of his cousin. "Maybe you would, if you didn't spend all your time hanging out with that loser Rudnicki," Ryan said, not unkindly.

Jeremy felt the sting of truth in his words, which only made him feel compelled to defend Rud. "You don't know him the way I do."

"I don't have to," Ryan replied, in a tone that meant Rud's reputation spoke for itself.

"Yeah, well, what's it to you? I don't see *you* breaking a leg to hang out with me."

"If you didn't have your head so far up your ass you can't see straight, you'd know why that is." Jeremy caught a flash of anger in his cousin's eyes. "*You're* the one who's always making excuses whenever I invite you anywhere."

With the last shreds of his dignity pulled around him like a tattered cloak, Jeremy informed his cousin, "Thanks, but I don't need your sympathy." The only reason Ryan had asked him along all those times, he was convinced, was out of a sense of familial duty.

Ryan smacked the flat of his hand against an open locker door, slamming it shut with a loud clang that echoed off the concrete floors and walls, causing Jeremy to start. "Jesus, you're a piece of work, you know that? Did it ever occur to you I might *like* hanging out with you? Or are you so busy feeling sorry for yourself you haven't noticed what a selfish prick you've become?" Jeremy opened his mouth to object, but his cousin was just getting warmed up. "Do you even care what's going on with me? That my mom's turned into a raving lunatic? Christ, she's talking about chaining herself to a tree! You'd think it was our own house that was going to be bulldozed, the way she's acting. Would it have killed you to stop by and talk to her? To see if maybe there was something you could do to help? She's been good to you, man. We *all* have."

Jeremy rose to his feet. "Thanks for the lecture. I don't feel so bad now about missing Mister G's class." He spoke with cool disdain.

"Are you even listening? Have you heard one thing I've said?" Ryan was visibly upset, his eyes flashing and his normally smiling mouth set in an angry line. Jeremy felt a small surge of triumph. He'd managed to get a rise out of his cousin. That was something.

He was about to walk away when his gaze dropped to Ryan's bare torso. With all the superiority he could muster, he said, in a voice very much like Rud's, "Dude. You should put some clothes on before you catch cold."

It wasn't until his anger ebbed that Jeremy was able to admit to himself that there was a grain of truth to what Ryan had said. More than a grain, in fact. How long had it been since he'd had dinner at their house or even stopped by to say hello? Aunt Denise was always inviting him over, but he'd given her nothing but excuses. Lately, he'd felt as if she and his mom were in cahoots somehow, both trying to get him to do stuff he didn't want to do, feel things he'd rather keep buried. Though hadn't he brought a lot of that on himself by volunteering to work for his mother?

He hadn't planned on it. It had just sort of . . . come up. And now, as he stood bent over in front of his locker, tying the laces on his gym shoes, a voice whispered in his head, *No one was twisting your arm*. Whatever his initial motives, though, he'd found that he *liked* working at the restaurant, even if it was just bussing tables. It was a point of pride, too, his wanting to prove to her that he was as worthy of her love as David, that the wrong son wasn't buried in the Episcopal churchyard where David had been laid to rest. Maybe then she wouldn't be so quick to leave, if it should come to that; maybe she'd even ask him to go with her. He wouldn't, of course. But it would be nice to be asked.

Something else occurred to him then, something that sent a chill shimmying down his spine: If anyone was going to be leaving, it would most likely be him, when they carted him off to jail.

Jeremy forgot his bad mood when he arrived at the restaurant later that afternoon to find most of the tables filled. The funereal atmosphere of the past few weeks had given way to a bustle of activity. Katie, sweeping past him in her waitress uniform, a forties-style gingham pinafore that his grandmother had sewn out of the leftover fabric from the curtains, seemed frazzled, her cheeks flushed and runaway strands trailing from her ponytail. Jeremy found his mother in the kitchen moving at the same warp speed.

"Amazing, isn't it?" she said over the machine-gun sound of her chopping. "It's been this way all day."

"Did something happen that I don't know about?" he asked, bending to pick up a piece of celery that had flown from the flashing tip of her knife onto the floor. He'd missed two days of work, due to a dentist's appointment and an overdue paper for English that he'd had to scramble to finish.

"We can thank Calpernia," Alice said. "Remember her uncle, from Memphis?"

Jeremy nodded. "The pit master." It was all his mother and Calpernia had been talking about for the past week or so.

"Well, he's here. And he's got the barbecue up and running."

"I thought I smelled smoke." Jeremy helped himself to a cube of bread she'd cut up for croutons.

"Well, apparently you're not the only one. It's been drawing in customers all day. It's like a miracle. Only who knew the burning bush would turn out to be Uncle Monroe's hickory chips?" She gave a breathless laugh, reporting, "We can hardly keep up with the orders. So much for *haute cuisine*. I guess *boeuf bourginon* can't compete with down home ribs."

"Be careful what you wish for, right?" said Jeremy, with a grin.

"No kidding. I never thought I'd be running a rib joint, but, hey, whatever works." Alice paused in the midst of her chopping to shake her head in wonderment, wearing a small, ironic smile. After a moment, she brought her gaze back to Jeremy. "If you're looking for something to do, you can start on those dishes," she said, pointing with her knife at the mountain of dirty plates in the sink. "Of all the days for Eduardo to call in sick!"

Jeremy reached for the apron on a peg inside the storage closet. He didn't mind being put to work, even a job as menial as loading the dishwasher. It warded off the black thoughts that flocked in his head like crows whenever he had too much idle time on his hands. Besides, his mom depended on him. It wasn't like with his old boss, Mr. Barbour, who could fire you one day and replace you the next as easily as changing a gasket on his car engine. His mother was just squeaking by, and even with the increased business it would be a while before she could afford to hire extra help.

He was scraping the last of the plates when Ryan's words floated back into his consciousness. Now he felt the slow burn of them in his belly. Had he been a selfish prick with his mother, as well? Seeing her through the eyes of a hurt, lonesome little boy instead of those of a nearly grown man? Punishing her for something that wasn't her fault?

Normally he would have scoffed at the idea, but the unsettling encounter with Carrie Ann and bruising he'd gotten from his cousin had shaken him up, made him reassess things. Not that he was ready to throw himself into his mother's arms and tell her all was forgiven. Just that it might not hurt to cut her a little slack.

Jeremy finished loading the dishwasher, then carried out the trash. He found Calpernia in the backyard conferring with an old guy, with hair like steel wool and skin the color and texture of beef jerky, the two hovering like a pair of conspirators over some backwoods contraption fashioned out of an oil drum fitted with what looked to be spare parts from the junkyard. Smoke curled from under its hood and from the length of stovepipe sticking up on top, like a mad scientist's experiment, the air around it shimmering with the heat it was throwing off.

"Jeremy honey, this here's Uncle Monroe," Calpernia introduced them. "I know he look like a dried up old thing can't lift a crate of marshmallows, but he as hardworking as any mule and ain't no ribs you ever tasted like his."

"Mouth on her like the *wrong* end of a mule, but she ain't half bad either." Uncle Monroe grumbled, turning to beam affectionately at his niece. He had to be close to eighty, skinny as the barbecue fork in his hand and missing one of his front teeth. He turned his attention back to Jeremy. "So what you think, son, ain't she somepin?"

For a moment Jeremy thought he was referring to Calpernia, then he noticed the old man gazing proudly at his contraption. "It's something, all right," he agreed. He just wasn't sure what. Yet from the enticing smells wafting his way, it was obviously doing the trick.

"'Course you got to have the touch," said the old man, lifting the lid to give the ribs sizzling on the grate a poke with his fork. "Ain't somepin you can learn overnight."

Calpernia turned to Jeremy. "He just holding out on me, is all. Don't want nobody knowing the recipe for his secret sauce. He say it's pro-*pri*-etary. Old fool don't even know what that word mean," she added with a throaty chuckle.

Uncle Monroe put on a mock injured look. "Do so. Looked it up in the dictionary."

Jeremy listened to their banter a few minutes longer. But if Calpernia's attempts to pry the recipe out of her uncle had been unsuccessful so far, Jeremy would bet a week's pay she'd get it out of him eventually. She wasn't the type to take no for an answer.

At first he hadn't known what to make of her. There weren't many black people on the island, and none like Calpernia King. In fact, she was unlike anyone he'd ever met: tough, streetwise, with a mouth that made Rud's seem tame. Nor did she seem all that interested in Jeremy's opinion of her, good or bad. But after initially being put off, he'd found himself intrigued. He even admired her in a way. She was unafraid and unapologetic. She refused to be defined by the bad hand life had dealt her.

The only thing that still seemed odd was the bond between Calpernia and his mom. In his fuzzy memories of childhood, the mother he had known would never have been friends with someone like Calpernia. She'd have been polite if they'd happened to meet, but that was about as far as it would have gone. Not because she was prejudiced, but because they had nothing in common—their skin color was the least of their differences. Whatever had happened to her in prison, he thought, it had made his mother a more interesting person.

Jeremy sampled the forkful of brisket Uncle Monroe had speared, which tasted even more delicious than it smelled. "Wow. That's amazing. You sure it's legal?"

Calpernia chuckled. "Better be, or I'm in trouble."

Jeremy lingered a few minutes more before saying reluctantly, "Well, I guess I'd better get back to work. My mom has her hands full in there. I've never seen it this busy."

"Son, you ain't seen nothing yet. We just getting warmed up," said Uncle Monroe.

Calpernia chimed in, adopting her uncle's Southern drawl, "Yeah, soon as this ol' fool teach me all his tricks, I be showin' y'all a thing or two." She chuckled, wagging her head, as if at some private joke.

Jeremy noticed the change in atmosphere as soon as he stepped back inside. A hush had fallen over the restaurant, and in the kitchen, with its counter that opened onto the dining area, his mother stood as motionless as a statue, gazing out at the packed tables.

"It's him," she said in a strange, flat voice.

"Who?" Jeremy felt his heart start to thump.

She turned to him, and he saw the fear on her face, the defiance too. “Mister White.”

Jeremy looked out into the dining area, where the mayor was seated at a table by the window. He looked perfectly at ease, as if he were any patron perusing the menu, trying to decide between a hot or cold appetizer. He was so inconspicuous Jeremy might not have singled him out if it hadn’t been for the wheelchair. That, and the sight of his mother, her face drained of all color, as she looked upon the man who had cost her everything she held dear.

CHAPTER TWELVE

April 1943

Eleanor Styles was holding up remarkably well, they all said. Though some privately speculated that the reason no one had seen her shed a tear might have more to do with her strange, proud ways than deep shock brought on by her husband's death. For while she'd joined the ranks of war widows, she kept mainly to herself. She was rarely seen about town and if she worshiped on Sundays it wasn't in any church. When someone did run into her by accident, turning down an aisle in Kingston Grocery or waiting in-line at Caldwell's Pharmacy, it was like glimpsing an apparition—a ghostly figure dressed in black, regal somehow in her mourning, often clutching the hand of her equally subdued daughter.

There was something about Eleanor that didn't invite conversation. Most of the islanders had known her since she was a little girl, but only a handful felt they had more than a nodding acquaintance with her. From early childhood on, the minister's youngest daughter had been set apart, by her beauty and by the rumors that later swirled around her: that she was fast, that she kept company with older men, namely one Lowell White. Even her marriage to Joe Styles had raised eyebrows. Why him and not one of the dozens of more suitable men her age who'd have walked over hot coals to be with her? More than a few had their suspicions about the timing of the union, given the arrival of Joe and Eleanor's daughter seven and a half months later, but Lucy had been a scrawny infant, weighing less than six pounds at birth, so she could indeed have been premature, as was claimed. And certainly no one could find fault with Mrs. Styles's conduct, which was beyond reproach.

Even her widowhood seemed more poignant somehow than that of others who'd suffered similar losses. Mourning had only heightened her pale beauty and made her more arresting in her quiet dignity. Those wives with husbands home from the war or on leave were secretly glad that Eleanor kept to herself, that she didn't partake in any of the social activities that might have thrown her into contact with them. For however bravely those men might have conducted themselves in battle, few would have been a match for Eleanor Styles. Without even meaning to, she could slay a man with a single glance.

One of those men approached her as she was collecting her mail at the post office one unseasonably warm morning in April, with the red-flowering currant in bloom and the gray whales making their annual pilgrimage to mate in the waters offshore. "Missus Styles," spoke a familiar voice in her ear. She turned to find herself face to face with her former lover. She'd spotted him in passing through the years, but they hadn't exchanged a word in nearly a decade. It was a shock now to see him standing before her, lean and louche as ever in a fedora and gray pinstripe suit too fine to have been purchased on the island. He smiled, the creases around his eyes and mouth deepening, as if with some private amusement. "Well, isn't this a nice surprise. It's been a long time, hasn't it?"

She froze for an instant, but quickly regained her composure, conscious of the postmistress's eye on her. No news by post or wire ever traveled faster than that carried by Edna Polhouse's tongue. "Yes, Mister White, it has. A very long time," she replied in a formal tone. "What brings you out this way?" Normally it would have been his secretary sending a package or collecting the mail, just as Eleanor had done on his behalf any number of times.

"Express delivery," he replied, producing a wrapped parcel from under his arm. "Wouldn't you know, everyone in my office is out sick with the flu. So here I am, left to fend for myself."

"Well, I'm sure you'll manage."

"And you? How are you getting along these days?" His jaunty smile gave way to an expression of sympathy. "Terrible about your husband. I read about it in the paper. Guadalcanal, wasn't it? "

She gave a stiff little nod of acknowledgment.

"I didn't know him well," Lowell went on, "but he did some work for me once. He seemed like a good man."

"He was." Eleanor cringed at the patent insincerity of his words. But she felt the hot fingers of her grief tighten their grip around her heart nonetheless, a grief magnified by the guilt she felt. For, as unreasonable as it was, she couldn't shake the suspicion that her love for William had somehow been the cause of her husband's death.

"Well, if there's ever anything I can do. Anything at all . . ." Lowell's eyes seemed to convey something more than sympathy.

Haven't you done enough? Her polite expression remained frozen in place, Eleanor wishing only for this unpleasant exchange to be over. What if Lucy had been with her? How awkward it would have been! And suppose someone had noticed the resemblance between father and daughter? Seeing them side by side, it would have been hard to miss. Eleanor grew cold at the thought.

"Thank you, but I'm managing just fine," she said. A lie really, but how was he to know?

She stepped past him to drop her mail into the slot: some overdue bills she'd finally been able to pay with the money from Joe's death benefit, and a letter to Joe's sister in Oregon, pleading the excuse of being under the weather to prevent her from visiting. Ever since word had come of her brother's death, Imogene had been insisting that she come, seeming to think Eleanor would benefit from the company of someone with whom she could share her grief, but Eleanor wished only to be left alone.

She was walking across the parking lot, headed for her car, when Lowell called after her, "Eleanor!"

She halted in her tracks. *He's going to say something about Lucy*, she thought. Her heart began to pound and wings of panic beat in her breast. It was a struggle to retain her cool demeanor, but somehow she managed it, pretending she didn't notice the purposeful way he was now planting himself in her path or the intensity of his gaze, which seemed intrusive somehow.

"Yes, what is it?" she replied somewhat impatiently.

"I just wanted you to know I truly am sorry. About your husband. About . . . the girl, too." In that moment, he almost seemed sincere.

Eleanor, though, was unmoved. She eyed him coldly. "She has a name. Lucy."

"Christ. You think I don't know? She's my daughter!" Lowell snatched off his hat, pushing a hand through his hair. The only other time she'd seen him this agitated was when she'd told him she was expecting. "You can't imagine what it's been like for me. So many times I've wanted to . . . to make it up to you somehow. But there was Joe. And if Dorothy ever found out, she . . . well, I'd rather she didn't."

Dorothy. His wife. The suitable match he'd made after he'd finished sowing his wild oats. Eleanor had read about it in the paper when the engagement was announced. Dorothy Jasper, daughter of Texas oil baron Henry Jasper and a graduate of Vanderbilt University, where she'd belonged to the Phi Delta Kappa sorority. Years later, upon Henry's death, the entire estate had gone to Dorothy, his only child, thus more than doubling Lowell's already vast wealth. But there was one thing he'd never lay claim to, and that was Lucy. Not as long as Eleanor had breath in her.

"How *is* your wife?" she inquired pointedly.

"Very well, thank you," he answered distractedly. "But, say, that's not why I—"

She plowed on resolutely. "And your children?" She'd seen them around town, a girl with her father's dark good looks, and a boy who was the image of his wan milk-skinned mother.

"Let's leave my family out of this, shall we." The faux warmth went out of his expression, and now he cast a furtive glance about the parking lot, as if suddenly becoming aware of being out in the open where anyone might have seen them. Luckily, no one was about. The only signs of activity were the bees bobbling amid the honeysuckle vines along the fence and the sparrows pecking at the blossoms that had drifted down from the maple tree overhead and were sprinkled in a fine gold carpet over the pavement. "Listen, Eleanor, I know this is awkward for you. It is for me, too," he said, adopting a more conciliatory tone. "Is there somewhere we can talk in private?"

"I don't see that we have anything to talk about," she replied.

"Look, I'm only trying to help. I know things have been rough for you lately."

"I don't need your help." She started to move past him, but he grabbed hold of her arm. She recognized the wild, unfocused look he wore, and she felt a flicker of panic. It was the same way he'd looked at her before kissing her for the first time.

His face was the same now as then, a bit more lined perhaps, yet it no longer held any appeal. There seemed something almost feminine in the brilliantined perfection of his dark, wavy hair, brushed now with gray. And in the harsh light of day, the pouches under his eyes that had once made him look excitingly decadent by candlelight merely made him look old.

"Don't be stupid, Eleanor. It's not going to be easy for you with Joe gone. I know. I checked your bank records." Her mouth fell open in shock, but he was unapologetic. "You don't have to look at me like that. It's not as if I was spying on you. Believe me, my only interest is in your and Lucy's welfare."

She quivered with indignation. "How dare you. "

"My point is," he went on, as if she hadn't spoken, "whether you like it or not, you're going to need money. And that, my dear, is the one thing I have plenty of."

"I don't want your charity!" she hissed.

"Call it a back payment on what I owe you then."

"Knowing you, you'd expect something in return."

He drew his head back to fix her with an injured look. "Do you really think as little of me as that? I'm not the terrible person you paint me to be. Honestly. The way things ended with us . . . I handled it badly, I'll admit. And don't think I haven't had my regrets."

Regrets? What did he know about regrets? "I stopped caring about all that a long time ago," she informed him coldly. "Really, there's no reason to trouble yourself on my account." She wanted no part of Lowell White, neither his money nor his belated regrets.

"We have a child. Isn't that enough of a reason?"

Blood surged up into her head, swelling against her temples, making them throb, but she managed to remain outwardly calm. "Lucy doesn't know anything about you. And I'd prefer to keep it that way." The thought of Lowell's getting anywhere near Lucy made her suddenly glad that Joe wasn't alive, for that would have killed him more surely than any bullet.

"She doesn't have to know," he said, wearing a cozily conspiratorial look that made her skin crawl.

Eleanor felt like screaming, *Enough*! She'd had her fill of secrets. First with Lowell, then with William. And, like toadstools flourishing in the dark, they had poisoned all that she'd held dear. In the case of William McGinty, by allowing feelings to grow where they shouldn't, which had very nearly led to an indiscretion. She shuddered now to think what might have happened, with Joe's body scarcely cold, if Captain Lewis from the home guard hadn't showed up at her door when he did.

She hadn't seen William since, nor did she intend to. The fact that it was torture to be apart from him only added to her resolve. She'd told him to stop coming to the house, and when he disregarded her wishes, she refused to let him in. Lately, he'd taken to leaving boxes of supplies on her doorstep. Eventually she would have to put a stop to that, too, but so far she hadn't had the heart.

Now she had Lowell to contend with.

"I see no point in continuing this conversation," she told him. "You've offered your help and I've told you I don't need it. Now if you'll excuse me, I have errands to run."

She attempted to move past him, but Lowell only tightened his grip on her arm. In the hard press of his lips against his teeth and cold depths of his eyes she saw his true nature: a man unaccustomed to being thwarted. "All right, we'll postpone the discussion. But you can't put me off forever, Eleanor. Don't forget, she's my daughter, too."

Eleanor reared back to fix him with a fierce look. "You don't want your wife to know that," she said in a low, warning voice. "It might not go over so well with her."

He laughed, as he once had at her provincial ways that he'd claimed to find so endearing. "You think I believe you'd say anything to my wife? Think what it would do to your reputation, my dear. You'd go from sainted widow to fallen angel overnight."

"I don't give a fig for my reputation."

"That much I believe," he said, eyeing her thoughtfully. "In fact, that's what I've always found so attractive about you.

You're not like the rest of them, are you? Not under the skin. You only pretend to be because it makes life easier. But I know what you're really like." He languidly traced a finger along her cheek, sending a shiver of loathing through her. He seemed to be enjoying her discomfort. "There's something you seem to have forgotten, though. If this gets around, Lucy will know, too. Are you prepared to take that risk?"

Eleanor felt all the fight go out of her. He knew her all right. He knew she'd do anything to shield her daughter from the truth. Lucy was having a hard enough time as it was dealing with Joe's death. This would devastate her.

"All right," she said, in a weary voice of defeat. "Pick me up outside your office tomorrow, before work. We'll go for a drive. We can talk then."

"No, someone might spot us. It's better if I come to your house."

She felt herself stiffen. "I'd rather you didn't."

"What, you don't trust me, Ellie? You think I'll try to seduce you?" He smiled, as if at her naiveté. "I suppose I should be flattered that you still think of me that way."

She hadn't considered that. She was thinking only of the danger to Yoshi. But what was the alternative? If she offered any further protests Lowell might grow suspicious and do some nosing around on his own. And at least in the privacy of her own home, surrounded by mementos of her life with Joe, a life that had been solid and good, she wouldn't feel so unclean.

Yoshi would just have to make himself scarce. There was an old, abandoned cabin along the trail up Spring Hill where she occasionally stopped to rest on long hikes. The boy would be safe there for the duration, well-hidden from view.

It was with trepidation nonetheless that she gave Lowell directions to her house. "Woodbury Lane, the last house on the left. You can't miss it."

His smile stretched into a grin that left her chilled, even as she stood in the warm spring sunshine with birds chirping in the trees overhead. "I know the way," he said.

The following morning Eleanor could scarcely concentrate on her chores, she was so wound up. She'd spent a restless night, thoughts of Lowell scampering through her head like the mice she could hear rustling in the walls as she'd tossed and turned in bed. Yet somehow she managed to get Lucy dressed and fed and off to school. She was in the midst of packing Yoshi off to the cabin, with explicit instructions that he was to stay put until she came to fetch him later on, when the boy hung his head, saying in his broken English, "I go, not come back. Better for you that way."

Eleanor's voice was firm as she told him, "No, Yoshi. You have a home with us, as long as you need it. And I promise it won't always be this way. This war can't go on forever. And when it's over, things will go back to the way they were before."

"Not same as before. Mister Joe not come back." Yoshi lifted his head to eye her mournfully. He'd loved Joe like a father and was taking his death hard.

"No, Mister Joe won't be coming back," she echoed sadly, her gaze drifting past him.

As she stood there, staring out the window, momentarily lost in thought, she was struck by the irony of it. Given how she felt about William, one might have thought a part of her would feel secretly liberated by her husband's death. Yet she missed Joe, more than she would have thought possible. She missed his kindness and his ready laugh, the unfailing courtesy with which he'd always treated her. Joe hadn't been a demonstrative man, but he'd always made sure she knew he loved her. Little things, like rising in the dark of winter mornings to get the fire started so the house would be warm when she and Lucy got up and driving into town to fill the car with gas whenever he knew she'd need to use it. What made it worse for her was that his body had yet to be recovered. According to Captain Lewis, he'd gone down with the *Hornet* when it was sunk.

She looked back at Yoshi. "Here. I packed you a lunch." She handed him the picnic basket she'd filled with enough provisions to last several days, including the little Japanese rice balls stuffed with bits of cooked fish and vegetables he'd taught her to make. "You might get bored, but at least you won't go hungry."

"I read book." He proudly held up the early reader, one of Lucy's old ones, with which Eleanor had been teaching him English.

She smiled at him. "I think you're ready for something a little more challenging than *Dick and Jane*." Yoshi might not have had the advantages of a privileged upbringing, but he had a quick mind and he loved to learn; in no time he'd mastered the alphabet and had worked his way through Lucy's primary and secondary readers. Now Eleanor plucked a tattered book off the bookshelf, one of Joe's old *Hardy Boys* mysteries, and tucked it into the basket, saying, "This ought to keep you busy for a while. Now scoot." She shooed him out the door, remaining on the stoop a while longer watching him trudge across the spring-blown yard: a slight figure in an old canvas jacket of Joe's that hung on him like a sail at half mast, his shoulders bowed, and his fine black hair falling over his forehead. When the war was over she'd miss having him around, she knew.

Yoshi darted a glance over his shoulder as he was nearing the gate that opened onto the field, and she saw the worried look on his face. He knew only that she was expecting a visitor, but it must have been obvious to him from how keyed up she'd been all morning that it wasn't just a social call. He might even have thought Lowell's impending visit posed some sort of threat, and he would have been right about that.

For while it was true that Lowell had a vested interest in letting sleeping dogs lie, Lucy was his child nonetheless, and where blood ties were concerned people had been known to act in ways that flew in the face of reason. So the night before, in the midst of her tossing and turning, Eleanor had come to a decision: If all Lowell wanted was to salve his conscience, she would take his money and hopefully that would put the matter to rest. Every cent would go into a savings account for Lucy, though.

What was less easily resolved was the matter of William. As she went back inside to finish washing up from breakfast, she thought that perhaps the real threat didn't come from her former lover but from her own wayward heart. Where she ought to have been on guard was in allowing herself to care so deeply for William. The fact that they'd never so much as kissed did nothing to erase the guilt she felt. For in her heart, she knew she'd betrayed her husband a thousand times over, with a married man no less. And now that Joe was dead, gone too was the chance to atone. The most she could do was banish William from her sight, knowing that otherwise she might weaken.

It was a wonder she was still functioning, really. It wasn't just her husband she missed, but William, too, with an acuteness that bordered on desperation, as if he were some essential element she needed in order to survive, without which she was slowly withering away. The only thing that kept her going was knowing she had to be there for Lucy.

An hour later Eleanor had finished tidying up and was tackling the ironing when she heard a car pull into the drive. She unplugged the iron and peered out the window. Lowell was striding up the front path, holding an enormous bouquet of flowers. The sight was at once absurd and deeply unnerving, causing her to let out a small cry, muffled by the hand she clapped over her mouth. What on earth . . . ? Why, anyone would think he'd come courting!

"Thank you," she said stiffly, as he handed her the bouquet. She left him standing in the entry as she hurried off into the kitchen in search of a vase, taking advantage of the opportunity to collect herself.

When she returned he was seated in the easy chair by the fireplace. Joe's chair. The sight of Lowell's brilliantined head resting against its high back, the spot left darkened by Joe's sweat—that of a working man who'd earned an honest wage, by his hands not his cunning—filled her with sudden rage. For a moment she was tempted to send him packing. But she reined in her emotions. The sooner they got this over with, the better.

From the pocket of her shirtwaist she produced a snapshot, which she handed to him. "Here. I thought you might like to have this." It was a photo of Lucy, taken the year she'd turned five, on a summer day when they'd all been out on Joe's boat. Eleanor had chosen it because Lucy, with her hair bleached several shades lighter by the sun and her face freckled from the outdoors, looked the least like Lowell than in any of the other photos. But Lowell only glanced at it before tucking it into his pocket, prompting her to remark, with barely contained contempt, "Don't you even want to know what she looks like?"

"I know what she looks like," he said.

Eleanor was taken aback, not only by his response but by the ease with which he'd spoken. It was as if he knew everything there was to know about Lucy. The unease she felt deepened, and for the first time she felt a flutter of real panic.

She lowered herself onto the sofa opposite him, smoothing her skirt over her knees. If he'd been an invited guest she would have offered him a cup of coffee or something to eat. But Lowell wasn't welcome, and she didn't care if he thought her rude. "Well. I suppose we should get this over with," she began, when it appeared he was in no hurry to leave. "I've given it some thought and, if you still insist, I'm prepared to take whatever it is you want to give me in terms of . . . of compensation. On one condition: This is in no way entitles you to anything as far as Lucy's concerned. You're to keep away from her." She fixed him with a hard, uncompromising stare. "Do I make myself clear?"

"Perfectly." A smile broke across his face. He seemed as relaxed as if he'd had it all planned out, right down to her response.

"You *do* understand, this isn't in exchange for visits . . . or anything of that nature," she emphasized.

He nodded, saying mildly, "I don't think that would be in either of our best interests."

"Well, then. I'm glad we can agree on that much, at least." Her fears should have eased, but for some reason she remained on guard. With Lowell's next words, she understood the real reason for this visit.

"You drive a hard bargain," he said, the smile lingering on his lips. "But that doesn't mean *we* can't see each other."

Eleanor was rendered speechless. It wasn't until Lowell rose from his chair and came over to where she sat, sinking down beside her on the sofa, that she found her voice. Jumping to her feet and pacing over to the fireplace, she said, "I think you'd better go."

Lowell stood up as if to leave, but instead of going to retrieve his hat and coat, he walked over to where she stood. "What's the matter, Eleanor? We're both adults, and it's not as though you'd be cheating on your husband." He cast a glance at the framed photo on the mantel, of Eleanor and Joe on their wedding day, Joe with his arm around her, appearing somewhat dazed, as if he still couldn't believe his good fortune, and Eleanor in her pale pink bridal suit, looking grimly determined to make a go of it. "Besides, we both know you wouldn't have married him if you hadn't been pregnant. With my child," he added, bringing his gaze back to her, his lips curled in a lazy, vulpine smile.

All at once Eleanor hated him, more than she had ever hated anyone in her life. "My husband was a good man. A good *father*," she said in a voice as cold as the ashes in the fireplace. "So I'll thank you not to drag him into whatever sordid little scheme you have in mind."

"Your loyalty is admirable, my dear," Lowell said, leaning with his elbow against the mantel, one ankle crossed insouciantly over the other, as perfectly at home in her house as if he owned it, "but I'm afraid your husband is no longer in a position to object."

Eleanor, seared by the callous insolence of his remark, lashed back. "He fought and died for his country! Which is more than I can say for you."

She could see that she'd hit a nerve—Lowell was at an age, late forties, when he was no longer eligible for the draft—for his smirk fell away. But he recovered quickly, giving a coarse laugh.

"Why go to war when there are so many pretty widows in need of comforting?"

He slid his arms around her waist, pulling her close. She was too stunned at first to resist, but she quickly recovered her wits and attempted to push him away, to no avail. He merely tightened his hold. She was only able to draw back far enough to take a swing at him, an open-handed blow that caught him clean across the jaw. He winced in pain, but it only seemed to inflame him further. He brought his mouth down against hers, not tenderly as in the past but with a roughness that was bruising.

Eleanor used all her might to wrench free. "If you don't leave this instant, I'm calling the police," she threatened with a bravado that might have been convincing if her voice hadn't been trembling. Lowell's response was to laugh. She glared at him. "You think I won't? Try me."

"Oh, I don't doubt you're capable of anything you set your mind to," he replied, in that lazy, mocking voice of his that was made all the more horrid by the knowledge that she'd once imagined herself in love with him. "But you don't really want the police in on this, do you? Think how it would look. The widow Styles entertaining her former lover when no one's home. People might get the wrong idea."

"You bastard!" she hissed, taking another swing.

He ducked, and she missed him. He straightened, forking back with his fingers the hair that had fallen over his forehead, which seemed as artfully placed as that of some movie villain: the heartless but irresistible rogue he no doubt fancied himself to be. His smile widened. "If I'm a bastard, there was a time it suited you just fine. I seem to recall, my dear, that before you joined the ranks of the respectable you couldn't get enough of this."

"Please. Just leave." It was more of a warning than a plea, for Eleanor felt certain that if he didn't something terrible would happen. Something irreversible.

"Gladly," he said. "But not until I've gotten what I came for."

With that, he fell on her.

Eleanor struggled against him, but it was useless. He quickly overpowered her. As she was dragged to the floor, her hip struck the end table by the sofa, and the lamp that stood on it came toppling down, its ceramic base shattering in an explosion of shards that dug into her like tiny sharp teeth when he threw her down on the rug. Then she forgot her pain, and there was only the terror, as Lowell straddled her, pushing her dress up over her thighs, tugging at her underpants. His breath came in hot little bursts against her face and neck, which made her feel dirtier somehow than what he was doing with his hands. She threw her head back and screamed but there was no one to hear. No one to prevent him from doing what no decent woman would have permitted, however foolishly she'd behaved in the past.

She didn't hear the car pulling up outside.

For William these past months had been a quiet agony. Eleanor had refused to see him and he hadn't been able to reach her by phone. He would have slipped a note under the door, but what if her little girl should be the one to find it? So in the end he'd said nothing, holding all his feelings inside, where they grew like a cancer, until he began to know the true meaning of heartsick. It wasn't just a figure of speech, it was a real sickness that left you weak and feverish. It robbed you of your appetite while at the same time eating at you until you could concentrate on little else. It left you lying awake, night after night, hating the wife sweetly slumbering beside you, whose only crime was in not being the one you loved. Whatever he'd felt for Eleanor before, it was magnified a thousand times over by his forced exile.

All he had left was the portrait.

These days, it was his sole occupation, devoting himself to it at the expense of commissions that would have brought in money. With painstaking brushstrokes, he went over each fold of her dress, the light illuminating her face, the dozen different shades of her hair, making sure it was rendered perfectly. It haunted him even when he wasn't at his easel. At night, it was there behind his closed eyelids, a gallery with but one work, a show of a single artist's obsession.

When he wasn't holed up in his studio, he was out walking the lonely stretches of shoreline that bordered his property. He would walk for miles, with no destination in mind, the dog his only companion. Anyone who might have happened upon him during one of those peregrinations would have been struck by the sight of him: a tall blade of a man with his unruly black hair blowing in the wind, lurching along the path with the aid of a walking stick, his border collie trotting at his side, William wearing a frown of concentration so fierce it made him appear slightly mad.

He knew he needed to get a grip. Martha had begun to remark on his odd behavior and frequent absences, and soon she'd wonder what he'd been doing holed up in the studio all those hours when he had nothing to show for it. But just as a man wracked with delirium must wait for the fever to break, so it was with him: He had no choice but to ride it out and hope this madness ended before any real damage was done.

The morning of Lowell's ill-fated visit to Eleanor's house, William had gone into town to pick up the gallon of turpentine he'd ordered from the hardware store. Martha had given him a list of items she needed as well, so afterward he headed over to the market. His mind was occupied, as usual, with thoughts of Eleanor. It had been several weeks since he'd been to her house, so he bought some things he thought she might need. If she wouldn't see him, then he could at least provide for her.

He understood the reason for his exile, that in her mind he'd somehow become tangled up in her husband's death, but that didn't make it any easier to bear. As he negotiated the winding roads to her house in his Packard he was thinking that if he'd been free to pursue her he'd have pounded on her door until she had no choice but to open it, torn it off its hinges if necessary. He wouldn't have allowed her to hide away, steeping in misguided guilt. But he *wasn't* a free man. He had a wife and son. And what right did he have to disrupt Eleanor's life any further when he had nothing to offer her but love?

He noticed the other car as soon as he pulled into the drive, a Cadillac convertible, midnight blue, with white-wall tires. Who did Eleanor know who would drive such a car? It must be someone on official business.

His first thought was that it had something to do with the bank loan she'd alluded to in one of their conversations. Even with Joe's military pay, she'd been having trouble keeping up with the payments. Was the bank coming to personally deliver the bad news of a foreclosure? He couldn't bear the thought of Eleanor and her daughter being forced out in the cold. Whatever he had to do, even if meant getting her to swallow that stubborn pride of hers and take money from him, he'd make sure that didn't happen.

He got out of his car and strode up the front path on legs that seemed to grow stronger with each step. He was barely limping by the time he reached the house. But there was no answer when he knocked on the front door. After a moment's hesitation he tried the knob, and the door swung open. He stepped inside and was about to call out her name when he heard a noise coming from the next room, a thump followed by a muffled sound that might have been a cry of distress.

William didn't stop to think; he acted on pure instinct, snatching the shotgun from atop the oak hall stand, where it was stowed. A woman all alone out in the country couldn't be too careful, Eleanor had reasoned, when he'd questioned its necessity. And he'd smiled at the time, thinking the threat of a wild animal or an intruder remote.

He wasn't smiling now.

As William catapulted into the living room, shotgun in hand, he encountered a scene that made his blood rise in a silent howl of outrage: Eleanor, in a welter of disheveled clothes and hair, held pinned to the floor by a large, dark-haired man. She was struggling to free herself, but she was no match for her attacker—he had to have outweighed her by at least eighty pounds. He was holding her down with one knee while reaching under her skirt to tug at her underthings, blind to anything but his sick purpose.

William froze for an instant, scattered bits of memory swirling in his brain, memories of the last time he'd held a shotgun in his hand, so many moons ago the smoothness of the oiled stock against his palm, the heft of the barrel along his forearm, shouldn't have felt as familiar as it did. In a series of rapid stereoscopic images, he saw the blood flowing from the wound in his brother's arm, blooming on his shirtsleeve like some hideous crimson flower; Stu, pale as birch bark, the doctor hovering over him; and the look their father had given him later on, as Stu lay dead.

William lifted the gun and fired.

CHAPTER THIRTEEN

Present day

He might have been any middle-aged man sitting there at the table in the window enjoying his meal—Judd Cove oysters, pan-fried flounder with butter-sage sauce, and a side of green beans. No messy ribs for him; he was too fastidious for that, Alice thought, watching as he delicately forked a piece of fish and brought it to his mouth. From where she stood, there didn't appear to be anything remotely threatening about Owen White. He wasn't big or menacing. If anything he appeared defenseless, sitting there in his wheelchair, his disproportionately muscular arms offset by the pampered softness of his belly. Next to the male visitors of her fellow inmates at Pine River, with their tattoos and piercings, their missing teeth and faces like roadmaps of their histories, he seemed almost comically bland.

But she knew what he was capable of.

Even as he sat minding his own business, his presence was creating a stir. He was like a stone plunked into a well, sending out ripples that could be felt from one end of the restaurant to the other. The other diners kept surreptitiously glancing his way and heads were bent together in whispered conversation. Soon they would be burning up the phone lines and everyone on the island would know.

But what would they know? Alice wondered. It didn't appear the mayor was here to make trouble. All they would see was a man willing to let bygones be bygones. More than that, one who was showing a generosity of spirit, not to mention a certain degree of trust, in partaking of a meal she had prepared.

Alice had a moment's doubt herself. Had she blown things out of proportion? Seen a conspiracy where there was none? Then the moment passed, and she knew with a certainty that had little to do with logic or appearances, one that was bone deep, that Owen was up to something. She was almost certain that he was behind what was happening to Jeremy. Why else would the D.A. be adopting such a tough stance, treating a sixteen-year-old kid whose worst offense until now had been talking out of turn in class, as if he were a hardened criminal? But if Owen was applying pressure, she wasn't sure what he hoped to gain. Was it pure revenge, using Jeremy to attack her in her most vulnerable spot? Or was it part of another, even more insidious plan?

All at once she felt as powerless as she had in prison, her body heavy with the same kind of inertia that had dragged at her those first months, when all hope for a retrial had faded and she'd had to accept that there was no way out. *Was there any way out of this?* Or was she doomed to have history keep repeating itself?

She became conscious of Jeremy edging up alongside her. She turned to find him eyeing her anxiously, and she was swept with a sense of déjà vu, thinking of the last time he'd been at her side and Owen within striking distance. Jeremy had to be wondering what her next move would be.

She knew one thing: She was not going to cower in the kitchen like a cornered mouse. Rearranging her features in what she hoped was some semblance of calm, she said, "I should go see what he wants."

"Maybe he's not after anything. Maybe he just heard the food was good." Jeremy sounded dubious even so.

"Maybe," she said. "But what do you want to bet it'll be the health inspector next. Looking for rats."

"The only rat I see is the one sitting over there," Jeremy muttered, casting a dark look at the mayor. Alice hadn't shared her suspicions with him, but it was clear he had his own feelings about Owen White. He hadn't forgotten that it was Owen who'd been the cause of his brother's death and of his mother's being taken from him.

As she pushed her way through the swinging doors into the dining area, Alice knew she had to be strong. If she failed by showing weakness, she'd be failing Jeremy as well. And that would be worse than anything Owen could dish out. Bolstered by that thought, she made her way over to his table.

At Pine River, she'd become a master at disguising her emotions. Cons had a nose like a bloodhound when it came to smelling fear or weakness, and they didn't hesitate to use it to their advantage, so it had been a matter of self-preservation. And now, even with her blood running high and fear pushing up from her sternum like something trying to claw its way out, the face she presented Owen was one of cool professionalism.

"Mister White. I hope everything's to your satisfaction."

He looked up from the roll he was buttering, seeming not the least bit surprised to see her. Obviously, he'd been expecting her. He swallowed the food he was chewing, his thin lips rolling back from his teeth in a smile that from a distance might have appeared sincere but that didn't match the cold look in his eyes. The smile of a politician making false promises or that of a CEO getting ready to eviscerate an opponent. Or a man with a secret who would do almost anything to protect it.

"Perfectly," he said, without a trace of irony. "In fact, that was the tastiest meal I've had in quite some time." In the hush that had fallen over the room, his voice seemed to carry, loud enough for all those listening in to hear every word.

She acknowledged the compliment with a little nod. "Thank you. I'm glad you enjoyed it."

"I must congratulate you, too, on what you've done with this place. It shows a lot of imagination." He cast an admiring glance around before leaning in to add, in a lowered voice that for all its manufactured warmth seemed to hold a note of menace, "But we all know that's something you're blessed with in abundance."

He was playing on Alice's biggest fear: that maybe she *was* crazy. After all, she'd suffered a nervous breakdown and it had been *her* behind bars, not Owen. How could she not have questioned her sanity? Yet, seeing him now, there was no doubt in her mind. She hadn't imagined any of it. For if Owen had nothing to hide, why was he going to such elaborate lengths to convince everyone of that? Aware that she was being scrutinized, she maintained a neutral tone, even with her heart pounding and every nerve quivering. "Is there anything else I can get you? Coffee? Dessert? We have an excellent crème brûlée today."

"Tempting, but I'm afraid I'll have to pass." He patted his belly. "I have to watch every bite. It's so easy to put on weight when you can't get around on your own two feet."

He spoke without enmity, but Alice knew that she was being reminded of the fact that she was the reason for his limited mobility. With a single, seemingly innocent remark he had her cornered. If she showed no remorse, she would appear heartless. If she displayed anger at the way she was being manipulated, she'd look vindictive, possibly even unstable. "Why don't I have Katie box something up for you, in that case," she told him, wearing a smile that felt as if it had been carved into her face with a box cutter. "Our mascarpone cheesecake. Compliments of the house."

She signaled to Katie, who hurried over at once. From the anxious look on her face it was clear she was aware of what was going on. The exchange between Alice and Owen had taken place without a raised voice or even a harsh word, but it had been a showdown nonetheless, and all those listening in—Joe Miner, from Island Excavating; the harbormaster, Roman Delgado, and his wife, Jan; Danica and Kurt Fellows, who owned the Old Depot Inn—to name a few—had to be conscious of that.

It wasn't until Alice was back in the kitchen that something in her let go and she began to tremble uncontrollably. When she went to pick up her knife, Jeremy reached over and gently pried it from her grip. "I can do that," he said. He seemed to eye her with new respect.

"Watch your fingers. It's sharp," she cautioned, as he started in on the scallions she'd been in the midst of chopping when Owen arrived.

He glanced up at her, wearing a funny little half smile. "Relax, Mom. I know what I'm doing. Who do you think fixed dinner all those nights Dad was on the road?"

His tone had been lighthearted, but for Alice it was yet another painful reminder of the years she'd been away and the family meals she'd missed. Jeremy and Randy, from what she'd been able to gather, lived like a pair of bachelors, without any of the comforts of a real home. All because of an act that had taken place in mere seconds and which had caused a lifetime of untold grief.

"I should go see how Calpernia's doing," she announced, after a minute or so of circling the kitchen aimlessly, looking for something to do that wouldn't result in a finger getting chopped off or third-degree burns.

"Mom?" She paused, turning to face him, expecting him to make some comment about Owen, but he only asked, "Have you talked to Aunt Denise lately?"

"Just the other day. Why?"

"I don't know. Something Ryan said. Sounds like she's pretty wigged about all this Spring Hill stuff. "

"Oh, that." Alice sighed. "You know her, she takes everything to heart." Alice felt bad about it, too. Like Denise, she'd have loved nothing more than to see the island's last true wilderness turned into a nature preserve. It had sentimental value for her, too; she had fond memories of catching tadpoles in the creek and of her grandmother taking her and Denise on hikes. But she had bigger worries at the moment than the impending development of Spring Hill. "What else did Ryan have to say?"

"Nothing much." Jeremy resumed his chopping. He suddenly looked preoccupied, and she wondered if his cousin had told him something that he didn't feel comfortable sharing. Something having to do with the tension she'd noticed lately between Gary and Denise.

"I'll call her tonight. See how she's doing," Alice said.

Jeremy shrugged, his head bent to his task. "Yeah, I think I will, too."

Excavation of the twelve hundred acre parcel slated for development on Spring Hill had begun the week before. The handful of activists who'd chained themselves to trees had only succeeded in delaying the inevitable. They might have held out longer but for the weather, which had turned suddenly nasty. With temperatures plunging and icy rain pouring down, even the most hardcore among them were forced to concede defeat before the police could move in with their bolt cutters.

Denise would have been among them, if at the last minute Gary hadn't put his foot down, saying he drew the line at having to arrest his own wife. In the end, Denise had backed down, but it had been a black day in their house nonetheless when the bulldozers rolled in. Their roaring could be heard all the way down to the main road as they bullied their way up muddy tracks made even slicker by the rain, uprooting trees and unearthing boulders that had sat untouched since their equally catastrophic formation a millennium ago in some mass, primordial upheaval. It had rained so incessantly that long-time residents whispered it was the curse of the Orcas Indians who'd once inhabited the island and who, it was said, had ancestors buried up on Spring Hill.

When, in the second week of the excavation, the bulldozers unearthed a moldering bundle of bones that proved to be human remains, it seemed the old-timers had been right. It wasn't until they were examined by a forensic expert on the mainland that it was determined they dated back no more than fifty or sixty years, and were those of a middle-aged man, a little over six feet in height, who'd died of a gunshot wound.

The consensus was that the unknown victim had been some vagrant passing through or perhaps an itinerant farm hand. Who else could it have been? Anyone else would have been reported missing at the time, and records showed no missing person who fit that description.

All except one.

When dental records established the deceased's identity as none other than the long-missing Lowell White, the news rocked the island with a force not known since the last earthquake, back in '88. Lowell, it seemed, hadn't gone off to some South American country to live like a king with his mistress. He'd been murdered.

Excavation on Spring Hill was brought to a temporary halt and the case was turned over to the police. Owen White made a public statement that, though saddened to learn of his father's death, he was gratified that the truth had come out at last. Even if the case was never solved, he said, at least his father's tarnished reputation had been restored.

Alice, meanwhile, was enjoying a temporary reprieve—the court date for the hearing on Colin's latest motion had been postponed due to a recent spate of arrests, those of protestors who'd attempted to block the excavation of Spring Hill. Taking advantage of the lull, on a Monday when the restaurant was closed, she decided to pay a visit to Colin. Since business had picked up at the restaurant she'd been so busy they hadn't had much chance to talk, except when meeting to discuss Jeremy's case. Conscious of the fact that he wasn't charging her for all those hours, she'd baked him a pie to show her appreciation. It was the least she could do, she told herself. Though deep down she knew that it was really just an excuse to see him.

Since that night at the restaurant when she'd sensed something between them, something so powerful it had left her shaken, she'd kept herself at an emotional distance. The last thing she needed right now was to add a whole new set of complications to her life by getting romantically involved, she'd reasoned. But that hadn't kept her from thinking about him. Again and again she'd replayed that charged moment in her mind, imagining what it would have been like if he *had* kissed her. It had been so long since she'd known a man's lips on hers, a man's touch against her bare skin, she scarcely remembered what it was like—at the age of thirty-nine she was like a virgin all over again. And now it seemed that part of her, buried for so long she'd almost forgotten it existed, was rising up in revolt. It invaded her thoughts and dreams, and it was what had propelled her out the door and onto the road to Colin's house, despite her asserting that she had absolutely no intention of sleeping with him.

She was passing the turnoff to Denise's house when her thoughts turned briefly to her sister and Gary. Her brother-in-law seemed particularly on edge these days. Alice recalled his hostile reaction when she'd approached him the other day, in the lingering hope that he'd be able to provide some scrap of information that would validate her suspicions about Owen.

"I'd drop it, if I were you," Gary had advised, eyeing her coldly. They'd gone for a ride in his cruiser, so they could talk in private, and were parked along a remote stretch of road out near Mountain Lake.

"Why? Is it so far-fetched?" she'd pressed on nonetheless. "Come on, Gary, we both know the reason I ended up getting the maximum sentence. Ten years, Gary. *Ten years*. I'd still be serving time, if I hadn't gotten paroled. You think I'd have been left to rot if it'd been someone other than Owen? He knows people. He knows which levers to pull."

"You want to blame someone, blame yourself," Gary had snapped. In the sunlight glaring in through the cruiser's windshield, showing off every smear and bug splat, his eyes peered from hollowed sockets, the skin around them bruised-looking. "You brought all this on yourself. And it wasn't just you who had to suffer. Christ, when I think of all the nights your sister cried herself to sleep. And your poor mom, having to cope with that while your dad was dying. Not to mention Jeremy."

Stung, Alice had been momentarily silenced. "I know I caused a lot of pain," she'd said softly at last, "and I'm sorry for that, truly I am. But if you care about Jeremy, don't you owe it to him to find out if there's any truth to what I'm saying?"

But this new Gary who'd taken the place of her normally considerate brother-in-law had merely given a scornful laugh. "So having me chase some paranoid delusion is your idea of helping? Jesus, Alice, sometimes I think the kid was better off with you in prison."

Alice had been more taken aback by the transformation in Gary than by his cruel words. In the old days, he never would have spoken to her like that. He'd always acted as the family peacekeeper, the calm voice of reason when Denise was on one of her leftist rants or when an argument between the kids needed refereeing. As a cop, he had a reputation for settling domestic disputes without further inflaming already sore tempers, and for cutting motorists a break if they had a good reason for going over the speed limit.

Even Gary had seemed to recognize that he'd gone too far, for he'd continued on, in a gentler tone, "Okay, let's just say, for the sake of argument, there's some truth to what you're saying. You start poking around where you don't belong, you could piss off some powerful interests."

Alice had grown suddenly alert. "So there *is* something to it."

"I'm not saying that," he'd said.

"What *are* you saying then?"

"Nothing." His mouth had settled into a grim line, as he'd stared out the bug-spattered windshield, as if seeing something other than the strip of gravel on which they were parked.

She'd placed a hand on his arm. His muscles were so taut they were almost vibrating, like an aerial cable in a high wind. "If you know anything, anything at all, please, you have to tell me. I promise no one will ever know where I heard it from. Not even Denise."

"So now you want me keeping secrets from my own wife?" With a violent twist, he'd thrown her hand off his arm, as if it had been a biting insect. "Christ, Alice. You should listen to yourself. You want people to forget about the past, stop acting like some crazy person. And stop hanging out with ex-cons, like your friend Big Mama."

With that, he'd slammed the cruiser into gear, sending it slewing over the gravel before it hit the roadway at a speed best suited for when the bubble light was flashing. Alice had been more confused and worried than angry. Gary was clearly under a tremendous strain. But what was causing it?

Did it have something to do with the way Denise had been acting lately? Or was it some work-related pressure?

When Alice arrived at Colin's house, there was a note pinned to the front door that read simply *Gone fishing*. She set off along the path that led down to the cove, using a hand to shield her eyes against the sunlight that seemed almost blinding after the spate of rainy days they'd had. The tide was out and the waters of the sound calm, glinting like so many capsized stars. Down below she could see Colin, in a hooded jacket and rubber boots, wading through the shallows, the lengths of PVC pipe he'd planted in evenly spaced rows stretching out before him like a field of newly sprouted cornstalks, while Shep watched from a safe, dry distance onshore. Colin spotted her and waved, sloshing his way toward her.

"Catch anything yet?" she asked, noting the plastic bucket he carried in one hand.

"Just starfish."

"I didn't know they were edible."

"I wasn't planning to make a meal out of them. In fact, they're the ones doing the eating." He explained that, to starfish and other predators, his fledgling oyster farm was nothing more than a giant snack bar. "I'm just thinning out the population to give my guys a fighting chance. Don't worry," he assured her. "They're not going to end up in some souvenir shop. I turn them loose in the bay." He pointed toward the larger body of water on the other side of the cove.

Colin's face was ruddy from working outdoors. He was looking more robust these days; not only that, more at peace with himself.

"Very considerate of you," she said, smiling. "It must help that they don't put up much of a fight. I mean, it's not exactly the battle of the *Old Man and the Sea* you're waging here."

"Oh, I don't know about that." He fished a starfish from the bucket and held it up, dripping, saying with a twinkle in his eye, "This guy looks pretty fierce. I wouldn't want to be at the receiving end of one of these suckers." He prodded an arm waving in sluggish protest before dropping the creature back into the bucket. "Now what do you say we take a ride over to the point and show these guys their new home?"

"I'm game, as long as it doesn't involve touching anything slimy."

"I promise to do all the dirty work," he said, as he started up the path, Shep at his heels. The border collie appeared to have settled into his new role as Colin's surrogate pet, as though he'd come to regard Colin, if not as his true owner, then as an ally at least. Shep waited politely to be invited along before hopping into the Volvo and settling onto the backseat.

The entire trip took less than half an hour, and they were back at the house by lunchtime. "You're not in any rush, I hope," said Colin, as they were getting out of the car. "I thought I'd fix us something to eat to go with that pie you brought."

"Why not? It's my day off," she reminded him. There were a million things on her to-do list, but at the moment she couldn't think of any better way to spend the afternoon than with Colin.

"I'm not as good a cook as you, but I make a mean shrimp salad," he said, as he led the way through the back door, pulling off his boots in the mudroom and slipping into an old pair of Weejuns.

In the kitchen, he set about assembling various bags of greens and bottles of condiments. "Anything I can do to help?" she asked.

"No, you sit. Can't have you working on your day off." He waved her toward one of the chairs at the old dinette, where she sat watching in amusement as he muddled through the process of tearing up lettuce, chopping vegetables, and peeling the cooked shrimp.

"Delicious," she pronounced, upon taking her first bite. "And the fact that I didn't have to lift a finger makes it taste all the better."

"You did your part. You brought dessert. How did you know pumpkin pie was my favorite?"

"Actually, it's sweet potato," she corrected him.

"Well, whatever, it looks good. I'll have to order it next time I'm in the restaurant."

"It's not on the menu, actually. I only make it for family."

He smiled at her across the table, a smile that caused a slow heat to rise in her cheeks. "In that case, I feel doubly privileged."

After coffee and pie, they headed back outside. It was chilly, but after all the weeks of dreary weather, the sunshine that had broken through the clouds earlier in the day was like an unexpected gift. Bundled in their jackets, they sat in the wicker chairs on the porch with their heads tipped back to receive it, like some sort of blessing or absolution, while Shep lay stretched out asleep on the old, scuffed floorboards at Colin's feet.

Talk turned inevitably to Jeremy's case.

"Cantwell's been applying pressure to set a date for the trial," Colin said, informing her of the latest. "I don't know how much longer I can stall. I filed a motion seeking a continuance to interview more witnesses, but I'm not sure the judge is going to grant it."

"And if he doesn't?" Alice felt a ripple of anxiety.

"We'll just have to hope that we have a strong enough case as it is."

His faintly troubled look prompted her to ask, "What is it? Is there something you're not telling me?"

After a moment's hesitation, he said, "I just got the results back on the rape kit from our own expert, the pathologist I told you about, in Spokane. It's nothing bad," he hastened to assure her. "It's just that I was hoping the findings would be more conclusive."

"But if they're not conclusive, doesn't that mean the D.A.'s case isn't very strong either?" she asked.

"It depends on which expert the jury finds more credible."

"So this doctor in Spokane, what's he like?"

"Actually, it's a she. And she strikes me as highly credible. She's a lot like you, in fact. Strong and decisive."

Alice gave a self-conscious laugh. "That's funny. Most days, it seems like I don't even know which shoe goes on which foot."

"Well, then, I guess appearances can be deceiving." Colin smiled at her, tiny lines radiating from the corners of his eyes.

Alice pondered his words, as though fingering some small, shiny treasure she'd accidentally stumbled across. Was she really that person he saw when he looked at her? It was almost too much for her to contemplate, so she brought the discussion back to Jeremy's case, asking, "What are his chances of a fair trial?"

"Depends." Colin gazed out at the cove, frowning in thought.

"On what?"

"On whether or not our suspicions are correct about your friend, Owen." He turned to face her. "Have you been able to find out anything yet?"

Alice thought once more about her frustrating conversation with Gary, and shook her head. "Nothing so far, but I'm still working on it." She'd put off going to Denise, in the hope that her sister would have better luck appealing to Gary, but Alice could see that she had no other choice. She sighed, adding, "The thing is, unless we can come up with some pretty compelling proof, no one's going to believe Owen's behind it. Especially now, with all this public sympathy over his father."

"That certainly adds a new wrinkle," Colin agreed.

"Do you think they'll ever get to the bottom of it?" she asked, out of curiosity.

A murder that took place half a century ago? With no weapon, no eyewitnesses, no suspect even." Colin shook his head. "You'd have better luck solving Amelia Earhart's disappearance."

"I suppose you're right. Still, I can't help wondering if he's somewhere on the island. The killer, I mean. Someone you might pass on the street and not think twice about. Someone we might even know." Suppose, like her, he wasn't a common criminal, but someone who'd simply snapped under pressure. In a peculiar way, she found the idea comforting. It meant she wasn't the only one capable of doing the unthinkable.

"If he's even still alive, he'd be pretty old by now," Colin said. "We don't even know if it's a he. It could be a she."

She nodded thoughtfully. "Maybe some woman he was involved with. He could have promised to leave his wife for her and when she found out he was just stringing her along, she went crazy and shot him. You know, like Jean Harris and that diet doctor."

He turned to her with a smile. "So you think it was a crime of passion?"

"From what I've heard, he was quite the ladies' man."

"If that's true, then your theory makes sense."

They lapsed into silence, and for a long while there was just the sound of the wind in the trees, a sound like the whispering of a thousand secrets, and the distant cries of seagulls. After a while, Colin remarked, "This was my grandfather's favorite spot. He used to love sitting out here after a day at his easel, especially in good weather."

"It must have been lonely when you weren't around," she said, thinking of the long winter months holed up in this remote place.

Colin shrugged. "I suppose. He never talked about it. He wouldn't have wanted me to feel guilty for not visiting more."

"What about your dad? Did he visit?" Colin seldom talked about his family, and now she realized how little she knew about them.

"No. Never." From the hardness of Colin's tone, it was obvious there had been some deep animosity. "My grandmother saw to that. She poisoned my dad against him."

Alice made a sympathetic face. "Their divorce must have been bitter." She was thinking of hers and Randy's, a dissolution that had seemed more of a sad withering than anything else.

"Yeah, but the weird thing is I never really knew why they split up. It's not something my grandmother likes talking about. In fact, to this day she refuses to have his name spoken in her presence. And my grandfather . . . well, he was too much of a gentleman to say anything that might have made her look bad."

"That must have been hard on your dad."

"It was." She could see the muscles tightening in Colin's jaw. "And after my grandmother moved to New York, William didn't have much chance to rectify the situation."

"Why was that?"

"For one thing, they lived at opposite ends of the continent. Travel wasn't so easy in those days. For my father it would have meant hours on an airplane, and he was just a little boy." Colin shook his head in regret. "By the time he came of age, it was too late, the damage was done."

"So how did you and William end up having a relationship?"

"That was my mom's doing. She thought it was a shame, us boys growing up not knowing their grandpa. She was the one who needled Dad into letting us visit. In the end, though, it was just me who went. My brother always had something going on. Little League, junior varsity, cross-country. Then once Patrick discovered girls you couldn't have pried him loose with a crowbar, especially not after he started having sex, and believe me, he didn't waste any time in that department. His wife was pregnant when they eloped, the two of them barely out of high school."

"That must have gone over well with your parents," she commented dryly, thinking about the current situation with Jeremy.

"No kidding. I thought they were going to go through the roof." Colin shook his head, chuckling as though at some private joke. "You'd have thought the odds of that marriage working were next to none, right? But amazingly, Pat and

Ginny are still together. They just celebrated their twentieth. Their oldest is in college and Mikey just graduated high school."

"Do you see much of them?"

"Not as much as I should. I was kind of out of commission there for a while. I even went a few years without seeing my grandfather, and by the time I was up to it, it was too late." A source of deep regret, she could see, from the sorrowful look that crossed his face.

"I didn't know your grandfather," she said gently, "but he sounds like the kind of person who'd have understood. The main thing is, you got sober. I'm sure he'd have been happy about that."

Colin regarded her for a moment, a small, considering smile on his lips. "You know a lot for a normie." At the puzzled look she shot him, he explained, "As in normal. It's AA speak for someone who's not an alcoholic."

She gave a wry laugh. "I'd hardly describe myself as normal. In fact, I'd say I'm anything but."

"Maybe that's what I like about you."

"Oh? And I thought it was just my cooking."

His smile widened. "That, too."

Alice noticed that the shadows had lengthened; the patch of sunlight in which Shep lay had shrunk to the size of a dollar bill, which glowed atop the furry hump he made curled there on the porch. Reluctantly, she said, "I should be going. It's getting late."

Colin didn't attempt to persuade her to stay, which made her wonder if she'd already worn out her welcome. As she rose to go, she felt strangely let down. She hadn't expected anything to happen—in fact, it was the last thing she needed—but foolishly she'd thought it might. Whatever she was feeling, it was clearly one-sided. Probably when he looked at her, he saw only a woman who'd spent her youth behind bars and who was now past her prime.

She'd turned and was about to walk away when she felt his touch against her elbow.

"Alice."

Just that, her name, spoken so softly it might have been a whisper, and she knew. It hadn't been her imagination after all: He wanted her. The knowledge brought a rush of joy so intense she needed a moment to compose herself before she could turn to face him.

Colin appeared uncertain, as if engaged in some sort of internal struggle. Then a corner of his mouth tipped up in a smile that was both hopeful and guarded. "I was just wondering what you would think if I kissed you."

Alice was rendered speechless. None of the old flirtatious comebacks came to mind, the coy lines from back in the days when such repartee had come as naturally as breathing. In the end, she simply spoke the truth. "Actually, I'm not even sure I remember how. It's been a long time."

"For me, too." He shoved his hands deep into the pockets of his corduroy trousers, as if suddenly not knowing what to do with them.

All of the perfectly valid reasons with which she'd been attempting to convince herself that now wasn't the time to be embarking on an affair, building her case as thoroughly as Colin had Jeremy's, vanished from her mind. She took a deep breath. "Well, then, what do you say we give it a try."

He took her in his arms, tentatively at first. She closed her eyes as his lips brushed over hers. So far, so good. Then the kiss deepened and all at once she knew she was in trouble. She had the sensation of falling, as if she were tumbling over and over in midair. Yet, strangely, it didn't terrify her. Instead, she only found herself wanting more.

She wound her arms around his neck, pulling him close. How was it possible she'd gone so long without this? That she'd shut down to such a degree that even the most basic human needs had come to seem like impossible luxuries? Now the rush of being liberated was almost overpowering.

She sensed that Colin, too, had been unprepared for the suddenness with which they were swept up in . . . whatever this was. His hands that hadn't known what to do with themselves were all at once taking charge, moving over her, touching her in places she hadn't been touched in so long his fingers might have been brushing over her bare skin, the sensations were so acute. He kissed her neck, her earlobes, the hollow at the base of her throat, where a runaway pulse would have given her away if her own hands and mouth hadn't already done so. The greedy kisses of a man who, like her, had been wandering in the desert for too long.

There, amid the lengthening shadows, they each found what they'd been looking for without realizing they'd been in search of it: a place to lay their burdens down, a temporary respite from the ghosts that haunted them. Love didn't necessarily enter into it. That could come later, she knew. Right now all that mattered was that, for the moment at least, they weren't alone.

"Shall we go inside?" Colin murmured when they finally drew apart.

"We'd better. Unless we want to give the neighbors something to *really* talk about," she said, with a breathless little laugh. Never mind the nearest neighbor was half a mile away.

Indoors it was quiet. There was only the slow ticking of the regulator clock on the mantel and a fly buzzing against a windowpane. Colin led the way into the bedroom, a room so full of history that Alice felt it settle over her like the thick down comforter Colin used to cover her as she stretched out on the old sleigh bed.

The last of the sunlight slanting in through the curtains had faded, but Colin didn't bother to switch on the lamp. In the soft gray light of dusk, he unbuttoned her shirt and eased off her jeans. With each new item of clothing removed it was as if she were being released somehow, from the chains that had held her bound for so long. For once, she wasn't fretting about what the future would bring. She wasn't questioning his motives or her own. She was too busy luxuriating in the feast of delicious sensations and in this new, giddy sense of freedom. She gave herself over to it, surrendering herself to his hands, as they moved over her naked body, and to his mouth that had kissed her so tenderly on the lips and was now exploring her with equal tenderness below.

She quickly grew acquainted with his body as well: the long, lean contours of his torso, the hair on his chest that tapered to a downy trail on his belly, his arms that had grown sinewy with muscle from all the outdoor work. Each crevice and plane and ridge was a fascinating new discovery. Colin was bigger than Randy, and adept in ways her husband hadn't been. In bed, he wasn't shy. Using his hand to guide hers, he showed her what pleased him and how she could let him please her.

Alice moaned as he pushed two fingers into her, rolling her hips up to bring them deeper into her. She felt as if she could come this way. And then she *was* coming, in waves so intense it was as though she were being turned inside out. When it was over, she fell back with a gasp. It was a moment before she could catch her breath and whisper, "Now you."

But Colin pulled away, murmuring, "Next time." He hadn't thought to buy condoms, he explained somewhat sheepishly. He hadn't exactly been planning to seduce her.

"You mean all you thought about was kissing me?" she teased.

"I didn't say that. But X-rated fantasies can't get you into trouble," he replied, nibbling on her ear.

He showed her then just how to pleasure him. An act she found more exciting, in its own way, than if they'd made love. Even then, it seemed they weren't done. He gently pushed her onto her back and gave her more of what he had earlier, only this time with his mouth. Afterward, Alice could barely move. She felt as though she'd been drugged.

At last she managed to roll onto her side, propping an elbow under her head. Colin was lying on his back, staring pensively up at the ceiling, wearing a satisfied smile, but already she sensed him beginning to withdraw.

Alice touched his shoulder. "You're not sorry, are you?"

He turned to look at her. "God, no. You?"

She should have felt reassured, yet there'd been something in the quickness of his response and the fleeting expression of guilt that had crossed his face that gave her pause. *He's thinking about his wife*. Even though she was dead and the woman lying next to him very much alive. More alive, in fact than Alice had felt in years.

She was quick to stow away her own emotions, not wanting to get hurt. "We're both adults and, as far as I know, unattached." She aimed for a light, laissez-faire tone.

Alice waited for him to respond, but he'd gone back to staring up at the ceiling, still wearing that pensive look. His thoughts taking him places where she couldn't follow. At last, he shifted so that he was facing her and reached up to smooth back a stray lock of her hair, saying, "That was amazing. But I should warn you, they don't encourage this sort of thing in the program, not until you've been sober at least a year."

"It's not as if we planned it," she said.

"I know. I just wanted you to be aware of what you're getting into. I'm not exactly prime relationship material."

The pleasure Alice had felt abruptly faded. "This is hardly the time for me to be thinking about getting into a relationship," she said, in the same airy tone, "so you can put your mind at ease on that score, at least. As lovely as that was, I'm not looking for anything permanent." It was the truth, she told herself, so why did she feel like a liar saying it?

Colin's expression softened. "Alice—"

She cut him off, peering at her watch and saying, "Will you look at the time? Now I *really* have to be going."

"So soon?" he asked, but at the same time she could sense that a part of him was relieved, the part that wanted to be alone with his thoughts.

"I'd love to stay, but I have some things to do at home," she said briskly, bending to retrieve her clothes, which were scattered over the floor. They both got dressed, an awkward silence settling over them. They didn't speak again until she was on her way out the door.

"Drive safely," he said, kissing her lightly on the mouth.

Alice nearly laughed out loud. Drive safely? He should have cautioned her about losing her heart.

For a long time after Alice had left, Colin sat on the sofa, absently rubbing his jaw as he stared off into space, mulling over what had just happened. It wasn't that Nadine wouldn't have given her blessing, he knew. In fact, whenever they'd played that particular game of *what if . . .* she would always teasingly run through a list of friends whom she thought would make compatible replacement wives.

No, he thought, if anyone had a problem with his being with another woman, it was him. He'd been unprepared for the slew of emotions that Alice had unleashed in him. It was as if, having thought he was dredged dry, no more tears left to be shed, he'd discovered there was a whole new level of grieving to be done.

The only other woman he'd slept with since his wife's death had been a one-night stand, after too much to drink at an office Christmas party. But the following day, aside from the usual free-floating morning-after shame, there had been none of the complicated feelings he was experiencing now. Because the woman hadn't been a threat to Nadine's memory.

Alice, on the other hand, wasn't just some warm body to distract him from his grief. She meant something to him. What exactly he didn't know, but one thing was clear: He didn't want to see her get hurt.

His sponsor had warned him about this. *After the first six months you think you got it made in the shade. That's when you* really *gotta watch out*, Dave had said. Dave Coffey, a big, tough, former biker with scraggly gray hair in a ponytail and more tattoos than Colin had ever seen on any one person. But he'd known what he was talking about.

Colin had let his guard down, allowed himself to believe he was out of the woods, and there, just as Dave had predicted, was that old, familiar thirst, rising up in him, with all the intensity of those first weeks in sobriety. His hands trembled with it and his throat was parched. He felt the old St. Vitus's dance start up in him, too, as if any minute he was going to jump out of his skin.

Colin eyed the antique cherry cabinet where his grandfather had kept a small supply of liquor for the occasional visitor. Colin didn't know how much, if any of it, was left; he hadn't bothered to check. It would have been tempting fate and he'd already had one too many rendezvous with that particular siren. But now he found himself wondering if the key to the cabinet was in the same place he remembered it being.

He squeezed his eyes shut, running through all the reasons not to get up and unlock the cabinet. It would wipe out eight months of sobriety, putting him back to square one, and once he started down that road the life he'd been struggling to rebuild would be washed away, too, like so much flotsam with the tide. Also, he'd be letting down people who had come to depend on him, like Alice and Jeremy, as well as destroying any goodwill he'd managed to cultivate among the islanders whom he'd gotten to know and like.

For what seemed like an eternity Colin remained motionless, his eyes shut and his hands balled into fists. A light sweat had broken out on his forehead and he was trembling ever so slightly. An image of Nadine rose up behind his closed eyelids, her angelic face with its devilish smile, her eyes sparkling with the come-hither look she'd worn on that last morning. He held on to it as long as he could and, even after it had faded, it was with the greatest reluctance that at last he opened his eyes.

With a deep sigh of release, or perhaps regret, he rose from the sofa and crossed the room to where the cabinet stood.

CHAPTER FOURTEEN

It was late in the day and the air cidery with the smell of apples rotting on the ground in the orchards along Fox Valley Road. The season had long since peaked, even for the later varieties, like Winesap. Though only a few short weeks ago, it seemed, the boughs had still been heavy with golden and red Delicious, McIntosh, Cortland, and Pippin. As he drove slowly toward home in his cruiser, Gary Elkin thought back to the days when he used to help out with the harvest in his family's orchard, before the rise of gourmet outlets had created a demand for newer varieties, many of them imported, that sounded more like fancy drinks—Pink Lady, Jazz, Gala—had pretty much kicked the bottom out of the market for what they'd grown. Between that and the industrial agrigrowers, which had further driven prices down, mom and pop operations like theirs couldn't compete. When Gary was in the fifth grade his parents had been forced to sell the farm.

He would never forget the day he'd arrived home from school to find his mom and dad seated at the kitchen table wearing shell-shocked looks, like after the barn had burned down a few years back. Their eyes stared out of suntanned faces the color of the milky tea in mugs before them. *Sit down, Gary. We have something to tell you*, his mother had said, in the same grave tone she'd used when informing him of Grandpa Eddie's death. She told him they were moving to California, where his father had found a job as foreman with a big grower in Bakersfield. They would be leaving as soon as they'd packed up.

What about the horses, Popcorn and Winkie, and the goats and chickens? Gary had wanted to know, not quite understanding what this was all about.

They'll be fine, his father had assured him. *Their new owners will take good care of them.* He'd explained that they hadn't had any choice in the matter; if they'd tried to hold on to the farm, the bank would have foreclosed. His dad had looked close to tears himself as he'd patted Gary's hand, saying with a bravado that was unconvincing even to an eleven-year-old, *Don't worry, son. It'll be all right, you'll see. In fact, it'll be an adventure. A brand-new start for us all.*

Only it hadn't been a brand-new start. Rather, it had been the end of an era. The end of living in a community where everyone had greeted him by name and most of his friends were guys he'd known since kindergarten; the end of lazy summer days waking up to the smell of fresh-mown grass and the crowing of roosters, with nothing more pressing on his mind than whether he'd be having pancakes or eggs for breakfast; of his dad letting him practice driving the tractor down the rows of trees, and of helping his mom peel the apples that would go into the pies she was always baking for various charitable causes, so many that their house had carried the faint scent of cinnamon and apples and golden sugary crusts year round.

In Bakersfield, in place of their roomy old farmhouse, he and his parents and two younger brothers had been shoehorned into a small, one-story house on a street lined with similar houses. The winters were so mild, it had been hard to work up much enthusiasm for Christmas, and the summers hot enough to turn the sidewalk in front of their house into a griddle. The produce on display at the neighborhood Safeway had borne little resemblance to the fresh-picked fruits and vegetables he was accustomed to. And in the school Gary and his brothers had attended, his classes had been made up largely of children of the migrant workers employed by farms and orchards like the one his father was foreman of, Mexicans mostly, among whom he'd been the odd man out.

He'd vowed to himself that as soon as he was old enough to earn his own living he'd return to the island. And so he had, going into the police academy right out of high school, then putting in two years with the California Highway Patrol, and biding his time until there was an opening here. Soon after that he'd met Denise and they'd gotten married and started a family. It wasn't life on the farm, no, but it was a good life all the same.

Or it had been up until now.

Lately, Gary had been feeling as if the carefully woven fabric of his life were starting to unravel. Or maybe it was just *him* that was coming apart. The very system that had crushed his parents was now crushing him: the incestuous union of commerce and government that he thought of as Them. The irony was that until fairly recently he'd been one of Them. Each morning when he'd put on his freshly ironed uniform he'd felt proud to be serving his community. Sure, he bent the rules from time to time, but always for a good cause. Like the other day, in not giving the Shepherd boy a ticket for speeding when he'd been going well over the limit, knowing that Marge Shepherd was in the final stages of terminal cancer and her husband Paul was working two jobs to make ends meet.

It had been just his luck that the only time he'd bent the rules for himself, he'd gotten caught. Now he was being blackmailed as a result. Whichever way you looked at it, he was in deep trouble. The kind that had him by the balls and was slowly squeezing him to death.

If his motivation had been pure greed, Gary might have felt he'd only gotten what he deserved. But he hadn't taken the money for himself. Ryan had so wanted to go on that summer trip to Paris with his French class, and Gary didn't have the heart to disappoint him. So when Buck Duggan, the owner of the Kittycat Club out on Route 6, had slipped him an envelope full of cash to turn a blind eye to the things that went on at the club that weren't strictly legal, he'd hesitated only briefly before accepting it, telling himself it was just the one time, that he wasn't the only cop on the take, that it wasn't wrong if it was for the right reasons. All the usual bullshit excuses, in other words. Then, a few months later, the transmission had gone out on Denise's ancient VW Rabbit, and Gary dipped into the well again—unaware that this time the entire transaction was being videotaped.

And now the mayor owned his ass.

In the beginning, Gary had naively thought that he'd eventually be let off the hook. But now he knew there was about as much likelihood of that as of peace in the Middle East any time soon. Instead, each time he did White's bidding, he only dug himself in deeper—not only in spying on his sister-in-law and keeping quiet about how his nephew was being railroaded, but in being forced to lie to his own wife. And that made him angry in a way that, with nowhere to go, was like acid leaking from a corroded battery. It had become a vicious cycle. Each time he lost his temper and lashed out at Denise or one of the kids, he'd hate himself even more, and that would only feed his anger.

Christ. If Denise only knew. If she'd had even the slightest inkling that he'd done his share of the dirty work in making sure nothing stood in the way of the Spring Hill development, by whispering in the right ears, by knowing which county commissioners to butter up and which ones needed a little extra persuasion in the form of a subtle threat. She might not divorce him—he didn't think she'd go that far—but life would never be the same. There were some things there was no coming back from and this was one.

Now all that was left for him to do was find a way to live with himself. If he could have talked to someone about it, it might have made it easier. But who was there to confide in? Not Denise. Not any of his fellow officers. And certainly not his parents, both retired now and living in Rancho Del Mar. It would have killed them to find out how far he'd strayed from the principles of honesty and integrity with which he had been raised. Principles that had been strictly enforced in their household. Like the time, when Gary was ten, that his dad had caught him pocketing a pack of chewing gum in Mr. Gowan's store. Gary had not only had to return the stolen merchandise, he'd had to spend the next two weekends helping out at the store. What would his father say if he were to find out about *this*?

Ironically, the only one who would have understood was Alice. The day she'd come to him, asking for his help, it had been all Gary could do to keep from spilling his guts. But she was the last person he could confide in. If she knew what he'd been up to . . .

Lost in thought, he was surprised to find himself turning into his driveway. He could have sworn it had been only minutes since he'd pulled out of his parking space behind the stationhouse. It was the story of his life these days. One of the guys would comment on something that had happened that day, something he'd apparently witnessed, and he wouldn't have the vaguest idea what they were talking about. Or Denise would remind him of something he'd promised to do that he had absolutely no memory of.

He suspected it was mainly because he hadn't been getting much shut-eye lately. These days, he'd wake in the middle of the night, his heart going a million miles a minute and his mind spinning like a wheel in a rat's cage, and there would be no getting back to sleep.

Well, he would just have to be a man and suck it up. Wasn't that what his father had taught him to do? And it had always served Gary well in the past: in school with the kids who'd bullied him, while in training at the police academy and later on, as a rookie cop with the veterans who'd made a sport of yanking his chain. This was *his* problem, one that he alone had created, not his wife's or kids'; there was no reason for them to be dragged into it.

He pulled up in front of the house and got out of the cruiser, his boots crunching on the gravel as he approached along the front path. It was the only sound other than the distant barking of a dog and the thump of hooves coming from the barn—Taylor's mare feeling her oats. Through the window, he could see Denise setting the table for supper. She had the phone pressed to her ear as she laid out forks and spoons, all the while talking animatedly to whoever was at the other end. The sight of her smiling and laughing like her old self caused his spirits to lift. Denise had been down in the dumps since excavation on Spring Hill had begun, and his own black moods hadn't helped. They'd been arguing a lot lately and he couldn't recall the last time they'd made love.

But the minute he walked in, it was as if a switch had been flipped. The light in her eyes dimmed and her expression became guarded, as she said a hurried good-bye to whoever she'd been gabbing with on the phone. Clearly she was still pissed off about the fight they'd had earlier in the day. A dumb argument over Taylor's wanting to wear a skirt to school that had showed off nearly every inch of her prepubescent legs, never mind she'd been wearing tights. Gary had refused to let their daughter out of the house until she'd changed into something more modest, and Denise had accused him of overreacting.

"Dinner's almost ready," she informed him now in the cool tone he'd become accustomed to of late. "Ryan's at football practice, so he'll be a little late."

"How's it going with that?" Gary realized with a guilty start that it had been a while since he'd gone to any of his son's games.

"The coach made him starting quarterback."

Gary broke into a grin, briefly buoyed by pride in his son's achievement. "That's great! We'll have to do something to celebrate. Maybe go out for root beer floats after supper."

His wife paused in the midst of setting out napkins to roll her eyes. "Root beer floats? He's six*teen*, Gary, not six. I think he's a little old for that."

"Same as Taylor, right?" The words were out before he realized he'd spoken.

Now Denise was squaring off, hands on hips, giving him that Look. "Are you going to start up with that again? I thought we'd settled it."

"Pardon me for thinking it's a big deal having our nine-year-old daughter walk around in public looking like a hooker," he said. *For Chrissakes, just let it go,* a voice pleaded in his head. But he couldn't stop. He was too revved up. "You know how many perverts there are out there just waiting to prey on little girls? The woods are full of them."

She gave a snort. "On Grays Island? Please."

"It happens. Remember the Gibbons kid?" he said. True, the guy hadn't exactly molested Joanie Gibbons, only flashed her, but even so . . .

"Gary, I know all about sexual predators," she said, in that excessively patient voice she used on kids who weren't paying attention in class. "But don't you think you're carrying this a little too far?"

He felt something shift in him, his anger turning ugly. Yet he seemed to have no more control over it than if it had been someone else's mouth the words were coming out of. "No, as a matter of fact I don't. What I think is that it's a good thing at least *one* of us cares what happens to our kids."

Denise's face went slack. She couldn't have looked more shocked than if he'd used his fist on her, something that in eighteen years of marriage he'd never even contemplated doing but which lately he'd been terrified might happen, if he didn't get a grip.

"I'm going to pretend I didn't hear that," she said.

Gary used a mental trick of his that had worked in the past, picturing himself pulling on the hand brake in one of those old-fashioned steam engines. But this time the brake was stuck and the runaway train continued to hurtle down the tracks. "Oh, so now I'm the bad guy? That's typical of you, Denise. You rag on the kids all day long. Do this, do that, don't forget to clean up your room," he mimicked in a whiney falsetto. "But I say one little thing to them and you're all over me like I'm some kind of dictator."

He could see that she was close to tears. "I never said—"

He smacked his fist down hard on the kitchen counter, causing her to jump. Some of the beer foamed up over the top of the can he was holding in his other hand, dripping onto the floor. "Don't contradict me! I'm still the man of this house, and what I say goes." Words that might have come straight out of his father's mouth and that shocked him as much as they surely had her.

"Gary, what on earth's gotten into you? Why are you acting this way?" Denise looked more worried than upset. Not just worried, scared. And for some reason that made him even angrier. Because he knew that *he* was responsible. He'd become a stranger to his own wife.

In a sudden fit of temper, he hurled the can at the wall. It landed with a hollow cracking sound, spewing a foamy geyser. For a long moment he just stood there staring at the beard of foam dripping down the light green wallpaper patterned with vines and miniature watering cans. Then, struck with horror at what he'd done, he sank to his knees with a groan, burying his face in his hands. He was scarcely aware of the puddle spreading across the floor and now soaking into the cuffs of his trousers; all he knew was that he was more scared than he'd ever been in his life: Another few inches and he'd have nailed Denise with that throw.

"Oh, Christ. I'm sorry. I didn't mean—" Dry sobs tore at his throat. Wrenched from him against his will, they were like the deep, hacking cough of a man choking to death. He was out of control and he knew it, but some part of him still insisted he could still get a grip if he just . . . if he just . . . rode this out a little while longer.

He felt Denise's hand on his shoulder and it was the last straw. He shook it off and lurched to his feet. He could barely see straight as he headed for the back door.

Through the roaring in his ears, he heard his wife cry out in alarm, "Gary! Where are you going?"

"I need some air." The words came out in a harsh rasp. "Don't wait up for me. I may be a while."

"What about supper?" She sounded panicked, and he knew it wasn't supper she was concerned about.

"You guys go ahead and eat without me."

He was letting himself out the door when he heard a small voice call after him, "Daddy?" He turned around to see Taylor poised there, in her leggings and Hello Kitty T-shirt, a worried look on her face.

The sight of her almost broke him, but he managed to pull it together just enough to say, "Everything's okay, sweetie. Daddy has to go out for a little while. I'll be back before you know it."

As soon as he stepped outside, Gary felt a strange calm descend on him. As he headed down the path, part of him marveled at the way his anger had magically dissipated, taking with it all of the tension that had been building over these past weeks. At the same time, the cop in him knew it wasn't unusual in situations like these. His years on the force he'd seen it all: bloody victims of accidents being carried off on stretchers, fretting aloud about some business meeting or lunch date they were going to miss; domestic disturbances where he'd arrive to find the wife casually making dinner or vacuuming the carpet, as though she hadn't just been beaten to a pulp; and once, memorably, a hit-and-run driver, who, when they'd finally tracked him down at his house, had calmly explained that he'd needed to get home and unload his groceries before the ice cream melted.

Psychiatrists had a name for it. It was called a Fugue state. But right now all Gary knew or cared about was that it was a blessed relief from the tension that had been building in him for weeks. As he settled in behind the wheel of his cruiser and turned the key in the ignition, he might have been dreaming; one of those dreams where everything seems so clear you almost imagine you're awake. And like in dreams, he hadn't the vaguest idea of what was going to happen next; he was in the driver's seat only in the purest physical sense.

Twilight was approaching and long shadows lay over the road. He drove slowly, mindful of the deer that had a habit of wandering onto the road this time of day. When he reached the outskirts of town, he found himself taking the turnoff for Killibrew Harbor. The road curved along a horseshoe-shaped stretch of waterfront that had a quaint little marina, where the people who lived in the fancy homes nearby kept their boats moored.

Owen White lived in one of those homes, a great sprawling monument to excess dubbed The Birches. Gary had been there only once, a cocktail party that had been held out on the lawn, some political fundraiser. On that occasion he'd spent almost the entire time jawing with Bud Hogan, who ran the chamber of commerce, but at one point, after he'd gone in to take a leak, he'd had a chance to nose around a bit inside the house. He recalled the general layout. He knew its vulnerable spots. In his mind he could see the wheelchair ramp that angled up along one side of the house to a sliding glass door opened by an electric eye. He could see the old, abandoned dog house, and the outdated security system that anyone with experience in law enforcement could have bypassed blindfolded.

As if this were a movie playing out toward its foregone conclusion, Gary saw himself turn onto the dirt road that serviced the private dock where at one time Owen's yacht had been moored. He switched off the cruiser's headlights, keeping a foot on the brake as he eased over the rutted surface in the near dark, watching for low-hanging branches. When he was within sight of the house, he shut off the engine and coasted the rest of the way.

He parked and got out, standing there for a moment, perfectly still with his head cocked, alert for sounds other than the hooting of owls and the hollow slap of waves against the dock. The Tudor-style mansion where Owen White lived with his wife of forty years sat on a low rise off to Gary's left, about a hundred yards or so from where he stood. As he set off in that direction, Gary's footsteps crunched pleasurably in the fallen leaves that littered the grass. He began to hum under his breath.

He was thinking about the time, when he was a kid, that he and his brothers had broken into an abandoned house down the block. They'd been hoping to discover something exciting, like a dead body or a dusty treasure, but all they'd found was a lot of broken glass and mice droppings. The excitement hadn't come until one of the neighbors, alerted by their flashlight beams, called the cops. Before they could make a getaway, they'd found themselves pinned against the outside of the house by a pair of headlights. Luckily, the officer, a big, burly Latino with a handlebar mustache who'd identified himself as Officer Ramirez, had gone easy on them. Even as he'd lectured them in a stern voice about trespassing, Gary could tell his heart wasn't in it. Afterward, he'd given them a ride home in his cruiser, agreeing not to say anything to their parents if they promised never to do anything like that again, a promise Gary had kept until now.

Now, thirty-some years later, here he was lurking about like a prowler. The part of his brain that was still functioning knew what he was doing was wrong, possibly even insane, and that if he were to get caught he'd lose more than his job. But in the Fugue state Gary was paying no attention to that small, faraway voice; it might have been a mosquito buzzing in his ear.

He hoisted himself over the low stone wall that bordered the grounds, then he was strolling across the lawn. Dusk had faded into twilight and a white ghost of a moon sailed on a thin raft of clouds overhead. In one of the ground floor rooms a window was lit, throwing a soft yellow light over the grass and shrubs below. Gary caught sight of a shadowy figure moving behind the curtains and he froze, reaching for the .38 on his hip. But no floodlights came on, no alarm sounded, and after a moment he relaxed.

Minutes later he was making his way up the wheelchair ramp, with its automated glass door that slid open easily at his approach. Islanders didn't bother much with locks; he probably could have strolled right in through the front door if he'd wanted. A snippet from the conversation he'd had with Bud Hogan, at the party, floated into his mind now. *Crime? Why, I tell them it's almost unheard of around here. You're more likely to get mugged at Disneyland.*

Gary smiled at the thought as he stepped through the doorway into a room cluttered with knickknacks, most with a nautical theme. In his old life, Owen, like his father before him, had been an avid sailor. In a display case filled with trophies won in various regattas, was a large framed photo of him at the helm of his yacht. There were a number of family photos as well. Gary paused before one of Owen as a young boy, standing with his father on the wide porch of their house, as pale and skinny as Lowell was manly and robust. Sailing must have been the only bond between them.

His thoughts turned to the bones that had been dug up on Spring Hill. The old man's bones. At first, Gary had seen it only as a bad omen. They'd mucked around where they didn't belong and look where it had led. Now he found himself wondering what it must have been like for that little boy in the photo, growing up without his father, not knowing what had become of him.

But those were only idle musings. And now the governor that had taken charge of Gary's faculties was giving him a gentle nudge, reminding him that he had business to attend to. Gary tiptoed into the hall. He could hear the muttering of voices in the next room, but as he drew nearer he realized it was only the TV. When he reached the open doorway, he eased his gun from its holster, and positioned himself with his back to the wall, twisting his head around to case the room for any sign of danger, as he'd been taught to do in training exercises at the academy but had had little call to employ since. A stance that, under the circumstances, struck him as more than a bit absurd, as his eye fell on the room's sole occupant: a balding man, grown soft around the middle, seated in the wing chair in front of the TV, his wheelchair parked a few feet away.

Owen tore his gaze from the evening news as Gary walked in, an expression of surprise dawning on his face. Sitting there in navy sweats, a tartan throw covering his lap, he looked old and defenseless. He must have been aware of the picture he made, for as soon as he'd recovered, he demanded, in his most authoritative voice, "Elkins! What are you doing here? Who let you in?"

"Good evening, sir." Gary didn't bother to illuminate the mayor as to how he'd gained entrance. He merely tucked away the useful bit of information he'd been given: That Owen was alone in the house. Or wouldn't he have assumed that someone else—the maid, or maybe his wife—had let Gary in? He went on in the same queer, flat tone, "I'm sorry to bother you at home, but I'm afraid it couldn't wait. There's something we need to discuss."

Gary saw Owen's gaze drop to the gun in his hand, and now he saw fear flare in those pale, shrewd eyes. Glimpsing his own reflection in the darkened window, he could certainly understand why: In his disheveled, beer-stained uniform, his eyes staring like a zombie's out of shadowed sockets, he was scarcely recognizable as the officer responsible for keeping the peace in this township. He almost had to admire Owen for the quickness with which he assessed the situation and attempted to defuse it.

"Well, in that case, don't just stand there," Owen said, his tone switching to that of a genial host. "Pour yourself a drink and sit down." He waved toward a burled-wood cabinet, atop which was arrayed a selection of liquor bottles and cut-glass decanters. "Please, help yourself."

Ignoring the offer, Gary calmly swiveled around and pulled the trigger on the gun, blasting a hole through the twenty-four-inch plasma TV. The sound and picture simultaneously died. "Beats remote control," he said, a maniacal giggle escaping his lips.

He heard a gasp and looked over to see that Owen had gone a pasty shade of gray. Owen licked his lips, asking in a noticeably less welcoming tone, "What . . . what is it you want?"

"What do I want? That's a very good question, sir." Gary appeared to ponder it a moment before replying with a touch more feeling, "For starters, you can stop fucking with me and my family."

The older man looked almost relieved. "Well, if that's all, consider it done. In fact, you should have come to me sooner. I'm not an unreasonable man, Gary, despite what you might think."

Gary laughed at the transparency of the lie. "I see. So all I had to do was ask nicely?"

"All right, you've made your point. Perhaps I *did* go a bit overboard," Owen hastened to concede. "But, where your sister-in-law's concerned, can you honestly blame me? She'd already tried to kill me once. How do I know she won't try something like that again?"

Gary wasn't buying it, though. "You know what I think? I think you were *hoping* she'd come back. I think you've been planning this for a long time. That's why you set me up, so you'd have someone to do your dirty work."

"Well, as far as that goes, you're free from any further obligation," Owen was quick to assure him. "In fact, you've served me and this community so well, I think a bonus is in order. Say, five thousand? Or, no, let's make it ten." Gary didn't react, which Owen must have misinterpreted to mean that he had some other compensation in mind, for he was quick to add, "Also, I can have the, ah, material in question delivered to you first thing in the morning." He tactfully refrained from referring openly to the incriminating videotape. "I'd give it to you now, but it's in a safe deposit box."

But it was much too late for that; Gary was too far gone. "You know, I think Alice had the right idea about you." He spoke in a queerly dispassionate voice. "The only problem was she didn't finish the job."

Calmly he raised the gun and pointed it at Owen.

Owen let out a little squeak. "Put . . . put that thing down. Please. Can't we discuss this like rational human beings? Really, Gary, there's no need for violence."

"What's there to discuss? As you can see, I'm the one holding all the cards." Gary advanced on Owen, a cheerless grin stretching across a face he wouldn't have recognized as his own just then. "How does it feel, now that the tables are turned? Not so great, huh? Well, here's the good news. You won't have to see the look on your wife's face when she finds out what an evil piece of shit you are. You'll be long gone by then. Just like your dad."

"Wait!" Owen shrilled, throwing up his hands. Hands that had once controlled Gary's every move and which now quivered pathetically. "Is it more money you want? I could call my bank, have them wire it into your account, if you don't trust me to write a check."

"Money? You think this is about *money*?" Gary gave a harsh laugh. He was feeling loosey-goosey, like when he'd had too much to drink, but he was perfectly lucid. He saw with sudden clarity that he'd been headed down this road all along, that all those weeks of agonizing had come from resisting what he'd known had to be done. Now that he'd given himself over to it, he felt strangely at peace. This wouldn't end well, but at least it would end. "You owe me more than that. I had to lie to my wife because of what you made me do. My own wife. She *cried* when those bulldozers moved in. She cried like a baby, and all I could do was stand there feeling sick to my stomach, knowing I'd had a part in it. And how do you think she'd feel if she knew that, on top of that, I was helping you drive her sister out of town?"

Owen lifted his chin in defiance. "That's putting it a bit too strongly, don't you think? All I asked you to do was keep an eye on Alice."

"That's not all, and you know it. You were out for revenge. An eye for an eye, right? Christ, don't you think she's suffered enough? And the kid, did you have to go after him, too?" Gary's voice rose.

"What happened to your nephew was entirely his own doing," the mayor protested.

"But you made sure they threw the book at him—an innocent kid."

"What makes you so sure he's innocent?"

"Because I *know* my nephew. He'd never do a thing like that, not in a million years."

"Given the right set of circumstances, people have been known to do a lot of things they might not have otherwise," Owen observed, giving him a pointed look that wasn't lost on Gary—wasn't he living proof of what a normally rational person was capable of when pushed too far? Now he saw that sweat had broken out on Owen's brow, making it gleam, and though the room was warm, he was shivering as if the temperature had plunged a good twenty degrees. As though from a distance, he heard the mayor go on, in a calm voice of persuasion that warbled only slightly, "Take you, for instance. I can see that I underestimated you, Gary. I failed to recognize your . . . your unique capabilities. In fact, Len's going to be retiring soon, and we could use someone with your leadership qualities to fill his shoes."

Gary shook his head in disgust. "Do you really think I'm stupid enough to think you'd make me chief of police? The minute I walked out the door you'd be on the phone with Len, and it wouldn't be to convince him to take an early retirement."

Owen slumped back in his chair, closing his eyes. He looked suddenly defeated. "All right, what do you want from me then? Anything, you name it. I'll do whatever you ask."

"What I want is this." Gary leveled the gun at his tormentor.

That was when he heard sirens in the distance. Apparently they weren't alone in the house after all—someone must have dialed 911. Gary felt a momentary pang of regret, thinking of his fellow officers, guys who'd have taken a bullet for him and vice versa, with whom he'd swapped shifts and joking insults through the years and unwound over beers after hours down at Frankie's, whose kids he'd watched grow up and whose wives called Denise when they needed advice. What would they think when they encountered *this?* But the concern quickly faded. He thought, *By the time they get here, it'll all be over.*

CHAPTER FIFTEEN

April 1943

They buried the body at nightfall. First loading it onto a handcart and hauling it up the hill as far as they could go, until the trail became impassable. There, at the bottom of a deep ravine, where hikers and picnickers were unlikely to find it, they dug a mean grave, William and Yoshi plying the earth with their shovels while Eleanor stood watch at the top of the ravine, her eyes carefully averted from the tarpaulin-wrapped bundle at her feet.

Later, when all this was over, she would allow herself to think about it, she would let the bloody, fragmented images whirling in her brain piece themselves into a gruesome whole. Right now, though, she needed to remain steady while they completed this unspeakable thing. Because no one must ever know. Lucy, most of all. If anything was keeping Eleanor sane, it was the knowledge that her daughter wouldn't be tainted by any of this. Earlier, Eleanor had phoned Sarah Donovan, the mother of Lucy's best friend, and asked if she could pick up the girls from school and keep

Lucy overnight, explaining that something had come up rather suddenly, some urgent business she had to attend to.

Bloody business, Eleanor thought, biting down on her lower lip to contain the hysterical giggle forcing its way up her throat. Far off in the distance she could hear the dogs baying in their kennel, almost as they sensed something or had caught the scent of blood. Dogs were smart that way. Maybe that was why she preferred their company to that of most humans. That, and because whatever your failings their devotion was unwavering. The way her husband's had been. And now Joe was dead. As dead as the *thing* (she couldn't bring herself to think of it as Lucy's father, the man she'd once believed herself to be in love with) lying at her feet.

The blood was what had brought it all home, as she'd rolled up the rug and scrubbed the floorboards on her hands and knees, wringing her cloth into a bucket of water gone red with the terrible fruits of her labor: Her husband hadn't merely ascended to some heavenly plane, he'd been shot to bits, or drowned, or, worse, left to a slow and agonizing death.

Now, staring down at the hole taking shape below, she began to tremble uncontrollably. She felt dizzy and realized she hadn't eaten since breakfast. The mere thought of food brought on a wave of nausea. Sick and shivering, she focused on the figures at the bottom of the ravine, bobbing in and out of the cone of light cast by the flashlight she was aiming their way, one tall and one slight, but at the moment more alike than they were different as they bent to their grim task.

The last bloody streaks of light had faded from the horizon by the time they were done, the ravine as deeply obscured from view as the town, on the other side of the sound, where the streetlights were dimmed and every shade pulled. Earlier in the evening, when Eleanor had gotten the blackout alert, three long and three short telephone rings, it had seemed like a signal from on high, some divine presence taking pity on her, for it meant that few would be out and about and the chances of their being discovered minimal. But now, as she helped the men drag the body down the steep, brushy slope, she felt only numb and exhausted.

She stumbled over a tree root and would have gone sliding the rest of the way down the slope if William hadn't caught hold of her just then. He held her tightly for a moment, so tightly she could feel the pounding of his heart against her ribcage. "Just a little more to go," he whispered. "Can you manage?" She knew that it wasn't just the distance to the bottom of the ravine he was referring to but the long and treacherous road she'd have to negotiate in order to get back to some semblance of normalcy.

She nodded, whispering back, "Yes, I think so."

She shone the flashlight on the men as they tipped the tarpaulin-wrapped bundle into the hole they'd dug. For the rest of her days Eleanor would carry that image in her head: of that crude grave hacked out of the earth, dirt-clotted roots protruding from its rough-hewn walls like skeletal fingers reaching out to reclaim their own, and Lowell's body rolling into the pit with a dull thud, amid a scattering of loose dirt and pebbles.

The men filled in the hole, tamping the dirt down as best they could, the night alive with the scrape of shovels, the ring of metal against stone. When the job was done they spread leaves over the grave to erase any evidence of their having been there.

The three were silent as they trudged back down the hill. Near dead with exhaustion, Eleanor clung to Yoshi's arm to keep from stumbling, as William led the way with the flashlight. She felt bad about Yoshi's being dragged into this and she would have spared him if he hadn't insisted on coming along. She was grateful to him at the same time, this boy whom some might have called an enemy and who'd proved his worth in ways that went beyond mere loyalty.

It was almost midnight by the time they reached the house. Eleanor could hardly see straight, she was so tired, but there was one thing left to do: They had to dispose of Lowell's car. William drove the Cadillac to the ferry landing while Eleanor followed in her car. Luckily, they encountered no other traffic, due to the blackout. In any event, anyone they should happen to have passed would have been hard-pressed to make them out, in the all-encompassing darkness, with their headlights dimmed.

At the ferry landing, William parked the Cadillac and got out. She watched as he walked to the end of the dock, limping more than usual, and hurled Lowell's key ring far out into the water—a glimmer of silver that was there and gone in an instant, like a falling star. Poor William, she thought. His only crime had been in coming to her rescue. Now he would spend the rest of his life looking over his shoulder. And what if he *were* to get caught? It wouldn't be just William who'd suffer; his wife and son would pay the price as well. He'd lose even his rightful place in history, remembered not for the brilliance of his work but as a murderer.

She would be held accountable, too, an accessory to the crime. And who would believe that Lowell had tried to rape her, with no one to corroborate it except William and the man who now lay buried in an unmarked grave up on Spring Hill?

She grew cold at the thought. This was all her fault. She'd been naïve to let Lowell come to the house, thinking that no real harm would befall her. Yet despite the horror of it all, she wasn't sorry he was dead.

William took the wheel on the ride home, Eleanor almost immediately falling into a deep sleep. She didn't wake until they reached the house, and even then William had trouble rousing her. He kept an arm around her waist as they made their way across the suddenly endless stretch of yard. As they were passing the barn, she saw that the window was dark—Yoshi must have gone to bed. She hoped she would be able to get some sleep as well. She would need to rest up for the sleepless nights to come.

As she stood on the doorstep fumbling with her keys, she wondered how she would get through this one—what was sure to be the longest night of her life. William must have read her mind, for he asked gently, "Would you like me to stay the night?"

Her eyes sought out his in the darkness. "What about your wife?"

"I'll tell her my car broke down." From the grim, exhausted look he wore, it was obvious he was past worrying about such a small lie, with the larger one of tonight eclipsing all else. "She won't suspect anything. She probably doesn't even know I'm gone."

Even so, Eleanor hesitated. What wife, however self-absorbed, would believe such an excuse? Martha would wonder why he hadn't telephoned earlier, and what kind of car trouble it was that would keep him away all night. No, she thought, it was far too risky. And he'd risked so much already. Still, she lingered on the doorstep. "I couldn't ask that of you," she said. "Not after . . . after what . . ." She swallowed hard, unable to complete the sentence.

He nodded gravely. He seemed to have aged a dozen years over the course of the day, his face all planes and shadows, his eyes glinting amid hollowed sockets. "Let's talk about it inside," he said, taking her by the arm and gently propelling her through the doorway.

This time Eleanor didn't protest. She allowed herself to be led down the hall and into the kitchen, docile as a sleepy child, her step faltering only once as they passed the living room that would be forever be stained with the blood of her former lover, if only in her mind.

"I think we both need a drink," he said, retrieving the bottle of whiskey from the cupboard by the stove and pouring them each a glass.

"What I need even more is a shower," she told him. "I feel as if I haven't bathed in a week. Do you mind?"

"Take your time. I'm not going anywhere," he said.

As she was undressing in the bedroom, she could hear him dialing the phone out in the hall, followed by the low murmur of his voice. She stood alert, listening for any change in its tenor that would signal an angry wife at the other end, but there was none, and after a moment she relaxed.

In the bathroom, as she stood in the old-fashioned claw-foot tub that Joe had fitted with a shower nozzle, hot water coursing over her skin, Eleanor marveled at the simple pleasure of it and the ease with which she found herself slipping back into routine, even after what she'd been through today. She imagined it must have been like that for Joe, too, that amid the horrors of war there had been days aboard ship with nothing to do but swap stories and play cards, when the only thing on his mind hadn't been getting home in one piece but how he was going to play the hand he'd been dealt. Was it really possible to go on as though nothing had happened? She would have to. For Lucy's sake. For her own, as well.

After she'd toweled herself dry, she dressed in a worn pair of Levi's and an old flannel shirt that had belonged to Joe. By the time she rejoined William, he'd drunk at least a quarter of what had been left in the bottle, though he seemed none the worse for it. If anything, it was having a salutory effect. Some of the color had returned to his face and he appeared more relaxed. He smiled faintly as he poured her a drink and pushed it across the table to her.

"Here. Drink up. It'll help you sleep."

"I don't think anything could help me sleep," she told him, reaching for the glass nonetheless.

They sat in silence, Eleanor sipping her whiskey. The house's usual nighttime noises wrapped themselves around her, the creak of it settling on its foundation and grumbling of the furnace in the cellar, the hum of the icebox and ticking of the clock over the stove. It hardly seemed possible that an hour earlier they'd been digging a man's grave.

"What did your wife have to say?" Eleanor ventured after a bit.

"I think she was more upset at being woken up than anything else. Which doesn't mean I won't catch hell later on." He spoke lightly, but she could see that he was troubled.

"I don't want this to come between you and Martha," she said firmly.

"I'm afraid it's too late for that." He gave her a long look, and in his naked, bloodshot gaze, stripped of all pretense by the day's ordeal, she saw the true depths of his feelings for her.

And, yes, Eleanor was glad, may her soul be eternally damned to hell for it. She was glad, and at the same time frightened, not wanting to cause any more damage than that which had already been done. "You can still make it right," she said. "You don't know until you try."

"I'm done with trying."

"You say that now, but you'll feel differently in the morning," she insisted. "You can't be thinking clearly right now."

"My head's as clear as it will ever be," he said, in that strange, hollow voice that seemed to rise from the bottom of a well, those burning eyes of his fixed on her with unwavering intensity.

Eleanor turned her gaze to the darkened window, a shudder going through her as the image of Lowell's leering face loomed before her unseeing eyes. She emptied her glass, in a single medicinal gulp that burned its way down her throat.

"Unless you have another bottle stashed away, I'm afraid that's the last of it," William said.

"Just as well. Any more and I wouldn't be fit for polite company." The idea of her being fit for any company whatsoever, polite or otherwise, struck her as funny, and she began to giggle. Before long she was doubled over with hysterical laughter, gasping for breath.

William rose and took her by the hand, pulling her to her feet. "Come, let's get you to bed."

With a last hiccough, all the hilarity went out of Eleanor, leaving her limp and drained. William guided her down the hall and into the bedroom, Eleanor teetering like a frail old woman. She fell onto the bed, not even bothering to undress. He drew a blanket over her, dropping a chaste kiss onto her forehead, and he was about to tiptoe out of the room when she caught hold of his wrist. In the light from the hallway that fell across his lean, hawk-nosed face she could see the worry in his eyes. It was the look of a man who knows his life is about to change, not for the better.

"Don't go," she whispered.

He shook his head, saying gently. "You get some rest. I'll sleep on the sofa."

"No. Please. I don't want to be alone."

Wordlessly, he nodded, then sat down on the end of the bed to pry off his shoes. As he crawled under the blanket and stretched out beside her, the comfort of his presence warmed her like the shot of whiskey, the bulwark of his body nestled against hers, his arm curled protectively about her shoulders. He smelled of tonight's clandestine activities—sweat and dirt and piney resin from the branches with which they'd covered Lowell's grave—but for some reason it only made her love him more.

She snuggled up against him, saying in a groggy voice, "It's strange, isn't it? The two of us in bed together. All the times I've thought about it, I never imagined it would be like this."

"Me either," he murmured thickly in her ear.

"So you've thought about it, too?"

"More than you want to know."

"Is there something wrong with us, do you think, talking like this after we've just buried a man?"

"I think we threw out the rule book a long time ago," he said, his fingers brushing her cheek in the darkness. His voice was scratchy with exhaustion and his breath smelled of whiskey. "Now why don't we get some sleep. We can talk in the morning."

She started to say something else, but William was already fast asleep, snoring lightly. Moments later Eleanor drifted off, too.

She slept straight through until morning, waking to the sound of the dogs barking outside. Even then, she kept her eyes shut, suspended somewhere between the blissful ignorance of sleep and the dark thing hovering at the edge of consciousness. Then, all at once, the memory of yesterday's events came rushing up behind her closed eyelids. For a moment, in her half-awake state, she felt sure that she must have dreamed it, then she opened her eyes and saw William lying wide awake beside her, in his dirty, rumpled clothing, sporting a day's growth of beard, and she knew that it was all too real.

"It really happened, didn't it? For a moment I thought I'd dreamed it," she said. He gave a somber nod, and she fell back with a low moan. What had seemed possible in last night's befogged state struck her now, in the light of day, as utterly insane. They would never get away with this. What had made her think they could? "So what do we do now?"

"The usual things. Get up, get dressed, have breakfast. Unless you have a better idea."

"I don't suppose there's any point in turning ourselves in."

"None at all."

"They might still track us down, you know."

"If they do, I'm the one they'll arrest. You did nothing wrong."

"Who would believe that?"

William brought a hand to her face, running his thumb over her cheek. "Don't worry, they won't find out. The last thing Lowell would have done was leave word with anyone about where he was going, so no one even knows he was here," he reasoned, with more conviction than she guessed he felt.

Eleanor, desperate to grasp at any straw, told herself he was right. She had to believe that. It was the only thing to hold on to at the moment.

"Even if we don't go to jail, we could go to hell," she said. "Some would call it a sin, what we did." Her father's image rose in her mind, his pious face and his hands folded about his bible.

William held her gaze, her chin still cupped in his hand. "When I pulled that trigger, the only thing I was thinking was that if I didn't aim straight he'd hurt you. I can live with what I did, Eleanor, but *that* would have been unbearable."

She saw the love blazing from his eyes, and it was almost more than she could absorb in her current, fragile state. Her throat seized up on her, and when she spoke it was in a choked whisper. "Oh, William. When I think what might have happened if you hadn't come along . . . "

She buried her face against his chest. He kissed her tenderly on the top of the head, then when she raised herself up, not so tenderly on the mouth. The shock of his lips against hers went through her like a bolt of lightning, igniting something in her, something beyond all thought and reason and more powerful than any whispered endearments.

Later on, Eleanor would have no recollection of either of them getting undressed. Their coming together happened so naturally, it was as if they'd been born again in each other's arms. With the morning sunlight warming their bare limbs, they made love with an urgency that was like a living thing apart from them. She was consumed by it. Biting and bucking, crying out with an abandon that would have shocked her husband.

William became a different person as well. Gone was the quiet, considerate soul she'd grown to love, in his place a man barely able to contain himself. A beautiful wild creature who saw nothing wrong with what they were doing, who in fact celebrated it. They clung to each other as if otherwise they might be swept away, their sweat mingling, his hands covering every inch of her that wasn't already covered by his body, his fingernails, still embedded with dirt, digging into her flesh, making her arch with pleasure.

Even when it was over and Eleanor utterly spent, she was left wanting more. And after a few minutes, apparently, so was William. The next time, they took it slow, exploring every inch of each other's bodies, reveling in the minutest of touches, the least little flicker of a tongue, each brush of lips over bare skin. Soon enough it would be time for William to go, but for now they were in their own world, lost to the one beyond these walls.

Finally he could no longer put off the inevitable. He rose from the bed and Eleanor reluctantly followed suit. She fixed breakfast while he took a shower and put on the clothes she'd given him to wear, an old shirt and a pair of trousers that had belonged to Joe. The shirt was so big it flapped on him, as if on a clothesline, and the cuffs of the trousers barely covered his ankles, but William didn't seem to mind; they were clean at least.

They ate their breakfast in silence, but it wasn't a heavy silence like before, more the intimate one of lovers for whom there was no need for conversation. And what was there to say? Words wouldn't have changed a thing. Yesterday she'd watched a man die and this morning she'd made love to a married man. Not the sort of things that made for a happy ending.

William attempted to put a good face on it nonetheless. "It doesn't always have to be this way," he whispered in her ear, as he was leaving. They were standing in the doorway, cheek to cheek with their arms wrapped around each other, William taking slow, deep breaths, as if he couldn't get enough of her scent.

Eleanor drew back, her eyes filled with tears. "Don't. You'll only make it worse."

"I could ask for a divorce," he went on in that same reckless tone. "Martha doesn't need me. She hasn't for a long time."

"What about your son? He still needs you."

"Danny knows I love him. Nothing will ever change that." William's voice grew hesitant nonetheless.

"Yes, and that means you'd cut your arm off before you'd see him get hurt," she said, thinking of the lengths she would have gone to protect Lucy. "Now go home to your wife and son." She gave him a none too gentle shove before she could weaken and give in.

"Will I see you again?" he asked, his eyes searching her face.

Eleanor longed to tell him what he wanted to hear, but they would only be fooling themselves, she knew. "I'm not sure that would be a good idea," she told him.

"Maybe not, but who gives a damn?"

"I do, and so will you, once you've had a chance to think it through."

He shook his head, pulling her to him, roughly almost. He was holding her so tightly she could scarcely breathe. "You really believe that? That I'll think better of it?" He gave a hoarse laugh. "God, I almost wish you were right. Life would be a damn sight easier. But don't you see? It's too late for that. I love you, Eleanor. I love you so much I can't bear the idea of us being apart. I want us to be together *always*."

Eleanor wanted nothing more at that moment than to remain in his arms forever, damn the consequences, but she drew back to give him a sorrowful look. "We don't have that luxury. It's not just your family I'm thinking of. If we don't handle this just right . . ." She didn't have to remind him that they weren't out of the woods yet as far as Lowell was concerned. If a search party was launched and his body discovered, people might start to put two and two together. Any suspicious behavior on their part would be noted.

They didn't say good-bye when he left. That would have been too final. For while Eleanor despaired of ever seeing him again, a part of her clung to the fragile strand of hope he'd held out to her. If he let enough time pass before asking his wife for a divorce, so no one grew suspicious, maybe, just maybe it could work. A little voice, scratching in the back of her brain like a stuck phonograph needle, insisted, *Stranger things have happened.*

He arrived back at the house to find no one home. William, braced for an angry tirade from his wife, felt the speech he'd been rehearsing on the way over die on his lips as he walked from one deserted room to the next, calling out her name. Danny and the dog were nowhere in sight, either. There was no reason to think it odd—Martha could have dashed off on an errand, leaving Danny with their neighbor—but with the house's silence coming at him like a reproach, William knew in his heart that something was wrong.

Finally, he thought to check the garage, where he found Martha's jaunty little red Austin Healy right where it always was. Baffled, he stepped outside, frowning. It occurred to him then that Martha might have decided to go for a walk—unlikely in this weather, for it had started to rain, but where else could she have gone? He was crossing the yard on his way to the path that led down to the cove when he noticed that the door to his studio was ajar. He halted in his tracks, a dull alarm sounding at the back of his brain. He was almost certain he'd locked up when he'd gone out yesterday. But so much had happened since then, he hardly felt like the same the man who'd last walked out that door less than twenty-four hours before. His head spun with images from yesterday and his body was like something loosely strung together with wire. In the midst of it all, like a quiet eye at the center of a hurricane, was the thought of Eleanor.

He pushed open the door. At first all he saw were the canvases stacked against the wall and the one on the easel, over which a cloth was draped. Then he spotted her, huddled in the old mustard armchair that she'd long ago banished from the house, her feet tucked under her and her arms wrapped around her knees, like a child left abandoned and shivering on some stranger's doorstep. In the soft gray light that filtered through the rain-streaked skylight he could see that Martha had been crying.

His first thought was of his son. "Martha. What is it? Did something happen to Danny?" he asked, rushing over to her.

"He's fine. Though I'm surprised you care enough to ask." Her voice was cold as the rain trickling down outside. "In fact, I don't know why you even bothered to come home."

"So this is about last night." He felt a heaviness settle over him, mixed with an odd sense of relief at knowing there was no further need for pretense.

"I know what you've been up to." Martha's face twisted into something ugly. "Oh, I had my suspicions all along, but I kept telling myself that was for wives who'd let themselves go, who'd turned their husbands away in bed. Then after you phoned last night I went through your things. I found what I was looking for, all right. It's *her*, isn't it?" She jabbed a finger toward the canvas on the easel, and he saw now that the cloth that covered it was askew.

He didn't bother to deny it. "I'm sorry you had to find out that way," he said quietly.

"So you were planning to break it to me eventually? Yes, I suppose that would be the honorable thing to do," she said, looking at him with contempt. "You probably even fancy yourself in love with her, and you think *that* makes it all okay. The great artist and his muse." She swept an arm out in a scornful gesture. "Well, you won't be making a public laughingstock of me, at least. I made sure of that."

He was gripped with a sudden sense of foreboding. He knelt before his wife, seizing her by the shoulders. It was all he could do not to shake her.

"Martha, what have you done?"

"What have *I* done?" she threw back at him, with a shrill little laugh. "I trusted you, that's what. I should have known better."

He knew there was no getting through to her right now, that she was in no mood for an explanation, but he made a clumsy attempt nonetheless. "I didn't go looking for it," he said. "It just . . . happened." He wanted to tell her about Yoshi, for her to know that his motives had been pure in the beginning, but that would only have made it worse.

"So now what? I suppose you want a divorce." She tossed her head, and he saw the challenge in her red-rimmed eyes. She wanted him to beg her to forgive him, to promise never to see Eleanor again.

But he couldn't do that, and the expression on his face must have told her everything she needed to know, for she began to weep.

"Martha . . ." He reached to console her, but she swatted his hand away.

"You're a coward, William. Not fit for duty, not even fit to be a husband. You couldn't even fight to save your own marriage."

What would she say, he wondered, were she to learn that last night he'd killed a man in cold blood? He smiled grimly to himself at the thought. Poor Martha. She really had no idea.

"I didn't see that there was anything left to fight for," he said wearily.

It was an honest response, not meant to be hurtful. In fact, it had surprised him to learn that Martha herself had thought there was something worth fighting for. Nevertheless, he could see at once that it was the wrong thing to have said.

His wife erupted off the chair, quivering like a drawn bow. "Are you insinuating that I drove you to it? How dare you! This is all *your* fault, William."

He sighed. "Honestly? I don't know anymore who's to blame." And right now he didn't care. His head throbbed and he wanted nothing more than to stretch out on the floor and close his eyes.

"Well, *I* know. And I'm not going to stick around and have you make an even bigger fool of me." She snatched up the sweater that she'd left neatly folded over an arm of the chair—even in despair, Martha didn't go about things sloppily—and tossed it over her shoulders. "I've already called Mother and Dad. They're perfectly happy to have us stay with them as long as we want."

We? William was at once on full alert. "You're not taking Danny with you." He was in no position to object, but all at once he knew with a sickening certainty that if he didn't put his foot down now, he could lose his son for good.

"Just try and stop me. I'll have my lawyer slap you with papers so fast your head will be swimming." Her eyes glittered with malice. William didn't think it was an idle threat. If Martha had gone off to battle in his place, the war would have ended by now, he thought.

"Where is he? Where's my son?" he asked, in a hard voice tinged with desperation.

Ignoring his plea, she said coldly, "I'll tell him you said good-bye." She stepped past him on her way out the door, pausing on the threshold to fire one last volley. "I'll spare him the sordid details, but make no mistake—Danny's going to know what kind of man his father is."

William stood there for a long moment after she'd gone, staring into space, listening to the rapid tap-tapping of Martha's heels as she hurried up the path to the house. None of it seemed real. Yesterday he'd shot and killed a man, and this morning he and Eleanor had made love. Now this. If a Japanese Zero were to have dropped a bomb on the island just then, it wouldn't have surprised him in the least.

Then he recalled his wife's words and raced over to the easel, snatching off the cloth. With a sinking heart, he saw how Martha had exacted her revenge.

The portrait of Eleanor was unrecognizable. It had been slashed with a sharp object until it was little more than shreds of canvas clinging to its frame. A low moan escaped him, and he slowly sank to his knees, feeling as if all the breath had been knocked out of him. She might as well have plunged a knife into his heart.

CHAPTER SIXTEEN

"You ain't be fooling me, girl. I know that look." Calpernia was giving her the eye, which meant not only was she on to you but you'd better not even *think* about trying to pull one over on her.

"I don't know what you're talking about," Alice said. She attempted to sidle past Calpernia on her way to check on the dough she'd left in the refrigerator to rise, but her friend shifted her bulk to block her path.

"The hell you don't." Calpernia was dressed in gray sweatpants and a warm-up jacket that looked as if it had come off an NFL linebacker, her braids gathered into a ponytail that bristled like a dried-flower arrangement. Alice had arrived home from Colin's to find her here. Calpernia preferred the restaurant, even when it was closed, to her studio apartment over Mrs. Meehan's garage, which she'd said reminded her of being in solitary. Suddenly, her fierce expression gave way to a grin. "Damn, girl, you done got yourself laid."

Alice threw her hands up in surrender. It would have done no good to deny it; Calpernia would have gotten it out of her one way or another. "Yes! All right! I slept with him."

"All I got to say is, it's about time." Calpernia just stood there, grinning.

But Alice was thinking about the look Colin had worn as they were saying good-bye. He'd been standing right in front of her, but he'd been somewhere else in his mind: If she was long overdue for this, then for Colin it might have come too soon. "Let's not make too big a deal out of it, okay?" she said. "It was fun, we both enjoyed it, end of story."

Calpernia watched, her arms folded over her chest, as Alice busied herself with the dough, dumping it onto the counter and carefully shaping it into loaves. Her friend had been cutting up onions when she'd walked in and now the sharp scent was making her eyes water.

"Want to know what *I* think?" Calpernia asked.

"Not particularly, but I'm sure you'll tell me anyway," Alice replied.

She glanced up to find Calpernia shaking her head, as if the diagnosis were grim. "Girl, you got it bad."

Alice, on edge, cried in exasperation, "What do you know? When was the last time *you* got laid?"

Calpernia tipped her head back in a haughty look, her eyes narrowing. "You think you the only one got it going on?"

Alice broke into a grin. "Why, Calpernia King. You've been holding out on me."

"A girl can't have some privacy 'round here?" Calpernia grumbled, pretending to be annoyed. "Bad enough you got me working myself half to death for shit pay make Mickey

D's look good. I get me some on the side, ain't nobody's damn business but my own."

Alice, used to these sorts of rumblings, asked in amusement, "Who's the lucky guy?"

Calpernia deliberated a moment, then she heaved a mock sigh. "Know that big dude come 'round couple times a week? Always order the same thing, ribs and slaw, baked potato on the side?"

Alice could hardly contain her surprise. "Ralph Dwyer?" Ralph owned his own tire shop, Dwyer's Tires. He was a nice enough guy, polite, even a little shy. But, leaving aside the fact that he was white, he was old enough to be Calpernia's father. It took her a moment to recover before she could remark, "Well, they say there's a lid for every pot. If it fits, I guess that's all that counts."

Calpernia gave a snort of contempt. "This ain't no Tupperware party. I ain't said I was planning on marrying the dude. But if the man's fool enough to want what I got to offer, which Lord knows ain't much, I ain't turning it down neither." She gave Alice a hard look no doubt meant to convey that Alice would be equally foolish to reject what Colin had to offer. But what exactly was Colin offering her? Friendship, with maybe a little something on the side. Hadn't he made it perfectly clear he wasn't interested in a relationship? No, it had been a mistake to sleep with him, she thought. One she didn't regret, but a mistake all the same.

And it wasn't just Colin. The timing couldn't be worse for her, either. She was just getting back on her feet and had enough to do rebuilding existing relationships, like the one with her son. Also, she would be making herself vulnerable in a way that was frightening to her, more frightening than any of the stumbling blocks she'd met with so far. If that was love, Alice wanted no part of it.

She was contemplating that when the phone rang. It was Denise.

After a minute or so of chitchat, her sister got to the real reason she'd phoned. "You haven't seen Gary, by any chance?" She affected a casual tone, but Alice could tell she was worried.

"Not since yesterday," she said. "Why? Is everything okay?" She kept her voice light so as not to add to Denise's worry.

Her sister was quick to reply, "Sure, fine. We just had a little tiff, is all. He took off about an hour ago, said he needed to cool off. I thought he might have stopped by your place."

"Do you need me to come over?" From the tension in her sister's voice, it was obvious it had been more than a little tiff.

"No, don't be silly. Everything's fine," Denise was quick to assure her. "I'm sure he'll be back any minute."

"Have you tried the station?"

"He got off duty a couple of hours ago."

"Still, it might be worth a call. Just to put your mind at ease." Alice knew what her sister was thinking: that he might have gotten into an accident. At least this way she'd be able to rule it out. If any 911 calls had come in over the past hour or so, the dispatcher would know about it.

Denise blew out a breath at the other end. "Yeah, you're right. If he's not there, I can always have the guys keep an eye out for him, if nothing else."

"Call me back as soon as you know anything," Alice told her.

"Will do."

Minutes later the phone rang again. This time all hell broke loose.

Colin heard a noise and glanced over to see the dog settling onto his haunches in the doorway to the living room. Briefly, Colin wondered how he'd gotten into the house. Until now, Shep had refused to leave his post on the porch whenever he wasn't keeping Colin company down at the cove. But in Colin's present state of my mind, the thought barely registered before fading from consciousness.

He stared at the bottle of cognac in his hand. Remy-Martin. The seal on the cap was still intact and a fine layer of dust had gathered around the neck. *A shame to let it go to waste*, Colin thought. He twisted the cap, his senses coming alive with the crackle of the seal as it gave way, and poured a generous shot into the glass he'd found on one of the cabinet's upper shelves. At the familiar sharp scent he felt a pleasurable rush, as if the alcohol were already insinuating its way into his bloodstream. He was lifting the glass to his lips when he happened to glance once more at the dog.

Shep seemed to eye him with reproach.

"What are you looking at?" Colin asked. "You've never seen anyone tie one on before?"

Shep cocked his head and let out a low whine. Colin felt a prickle along the back of his neck, and in that instant he could almost imagine that it was his grandfather's spirit inhabiting the dog. And what would William make of the current situation? No doubt that his grandson was as much a disappointment to him as his son.

Colin's gaze was drawn to the portrait over the mantel. "You, too?" he asked of the woman looking down at him, with her Mona Lisa smile and melancholy eyes. In the soft lamplight, she appeared almost lifelike, and he had the eerie feeling that if he had brought his fingertips to that glowingly rendered flesh, it would be warm to the touch.

Ghosts. The world was full of them, and he'd best make peace with that fact or remain doomed to a lifetime of stumbling each time he tried to get past his. *Here's to you, my sweet,* he toasted silently, lifting his glass. His wife's spirit he felt most strongly of all. Yes, Nadine would have understood about Alice. But she'd known him well enough to also know that it could never be. What could he offer Alice other than his legal services, when he scarcely knew what to do with himself?

The rim of the glass pressed to his lips was the sweetest of kisses, the sharp, fruity scent filling his nostrils more tantalizing than any perfume. He closed his eyes in a kind of swoon and was tipping the glass back when he abruptly froze. In a sudden flash, he saw what he was doing as clearly as if he'd been standing outside of himself, a neutral observer to the scene. *You can rationalize it all you want,* spoke the other, clear-eyed Colin, *but what it really boils down to is that you're just looking for an excuse to drink.*

With a trembling hand, Colin lowered the glass. Quickly, before he could think better of it, he dashed into the kitchen and poured its contents down the sink. Afterward, he stood bent over, gripping the edge of the counter, as weak as all the times he'd been sick to his stomach after too much to drink. He was filled with despair, not just because he'd come close to throwing away nearly nine months of sobriety, but because even now a part of him cursed the waste.

Disgusted with himself, he turned away and shuffled back into the living room, where he sank heavily onto the sofa. He knew he ought to phone his sponsor, but he couldn't seem to summon the energy even to pick up the phone. He was wondering how he was going to white-knuckle it until the next AA meeting when a low, doggy whine momentarily distracted him from his thoughts. He turned his head to find Shep standing before him, regarding him with worried eyes. He nudged Colin with his nose and, when that brought no response, he pawed at his arm. Colin absently stroked him between the ears, saying in a weary voice, "Yeah, I know. I miss my wife, too. But it's just you and me now. Misery loves company, right?"

The dog settled onto the carpet with a grunt of what might have been affirmation. Colin's thoughts turned to Alice and how much fun they'd had today, particularly in bed—that is, until his dark ruminations had spoiled the mood.

The phone rang, startling him. For a moment he thought it might be Alice and, as he went to answer it, his spirits picked up.

But it wasn't Alice; it was her son. Jeremy sounded in a panic. "I didn't know who else to call. My mom's not home and I couldn't get a hold of my dad. It's bad, Mister McGinty. Real bad . . . "

The boy's panic had a strangely calming effect on Colin. He found himself saying in a voice of cool-headed authority, "Slow down. Now tell me what this is all about?"

The words tumbled out in a breathless rush. "My uncle Gary . . . he . . . he . . . it's like he's gone crazy or something. He's holed up in there with his gun and he says he'll shoot if anyone tries to come near." He let out a groan. "Oh, God.

It's like it's happening all over again. Like when my mom—" He broke off with a choked sound.

"All right, take a deep breath and start at the beginning." Colin spoke in a calm, reassuring voice.

Colin listened to Jeremy's garbled secondhand version of the story, which he'd apparently gotten from his cousin Ryan. Something about his uncle's going over to the mayor's house and the two of them getting into an argument—that was the theory, at least, no one knew for sure—during which Gary had pulled his gun on the mayor, who at the moment was being held hostage. What would have been routine stuff during Colin's tenure in the Manhattan D.A.'s office, one more act of desperation in a city full of people living on the razor's edge, but which struck him now, in the context of this sleepy backwater, as almost too bizarre to be believed.

"Where's your mom?" he asked.

"She and Aunt Denise are on their way over there now."

"If I come pick you up, can you take me there?"

"Sure. I know the way. Just please hurry."

The first thing Alice noticed, as they turned onto the private road to the mayor's estate, was the patrol car blocking further access, its radio squawking and the blue glare from its bubble light careening off the surrounding trees and shrubbery. An earnest-looking young officer climbed out. From the manner in which he approached, one hand held up like a stop sign and the other on his holster, it looked as if he'd seen one too many cop shows.

Denise rolled down her window and stuck her head out. "It's okay, Tony. It's just me."

His hands dropped to his sides and his face reddened. "Missus Elkins. Sorry, I didn't know it was you." Somewhat apologetically, he informed her, "I'm afraid I'm still going to have to ask you to turn around. The chief told me not to let anyone through."

"Well, as you can see, I'm not just anyone." Denise's voice was remarkably calm, Alice thought, given how upset she'd been on the way over. "Now, are you going to let us by, or do I have to phone the chief myself?"

Minutes later, after a hasty consultation with the chief on his two-way, he was pulling off to the side and waving them on.

After a quarter of a mile or so the road came to an end. Several more patrol cars were parked along the grassy verge that gave way to the more manicured grounds of the White estate. What looked to be half a dozen policeman were circulating about, and though there was clearly someone in charge—she recognized the chief of police, Len Chambers, a burly gray-haired man leaning against the open door of his patrol car, one foot propped on the running board, as he carried on a tense conversation over his cell phone—there seemed to be a general sense of confusion nonetheless. In the harsh noonday glare of the floodlights that had been set up along the perimeter, Alice could see the tense looks they wore as they conferred with one another in little huddles, the frosty plumes of their breath punctuating the air. It was obvious these guys had never before experienced anything like this, at least not on the island. Their gait seemed awkward and their movements stiff, as if even the Kevlar vests they wore over their uniforms had yet to be broken in.

Denise must have noticed it, too. She reached for Alice's hand, squeezing it tightly, the worry lines on her forehead deepening.

As soon as he'd gotten off the phone, Len jogged over to them. "That was Gary," he informed Denise, his square-jawed face set in stern lines. Len, paunchy with age and the mostly sedentary position he now enjoyed, made Alice think of a retired combat veteran, past his prime, pressed into service once more. "The good news is he sounded calm and coherent, so I don't think there's any immediate danger." He placed a hand on Denise's arm, saying in a gruffly reassuring tone, "Believe me, Denise, we're doing everything we can to make sure no one gets hurt."

"Let me talk to him," she said. It wasn't so much a request as an order. Len wordlessly handed her the phone. Denise punched the redial button and stood for a moment with the phone to her ear, then she let out a muttered curse. "Damn. I got cut off." The island's spotty cell phone service had never seemed more maddening. Not to be deterred, she thrust the phone back at Len, saying, "That's it. I'm going in."

The chief shook his head, his short gray hair bristling like the fur of some nocturnal creature caught in the floodlights' glare. "I know you're upset, Denise, but we can't have anyone panicking here." He spoke in a tone Denise herself might have used on a student who was being disruptive in class. "Now what I'm going to ask you to do here is to stay calm and let us handle this. We've got things under control."

"Len, that's my husband in there, so unless you plan on arresting me, I'm going in whether you like it or not." Denise's voice rose on a high, frantic note, her gaze sweeping the floodlit perimeter as if she were already plotting her route.

The chief remained firm. "I'm afraid I can't let you do that, Denise. It's too risky. It's not just you and Gary—I have the mayor to think of, too."

"For God's sake, Len, I'm his *wife!*" Denise was near tears.

"All the more reason. Gary's in a highly emotional state right now. If you go in there, it might just push him over the edge." Len wore a look of profound sympathy. "I know you want to help, but trust me, this isn't the way."

Alice chose that moment to step forward. "Let me go instead."

The chief turned to look at her, as if just then becoming aware of her presence. Now his gaze clicked in: hard, cop's eyes. Len Chambers had been the arresting officer that long ago day when it had been her, not Gary, who'd been the cause of so much police activity. Clearly, Len hadn't forgotten it either.

Before he could object, Alice hurried on, "It makes sense. I . . . I know a little something about what he's going through right now. Maybe I can reason with him. It's worth a try." She knew it was reckless, possibly suicidal, but right now all she could think about was Denise. Her sister had always been there for her; now it was time for her to repay that debt.

"No." Denise gripped her arm. "Len's right. It's too risky."

Alice placed a hand over the fingers clenched about her arm. "Please. Let me do this."

They exchanged a long look, that of sisters for whom words weren't necessary, then Denise dropped her hand from Alice's arm and turned to Len with a questioning look. He appeared dubious, but clearly he'd run out of other options, for after pondering it a moment he said, "It could work. He knows you. More importantly, he knows your history."

Alice hugged Denise long and hard. Her sister smelled of the shampoo she bought at Costco in economy-size bottles and underneath, the sour sweat of fear. "It'll be okay, I promise," she whispered. "I'll be back before you know it." As they drew apart, she saw a queer look cross Denise's face. "What?" she asked.

Denise gave a small, humorless smile. "That was the last thing Gary said before he left."

Alice was being fitted with a Kevlar vest by the lone female officer, a slender red-haired woman about her size, when she heard a familiar voice call out her name. "Alice!"

She swung around, surprised to see Colin. He was approaching on foot, Shep trotting at his side and Jeremy bringing up the rear. They must have parked out on the main road in order to slip past the roadblock. Alice felt something hot and quick leap in her chest. Colin had on the same flannel shirt and corduroys he'd been wearing when she'd last seen him—hours ago that felt more like days—only there was something different about him. Gone was the preoccupied look he'd worn then. He was looking straight at her as he walked toward her with a purposeful stride, his expression that of someone determined not to let her slip through his fingers a second time.

"You're not going in there alone," he told her. "I'm going with you." Alice opened her mouth to protest, but he cut her off before she could get a word in. "I happen to know a little something about hostage situations. And right now," his gaze dropped to the Kevlar vest, "it looks as if you could use someone to watch your back."

Alice was about to refuse—she couldn't let him risk his life—when she noticed the stricken look on Jeremy's face. He was staring at her, his face paler than usual, his eyes huge beneath the dark hair falling over his forehead: that of the little boy who'd watched his mommy being led away in handcuffs. "Mom," he said. Just that, a single plaintive note.

Alice hesitated, feeling her resolve weaken. She took Jeremy aside, saying in a low voice, "If you don't want me to go, I won't." If she got killed going in, she'd be abandoning him a second time. And as dearly as she loved her sister, her son came first.

Jeremy licked his lips, darting a look toward the house where his uncle was holding the mayor hostage. "Do you really think Uncle Gary would . . . would do something to hurt you?"

She could have soothed his fears, as she had when he was little in reassuring him that there were no monsters in the closet, but they'd been through too much for her to be less than honest with him now. "I'd like to believe he wouldn't, but right now I don't know what he's capable of," she said.

Jeremy thought for a moment, then seemed to come to a decision. "If you don't go, he might hurt himself." He glanced over at Denise, as if thinking about her being widowed and his cousins without their father. "It's all right," he said, giving Alice a brave smile that would have been more convincing if he hadn't looked so pale and shaken. "Do what you have to do. I know Mister McGinty won't let anything happen to you."

She nodded, not trusting herself to speak. She was about to walk away when, without warning, Jeremy launched himself at her, throwing his arms around her in a fierce hug that nearly knocked her off balance. In that moment she knew it was all worth it. If she died in there, it would be with the knowledge that her son still loved her.

Minutes later, she and Colin set out across the lawn, stepping from the hard white glare of the floodlit perimeter into the near black of the starlight night. It was a moment before Alice's eyes adjusted, then she was guided by the light of the full moon, which hung low in the sky, casting an almost diurnal glow and turning the grass over which they walked pale, as if with morning frost. They moved in silence, each lost in their own thoughts, the lovemaking of just hours before a memory from another lifetime. A short distance away, at the top of a grassy knoll, the house rose up out of the darkness, its lone illuminated window staring out at them like an unblinking eye. Its peaceful façade seemed to mock them somehow, as though the drama taking place inside were nothing more than a false rumor.

They'd nearly reached the house when Alice heard a high, agitated yip and turned to see the dog, whom Jeremy had been holding by the collar, break away and come streaking across the lawn toward them, a furry black and white projectile, the white blaze on its chest all that was visible as it was swallowed up by the surrounding darkness.

The automated door slid open at their approach, just as it had for Gary. Inside, they were greeted, not by gunfire, but by utter silence, which in its own way was more unnerving.

As Alice and Colin made their way through the deserted trophy room and into the hallway beyond, accompanied by the dog, the quiet was broken only by the muffled tread of their footsteps and the low growl emanating from Shep. Alice glanced around, taking in the palatial surroundings. So this was how her son's killer had lived, while David had lain cold in his grave and she'd occupied a six-and-a-half-by-nine-foot cinderblock cell. She felt her blood rise and tasted bile at the back of her throat. But she quickly pushed the thought away. She couldn't afford to dwell on that now.

Colin must have sensed something, for he turned to her and whispered, "You okay?"

She nodded and they continued on. Light poured from an open doorway down the hall and, as they entered the room, the first thing Alice noticed was the blasted-out TV screen, broken glass littering the oriental carpet around it. When her gaze fell on her brother-in-law she almost didn't recognize him at first. Gary's eyes stared vacantly from hollowed sockets and the unhealthy pallor of his skin was that of cancer wards and plants robbed of sunlight. He was seated on the leather settee across from the mayor, holding his gun loosely on one knee and wearing the look of someone who'd stumbled into the situation quite by accident. Owen, slumped in his chair, merely looked drained.

She spoke softly. "Hello, Gary."

His head swiveled slowly toward her. He stared at her uncomprehendingly for a moment before a faint smile of recognition surfaced. "Alice. What are you doing here?"

"We came to see you. You remember Colin, don't you? Jeremy's lawyer?" She gestured toward Colin, who nodded at Gary, his expression carefully neutral.

"You think I need a lawyer?" Gary gave a scornful little bark of a laugh. "Not where I'm going. I'm afraid it's a little too late for that."

"It's not too late until you pull that trigger," Colin observed in a mild, conversational tone, gesturing toward the gun. "Take it from a guy who knows. Only in my case, the weapon of choice was a quart of booze a day."

"Well, in that case, by all means help yourself." Gary waved magnanimously toward the burled wood bar. "I'm afraid the party's already begun, but the more the merrier." His voice carried a note of almost manic glee. There was a strange kind of exhilaration, Alice knew, in releasing your hold on sanity and throwing yourself into the void. "You know our host, Mister White." He gestured toward the mayor, who, though clearly frightened, wore an oddly defiant look. "As a matter of fact, we were just talking about you, Alice. Mister White here seems to think your son could benefit from some jail time of his own."

Alice sucked in a breath. It was all she could do to keep her eyes averted from Owen, fearing that if she were to so much as look at him her already thinly stretched composure would desert her altogether. And Gary didn't need any further provocation right now. "You're not telling me anything I don't already know," she told him, struggling to keep her voice even.

"Yeah, but you don't know the half of it," Gary went on. "Nobody in that office takes a piss without his permission."

Colin stepped in, saying, "Why don't you let us handle it, Gary? There's no reason for you to get involved."

Gary gave a high, lunatic's cackle, and the dog, alert at Colin's side, let out another low growl. "Involved? Christ, I'm already in up to my eyeballs. He made me do things.

Things I'm not proud of." Something glimmered in his blank-eyed expression, like a faulty bulb flickering to life, and the familiar face of her sister's husband briefly emerged. "I'm sorry, Alice. You deserved better." His voice cracked. "I never meant to hurt you. I was only trying to protect my family."

So Gary had been in this, too? Alice felt more than betrayed; she felt ashamed, thinking of all the times he'd stopped in at the restaurant when she'd naïvely believed it was to show support. How stupid she must have seemed, pleading for his help! It was all she could do to speak calmly to him now. "No one blames you, Gary." She kept her thoughts focused on Denise and how terrible it would be for her and the kids if this were to end in tragedy. "All we want is for you to come home."

Gary gave her a pitying look, as if she were the one who'd lost all touch with reality. "I can't. Don't you see? It wouldn't be the same. You, of all people, should know that."

Alice took a step closer to him. "I understand, Gary, believe me I do. But for me there really was no going back. You haven't crossed that line yet. You can still do the right thing."

Gary shook his head, tears coming to his eyes now. "Denise and the kids will be better off without me."

"That's not true. They'd be devastated." Alice's anger gave way to compassion. She knew the special brand of agony he was in; she knew what it could do to you. "Think about Ryan and Taylor growing up without their dad. And Denise . . . she'd never get over it. She loves you, Gary."

"She wouldn't, if she knew what I've done."

"You're wrong about that," Alice forged on. "There's nothing she wouldn't forgive you for. Yeah, she'll be pissed off and you might have a few uncomfortable days." Here, Gary cracked a small smile. "But you know her. She always comes around in the end."

"Like Randy did with you?" he said, with irony.

"It was different with us," she said. Or maybe it had just been different circumstances, their love for each other strained to the breaking point by David's death. "You and Denise . . ." She reached for the word that had best described them, before all this craziness. "You're solid. I used to envy that about you. The way you always worked as a team. One of you picking up the slack when the other was too busy or stressed out. Not like it was some big favor, but because that's just what you do when you love someone."

Some movement out of the corner of her eye made her glance over at Colin. But he was standing perfectly still, and she realized it was his gaze that had drawn her attention; it was concentrated on her with an intensity that was almost physical.

She thought about all he'd risked for her sake and knew it was time for her to take some risks of her own. She held out her hand to her brother-in-law. "Give me the gun, Gary. Please. You don't want to do this. Think of your family."

"They'll be better off," he insisted, shaking his head.

"No. They won't." She was thinking of David and how she would have done almost anything to have him back. She took another careful step forward. "Now give me the gun."

The moment stretched on, Gary staring at her without seeming to see her, as though looking inward. The only sounds were the low growl coming from Shep and the distant sounds of activity from outside. For Alice, it might have been taking place in slow motion. There was none of the stunning swiftness with which her own sanity had been hijacked on a day very similar to this one, a day when all the ones leading up to it had coalesced in a single flashpoint that had sent her spinning over the edge. It was as if time were standing still. There was only the silence and the sight of the tortured man before her, who had no idea what he'd be taking with him should he end his life.

"Please, Gary," she cajoled, her voice breaking.

But he went on shaking his head, those sightless eyes fixed on her like those of someone already dead, repeating, "I can't. You know what prison is like. I can't go there."

"You may not have to. I'll talk to them, explain it so they'll understand. What you need right now is a doctor. You're sick, Gary, but you can get better. Trust me. *I* did."

He focused in on her, as if seeing her for the first time. Not as the ex-con he'd been spying on or his wife's crazy sister, but the strong, decisive woman she was in Colin's eyes.

Then Gary's shoulders slumped, and when she reached down to pry the gun from his fingers, he didn't resist. Delayed shock hit her then and for a long moment she just stood there, the warm weight of the revolver against her palm the only thing anchoring her in reality. She watched, as if from a distance, as Colin moved in, accompanied by the dog, helping Gary to his feet and guiding him out the door, Gary shuffling along beside him like an old, old man. By the time she came to her senses, the room was empty except for her and Owen.

The awareness, when it came, was like someone stealing up on her from behind: *I could kill him.* She could claim it was an accident, that the gun had simply gone off in her hand. And why not? It couldn't be mere coincidence that she happened to be standing before him, holding a gun, with no one to bear witness. Perhaps she was even the instrument of some divine retribution.

"Go ahead. You'd be doing me a favor."

Alice started at the sound of Owen's voice, rousing from her thoughts as if from a dream. When she focused in on him, she saw that the spark of defiance was gone from his eyes; they were as bleak and empty as Gary's had been. The man who had once seemed so powerful looked small and shrunken to her now, a pale reflection of his former self, the faint rise and fall of his chest as he took in breaths the only thing marking his existence. She realized, to her amazement, that she was no longer afraid of him. She didn't even hate him—that would have been giving him too much. All she wanted was to be free of him.

Still, she found she was unable to walk away. David wouldn't let her. "I just want to know one thing. Why?"

He gave an almost imperceptible shrug. "You want reasons? I'm afraid I can't help you there, my dear. It was an accident, just like I told the police. The only detail I left out was inconsequential really. It wouldn't have brought your son back for it to have been made public. And, if it helps any, I haven't touched a drop since." He regarded her for a moment, then he sighed and said, "No, I don't suppose it does." He spread his hands in a helpless gesture. "And there you were again after all those years, turning up like a bad penny on my doorstep. Just when I was beginning to think I could put it all behind me. So you see, you left me with no choice. I had to do whatever it took to get rid of you."

"Even if it meant sending an innocent boy to prison?"

"I wish your son no ill," he said. "He seems like a nice boy. A bit confused perhaps, but I suppose that's to be expected."

Something twisted in her chest. "Not surprising, considering he grew up without a mother."

Owen shrugged again. "As for that, I'd say I paid just as steep a price." He glanced down at his lifeless legs, canted at a funny angle that made them seem unconnected to the rest of him. But there was no self-pity in his voice and the look on his face was oddly dispassionate, as if this final outcome to the drama that had been playing out between them for years was to be expected, and in some ways would be a relief. "But you feel differently, I know, so go ahead, shoot me. You have nothing to lose. I'm sure your lawyer friend will find a way to get you off."

Nothing to lose? "You're wrong about that," she said. There was one thing left for her to lose; something that neither he nor the nine years she'd spent in prison had managed to take from her: her humanity. Carefully, she lowered the gun onto the end table next to the settee. She stared at it for a moment, the hard fact of it more real somehow than anything that had led up to this moment. Then without another word, she turned and walked away.

CHAPTER SEVENTEEN

July 1943

The war that had posed but a distant threat took a new and alarming turn when, in May, the same week as the pivotal battle at Midway, the Japanese invaded the Aleutians, off the coast of Alaska, seizing control of two of its islands. On Grays Island, this worrisome development brought the war even closer to home—it was practically in their backyard!—galvanizing them into new heights in their war relief efforts. Bond pledges reached a record high and as did yields for scrap metal, paper, and rubber drives. The home guard redoubled their efforts and a two-man watch system was instituted for the bunkers out at Pigeon Point, so there would be someone on the lookout round the clock for any signs of suspicious activity. This resulted in a few mishaps, nerves being as frayed as they were, such as when Arnie Sykes's trawler was mistaken one morning for a Japanese sub in the midst of a dense fog. Poor Arnie had the fright of his life when the fog lifted and he found himself surrounded by Navy coast guard cutters.

But the threat proved short-lived. Within weeks American troops regained control of the Aleutians. During that same period a much smaller drama was taking place on Grays Island. One of the dozens of uninhabited little atolls dotting its coastal waters, a scrubby knuckle of rock and pine, gained temporary prominence when the chamber of commerce successfully petitioned the governor of Washington State to have it renamed, due to its unfortunate moniker—Jap's Island. There was some debate over what the new name should be, and it wasn't until summer of that year that one was finally decided upon. Henceforth it would be called Victory Island, a tribute to all the men and women on Grays Island who'd loyally served their country.

One of the few on the island who didn't attend the official ceremony at the dock, which included speeches by the mayor and harbor master, was William McGinty. It had been some weeks since his wife had taken their son on what was billed as an extended trip to New York to visit her parents, and he'd grown tired of the endless inquiries about when they were coming home. Tired, too, of giving excuses that would seem all the more pitiful once the truth came out. For there was no longer any doubt in William's mind as to how this would end. In the few terse phone conversations he'd had with Martha, she'd made it clear that a reconciliation wasn't forthcoming, and William was past the point of trying to convince her otherwise.

He would have been able to make peace with that if not for Danny. William couldn't bear the thought of being such a distance from his son. For that reason alone he'd begged Martha to see reason, offering her the house, along with a generous share of his earnings, if she'd come back to the island. But she'd refused to even consider it. She and Danny would be staying on at her parents' indefinitely, she'd informed him, adding that, in the future, if he had anything to say to her, he could speak to her lawyer.

The only thing that kept William from utter despair was knowing that when all this was over he'd be free to marry Eleanor. In the meantime, they'd agreed not to see each other until the dust had settled. It wasn't just his impending divorce. The island was still buzzing with rumors about Lowell White's disappearance. Some speculated that he'd fallen overboard and drowned while out sailing, though that was unlikely given that his boat was found moored at the marina and his car parked at the ferry terminal. A likelier theory was that Lowell, a known womanizer, had run off with a mistress. A suspicion that was confirmed in their minds when the *Seattle Times* brought news of a thirty-year-old woman in Port Townsend who'd gone missing, accompanied by a photo of an attractive blonde.

In time the talk would die down, William knew, only to be replaced by a new flurry of gossip when his intentions toward Eleanor became known. He would no doubt be portrayed as a philandering cad and Eleanor as a merry widow. They would have to take it slowly so as not to fan the flames (he didn't give a whit about his own reputation, but they had their children to think of). But eventually that, too, would fade. What would take longer was their children's accepting the new reality. He didn't fool himself into thinking Lucy would be quick to embrace him, given how devoted she'd been to Joe, any more than Danny would Eleanor. But in the end, he believed, his and Eleanor's love would prevail. Until then, he'd just have to be patient.

Which was easier said than done, for he missed her more than he would have thought possible. He didn't even have her portrait to fill the empty hours. In fact, he hadn't picked up a brush in weeks. It was as if Martha, in destroying the one thing he'd cared about, had robbed him of his creativity as well. All he had left was Laird, though Martha would have taken him, too, if her mother hadn't been allergic to dogs. For William, the dog's presence was a comfort. Laird seemed to have an almost human understanding of the torment he was in and seldom let William out of his sight. No day ended without the dog curled at his feet, his furry black and white head resting on his master's feet.

Then one morning Eleanor phoned him out of the blue and asked if she could see him. It had been weeks since they'd last spoken and the sound of her voice acted on him like tonic, bringing a bracing rush of adrenaline and clearing his mind of its cobwebs. He would have driven over to her place right then, but she insisted on coming to his house instead.

William, spurred by the prospect of her visit, was tackling the weeds in the garden, which he'd neglected these past weeks, when she came rattling down the drive in Joe's old Ford pickup. From behind a clump of tall hollyhocks that partially screened him from view, he watched her step down from the cab. She wore a yellow checked dress faded from too many washings, her hair untidily pinned up atop her head, stray tendrils chasing the dappled sunlight that played over her cheeks and neck. She looked as beautiful as ever, yet from the shadows under her eyes, it was obvious the strain of these past weeks had taken their toll. Partly because of Lowell, he knew. Also, he suspected, because she harbored some guilt about Martha.

"Eleanor!" he called out her name.

She came to a halt on the path, her eyes darting about before she finally spotted him. William rose from his knees, brushing the dirt from his khaki trousers, while cursing his stupidity in not having changed into something less disreputable—he'd been so preoccupied he hadn't thought to do so.

He hurried over to meet her. "I wasn't spying on you," he said, with a grin, noting the faint look of reproach she wore. "Just enjoying the sight of you strolling up my path. You look right at home." He longed to take her in his arms, but something in her expression warned against it.

"And *you* look much too thin." Eleanor's fingertips brushed over his arm, a touch so light he barely felt it through the sleeve of his shirt. "How are you holding up? It must get pretty lonely out here."

She was smiling, but she looked troubled. A little sliver of worry nicked at the edges of his consciousness. Was it possible her feelings toward him changed? He dismissed the thought at once, telling himself it was just the workings of his fevered brain.

"It does at times," he confessed, "but I'm not exactly alone." He turned to look at Laird, lying in a patch of sunlight on the porch, his head resting atop his paws, snoozing, as was his habit, with his eyes half open so as to track William's movements. "You did well when you chose him for Danny. Only how did you know he would end up being my dog?"

She regarded Laird, hands on hips, her head cocked slightly. "I can't take credit for that. He did the choosing, not me," Laird picked his head up off his paws, as if he knew they were talking about him. "Some dogs are like that. They're bonded to only one person, and it's for life."

Her eyes met his, and William could see that she wasn't just talking about the dog. He felt a surge of relief. In her oblique way, she was telling him she loved him, that nothing had changed. "Shall we go inside?" he asked.

"Is it all right if we sit out on the porch? It's so nice out."

She settled into one of the wicker chairs on the porch, while William went to fetch them something to drink. When he returned she was sitting with her eyes closed and her head tipped back, savoring the sunshine. Summertime was when the rains that drizzled down throughout most of the year gave way to clear skies and dry, sunny weather, and today was no exception. The sky was a deep cobalt above the cathedral spires of the pines along the ridge and out beyond the cove the waters of the sound sparkled with pinpoints of reflected light. She opened her eyes at his approach, darting him a sheepish look, as if she'd been caught indulging in something she shouldn't.

"I hope it's not too sweet for you," he said, handing her a glass of lemonade and settling into the chair across from hers. "I made it myself, and I didn't know how much sugar to put in."

She took a sip, pronouncing, "It's perfect. Just the way I like it."

So polite. As if they hadn't made love. As if the man he'd killed for her sake weren't buried on the hill behind her house.

"How's Lucy?" He played along with the ruse, if that's what this was, that they were just a pair of old friends catching up after a long absence.

She smiled. "Getting taller by the day."

"And Yoshi?"

"As hardworking as ever. In fact, I'm already wondering how I'm going to manage without him once this war is over." She turned to William, wearing a look of polite interest that didn't quite disguise the troubled expression he'd noticed earlier. "And you? You must miss your family."

"I miss Danny," he said, not wanting there to be any confusion about where his sentiments lay.

She took another sip of her lemonade. "How's he taking it?"

"When we talk on the phone, he doesn't say much, so it's hard to tell. But it has to be tough on him, and Martha isn't making it any easier."

"She's hurt. She wants to punish you. Once she comes to her senses . . ." Eleanor trailed off at the perplexed look on William's face.

What was she getting at? he wondered, in a mild panic. Did she *want* him to reconcile with his wife? The only reason she would wish for that, he realized with a sinking heart, would be if her feelings toward him had changed. Suddenly he was afraid to find out what she'd come to tell him.

The telegram in Eleanor's pocket was like a hot coal burning through the fabric of her dress. It had arrived the day before yesterday, and since then she'd been in a state of turmoil, pacing about, unable to sit still for more than few minutes at a time, happy one moment and miserable the next. Just when she'd see her way clear, it would grow murky again and she'd be back to plowing little furrows in the rug with her restless feet. It wasn't until this morning, after yet another sleepless night, that she'd come to a decision. That was why she was here. To tell William.

Only he wasn't making it any easier. In a firm voice, he declared, "It's over with Martha and me." He eyed her across the small wicker table on which his glass of lemonade sat untouched. He appeared puzzled and more than a little worried, as if wondering what could have brought about this sudden change of heart on her part.

Eleanor sighed. She'd been afraid of this. "You don't know that for sure."

Comprehension dawned in his blue eyes. "This isn't about Martha, is it?" he said softly.

She dropped her eyes, answering, "No." In that moment, with his eyes burning into her, she found her resolve weakening. But she knew there was no other way. "This came the other day." With a deep sigh, she withdrew from her pocket the flimsy yellow slip of paper, folded and refolded so many times it was coming apart at the creases. She held it out to him. "They found Joe. He's alive."

William gaped at her. "But how . . . ?"

"He was in the hospital all this time, but it was a while before they could identify him," she explained. "He'd lost his dog tags and most of his memory it seems. The doctor I spoke with is hopeful it'll come back, but no one knows for sure. He's well enough to be shipped home at least. They're transferring him to the Naval hospital in San Diego. Lucy and I are taking the train down. We leave first thing tomorrow morning."

"So that's it then." William spoke in a queer, flat voice.

She nodded, her throat tight.

She could see a battle being waged in his anguished face, between what he knew was the moral thing to do and what he selfishly wished for. Finally his mouth shaped itself into some semblance of a smile. "I suppose I should offer my congratulations, but right now I'm finding it difficult."

Eleanor's eyes flooded with tears. "This has nothing to do with you, William. You have to know that. I'm . . . I'm grateful Joe's alive . . . but I would give anything if it didn't mean—" She broke off, finding it suddenly difficult to speak.

Abruptly he jumped out of his chair and began pacing back and forth. Laird brought his head up, ears pricked at the sight of his master in such a state of agitation. Eleanor had never seen William this way either, not even the night they'd buried Lowell. She watched him rake his fingers through his hair, which had grown long in the weeks they'd been apart. His eyes seemed to leap like flames from the bony planes of his face when at last he swung around to face her. "Don't do it. Don't stay with a man just because you pity him. From everything you've told me about Joe, he wouldn't want that either."

Slowly she shook her head. "I couldn't do that to him. Not after what he's been through."

But William was too crazed to listen to reason. "Haven't you sacrificed enough? My God, Eleanor, you don't even love the man!"

"You're wrong about that. I *do* love him." She spoke with quiet finality. "Maybe not in the same way I love you, but enough to know I could never hurt him. Whenever I think I can't live without you, I wonder how I'd live with myself if I were to leave Joe, especially now when he needs me most." She seized hold of William's hands, tears spilling down her cheeks. She didn't bother to wipe them away. "Haven't we done enough harm? Look at you and Martha. And what about Lowell's family? How can we possibly destroy another man's life on top of all that? And my little girl? Lucy would never forgive me." This morning it had been something Lucy had said to her that had solidified her decision. *When Papa comes home I want to sleep in your room, so I'll always know where he is.*

But William only shook his head, unwilling or unable to accept what she was telling him. "No. I can't lose you. I *won't* lose you." He spoke through gritted teeth, his eyes hard and bright with tears that he refused to let fall. "You think something like this will ever come again? It's once in a lifetime. I had to wait almost forty years to find it and if I live another forty without you, I'll die a lonely old man. And you, Eleanor . . . every night you lie down next to Joe, you'll be thinking of me. Is that really what you want? Is that how you see this ending?"

She rose to her feet, reaching up to cup his dear face in her hands, feeling the warmth of his skin and the tensed muscles flickering underneath. "That's what makes this so hard. If it were any easier, it would be because I didn't love you so much."

Everything about him seemed to cave in at once, his shoulders sagging in defeat and his tall, bony frame swaying like a tree in a high wind. Eleanor felt unsteady, too, thinking that if she didn't go now, this very instant, she wouldn't have the strength later on.

William's anguished gaze met hers, stripped of all hope but showing the glimmerings of understanding. As he took her in his arms one last time, holding her tightly, she could feel the muffled beating of his heart through the soft fabric of his shirt, a heart that would stubbornly go on beating long after this was over. Life would go on, too. Maybe not as they wished it. But, in one form or another, it would go on all the same.

"Good-bye, William." She pressed her lips to his in the most fleeting of kisses. Moments later she was darting down the path, the honeysuckle that grew along the hedge assaulting her with its sweet scent as she raced past, blinded by her tears. She never looked back.

CHAPTER EIGHTEEN

The phone was ringing. Colin could hear it all the way back from the shed, where he was stowing away his equipment. He'd spent most of the morning repairing the damage done by the storm that had rolled in the night before last, pounding in stakes that had come loose and digging out lines that were buried in silt. It was filthy, backbreaking work, with little reward, but the sight of the lines strung out in neat rows, the fledgling oysters clinging to them with the same tenacity he'd shown in his own efforts, was deeply gratifying to him in a way that he couldn't have put into words. Out on the flat with the tide retreating, his conscious mind seemed to recede as well. There was just the sun and the wind and the reedy calls of the seagulls circling overhead.

He was thinking of Alice, as he often did these days, as he walked toward the house to check the answering machine. He hadn't seen her since the night at Owen's, more than two weeks ago, and they'd only spoken on the phone a few times since, most recently when he'd called to let her know Jeremy's trial date had been set. They were both keeping their distance, backing away from the intimacy of that strange day, as if from a too hot fire. Colin ate most of his meals at home these days and Alice was so caught up in her work and in helping her sister cope with Gary's breakdown, she didn't seem to notice that he hadn't been to the restaurant in a while.

The moment of truth for Colin had come, oddly enough, when the hostage crisis was past, after he'd handed Gary over to the police. Looking around, he'd realized, to his horror, that Alice was still in the house. With Gary's gun . . . and the man she had every reason to want to kill. The scenario had spun itself out in his head, with all its frightening possibilities, and he'd been gripped with a terror greater than any he'd felt going in. Then, suddenly he'd caught sight of her, walking toward him across the lawn, a slender figure silhouetted in the moonlight. In the darkness, from that distance, she could have been anyone, and for a heart-stopping moment, in his nerve-shot state, he'd even imagined it was Nadine. Nadine emerging unharmed from the rubble of the Twin Towers, as he'd watched her do a thousand times in his dreams.

When Alice had finally stepped into view and he'd seen no evidence of the terrible things he'd been imagining, Colin had felt a rush of relief at knowing she was safe. And something else as well: the knowledge that he didn't have the strength to sustain another loss. The next time he wouldn't be able to pull himself out of the abyss.

When she'd phoned the next day to give him an update on her brother-in-law, Alice, perhaps picking up on his mood, had been guarded as well. The conversation, while friendly, had had the feel of a missed connection. No one listening in would have guessed they'd ever been intimate.

"Gary's lucky in one sense," she'd said. "If he hadn't been one of their own, he'd be in jail by now." Instead, Gary had been taken to a psychiatric hospital in Bellingham, she informed him.

"What do the doctors say?" Colin had asked.

"He should pull out of it. He's still pretty depressed, but they think the psychosis is only temporary."

"Which means he'll be declared fit to stand trial." Colin had found himself slipping on his lawyer's hat.

"I'm not sure it'll come to that. I can't imagine he'll get off with just a slap on the wrist, but Gary has a lot of influential friends. They'll bend over backward to cut him a break."

"Even if it means making an enemy of the mayor?"

"I don't think we'll have to worry about him anymore."

"What makes you say that?"

"Just a feeling," she said after a pause.

Colin had found himself wondering once more what had happened in those few minutes when she'd been left alone with Owen. But she hadn't volunteered any more information and he hadn't pressed her. "How's your sister holding up?" he'd inquired.

"Not so good. But she's keeping it together for the kids' sake. And I know she'll get through this. She's a survivor."

"It must run in the family," he'd said. And she'd laughed knowingly.

After they'd hung up, Colin had begun thinking about his own family. How long had it been since they'd had anything of real substance to say to each other. When he'd been in rehab, his parents and brother had dutifully attended family week, but in the end none of them had been willing to admit their own role in his dissolution. During the worst of his drinking, his mom would declare staunchly to anyone who even hinted that he had a problem that there was nothing wrong with her son that a new wife wouldn't fix, and Pop had always been quick to pour him another drink and point to Patrick, who could put away more beers on a Friday night than any man standing and who hadn't let it interfere with his life. It had taken a full flameout on Colin's part for them to finally accept that he was an alcoholic, and now that he was sober they referred to it only in the past tense, as if alcoholism were a curable disease, like meningitis.

He didn't blame them, though. God knew he hadn't made it any easier for them. Besides, they had their own troubles. His grandmother, for one. Marma, as she'd been nicknamed by Patrick at an early age when he couldn't pronounce her full name, Martha, was a bit of a terror. For years she'd had one or both of his parents running over to her house at least once a day, on some pretext or other. Things had improved somewhat since she'd moved into an assisted living facility, but she hadn't abandoned her martyr role and no visit with her was complete without a litany of complaints.

Colin knew he owed her a call, and minutes later, when his mother's voice on the answering machine reminded him that it was Marma's birthday tomorrow, her ninetieth, it only increased his guilt. He'd been so preoccupied lately, he'd forgotten all about it. He phoned his mother back at once.

"I wish you could be here for it," she said, after the usual pleasantries, when talk turned to his grandmother's birthday. "It would mean so much to Marma. We're throwing her a little party. I'm making all her favorite foods."

"I wish I could be there, too," Colin lied.

There was a sigh at the other end. "Who knows how many more birthdays she'll have?"

Colin laughed. "You're beginning to sound like Marma."

His mother gave a mock gasp. "Am I? Oh, God. It must be rubbing off."

"Don't worry about Marma. She's a tough old bird."

"I won't deny that." His mother chuckled knowingly. "But, really, Colin, it wouldn't hurt you to come for a visit. It's not just Marma. We *all* miss you."

"I know, Mom," he said, with a sigh. He missed them, too, in a way. At the same time, he found the mere thought of his childhood home in Queens, with its little patch of grass out back that only a fast-talking realtor would call a yard, and its walls permeated with the smell of every meal that had been cooked in it for the past three decades, profoundly depressing.

They chatted a while longer, his mother giving him the latest status report on his dad's sciatica and telling him all about the house his brother and sister-in-law had bought in the Poconos. Colin provided a brief, generalized update on his own activities, leaving out any mention of Alice. His mother lived in perpetual hope that he would remarry one day and he didn't want her to be disappointed when she learned that no wedding bells were in the offing.

After they'd hung up, he phoned his grandmother. For all her contrary ways, he admired the old gal. Forever blond and always dressed to the nines, in full make-up, she was the siren of Heritage Manor, where she reputedly had the men who were still sentient lusting after her. Last year for her birthday Colin had given her a subscription to *Glamour* magazine, and when she'd declared it to be her favorite present of all, he'd known she'd meant it.

"Did I wake you?" he asked, after she'd answered the phone in a groggy voice.

"In the middle of the day?" She snorted at the absurdity of such an idea. "Don't be silly. I was only resting my eyes."

"There's nothing wrong with taking a nap," he told her.

"Sure, if you're an old lady. I'm not old, I'm just getting on in years. There's a difference."

"You'll never be old, Marma," he agreed. "You're too busy keeping the rest of us on our toes."

She laughed heartily. Colin was the only one in the family who could get her to laugh like that. They didn't always agree, but the bond between them was tight. "Like you would know. I haven't heard from you in ages," she chided. "What are you doing out there that's so important you can't give your grandma a call now and then?"

"Not much," he admitted. "But that's sort of the point."

"How's the oystering business coming?"

"I'll let you know as soon as I have something to show for it," he said. "Right now, it's not much to look at."

"Never mind. Mister Deets would be proud. He was an old coot, but he knew his stuff. We had so many oysters they were coming out our ears. I used to make oyster stew every Sunday and feed what was left over to the dog. Imagine! How's the old place holding up?"

"I've had to do a few repairs, but all in all it's in surprisingly good shape."

"You don't get lonely rattling around in it?"

"At times, but I kind of like it. Seems a shame, though, that I'm the only one who gets to enjoy the view. It's pretty spectacular, especially on clear days."

"I remember it well." Her tone turned wistful.

On impulse, he said, "You should come out for a visit. Seriously, Marma. I'll even send you a ticket." He'd sold some of the antiques to finance the oyster farm and cover his living expenses: a pair of Tiffany lamps and the dining room sideboard, which had turned out to be a signed Stickley. He wasn't rich but he could afford the airfare.

There was a long pause in which he could hear the rustle of her breath, a sound that made him think of yellowing pages being turned in an old book, before she answered with regret, "Thank you, dear. It's sweet of you to offer, but I don't think I'd be up to it."

"Arthritis acting up again?"

"It's not that, and you can stop pretending you don't know perfectly well what the reason is," she said somewhat tartly.

"Actually, I *don't* know. We've never really talked about it." Normally he would have dropped the subject, but he wasn't backing away this time. Being in this house had made him wonder more and more about the circumstances of his grandparents' divorce. And now he could feel his grandfather's spirit chafing at the dishonesty and unspoken resentments that had been so corrosive to their family.

"I can't see what possible interest it would be to you. It's all ancient history," his grandmother said in a dismissive tone. "Anyway, if you'd wanted to know so badly, you should have asked your grandfather about it while he was alive."

"We never talked about it, either."

"I find that hard to believe." She spoke with a bitterness that was undiminished by the years. "I'm surprised he didn't fill your ear with tales about what a rotten wife I was."

Colin was amazed that his grandmother would think that. Clearly she hadn't known William as well as she thought. "Actually, he never had a bad word to say about you or anyone. All he ever told me was that you and he disagreed on how Dad should be raised."

Marma snorted in disdain. "He was upset because I took Daniel to live with my parents. But, honestly, what choice did I have?"

"You could have stayed on the island."

"What, and have everyone feeling sorry for me? Poor Missus McGinty, whose husband made a fool of her!"

"So it was another woman." Colin had guessed as much.

She hesitated before replying, as if realizing she'd already said too much. At last, she heaved a sigh that seemed to come down the long tunnel of years. "Yes. Her name was Eleanor."

"The woman in the portrait."

There was another long pause, and for a moment he wasn't sure she would reveal any more than that. But maybe it was the advent of another birthday, a reminder that she didn't have many more years left, or maybe that she'd simply decided the statute of limitations on his grandfather's crimes was up, for she replied, "It wasn't just an affair—I might have forgiven him that. He loved her."

"Did he tell you that?"

"He didn't have to. The portrait said it all."

"I always wondered about that, why he never sold it." Taking advantage of his grandmother's unexpected candor, he asked, "Why did you leave him? Was it because he refused to give her up?"

"Partly, though I probably could have persuaded him to—for Danny's sake, if not mine. But I had too much pride.

And I loved him too much to stay, knowing how he felt," she said, in a strange, hollow voice. "Of course, I never told him that. He wouldn't have believed it, if I had. Our life had become . . ." Her voice trailed off. "After you've been married a while you get into a routine. And it was the war. I was doing my part along with everyone else. I suppose I wasn't paying as much attention to my husband as I should. And your grandfather . . . he did what men do. He looked elsewhere."

Colin found himself gazing up at the portrait that had stood at the center of his family's mystery and that even now carried a hint of intrigue. "So why didn't he marry Eleanor?"

"She was already married, for one thing. Her husband was off fighting in the war when they met. For a while everyone thought he was dead, but it turned out he'd only been missing in action." Colin listened raptly as the tale grew even stranger. "He was wounded pretty badly, from what I heard, and I suppose she couldn't bring herself to leave him."

"Once you found that out, you never considered going back?"

"No." Another deep sigh. "Even if I'd been able to forgive him, I doubt he would have forgiven me."

"Because of Dad?" Colin asked, knowing the bitterness it had caused when she'd taken their only child away.

"No, he'd have done almost anything to get Daniel back. It was the portrait." She seemed reluctant to continue.

"What about it?" Colin prompted, gazing at the portrait as he puzzled over her cryptic words.

After a moment Marma said, "That's how I found out about the affair. I came across the portrait in his studio, where he'd been working on it in secret. I knew the moment

I laid eyes on it, of course." Her voice was soft with a kind of wonderment, as if she were surprised to find those memories, locked away all these years, still alive and intact. "No one but a man in love could have painted her like that. Almost as if she were glowing. I couldn't bear it, so I grabbed the first thing I could get my hands on—a pair of scissors. I wasn't thinking clearly at the time. I'm not even sure how it happened." She faltered a bit before going on. "By the time I was finished, there was nothing left of it."

Colin struggled to make sense of what his grandmother was telling him. "So the one he left me isn't the original?"

"He painted it again from memory. Every detail, exactly as it was. *Better* even." He heard the bitter pride in her voice. She might have scorned William in private, but she'd always seen the value in being Mrs. William McGinty. Why else keep his name? "When I saw it, I could hardly believe my eyes. I'd gone to a show of his works, at the Brooklyn Museum. More out of curiosity than anything. And there it was, up on the wall bold as you please. Like I'd only dreamed that I'd hacked it to pieces. Like . . . like I'd never existed. It wasn't until later on that I figured out what must have happened."

"That's quite a story." Stunned, Colin stood there shaking his head. He couldn't quite picture his grandparents as those younger people embroiled in all that drama. Briefly he thought about mentioning that he'd become friendly with Eleanor's granddaughter—more than friendly, in fact—but he decided against it. It would have been too much for Marma to handle.

"Well, now you know. I hope you're satisfied," she said.

"I'm sorry for dredging it all up," Colin apologized.

"Oh, I'll survive. I have so far. You don't get to be my age without your share of hard knocks. I might have had more than most, but I'm still here, aren't I?"

"That you are." Colin smiled. "Happy birthday, by the way. I'm sorry I didn't send you anything."

"Never mind. You've given me something far better than anything money can buy." From the note of affection in her voice, he knew that he was forgiven.

"What's that?" he asked.

"You didn't let the fact that I'm old and sick stop you from speaking your mind."

Colin chuckled. "Well, Marma, maybe it's because I don't think of you that way." More soberly, he added, "Anyway, I'm the one who should be thanking you. This explains a lot. Not just about Grandpa, but about our whole family."

"I'd rather you didn't mention to your father that we had this little chat," she said. "You know how he feels about your grandfather. It would only get him worked up."

What Colin knew was that if his father harbored ill will toward William, the seed had been planted there by Marma and nourished through the years until it could flower on its own. But there was no point in dredging up that, too. It wouldn't have done any good.

"I'll try to make it out next year for your birthday," he told her, as they were saying good-bye.

"If I live that long," she muttered.

"Marma, you'll outlive us all," he said, with a laugh, almost believing it at that moment.

The house seemed quieter than usual after he'd hung up. He sank down on the sofa, his gaze drawn once more to the portrait. His grandmother had told only one side of the story—the rest William and Eleanor had taken to their graves—but she'd provided a crucial detail. Her words came back to him now. *He painted it from memory. Every detail. Even better than before.* A revelation that had rocked Colin to the core, for it spoke of a love so powerful that nothing, not even time, could diminish it. A love that had enabled William to see Eleanor through the eyes of memory, as clearly as when he'd painted her in life. The kind of love that could only be when you know you're loved as deeply in return. Colin had seen it on his grandfather's face the one time he'd asked about the woman in the portrait: He'd been true to Eleanor till the end.

Colin could only imagine the exquisite hell of their living so close to one another yet so far apart. And yet both had stayed on the island. Maybe because to have moved away would have been even more unbearable. What would those two have made of the friendship, for lack of a better word, between the children of their offspring? That the happiness that had eluded them could have been his and Alice's for the taking? Might they even have had a hand in their being thrown together? Colin didn't believe in ghosts, except the ones of his own making, but at the same time he was having difficulty *not* believing that there was something more at work here than mere coincidence.

He thought now of Alice, warming at the memory of their lovemaking. This time it wasn't clouded by thoughts of Nadine. As if a fog had lifted, he saw Alice as clearly as the image in the portrait, to whom she bore such a striking resemblance, an image that shone now like a lighted window materializing out of the darkness at the end of a long journey, guiding the way as he searched for what was in his heart.

Denise sat on the edge of the bed, plucking absently at the balled-up Kleenex in her lap. "It's just so hard sometimes," she said, looking more dispirited than Alice had ever seen her. "Life doesn't just stop when something like this happens. Even when you're dying inside, you still have to get up and go to work every day. You have to put a smile on your face for the kids' sake, and so people won't be talking about you behind your back any more than they already are. Oh yes, I know there's been talk! They're saying our family is cursed." She turned swollen, bloodshot eyes to Alice. "What if it's true? What if we *are* cursed?"

"That's ridiculous, and you know it," Alice told her. "There's a perfectly good explanation for everything that's happened." Owen White had been at the root of it all.

She waited for that clenched feeling she always used to get whenever she thought of him, but it didn't come. It was as if, in confronting him, some burden had been lifted from her. He wasn't a monster, she'd realized, just a man so twisted inside he'd resorted to monstrous acts.

"That's a comforting thought," Denise said sarcastically.

Alice placed a hand over her sister's. "It's not the end of the world. It just feels that way right now."

Denise shook her head, refusing to be consoled. "It's like I don't know my own husband anymore. It's like visiting some sick relative I have to try to cheer up."

"I know you don't believe it right now, but you'll get through this, trust me."

"The question is *how*."

Alice got down to practical matters. "What does Gary's lawyer have to say?"

Denise brightened marginally. "Steve worked out a deal. Gary gets off with a suspended sentence, as long as he remains under a doctor's care. Brett Loggins," she said, referring to the assistant D.A., "is an old school friend of Gary's. They'd get together for a beer now and then." She paused, adding in a softer voice, "I suppose those days are over."

"You can't think that way. Some people will have a hard time understanding, sure. But when Gary gets home I think you'll be pleasantly surprised to find out just how many friends he has." Alice said, reminded of the old friends and acquaintances who'd supported her.

"Maybe, but that's only the half of it. What's he going to do for work? What about *us*?" Denise moaned.

"Have you two talked? I mean, *really* talked."

Denise shook her head. The Kleenex she'd been mangling had disintegrated, and now she stared down in misery at the tiny pieces scattered like snowflakes over her lap. "The doctor doesn't think it's a good idea to get into any of that stuff right now. He says Gary is still too fragile. But I know something's on his mind. I can sense it. What I can't figure out is why he's keeping it from me. We've always shared *everything*."

"Maybe he's afraid."

Denise's head jerked up, her eyes widening. "Afraid of what? Me? I'm his wife."

"It's the people you love the most that you least want to hurt," Alice said gently. She hadn't told her sister any of the things Gary had revealed to her that night. It would be better if she heard it from Gary. "Maybe he's only trying to protect you."

"Protect me from what? I already know the worst."

"Just let him know you'll love him, no matter what. Maybe that's all he needs to hear." She'd long since forgiven Gary herself, knowing the kind of pressure he'd been under.

Denise nodded slowly, her mouth turning up in a small half smile. "Just like the old days, huh? You giving me advice. Only back then I thought you had all the answers."

Alice gave a rueful laugh. "Not even close."

She was thinking of Colin, how wrong she'd been about him. That night, she'd felt the connection between them more strongly than ever. No man had ever gone out on a limb like that for her, not her husband, not even her father when he was alive. Moving side by side through the shadows, she'd felt closer to him than she ever had to another human being, almost as if they'd been one. She'd felt his strength flowing into her, giving her the courage to do what she'd needed to do. All her earlier fears and misgivings about him had faded away. *This must be what love is*, she'd thought, marveling for an instant, in spite of the trepidation she'd felt at the prospect of what lay ahead, that it had taken her this long to find out. Love was someone who knew instinctively what you needed and gave it without being asked or expecting anything in return.

But ever since then he seemed to have retreated back into his shell. Hurt, she'd kept her distance as well, wondering how she could have been so mistaken about him. No, clearly she didn't have all the answers. Who, after all, was she to give advice?

Denise rose heavily to her feet. "Well, I guess I should get started on supper. Though if it weren't for the kids I probably wouldn't bother. I don't seem to have much of an appetite these days—silver lining to every cloud, right?" She glanced down at her slacks, which drooped around her hips, she'd lost so much weight. She paused to ask Alice, as she was making her way to the door, "Should I set an extra place?"

"Thanks, no. I'm taking Jeremy out for pizza tonight." Just saying the words brought a little glow of satisfaction. Such an ordinary thing, yet for her it was anything but ordinary.

"Don't you have to work?"

"I'm taking the night off. Calpernia's holding the fort down, and that new guy we hired seems to be working out." Usually, Alice only took Mondays off, when the restaurant was closed, but business had been picking up lately—word was getting around and they'd had a nice write-up in the *Seattle Times*—so she could afford to take an extra day now and then. And she'd wanted to go out on a night when Jeremy didn't have school the next day, so he could enjoy their time together without worrying about his homework.

Denise hugged Alice as she was leaving. "Thanks. I don't know how I'd get through this if it weren't for you."

Alice thought again of all that Denise had done for her. Her sister had never stinted, not once. "Consider it payback."

"Okay if I tag along?"

Randy spoke casually, as if it had been a spur of the moment thing, but Alice could tell from the way his eyes cut away that he'd had it in mind it all along. Her heart sank. She'd been so looking forward to the time alone with her son. But, conscious of Jeremy watching them, waiting to see how she'd react, she tried not to let her disappointment show.

"Fine by me. If it's okay with you." She turned to give Jeremy a questioning look. He stood slouched in the doorway to the living room, a study in teenage insouciance, in his baggy cargo pants and Mariners sweatshirt at least three sizes too big, except for his eyes, which flicked back and forth between his parents, keenly attuned to their every nuance.

"Whatever." He shrugged, but she thought he looked pleased.

"All right then. Shall we?" She put on a smile that she hoped didn't look manufactured.

On the drive into town, the conversation was a bit strained. She couldn't remember the last time they'd all gone on a family outing. Her memories of the events that had taken place in the months after David's death all ran together in her mind like colors on a child's finger painting. Now, here they were together again. Alice felt sad, thinking of all the wasted years.

"I'm glad we could do this," said Randy, later on, as he was tucking into the last slice of pizza. Jeremy had run into a couple of friends from school—not the ones he usually hung out with, she'd been relieved to see—and after finishing his pizza he'd gone off with them to the video arcade in back. "I've been wanting to tell you how bad I feel that I wasn't around during that whole business with Gary. You shouldn't have had to go through that alone."

Her thoughts turned once more to Colin. "I wasn't exactly alone."

"Yeah, I know. Jeremy was pretty shook up," Randy said, clearly unaware of Colin's role in it. "How's Gary doing?"

"Better. He seems to be responding to his treatment."

"Poor guy." Randy shook his head in sympathy. "It has to be tough on Denise, too."

"It is, but she's hanging in there. Mainly, she's worried about how they're going to manage if he can't find another job."

"Maybe I can help with that."

"Really?" Alice perked up.

"I know a guy who manages a department store in one of those big shopping malls. They're always looking for security guards. I can probably get him to hire Gary."

"That would be great." It might not be ideal, but it was a job.

"I'll give the guy a call, see what he can do." Randy paused, frowning in thought as he chewed on a mouthful of pizza. "Of course, they'd have to relocate. How would they feel about moving off the island?"

"I'm sure they wouldn't be too happy about it, but they may not have a choice." It might even be preferable in a way. Life in a small community could get pretty uncomfortable when you were the subject of scrutiny, Alice knew from her own experience. Touched by the unexpected show of support from her ex-husband, she reached across the table and squeezed his hand. "Thanks, Randy. I really appreciate this."

He smiled at her with more warmth than usual. "No problem. Happy to do what I can." He pushed aside his half-eaten slice of pizza. "You know, Alice, we should do this more often."

She wasn't sure what he was getting at and didn't want to read too much into it, so she said lightly, "You're right, we should. I'm sure Jeremy would like that."

Randy gave her a meaningful look. "I wasn't just thinking of Jeremy."

"Oh." She felt heat rising in her cheeks. She dropped her voice, asking, "What exactly are you getting at, Randy?"

He took a deep breath and exhaled slowly. He appeared nervous for some reason. "Look, Alice, I've been thinking a lot lately. About us. I'll be honest with you. I'm not proud of the way I handled things in the past. But whatever you might think, I wasn't trying to punish you. I was only looking out for Jeremy, doing what I thought was best for him. For whatever it's worth, I was wrong. And I wouldn't blame you if you can't find it in your heart to forgive me. But if there's a chance, even a slight one, that we can put all this behind us and make a fresh start, don't you think we owe it to ourselves, and to Jeremy, to at least try?"

Alice was speechless. How could she have been so blind to the signals? There was a time she'd known Randy's every tic: that certain look he got in his eyes when he was being less than honest; the way the tips of ears reddened when he was feeling amorous; the heightened pitch of his voice when he was winding up to make a case, usually for expensive things they couldn't afford—a Minolta camera, a trip to Hawaii, a new propane grill. And even when she'd known he was lying or when she didn't feel like making love or was annoyed at his spendthrift ways, it had been a reminder of how close they were. They'd been high school sweethearts. He was the first boy she'd kissed, when she was fourteen, under the bleachers after the homecoming game. The first boy she'd had sex with. In college there had been other guys and, she knew for a fact, other girls for Randy, but in the end they'd always come back to each other. Even if she hadn't gotten pregnant in her sophomore year, marrying Randy would have been a foregone conclusion.

Those old memories washed through her, but underlying them, like gritty sand, was the knowledge that Randy hadn't been there for her when it counted most. After David died, she had felt as if she'd lost her husband, too. But though he'd been wrong in keeping Jeremy from her, she knew he'd meant it when he'd said he had only done what he'd thought was best. She couldn't lose sight of the fact, either, that Randy had been there for Jeremy all those years when she couldn't be. He'd been a good dad, even if he'd made mistakes as a husband.

She found her voice at last. "I don't know what to say. I didn't see this coming."

He was gazing at her intently, his eyes bright with expectation, as if it were possible to get the answer he wanted through sheer force of will. "Will you at least think about it?"

"All right. I'll think about it." Maybe Randy was right. Maybe they owed it to themselves to try. It might be the best thing for all of them, not just Jeremy. But she wasn't ready to commit to anything just yet, so she cautioned, "Don't say anything to Jeremy just yet. I don't want him to get his hopes up."

"I won't say a thing." Randy smiled as if it were already a done deal, his eyes remaining locked on hers. She noticed, to her embarrassment, that the tips of his ears were pink. "I was thinking next time, it could be just the two of us. Someplace nice, with candles." He glanced up at the string of red lights in the shape of chili peppers strung along the exposed brick walls, and they shared an amused look. "I can always make up some excuse, tell Jeremy I'm going bowling with the guys or something."

"You don't bowl," she said, smiling.

"True, but I could always learn."

Alice thought about how long it had been since she'd been on a real date. Even if it was with her ex-husband, it would be nice to dress up, put on high heels for a change.

An image of Colin intruded once more. The tenderness with which he'd kissed her when they'd parted at his house, as if he'd known it was the last time. As if he'd already made his decision, a decision that, even though it pained her, Alice could respect. For didn't she feel the same pull of the past with Randy? Letting go was hard, even when all you had to hang on to was memories.

Jeremy reappeared at the table just then. His face was flushed and he looked more at ease than he had in a while. Alice smiled up at him. "Having a good time?"

He grinned in reply. "Kent and Tyson are heading over to Bucky's. There's supposedly a good band playing tonight. They want me to go with them. Is that okay?"

"As long as you promise not to stay out too late," Randy told him. "I want you home no later than midnight."

Jeremy looked a little surprised, as if it had been a while since he'd had a curfew, but he played along. And although it was clear to Alice that Randy was only exercising his authority in order to impress her with his parenting skills, she was touched by the effort.

"Mom?"

Alice became aware of Jeremy's eyes on her. She realized with a start that he was asking her permission as well—his way of letting her know that she was still his mother, no matter what. Her throat tightened, but she didn't want to embarrass him with a show of emotion, so she merely said, "Okay with me. Just remember, tomorrow's a work day."

Watching him bound off, like any teenager eager to get back to his friends, his impending trial seemed to her a distant threat.

CHAPTER NINETEEN

It hit him as soon as he walked through the door, a solid wall of sound, its pulsing beat seeming to surge up through the soles of his feet, filling him with excitement and a wild sense of possibility. Jeremy waited in line to get his hand stamped, but when he turned to his friends, Kent and Tyson were already moving off in the direction of the dance floor. Kent called something over his shoulder to Jeremy that he couldn't hear, then the two were swallowed up by the crowd. Jeremy started after them, but by the time he'd made his way through the crush of bodies, he'd lost them.

He hadn't known either of them that long. Kent Park was his lab partner in bio, a quiet-seeming Korean kid who'd turned out to have an offbeat sense of humor—Jeremy had arrived at class one morning to find the frog they were supposed to dissect arranged in a prayerful pose, as if pleading to be spared. Through Kent, he'd gotten to know Kent's best friend, Tyson Fowler. They weren't the coolest kids in school, Kent a self-proclaimed tech geek and Tyson president of the chess club, but they weren't off the grid in terms of popularity, either; Jeremy's reputation wouldn't suffer from hanging out with them. Not that that was such a big deal to him any more; stuff like that had stopped seeming so important after he'd learned the hard way what it took to get noticed. And with Kent and Tyson he could be himself; he didn't have to put on an act to try to look cool.

Occasionally he still ran into Rud and his posse. They would always greet him with hooting calls and pump their raised fists at him, their idea of a friendly gesture, and he'd always wave in return. But on those occasions he didn't automatically fall in with them as he had in the past. Instead, he'd find himself noticing things he hadn't before, like the other day when he'd observed with a mild shock that Rud's hair was thinning, his pale pink scalp visible through the gelled spikes of his albino hair—*He'll be bald by the time he's thirty*, Jeremy had thought—and the time they'd walked past Bettina Stromberger and she'd screwed up her face and flapped a hand in front of her nose in their wake, at the stench from the smoker's pit that followed them everywhere they went.

Jeremy would marvel then that he had ever thought they were "dope," as Rud would have put it. His dad had been right about them. *You hang out with losers, you'll become one yourself*, Randy had cautioned. And by the time Jeremy was his dad's age, he sure as shit didn't want to be pushing a broom for a living or reading his name upside down off his shirt pocket. He had bigger plans for himself.

Then, inevitably, would come the sudden, sickening sensation in his gut, the realization that instead of going to college he could be spending the next few years behind bars. It was like his shadow, something he wasn't aware of most of the time but which followed him everywhere he went.

For a while he'd fooled himself into believing the whole thing would get buried in the shit storm over his uncle. But that wasn't proving to be the case. The same D.A. who'd come down so hard on Jeremy had been a soft touch with Gary. The matter had been handled quietly, and though his uncle wouldn't be returning to his job any time soon, he'd been spared a trial.

It helped that the mayor hadn't pressed charges. He'd been quoted in the newspaper as saying that, while Gary Elkins's actions had caused him and his wife a good deal of trauma—Mrs. White had been holed up in her room the whole time; it was she who'd called the cops—he understood that there had been no criminal intent; the former deputy chief of police had merely been reacting to the "mental stress" he'd been under.

Jeremy knew, from listening in on his mom's and Colin's conversations, that the old man had had something to do with his uncle's crackup and that he was in some way responsible for the D.A.'s coming down so hard on *him*. But they couldn't prove it, so nothing had changed as far as he was concerned.

While he was contemplating this, as he pushed through the crush at Bucky's he ran headlong into Carrie Ann Flagler. She was carrying a large plastic cup of what looked to be Coke—they only served non-alcoholic beverages on teen Fridays—and when he accidentally plowed into her, some of it splashed over onto her top. He froze for an instant, staring at her in horrified disbelief, before he managed to fumble out an apology.

"Shit! I'm sorry. I didn't see you."

Ignoring his apology, she began furiously dabbing at her top with the napkin in her other hand. In the dim light, he wondered for a second if she'd even recognized him. Then her head jerked up and she glared at him. "So, what, are you, like, *stalking* me or something?" she demanded, raising her voice to be heard above the loud pulsing of the music. Silvery flecks of light from the twirling mirror ball overhead funneled down like snowflakes, catching in her light brown hair and bouncing off the spangles sewn onto the scooped neck of her top, which showed a fair amount of cleavage. The spillover from the dance floor crowded in around them, gyrating couples bumping up against them, pushing them closer together, close enough for Jeremy to catch the scent of her perfume—something light and grassy that smelled like a meadow after a rainfall.

Jeremy shouted over the music, "Can I get you another one?" He pointed at her half-empty cup.

Unexpectedly, she shrugged in what he took to be an assent. They made their way through the crowd to the bar, where he bought them each a Coke. The situation was already so surreal that when she suggested they go outside, where it wasn't so noisy, it didn't seem all that strange.

Outside, she used a fresh napkin to dab once more at her top. "Shit, I think it's ruined. And this is only the first time I've worn it. What do you think, is it too late to exchange it?" She looked up at him, and he saw a small smile peeking from under her frown. "A joke," she said. "It was a joke."

He wondered if she also considered it funny to be falsely accusing someone of rape. "I get it," he said, in a surly voice.

Her smile abruptly fell away. They were standing on the concrete landing above the steps that led down to the parking lot. He could hear the music, muffled now, thumping on the other side of the door through which they'd just exited and smell the after-hours punch-bowl odor of empty cups and rotting fruit that drifted up from the Dumpster below. A breeze was blowing, lifting the hair off her face, lifting it and gently lowering it again. In the light from the quarter moon caught in the trees branches overhead, her eyes, ringed with mascara that had already begun to smudge, were bright as they fixed on him with the same look of faint bewilderment that Jeremy imagined he wore.

"This is weird, isn't it? If my dad could see us, he'd be calling the cops right now." A note of defiance crept into her voice, as if she were somehow thumbing her nose at her father, and Jeremy noticed that her words were slightly slurred. She'd been drinking. He knew that some of the kids who came to these things brought their own booze, which they either smuggled inside in flasks or drank outside in the parking lot. She wasn't drunk, though, like on the night they'd had sex. The mere thought of which made his dick stir.

What made him even angrier than what she'd done was that he could still be even remotely attracted to her. "Why, you scared I'm going to rape you?" he said sarcastically.

"I didn't say that." Now her defiance seemed directed at him.

"You didn't have to."

"It's not all my fault, you know."

"Oh, and just whose fault is it then?" Throwing aside every caution, from Mr. McGinty, from his mom and dad, he spoke his mind. "You fucking *lied*. You know what really happened, but that's not what you told the police."

A sullen look came over her face. "You're making it sound like it was on purpose. It wasn't like that."

He pounced. "So you admit you lied."

"That's not what I said. You're twisting my words."

Jeremy pressed on. "What I want to know is *why*. Why did you do it?"

Her eyes met his then, and he saw the confusion in them. "I don't know," she said, with a small shrug. "It just . . . kind of got away from me, I guess. Once my parents got the police involved, it turned into this whole big deal. Like, it wasn't really about *me* anymore, you know?"

"Not really," he said coldly.

"If it means anything, I'm sorry."

He felt a surge of hope. "So you'll tell them I didn't do it?"

She shook her head slowly, and tears welled in her eyes, making them shiny as newly minted nickels in the moonlight. "I can't. My dad would kill me. That's how this whole thing started. That night, when he caught me sneaking into the house, he went ballistic. It wasn't just that I'd been drinking. It was like he *knew* what had happened, like he could smell it on me. I was crying, my mom was crying, and somehow it all came out. I guess I must've made it sound like it was all you—shit, I had to tell him something, didn't I, or he'd have blamed *me*—and before I knew it, he was on the phone with the cops. What was I supposed to do?" Her eyes pleaded with him to understand.

But to Jeremy it wasn't at all complicated. "You could have told the truth."

"You don't know what my dad's like when he gets like that. He's scary. If I told him I'd made the whole thing up, I . . . I don't know what he'd do." She hugged herself, shivering, and Jeremy could see, from the look on her face, that it wasn't just from the cold.

Strangely, he wasn't unsympathetic. He used to think his family was more screwed up than anyone's, but lately he'd begun to realize that there were families worse off than his, like Carrie Ann's. He couldn't let that get in the way, though. She might be too scared to stand up to her father, but Jeremy was equally afraid of what would happen to him if she didn't. "There's got to be somebody you could talk to. A teacher, or maybe Mister Bradley," he urged her, thinking of their school guidance counselor, who really did listen and who didn't talk down to you. "If things are really that bad at home, there are people who can help."

It was the wrong thing to have said, he could see that at once. Her face closed off as suddenly as a door slamming shut. "You make it sound like he'd actually hurt me or something." Her tone turned belligerent. "Just because my dad has a temper, it doesn't mean he's some kind of psycho. Anyway," her eyes narrowed, "it's not like *you're* so innocent. How do I know it didn't happen the way I said? We were both pretty drunk that night."

"Because," he said, "If I *had* raped you, you wouldn't be talking to me right now."

Even Carrie Ann couldn't argue with that logic. She went on glaring at him, though, wearing the sullen expression that made her look closer to six than sixteen. In the parking lot below, he heard the sound of an engine roaring to life. As the car swung around, the glare of its headlights caught her full in the face. In that instant he saw in her eyes that she was torn, between what she knew was the right thing to do and her desire to protect herself and her family. He understood that desire. After his brother died, Jeremy had tried to protect his mother from the grief that he could see, even at such a young age, was tearing her to bits, and he'd failed. It was part of the reason he'd been so angry all those years. He'd been angry at himself as much as at her, for letting her down.

Then all at once Carrie Ann's face crumpled and tears began rolling down her cheeks. "I'm sorry," she said, in a low voice that was almost a whisper. "Please don't hate me."

He didn't know if she was sorry for what she'd done or if it was because she lacked the courage to make it right. But Jeremy recognized that there was nothing more he could do, at least not tonight. Tomorrow, when she'd sobered up, he'd try again. He touched her gently on the arm. "Come on, let's go back inside. You must be freezing."

"I feel like dancing. Will you dance with me?" She blew her nose into the crumpled napkin and a wobbly smile surfaced on her tear-streaked face.

"You're not afraid of what people will say?" he asked.

"Fuck it," she said, and laughed.

Then they were plunging back in through the fire exit, into the pulsing heartbeat of the music and the heat of all those bodies crammed together, into the mingled smells of sweat, perfume, sticky spilled drinks, and the burnt-toast stink of overheated amps, as if he and Carrie Ann were being swept along by a riptide, with only each other to hold on to.

CHAPTER TWENTY

Alice had been mulling over Randy's proposal for more than a week when her mother stopped by the restaurant one morning to drop off the last of the rosemary from her garden. Lucy stayed to chat while Alice cracked Dungeness crabs for the stuffed tomatoes that were today's appetizer special. It wasn't until she was getting up to leave that she happened to mention, "I don't know if you've heard—Nana's old place is up for sale."

Alice paused in the midst of her cracking, brushing bits of shell and crabmeat from her fingers. "No, I hadn't heard," she said, looking quizzically at her mother. "I thought the people who bought it were planning to stay there until they retired."

Lucy shrugged, reaching for the blue quilted bag she carried with her everywhere she went. In it, along with the usual items, like wallet and checkbook and keychain, was a small arsenal of emergency supplies: breath mints and dental floss; ibuprofen and gum for when her ears plugged up on airplanes; a pocket-size Kleenex dispenser and little foil packets of pre-moistened wipes; a pen light, should she happen to get lost while driving after dark and need to consult a map (though there was little likelihood of that, on an island where she could've found her way around blindfolded); a small spiral-bound notebook with a pen clipped to it; a collapsible umbrella and a rain slicker that folded up into a pouch, in the event of a downpour. Her mother was too much of an optimist to live in fear of the sky falling, but should that ever come to pass she would be more than prepared.

"Herb Crenshaw? He'll never retire," she said, with a dismissive wave of her hand. "He can't afford to. I'm sure that's why they're selling. Don't repeat this to anyone," she dropped her voice and leaned in close, "but Darlene Overby, down at the savings and loan, let it slip that they're behind on their payments." Lucy prided herself on being the kind of person who minded her own business, and when passing on such tidbits of information she was fond of prefacing it with *Now you know I'm not one to gossip*, but very little happened on the island that she didn't know about.

"I wonder what they're asking for it," Alice mused aloud.

"The land alone has to be worth a fair bit. Prices have really gone up. I should probably think about selling myself. I could always get one of those nice little condos." Ever since Alice's dad died, Lucy had been talking about selling her house and moving into something smaller, but Alice knew it was just talk—when her mother moved, hopefully a long time from now, it would be to the burial plot next to her husband's. "Well, I've got to run. I have to get those jars of piccalilli over to Cora's. Did I tell you she's one of the judges this year?" Lucy hoisted her quilted bag onto her shoulder, waving good-bye to Calpernia, who was busy washing lettuce at the sink.

Alice recalled that today was the cutoff date for entries in the annual winter crafts fair, held ever year at Christmastime. Along with the crafts and edibles for sale, there was a booth displaying various baked goods and homemade preserves that had been submitted for judging. At last year's fair, her mother's pumpkin streusel tart had taken home the blue ribbon in the pie division.

"Then you can't miss," said Alice, with a smile. Cora Bradley was one of her mother's oldest friends.

Lucy pretended to be appalled that Alice would even suggest such a thing. Cora wouldn't let friendship sway her opinion, she declared staunchly. And while Alice thought that might be true, it was also true that, here on the island, it was all about who you knew.

Watching her mother fly out the door, clutching her coat with one hand and holding onto her quilted bag that held the cure for every one of life's ills with the other, Alice was thinking that the network of old ties and alliances by which business was conducted on the island had a dark side as well. One that Owen White had used to his advantage. He'd been like a spider sitting in the middle of his web, a web he himself was now snared in. For, just days ago, Gary had made a full confession. Not only owning up to the bribes he'd taken, but the mayor's role in it as well, how Owen had used the evidence that would have incriminated Gary to blackmail him into doing things that, if not exactly illegal, were highly unethical. In the firestorm that ensued, Owen had been forced to resign. Construction on the Spring Hill project had also ground to a halt, pending an investigation.

Unfortunately, none of this had altered Jeremy's case. Gary would testify on his behalf, of course, but he had little to offer that wasn't hearsay. Besides, in Gary's present condition, how credible a witness would he make? Now, with the trial date just weeks away, she'd given up hope of an eleventh hour save. They'd simply have to see this through to the end and pray that the jury would believe Jeremy's side of the story.

Alice's own attempts to do an end run had only made matters worse. The other day she'd driven out to the Flaglers's thinking that if she could appeal to Mrs. Flagler, one mother to another, she might still be able to short circuit this whole thing. But Warren Flagler had arrived home as she was winding up to give her pitch, and had all but physically ejected her from the property. *You have a lot of nerve, lady*! he'd shouted, thrusting his angry bulldog's face into hers. *You and that kid of yours, you're two of a kind—a couple of bad apples. If I ever catch either of you anywhere near my family again, I'm calling the cops!*

But it wasn't all doom and gloom. At least now she knew Jeremy would be getting a fair trial. For one thing, the D.A., rather than currying favor with the mayor, would be distancing himself instead. For another, Judge Voakes had just this past week resigned, purportedly for health reasons (though Colin believed it was because he'd been in tight with the mayor and was looking to avoid being tarred by the same brush) and a new judge had been assigned to the case, whom Colin seemed to think would be more sympathetic.

Colin. As always, the thought of him brought a keen sense of regret. But maybe it was just as well that nothing had come of it. Maybe it was Randy who she was meant to be with. Could that be why he'd never remarried? Because deep down he'd been waiting for her all this time?

She was roused from her thoughts by Calpernia, who'd planted herself in front of Alice. Calpernia waved her arm in a shooing motion. "Go. Get. Baby, if you don't take a break, get yourself some R and R, you gonna trip on that long face of yours."

Alice shook her head and smiled, pretending to search for her claw cracker amid the pile of shells on the counter. Was she that transparent? With Colin, too, her feelings must be written all over her face. The realization made her cringe inside, feeling as vulnerable as she had in prison when her cellmate, Norma Fuentes, had gotten hold of her journal and read passages aloud.

When Calpernia showed no sign of backing off, Alice protested, "I can't just *leave*. What about all this?" She gestured to take in the crabs still to be cracked, the vegetables to be chopped, the chickens breasts to be butterflied. And that was just for starters.

"I ain't exactly sitting here on my butt." Calpernia planted her hands on her hips, wearing an obstinate look. The word no wasn't in her vocabulary. "And if that homie can't handle a little heat in the kitchen, he in the wrong profession," she said, referring to Terrel Louis, the short order cook who'd responded to the Help Wanted ad they'd placed and who, according to Calpernia, was the only other black person on the island. So far he was proving to be a good hire, but at the moment he was in town on an errand; he wouldn't be back for another hour at least. And Alice still had so much work to do . . .

"Really, I can't. I've taken so much time off already," she insisted, thinking of all the hours lost due to court appearances. It was amazing she was still in business.

"An hour or two won't kill you. Won't kill folks' appetite none, either. They be eating that food, same as always, if it was the devil himself who cooked it."

Seeing that her friend wasn't going to budge, Alice gave in at last. "All right. I'm going. But if we fall behind on orders, it's on you," she grumbled, slipping out of her not-so-white chef whites.

"Fine. Just tell me where you goin' off to, 'case we accidentally set the place on fire or something and need to reach you." Calpernia flashed her a wicked grin.

Alice had no idea where she was going, but on a whim, she said, "I may take a drive out to my grandmother's old place. I hear it's for sale."

She'd hadn't been back since it was sold, years ago, and as she headed out back to where her car was parked, she was reminded of all the happy times she'd spent there. Her nana hadn't been one to sit still—the only times Alice could remember her being off her feet was when she was knitting or sewing, and even then her hands had never stopped moving—but she'd never been too busy for her grandchildren.

Alice smiled, as she climbed into her car and turned the key in the ignition, thinking that if she knew how to cook, it was mainly due to her nana, who'd taught her to trust her instincts. She recalled her first attempt at making cornbread, when she was nine, with Nana supervising.

How much flour, Nana? she'd asked, poised on the step stool at the kitchen counter.

Oh, I always put in a couple of handfuls, Nana had said, standing at her elbow, wearing the flowered apron, faded from many washings, that had seemed as much a part of her as the hand reaching into the flour bin.

But my hand is smaller than yours, Alice had replied, frowning down at her stubby fingers.

That's why we have eyes and mouths. Nana had smiled and tapped the side of her head, where her crinkly hair that was the color of old pennies was growing gray. *You don't become a good cook by following recipes, Allie*—Nana was the only one who'd called her that—*any more than you can learn to ride a bike by reading a manual. It's about feel and taste, and having the courage to experiment*. When the batter was ready, she'd had Alice dip a finger in to taste it. *Now tell me, quick, does it need more salt? Is that the right amount of sugar?*

Alice had told her it could use a bit more salt and Nana had beamed at her as if she'd solved a difficult math equation. *You see? You're a natural. Next time, you won't need my help*.

Thinking back on it now, Alice realized that it had been a lesson in more than cooking. Her nana had wanted her to have the courage to experience life in the same way. Maybe because her own had been one of compromises. Alice pondered that as she made her way in her car along the familiar winding road to Eleanor's house, a road lined with trees—Douglas firs, madronas, maples—that grew as thick as the memories crowding her head. Memories she'd drawn strength from while in prison, for that was what had been at the core of Eleanor's strength as well: She'd endured. Not only the war and the loss of her husband (for the man she'd seen off to battle wasn't the same man who'd returned) but the greatest loss of all, that of her true love.

Alice remembered the far-off look her nana would sometimes get. She'd be in the midst of some task, peeling potatoes or pulling weeds in the garden, when suddenly she would pause to gaze sightlessly out the window or to rock back on her heels on the loamy ground, staring off into the distance. The muscles in her face would loosen, and it would grow soft, girlish almost, with the same dreaming-awake look she'd worn in the portrait William McGinty had painted of her.

It was the portrait that had provided the final clue to the mystery. Now, piecing it together with what she'd learned, Alice finally understood: It was William for whom Eleanor had yearned.

There might still have been a chance for them late in life, but, sadly, when Grandpa Joe died of a stroke, in '86, Eleanor had followed shortly after. There had been a small tumor on her liver that her doctor had been keeping his eye on. While she'd been caring for her husband, it had remained inactive, neither growing nor shrinking, but as soon as she was no longer responsible for him it had begun to metastasize at an alarming rate. Almost as if, having willed it into submission, she could finally let go of her grip. Within six months, she was gone, buried beside her husband in the small graveyard behind the church of which her father had been pastor.

Alice wondered if it was the same graveyard in which William had been lain to rest. It would be fitting somehow, that the lovers be reunited in death. Though from what she knew about William, it would have been more his nature to have been cremated, his ashes scattered over the ocean or the wild, windswept cliffs he'd captured so vividly on canvas.

Half an hour later she was pulling into the drive at her nana's house. It was overgrown in spots with the brambles and weeds her grandmother had battled in her lifetime, now run riot, though the potholes she remembered had been filled in. In the field off to her right, she saw a flash of red amid the brown grass—a crossbill. She remembered that crossbills didn't fly south for the winter, a fact she'd learned from her grandmother. The long walks they used to go on had been more than recreational, Nana calling out the name of every plant and bird, animal and insect; pointing out a bald eagle riding the thermals, or pulling a branch out of a pond to show her the jellylike sac clinging to it, dotted with black specks that would become salamanders.

It's just nature. Nana would say with a laugh, when Alice wrinkled her nose in disgust. *It's not always pretty, but it always has a purpose. And what could be more beautiful than that?*

Her nana had taught her to listen for the frogs that heralded spring, and to appreciate the music they made, chorusing in the ponds and marshes; to spot the dark flash of brown bats diving after insects in the twilight and the woolly bear caterpillars that clung to the undersides of leaves, soon to morph into tiger moths. In winter, there had been lessons in picking out various animal tracks from among the delicate tracery that crisscrossed the snow.

The modest house at the end of the drive seemed almost an afterthought, tucked behind a curly-barked madrona twisted with age, a tree that had always reminded Alice of a wizened old man, his back bent under a heavy load. A new-model Plymouth was parked in the turnabout. She pulled to a stop behind it and was climbing out of her car when a woman emerged from the house—petite with short blond hair, smartly dressed in a pantsuit and low-heeled pumps. The realtor, no doubt. With her was a middle-aged couple, prospective buyers presumably. She caught sight of Alice and paused to murmur something to her clients before walking briskly toward her.

"Hi! Are you here to look at the house?" she asked, when she'd caught up.

"Actually, no. This used to be my grandmother's place," Alice told her. "I heard it was for sale and I happened to be driving past . . . "

The woman brightened. "Oh! You must mean Missus Styles."

Alice nodded. "She was here a long time, over fifty years." Eleanor had seemed as much a fixture as that old madrona. So much so that when the house was sold after her death, the sense of loss Alice had felt had been almost as acute as when she'd watched her nana's coffin being lowered into the ground.

"Sylvia Brenner," the woman introduced herself, putting out a manicured hand. "Let me give you my card." She reached into the oversize leather bag slung over one shoulder.

Alice tucked it into her pocket, saying, "Do you mind if I take a look around?"

Some of the wattage went out of the realtor's smile and she glanced discreetly at her watch. Then her saleswoman's instincts kicked in, and Alice could almost hear her thinking, *You never know. It could lead to something.* "Not in the least," she said. "Why don't you have a look around inside while I show these folks the rest of the property. The front door's unlocked."

Moments later Alice was stepping through the door, assailed by the scents she associated with visits to her grandmother, that of old woodwork steeped in lemon oil, pine logs and smoke-blackened chimney bricks . . . and the dogs, of course. She didn't know if the current owners had pets, but that doggy smell, as musky and familiar as the old blanket by the stove that her nana's border collies used to sleep on when they were allowed inside, was so distinct she half expected that any minute she'd be greeted by a wet nose and a wagging tail.

The house, too, was pretty much as she remembered it. The knotty pine walls in the living room and brass chandelier suspended by a dusty chain from the crossbeam; the river rock hearth where they used to pop popcorn over the open fire in a long-handled wire basket. As she wandered from room to room, she could see that the current owners had made some changes, such as replacing the old chiffarobes in the bedrooms with built-in closets and updating the thirties kitchen cabinets, but the essential spirit of the house was the same. It was in the kitchen that Alice felt her grandmother's presence most strongly. The curtains drawn over the open window might have been fluttering with the air stirred by Eleanor's ceaseless motion. Alice could almost see her pacing back and forth between the table and stove as she laid out supper, a path she'd traveled so many times her feet had worn away the linoleum in spots. She'd never appeared frazzled or in a hurry, but the sheer volume of what she had to accomplish in a day seemed staggering to Alice now, looking back on it through the eyes of an adult.

First thing each morning there had been Grandpa Joe to bathe and dress, a task he hadn't made any easier when he was having what Eleanor had called one of his "spells." If he'd had an accident in the night, which he became prone to in his later years, she would have to strip the mattress and put it out to air. All that before she'd even gotten breakfast on the table. The rest of the day, when she wasn't tending to her husband, was spent cleaning house, cooking and sewing, and gardening in summer. Sunday had been the one day of the week when she'd rested, after a fashion. Alice couldn't remember her ever going to church—that hadn't been Nana's style—but on afternoons when Grandpa Joe was napping she would go on long walks, taking Alice and Denise along if they happened to be staying over.

By that time, she'd long since boarded up the kennel, keeping only a few dogs as pets—Rufus and Checkers, and their mother, Jewel, a sweet old thing who'd been named after a rhinestone collar she'd been given as a puppy. Alice remembered when Jewel died, how Nana had wept as though her heart would break. Alice had been stunned to come across her stretched out on the bed in her room with her face buried in the pillow to muffle her sobs. She'd never before seen her grandmother cry. Come to think of it, Alice couldn't recall ever having seen her lying down in the middle of the day.

Nana had sat up, patting the space beside her, and Alice had climbed up onto the bed. "Are you sad about Jewel?" she had asked.

Nana had brushed at the tears on her cheeks with an age-speckled hand. "Yes, honey, I'm sad about Jewel."

She'd started to choke up again, and Alice had put her arms around her, beseeching, "Don't cry, Nana."

Nana had stroked her cheek, smiling through her tears. "It's good to cry, Allie. It helps you remember."

"How does it do that?"

She'd paused, as if searching for the right words. "When you mourn for someone you loved, it's like they're still a part of you. The only way you can really lose someone is if you forget them."

It all made sense to Alice now: She'd been talking about William. She shivered now, in the cool of the old house, which even in summer didn't retain heat. Poor Nana. How had she been able to bear it, knowing the man she loved was so close yet so far from reach? There must have been times she'd longed to run away from her responsibilities, run to William. Especially once Lucy was grown. But she'd stayed, and by the time she was free of those responsibilities, it had been too late.

Alice's reverie was broken by the sound of a car pulling into the drive. Another prospective buyer, no doubt. Minutes later the old strap hinges on the front door let out a squeal, and Alice looked up to see an elongated shadow fall over the scuffed floorboards of the entryway. It was followed an instant later by the figure of a tall, black-haired man, world weary but handsome in a tortured-hero kind of way, with eyes the blue of a banked fire and the kind of face you could never grow tired of looking at.

"Colin," she cried softly. She'd been so wrapped up in thoughts of William and Eleanor, it was almost as if she were seeing a ghost. "What are you doing here?"

"I could ask the same of you," he said.

"This was my grandmother's house," she told him. "I'd heard it was for sale, and I wanted to see it one last time." Her gaze traveled about the room. For some reason, she was finding it difficult to meet his gaze.

"It's charming," he said, looking around.

"You still haven't told me what you're doing here," she said. "Don't tell me you're in the market for another house."

He shook his head. "Calpernia told me where to find you."

"You could have called me at work and saved yourself the trip. What was so important you had to drive all this way?"

"I wanted to give you the news in person." Alice felt herself tense, but he was smiling, so she knew that it couldn't be bad.

"I got a call from the D.A.'s office a little while ago. They've decided to drop the charges against Jeremy."

Alice was so stunned that for a moment all she could do was gape at him. "But how . . . ?"

"It seems Carrie Ann changed her story," he explained. "Without her testimony, there would be no case. Also, I suspect it had become a political hot potato."

It finally sank in, and Alice let out a whoop, jumping up off the sofa and throwing her arms around Colin. She might have been dreaming, if not for the very real presence of Colin in her arms, as solid and comforting as this house. With an effort, she drew back to ask, "Have you told Jeremy?"

"Not yet. I wanted you to be the first to hear it." Colin was grinning.

"I think I need to sit down." The muscles in Alice's legs gave way, and she plopped back down on the sofa. Colin sat down beside her. "Does this sort of thing happen very often?" she asked.

"Actually, it's pretty rare," he told her. "Usually they'll go for a lesser charge in exchange for a reduced sentence, if the defendant agrees to plead guilty. Sometimes, if it's a bigger fish they're after, they'll give immunity. But I've only seen them drop the charges this late in the game twice in my whole career. All I can say is, Jeremy's one lucky kid."

"Do you think it was just luck?"

"Who knows? He said something about having run into Carrie Ann at Bucky's the other night. Maybe that had something to do with it."

"Funny, he didn't mention it to me."

"He probably didn't want to worry you. You know, in case she took out a restraining order or something."

"Am I that much of a worry wart?"

He smiled. "You're a mother. It's your job to worry."

She hadn't thought of it that way. *My job*. The realization drifted down through old, encrusted layers of guilt and self-recrimination. "Thank you for coming all this way to tell me," she said, her throat tight.

"My pleasure, but I'm afraid my motives were more personal than professional."

Alice saw from the look on his face that something had changed for him, that whatever he'd been struggling with before, it had lifted. She felt herself grow still, and she had a sense that things were about to change for her, too.

"I've been doing a lot of thinking," he went on. "Mostly about the ways I've screwed up, but about my grandfather too. How sad it must have been for him, losing the two people he'd loved most in the world. There was nothing he could have done about Eleanor, I suppose. But he tried hard with my dad. I think if he were here now he'd give me the same advice. He'd tell me not to give up on something this good before I'd even given it a chance."

She knew then that she hadn't imagined it: The connection between them was real. As real as the man sitting beside her now. "Your grandfather sounds like a smart man," she said.

"He was. Just unlucky in love."

"And you?"

Colin took her hand, lacing his fingers through hers. "I'm two down in the ninth inning, but the game isn't over yet."

"I didn't know you were a baseball fan," she observed, with a giddy little laugh.

"Growing up in my house, it would have been hard not to be. Though I think I was the only kid in Bayside who couldn't hit a fastball to save his life." His expression turned serious. "Look, Alice, I know I'm a little late to the game on this one. I was so busy feeling sorry for myself, I couldn't see what was right in front of my nose. But I realized something the other day—that we don't always get a second chance in life. I don't want to lose you, too." In a more formal tone, he added, "I guess what I'm asking is, if you're willing to take a chance on a down-and-out lawyer with nothing to show for himself except a dog that doesn't belong to him and an oyster farm that so far hasn't made a dime."

"I happen to love oysters," she said. "I love dogs, too."

"Should I take that as yes?"

Her heart was so full that she had difficulty finding the words. Then together they rose, unbidden, as though it were scripted by an unseen hand. "Don't you know? You've already given me more than I could ever ask. All that matters to me is that you haven't given up, on yourself . . . on us. I can live with just about anything else, as long as I have that."

His face was that of a man who'd emerged from the shadows into sunlight, clear of any doubt. As he drew her into his arms in a slow kiss that seeped through her like water through porous rock, a memory stirred in her: how it had felt stepping out of the prison walls after her release, how she'd stood there a moment on the sidewalk with her eyes closed, feeling the sunlight on her skin and taking in deep breaths of air that had seemed newly invented just for her. Alice felt that way now, as though she'd been set free.

Sylvia, the realtor, chose that moment to poke her head through the doorway. "Oh!" she cried, looking startled and a little embarrassed to have found Alice kissing a strange man, as if it were their house and she the interloper. "I'm sorry. I came to lock up. Would you and your husband like to make an appointment to come back another time?"

Husband. Alice and Colin exchanged a smile at the misunderstanding. Not yet, she thought, and maybe not for a long, long while. If ever. But it had a nice ring to it.

EPILOGUE

One year later

From the backseat of the cab, which was stalled in midtown traffic, Colin peered up at the Swarovski crystal snowflake suspended high above Fifty-Seventh Street, twinkling like the Star of Bethlehem. It filled him with holiday cheer, as did the street below, with its festive displays and fairy lights illuminating the trees and storefronts. Christmas in New York. He hadn't realized until now how much he'd missed the city, especially this time of year.

He turned to Alice. "You okay?" She'd been so quiet all evening, he worried that she might be finding this all too overwhelming.

She nodded and slipped a gloved hand into his. "I was just thinking that we have a lot riding on this."

He smiled, giving her hand a little squeeze. "First-time jitters. Don't worry, it'll pass."

He ought to know. He'd been to enough auctions with his parents through the years. William had been generous in sending them paintings from time to time, and whatever hadn't been sold to dealers was auctioned off. Colin felt a pang of regret now, at how those gifts had been cashed in, seemingly without a scrap of sentiment. But he supposed that had been William's intention, and the money had always been put to good use. It had tided them over during the period his dad had been out of work with a bad back and paid for Colin's college education.

Colin's own decision to auction off William's last remaining work had nothing to do with economic need, at least not his own—though he could have used the money. It had to do with Spring Hill. The big money interests behind its development, seeing that it would likely be tied up in court for the foreseeable future, had done the sensible thing in offering to sell it to the county, for the "rock bottom" sum of fifteen million. Local conservancy groups had done their part in raising some of the money, with corporate sponsors and a few wealthy benefactors kicking in, but that still left a shortfall of several million. The money realized from the sale of Eleanor's portrait, if it sold for anything close to the estimate, would cover a good portion of that.

That was where they were headed now, to Sotheby's. The auction, for works of important twentieth-century artists, would draw wealthy art patrons, museum curators, and dealers from all over the world. *Woman in Red*, featured prominently in the catalogue, had already garnered a fair bit of interest, and hopes were high for a price that would break the record for previous sales of William McGinty's works.

It seemed fitting to Colin that the money go to such a worthy cause. It was what his grandfather would've wanted, for it would provide in death what had eluded William in life: It would bring him closer to Eleanor in a way, in helping preserve the land she'd loved. A bittersweet resolution that had Colin closing his eyes for a moment, reflecting upon all that had happened over the past year. When he opened them again, he found Alice looking at him in consternation.

"Country life must seem pretty quiet compared to this." Her tone was light, but he knew she was wondering how much of this trip was, for him, tied up in memories of Nadine. "Do you miss the bright lights?"

"Not a bit. For one thing, I don't know that I would've stayed sober here. Also, more importantly, I wouldn't have met you." He kissed her lightly on the lips, thinking she'd never looked more beautiful. Like the portrait whose image she resembled, she glowed in this setting, a rare gem in a vault of more ordinary ones.

"Good answer." Her face relaxed in a smile. "Though I wouldn't mind staying an extra day or two. I feel like we've barely made a dent."

"We have all day tomorrow," he reminded her. "If the weather's nice, I'll take you to the top of the Empire State Building. The view is pretty amazing. You can see all the way to New Jersey. Unless there's something else you'd rather do," he added, noting the uncertain look she wore.

She was silent for a moment before venturing, "I thought you might like to visit Ground Zero."

Now it was his turn to fall silent, the memories crowding in on him. At last, he shook his head, saying, "This may sound strange, but for me it's just a hole in the ground. Wherever Nadine is, it's not there." He was surprised by the ease with which he was able to talk about his wife. There had been a time, in the not-so-distant past, when the mere thought of her would have sent him reeling into darkness . . . typically the darkness of the nearest bar.

She would always be a part of him, he knew, but what had changed was that he'd stopped believing his own life had ended that day. Alice was living proof of that. With her, he'd rediscovered the wonder, not only of loving again, but of being alive.

Marriage was still a ways off, but he was working on that. First, he had to convince Alice to move in with him. So far she'd resisted, arguing that she needed to focus on Jeremy right now, but lately Colin had sensed he was wearing her down. They were talking about taking a trip to Italy next summer, all three of them. Jeremy was excited by the prospect. Jeremy also had his eye on the spare room Colin had subtly hinted could be his.

"Your dad ever get back to you about tonight?" she was asking him now.

Colin felt a familiar tightening inside, like he always did whenever the subject of his family arose. "Yeah, he's not coming." A bitter note crept into his voice. "His excuse is that Marma's sick and he wants to stay nearby in case she needs anything."

"What about your mom?"

Colin shook his head. "If she came without him, she'd never hear the end of it."

"Don't be too hard on them," Alice said gently. "They're not doing it to hurt you. It's just . . . they have a vested interest in keeping things the way they are. Anyway, I'm glad I got to meet them, at least."

Colin brightened, thinking about the afternoon they'd spent over at his parents' house. Alice had gotten along with everyone, forever endearing herself to his mother by lending a hand with supper and the cleanup afterward, and winning points with his dad and his brother by showing interest in their favorite subject: sports. Even Marma had been won over, though there had been a tense moment in the beginning, when he'd introduced them and his grandmother had just stood there, staring at Alice as if at a ghost. But she'd rallied, for his sake more than anything, Colin suspected, and before long the two had been chatting like old friends.

"Speaking of which," he said, "Dad wanted me to know they all think you're something special." Not that Colin had needed to be told. "But I'm warning you. Now the pressure will be on. Don't be surprised if your Christmas present from my mom is a subscription to *Bride* magazine."

"I think I can handle it," she said with a laugh, not committing herself one way or the other.

Colin suppressed a sigh. He'd just have to be patient. She would come around eventually. In the meantime, life was good. He was still sober: In three month's time, he'd be getting his two-year chip. And the oyster farm was coming along nicely; already he had orders for his first harvest.

Before long the taxi was letting them off at the corner of East Seventy-second and York, where Sotheby's was located, a modernist cube of a building with a sheer expanse of glass in front that, lit from within, lent it a theatrical glow. Chauffeured limos were double-parked along the curb, clouds of vapor rising from their tailpipes in the frosty air, with more pulling up every minute. Colin helped Alice negotiate the icy sidewalk in her high heels, which she was unaccustomed to wearing, as they made their way toward the entrance, picking their way around the clumps of dirty snow left over from the storm that had dumped six inches on the city the week before.

Inside, they found themselves caught up in the crush of people gathered near the coat check. As they waited in line, snatches of conversation rose in the heated air, along with the mingled scents of perfume. . . . *The Noguchi alone has to be worth . . . Not one of her better works, in my opinion . . . Did you catch the exhibit at the Whitney?* After they'd handed over their coats, they made their way into the lobby, where they were greeted by an attractive young woman in a slim-fitting skirt and cowl-necked sweater, who directed them to the gallery on the second floor.

Yesterday, one of the senior directors at Sotheby's, an elegant bow-tied gentleman by the name of Spencer Morton, had given them a guided tour of the works that were to be auctioned off. When they had reached the portrait of Eleanor, he'd paused, commenting in a hushed voice, "The photos don't do it justice. It's truly magnificent. I wouldn't be surprised if it goes to one of the museums. Several have already expressed interest."

"I wish Denise could see this," Alice had remarked to Colin, after Morton had been pulled away to attend to some other business. "She always said our grandmother deserved to hang in a museum, after all she'd been through. Though knowing Nana, she'd have hated that. She didn't like drawing attention to herself. And the worst thing for her was sitting idle."

"Your sister would know a thing or two about that." Colin had smiled, thinking about the fact that it was partly due to Denise's efforts that Spring Hill had been saved.

"She certainly has her hands full at the moment," Alice had said, with a sigh. "The last time we spoke she sounded like she didn't know if she was coming or going."

"It takes a while to settle into a new place." Not only that, a new job—she'd found a teaching position at the local elementary school—and a husband who was still getting back on his feet. "I'll bet it would cheer her up if you came for a visit. In fact, if you want, we could stop on the way back." They could rent a car at SeaTac and drive to Spokane, he told her.

"I keep offering, and she keeps putting me off." Alice had worn a look of sad resignation. "She'll have me come when she's ready, I suppose." She missed her sister, he knew, but she also respected Denise enough to allow her the space she seemed to need.

Now, as he and Alice made their way through the gallery in search of empty seats, Colin thought that it was a miracle any of them were still standing. But here they were, and from the sizeable turnout, it looked as if their fortunes were about to improve even more. Luckily, they found two seats near the front, where they wouldn't have to crane their necks to see over people's heads. As Colin settled back in his chair, it hit him that this was it, no turning back now. His grandfather's most prized possession—more than that, his paean to his lost love—would soon be in the hands of a complete stranger, someone who would know nothing of its history, of the tortuous route it had traveled to arrive at this point. Colin felt a twinge of regret, and at the same time he knew that it was for the best.

The bidding commenced with a minor work by Egon Schiele followed by an Andy Warhol sketch. Both went for prices higher than their estimates, the Warhol to an anonymous bidder over the phone. The entire transaction had been conducted without so much as a hair being turned. The stylish older woman taking bids over the phone had only subtly lifted a finger with each new bid before finally, when the bidding reached its climax, confirming the buyer's intentions with an expressionless nod. She hadn't spoken a word, but every eye in the room had been fixed on her, as if on an actress doing a solo performance.

It was theatre, this business of auctioning off fine art, Colin thought. The auctioneer, a Brit from Central Casting, heralded each lot, as it was reverently placed on the spot-lit easel on the podium, in a voice like a drum roll. The hushed tension of the crowd, the hands going up holding their numbered paddles, as sums that would have dwarfed the average person's annual salary climbed ever higher into the stratosphere. Then the final moment when the auctioneer's gavel came down and the tension would go out of the room like an exhaled breath, replaced by a ripple of excited commentary, a smattering of applause.

Woman in Red came up in the second hour. The auctioneer gave his spiel, informing the audience of what they could see with their own eyes: that it was William McGinty's masterwork. The fact that it had been in private hands until now only added to its luster and to the air of mystery surrounding it. Colin, seeing it anew through their eyes, noted how it glowed in the spotlight, its colors as vibrant as when first painted, its subtle flesh tones breathing life into its long dead subject. As much a tribute to Eleanor as a work of art.

". . . Seventy-five thousand from the gentleman in the back . . . Do we have eighty?. . . A hundred. . . ?" The ever escalating numbers rolled smoothly off the auctioneer's tongue. He scarcely paused to take a breath as they rapidly went from high five to six, then seven figures.

Colin wasn't aware of how tightly he'd been holding Alice's hand until she winced at the pressure of his fingers.

She leaned in to whisper, "Who has that kind of money? Who *are* these people?"

One by one the bidders dropped out, until finally it was down to an anonymous phone bidder and an older Asian man in back whose paddle rose and fell as the numbers climbed to well over a million. Colin twisted around in his seat, trying to make him out amid the shifting sea of bodies—a round face, white hair combed straight back, a back as erect as the cane he clutched in his other hand. Colin could feel the tension around them mounting as the quietly fought battle continued, its intensity seeming to grow in inverse proportion to the languid hand movements of the Asian man and that of the Sotheby's employee acting on behalf of the phone bidder.

Colin was so tense himself he could scarcely draw a breath. Two million . . . three . . . three and a quarter. Finally, at just shy of three and a half million, the Asian man, wearing an impassive face, raised his paddle one last time. A hush fell over the room, all eyes now on the woman manning the phone. She murmured something to the person at the other end, and there was a pause during which Colin felt his heart buck up against his ribcage, then she shook her head to indicate that her bidder was withdrawing.

The auctioneer's gavel came down. Sold.

Alice looked as stunned as Colin. Before bidding commenced on the next lot, they quietly rose from their seats and made their way into the anteroom beyond, where they could talk in relative private.

"I can hardly believe it," she said. "My God, all that *money*. The guy must be seriously rich."

"Either that or he's representing someone who is," Colin speculated.

"I wonder what he plans on doing with it."

"Who knows? Lock it in a vault maybe." Colin certainly hoped that wouldn't be the case.

"Well, I just hope he appreciates the sacrifice, whoever he is."

They were heading for the stairs to the lower level when they noticed their mystery buyer waiting by the elevator. Up close, he looked even older, as he stood there leaning on his cane. And although the suit he wore was well-cut and his watch expensive, there was something humble about his appearance. He didn't look the sort to be throwing around millions.

His eyes lit up when they introduced themselves. "Ah, yes. I was hoping I would have an opportunity to meet you," he told Colin, speaking in perfectly enunciated English. "I am Mister Yamamoto. And you," he said, directing his smiling gaze toward Alice, "are the image of your grandmother."

"You knew her?" she replied, her eyes widening in surprise.

Mr. Yamamoto inclined his head in a reverent nod. "She was a great lady."

Alice shook her head in disbelief. "What an amazing coincidence." Then comprehension sank in, and she said, "It wasn't a coincidence, was it? That's why you're here."

Mr. Yamamoto inclined his head again. "You guessed correctly. And I will treasure your grandmother's portrait all the more because of our friendship." He turned to Colin. "I knew your grandfather as well. A good man. As kind as he was gifted."

"How did you come to know them, if you don't mind my asking?" Colin said.

Mr. Yamamoto smiled, a slow, remembering smile that transformed his wizened face into that of a much younger man. He said, "Please, if you are not in a hurry, come have a drink with me at my hotel. I will be flying back to Tokyo tomorrow, and there is much to tell."

Alice leaned forward impatiently. "Mister Yamamoto . . . "

"Yoshi, please," he corrected her. "Your grandmother always called me by my first name. She was like a mother to me, and now to my wife and children, whom I have taught to revere her memory."

"I don't understand. If you were so close, why is this the first I'm hearing of it?" Alice asked, looking perplexed.

The elevator pinged just then and its door slid open. With a smile, the old man took Alice by the elbow and gently but firmly steered her into the elevator, Colin stepping in behind them. "Come," he said. "Let us sit and discuss this at leisure. It's a long story."

Coming Soon from *New York Times* Bestselling Author,

Eileen Goudge

Once in a Blue Moon

HARDCOVER • OCTOBER 2009

Once in a Blue Moon is a new, emotionally-charged family drama, focusing on two sisters and their turbulent lives, both together and apart. In a dramatic conclusion that will forever alter both women's lives, Lindsay and Kerrie Ann are forced to unite against all odds, restoring belief in the unshakable bond of family and proving unequivocally that blood is thicker than water.

ISBN: 978-1-59315-534-6 • $24.95 US/$31.95 CAN

Now available in trade paperback from
New York Times Bestselling Author,

Eileen Goudge

Domestic Affairs

TRADE PAPERBACK

"Eileen Goudge deftly weaves multiple storylines into a seamless page-turner propelled by juicy secrets, skeletons in the closet, stunning betrayals and heart-wrenching reunions."

—WENDY CORSI STAUB, *New York Times* bestselling author of *Dead Before Dark*

"This is the ultimate indulgence—dramatic, involving, and ringing with emotional truth. This is a top-drawer author at the top of her game."

—SUSAN WIGGS, *New York Times* bestselling author of *Fireside*

ISBN: 978-1-59315-533-9 • $15.95 US/$20.00 CAN

Also available from *New York Times* Bestselling Author,

Eileen Goudge

The Diary

"I've always loved reading a good romance and this one . . . oh, this one, is special. The Diary is a lovely book, tender, poignant and touching. It really comes from Eileen's heart."

—Debbie Macomber
New York Times bestselling author of *Summer on Blossom Street*

TRADE PAPERBACK	HARDCOVER
978-1-59315-529-2	978-1-59315-543-8
$12.95 US/$15.00 CAN	$19.95 US/$23.00 CAN

THE SEEKERS

They found a land that was eager to accommodate their most wilful mistakes, their undenied weaknesses, their uninhibited attacks upon a destiny that must conquer and reject before it can make its chosen nation great.

The Boston of publishers and political squabbles . . . the society of George Washington as President and Thomas Jefferson as the sage of Monticello . . . the duty and sacrifice of war that becomes in only a few years the trials and terrors of the settlers, the pioneers of a West on the move . . . the homesteads oppressed by Indians . . . the crude opportunists from Tennessee to Ohio . . . drink, excess and disease . . . and new life, new hope, waving its pennant aboard the *Constitution* off Boston and from the home of Old Hickory in the South . . . Beleagured gentry—soldiers of fortune —women in love and with children—the Seekers find them all, stars in a panoramic sky that, quite literally, knows no charted nor settled horizon.

The Seekers

THE KENT FAMILY CHRONICLES VOLUME III

JOHN JAKES

A JOVE BOOK

Produced by Lyle Kenyon Engel

Twenty-four previous printings
First Jove edition published August 1978

10 9

Library of Congress Catalog Card Number: 75-21695

Printed in the United States of America

Jove books are published by Jove Publications, Inc.,
200 Madison Avenue, New York, NY 10016

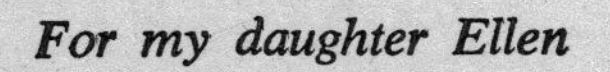

For my daughter Ellen

"Ask these Pilgrims what they expect when they git to Kentuckey the answer is Land. have you any. No, but I expect I can git it. have you any thing to pay for land, No. did you ever see the Country. No but Every Body says its good land . . .

"Here is hundreds Travelling hundreds of Miles, they Know not for what Nor Whither, except its to Kentuckey, passing land almost as good and easy obtained, the Proprietors of which would gladly give on any terms but it will not do . . . its not the Promised Land its not the goodly inheratence the Land of Milk and Honey."

1796:
Moses Austin,
founder of Texas,
writing of a journey
from Wythe County, Virginia,
to Louisiana Territory.

"I of course expected to find beaver, which with us hunters is a primary object, but I was also led on by the love of novelty common to all, which is much increased by the pursuit of its gratification . . ."

1827:
the journal of
Jedediah Smith,
mountain man.

Contents

Book Three

Voices of War

Book Four

Cards of Fate

The Seekers

Book One

Kent and Son

CHAPTER I

Battle Morning

ABOUT FOUR O'CLOCK Abraham Kent woke from a fitful sleep and realized he couldn't rest again until the day's action was concluded, in the Legion's favor or otherwise.

His heart beat rapidly as he lay sweating in the tiny tent. He heard muted voices outside; saw a play of flame and shadow on the tent wall. Campfires; burning brightly in the sweltering dark. No attempt had been made to conceal the presence of three thousand men on the north bank of the Maumee River. The Indians already knew that the general who commanded the army of the Fifteen Fires had arrived, and meant to fight. The only question was when.

Abraham had learned the answer to that the preceding evening. Sitting his mare in formation, he'd listened to the reading of the general order that announced a march at daybreak. Men cheered—principally some of the less disciplined Kentucky mounted militia, whose ranks numbered close to fifteen hundred.

On hearing the order, Abraham Kent felt both relief and sharp fear. Relief came from knowing that nearly two years of preparation, marching, fort-building in the wilderness of the Northwest Territory was finally reaching a climax. The general had repeatedly sent messages to the tribes, urging peace and conciliation even as he drove his Legion of the United States deeper into the lands north of the Ohio, constructing stockade after stockade en route. The reply of the tribes to the last message had been equivocal. So the general had let it be known he meant to attack.

Abraham Kent experienced fear on hearing the order because he'd never taken part in an actual engagement; not in all the twenty-four months since he'd arrived in Pittsburgh in response to the recruiting notices in Boston. Those notices declared that the United States was raising a formal army for the first time since the Revolution.

There had been engagements as the American army twisted back and forth across the hostile country, earning the general the name *Blacksnake* from the Indian spies who watched the army's progress. Earlier in the summer, for example, a Shawnee war party had launched a ferocious attack on newly built Fort Recovery. When it happened Abraham was on duty at the general's base, Fort Greenville, a day's ride south. So he had yet to be blooded.

Today, the twentieth of August, 1794, that situation was likely to change.

He crawled out of the tent, his linen shirt and trousers already plastered to his body. For a moment he wondered whether he would see the dawn of the twenty-first.

Scouts had brought reports into the camp beside the river that upwards of two thousand Indians had gathered some seven to ten miles northeast, near the rapids of the Maumee where the British had brazenly erected a fort close to McKee's trading station. Warriors from all the major tribes had come: Blue Jacket's Shawnee, including the young warrior with the fierce reputation, Tecumseh, who had led the unsuccessful attack on Fort Recovery. Little Turtle's Miamis were there. The Wyandots under Tarhe the Crane. Captain Pipe's Delawares.

All united to resist the Americans who were bent on taking the Indians' land—

Not a man in the Legion of the United States considered it anything but American land, of course. The vast expanse west of Pennsylvania, east of the Mississippi, north of the Ohio and south of the Lakes had been ceded to the new nation by Britain as part of the peace treaty of 1783. Yet in the following decade, the British continued to maintain their posts in the surrendered territory; kept urging the Indians to demand that the northern border of American expansion remain the Ohio River.

Small expeditionary forces had marched into the Northwest before, to try to settle matters. One, St. Clair's, had met death along the bend of the Wabash tributary where Abraham's commanding general had built Fort Recovery the preceding winter. Yawning and stretching as he walked past the men talking around the campfires, Abraham vividly recalled the stone-gray winter's day he had ridden as one of the eight hundred pressing forward to the site of St. Clair's defeat—

In the first drifting snowflakes, he had seen skulls and bones protruding from the frozen ground. As the new fort rose on the site during the early months of 1794, men working the earth dug up and counted the human skulls. Over six hundred of them. Six hundred of General Dicky Butler's soldiers, slaughtered—

Abraham ambled on through the steamy darkness, breathing the acrid wood smoke; listening to the strained, subdued conversations; seeing here and there a surreptitious jug passed, in violation of the general's edict forbidding use of alcohol in camp or on the march. Nineteen years old, the young soldier had wide shoulders and a stocky build; heavy brows and the dark eyes of his parents. He'd also inherited their dark hair, which he never bothered to dress since dashing about on horseback loosened all the powder. He stood five feet ten inches, taller than his father.

Abraham passed the end of an earthwork. Behind it, the general had deposited the army's baggage and wagons, in case they needed to be defended during a retreat. Outside a command tent Abraham saw aides conferring with Captain Zebulon Pike, who'd been put in charge of the rear position. He strode by the circle of lantern light, swatting mosquitoes that deviled his neck, and soon reached the picket lines where the dragoon horses fretted and stamped in the pre-dawn heat.

A sentry thrust out his musket:

"Who goes?"

"Cornet Kent. I want to see to my mount."

The sentry saluted the junior officer, stood aside. Abraham ducked between two nervous stallions, found his mare at her tether, ran his hand down her neck, soothing her as if she were human:

"I hope they fed and watered you well, Sprite. You'll need to be lively when the sun's up. They say the Indians have taken positions among some fallen trees destroyed by a storm a long time ago. That'll be hard ground for galloping and jumping, my girl—"

The mare nipped at his caressing hand, but not viciously. Abraham smiled. In two years, he and the mare assigned him at Cincinnati had established a bond between them; the kind of bond infantrymen and other, lesser orders of human beings could never comprehend. Like the other dragoon officers, Abraham talked to his horse frequently. He knew Sprite recognized his voice if not the sense of his words. Now he almost spoke his fear aloud to the animal; almost launched into a monologue concerning the special reason he was apprehensive about the coming battle. He had admitted the reason to few other human beings; he admitted it to himself only with some shame—

Oh, he was a good enough soldier, he supposed. But his motive for enlisting—for making the difficult overland journey to Pittsburgh—had not been purely patriotic. He had no desire for glory in battle, and hence feared combat perhaps more than some officers did—

Noticing the sentry watching him, Abraham kept it all to himself. After one more stroke of Sprite's sweating neck, he turned and made for the river, feeling a steady pressure in his loins.

He was again thankful that his father's business had prospered sufficiently to permit him to go riding on the Common on a fine hired mount when he was growing up. Abraham was likewise thankful that his stepmother had encouraged the lessons in horsemanship. Except for that, he would never have been accepted for the dragoons.

But astride Sprite, and commanded by an excellent officer—a captain with the peculiar name Robert Mis-Campbell—Abraham knew that in the coming battle, he would be less of a target than those in the four Sub-legions who advanced on foot with bayonet-tipped muskets. Whether the general's combined infantry and cavalry stood a chance against the untrained but elusively swift tribesmen waiting somewhere up the Maumee, he couldn't say. That made him even more glad that he was going into danger on an animal he loved and trusted.

A trampled patch of corn and the charred smell of a burned Indian lean-to told him he was nearing the shore. He smelled the wet loam of the bottoms; heard night birds crying among the rushes. The stars were lost in a humid haze. He unfastened the buttons of his trousers and started to urinate in the river.

While in this prosaic but somewhat restrictive position, he heard slow footsteps along the bank.

He turned his head, choked back an exclamation as

he recognized the man limping out of the darkness, a rangy silhouette against the distant fires.

Faced with the choice of saluting or closing up his trousers, he decided on the latter. Only afterward did he whip up his right hand in the respectful gesture due the tall, somewhat rotund officer whose left boot and pants leg were almost entirely swathed in strips of flannel.

Major General Wayne—admiringly called Mad Anthony ever since his daring seizure of the British fort at Stony Point during the Revolution—rested a hand on the butt of one of the two pistols thrust into his belt and stared at Abraham Kent, whose face all at once felt hotter than ever.

ii

The general, appearing rather bedraggled in his old blue coat, leather sword belt and leg-bandages, smiled at last:

"Cornet Kent. Good evening to you. Good morning, rather."

"Good morning, sir," Abraham managed to say in a reasonably calm voice.

Wayne hobbled toward him; Abraham guessed the general must be close to fifty now. Supposedly his left leg still contained a piece of ball lodged there during the Virginia campaign at the close of the War for Independence. He had been called out of retirement to head the army sent west by President Washington to quell the Indian threat in the Northwest Territory once and for all.

Wayne's men loved him; Abraham was no exception. The Indians dreaded him because it seemed that he was never off guard; never slept; knew everything that transpired for miles around whatever position he happened to be occupying.

In gentle reproof, Wayne said, "I urged my men to

get as much sleep as possible, Cornet. All my men."

"Yes, sir, but—well, sir, that's hard, facing an engagement as we are—"

To Abraham's relief, Wayne nodded. "As you can tell from my presence here, I understand perfectly. I hope our red adversaries aren't resting. I know they're not eating," he added with a thin smile.

Abraham knew the meaning of Wayne's last words, of course. The general's stratagem had been the talk of the camp for two days:

Via his scouts, Wayne had let slip word that he intended to fight, knowing full well that, by custom, the Indians would never eat on the morning of a battle. For that reason Wayne had carefully refrained from mentioning exactly when he intended to engage. Thus the enemy had probably taken little or no nourishment for almost forty-eight hours.

Wayne stumped closer. As always, the general's limp reminded Abraham of his father's, the result of a hit by a musket ball at the battle of Monmouth Court House. The general asked:

"Did the last pouches of mail from Cincinnati bring any word of your father, Cornet?"

"Yes, sir, I had a letter. He's recovered from the grippe that kept him in bed for a time. His business continues to do well."

"Success evidently runs in the family. Captain Mis-Campbell informs me you're an exemplary junior officer."

"That's good to hear, sir—thank you for telling me."

Wayne had acknowledged his acquaintance with Abraham's father when Abraham first reached the training camp at Legionville, down the Ohio from Pittsburgh. Part of Abraham's reverence for the general was due to his father having fought beside Mad Anthony in the Revolution. During the retreat after the American defeat at Brandywine Creek, Philip Kent had joined the reckless young officer in a charge against some Hessians harrying the retreat route. And Philip often referred with pride to standing with Wayne a second time at Monmouth Court House.

Wayne stared at the dark-flowing river. "May I ask you a personal question, Cornet?"

"Of course, sir."

"It comes to mind because you are an excellent officer, and because I remember your father so well. Do you intend to make the army a career?"

Abraham hesitated a moment, then decided to answer truthfully:

"No, sir. I imagine I'll go back to Boston when the campaign's over."

"Perhaps that will be accomplished by this time tomorrow. There is a very great deal at stake in the next few hours—"

"I'm aware of that, sir."

So was virtually every man in the Legion. The Northwest Ordinance, passed by the Congress in 1787, had wisely promised the creation of new states—no less than three, no more than five—once the territory was pacified and settled. Each new state would be fully equal with those fifteen already established under the country's federal Constitution, which had become law when the ninth of thirteen original states, New Hampshire, ratified it in 1788. Abraham knew that thousands of settlers were waiting along the eastern seaboard for the chance to start new lives in the western territory. But they were held back by fear of the Indian menace.

Just as important, President Washington had recently sent Chief Justice John Jay to England to attempt to negotiate a new treaty with the king's ministers. The status of the Northwest was one of the points at issue. Under the peace settlement, the territory unquestionably belonged to America. But if Britain could in effect hold it illegally—hold it by means of Crown agents inciting the tribes in order to prevent an inrush of settlers—Jay could never hope to gain a re-confirmation on paper of America's claim to the land.

Picking up the conversation, Wayne said, "I'm sorry to hear the military will eventually lose your services, Cornet. Still, I'm not entirely surprised. Ever since you enlisted, I have frankly wondered why a young man of your background—your prospects for the future—would risk himself in an enterprise of this sort."

Caught off guard, Abraham replied haltingly, "Someone must if the territory's to be secured—"

"Oh, I'm not questioning your patriotism. But I've found that in the Legion, most of the men have at least one other motive for joining our hazardous venture. Wives they regret marrying, for example—"

"I'm single, General."

"Debts, then."

"No, I haven't that problem."

"I should imagine not." Bleak, tired eyes ranged the murmuring river where a heat mist was beginning to form. "Sometimes the motive for a man staying in the army is simply an inability to endure other, comparatively tame endeavors once the man has tasted battle—" That, Wayne's officers well knew, was the general's own spur.

Wayne turned slightly, his eyes reflecting the distant fires. Those glowing eyes prodded Abraham to another honest reply:

"Well, sir, in my case that doesn't apply either. I left home because my father and I were having our differences."

"Over what, may I ask?"

"My future. Specifically, my future with the family printing house. My father wanted me to study at Harvard a year or so, then join him in the business. I honestly couldn't decide whether I wanted that. With so much happening in the country—all this new land opening—it seemed, to use your word, a tame alternative."

"So you chose a period in the army to think things over?"

"Exactly, sir. I'm afraid my father and I had quite a few loud and lengthy arguments on the subject. On many other subjects, too. We don't see eye to eye on politics, for instance."

Wayne nodded. "I'm familiar with Kent and Son publishing tracts in support of Mr. Hamilton's Federalist views."

"Quite right, sir. And if you'll forgive my saying so, it's always struck me as damned odd that men who were so violently anti-British twenty years ago are now anxious to establish strong commercial and political ties with that country."

"A matter of economics," Wayne shrugged. "Think of the market in England for ship's timbers, for instance. Good northeastern oak and pine to build dreadnoughts for the most powerful navy in the world—who wants to lose trade like that? No wonder nearly all of New England's gone Federalist—"

"I'm a New Englander and I haven't, sir. I personally see nothing wrong with Mr. Jefferson's support of the revolution in France."

"You'll have to agree it's fallen into bloody excess."

"Yes, but—"

"And still Mr. Jefferson and many of the others in the Virginia junto continue to champion its democratic principles. If they exist any longer!—which I doubt. Ah, but let's not debate that. We have a more immediate enemy—"

Abraham wasn't quite ready to drop the subject, though:

"Part of the trouble at home comes from the fact that my father's grown wealthy. Achieved a status that encourages him to think like an aristocrat—"

"The father's a Federalist, the son isn't—and under those circumstances, a term of service in the army seemed prudent in order to maintain the domestic peace?" Wayne's voice had a wry sound. But Abraham's answer was straightforward:

"Exactly."

And that one word concealed much: the turmoil, the rancor that had shaken the Kent household until Philip had finally given grudging permission for his son to enlist under Wayne's command. Something compelled Abraham to add:

"The solution's only temporary anyway. I'm sure that when I go home, the arguments will start all over again."

Wayne didn't comment immediately. With a touch of chagrin, Abraham realized he had already poured out a good deal of what ought to be considered private information. But as long as the general was willing to listen, Abraham supposed the talk didn't hurt. In a way the confession relieved him. He seldom had a chance to air the problem that continually nagged at his mind. As he'd intimated, it was a problem for which a permanent solution would have to be found eventually.

Wayne brushed a hand absently over one cheek, squashing an insect. He smiled that weary smile again:

"Fathers and sons at loggerheads—that was the central issue of the war for independence, you know. The right of the new blood to run its own course—freely. Well, Cornet, if the army doesn't suit you as a career, and if you've no heart to spend your days in a prosperous Federalist printing firm—"

"I just haven't decided, sir," Abraham broke in. "My

father wished for me to do so immediately. That's why I had to strike out on my own for a time."

Once more the relatively glib explanation hid other meanings. Abraham felt a momentary sense of his own shameful, innate weakness—

No, no, that was the wrong term. Unbearably demeaning. Call it not weakness but indecision born of family loyalty. He loved his father even though he resented Philip's strong opinions. And, deep down, Abraham supposed he'd eventually succumb to his father's wish that he join Kent and Son. But at his young age, he didn't want that decision forced on him by fiat—

So he'd run away. No other description would do. Again he was face to face with a suspected failure of character that troubled him often; a failure he struggled to rationalize away by convoluted explanations involving family love and devotion—

Listening to the night insects, he recalled abruptly where he was, and why. A coldness filled his belly. The question of his future might soon become entirely academic. There was a battle to be fought. Men died in battle.

As if hunting for stars behind the sky's haze, Wayne tilted his graying head back. "I can suggest an alternative to commerce or the army, Cornet. You could settle out here."

Mildly astonished, Abraham replied, "Why, yes, sir, I suppose I could. Truthfully, that's never occurred to me before."

"When we raised the stockade at the confluence of this river and the Aux Glaize—" The general was referring to the fort he'd christened Defiance. "—I was struck by the remarkable beauty and fertility of the land. Nature's dealt bountifully with it. A man could hew his house from these forests. Fill his table from the trails and streams—" A boot scraped a furrow in the loam of the bank. "—raise enough crops in this soil to provide for his household and have ample corn meal or flour left to transship across the Great Lakes, or back up the Ohio in exchange for the manufactured goods he needs. You know what they call me these days. One of the old Revolutionary war horses. I suppose I'll never shed the label—nor lose the urge to lead men. But I've found that life on the land can be very good. Very good. I own a rice plantation in the south—Hazzard's Cow-pen, it's called. A gift of the people of the state of Georgia for my services during the rebellion—" His voice had grown dreamy, remote. "Yes, a man could do far worse than to stay here when the battle's done—"

Abraham had to admit the idea was intriguing. Escape to a homestead in the Northwest Territory would solve his problem with his father. As Wayne said, a man could live well. *If* the Indian threat were gone—

Abraham's brief enthusiasm faded as footsteps approached. Northward along the Maumee, his whole life could be decided in an instant. It could end in an instant. The recollection of that set his palms itching and started rivulets of sweat trickling down his neck to his linen collar.

He'd been foolishly carried away by Wayne's remarks. Even if he survived his first test in battle, the chance of pulling away from his father was a slim one. Philip Kent would not easily loose his hold on his son—

Abraham put the whole vexing question out of mind, turning along with Wayne as a wiry young officer approached. The officer carried his cockaded bicorn hat under his arm. Despite the semi-darkness, Abraham recognized one of the general's aides, William Henry Harrison.

Harrison saluted. Wayne returned it smartly. "What is it, Lieutenant?"

"The barber has arrived at the headquarters tent, sir."

"Ah, yes—" Wayne smiled again. "I don't want to lead the Legion with my hair unpowdered and disarrayed." The general's vanity, like his courage, was familiar to the men he commanded. But on the wilderness march, he'd had few chances to indulge his penchant for elegance. Care of his hair was one of the rare exceptions.

Stifling a groan and clamping a hand around his bandaged left leg, Wayne started to hobble off. The mist hanging over the Maumee had begun to turn a pearly color. A few drooping willow branches were discernible in the murk now. Dawn—

Wayne stopped, glanced back.

"Whenever I've had the opportunity to speak privately with one or more of my officers, I have acquainted them with a letter I recently received from the secretary of war—"

"General Knox is a friend of my father's, sir."

"Then your father is fortunate. Henry Knox is a sagacious man. He wrote to say that the nation has waited two years for this morning. So have the hundreds of thousands seeking to leave the seacoast. And those six hundred brave men whose remains will stay forever along the Wabash—they're waiting too. I trust each officer will carry that thought in his heart today."

Abraham could only give a quick nod as Mad Anthony leaned on William Henry Harrison's offered arm and labored back toward the camp where men were rousing around the fires. In the gray light Abraham heard the first drums beating.

iii

On the way back to his tent for his sword and pistols, Abraham Kent was hailed from an officer's tent belonging to the Third Sub-legion. He angled through the noisy press of men turning out with their muskets and approached a handsome twenty-year-old. The officer held his spontoon in one hand while he crooked the index finger of the other.

On his blond head the young man wore one of the shaggy fur caps designed at Wayne's request by the tailors at Legionville. The cap in this case was decorated with a plume of the Third Sub-legion's particular color —yellow. The lieutenant kept beckoning with his finger:

"Come here, dragoon. We've a present for you."

"Not now, Meriwether—they're beating assembly."

But Lieutenant Meriwether Lewis, whom Abraham had frequently engaged at cards in winter quarters back at Greenville, set his spontoon aside and practically dragged the junior officer to the tent entrance:

"I hear. But you're out-ranked, Cornet. You're not permitted to reject a gift from a couple of Virginians who've taken so much of your pay."

"Stolen would be a better word," Abraham said with a grin not completely genuine.

Lewis spoke to someone inside the tent:

"This horse soldier's questioning our integrity, William. Suggesting we deal with sharp's cards—"

"Didn't know New Englanders were that astute," came the laconic reply of another lieutenant, a tall, red-haired fellow some four or five years older than the other two. Abraham was pushed bodily into the tent.

"Shut the damn flap before we're all cashiered!" the red-haired officer whispered. As he rummaged through the folds of his blankets, he added, "Don't tell me you're going to refuse a tot of prime Kaintuck whiskey."

Abraham's grin looked less forced. "I didn't realize that was the gift you had in mind, William."

Lieutenant William Clark, youngest brother of the famous frontiersman George Rogers Clark, displayed his jug:

"Most carefully smuggled in—at a cost of five new dollars per gallon."

Clark walked toward Abraham, stepping over the pile of sketch pads he was using to develop his natural aptitude for drawing and map-making. Clark's intelligence reports, illustrated with small charcoal scenes, were well known in the Legion—and reputedly brought General Wayne diversion while increasing his regard for the junior officer.

Clark propped a boot on one of two brass-latched wooden cases in which his friend Lewis, almost his match in height, collected mineral and botanical samples. Clark waggled the jug at Abraham again, his eyes losing a little of their mirth.

"If you can't use a couple of swallows on a morning like this," he said, "I'll be happy to down your share."

"Or I," Meriwether Lewis said.

Touched by the gesture of friendship on the eve of battle, Abraham looked at the two officers from Virginia—men with whom he'd spent many an enjoyable, if unprofitable, hour over the past twelve months. A shiver chased down his backbone as he thought of the massed might of the tribes awaiting the Legion to the northeast. He grabbed the jug.

"Yes, I can use it—on a morning like this," he said.

Somber-eyed, he drank while the Legionary drums beat steadily louder in the dawn heat.

CHAPTER II

The Charge

SHORTLY AFTER SEVEN, with the sun spearing oblique shafts of light through the mist on the Maumee, the Legion of the United States assembled for the attack.

The Legion itself, four Sub-legions of foot preceded by a small mounted patrol, formed in columns of fours on the right flank, close by the shore of the river. Scott's Kentucky mounted militia would advance along a parallel route on the left flank, through the cornfields that stretched northeast between the river on one side and thick woods on the other.

Mounted on Sprite, whose restlessness seemed to match his own, Abraham gathered with the rest of MisCampbell's dragoon officers at the rear of the Legion columns. The commanding officer explained their orders in a few words:

"We'll be held in reserve, behind the lines, and ordered forward if they need us."

On hearing that, Abraham gave voice to the annoyance most of the officers expressed with scowls and grumbles:

"Sir, if the Indians are really waiting for us upriver—"

MisCampbell swiped at his perspiring cheek. "We believe so, Kent. But we're not positive. They were seen there on the eighteenth. They may have pulled back to the British fort."

"Even so, shouldn't the horse be going in first? If the terrain's as rough as I hear it is, columns of foot can hardly maneuver there."

"To the contrary, Cornet. Only columns of foot can maneuver well on such ground. A head-on cavalry charge with all those fallen trees lying every which way would be impossible. Perhaps General Wayne will utilize us for an assault on the flank—"

The captain's stern eyes softened, cynically amused. "Don't be so anxious to shed blood. I've done it, and it's far from pleasant."

Abraham saw some of his fellow officers grinning and turned red. He was the greenest of the lot, and he'd unwittingly demonstrated it. Fortunately discussion was cut short. MisCampbell shouted:

"Prepare your troops to advance and await the command!"

Tugging Sprite's rein, Abraham turned the mare back toward his men. All were dressed much as he was: shirt, trousers, boots. Sabers hung from leather belts. Pairs of primed and loaded pistols were snugged in saddle holsters. At least the Americans had learned something from the agonizing years of the Revolution. Wayne suited the army's clothing and equipment to the country and the temperature; there was no laboring under monstrously heavy packs and blanket-rolls, as Abraham's father said the British infantry had always done during the Rebellion.

The foot too were lightly dressed this morning, carrying only canteens and weapons. The trappings of rank—waistcoats, epauletted outer coats—had been left in heaps behind Captain Pike's earthwork.

The Indians fought with even less equipment, Abraham knew. They wore only hide trousers or waist clouts, and moccasins.

And paint.

He'd listened to descriptions of those ugly slashes of color with which the braves decorated their faces, arms and torsos. This morning, he'd probably see war paint with his own eyes—

Head aching from the heat and the whiskey he'd drunk with Lieutenants Lewis and Clark, he swung Sprite into line behind his troop's senior officer, Lieutenant Stovall. Abraham didn't care much for the chubby Marylander, reputed to be a sodomite. Stovall had made one advance, months ago, but Abraham's gruff reply and clenched fists quickly persuaded the young officer from Baltimore to seek his pleasure elsewhere.

Stovall occasionally bragged that his parents had hustled him out of his home city and into the army because of a scandal whose enormity remained a source of amusement to him. Abraham never learned the full nature of the scandal, but an incident a few weeks prior to the abortive seduction gave him a clue.

One of Stovall's treasured possessions was an expensive, rather large oval locket on a chain. A woman's locket; a curiously effeminate souvenir for a man in the army. In a rare hour of drunken camaraderie, Stovall had opened the locket and shown Abraham a miniature which even the young Bostonian, no prude, found shocking because it represented something he had never seen before: a full-figure miniature of a dark-haired young woman reclining on a drapery, nude.

One coy hand partially concealed a dusty triangle, which the anonymous artist had detailed with the same attention to eroticism he'd given to the young woman's somewhat sleepy eyes, her wide mouth and her large breasts, carefully reddened at the tips.

The young woman in the portrait—she could be no more than sixteen or seventeen—had a voluptuous, puffy decadence that disgusted Abraham even while it aroused him. As Stovall snapped the locket shut, Abraham offered the expected ribald compliment, then asked:

"Is that your mistress, Lieutenant?"

Stovall chuckled, using his amusement as a pretext to touch the back of Abraham's hand:

"A gentleman never compromises a lady by answering such a question, dear boy. It's sufficient to say the locket was given to me by a charming creature who loves me deeply, and whose love is reciprocated."

Days later, Abraham brought up the locket in conversation with another officer. His scalp crawled when the officer identified the girl in the painting:

"His mistress? Yes, he intimates she is. She's also his sister, Lucy Stovall."

"Good Christ! I thought his remarks about a scandal in Baltimore were only boasts."

"To the best of my knowledge, I'm right in the identity of that pretty whore he carries around in his breeches. There was a scandal, and a juicy one. The girl's married now, to some chap named Freemantle—Stovall fairly seethes whenever he mentions him. In case it's not clear, Cornet, Stovall is a libertine of the worst sort. Don't let him catch you alone! I understand his family's damned rich, by the way. That probably helps buy official silence about his little escapades—"

"And helps bribe recruiting officers to look in the other direction?"

"And sign his papers in haste—yes."

After that, Abraham avoided the lieutenant, save for the one time he was unavoidably alone with him, and slyly propositioned.

Stovall's unpopularity was heightened by a condescending manner he displayed even to superiors—and to Abraham this morning:

"Damned silly of you to run about pretending to be a bloody firebrand, Kent." Stovall sometimes affected diction he imagined to be British; Abraham considered it a sign of Federalist leanings. "I've no desire to be potted by a bloody lot of howling heathen. Riding in the rear suits me admirably—"

Abraham couldn't resist a jab at the soft-featured officer:

"Off the field as well as on, eh, sir?"

Stovall colored, started to retort. MisCampbell's shouted command distracted him. Stovall reined his horse around and repeated the order loudly:

"For-aaard!"

In a moment they were moving with a jingle of metal, a slap of leather, a plop of hoofs in the black earth leading to the slope that angled down into the cornfields. Abraham still felt foolish because of his comments to MisCampbell. Perhaps that was the reason he'd dared to jape at a senior officer.

Why *had* he made those idiotic remarks about wanting to be first to charge the enemy? Was he secretly afraid he lacked courage? Yes, that might be the reason—

But admitting it didn't help his spirits one whit. A heavy lump had formed in his throat. Sweat continually blurred his eyes. Off to the far right, the Legion columns shimmered in the heat, their fur caps with different-colored plumes the only concession to military dress. Abraham felt heavy sweat on his chest and under his arms as MisCampbell led the dragoons down into the tasseled corn planted by the Indians.

As he rode, Abraham's thoughts turned inward again. He knew why he hoped to do well in the engagement. He wanted some record of accomplishment, however slight, from which to draw the strength of experience if and when he confronted his father in a much different sort of conflict.

Once he acknowledged this in the silence of his mind,

he felt a little better—though no less nervous. Guiding Sprite over the edge of the gentle slope, he noticed activity in a grove to the left. He saw General Wayne trying to lift his foot to his stirrup. Bending the flannel-swathed leg brought a grimace to Wayne's face, then tears. Two servants rushed forward to boost him up. Abraham distinctly heard Wayne's gasp of pain as he mounted.

But once in the saddle, the general looked fierce and formidable. No trace of the tears remained. The hilt of his sword and the metal-capped butts of his pistols twinkled in the dappled sunlight of the grove.

Abraham coughed in the dust raised by Stovall's gray just ahead. He felt a sudden pride in serving with Anthony Wayne. If he were to die this morning, at least he wouldn't be dying for a coward or an incompetent—

Or a sodomite, he thought, making a disgusted face as Stovall wiggled his fat rump in his saddle and complained loudly about the heat.

ii

The sun climbed higher as they advanced. Stovall owned a precious wilderness rarity, a pocket watch with a cheerfully painted sun face on its dial. He kept close track of the time.

Eight o'clock.

Nine o'clock.

Nine-thirty—

Lulled by the rhythm of posting, Abraham grew drowsy in the heat. Sprite's flanks glistened with lather. He and the mare—in fact all of the dragoons and their horses—exuded a stench that grew riper with every passing moment.

Ahead and to the right, half the Legion had already vanished into a line of trees running at a right angle between the woods on the far left and the river. The trees, a living wall that hid all the terrain beyond, marked the end of the corn bottoms. As the Legion foot disappeared into the dark green gloom, MisCampbell called a halt.

The dragoons reined their horses. General Wayne and his command staff cantered past on their left, soon gone into the trees after the others. Lieutenant Stovall tugged out his pocket watch again.

"Ten o' the clock. The hostiles must have turned tail. Suits me perfectl—"

Abraham stood up straight in his stirrups as Stovall's sentence was punctuated by a rolling thunderclap of sound from the other side of the line of trees. Frantic orders rang along the end of the column of foot. The last of the infantrymen plunged into the woods at quick-step. Abraham saw smoke rising above the trees, but those same trees barred the dragoons from seeing the source of the firing.

"Turned tail?" a dragoon jeered at Stovall. "Doesn't sound like it!"

"No, I don't imagine Mad Anthony ordered musket practice just to while away the time," said another. Stovall jammed his watch back in his trousers pocket, looking petulant.

That muskets by the hundreds were exploding beyond the trees was not in question. But suddenly a new sound was added to the din: massed voices—yells—of infantrymen charging.

A third sound made Abraham's scalp prickle. Wild, ululating yells that could only come from the savages entrenched in the fallen timbers. The battle had been joined—

A horseman burst from the trees, galloping straight toward MisCampbell. Bringing orders? So it appeared. Abraham's belly knotted. His palms turned cold despite the heat.

MisCampbell conferred with the arriving officer, then stood in his stirrups and drew his saber.

"Listen to me!" he shouted, pointing his blade at the river. It shone like a brass mirror now that the mist had burned away. "There's another cornfield along the bank beyond those trees. We're to advance, drive into the enemy's left flank and turn it that way—" In a shimmering arc, the saber flashed toward the forest on Abraham's left. Smoke rose from its depths too. More muskets crashed. The Kentuckians had engaged.

MisCampbell bent to listen to the courier again. Then:

"The foot's already in trouble among the fallen trees. So once we're in there, formations be damned. Just kill the red whoresons." Up went his saber, then down. *"For-aaard—!"*

The dragoons thundered toward the trees nearest the river. Abraham breathed loudly through his mouth as his rump bounced up and down in the saddle. Sprite's plaited mane stood out in the wind. She seemed eager to run—

MisCampbell plunged into the trees, a gloomy place made gloomier by drifting smoke. Above the drumming of hoofs Abraham once more heard sounds on his left. Muskets. Men shouting and cursing in English. Other voices screaming in tongues he didn't understand—

The line of trees was not deep. MisCampbell's men rode through in a matter of a minute or so, bursting onto level ground thick with ripe corn that grew nearly to the water's edge. The world seemed to race by as Abraham's mare carried him from semi-darkness to blinding sunlight. He gasped at the incredible scene of confusion and carnage on his left.

A vast area of the bottom was covered by the immense trunks of uprooted trees, some nearly rotted away. Here and there, two or three of the storm-blasted trunks lay across one another, creating natural barricades six to eight feet high. Among this titanic natural wreckage, men struggled; men with white skins, and others much darker—

Abraham saw bayonets flashing as whole squads clambered over the huge horizontal trees; saw red faces contorted in rage; red hands swinging war clubs and tomahawks and even firing muskets. The Legion and the Indians fought hand to hand in near-total disorder—

At least a thousand to fifteen hundred men were battling, Abraham guessed. He was barely able to hear MisCampbell's bawled orders in the din. Past the fallen timbers, the smoke thickened above the woods where the Kentuckians fought.

Screaming commands, MisCampbell turned the column's head, charging the dragoons left toward the nearest uprooted trees. As Abraham pulled his saber, Stovall swung left in turn. Abraham followed—and got a horrifying view of hard-planed, reddish-brown faces waiting behind the natural fortifications; faces marked with slashes of yellow and vermilion.

Heads shaved save for single oiled scalplocks trailing down their necks, the Indian defenders—of what tribe, Abraham didn't know—raised muskets and aimed at the attacking cavalry.

Abraham bent low over Sprite's neck. He realized the dragoon formation would disintegrate the moment MisCampbell reached the first great trunks. So he chose a route for himself: a natural lane between two destroyed trees. The lane angled away to his left. Riding hard, he turned Sprite in that direction.

The smell of powder was chokingly strong. He heard the Indian muskets erupt, raised his head just a little as a sheet of flame leaped out directly in front of the first dragoons. MisCampbell's chest seemed to cave in, the white of his linen shirt stained with red blotches as several balls struck him at once. He pitched from his saddle, trampled by his men galloping behind him—

Then the first riders were into the trees, each man charging in a different direction, choosing his own enemy. Never before had Abraham heard such noise: the muskets blasting; the American foot soldiers grunting and cursing as they clambered over the tree trunks; the earth-shaking hoofbeats; the war cries of the Indians—and the shrieks of men on both sides dying of a ball or a bayonet or the blade of a scalp knife—

Abraham's mare dashed into the head of the lane he'd picked out. Stovall was racing down the same lane directly ahead. Sprite's flank scraped one of the tumbled trees. She almost fell. On the far side of the tree, two clouted Indians struggled with an officer of the Fourth Sub-legion. The man was fending off the savages with thrusts of his spontoon.

Abraham reined in, reached across the trunk, hacked down and sideways with his saber. The blade struck flesh. With a kind of hypnotic fascination, he watched the brave's neck spout blood over the beleaguered officer. The American took the hideous drenching—and grinned.

The other Indian tried to scramble away over the next tree. The officer ran him through the back with the long spontoon. Abraham's bowels felt watery as he nudged Sprite ahead, the dying Indian's cries of agony loud in his ears.

Abruptly, on his right a brave leaped to the top of another fallen tree. Abraham realized the warrior must have been crouching down—awaiting a victim. The Indian was tall, in his late twenties, with a distinctively handsome face and baleful eyes. He swung his spiked war club straight at Sprite's neck.

Abraham jerked the rein savagely. The mare reared,

front hoofs tearing at the sky. The spike missed her by a fraction.

Sprite came back to earth with a terrific jolt. The Indian found a new, more convenient target: Lieutenant Stovall. A few yards ahead, his gray's front hoof had caught in a tangle of exposed roots. The Indian ran gracefully along the tree trunk, leaped as Abraham shouted:

"Stovall! Behind y—"

Stovall took the spike of the war club in the nape of his neck. He screamed a name—Lucy, Abraham thought it was—as he slumped over. His corpse bounced in the saddle.

Abraham kicked Sprite ahead, hatred dizzying his mind. Stovall was a despicable young man. But he was also a United States soldier, and he had been foully murdered. Holding his seat by clenching his knees against Sprite's heaving sides, Abraham jerked out one of the dragoon pistols and fired.

When the smoke cleared, Abraham saw the Indian laughing at him from the other side of Stovall's horse. Fresh blood stained Stovall's shirt where the pistol ball had struck. The Indian had maneuvered Stovall's corpse as a shield.

Eyes glittering with hateful mirth, the Indian reached up as Stovall's boots came loose from the stirrups. He tangled his fingers in Stovall's blood-slimed hair, jerked, flung the body on the ground. In a moment the Indian was mounted and riding away, bent close to the animal's neck as he beat the gray's ribs with moccasined feet. Abraham pulled his other pistol, shot—but the fleeing savage was already out of range.

Soon the Indian was gone in the smoke. Abraham rode past Stovall's corpse, unable to look at it. Vomit filled his throat. He swallowed several times and that way kept from getting sick. But nausea still churned his middle.

Pistols empty, he had only his bloodied saber for a weapon—and precious few enemies to use it on, he discovered. The Indians had withdrawn from the immediate area. In fact, as he reined in again, he saw scores of them retreating in a frantic scramble through the timbers at the far side of the battleground. Legion soldiers with bayonets gave chase, stabbing the fugitives in the back or shooting them.

Abraham began to shake. He controlled the violent trembling only with great effort. He'd been in combat five minutes or a little less, and already the field was clearing. As he scanned the tumbled trees, he realized that the cavalry charge against the Indian flank had been largely responsible for the sudden retreat. Wayne's strategy had been sound after all.

He heard a lieutenant calling for the dragoons to assemble in a relatively open area a short distance away. He spoke to Sprite to send her forward. The firing was diminishing quickly, but great blue layers of smoke still lay over the blasted trees. The grotesque and gory bodies of Americans and Indians were hideous to look upon.

As Abraham rounded the split end of a rotting tree, he heard a muffled groan, glanced down—

He saw an Indian, hardly older than he was.

Hunched over in pain—gut-shot—the young brave stared up at Abraham's bloodied sword, expecting death. Abraham's eyes locked with the brave's. Agony and humiliation filled those eyes, but no hatred. The Indian was dying.

Abraham had no stomach for administering a final stroke, merciful or otherwise. He rode on. The young warrior began to chant, a mournful, sing-song melody. A death-litany—?

The sight of the dying warrior lingered in Abraham's mind, sad and ugly. He felt ashamed as he remembered his foolish bravado earlier in the morning. To take pleasure in the death and suffering of battle struck him as inhuman, no matter how important or righteous the cause of either side seemed. He was oddly proud of having survived the short but fierce engagement. Yet at the same time he was sickened and shaken by everything he had seen and done.

iii

The battle along the Maumee was won in under half an hour. It was won by superior numbers and, specifically, as Abraham had suspected, by the dragoon charge against the Indian flank. When Abraham rejoined his troop, he found that seven or eight men he knew well had died somewhere in the fallen timbers.

Not long afterward, he and the other dragoons found themselves in high grass overlooking a stockade beside the river. Above the fort, a British flag flew.

Closer to the hilltop position, McKee's trading station stood among a collection of deserted Indian huts and lean-tos. One of the men in Abraham's troop pointed in surprise:

"Stripe me if the yellow British ain't going to keep the damn gate shut."

He moved forward for a better look. About two dozen Indians, most of them wounded, were howling and beating on the entrance to the log fort. Red-coated sentries on the ramparts motioned for them to go away. That set the Indians to howling all the louder. Abraham recognized one of the angriest fugitives.

"See that one who's bloodied his hands hammering the gate?" he asked the officer beside him. "Unless my eyes are tricking me, I came close to killing him back in the timbers."

The bedraggled officer answered, "Don't you know who that is?"

Abraham shook his head.

"A scout pointed him out to me. He was fleeing like the very devil. On horseback."

"But who is he?"

"The Shawanese, Tecumseh. One of Blue Jacket's hottest bloods."

"I'm sure he's the one I shot at—"

"And missed, obviously."

"Yes."

"Too bad. A ball in his brain would have saved every white man on the frontier a mighty lot of grief."

Hardly hearing, Abraham continued to stare at the appalling sight of the allies of the Indians refusing them sanctuary in the fort. Presently the enraged braves slipped out of sight in the woods beyond the log stockade. Wayne had passed an order that they were not to be fired on.

That angered a great many of the Americans. Abraham felt only a profound sense of sorrow. The tribes of the Ohio country might be enemies, but you could only pity men whose pretended friends abandoned them in such fashion.

iv

Boldly, General Anthony Wayne remained camped in the meadows half a mile from Fort Miami. Although the British commandant refused Wayne's demand for surrender, the redcoats stayed safely behind their palisade and didn't fire even a single shot when Wayne ordered McKee's station burned.

Next the Americans burned the huts around the trading post. Finally they set fire to the gardens and cornfields where the Indians raised their food for the winter.

On the way south again in the rain, the army still managed to light enough firebrands to start the cornfields along the Maumee blazing. While the wagons carrying wounded creaked and oozed through the muddy bottoms, pillars of black smoke climbed to the drizzly sky. Wayne had not only vowed to defeat the federated tribes—which he had done in thirty minutes—but also to leave them no means of survival.

Abraham rode Sprite through the rows of ripened corn, setting the tall stalks alight with a sputtering torch. His emotions were in turmoil. He knew that destroying the corn was a military necessity. Yet doing it somehow made him miserable.

He felt that during the brief battle, he had come a little closer to full manhood. But the experience was not nearly as glorious and gratifying as he'd imagined it would be. He found himself thinking frequently of his family. Found himself calling on Lieutenants Clark and Lewis whenever he had a free moment, helping himself to quantities of their whiskey.

And he always avoided looking back at the smoky horizon as the triumphant army marched south in the waning summer.

V

A commotion brought Abraham running from his barracks at Fort Greenville one brittle gray afternoon late in January. Dull silver light tinged the western horizon. Lamps had already been lit in General Wayne's neat house with its border of white picket fencing. On the ramparts, sentries were hallooing while other men lifted the great log bar that held Greenville's gates shut from the inside.

Crowds of soldiers had already gathered. In one of them, Abraham found red-haired Lieutenant Clark.

"Why all the excitement, William?" Abraham asked, shivering in his all-too-thin dark blue winter coat. He blinked as a couple of snowflakes tickled his eyelids.

"Party of red men coming in," Clark answered in his soft Virginia speech. Several officers dashed to the porch of Wayne's house. One pounded on the door.

The fort gates swung inward. A strange silence fell, broken only by the wind's whine. A file of about three dozen Indians straggled into the fort, looking considerably less prideful than their peers at Fallen Timbers. In fact Abraham had seldom seen so pathetic a sight as the half-dozen hunched old men who led the procession on horseback.

The protruding ribs of the horses testified to their near-starvation. The men wore ragged blankets, or filthy cast-off British army coats. They huddled together while an American interpreter in buckskin spoke to the leaders with words and signs. Among the soldiers gathered on the perimeter of the parade area, there were brief outbursts of contemptuous laughter, and a few obscene jests. The laughter soon died. The jokes drew little response.

How different from the day in late December, Abraham thought. Wayne had assembled the Legion and the Kentuckians in the post-Christmas cold to hear a reading of a proclamation from Philip Kent's old friend Knox, head of the Department of War. The proclamation said President Washington and the Congress *joined in commending Major General Wayne's men for the good conduct and bravery displayed by them in the action of the twentieth August last, with the Indians—*

Afterward, the cheering was long and loud.

Now some of those same Indians, hollow-cheeked and shivering, stood helplessly in the midst of their enemies under the lowering winter sky. They awaited the emergence of the White Captain from his cozy house. Abraham remembered the dreadful harvest of skulls on the Wabash; reminded himself that perhaps some of these very chiefs had caused that slaughter—

Yet he understood their reasons. Pitied them again as he recalled the way their erstwhile friends had denied them sanctuary after the battle. Ever since that simmering morning in August, he'd scorned himself for ever thinking that war, in whatever cause, could be ennobling.

Necessary, perhaps. But ennobling? Never.

Men drifted from group to group, identifying members of the Indian party:

"That's Half King's son, the Wyandot."

"And the Delaware, Moses. The only English letter he can write is M, they say—"

"Well," remarked Lieutenant William Clark, "this is what the general wanted. Beating them in the field wasn't enough. They had to be beaten in their bellies and their hearts and their minds before this country could be pacified. I'll venture this is only the start, Abraham—the first trickle."

"You mean more of the chiefs will come?"

Clark nodded. "Wayne will have a treaty with all the tribes before the year's out, mark my word."

"That'll mean furloughs!" a soldier behind them exclaimed. "Damme, I can't wait to fuck one of those Cincinnati whores, never mind how bad they smell—"

Someone else snickered. But only for a moment.

Abraham was thinking of something other than women. He was thinking that if the Northwest had indeed been secured, he could return home when his enlistment ran out at mid-year. The realization triggered a memory of Wayne's remarks about the opportunity in the new land.

But Abraham knew himself reasonably well now. He couldn't simply defy his father and never go home. He'd have to return to Boston at least for a short time.

The thought of the homecoming filled him with conflicting emotions. On one hand he longed to be among familiar comforts and familiar people again; on the other, he dreaded facing the owner of Kent and Son.

He dug his hands deeply into the pockets of his thin coat. The more he thought about Wayne's words that stifling morning beside the river, the more he questioned them. At the moment he could see very little in this western frontier that was attractive. Memories of shimmering meadows, abundant forests, white-water brooks and plentiful wildlife all seemed lusterless here in the dull silver light of a January afternoon—

The front door of Wayne's small house opened, spilling lamplight in which a shadow loomed. The general hobbled out, tall and somehow awesome in spite of his infirmity. The Indians drew closer together.

"Yes, it's the end," William Clark said. He sounded relieved. A moment later he clapped a hand on Abraham's shoulder. "Care for some whiskey by way of celebration?"

"Very much so," Abraham answered, with more feeling than his friend understood.

vi

Some thirteen months after the defeat of the federated tribes, with the great treaty signed in Greenville's council house, men began to be released from Wayne's command. Abraham Kent was one.

Turning Sprite over to the new cornet whose mount she would become, he spoke with the unconsciously condescending air of the veteran addressing the green replacement.

"Take care of her. She's a splendid campaigner—" His natural manner broke through the feigned superiority; he smiled in a rueful way. "—better than I am, in fact. There's a great deal to recommend this western country, Cornet. But I don't have much fondness for the human price paid for settling the question of its ownership. I mean the price on both sides."

The new junior officer merely looked puzzled.

"One final word of advice," Abraham added, with a broad wink. "It's in reference to the whiskey they freight up from Kentucky. Or Kaintuck, if you prefer. If you can survive the first few sips—and develop a fondness for it—you can face the worst life has to offer out here. The Kentucky brew, in case I don't make myself clear, is potent as hell. It's also necessary as hell."

He was only partially joking.

CHAPTER III

Clouds at Homecoming

AFTER THE MAGNIFICENT dinner, Abraham held forth for a quarter of an hour.

He described how more than eleven hundred braves and sachems of the northwestern tribes had come to Greenville the preceding August to listen to Wayne's passionate, if lengthy, speeches of persuasion. Dressed in a fine suit of brown New England broadcloth, he jumped to his feet as he launched into the closing of the general's last speech, which he'd memorized:

"*—I now take the hatchet out of your hands—*"

Abraham added gestures to the recitation, aware that four pairs of eyes were focused on him with varying degrees of attentiveness. One pair particularly—eyes at which he dared not glance—stirred him in a strange and surprising way. His voice strengthened:

"*—and with a strong arm throw it into the center of the great ocean, where no mortal can ever find it!*" A mimed throw dramatized the line. "*And I now deliver to you the wide and straight path to the Fifteen Fires, to be used by you and your posterity forever. So long as you continue to follow this road, so long will you continue to be a happy people. You see it is straight and wide—and they will be blind indeed who deviate from it!*"

Flushed, Abraham paused. He'd jumped up almost unconsciously, carried away with excitement. He sat down before going on:

"That was virtually the end of it. Wayne had won them—every important chief and brave in the Northwest Territory except one. A Shawnee named Tecumseh. He refused to come to Greenville because his father was shot to death by white hunters when he was a boy—and he saw his village burned on orders of George Rogers Clark just a couple of years later. The day after Wayne's speech, the chiefs began signing. They're to receive twenty thousand dollars this first year, half that in succeeding years in return for the land they've given up. I've heard the area amounts to as much as twenty-five thousand square miles. The treaty line runs roughly east to west, from a river called the Cuyahoga to Fort Recovery. There, it angles down toward the Ohio. Everything south and east of the line is reserved for white settlement. The Indians must stay to the north and west—but Wayne very cannily granted the tribes the right to hunt and fish all the way to the Ohio so long as they conduct themselves peacefully. At the same time, he negotiated U.S. possession of sixteen choice parcels *within* the Indian territory. Altogether, the terms were complex to explain to the sachems. But they were eager to sign when the general finished speaking. I was listening outside the council house a good part of the time, and I've never heard such eloquent delivery."

"Nor I," said Elizabeth, seated on Abraham's right. He couldn't help turning red again.

He wanted to look into the girl's pale blue eyes; wanted to savor the sight of her fair, perfectly coiffed hair and the fetchingly rounded breasts that had barely been visible on her slim body when he left for Pittsburgh three years earlier.

But Abraham Kent had served in the army. He could discipline himself. Instead of making a show over Elizabeth's admiration, he acknowledged his stepmother's smile from the lower end of the table, and kept his eyes on her as she spoke:

"I agree, Elizabeth. We may have raised an orator as well as a soldier."

Peggy Ashford McLean Kent's smooth white hands rested on the polished surface of the great dining table imported from Mr. Phyfe's increasingly popular—and immensely expensive—New York shop. When Abraham departed for the west, the family had only been settled six months in the new home on Beacon Street overlooking the Common. Since his return a week ago, he had been dazzled by the opulence of the furnishings added in his absence.

"A soldier I'll never be, mother," he said now. Out of politeness, he always referred to the dark-haired, graceful woman from Virginia as mother, even though she was his father's second wife.

Peggy Kent had a gentle, lovely face, and eyes that occasionally revealed some private sorrow Abraham had never fully understood. She was taller than his father, but that hadn't proved an impediment to a happy marriage. Philip, the head of the household who was sitting silently at the other end of the table, more than made up in strength of personality what he lacked in height. Abraham fidgeted, aware of Philip's unblinking gaze.

Across the table from Abraham, thin and sallow little Gilbert, going on twelve, leaned forward and exclaimed:

"Tell us again about the fight at Fallen Timbers, Abraham."

"Come, I must have recited that four times already this week," Abraham grinned.

Gilbert was Abraham's half-brother, the only child of Philip Kent's second marriage. He had a fragility to his bones and a luminosity in his eyes that showed him to be his mother's child. The brightness of his mind somewhat compensated for his lack of size and stamina.

He answered Abraham with a gay smile:

"Actually it's five. But I don't tire of it."

"Let's spare the family, then, shall we? I'll repeat the story in private."

"A promise?" asked the boy. He'd been named for his father's life-long friend Lafayette, the French nobleman who had fought valiantly for the American cause during the Revolution.

"A promise," Abraham replied.

"Abraham."

The voice from the head of the table was quiet yet commanding. Abraham turned, almost dreading to meet his father's eyes.

At forty-two, Philip Kent's strong features had acquired some of the lines of age. His neatly tied hair showed gray streaks. Abraham could never remember Philip using powder, or covering his hair with one of the wigs now rapidly passing out of fashion. This evening Philip wore an expensive suit of deep emerald velvet, a fawn waistcoat and snowy linen. He'd returned late from his business establishment—it occupied three floors in an old building near Long Wharf, and was already outgrowing the space—and hadn't bothered to remove traces of ink from beneath his blunt fingernails. Owner of the highly successful printing and book publishing firm of Kent and Son, Philip was by no means an absentee manager.

"Yes, papa?" Abraham said.

Philip continued to scrutinize his older son. There was something a bit forbidding in that stare, Abraham thought.

Or was that only his imagination? His guilt? In the short time he'd been back in Boston, he had seen Philip but briefly; the inevitable subject of Abraham's future hadn't yet arisen.

At last Philip spoke: "You favored us with some interesting accounts of your time in the west. But you'll forgive me if I observe that very little of what you've said is anything more than superficial."

Abraham frowned. "I don't understand, sir."

"Well, for instance—during the charge, were you frightened?"

Peggy clasped her hands together. "Oh dear, Philip, must he answer? You've a way of tossing people straight onto the griddle with your questions."

"My thought exactly!" Elizabeth agreed.

Her words drew a frown from Philip. But that wasn't all:

"Young woman, I believe I've made it abundantly clear that you have a great many thoughts of which I don't approve." His glance leaped to his wife. "Have you seen to the disposal of that trashy novel Elizabeth brought into the house?"

"Yes, she did," Elizabeth said, angry. With a slight turn of his head, Abraham saw the fire in the girl's blue eyes. Almost reckless, those eyes. An inheritance from her father, the family had long ago concluded—

Elizabeth's father had been a Virginia gentleman of good background but poor character. On the rare occasions when he was discussed in the Kent house, it was said that he'd been given to heavy drinking, and furious rages. Now Elizabeth showed more of that inheritance. She pouted; struck the table with one dainty fist:

"I should think at seventeen, I might read what I please."

"Not Mrs. Rowson's sinful novel," Philip declared. "*Charlotte Temple* is sentimental tripe. It dwells excessively on seduction, and is therefore unfit for young women of breeding. The book may have enjoyed a vogue in England. But I refused the opportunity—if you care to call it that—to bring it out in America under the

Kent imprint. That summarizes my opinion, I believe." He addressed his wife again. "Is it gone?"

Peggy smiled a tolerant smile. "Yes, what Elizabeth told you is correct—I've seen to it."

"Good."

Abraham kept a straight face. The little dialogue just concluded only demonstrated again the thickness of the shell of conservatism that had hardened around his father in the latter's advancing years.

Philip said, "Now, Abraham, back to the question—which I didn't mean unkindly, by the way."

"I realize, sir."

"A man who goes into battle without fear is the worst sort of fool."

"Then, happily, I guess I'll escape that label. I was terrified."

Gilbert's worshipful expression vanished. "You were?"

"Of course. At the same time, I still wanted to do well—wanted to acquit myself honorably." That pleased Philip. "But after ten minutes in the thick of the fighting, I'd frankly had enough to last me the rest of my life. I discovered there's nothing pleasant or uplifting about killing another human being."

"Yes, I discovered the same thing. On several occasions," Philip added, letting it go at that.

Abraham naturally knew most of the details of his father's history. Philip Kent had emigrated from England before the Revolution, as a result of trouble over an inheritance from his father—an English peer dead almost six years now. The duke had never married Philip's mother, a French woman of great beauty but low birth who had been an actress in Paris for a time. Philip frequently intimated that he'd had to defend his own life more than once in the uncertain years before he gave his wholehearted support to the cause of the Boston patriots. Philip's struggle for survival as a young man—and perhaps his bastardy—explained to Abraham why his father had acquired an aura of confidence, power, even arrogance that often intimidated others of his sex—his sons included.

Not that Philip was overtly truculent. The quiet air of absolute authority was simply part of his makeup. It showed in the challenging quality of his next remark:

"You've decided that soldiering is not a career you'd want to pursue, then?"

Abraham nodded. "Very definitely."

"So that leaves your future open to discussion. Excellent."

Abraham tried not to show how great an impact those words had on him. He felt as if a huge weight, long suspended over his head, had crushed down on him at last. He'd known he couldn't indefinitely postpone talking about what he intended to do now that he was home. Philip had just made that doubly clear.

But Gilbert didn't want to abandon war stories quite so quickly. The adoring look stole back into his eyes as he said to his half-brother:

"How many of the red men did you kill, Abraham?"

"I don't know."

"Didn't you count?"

"No," Abraham answered, curtly. He saw agonized faces; heard screams—

Elizabeth tossed her fair hair. "I'd like to know which is more immoral—Mrs. Rowson's novel of seduction or all this gory talk of slaughtering Indians!"

Philip shot the girl another irritated glance. Peggy, always the mistress of tact and diplomacy, rose from her chair before he could speak:

"Neither is appropriate at the moment, my dears. I'm sure the servants are anxious to clear away. Shall we take tea in the music room? Abraham, you haven't heard Gilbert play the harpsichord—"

Gilbert made a disgusted face.

"I'm looking forward to it," Abraham said.

"You'll be delightfully surprised. Gilbert can perform most of the hymns and fugues in Mr. Belcher's *Harmony of Maine*. Or any of Mr. Kimball's popular songs from *The Rural Harmony*—he's really quite accomplished."

Philip stood up. "I prefer that Gilbert concentrate on his study of mathematics. If he continues to show the aptitude he's demonstrated so far, our business will never lack for managerial talent. In fact I've given some thought to having the sign repainted."

Peggy looked startled. "In what fashion?"

"So that it reads *Kent and Sons*—plural." With affection, Philip reached out to tousle Gilbert's curly hair. For a moment his stern countenance softened noticeably.

Gilbert smiled in a forced way. He appeared to accept the channeling of his life into a pre-determined course with almost complete resignation. But he grew a little more cheerful when Philip said to him:

"Let us postpone the concert, shall we?"

"Anything you say, father!"

"Why can't Gilbert play?" Peggy asked.

"Because I want a word with Abraham alone—over a glass of port in the sitting room."

Again it was more of a command than a statement, and it didn't sit well with Abraham, rankled as he was by Philip's remark about re-naming the firm. Elizabeth rebelled too, though against something else:

"I despise this ridiculous tradition of the gentlemen retiring behind closed doors!" She rose, flinging her linen napkin on the table. "Mama and I are expected to be docile slaves simply because of our sex—"

"Elizabeth!" Peggy warned. "You will refrain from the use of that word in conversation."

"Oh, mama, stop!"

Peggy glanced pointedly at Gilbert. "Please consider who is present—"

"Do you honestly suppose Gilbert hasn't seen the dogs coupling in every alley in Boston?"

"Of course I have," Gilbert grinned.

Already scarlet, Peggy gasped, "Young man—!"

"This pious sham of not using certain words is disgusting!" Elizabeth cried.

Philip's eyes were thunderous—like his voice:

"Nevertheless, you will not use them in Gilbert's presence—your mother's presence—or mine! This is my house, and it's my decision."

"Yes, you make all the decisions, don't you?"

"See here—!"

"You also make it quite apparent that I'm an outsider."

"Oh, Elizabeth, that's altogether unfair and unwarranted," Peggy said in a saddened tone.

"Is it? I don't believe so!"

The candles in the chandelier put glistening highlights in Elizabeth's pale blue eyes. Yet Abraham had the uncanny feeling that her tears were artifice. If so, they still worked. Philip looked taken aback:

"My dear child, your mother's quite right. You're as much a part of this family circle as any other person at the table. But the fact remains—you're much too forward and free-thinking."

"I suppose next you'll be calling me a mad, bloodthirsty Jacobin!" Elizabeth wailed, starting to rush out. As she left, she contrived to brush against Abraham. His arm tingled at the touch of her muslin-covered breast.

They all listened to Elizabeth clattering away upstairs to her room just down the hall from Abraham's on the third floor. A door slammed distantly. Philip sighed. Then:

"Peggy, will you please go to her? She continues to harbor the misguided notion that because I'm not her father, I care the less for her."

Peggy said softly, "We both know that's not true."

"At the same time, I demand decent behavior. Elizabeth quite often seems totally incapable of it."

"She just doesn't want to grow up and be ladylike," Gilbert said with a tentative smile.

No one responded. His large eyes lost their glow. His face fell.

Abraham knew full well that the problem was much deeper than Gilbert's over-simplification suggested. Elizabeth bore her father's last name, Fletcher. That she was illegitimate was no secret within the Kent family. The circumstances of her conception, however, were largely unclear to Abraham.

He did know that his stepmother had met Philip only after she had placed her infant daughter in a foster home here in Boston. Evidently Peggy hadn't wanted to expose the child—and herself—to scandal in her native Virginia. Beyond that, Abraham had pieced together certain other information from chance remarks at the family table or hearthside:

Peggy's first husband had been a Virginia planter named McLean. He was butchered in a short but apparently harrowing slave rebellion that swept Peggy's home district along the Rappahannock River in 1775. Elizabeth, born in 1778, had therefore been fathered by this Fletcher fellow after Peggy became a widow.

Sometimes Abraham wondered whether that slave uprising might be the cause of the silent grief that seemed to grip his stepmother occasionally. Walking abroad in Boston, he had seen Peggy turn pale at the sight of a free black man.

Philip had once confided to Abraham that Peggy had indeed suffered physical harm in the rebellion. To what extent, he didn't say. Abraham had speculated on the possibility of rape. That would account for Peggy's pallor and the sudden nervous starts which automatically —and unfairly—lumped all Negroes into a single category: persons to be feared.

If Peggy Ashford McLean Kent's past did include ravishment, how it had affected her intimate relationship with Abraham's father remained a mystery. He knew they shared one large bed. And his stepmother hadn't been so devastated that sexual congress was impossible for her. Gilbert was proof of that. Beyond the obvious, however, Abraham didn't deem it his business —or, to use Philip's word, decent—to speculate.

He did know that no children had come of Peggy's union with the murdered McLean. Growing up, he'd asked his father questions about the whole puzzling business. Philip refused to reply to most of them, stating that he did so out of respect for his wife's wishes. The past was buried and would remain so.

No one was forbidden from talking about Elizabeth's real father—though no one dwelled on him especially either. Over the years, Peggy had let slip a few tantalizing details about the man. The one mentioned most often—and most proudly—was that he had been shot to death in Pittsburgh in 1778, by an Indian spy attempting to abort George Rogers Clark's march to capture British forts in the Northwest Territory.

It seemed clear that the man had indeed possessed an unstable nature. It showed up, as it had for as long as Abraham could remember, in Elizabeth's dislike of Philip's discipline, and her occasional outright rebellion against it. That was one thing in the household that hadn't changed in Abraham's absence—even though Elizabeth's appearance had changed remarkably. She had quite literally grown up. Filled out. Become almost beautiful.

She was no blood kin of Abraham's. Yet he still felt vaguely guilty over the sensual thoughts she inspired. Her frank glances had stirred him often during the short time he'd been home.

Responding to Philip's request, Peggy said in a weary tone, "Yes, I'll go to her—though I doubt my admonitions will have much effect. They seldom do any more. Gilbert, you see to finishing your studies for the day."

Gilbert stuck out his lower lip. "I'd rather talk to Abraham about Indians."

"Your brother is going to talk to me," Philip said, starting from the dining room. With each step, his right shoulder drooped a little—the result of the wound he had suffered at the battle of Monmouth Court House. The way he had limped ever since had also played a part in making him an assertive, sometimes domineering man, Abraham suspected.

Reluctantly he followed his father into the front sitting room. Servants had already lit a fire against the December darkness. Philip warmed his hands in front of the blaze. He didn't once glance back to see whether Abraham had followed. He expected Abraham to be there, and Abraham was.

ii

Over the mantel hung a long, beautifully polished and oiled Kentucky rifle that Philip had acquired in the war. Above that, a focal point of the room, shone the grenadier's sword given him by Lafayette. They had known each other as young men in the French province of Auvergne; then, Philip's name had been Phillipe Charboneau. He had adopted his new one on the voyage to America.

Gazing at the sword, Abraham recalled what his father had recently told him about its famous donor. At first a supporter of the French Revolution, the Marquis de Lafayette had lately rebelled against the savagery of the Jacobins. He was now imprisoned somewhere in Europe —Prussia or Austria, Philip believed. It was an irony of the great political upheaval that had polarized not only Europe but the United States that Lafayette, finally rejecting the revolution, had still been clapped into irons by its enemies because of his position before he changed his mind.

Below the rifle and sword on the mantel proper stood a small green glass bottle with a quantity of dried tea leaves in the bottom. This Abraham's father had acquired on the night of Mr. Samuel Adams' famous tea party in Boston harbor.

The tea had accumulated in Philip's boots during the opening and dumping of the chests. Later that same night he had put the tea in the bottle, to save as a family souvenir. Years afterward, he'd adopted the symbol of the partially filled bottle for the signboard identifying Kent and Son.

Despite the crackling fire, the sitting room was chilly. All at once Abraham noticed the tea-bottle symbol on the masthead of a single-sheet, four-page gazette lying on a small table. The title of the paper was the *Bay State Federalist.* That and a quick glance at its columns identified the paper's slant; Abraham noted an unfriendly story referring to the ex-secretary of state, Mr. Jefferson, and his *Jacobin cohorts.*

"I've a great deal to catch up on," he said while Philip poured two glasses of port. "No one's bothered to tell me you've gone into the newspaper business as well."

Philip handed a glass to his son. "It's merely a weekly at the moment. Still, the more voices speaking out against these imbeciles who'd entangle us with the French, the better."

Abraham laughed.

"Pray tell me what's so amusing," Philip snapped.

"Forgive me, papa—it's just that your attitude's a bit surprising. I mean, you *were* born in France."

"The people living there now have collectively lost their minds. And some of the revolution's friends in America are in equally pathetic shape. I've heard educated gentlemen who should know better aping the French barbarians by addressing one another as 'citizen.' Proudly! Can you imagine—?"

He capped his little oration with a scornful sniff. Abraham sipped his port, then said:

"So your sympathies are entirely with Mr. Hamilton and his faction?"

"Indeed they are. Alexander Hamilton is the one authentic genius in the president's cabinet. An absolute master of financial affairs. It's Hamilton who untangled the debt mess left at the end of the war, you know. He and he alone put this nation on a sound monetary basis. I agree wholeheartedly with his contention that we must strengthen our commercial ties with England now that we've settled our differences."

"I'm not sure they're settled."

"You're wrong."

"No, papa. For one thing, the British haven't yet withdrawn from their forts in the northwest."

"But they signed Mr. Jay's treaty last year, agreeing to do so! They can't delay forever," Philip declared, seating himself as if the subject was closed. Abraham still looked skeptical:

"The treaty is all right as far as it goes. But as I understand it, the treaty said nothing about some vital issues still outstanding. Interference with our shipping—that absurd ploy of boarding American vessels to hunt for British seamen who've deserted. The real object as everyone knows is to seize Americans to fill the Royal Navy's press gang quotas."

"The treaty may have its weaknesses," Philip said, somewhat huffily. "But by and large, I approved of Mr. Jay's endeavors."

"I heard that others didn't. Quite a few others."

Philip waved. "Ignorant rabble."

"Is it true they burned Jay's effigy in various cities?"

"Yes, and stoned Hamilton when he spoke for the treaty in New York! But I can cite you an outrage closer to home. Do you know what those filthy Francophiles painted on the wall of my own establishment—right here in Boston? *Damn John Jay! Damn everyone who won't damn John Jay—!*"

Philip noticed his son smiling again. "You are easily amused, Abraham. Such outbursts against public order—deprecations of the effort of decent, patriotic men—they're a disgrace!"

He lowered his voice until it sounded almost threatening:

"I trust you haven't acquired a different view. Haven't fallen in with a pack of republican radicals during your army service."

Straight-faced, but marveling anew at the way wealth and position could alter a man's politics and tame his passion for upsetting the status quo, Abraham answered:

"I don't believe so, sir. We were a little too busy with the tribes to discuss political theory."

"I had some doubts about permitting you to go off to military duty—as you well know. I allowed it because I suspected the outcome—that you wouldn't find it to your liking."

"You knew that ahead of time? How?"

Philip shrugged, as if the answer was obvious:

"I never liked soldiering either."

"I see." Again Abraham wanted to chuckle. But he didn't. Philip went on:

"I confess I'm not entirely happy to see the new territory secure. It only means the creation of new states. The settlers will be nothing but farmers—artisans—"

"Mr. Jefferson's sort of people," Abraham returned wryly.

"The fool is wrong to believe government should rest in the hands of all! Hamilton sees the issue correctly—"

"Only the rich—the well-educated—are competent to administer the affairs of the nation? Forgive me a second time, papa, but I thought that was exactly what you fought against in the late war."

"Times change! So does a man's thinking. However, I don't wish to discuss my views. I wish to discuss your future."

"I've only been home a week—"

"And I expect to give you sufficient time to acclimate yourself to civilian life. But I do want to inform you of one fact, Abraham." Philip looked so serious, Abraham lost even the slightest desire to laugh. He asked:

"What fact?"

"I am relying on you to join the printing house as soon as possible. I'll give you as much responsibility as I think you can handle, and—"

Quickly, Abraham raised his glass to interrupt:

"Papa, papa—wait! I'm not certain that's what I want to do with my life."

"A career with Kent and Son offers you everything!" Philip exclaimed. "Why wouldn't you want a comfortable, secure existence? Influential friends? A position of respect within the Federalist community—?"

"Perhaps because I'm not yet a Federalist."

"You'll change."

"How can you be so sure?"

The dark eyes caught the hearth's glare. "You are my son."

Softly, but without hesitation, Abraham said, "Yes—and that's the very reason I prefer to do exactly as you did."

"What do you mean?"

"The story, papa."

"What story?"

"The one you told me so often when I was growing up. How you refused to accept what was planned for you by your mother—how you struck out on your own instead. Made your own way. Will you deny me the same opportunity? It's a tribute to you that I want it that way—"

"I do *not* consider it a tribute," Philip said. Abraham felt a sudden hurt. "I will be exceedingly disappointed if you refuse to come into Kent and Son as your half-brother will surely do."

"Gilbert's a different case. Bright, but too frail for any kind of work except commerce. In a business he can use his true strength—his mind."

Philip sat in stony immobility for a moment. Then:

"If you don't care to accept my suggestion, be kind enough to tell me what alternative you've chosen."

"The truth is, I can't."

"And why not, sir?"

Silence.

"Answer me! *Why not?"*

"I—I just haven't found it yet. The alternative—"

Abraham's sentence trailed off in lame fashion. Philip's lip showed his scorn—and perhaps concealed pain as deep as Abraham's own. Philip turned defensive, sarcastic:

"You don't know what you want to do, yet you already know my proposition is unsatisfactory. Odd—"

"Papa—"

"*Damned* odd!"

Abraham set his unfinished glass aside. "Sir, I'd like to ask that we postpone the rest of this discussion."

"Until when?"

"Until I've had a chance to think things out."

Abraham was uncomfortable in the evasion. But he couldn't bear to continue the talk—the argument—now. His father was growing too angry. It showed in the seethe of his next sentence:

"I do hope you haven't entirely closed your mind against me."

"No—" Abraham faced away quickly to conceal the lie. "—no, of course I haven't. Goodnight, papa."

Philip rose and walked into the shadows near the front windows. He remained gloomily silent as his son left the room.

iii

"Good night, Mr. Abraham," said the nasal-voiced octogenarian who served as footman in the Kent house. Climbing the stairs to his old room in the third story—a room only occupied for a short time before he left for Pittsburgh and Wayne's service—Abraham called a reply over his shoulder. The reply was more grumble than anything else.

Yes, he had lied to his father. No point in denying that. On the long, arduous journey home, he had thought a good deal about the future. He wasn't content to fit pliably into the mold prepared for him by Philip Kent.

In many ways service in the northwest had been an unsettling experience. It had shown him the world was not confined to paper and presses—all he had known as a child. His most vivid early memory of his father was sensory: the smell of ink in the first loft Philip had occupied; a loft above the chandler's store operated by the patriarch of the powerful Rothman family, now respected Boston bankers.

Some of what Abraham had told his father was true. He didn't yet know what he wanted to do with his life. Not in detail, that is. His central goal was much as he'd stated it: to strike out on his own. That was clearly imitative admiration of Philip—though he realized his father would always refuse to see it as such. God, how the man had changed in just three years—!

During Abraham's first twenty-four hours in the house, he'd literally gaped at the lavish new furnishings—the obvious signs of Philip's continuing ability to pyramid his profits from his initial business venture: an investment in shares in privateering vessels during the Rebellion. The venture had cost Abraham the mother he didn't remember. She had been abducted by one of the privateer captains, and had perished at sea trying to escape from her kidnapper.

Abraham really hadn't appreciated how rich Philip had become until he'd been away from Boston a while, living in altogether different and less luxurious surroundings. Following his return, however, he very quickly found the wealthy household stultifying; too formalized and proper. That spurred him to make up his mind to go his own way.

Because he didn't want to hurt his father, he had tried to hide that truth just now. But he couldn't hide it from himself. So there remained two obstacles for him to overcome:

The immediate one of convincing Philip that he deserved the right to shape his own destiny.

And the more difficult because less clear-cut one of determining what that destiny ought to be.

With a shake of his head, Abraham realized he'd paused on the second-floor landing. As he started up toward the third, he heard his stepmother's voice murmuring in Gilbert's room. He called the obligatory good-night. Then, aware of Peggy hurrying to the door to speak to him, he rushed on up the steps into the relative gloom of the cramped upper story.

Peggy didn't call out to summon him. She was a wise woman, and he admired her wisdom. She would sense from his quick passage upstairs that the interview with Philip hadn't gone well, and he wanted to retire undisturbed.

Servants had lit a small fire in the grate in his room. He could smell the wood smoke as he touched the latch, thrust the door inward—

"My God—!"

"Sssh!" Elizabeth Fletcher put a warning hand to her lips. "Don't be a ninny and make noise or you'll spoil everything."

Shaking a little, Abraham stepped into the room, closed the door.

"What the devil are you doing here, Elizabeth? Dressed like that—it—it isn't proper."

"Oh, don't start talking like the others!" Elizabeth exclaimed. "I've already had another tedious lecture from mama this evening."

She was standing barefoot before the hearth. Thus Abraham could see—most disturbingly—the details of her figure through the filmy material of her nightdress. Her young woman's breasts were clearly defined, nipples and all. And—was her pose deliberate?—he even glimpsed the area between her legs where the clearer outlines of her thighs joined, blurring into a hint of—Quickly, he looked away.

"Please do keep your voice lowered," she whispered. "Before I crept down the hall, I shut my own door with a great show of going to bed."

She walked slowly toward the turned-down coverlets,

plumping herself on them. "Anyway, why shouldn't I be here? We're not brother and sister."

"I know, but—"

"And I'm already condemned as perfectly scandalous by the rest of them—" The pale blue eyes challenged him. "Excluding you, I trust."

"Yes. Yes, certainly," Abraham told her, dissembling desperately. He felt both awkward and terrified.

She patted the bed next to her leg.

"Then sit with me, and talk. There's no one else I can talk to in this house, you know."

He continued to stand motionless. She brushed back a lock of fair hair, her expression by turns defiant and devilish:

"Don't tell me you've never been alone with a woman, Abraham Kent. Not after three years in the army."

"Why, I—I've been with a woman several times." The truth of it was, it had happened just once. In the village of Cincinnati, on his way home, he had paid a whore. At the time the whole business had been quick and embarrassing, though in retrospect it had a certain nostalgic charm.

"So do sit down!"

He stared at her a moment longer, seeing something strange, even wicked, shining in her blue eyes. It was a reckless unconcern for propriety that lent her lovely face an almost unholy radiance in the flicker from the grate. Was this what she'd inherited from the Fletcher fellow who had carried on so disgracefully before his death?

The thought frightened Abraham all the more. Yet he didn't pull away, or order her out. Instead, he eased himself gently onto the bed. Elizabeth seized his cold hands in her warm ones. He felt the first hardness of arousal.

"Abraham," she said, her face close enough so that

he could smell the sweetness of her breath, "you understand what they're trying to do to both of us, don't you?"

"They?"

"Well, chiefly your father. I didn't understand it myself for the longest time. Then, the older I got, the clearer it became. I've known the truth for—oh, almost two years."

"The truth about what?"

"About what your father wants. It's very simple. He wants everyone who lives under this roof—me, and now you—to bend to his notions of respectability. I admit he's been kind to me over the years. Yet in a way, I hate him."

"Elizabeth, that's a damned ghastly thing to say—"

"I can't help it, that's how I feel. Don't you realize he wants to trap both of us in the same trap? Neither of us must let that happen—we're not cut out for it!"

"What do you propose we do, may I ask?"

"We must fight him, Abraham. Secretly. Together—"

Suddenly she leaned against him, letting him feel her breasts through the thin gown.

Then she took his hand and placed it over one breast and squeezed his fingers, all the while staring at him with those strange, pale eyes.

iv

That moment destroyed any doubts Abraham Kent might have had about Elizabeth's purpose in coming to his room so furtively. By means of an act Philip would be sure to find reprehensible, she would defy the authority he sought to exert over her.

Abraham had felt some of the same pressure in the painful interview with his father. Thus he was quite willing to let the eager instincts of his young man's body have their way, joining the girl in this private, ultimately pleasurable form of protest.

To his surprise, he discovered she wasn't a virgin. Her gown tossed aside, her pale thighs spread to reveal a gilded place, she kissed and teased him as expertly as that Cincinnati whore. She drew him down, then guided him with practiced hands curled around his maleness. As the rhythm of the coupling intensified, she groaned louder and louder against his ear. Wantonly, she locked her legs around the small of his back. The ferocious outpourings shook them both almost simultaneously.

Afterward, under the coverlets, she nestled naked in the curve of his arm. When he questioned her about her experience, she only laughed brightly and said it was of no importance. She rolled against him, gripping his cheeks with both palms while those intense blue eyes probed:

"We mustn't let them destroy us, Abraham. *We mustn't.*"

Limp from their union and captivated by her presence, he found it easy to say, "We won't."

"Promise?"

He heard a grotesque echo of Gilbert's voice when she spoke; another echo in his own reply:

"Yes, Elizabeth. I promise."

She uttered a small, satisfied laugh and leaned back against his arm.

She stayed with him an hour or more, until the house was utterly still, and then stole away. In the weeks that followed, as the new year of 1796 opened, she visited him by night whenever she could. No one in the house seemed to suspect, because the lovers carefully avoided one another except at those times when normal household activities such as meals brought them together.

But not many days had passed in January before Abraham realized that his problems had taken on a new dimension.

He was no longer merely defying his father.

He was falling in love with Elizabeth Fletcher.

CHAPTER IV

The Storm Breaks

DURING LATE JANUARY and into February, Abraham's relationship with his father remained in a state of truce. He agreed to work regular hours at Kent and Son—the firm was expanding so fast that sufficient help couldn't be found—but at the same time, he made clear to Philip that his decision shouldn't be construed as a permanent one.

To reinforce the point, Abraham insisted on menial work and menial wages. He didn't want other employees thinking he was taking advantage of his status as the owner's son.

Despite all the conditions Abraham set, Philip seemed happy with the arrangement. His face showed his pleasure whenever he walked into the press room and saw Abraham black-handed and smeary-cheeked from manipulating the leather balls that inked the type forms, or lugging huge stacks of newly cut paper.

Although new inventions were being introduced at an astonishing rate—duly reported in the columns of the *Bay State Federalist*—the equipment of Kent and Son remained similar to that on which Philip had first learned his trade in a shop in London in the 1770s. Kent's now owned four large flatbeds, each driven by human muscle applied to a screw lever. The presses were located on the first floor of the three-story structure near Long Wharf. Their weight had already caused a noticeable sag in the floor.

On the second story Philip maintained his own bindery, plus warehousing space. Kent and Son had just printed an inexpensive edition of Mr. Noah Webster's *Blue-Backed Speller*. This instructional book for school children was already more than a decade old. But it showed every sign of remaining the standard text for generations to come, and the warehouse was piled high with copies of the Kent version.

The building's third floor held Philip's cramped, rather dingy private office, a smaller press for his weekly newspaper, and another, even dingier cubby occupied by the paper's editor, Mr. Supply Pleasant.

Mr. Pleasant had advanced to journalism from a career as a public letter-writer hired for a few pence by the illiterate, or by those who wanted their correspondence inscribed in a fine, graceful hand. Abraham quickly developed a liking for the graying, pot-bellied editor. Whenever he had a free moment, he climbed the stairs to talk with Pleasant and scan the stories being set in type by Pleasant's one assistant.

Pleasant, in turn, soon sensed Abraham's dissatisfaction with his work downstairs. He raised the subject one blustery day in February:

"Your father's delighted that you're working for Kent's, Abraham."

"It's only temporary, I assure you."

"The book trade isn't to your liking?"

"No, that's not quite it. What I don't like is being expected to spend my life in the book trade."

Supply Pleasant leaned back in his chair, scratched his nose with a quill that left an ink stain between his eyes. He peered over the top of his steel spectacles:

"Then what career do you have in mind? Medicine? The law?"

"I don't know."

"A year's study at Harvard might help you decide."

"I doubt it."

"Well, many a young man takes a while to find his way. But surely you have some idea—"

"Frankly, Mr. Pleasant, about all I've been able to determine so far is what I don't want. I know I'm not a bookman or a scholar. I'm damned if I'd make a good soldier, either—"

Admitting all that was hard. In fact, he was vaguely ashamed that his accomplishments in Boston thus far consisted of doing his job without too many mistakes, and conducting half a dozen furtive meetings with Elizabeth. That last, and the attendant deception of his father and stepmother each secret hour required, were hardly things to be proud of; yet he was so completely and dizzily in love with the fair-haired girl, all else seemed unimportant.

Supply Pleasant chewed the stem of his quill a while, then picked up a stack of neatly inked foolscap sheets:

"Strikes me you're like a beggar at a banquet, Abraham."

"How so, Mr. Pleasant?"

"You're confronted with so many rare dishes, you don't know which to pick first. The country's a veritable cornucopia of opportunity—a veritable cornucopia!" Pleasant had a passion for flowery phrases, in conversation as well as in the paper. He wrote every word of the five columns on each of the four sixteen-by-twenty-inch pages of the *Federalist*.

He handed the foolscap sheets to the younger man: "Sit ten minutes with this. You'll see what I mean."

"What is it?"

"A feature I've been preparing for some time. A review, if you will, of the remarkable accomplishments of our young country. Of course," Pleasant added after another bite of the quill, "my employer exercises his right to edit my copy. There *are* subjects which can't be mentioned. The very sensible metric measurement system, for example. It's certain to become a world standard—certain! But it's deemed an invention of the devil by good Federalists like your father. While other nations go ahead and adopt it, I predict we shall not—simply because the French Jacobins thought it up. Also—"

He pointed at the sheets with his quill.

"Mr. Jefferson's new plow. Experts claim it will revolutionize farming. Not only does it break the soil, it lifts and turns it aside more efficiently by means of the moldboard Jefferson added. I've put in some copy on the plow, but I'm sure Mr. Kent will scratch it out."

"Don't you resent that sort of interference, Mr. Pleasant?"

"Naturally I resent it."

"Then why don't you protest? Or quit? The first amendment to our Constitution in 'ninety-one guaranteed a man's freedom to speak—or publish—what he wishes."

"That's exactly how it is—Mr. Kent publishes what he wishes," Pleasant said with a resigned smile. "I don't quit because I like newspapering. And I'm not shrewd enough on matters of financing to operate my own gazette. You're too young to realize that much of life is compromise, Abraham. My idealism doesn't extend to my belly, which is empty several times a day, regular as a clock. Besides, your father and I have reached a state of accommodation. He only interferes on subjects related to politics."

"But slanted news is dishonest!"

"No doubt you're right. However, don't forget it was propaganda, not straight news, that rescued us from the morass of the unworkable Articles of Confederation and gave us our Constitution. If Messrs Jay and Hamilton and Madison hadn't published their eighty-odd *Federalist* essays in the New York papers a few years ago, we might still be a gaggle of fractious states instead of a reasonably stable federal union. Like all things, journalism has both its lofty and ignoble sides."

Abraham wasn't persuaded. But he was interested in the article Supply Pleasant had handed him; intrigued by its title and sub-headings:

THE YOUNG COLOSSUS!
A Succinct Review of the Conditions
Generating Unparalleled Prosperity
Under Our Federal Government!
Amazing Advancements
In The Mechanical Sciences!
Expansionist Fever Points To
Vast Population Increase!

"To return to my original point," Pleasant said, "there is enough happening in the United States to provide a young fellow with twenty lifetimes of satisfying labor. Give that a scan and you'll see I'm right. Now I must get to work and finish this review of *The Mysterious Monk*. I saw it last night at Powell's theater. A most diverting Gothic melodrama—"

Abraham hardly heard. Carrying the sheets in his blackened fingers, he retired to the back stairs of the building, found a little light under a grimy window, plucked an apple from his leather apron and began to read.

For a while he couldn't get past the opening sentence. He kept seeing Elizabeth's lovely and defiant blue eyes.

ii

Finally Abraham managed to read the article to the end. Mr. Pleasant's piece was indeed a paean to the prosperity and intellectual achievement that seemed to be sweeping the nation.

Pleasant began by noting that the first census, authorized by Congress in 1790, had discovered a population nearing four million, of which, he reported in a dour aside, almost seven hundred thousand were slaves. The editor predicted that by the time of the next census—the year the new century opened—the country would probably grow to an astonishing five or six million people, particularly since there was now more room in which to raise families. The treaties maneuvered through the ministries of England and Spain by Mr. Jay and Mr. Pinckney had at last resolved some territorial disputes and brought a measure of stability to the northwest.

Jay's treaty had removed or reduced the British threat on the country's northern and western borders. Pinckney's Treaty of San Lorenzo, signed in Madrid, had established the Mississippi as the offical western limit of the country—set the southern boundary at the thirty-first parallel—and, most important, given America free navigation of the river and free deposit of goods—the right to store and re-ship them without paying duty—at Spanish-held New Orleans for an initial period of three years. Settlers raising crops for profit would now have a secure and easy route to a major port.

The nation had adapted with reasonable ease to the new coinage of 1786. Abraham smiled at Pleasant's deliberate inclusion of the fact that Mr. Jefferson had thought out the system, based on the Spanish milled dollar; the editor wasn't as pliant as he pretended.

A general economic boom was accelerating the pace of commerce and invention. Mr. Whitney of New Haven, for instance, had virtually eliminated the old, tedious process of cleaning green seed cotton. His new gin enabled a single slave to separate out a remarkable fifty pounds of staple per day. As a result, the entire south was turning to a cotton economy; the commodity had at last been made profitable. At the same time, the luckless Whitney was spending a fortune to defend his patent against infringements by rival manufacturers.

As for "expansionist fever"—well, a whole array of startling developments had made it possible for immigrants to travel into the newly won west faster and more safely than ever before.

Highways were a-building; a turnpike modeled after those in Britain had been opened between Philadelphia and Lancaster, Pennsylvania. Boone's Wilderness Road had been widened to accommodate wagon traffic. And the waterways swarmed with one-way flatboats and keelboats. Families going west gathered on the Pittsburgh docks faster than craft to transport them could be constructed. Wayne's victory had made a journey down the Ohio relatively safe.

Mr. Pleasant touched on other trends that promised to quicken the pace of migration even more. Men were talking of canal systems. Steam power was being harnessed for river boats. Fitch and Rumsey had already launched trial vessels on the Delaware and the Potomac—

With a sigh, Abraham turned over the last sheet. The editor had indeed painted a glowing picture. But in it, he still saw no definite place for himself.

He carried the article back to Pleasant's office, hearing and feeling the thud and vibration of the building's presses. That noise, that motion was a manifestation of his father's power. It brought on the pessimistic thought that perhaps he never would find what he wanted.

On top of that, what he wanted most was something he probably wasn't supposed to have—

Elizabeth.

iii

The shame of conducting an illicit relationship and the intolerable sameness of the work at Kent and Son finally drove Abraham to decisive action. One balmy Sunday in March, he surprised the family at dinner by announcing that he and Elizabeth were going walking in the afternoon.

As he said it, he caught Elizabeth's quick, glowing glance of admiration. Immediately, his stepmother gave all her attention to the plate in front of her.

But to Abraham's surprise, Philip's reaction was exactly the opposite of what he'd expected:

"Certainly, if you wish." Philip smiled at his son. "I'm not quite the blind, insensitive fellow I'm sometimes credited with being. The interest you two have shown in one another hasn't passed entirely unnoticed."

In a panic, Abraham wondered how much his father knew. Peggy partially answered that:

"We've noticed how you gaze at each other at mealtime."

Abraham was still nonplussed, as was Elizabeth. Philip seemed almost as delighted as little Gilbert, who stared at Abraham with worshipful eyes. Abraham could no longer count the number of times he'd described the charge at Fallen Timbers to his half-brother.

"Have you strolled by Hartt's as yet?" Peggy asked her stepson.

"No—"

"It's quite the attraction, even though work on the frigate has been suspended." She was referring to the shipyard where the keel had been laid in 1794 for one of four large warships put under construction by the government. The ships had been ordered as a response to a threat to American commerce in the Mediterranean. Pirate vessels of the Barbary states had taken to harassing U.S. merchantmen. A tenuous settlement had finally been reached with Algiers; it amounted to paying tribute in return for safe passage of American vessels in the area. At that point, work on the frigates being built at Boston, New York, Philadelphia and Norfolk had been stopped.

Still struggling to fathom Philip's easy compliance, Abraham said, "Where we go is less important than—certain things Elizabeth and I need to discuss."

"Then by all means discuss them," Philip exclaimed. "I'm delighted to see you giving some thought to the future. Along with these personal matters, I imagine you'll want to consider a decision about your livelihood."

Peggy shot a warning glance at her husband. Philip ignored it:

"Naturally I hope that will also be resolved in favor of a family association."

So that was the trap! Philip was confident that if Abraham settled down with a wife, he would instantly surrender—join Kent and Son. Abraham's jaw muscles hardened as he put down his napkin and rose abruptly.

"One decision won't necessarily lead to the other, sir."

Stung, Philip turned red.

"Then you are a damned fool, sir!" he shouted as Abraham left the room.

Too overwrought to look back, Abraham heard Elizabeth hurrying after him. He paused in the hall to get control of himself. Elizabeth rushed to his side, grasped his arm in silent approval. As they left the house and turned down sloping Beacon Street, both could hear Philip's voice raised in angry argument with Peggy.

iv

In the sunny warmth of the afternoon, they did wend their way to Hartt's. Abraham perched on a rotting nail keg, barely seeing the huge frigate sitting unfinished on the ways that ran down to the lapping water.

The great hull, over two hundred feet long, was only partially sheathed in the copper supplied by Philip's old friend Mr. Revere—the same gentleman who, years ago, had fitted Philip with a hand-carved replacement for a broken front tooth. Abraham's father now and then liked to show off his tooth of African hippo tusk. Revere had been able to complete that small project—which couldn't be said of his metalwork on the frigate.

Rated at forty-four guns and estimated to cost a staggering three hundred thousand dollars or more, *Constitution* sat in lonely splendor, guarded only by a couple of elderly watchmen. They paid no attention to the dozen people wandering through the yard to admire Boston's would-be contribution to national defense.

Abraham took Elizabeth's hand, stared into those blue eyes that, by turns, could be so intemperate and so loving:

"I wonder how long father and mother have suspected."

"What difference does it make, Abraham?"

"None. Actually, I'm glad the secret's out. Now I can talk to them about my intention."

"Which is—?"

"To marry you, Elizabeth. With their permission or without it."

She bent to tease his mouth with her lips, caressing him briefly with her tongue. A middle-aged couple hurrying by with two children loudly expressed their outrage.

"You still want to marry me even after enjoying what most men want from a wife?"

"How do you know so much about what most men want?"

"La, Abraham, don't be so frightfully stern! I'm fairly suffocated by all the righteousness in the Boston air! And the thickest cloud hangs over Beacon Street—as you well know. I want to get away from here." She touched his cheek. "With you."

Abraham pondered silently a moment or two.

"Elizabeth—I must ask you a hard question."

Her eyes clouded. "Ask it, then."

"I know growing up in the Kent house hasn't been easy for you—"

"Easier than running the streets and alleys, I suppose. But no, it hasn't. Your father isn't my father. Yet he insists on acting like—I'm sorry. What did you want to ask?"

He hesitated. She stamped her foot:

"Go on!"

"All right. My question is this. Would you marry me just to escape?"

"Good heavens, that is a foolish question! Please don't think me too conceited for saying this, but do you fancy you're the only man I *could* marry?"

He sighed. "No. You're a lovely girl. I've noticed the looks some of papa's gentlemen friends cast your way. I realize you could have your pick of husbands."

"Doesn't that answer your question, my darling?"

He shook his head. "Not entirely. I wouldn't want you to say yes in order to spite father—"

"Impossible! You saw his reaction at the table. I think he'll approve of the match."

"Oh, no. Not unless a commitment to Kent and Son is part of it."

"But it isn't, is it?"

The intensity of her whisper bothered Abraham; revealed again the depth of her dislike of Philip. Still, he said:

"No."

"Then don't make me out to be more wicked than you are, please."

"I don't understand."

"Are *you* thinking of marrying me because it would help you break with him?"

Chilled, he realized how accurate her question was. All the turmoil of the past weeks seemed to clarify in an instant. He understood at last, completely, that Elizabeth's pleas about resisting his father would never have taken root had not the ground been fertile. He needed a force to propel him to action; to help separate him from what he didn't want—even though he still had no clear goal to pursue afterward.

Glumly, he admitted, "Yes—in part. Don't misconstrue that. I do love you. Very much."

"And I love you, Abraham. You needn't be ashamed of admitting we need each other because neither of us can fight him alone."

"He isn't trying to influence me to join the firm out of malice—"

Her features froze. "Since he's your father, you're free to hold that view. But I see it differently. I'm not his child—and I refuse to jump at his every order."

He was tolerant of her last remark. Her reaction to Philip wasn't tempered by natural love, as his was. Yet even he could never remember a time when his father hadn't terrified him just a little. Philip was a formidable person; a penniless bastard boy who, by sheer will and luck, had elevated himself from nothing to a position of importance in Boston. Abraham recalled one dreadful period of double intimidation; a dim time when Philip's authority had been supported by a harridan housekeeper.

A woman named Brumple, long dead. Under Philip's orders, she had pushed Abraham this way and that—

He shook his head again, as if clearing his mind. There was no doubt that he had to escape Philip's dominance, or perish.

Once more he clasped Elizabeth's hand. He was heartened by the responsive pressure of her fingers. And her soothing tone:

"It's all right, Abraham. Marrying to escape him is no sin—"

He didn't answer. His gaze drifted back to the copper plating on *Constitution*'s lower hull. A highlight from the sun blinded him a moment. In the glare he saw a ghost-image of Elizabeth's blue eyes. Unsettling; defiant—

He loved her in spite of all he knew about her: that she'd been born with rebellious blood; a temperament that delighted in defying accepted standards and conventional family authority. It didn't pay to dwell too long on that side of her character. He had to remember only that she was lovely, and said she loved him—

"What we've decided raises another issue, though," he said. "I must support you, but I have no trade."

"We're both young and strong—" She clapped her hands and threw her arms wide. "We can do anything we wish! The country's vast now. There's room for us to search for the kind of life that suits us. I honestly don't care where we live so long as it's not Boston."

Abruptly, his mind jumped to a memory of Anthony Wayne's musings about the promise of the northwest, then to the article by Mr. Pleasant; specifically, his comments on the tide of migration sweeping through Pennsylvania and down the Ohio to the territory east of the Mississippi. Speculating aloud, he described what Wayne had said about the opportunity in the lands now largely cleared of Indian menace.

As he spoke, Elizabeth watched him with total attention. When he finished, her voice was hushed:

"My father felt just as General Wayne does, Abraham. You know he was a lifelong friend of George Rogers Clark—"

"Yes."

"Mother's told me Clark wrote him many letters about the west. But he only got as far as Pittsburgh. We—we could go farther. Build our own home—why, I've read you can buy an acre of ground out there for as little as two dollars!"

"If you attend an auction sponsored by one of the speculation companies. They've grabbed up a lot of the acreage." His speech quickened, just as hers had a moment ago. "There are other ways—"

"Tell me!"

"Men who fought in the Revolution can claim parcels of western land the government reserved for veterans."

"Does your father own land like that?"

"I've no idea. I suppose if he ever did, he's sold it by now."

"Even if he hasn't, he'd never give it to us."

"You're probably right. Better we don't even raise the subject with him. Besides, when I was in the army, I saw a few people who simply moved in and settled where they wished. Squatters, they're called. They choose their land first and worry about filing a claim later. If you go far enough west, you see, you'll find territory that hasn't been laid out into townships—or even surveyed as yet. Pick a parcel like that, and if you're lucky, no speculators will ever leave their comfortable eastern parlors to dispute your title—" He sighed all at once. "It's an exciting idea."

"Oh, yes!"

"But there's a drawback."

"I don't see any."

"The one I mentioned before. I've no trade I could practice out there."

"You know how to run a printing press."

"I've no particular desire to be a printer. Besides, it'll be a while before the west is civilized enough to want many newspapers and handbills."

"Frankly, I don't care what you do. Keep a store. Hammer at a smith's forge. Farm—"

"I doubt I'd be too successful at farming—"

"How do you know till you've tried? You're certainly bright enough to learn anything you want to learn. *If* you want it badly enough."

Standing, he put both hands on her waist. "I want only you. Let the rest happen as it will."

Again he thought he detected that strange glint of malicious delight in her sunlit eyes. He resolved not to worry about it. Who ever understood all the motives behind any action or decision? He was content that her passion matched his.

In a moment, emotion swept practical considerations out of his mind. The thought of the two of them launching out together beyond the mountain barriers had an almost magical attraction—

"All right," he said abruptly. "We'll try the new country."

She fairly leaped into his arms, hugging him while scandalized heads again turned their way. He felt the warmth of her mouth near his ear:

"Do you know a secret? I despise wearing stockings and shoes—isn't that funny? In the west, I won't have to, will I?"

"No." He laughed. "No, you can run barefoot any time you please."

Happy and confident, they rushed back to the Kent house to break the news.

V

When Philip heard Abraham's breathless declaration of the young couple's plans, he reacted swiftly and emphatically:

"Madness! Absolute *madness!*"

His strong, blunt jaw had drained of color. He stalked back and forth in front of the windows overlooking the street and the Common, where noisy children played in the sunlight. A chill had enveloped the sitting room all at once, it seemed to Abraham.

Peggy Kent, seated, tried to temper her husband's rage:

"Perhaps we should discuss the whole subject later, Philip. When everyone's a bit calmer—"

"What is there to discuss, woman? The very idea's preposterous!"

Consigned to a corner of a settee, Gilbert bounced to his feet:

"I think it's splendid, papa. I've read Mr. Pleasant's articles in your paper—men will be needed for all sorts of work in the west."

"Be damned to your impertinence!" Philip shouted. Gilbert turned white. Philip shot out one hand, pointing. "To your room—immediately!"

Hurt, Gilbert rose and hurried out.

Philip limped over and slammed the doors. Then he whirled to face his son. In moments, Philip had almost destroyed Abraham's confidence. But Elizabeth looked as determined as ever; and almost as angry as the head of the household.

Before she could say anything, Philip shook a finger in his son's face:

"The time to abandon this lunacy is *now,* young man!"

"No, I won't—"

"*Yes!* You're being totally impractical!"

"Papa, I refuse to listen to—"

Philip drowned him out: "Precisely what do you plan to do after you complete this romantic pilgrimage? Become one of Mr. Jefferson's noble and impoverished dirt-farmers?"

"By God, sir," Abraham said, reddening, "there's no shame in any kind of work so long as it's respectable."

"Respectable poverty, that's what you want?"

"I want to make my own way! Thousands of others are doing it—with fewer wits and less strength than I have!"

"I question your statement about wits," Philip sneered. "You've lost yours." He faced Elizabeth. "This is entirely your doing."

"Philip, don't—!" Peggy began. Elizabeth broke in:

"You're vile to suggest that!"

"Do you deny it?"

"I won't deny Abraham and I want to leave Boston and live our own lives—"

"In preference to staying here and enjoying security? Wealth? The chance to mold opinion—the very course of this nation? You're a fool—" Philip spun to his son. "And so are you. At Kent's you have every opportunity to be of real service to the country—*and* earn a handsome profit at the same time! I—"

Suddenly Philip drew a deep breath. His anger seemed to melt just a little. He ignored Elizabeth standing beside Abraham, gripping his arm. His eyes sought his son's, imploring:

"—I beg you to recognize what you're throwing away."

"We're throwing away *nothing*!" Elizabeth exclaimed. "Arguing is useless. We plan to be married and go where we will!"

Again Philip started to yell, restrained himself only

with obvious effort. While Peggy watched anxiously, he took a different tack. His voice shook as he raised both hands:

"A compromise, then—"

Abraham looked stunned when he heard the words. They were natural enough coming from a poor man like Supply Pleasant. When Philip used them, it signaled panic.

"No compromise," Elizabeth said.

"You must give me a fair chance to present my side. Abraham? You must!"

Abraham hated to see his father plead. It was sad and degrading, somehow. And yet, one tiny part of his mind took pleasure in it.

He said to Elizabeth, "We should at least be courteous enough to listen—"

"*No!*"

"Yes," Abraham said, with firmness.

"Thank you," Philip said. "If—if you've failed to see the sort of future you could have, the fault's mine. I must rectify that. Elizabeth—"

Forcing himself to ignore her hostile glare, he moved toward her, his right shoulder sagging at every step.

"—you've never been outside Boston. Abraham has seen nothing but the back roads and rivers between here and that damned godforsak—between here and the west. Let me show you what you'll be rejecting if you pursue the course you've set—"

Sounding more confident, Philip straightened his shoulders, even attempted a smile:

"I think after I've laid the alternative before you both, you'll quickly choose it in preference to your own plan."

Quietly, Peggy said, "Philip, I am not sure what you *are* proposing."

"A tour! A holiday! To the capital—perhaps even as

far as your home state of Virginia—" There was a falsity to Philip's enthusiasm that still saddened Abraham. But he listened without comment as the older man rushed on:

"I'm in need of a change of scene anyway. The good weather is coming—the roads will be passable—we'll show these young people where the future of America really lies. In the cities! The solid seats of power along the coast! By God, I'll even write my old friend Henry Knox and arrange for Abraham and Elizabeth to meet the president himself! What do you say, Abraham?"

The son hesitated, sickened to see his father so desperate. At the same time, he was conscious of Elizabeth's tension as she held his arm. Her fingers dug into the fabric of his sleeve.

"I say nothing can change our minds," she told Philip.

"Not the prospect of being well off? Influential? Ah, we'll see. We'll see—!" He looked straight at Abraham. "As my son, I think it is your duty to grant me the right to prove my case."

"Oh, that's unfair, sir!" Elizabeth cried. "To play on his emotions—" She would have said more, but Peggy's sharp glance silenced her.

There was a long moment in which no one spoke. Then, very quietly, Philip said:

"Abraham?"

Abraham knew even before he replied that his father had outwitted him—because Philip knew his son couldn't refuse a plea of family love, family duty—no matter how expedient or meretricious its invocation. With mingled feelings of outrage and pity, he answered:

"All right, we'll accede to your wishes, papa."

"Splendid, excellent! We'll leave within a week."

"But don't expect miracles," Abraham cautioned. "Our minds are made up."

"Ah, we'll see!" Philip repeated, trying to restore a measure of gaiety to the discussion. Elizabeth's blue eyes burned with resentment.

As his anger drained away, Abraham was saddened by a new thought. The Bible, which Peggy had insisted he study as a boy, said something explicit about a man taking a wife, and cleaving to her, and leaving his father's house forever. He'd come to that watershed—and at the last moment, refused to cross.

Seated beside Peggy, Philip was already outlining his plans for hiring carriages, packing their belongings. He acted supremely confident. For a moment Abraham thought that his father might be right. Perhaps he *was* a fool to throw away so many advantages—

As if sensing his indecision, Elizabeth dug her fingers still deeper into his arm. Abraham looked at her, then away. The savagery of her glance terrified him.

CHAPTER V

"Scenes of Life Among the Mighty"

WHEN EDITOR PLEASANT learned of the forthcoming trip, and heard Abraham describe its purpose, he broke out laughing:

"Why, it's almost as if he's taking you to a great museum, isn't it? One in which you'll be expected to sigh and gape respectfully at scenes of life among the mighty—"

Pleasant sobered, raised a hand. "I don't mean to mock your father, Abraham. He's treated me well. But he's as stubborn as sin—and remarkably canny, as you'll discover if you haven't so far. Prepare yourself for a dazzling exhibition. 'Scenes of life among the mighty'—"

He scribbled it down with his quill.

"I rather like that. Damned if I'm not a shade jealous at being left behind!"

Pleasant's phrase stuck in Abraham's mind, constantly emphasizing the contrivance of the trip and tainting his attitude toward it. He didn't mention the remark to Elizabeth. He was afraid she might taunt Philip with it. That could earn Pleasant a reprimand, a cut in salary, the loss of his job, or, if Philip were really exercised, a thrashing. From his boyhood Abraham remembered a couple of occasions when Philip struck employees who displeased him.

The family set out in mid-April, in two carriages.

Each carriage had its own driver and postillion. Luggage was lashed in place on top. An armed guard rode ahead, another behind; ugly fellows, but necessary because the rutted highways were known to attract thieves who preyed on rich travelers.

Gilbert was delighted by every new vista along the route. But Elizabeth complained constantly about the jars and jolts. At their overnight stops, she seldom ate more than a few mouthfuls of the evening's meal, and retired early. Her pale blue eyes sought Abraham's often, silently imploring him—warning him—not to be seduced. He had few chances to speak to her in private, and reassure her that he was on his guard.

As Elizabeth suffered under the rigors of the journey, Philip's spirits, by contrast, grew more and more ebullient. He was positively gay as they neared the nation's temporary capital, Philadelphia.

On their first full day in that splendid and impressive city, they drove out to see some of the fine Georgian homes, as well as the newer, neo-classic ones designed in what was coming to be called the Federal style. They visited Congress Hall, where the two houses of the legislature sat while in session. They returned to their lodgings to find a beautifully inscribed invitation from the appointments secretary of the chief executive of the United States.

President and Mrs. Washington would be delighted to receive the family of Mr. Philip Kent, the noted Boston publisher, at their quarters in the Morris mansion on High Street at four P.M. Thursday.

At last, Elizabeth seemed a bit impressed by the ease with which Philip's long-time friendship with the Boston bookseller Henry Knox, now retired as Secretary of War and gone to Maine, had opened the doors that shielded the mighty from those Philip scorned as "Jefferson's democratic-republican rabble."

ii

Robert Morris had signed the Declaration; managed the fledgling nation's finances during the Revolution; founded the national bank. He was called the wealthiest man in the country. His house, turned over to the president and first lady for their own use, was a magnificent three-story brick mansion. In it, people said, everything glittered, as befitted an American Midas. The lamp fixtures outside glittered; the furniture and mahogany woodwork glittered; the largest brass door-hinge and the smallest bit of brass cabinet hardware glittered. It was no wonder the entire Kent family was in a state of nerves when their carriage pulled up in front of the Morris house at the appointed hour.

With obvious trepidation, Peggy remarked on the presence of half a dozen even more sumptuous coaches, and many servants lounging around them. Even Elizabeth's eyes sparkled at the sight.

Elizabeth had dressed with special care, as they all had. Her gown of white brocade silk shimmered in the mild sunlight of the spring afternoon. In her excitement, she stumbled going up the walk, losing one of her silver-embroidered high-heeled shoes, which Abraham gallantly retrieved.

Servants ushered the visitors into the parlor. Abraham's nervousness grew as the elegantly groomed guests, a dozen ladies and gentlemen, turned toward the newcomers.

The aging president approached the Kents, a small, plump woman at his side. Martha Washington exchanged curtseys with Peggy and Elizabeth while the tall Virginian who preferred Mount Vernon to Philadelphia greeted Philip and his party with impeccable politeness:

"I'm honored to welcome so distinguished a family,

Mr. Kent. When General Knox wrote that you planned a tour, I decided we must surely meet—for social as well as for somewhat more practical reasons."

Washington, Abraham noticed, had an odd, rigid smile. Except when speaking, he kept his lips compressed. The gossipmongers said this was to hide false teeth that fit poorly, causing him continual discomfort. According to Supply Pleasant, a New York dentist had carved the president's dentures out of hippotamus ivory, the same material Revere had used for Philip's false tooth. Washington's were reportedly attached to metal bars that gouged his gums and lent his lower face a swollen look.

Philip said, "The honor is entirely ours, Mr. President."

"Come, let me present you to the rest of the gathering," Washington said. His lips parted sufficiently for Abraham to see that something—wine or tea—had badly blackened the artificial teeth.

Among men who were taller than he, Philip always seemed to stand more erect. That was the case now. His limp was hardly noticeable as he walked at Washington's side.

Abraham and the others met Robert Morris and his wife, then the tubby vice president, John Adams, and his wife Abigail. Philip and Adams reminisced briefly about their long acquaintance; it had begun in Boston, before the Revolution.

The famous Philadelphia socialite and beauty, Mrs. Bingham, was presented next. She graciously drew Peggy and Elizabeth into conversation after apologizing that her wealthy husband was indisposed.

Servants brought in refreshments—tea, port and trays of sweet little cakes. Before long, the gentlemen were gathered in one group, the ladies in another. The president led Philip and the others to a large, ornate key which hung on one wall of the parlor.

"I'm reminded that you are a good friend of the Marquis de Lafayette, Mr. Kent."

Philip didn't seem the least overawed by the towering president. Giving a crisp nod, he replied, "Perhaps you also recall we met when we were quite young, in our native province of Auvergne, in France."

Washington nodded. Then his gaze turned toward the great key. "My sympathies were with the revolutionaries for a time. As were those of our mutual friend." He gestured. "That is the key to the Bastille. Lafayette obtained it the day that evil fortress was destroyed, and later sent it to me."

"I understand the marquis is being reasonably well treated in prison," Philip said.

"Yes, so I've heard. But his circumstances grieve me all the same. France was our great ally once. Now I believe our courses have separated—perhaps forever."

The president was alluding to the political rift between the Federalists—some said they controlled Washington's thinking through Alexander Hamilton—and Jefferson, the Francophile, who had resigned his position as secretary of state and gone home to Virginia.

"Experience is a good teacher, if she is only heeded," Washington continued. "I would hope the next president of these states would avoid permanent alliances of any kind. Even though conditions have changed radically in France in twenty years, she still expects us to grant her favored status because of her past support. Our refusal may pose difficulties for us."

Philip set his port aside. "You refer to the next president, sir. The reports are true, then? You won't relent and seek a third term?"

Washington shook his head. "When a man passes sixty, a certain vigor departs. But I am sure your widely read newspaper, as well as you personally, will stand behind the gentleman I hope to see elected by year's end."

He laid a hand on the shoulder of the preening Adams.

"Among men of Federalist persuasion, Mr. Adams has no peers and no rivals," Philip answered smoothly. "Of course my paper will endorse his candidacy."

Robert Morris—and even Adams himself—murmured their approval.

Abraham was beginning to understand the pleasure his father took in associating with these opulently dressed, rather aristocratic gentlemen. They were the movers of the new nation. Abraham sensed an unspoken bond between them. They shared, and enjoyed, power. Philip was happy to be included.

President Washington faced Abraham. But his words were for the older Kent:

"And your son? Does he intend to carry on the family endeavor? Will my successor have his support along with yours?"

Philip's glance challenged Abraham. "I have every hope the answer to both questions will be affirmative."

Abraham's jaws clenched. A burst of laughter from the ladies kept him from speaking up, and mentioning his plan to travel west. With the rest of the gentlemen, he turned toward the women. He saw Elizabeth chatting in lively fashion with the beautiful Mrs. Bingham. He was delighted to see color back in her cheeks—

He decided not to re-open the argument with his father in such dignified surroundings.

iii

The Kents stayed a week in Philadelphia, attending the theater and visiting tourist attractions such as Bartram's famous botanical gardens, the Charles Peale museum with its amazing display of mastodon bones, and the old State House where the Declaration had been presented by the self-exiled Mr. Jefferson. Then the two carriages resumed their journey south. Peggy had persuaded Philip to follow through on a chance remark the day the trip first came up. At her request, Philip intended to show the young couple the prosperous, populous state of Virginia where Peggy had spent much of her life.

The spring weather turned stormy. The roads became bogs. Progress was slow and the carriages stopped frequently. Alarmed, Abraham watched Elizabeth growing pale again. She was unable to travel for more than a few hours without succumbing to fits of nausea.

For the first time, he wondered about her health. She had always been slender and somewhat delicate. Now he asked himself whether she was suited for a long trip west, not to mention the hard work that would follow. Perhaps he shouldn't be so quick to reject his father's offer of a good job—

He didn't express his doubts to the girl. They were having enough trouble just making a few miles a day on the wretched roads.

Their route took them near the ten-square-mile tract of land straddling the Potomac River where the capital would eventually be located. The site had been chosen in a political horse trade. Former Secretary of the Treasury Hamilton had been instrumental in moving the permanent seat of the nation's government below the Mason-Dixon survey line in return for southern votes for some of his financial measures.

The special district, two-thirds in Maryland, one-third on the southwest side of the river in Virginia, was already being informally called "Columbia," in honor of the Italian navigator who had reached the continent in the fifteenth century. A French-born engineer named

L'Enfant was drawing up plans for a modern city which everyone hoped could be occupied by the turn of the century.

Abraham found Virginia a green and pleasant state, full of handsome homes, large tracts under cultivation —and scores of black men and women owned outright by white planters. Though he was well aware of slavery's existence, seeing it first hand was something of a jolt. He'd been brought up in the only state in the union which had reported a slave population of zero in the 1790 census.

As the weather improved, so did Elizabeth's health. The Kents spent an enjoyable week and a half at an inn in Caroline County, responding to invitations from families who remembered Peggy and her second husband from their trip to Virginia shortly after their marriage in 1781. The family even received a note by courier from a totally unexpected source: a gentleman who had heard of their presence from mutual friends with whom they'd dined.

When Peggy read the gracious note, Philip exploded: "*What?* Visit that damned republican devil? I'd sooner take a vacation in hell!"

"Come, come, dear," Peggy soothed. "Mr. Jefferson is an old, old friend of my parents. It would be rude to refuse his invitation to Monticello." She teased him: "Are you afraid your principles would melt away in his presence?"

"I am afraid I might not be able to contain my temper!"

"I think we should go, papa," Abraham said.

"The decision is not yours," Philip answered in a brusque way. But after twenty-four hours of grumbling, he gave in. He justified his turnabout by saying a man should know his enemy.

The two carriages left the Rappahannock and turned

westward toward Mr. Jefferson's country seat in Albemarle County. There, on the eight-hundred-foot *monticello*—little mountain—near Charlottesville, Philip confronted his intellectual adversary.

He soon had cause to regret agreeing to the excursion.

iv

Never in his life had Abraham inhaled such a heady combination of fragrances—nor seen so many different kinds of trees.

Mr. Jefferson had arranged to receive them in the garden adjoining his orchard. A burly black servant who met the carriage pointed out the varieties: walnut and peach; plum and cherry; olives and almonds and figs. There were even a few of the exotic orange trees from the far Floridas. Deer could be glimpsed grazing here and there in the orchard. Only Peggy acted uninterested. She gave the slave guide a peculiar, nervous look from time to time.

On the carriage ride to the hilltop, Abraham had been startled to see that Monticello seemed to be in a state of disrepair. Now, at close range, his original impression was confirmed. Scaffolding rose everywhere. Slaves pushed barrows of bricks from the kilns on the property. Carpenters' tools made a racket in the soft morning air. Peggy explained that since the death of his wife and the decline of his political fortunes, the man who had played such a large role in shaping the new country had withdrawn from public life and now occupied himself with his two passions—architecture and agriculture.

Abraham touched Peggy's arm. Was the man approaching through the orchard Mr. Jefferson? Yes, she said, it was. The man's clothing instantly drew a disdainful comment from Philip, who was formally dressed. Jefferson, ten years younger than the president, and standing well over six feet, wore a linen shirt sticky with sweat, and workman's trousers tucked into dusty boots.

Jefferson's face had a gaunt quality, as if from illness or personal strain. But he greeted Abraham's stepmother warmly, taking both her hands in his:

"My dear Peggy! How wonderful to see you! When I heard you'd come home, I wanted to welcome you in grand style—" Chagrined, he indicated his filthy clothes. "—and look at me."

"You're remodeling the house, Tom—"

"Again," he said, and pointed. "Tearing down most of the façade. There'll be a new foyer and balcony, and an octagonal roof I've patterned after the Roman temple of Vesta. Unfortunately, a scaffolding collapsed yesterday. One of my nigras—the husband of my cook—nearly lost his life. We've been in a turmoil—so all my plans for setting you a good meal inside have gone away."

In the sunlight, Jefferson's graying hair still showed faint glints of its original red. He swung toward Philip, who was gazing at the blacks pushing the barrows. Jefferson had often spoken out against the evils of slavery. Yet he continued to keep slaves on his own property, making him vulnerable to the criticism of New Englanders.

If the former secretary of state understood the meaning of Philip's pointed stare, he was polite enough to overlook it.

"And this is your husband—" Jefferson reached Philip in two long strides, grasped his hand. "My honor, Mr. Kent."

"Mine, sir," Philip said.

Peggy introduced Abraham and wide-eyed Gilbert. Then she resorted to the convenient falsehood used by the family:

"And my niece who lives with us, Miss Elizabeth Fletcher."

Jefferson raked a muscular wrist across his sweaty jaw. His eyes lingered on Elizabeth's face. "Fletcher," he repeated. "A familiar name in the district where you grew up, Peggy. The Fletchers of Sermon Hill come to mind—"

Pale, Peggy answered, "There is no connection other than coincidence, Tom. Elizabeth is kin to my mother's people in Massachusetts."

"Yes, I suppose we have no monopoly on good English names in Virginia," Jefferson smiled.

Philip shifted from foot to foot, uncomfortable. Abraham had been a bit startled at his stepmother violating protocol by introducing Elizabeth last rather than first. Now he suspected the reason—fear. He recalled that Elizabeth's father had spent a short time in the Second Continental Congress, as an alternate for his older brother. Jefferson, attending the same Congress—had he known the long-dead Judson Fletcher? If so, it might account for his momentary surprise when Elizabeth was presented.

But any echoes of the past had been stilled by Peggy's statement and Jefferson's tactful acceptance of it. He led his guests to benches in the breezy shade. A moment later, a huge-breasted black woman brought a tray of refreshments into the garden. Abraham took a crystal goblet of tea with chips of ice floating in it. Philip gave Gilbert permission to run off and explore the orchard, but warned him to avoid the frantic construction activity near the house.

Jefferson sat down, resting his elbows on his knees and lacing his fingers together beneath his chin. Philip remained standing. Jefferson said:

"Your newspaper is well written, Mr. Kent."

Now it was Philip's turn to be startled. It took him a

moment to reply, with a shrug whose involuntary impoliteness made Peggy frown:

"The *Bay State Federalist* is only a minor part of the activities of Kent and Son, Mr. Jefferson."

"Yes, but politically, it's the most important part."

"I'm surprised the paper has circulated this far south."

Jefferson's smile was vaguely pained. "Why, Mr. Kent, I never close my mind to the views of the opposition."

"A noble sentiment," Philip mumbled, put off by the other man's polite and winning manner.

"Not a sentiment—conviction!" The tall Virginian stood up. "The basis of our government is the opinion of the people, Mr. Kent. *All* the people—"

Philip stiffened. Jefferson returned the pugnacious stare with an equally steady one. He immediately began to undercut Philip's obvious irritation:

"So the very first object of government must be the maintenance of free circulation of ideas. From all quarters. If it were left to me to decide whether we ought to have a government without newspapers, or newspapers without a government, I shouldn't hesitate a moment to prefer the latter." He smiled that charming smile again, and drank his tea, leaving Philip nonplussed.

Jefferson turned his attention to Abraham:

"What's your role in Kent and Son, young man? Are you connected with the book side? Or the newspaper?"

"I work in the book printing department. But I don't have an official position. My—" He decided to test the water. "—my presence in Boston is only temporary."

"How so?"

Ignoring Philip's hostile stare, Abraham went on, "I served with General Wayne's Legion in the northwest. I was taken with the spaciousness and abundance of the country. I find the idea of settling where there's plenty of land—and few people—more appealing than city life."

He was about to add that the girl Peggy presented as her niece shared that opinion, and would share whatever future it led him to as well. But since neither Philip nor Peggy had raised the subject of marriage, he held back; the introduction of one more irritant wouldn't help the already strained situation.

"You plan to take up farming, then?" Jefferson asked.

"Quite possibly."

"Do you know anything about agriculture?"

"No. But I imagine a man can learn that, can't he?"

"Indeed he can—if he has the back for it."

Peggy's soft laugh was forced. A bird rilled in a nearby walnut tree. Philip didn't bother to hide his unhappiness over the course of the conversation.

Jefferson, however, showed genuine enthusiasm all at once. He snatched up a stick, sat down and started to trace a rectangular shape where the grass had worn away in front of his bench.

"I'm glad to hear your plans, young man. I think they're praiseworthy." As he talked, he changed the outline of the rectangle, angling it here, adding a jutting peninsula there. All at once Abraham realized Jefferson was drawing a crude map of the North American continent.

"We must fill the west with settlers as fast as we can. In the west, there's room for families to multiply. And an increasing population of farmers and craftsmen will strengthen America immeasurably."

"That is the democratic view," Philip said in an arch way. "The French view."

Jefferson didn't rise to the bait:

"Unfortunately, the French have carried liberty to the stage of license—but yes, you're quite right. They have also shaped my views—as perhaps mine shaped theirs."

Drawing a vertical slash from the bottom of the rectangle two-thirds of the way to the top, he tapped it with the stick, saying to Abraham:

"Our boundaries extend only this far—the Mississippi. But beyond—" He moved the stick left, toward the irregular coastline. "—the land mass is immense. All of this territory is currently the property of Spain. In fact, a Franciscan named Serra has established missions all up and down this shore—"

He jabbed several times at the western perimeter, then moved the stick back to the right.

"But it's my conviction that the Spanish lands physically connected to these United States must one day belong to the United States. Somehow, somehow—!"

"And what about British land, sir?" Philip demanded. "What about Canada? Would you covet that too?"

"I might."

Jefferson cast the stick aside, standing again, splendidly tall and commanding:

"At very least, we must know for certain what natural riches lie between the Mississippi and the ocean. I've tried for almost a decade to generate funds for a transcontinental exploration—all the way to the Pacific. A few years ago, I almost succeeded. The Philosophical Society agreed to send Michaux, a French botanist. The president himself gave the largest single contribution—twenty-five dollars. Which shows you the popularity of exploration. Or should I say the insularity of those of us who live east of the mountains?"

"I'm not surprised you had trouble raising the money," Philip told him. "Such exploration is absolutely pointless."

"Indeed? Spain doesn't think it's pointless. She's been at it for several centuries."

"America's prosperity rests on the continuing development of eastern commerce."

"Partly, only partly," Jefferson argued. "A contemporary man must have manufactured articles—including a shirt on his back. But he also needs food in his belly. The northeast is poor farmland, and the south is going to cotton. The west, by contrast, is unbelievably fertile. We simply can't ignore that kind of natural wealth—"

As he spoke, his gaze lingered on the hazy blue hills in the west. Then he smiled again:

"But let's not quarrel over honest differences of opinion, Mr. Kent. The fact is, many Americans feel just as you do. That's why I wasn't able to implement my trans-continental plan in '93."

Philip said, "I also recall Michaux proved to be a spy intent on causing friction between America and Spain."

Jefferson looked rueful. "That's correct. When the less than pure-hearted botanist was recalled by President Washington, we had something of a scene about it. Just one of many," he added, with a trace of sadness. "Still, if I'm ever in a position to encourage a similar venture, I will. I believe our country's true future lies not in the east but the west."

For the first time, Elizabeth broke from the expected feminine role of polite listener:

"That's exactly what Abraham has been saying, Mr. Jefferson!"

"Then I'd encourage you to follow your instincts, young man. They're correct."

"I am *dis*couraging him!" Philip exclaimed, limping off to emphasize his pique. "I think the idea is utterly foolish."

"I don't know that either of us will have much of a hand in the decision, Mr. Kent." Jefferson nodded to Abraham. "Youth must be given its day—and its freedom to choose. Ah, but I think we've quite covered the subject—let me give you a tour of the grounds. And then, if you don't mind the dust and noise, I'll show you a little of the house, too."

He lifted one hand toward Philip, palm up; it was both an invitation and a gesture of conciliation. Although Philip still looked flushed and upset, he didn't prolong the argument. He fell in step beside his wife as Jefferson led the way.

Abraham and Elizabeth dropped a few steps behind, allowing their hands to touch. She whispered softly:

"Mr. Jefferson said exactly what I hoped to hear, Abraham."

"And I."

"Those dreadful, stuffy people in Philadelphia—so rich and smug—I don't want to be like them. I don't want to spend my life in drawing rooms—or on a plantation veranda, for that matter—murmuring lies with a smile on my face."

"Speaking of lies, I had the eerie feeling Mr. Jefferson recognized you."

"I suppose he would have known my father, and I'm told I resemble him."

"I feel a little sorry for papa. I expect he's kicking himself for his decision to come here."

"He only did it as a courtesy to mama," Elizabeth sniffed, scornful. "Your father was positively rude. There's no other word for it."

"Rude because he fears Jefferson's right," Abraham said. His eyes were drawn to the blurred hills of the Blue Ridge in the west. But his mind went back to Supply Pleasant's mocking comments about the little series of exhibitions arranged for his benefit. How true the editor's jibe had turned out to be!

Ah, but Jefferson had given Philip a comeuppance.

Under the spell of the Virginian's words, with Elizabeth at his side in the sweet-smelling lane between rows of trees, Abraham abruptly voiced a decision:

"I wavered a little in Philadelphia. But now I'm convinced we should do what we talked about doing in the first place."

"I am too, my darling."

He turned, noting that his father and stepmother were a good distance away in the orchard's dappled shade. Mr. Jefferson was pointing out something up in the branches of a cherry tree. But Philip was staring back over his shoulder at the young lovers who stood close together beneath leaves that seethed softly in the warm wind.

Abraham began, "I have only one reservation—"

Her blue eyes flared. "You're afraid to inform your father of your decision, is that what you mean?"

He was, a little. But it wasn't what troubled him:

"You haven't been in the best of health on this trip. A life somewhere other than a comfortable city might be too difficult for you."

"Abraham—"

"No, hear me out. If I were responsible for putting you into unhappy circumstances, I'd carry it on my conscience all my days."

"I am strong and completely healthy!" Elizabeth said, with such fervency that Abraham was alarmed. She protested too much. It was another indication of her almost fanatic desire to escape the confinement of the Kent house.

She seized his hand. "I'll go with you anywhere you want to go. And I'll thrive, I promise you. I'll thrive!"

What she said failed to put all his fears to rest. But her expression was so intense, he didn't dare voice further doubt.

So, with part of the burden temporarily lifted by her declaration, he closed his fingers around hers. Together they hurried to catch up to the older people.

V

That night, in the sitting room of the suite they had taken at the best lodging house in Charlottesville, Abraham and Elizabeth announced their determination to stick by their original plan.

Again Philip burst into a rage; again he hammered them with the same arguments. Hadn't they seen the desirability of being welcome among the rich and powerful—?

Losing his temper, Abraham admitted that such a life had its charms—for those who valued them:

"Perhaps there's a reason you value them more than I, papa."

"Explain that remark!"

"There's still a touch of the aristocrat in your blood. Your father *was* an English lord, after all—"

Livid, Philip whirled on Peggy. "This is your fault!"

"Just a moment, sir—!" she exclaimed.

"Don't deny it! You permitted him to be exposed to Jefferson's democratic rot—!"

"You agreed to come, Philip! No one coerced you!"

"Don't blow Mr. Jefferson's part in this all out of proportion," Abraham put in. "He did no more than articulate what I've been thinking for a long time."

"He did more than that," Elizabeth said. "He told the truth!" To Philip: "Which you, in your narrowness, can't stand to hear!"

Philip glared. *"You damned, ungrateful—"*

"Stop it, sir!" Peggy cried, jumping up. She was angrier than Abraham had ever seen her.

Philip limped to Gilbert, who sat on a cane-backed

chair, huge-eyed and frightened. He slipped his arm around the boy's shoulders:

"At least I've one son who won't turn his back on me."

"Oh, God, sir—that's *vicious!*" Elizabeth practically screamed. "The closer you come to being defeated, the more your cruel, vindictive nature reveals itself!"

Philip's hand whipped upward, as if he meant to strike her. She ran to Abraham. Slowly, and with obvious effort, Philip lowered his hand to his side.

"Cruel?" Philip repeated in a strangled voice. "Vindictive—? I thank you for your compassionate judgment. For your gratitude—" His glance at his older son was scathing. "I thank you both. Gilbert, come with me."

"Where, papa?"

"Downstairs. I'll buy you a sweet from the landlord before you're tucked in."

Stunned and hurt, Abraham watched his father limp out with the boy. Peggy began to cry softly.

Elizabeth moved closer to Abraham, pressing her breast against him. She slipped her arms around his waist, squeezed hard, making a strange little sound in her throat. A suppressed laugh? he thought, horrified. No, surely not—

She buried her head against his chest. He couldn't see her eyes, ugly with triumph.

Philip didn't speak to either of them for the first forty-eight hours of the dismal journey home.

CHAPTER VI

Wedding Night

IN HIS YOUTH, Philip Kent's connection with a religious faith had been all but nonexistent. Because of her brief career as an actress in Paris, his mother was automatically excommunicated from the Catholic church.

Philip's first wife, Anne, the daughter of a Boston lawyer, was a Congregationalist. But she and her husband had seldom attended services. His second wife had been raised in Virginia's aristocratic Episcopal church, but had adopted her first husband's faith—the dour Presbyterianism of the Scots—following her marriage.

Thus it was another sign of Philip's rising status and growing conservatism that by the time Abraham and Elizabeth were married in midsummer of 1796, Philip had reverted to British-rooted Anglicanism. The Kents owned a high-sided box pew directly across the aisle from the one belonging to the family of Mr. Revere's eldest son in the small but lovely Christ Church in the city's North End.

Here, on a mellow Saturday in late July, the rector united Abraham Kent and Elizabeth Fletcher, watched by an impressive gathering of notables.

Elderly Mr. Revere sat in his son's pew. Philip's friend General Knox, the obese ex-Secretary of War, had traveled down from Maine. John Adams and his wife Abigail, just returned from Philadelphia, were present. So was the head of the Rothman house, dark-eyed and handsome Royal, and his attractive Jewish wife.

A wealthy iron-maker named George Lumden had come all the way from Connecticut, along with his red-haired, bright-cheeked wife Daisy. The bridal couple understood Philip had helped Lumden desert from his British regiment during the troubled days before Lexington and Concord. Lumden had been quartered in the house of Abraham's mother, where Daisy was a lowly cook. Now she was rich.

Christ Church, in short, was so packed with persons of wealth and influence that ordinary well-wishers such as Mr. Supply Pleasant were hard put to find a single seat in a rear corner.

Abraham hardly noticed the dignitaries, however. His attention was divided between Elizabeth and his father.

Elizabeth's bridal gown and veil were the most expensive obtainable. Yet beneath that veil, her cheeks lacked color, as if the wedding were more strain than pleasure.

Philip looked just as he had for weeks—glum and displeased.

Peggy had been responsible for virtually all the wedding arrangements. She sat in the family pew with perfect poise. Yet her face showed signs of fatigue and tension. Philip's face might have been hewn from Maine granite as he performed the novel function of giving Elizabeth away to his own son and then retired to the pew, limping yet somehow haughty.

Only thirteen-year-old Gilbert seemed totally delighted. Gilbert had shot up in height without adding weight. His skin was the color of parchment. People often commented privately that Gilbert Kent resembled a worried, emaciated old man more than he did an adolescent.

But all that dimmed from Abraham's awareness as he stood beside Elizabeth. Her eyes sought his from time to time, large and startlingly blue despite the gauzy veil covering her face. He wished he could speak to her. Comfort her. Instead, he was forced to stand rigid, then kneel, then rise again while the rector droned his way through the service.

Unhappy about his father's attitude and concerned for his bride, Abraham got a jolt as the rector began reading scripture:

"So ought men to love their wives as their own bodies. He that loveth his wife loveth himself."

The words struck a responsive chord in Abraham's memory. Wasn't that the very passage he'd tried to recall months ago? At the time, he'd been unable to remember either the precise text or its source—Saint Paul's epistle to the Ephesians. A slight flush tinged his cheeks as he realized how widespread the knowledge of his rift with his father must be. Otherwise, why would the rector have selected this particular passage?

Sunshine slanted through large windows into the white-walled brilliance of the sanctuary. Elizabeth's fair hair shone beneath her veil. Her quick, sidelong glance told Abraham she too understood the significance of the text—and his discomfort.

"For this cause shall a man leave his father and mother, and shall be joined unto his wife, and they two shall be one flesh—"

Abraham longed to turn and see how Philip was taking it. He didn't dare.

"—let every one of you in particular so love his wife even as himself, and the wife see that she reverence her husband."

The rector closed his Bible, began to pray. In a tangle of emotion—soaring love, depressing guilt—Abraham steeled himself to endure the rest of the ceremony. He wanted it over so that he could speak to his father. The need had all at once grown almost compulsive.

The rector might as well have been praying in a foreign tongue for all the attention Abraham paid. Something else was troubling him now.

Shame.

Here he was, standing in God's house accepting a white-gowned young woman as his spouse—and he had already known her carnally. Sinfully, the rector would declare. The mere thought undercut the joy of the occasion, and increased his uneasiness.

Well, he said to himself at last, *I suppose even among these respectable people, there are few who have totally clean hands and a spotless conscience.* His father, for example, had killed other human beings in order to survive. Didn't the Bible promise that Christ would forgive error? Bless those who came to His altar with a humble and contrite heart?

Never what could be called a devout person, Abraham still found himself saying a short, fervent prayer. A prayer begging Heaven to grant him forgiveness and, more important, a good beginning to his life with his new wife—

The organ pealed. Lifting Elizabeth's veil to give her a decorous kiss, Abraham saw her lids flutter, as if she were faint. When he touched his mouth to her cheek, he was shocked by the chill of her skin. And he felt her trembling.

As he stood back, she smiled, but wanly. With a stab of dread he wondered whether his prayer would go unheard because they had both sinned.

ii

In the dusk, the house on Beacon Street blazed with lamplight; rang with the voices of the guests. The voices grew louder with every quart of rum added to the great crystal bowls of punch. In a corner of the dining room, a small string orchestra scraped away, adding to the din.

Abraham paced back and forth in the downstairs hall. He was dressed in his best suit. From time to time he glanced anxiously up to the second-floor landing.

Luggage had already been carried to the hooded chaise awaiting the young couple at the ring-block out in front. Abraham had intended to pay for all expenses connected with their wedding journey. But through Peggy, he discovered that Philip had hired the chaise himself, just as he was financing this large, noisy party.

Since leaving Christ Church, Abraham had had no good opportunity to speak to his father. Outside the church, Philip had shaken his son's hand, murmured some word of congratulations, and gone immediately to his own carriage. Once the party started, Philip seemed to be everywhere—except alone, where his son might catch him for a private word. Abraham was hurt and angry at the way Philip seemed to be withholding his emotions—his affection—while he displayed his material generosity.

Through a doorway, Abraham could see his father's back. Philip was in the midst of a heated discussion with huge-bellied General Knox, Lumden the iron-maker, and the slender, elegantly dressed banker, Royal Rothman. Suddenly Abraham felt a tug on his arm. Startled, he turned to discover Gilbert—at thirteen already taller than his half-brother.

"Aren't you anxious to be away, Abraham?" Gilbert asked, trying to invest the question with a manly wickedness.

Abraham put on a smile he didn't feel. "Of course I am."

"Where are you and Elizabeth going?"

"That, Gilbert, is our secret."

"You must be sure to speak to papa before you leave."

Abraham frowned. "Yes, I do wish he'd take the trouble to say goodbye—"

Philip's haughty back—and his loud harangue about the danger of Jefferson standing for election and receiving enough votes to become vice president or, worse yet, president—gave him little encouragement.

"Oh, he definitely wants to speak with you." A mischievous smile curved Gilbert's colorless lips. "I have it on mama's authority."

But Philip still showed every sign of being engrossed. The older brother shrugged in a weary way:

"Mama may be expressing a hope, not a fact."

The slim, white-faced boy stepped closer. His expression showed a maturity beyond his years as he asked:

"You're unhappy with papa, aren't you?"

"I'd say it's the other way around."

"Well, I want you to know I think it's splendid you and Elizabeth made a match. Just splendid."

"Thank you, Gilbert. You're the first person to really sound sincere about it."

"You'll be a good influence on her, too."

"What?"

"I mean you'll keep a good tether on her, so she won't grow moody and tearful, and fly into her rages—yes, it's all turned out very well."

Abraham failed to share Gilbert's enthusiasm:

"I don't believe papa sees it that way. He still blames Elizabeth for our plans to move west."

"I think it's wonderful you're going." Gilbert's eyes brimmed with admiration. "I just wish I were strong enough to see the new country. I know I'm not. So I'll help papa look after Kent's. It's probably the only sort of life I'm cut out for anyway—" He touched his half-brother, fondly yet with a certain shyness. "I'd like to be as big as you—"

"You're taller."

"As strong, I mean. With good shoulders. Hands that can chop wood, or plow—"

"A fine compliment! Comparing me to a plow horse!"

Gilbert reddened. "I know I'm not saying this exactly right—"

"I'm only teasing."

"I just don't want you to have any bad feelings about leaving. You're doing what you were meant to do—"

"Let's hope so," Abraham said, uncertain.

"There's only a problem because papa needs someone to carry on the business. I'm the one. He'll get used to it one of these days, don't you worry."

Abraham was touched by his half-brother's words, even as he was a little saddened by their hint of sorrow. Suddenly Gilbert's eyes flashed past Abraham's shoulder.

"I told you!" he hissed. "Papa's coming—"

Abraham didn't face around. He waited, feeling his father's presence almost like a physical force. He prayed there would be no stormy scene—

Moments later, in response to Philip's toneless request, Abraham followed the older man past groups of boisterous well-wishers to the library. There, Philip closed the double doors. He swung to face his son.

Philip's dark eyes caught light from the single lamp on a small Phyfe table. Without knowing precisely why, Abraham shivered.

iii

Philip spoke a low voice:

"Before you and Elizabeth leave this house, Abraham—"

"Don't sound so grim, papa. We'll be back after our honeymoon."

"Only for a short time. This is a day of parting. Because you're my son, I felt we should have a moment alone. In addition to all the items your stepmother has provided for your new household, I am adding a family gift." He paused only a moment. "The sum of five hundred dollars."

"Five hundred—!" It took Abraham a few seconds to recover. "Sir, forgive me, but I don't understand."

"What is it you don't understand?"

"A gift like that. You don't approve of this match."

"Perhaps not," Philip agreed. He rolled his tongue in his cheek, and nearly smiled. "However, I'm not so insensitive that I failed to grasp the meaning of the rector's text. I'm sure he chose it deliberately. But let's not discuss that. The reason for the gift is very simple. Eventually you'll need funds to purchase land. Just as important, you'll need money for transportation. Wagon travel, river travel—I am informed they're not cheap."

"I've put aside most of my cornet's pay from the army for that, papa."

Philip stiffened. "Are you trying to say you refuse the gift?"

Abraham swallowed. "No, sir, of course not. I'm extremely grateful for—"

He hesitated over the rest. Emotion brought it forth: "—for an expression of your love."

Features still stony, Philip seated himself in a chair. He placed his hands on the knees of his fine gray breeches. "I won't pretend I believe you're doing the right thing. Nor will I deny I want to keep you here for selfish reasons."

"Gilbert has a much quicker mind than I do. He'll be an asset to the firm after he gains a little experience. He'll be able to discuss finances with men like your friend Mr. Rothman, for instance. I get lost just doing a few simple sums—"

"Yes, even as young as he is, Gilbert shows great promise. But he is also not in the best of health. That may reduce his value to Kent's, though I sincerely hope not—"

Philip's dark eyes locked with his son's.

"I not only wanted to keep you in Boston for my own sake, but for yours. You have great strength and vitality, Abraham. But enthusiasm often blinds a young man's eyes to hard reality. I do believe you underestimate the rigors of life in the west. You yourself may be fit enough for it. But you are not one person any longer. You are two. A family—"

Refusing to dodge the issue, Abraham blurted, "Papa, this is no time for anything less than complete candor. Do you dislike Elizabeth so much? Would you rather I not have married her?"

Philip glanced away. "That choice wasn't mine to make."

"Please answer."

"No. To do so might be uncharitable."

"That makes it very clear that you—"

"Permit me to finish. I took your wife into my house when I married Peggy, and I have tried to give her every advantage you and Gilbert have received. I have tried to give unstintingly—regardless of my feelings. Elizabeth has good qualities. She's certainly beautiful, and I can readily understand why you would fall in love with her. But she's frail, like Gilbert. And sometimes her behavior, as you've seen for yourself, suggests a reckless, even unstable temperament. I don't mean any unkindness when I say she may be quite unsuited for the sort of existence you've both chosen."

Abraham struggled to forget that the same suspicion had troubled him on the family trip. He shook his head:

"I'm sure she'll get along with no difficulty, papa. We both will."

Philip sighed. "Youth's optimism. Seldom tempered by reason until—" He seemed to grieve as he studied Abraham. "Until it's much too late."

"Papa, I've said I appreciate your gift. But to present it along with these dire warnings—"

Philip held up his hand to interrupt: "Don't be angry with me. I realize the decision's made. I accept it. I would have struggled even harder—kept trying to persuade you to change your mind—except for one fact."

His eyes drifted toward the windows overlooking the dark Common.

"I would have been forced to employ the same weapon my mother employed with me. The bribery of love. And you needn't say I *have* employed it, because I know I have. But not to the extent—well, someday I'll tell you the story of what she wanted for me. How she almost destroyed me as a man by insisting I would destroy *her* if I didn't follow her plan for my life. Much as I loved her, I couldn't allow that, because I *was* a man. Experience does knock a few lessons into thick old heads, you see. Difficult as it is—"

Philip's voice had grown almost hoarse. He rose, limped toward his son, suddenly gripped his shoulders.

"—I let you go. With bitterness, yes. With regret, yes. But also with the deep and honest hope that your dreams won't be shattered. I can't help how I feel, Abraham—even as you can't help going your own way. We are all guilty of being human. If I have committed any sins against you, I have committed them only out of love—just as my mother did. What a paradox, eh? What a damned, terrible par—"

His voice broke. He embraced his son.

Head bent against his father's shoulder, Abraham heard the tears in the older man's voice:

"God keep you, Abraham. God keep you *and* your dreams."

With sadness and a strange sense of foreboding, Abraham held Philip close for a long, silent moment.

iv

While Peggy cried and Gilbert capered and a crowd of guests shouted good wishes along with a few somewhat ribald encouragements for the evening, Abraham and Elizabeth hurried into the hooded chaise for the start of their wedding journey. Abraham whipped up the horse and they rattled off through the summer dark with the shouts and laughter dwindling slowly behind.

Abraham's new sense of responsibility sat heavy on his shoulders for a little while. He was launching out on his own at last. And, as Philip said, he was a new, different man. He was accountable for his wife's future as well as for his own—

But with Elizabeth close beside him in the bouncing chaise, chattering gaily and caressing his arm from time to time, the responsibility quickly changed from an ominous burden to a joy. He tingled when Elizabeth pressed her lips to his cheek and whispered that she hoped they wouldn't take too long to reach the night's stopping-place.

Their eventual destination, some miles northeast along the coast, was the town of Salem. They planned to spend a week at the town's best inn, enjoying the sea air and taking in the sights of the booming seaport.

Salem's harbor was crowded these days with tall-masted ships whose enterprising captains were carrying the country's flag and the country's products to Europe and around the world. Some of the ships that transported beer brewed in Philadelphia and butter churned on

Massachusetts farms voyaged as far as the Chinese port of Canton, there unloading another part of their cargo —American-grown ginseng, an aromatic root highly prized by Oriental physicians.

The same ships often returned to Massachusetts bearing Chinese opium for the valises of American doctors, as well as pepper, madder dye, Turkish carpets, figs and other exotic goods from ports along the way. People said marvelous curiosities such as African monkeys could be seen on the Salem docks—and, nearby, evidence that the thriving ocean trade was creating fortunes overnight. Mansions were being raised by captains or ship-owners who often realized as much as a seven hundred percent profit on a single voyage.

Both Abraham and Elizabeth had considered Salem an ideal spot for a honeymoon. This evening, however, they only planned to go part of the distance, to a country inn where Abraham had reserved a sitting room with adjoining bedchamber. Amused, he supposed that when they got there, they'd probably find Philip had pre-paid the bill.

As the ferry bore them across the Charles to the peninsula, Elizabeth seemed to grow less animated. At one point, she pressed a hand to her stomach.

"Elizabeth, are you feeling poorly?"

"No, darling, don't worry."

He peered at the dim oval of her face, beautiful under the summer stars. "You're not telling me the truth."

"Only a minor dizziness. It will pass." She tried to smile. Her eyes reflected the glint of the rising moon on the river. "Caused, I'm sure, by the excitement of finally being married—"

But her face remained white. Abraham saw that when the ferryman lifted his lantern and motioned the chaise forward across the end of the scow that had dropped down to rest on the dark shore.

V

Abraham leaned over and blew out the lamp.

He heard rather than saw Elizabeth slip toward the bed from the concealment of the screen where she'd retired to remove her traveling clothes. The country inn was quiet, save for one last customer bidding the landlord a tipsy farewell beneath the open window.

The summer air was fragrant with the smell of scythed grass. The brilliant moon turned the planes of Abraham's chest white above the coverlet drawn to his waist. Expectantly, he swung toward the whisper of Elizabeth's bare feet—and caught his breath.

Her hair hung unbound, a waterfall of gold across her shoulders. The moon lit her eyes until they glowed like blue gems.

Her breasts, remarkably large and firm for one so slender, bobbed as she neared the bedside. The moonlight burnished the soft golden thatch below her smooth stomach.

Without embarrassment or hesitation, she raised the coverlet and slipped in beside him. Her bare hip touched his, a velvety sensation. Her hand stole over to grasp him as her other arm slipped around his neck. He pressed her to the pillows, his lips eager, hers responding, opening—

Transported beyond himself by the sweet smell of her clinging mouth, he seemed to float in a dazzle of summer moonlight that spilled over the bed. He stroked her body with mounting excitement. Felt the heat of her flesh as it warmed—

"Elizabeth. Elizabeth, dear heaven, how I love you," he murmured. His mouth sought her breasts as she caressed the back of his head.

"And I love you, Abraham. Husband," she laughed.

"Isn't that a grand word? I love to say it. Husb—*ah!*"

She arched her back, rolling out of his embrace. Her left arm came up across her forehead, her wrist resting over her eyes. When he reached for her face—"Dearest, what is it?"—he felt an unexpected clamminess on her skin.

"A little dizziness again, that's all."

"The same as you felt on the ferry?"

"Yes. I'm sorry. The rains last week made the roads so rough—"

"And in my haste to get you here—" He tried speaking lightly, to hide his dismay. "—I drove too fast."

"I seem to be a poor traveler, don't I?"

"All the furor of the wedding—it's bound to be tiring—"

He tried not to let her hear his disappointment. But his body registered that disappointment. Reacted by cooling; changing; diminishing—

"Abraham, I wouldn't spoil tonight for anyth—"

He pressed tender fingers against her mouth. "Hush, hush. Don't fret about that." Again he feigned lightness. "It's not as if we're missing something we've never tried before."

"Yes, I realize. But even though we've been together, tonight is—well, important."

"Of course it's important. We're married at last. Here—" He shifted his body to let her rest in the crook of his left arm. "Lie back. Be comfortable. We have the whole week—and all our lives—for making love. One night missed isn't that important."

"Yes it is. I'll be fine in a few minutes," she promised.

"Elizabeth, don't worry!" he said, ashamed of his own inward bitterness.

He found himself wondering where she'd come by this physical weakness. Did it spring from the same source as her passion for rebelling against authority? From the same source as her vindictive streak?

From her father, that unstable man who had lived a profligate life, and only cleaned up a little of the blotted ledger by the manner of his dying?

Abruptly, he was ashamed of the speculation too. Yet he couldn't help feeling that something had robbed him—and Elizabeth—of the mutual joy that should have been theirs this evening.

Presently she stirred; started the love-play again. It lasted only a minute or so. She gave a small, and unhappy cry when her hand glided across Abraham's lifeless loins.

Without warning, whatever pain had seized her before struck her again. She doubled over, knees clenched against her belly, hands locked around her legs. For a confused moment, he thought of one possible answer. Pregnancy.

No, that was absurd. They'd had no opportunity to be alone since well before the southern tour. And once they agreed to marry, she stopped visiting his room secretly—as if the defiance that had driven her to his bed in the first place was no longer necessary, or even quite proper.

In misery, Elizabeth straightened her legs. She clutched her naked stomach, cried out. Then she began to sob an incoherent apology. Abraham didn't know what to do.

All at once she struggled up to a sitting position, left the bed. She staggered toward the screen on the far side of the room.

Abraham raced after her, reaching out to steady her. Almost screaming, she threw off his hand:

"I don't want you to touch me when I'm this way!"

He stepped back, horrified by the ferocity of her cry. Still hunched over, she started to weep in earnest:

"Abraham, I'm sorry. I didn't mean to raise my voice. But I'm ill. I can't bear for you to see me—oh, I'm so ashamed—"

She disappeared behind the screen. Abraham watched it totter and almost topple before she caught it. A moment later, he heard the ugly sounds of his wife being sick in a basin.

Standing naked in the moon-glare at the foot of the bed, he felt as if winter had closed in outside the open window. He recalled his father's warning, and experienced a consuming fear that Philip was right: Elizabeth *was* entirely unsuited to the sort of life awaiting them in the Ohio country—

Even more appalling was his certainty that he'd never be able to change her mind about the future.

He could hint, argue, plead—and he would. But he knew her nature; knew his efforts would prove futile in the end.

Frozen and frightened, he stood staring at nothing, listening to the terrible sounds of sickness from behind the screen.

CHAPTER VII

Wagon Road

THE WAGONER'S NAME was Leland Pell. He stood nearly a head taller than Abraham, thin but broad-shouldered, with immense, dirty, scarred hands. Wind and weather had burnished his cheeks to the color of mahogany. His eyes were brown, his hair the same, sleek and pushed straight back over his high forehead. Abraham judged him to be about forty. White stubble showed against the dark skin of his jawbone.

Pell's clothing certainly didn't justify arrogance. He wore old leather boots, linsey trousers, a faded blue flannel shirt, a broad-brimmed wool hat heavily stained with grease. At his feet crouched the fattest, ugliest bulldog Abraham had ever seen. The dog's wet eyes and underslung jaw looked downright threatening.

When Abraham first approached Pell in the tavern yard, the wagoner struck a pose. Thumbs hooked in his belt, he gazed at the sky with lofty indifference. Fortunately, Abraham had been warned to expect such behavior. A passenger in the coach from Lancaster to Harrisburg told him the wagoners considered themselves "sea captains of the road."

Instead of an answer to his question, Abraham got a continuation of the pose. Irked, he said:

"I asked you the price, Mr. Pell."

Silence.

Abraham shivered in the chilly autumn wind. Nearby, the Susquehanna flowed with a cold yellow sheen. Beyond, the western hills rose black against the clear blue sky of the changing season.

Pell's cronies inside the tavern shouted for him to come share whiskey and cigars. The wagoner ignored the shouts, but finally deigned to glance at Abraham—then past him, to Elizabeth. Bundled in her heaviest traveling clothes, including a shawl and bonnet, Abraham's wife still looked frozen as she waited beside the five large trunks stacked under the tavern wall.

"Six pieces of baggage," Pell said, then grinned. "Counting your missus, I mean to say. She's the handsomest piece o' the lot."

Angered by Pell's insolence, Abraham pivoted away. "I'll find someone who wants to discuss business, not crack jokes."

"Suit yourself," Pell called as Abraham walked off. "But there ain't a wagoner on the old Forbes Road who'll take you on—haul you to Pittsburgh before the snow comes down. I know every one of 'em. Passengers ain't their business—and they all got full crews."

Abraham halted as Pell took a couple of steps in his direction:

"Only reason I'm even botherin' to talk is because my Conestoga needs two men. My second—he got a mite chopped down a while back. So far I ain't found a new second, y'see—"

Reluctantly, Abraham went back. If this was an elaborate game, he supposed he had to play it if he wanted to make a deal.

"What do you mean, he got chopped down?"

"Cut." Pell showed his right hand. "Lost three fingers in a fight. Dumb son of a bitch was nineteen years old. But up here—" He tapped his head. "More like six. Shoulders like an ox, though. I was right sorry to lose him."

Pell wiped his nose with the back of his hand, eyed Elizabeth again. "You was askin' about the price—"

"Several times."

"First of all, you realize no coaches can make it over the mountains to Pittsburgh?"

"That I already know. What's your price?"

But the wagoner wouldn't be hurried:

"And you also got to realize I'm a regular, not a sharpshooter. I get you there in good shape, fifteen steady miles a day. I don't shake your teeth out like them gypsies that pull a farm wagon outa the field and try to turn a fast dollar pushin' twenty, twenty-five miles a day—wreckin' everything aboard. Besides, don't look to me like too much speed would suit the lady. She don't appear any too strong."

By now Abraham's temper was raw:

"I want your price, Mr. Pell, not a discourse on customs of the road."

" '*Dis-course!*' I don't believe I ever heard that word before. You must be a mighty educated young fella—"

"*Your price!*"

When Abraham shouted, Pell's brown eyes grew unpleasant:

"A hundred dollars. Cash."

"Ridiculous!"

Pell shrugged. "Shit, nobody's forcin' you."

"A hundred dollars—" Abraham repeated. "That's four times what it should be—"

"Sure, based on the fare from Lancaster to here," Pell agreed with a frigid smile. "But they's hard country 'tween Harrisburg and the old fort at the Ohio. You want to get to Pittsburgh 'fore next spring, mister, you ain't got but three choices. Shank's mare. Buy your own wagon and team—which'll cost you plenty more'n a hundred. Or pay my price. I'm doin' you a favor the way it is—"

From his height, he downgraded Abraham with a single glance:

"I ain't even sure you're big enough to handle the chores on a Conestoga. Well, it's up to you. I already got nigh to a full load of freight, so you won't skin my ass any if you say no."

The frosty smile revealed a mouth with only half the teeth left; and those were browned by tobacco. With another look at Elizabeth, Pell added:

"I need some segars. I'll be inside if you want me. Come on, Chief."

He ambled toward the tavern door, the bulldog at his heels. Drool dripped from the dog's lower jaw. Pell paused at the entrance for one last bit of persuasion:

"You want to try to hire a smaller rig for them rough roads up ahead, go on. But I warn you, you'll spend six or seven times what I'm askin'. And you're liable to get to Ohio two years from now—and find somebody else squattin' on them twenty acres you say you bought. Your business, I guess—"

Shrugging again in that arrogant way, he started inside. The bulldog got between his boots. Pell kicked the dog's ribs. Chief yelped, fell, but finally trotted after the tall man as he vanished into the tavern's yellow haze.

Abraham stuffed his hands in his pockets, walked morosely to Elizabeth.

"You look cold," he said.

She tried to smile. "I'll be glad to reach the lodging house."

"That man wants—"

"I heard. Abraham, let's find another way. He's loathsome."

"But from what I've observed, he's not much different from any other wagon driver."

He knew he was trying to convince himself. He could hardly blame Pell for staring at his wife. In spite of her pallor, Elizabeth was by far the prettiest woman he'd seen since the coach pulled into Harrisburg. Just about the only young woman, in fact.

He thought of Pell's warnings about squatters. Thought of his auction deed to twenty acres of prime bottom land on the Great Miami near Fort Hamilton. The deed would be next to worthless if he and Elizabeth found other settlers already occupying the tract of ground. Forged deeds weren't uncommon. It could take months—even years—to validate his claim in the frontier circuit courts.

Reluctantly, he said, "I'm going to accept his offer."

"No. No, Abraham!"

He touched her arm. "We'll be all right."

But Elizabeth wasn't reassured. She closed her eyes, shivering in the autumn wind.

Swiftly, Abraham stepped forward, supported her with both arms. "You'd better sit down a minute. I'll find a boy to help with the trunks. I can come back and see Pell later. Sit down, Elizabeth—we'll be at the lodging house soon. Then you'll be warm."

"I don't think I'll ever be warm again," she said. The forlorn look in her blue eyes chilled him more than the wind off the river.

ii

Only a closed pan of coals warmed the bed, and the lodging-house room, that night. Elizabeth put on a second bedgown over her regular one, then snuggled in the curve of Abraham's arm.

They had been traveling since early September, down to Philadelphia and then westward. But the hardest terrain lay ahead. He still questioned whether they should go on.

Elizabeth had already been stricken with spells of

nausea and abdominal pain. Each time, for his benefit, she tried to conceal or minimize her discomfort. But she couldn't conceal the fact that she was losing weight. The coarse fare served at the coaching stops wasn't to her liking.

So, as they huddled together with their feet near the warming pan, he voiced his doubts:

"Perhaps we should turn back."

"My answer to that is the same as it was in Salem. Nonsense. I'm stronger than you think. I'll prove it."

"But things seem to grow a little more difficult every day. Dealing with clods like Pell doesn't make it any easier—"

"Are you saying *you* want to turn back, Abraham?"

Shamed, he answered quickly, "Only for your sake."

"Put it out of your mind, then. I'm sorry I carried on at the tavern. I was just tired. That Pell fellow is probably all bluff and boast."

In his mind's eye Abraham saw the arrogant brown eyes and thought otherwise. Elizabeth's first assessment had been the correct one. But he said nothing.

"We can deal with him," she went on, her voice firm. "With him and with any other difficulties we encounter. I want our children to be born out here, Abraham. It's beautiful country. Beautiful—"

Murmuring, she drifted off.

Abraham lay awake for more than an hour, listening to the noise drifting from the Harrisburg riverfront. Elizabeth had inadvertently raised another troubling question. Thus far, their efforts to conceive a child had failed.

Lately, he had even grown hesitant about making love to his wife, much as his body urged him to it. He was afraid that on top of the other rigors of the journey, the burden of carrying a baby would prove too much for Elizabeth.

Tormented by his anxieties, he stared into the darkness. His father's gift of five hundred dollars was dwindling. Another hundred paid to Pell would leave only three hundred and fifty in reserve.

And even if they got to Pittsburgh, there were many long, arduous miles yet to travel before they reached the land whose deed was tucked away in one of the trunks.

They had to make a start before bad weather closed in. Much as he disliked the idea, he'd look Pell up in the morning.

iii

Leland Pell's Conestoga wagon measured twenty feet along the top, fourteen feet along the bottom, and could, he boasted, bear up to ten tons of crates and barrels through the Pennsylvania wilderness.

The wagon had huge, iron-tired wheels. The axles sat high off the ground, so they'd clear the stumps left standing in the cleared track that passed for a road west of the Susquehanna ferry. Inside, the wagon was comfortable enough. The heaviest goods were packed toward the middle, and the whole was covered over by tow-canvas stretched on twelve large hoops.

The German craftsmen of eastern Pennsylvania who built the four-wheeled land arks decorated them in cheerful colors. The wagon proper was painted bright blue, with flame red used on the gear, including the lazy board and the grain box. This box hung under the tailgate during the day. At night it was opened and placed on the tongue.

Pell owned not only his wagon but the six great black horses that pulled it. A couple of the horses weighed over three-quarters of a ton. Pell's pride in the animals was evident in the way he decorated them. Their chain-link traces were wound with bright red yarn. Five small bells hung from a wrought iron arch that rose above the hames of each horse. On the road, the thirty bells all chiming at random made a strange, wild music.

The horses were hitched in tandem. Altogether, wagon and animals stretched more than sixty feet. When the wagon was moving, the bulldog dashed back and forth beneath the bed, barking at the horses to urge them along.

Elizabeth spent most of her time in a nook Abraham had arranged inside. He rode the lazy board, a piece of stout white oak that pulled out from the wagon's left side to make a projecting seat. The seat was handy to the long lever which controlled the brakes for the rear tires; brakes that set the iron squealing and sparking when Pell screamed for more pressure on a steep downward grade.

No wagons overtook them. Pell knew his business. He clipped off fifteen miles almost every day, regardless of delays from fording streams or climbing and descending mountainsides.

Once or twice a day they did encounter freighters returning east. Pell greeted some of the drivers with an obscenely cheerful hail. Others he ignored: the despised, unprofessional sharpshooters. He never relinquished his position on the right side of the rough dirt road. Professional or sharpshooter, it was the other wagon that always pulled aside to let Pell pass. That said a lot about the man and his reputation.

After no more than a few days of travel, it became evident to Abraham that his wife was terrified of Leland Pell. Terrified even though the wagoner's behavior was fairly restrained when they made their night camps.

The camp routine seldom varied. First the horses were unhitched and tied to the tongue, three on each side, and the grain box was set out to feed them. While Chief barked at noises in the forest, Abraham and Pell gathered wood for a fire. Conversation during the meal was fitful.

Pell actually boasted about his illiteracy. He needed no education to turn a profit hauling freight back and forth across the mountains!

The wagoner knew the United States had won the war with Britain—he hadn't bothered to volunteer for the army, he announced—and he knew the president's name was General Washington, and that he'd fought along Braddock's old Pennsylvania road at some dim time in the past. Over and above those meager facts, Pell's knowledge of national affairs was scanty, and his interest nonexistent.

In one way, though, he was completely typical of people in all social classes, Abraham noticed. Pell still wasn't accustomed to thinking of the country as a single entity. Once or twice when he mentioned the United States, he did so in the plural—"The United States are mighty big now, I reckon"—which was the common way.

Pell's chief recreation seemed to be smoking the long, thin, villainously black four-a-penny cigars favored by the Conestoga drivers. When the travelers sat beside the fragrant evening fire, Pell would light up one of the foul-smelling stogies, then flourish it or tilt it up between his clenched teeth as though it lent him a dashing air. Through the blue haze, his eyes frequently darted to Elizabeth's breasts.

Those sly glances angered Abraham. But since the wagoner did nothing more overt than that, he restrained his impulses to speak out. He and Elizabeth were dependent on Pell, after all.

Abraham had to admit Pell's physical strength was admirable. The tall man handled the sets of gears for each horse as if they were a fraction of their actual weight. Abraham panted and grew slightly dizzy the first time he tried to help Pell with the fifteen-inch back bands and ten-inch hip straps.

He'd gained weight and lost muscle tone during his months in the east—and this despite the hard work in Philip's press room. Good food and home comforts had taken their toll. But as they put more and more miles behind the wagon, Abraham's skin darkened, his belly flattened, and his general fitness improved. The winy October air, the rich blue skies, the bursts of autumn color on the hillsides lifted his spirits. Elizabeth too seemed invigorated; less pale.

Still, her presence clearly gave Pell something to think about.

"Kent," he said, scratching his crotch unconsciously, "you s'pose you'd let your wife have a dance with me tomorrow night?"

It was a brilliant morning. Abraham was walking beside the left-hand wheel horse. Pell drove from a saddle on the horse's back, jerkline in one hand, long blacksnake whip in the other.

Abraham stared upward, studying the odd smile on the wagoner's face. Thanks to Abraham's hard work, Pell had lost some of his contempt for the younger man. Some, but not all.

"We going to be someplace where there's dancing?" Abraham asked.

"Yep. Figger we'll be in the next settlement by dark tomorrow. Hell, we're gettin' near Pittsburgh—ain't you noticed the eastbound traffic heavyin' up?"

Abraham nodded to indicate he had.

"We only got one more crick to ford. There's some cabins and a dandy tavern just this side. I usually find lots o' my friends there. And when a bunch o' wagon men stop at the same place, we have dancin' with our whiskey. Provided we can rustle up a fiddle player, 'course."

"What about women? They aren't necessary?"

"Sure. But we'll dance with each other if they ain't any whores around—wait a minute, now! Don't take on! I ain't puttin' your wife in the same stall as whores—"

"Thanks very much." But the sarcasm was lost.

"Yessir, I'd surely like to have a whirl with your missus. A real, clean-smellin' lady—"

Pell grinned, jerking the whip back over his shoulder, then laying it into the air above the heads of the lead horses. Pell was expert with the whip. He could give it an explosive crack—accompanied by an obscene bellow—inches from the horses' ears, never touching them.

"Well, Kent, what d'you say?"

"It's not up to me. It's up to the missus, as you call her."

"Yeh, but I want you to ask her. She won't pay me any mind."

"I'll ask her," Abraham agreed. *And you'll get set on your butt by her answer, my friend.*

The wagoner rubbed his crotch again. "Good. I figgered I ought to have your permission first. Sure wouldn't want to tangle with an educated eastern feller—I might get hurt, y'know? Talked to death by all them ten-penny words—"

Laughing, he popped the whip again. Abraham stopped to wait for the lazy board, furious at Pell's heavy-handed contempt.

iv

That night Abraham mentioned Pell's request to Elizabeth as they bedded down inside the wagon. Pell slept outside, wrapped in blankets, with Chief keeping watch.

Elizabeth's reaction was just what Abraham expected:

"I wouldn't let that filthy, illiterate ruffian touch me."

He chuckled, moving close to her for warmth. "That's why I didn't write his name in your program."

"As for this—celebration he's planning, I refuse to have any part of it. I'll spend the evening right here in the wagon. Have you noticed Pell's behavior the last couple of days? Somehow he acts almost—oh, I don't know. The best word I know is feverish."

"I expect he's just ready to tear loose and kick up his heels."

"In that case I suggest we have some protection handy. One of those pistols from the trunk—"

"I doubt if that'll be necessary," Abraham said. But next day, he wondered.

Smiling, he broke the news that Mrs. Kent didn't plan on dancing in the settlement tavern. Pell scowled:

"I don't smell good enough for her, mebbe?"

Abraham met the ugly brown eyes under the wool hat brim. "I didn't ask. I suggest that you don't either."

"Fuckin' high and mighty easterners," the wagoner muttered, lashing out with the whip. This time, accidentally or otherwise, he nicked the neck of one of the lead horses, drawing blood.

They rolled into the little settlement just before sunset. Pell cursing and stormed about, flinging off the gears and manhandling the six horses up to the tongue. While Abraham and Elizabeth ate a meager supper at one of the tavern's greasy tables, they could still hear Pell's profanity.

They left the table and started for the wagon just as Pell came in. The wagoner was greeted by shouts from half a dozen of his road cronies gathered at the plank bar.

All during the meal, Abraham and his wife had been conscious of the men staring. Pell's glance as he approached the couple just inside the doorway was more angry than lascivious. Abraham whiffed liquor. He took Elizabeth's elbow—and struggled to keep his temper when Pell jostled him.

Fingering the coiled whip at his belt, Pell stalked on toward the bar:

"Somebody drag that fiddler-boy's ass out of the woodshed. I been bouncin' on the road for days. I aim to stomp a little."

Stomp he did, along with the others, while the fiddle squeaked frantically. The laughter and boot-thuds grew louder, the oaths more florid as midnight approached. Elizabeth fretted and tossed under the blankets, trying to sleep despite the racket.

Abraham sat up for a while, then crawled in beside his wife. He dozed off, only to be wakened by a shrill cry.

He bolted upright, shot out his hand—

Elizabeth was there.

He wiped his perspiring forehead. Torchlight flared in the tavern yard. As he scrambled out of the Conestoga, Chief barked at him. He shied a stone at the bulldog and trotted toward the confusion of firelight and shadow-figures around the tavern door.

Pell had parked the wagon a good distance from the building. So it took Abraham a moment to see what was happening. The drunken wagoners, their clothing in disarray, formed a ring around someone. One of the men held the torch, and by its light Abraham finally identified the person in the center of the circle. A tow-haired boy. He realized he must have mistaken the boy's high-pitched voice for a woman's.

Held by a couple of the wagoners, the boy struggled to break loose. He couldn't. All at once Abraham saw a demijohn dangling from the boy's right hand.

Hatless, Leland Pell staggered forward, flipping away the stub of a stogie. He backhanded the boy across the cheeks.

"Nothin' worse than a whiskey thief."

"Leave me go!" the boy squealed. "Ain't but a quarter of a jug left in here—"

A man jerked the demijohn out of the boy's fingers, shook it. "Goddamn liar. She's nearly full."

Another wagoner grabbed the boy's hair. "Full or empty, don't make no difference. You was sneakin' out with it—"

"Call the landlord," the boy pleaded.

"He's dead drunk," a third man said. "And you, you little shithead, you're stealin' the liquor we paid for!"

"I played for you all evenin'! I'm entitled—"

Leland Pell's voice was slurred: "You played for free 'cause we said so. You're entitled to *nothin'*—" He drove his fist into the boy's midsection.

The boy doubled, retching. Pell seized the whiskey jug.

"You ever been to Pittsburgh, boy? You know how they take care of whiskey thieves in Pittsburgh? I'll show you. Sam, bring me a stick from the fireplace."

"What the hell you fixin' to do, Leland?" one of the drivers asked, apprehensive suddenly.

Pell weaved on his feet. "You shut up."

Abraham had jogged through the darkness and stopped near the group. All at once Pell saw him. Pell's stubbled mouth wrenched.

"An' you better crawl back to your wagon, Kent. This might be a little too strong for your lah-de-dah eastern belly—" Spittle flew from his lips as he wheeled around: "Sam, go get that stick 'fore I take after you with this whip!"

Terrified, Sam bolted inside.

Pell uncorked the demijohn, poured its contents over

the writhing boy. Abraham's stomach flipflopped as Sam appeared with the stick. The end was afire—

He'd taken just one long step when Pell motioned the boy's captors away and touched the stick to the boy's soaked shirt. The alcohol ignited.

The boy shrieked. The shirt was afire across his shoulders. The flames leaped down his back, into his hair, as Pell laughed uproariously. Two of the wagoners stood aside to let the boy dash toward the nearby stream.

Abraham's mouth hardened. Pell didn't see. He was collapsing with mirth on a bench beside the tavern door.

The boy's screams pealed, even as the blur of orange grew smaller in the darkness. One of the wagoners was shocked to sobriety:

"That warn't called for, Leland."

Wiping tears from his eyes, Pell told him what he could do with his opinions. Abraham yelled at the men:

"Why are you standing there? Let's go help the boy!"

He started running toward the orange glow. Suddenly it dipped toward the ground; the boy was frantically trying to extinguish the flames by rolling along the creek bank.

Three of the wagoners responded to Abraham's shout, followed him. Two others drifted back inside, not quite sober enough to be ashamed. Pell's laughter boomed.

Halfway to the stream, Abraham heard another keening cry. This one he recognized instantly:

"Elizabeth—!"

One of the wagoners running beside him panted, "That's your wife's name, ain't it? Pell's been talkin' about her all evenin'. Dirty talk—"

"You see to the boy," Abraham shouted, pivoting and racing back toward the tavern.

The two wagoners had come outside again. Beyond

the shifting circle of light from the torch one of them held, Abraham saw only the tethered horses. The Conestoga itself was deep in shadow. But he was sure the cry had come from within the wagon. He heard it again as he pounded across the tavern yard.

"He warned us to stay away," called one of the wagoners by the doorway. "You better too. He's murderin' drunk—"

Hardly hearing, Abraham dodged the bulldog snapping at his boots. From inside the wagon came sounds of a struggle—thumps and thrashing. Elizabeth screamed a third time.

Abraham hauled himself up the wagon's high raked front, tasted sourness in his mouth as Pell wheezed in the darkness:

"Come on, you sassy little bitch. Jest feel it once. Gimme your hand—"

Abraham bellowed, *"Goddamn you, Pell—"*

He started to climb inside, marginally aware of a body falling—Elizabeth?—then Pell's sudden, strident breathing. With one leg hooked over the end of the wagon, he could still see nothing of the interior. But he realized with quick terror that Pell could certainly see him against the glare of the torch.

Pell laughed again; a flat, wicked sound. A slithering noise warned Abraham to jerk his head aside—

Crack!

Had he not reacted so fast, the tip of Pell's blacksnake would have put out an eye. As it was, he hung on the end of the wagon with his left cheek laid open, pouring blood.

The pain overwhelmed him in an instant. He fell toward the tongue and the hoofs of the snorting, stamping horses.

V

The back of Abraham's head slammed against the wagon tongue. His vision blurred. One of the frightened horses kicked his ribs.

He rolled away, toward the front wheels, just as Pell leaped down, his boots stirring little clouds of dust when he landed.

Abraham couldn't see clearly. He was dizzy. Blood from the whip cut leaked into his left eye as he groped for the front axle, frantically dragged himself under the wagon bed just as Pell brought the whip down with maniacal force.

Abraham jerked his legs out of the way just in time. The whip raised another dust cloud. Distantly, Abraham heard men yelling and running; heard doors crash open. Residents of the settlement coming from their cabins. Overhead, Elizabeth screamed again.

In a moment of terrible lucidity, Abraham understood that most of the wagoners were too afraid of Pell to interfere. The same probably held true for the settlers. And he was certain Pell meant to kill him.

He shook his head, trying to overcome the dizziness. At the front end of the wagon, Pell dropped into a crouch, gesturing at Abraham with the whip.

"Come out from under there, you yella bastard!"

Pell was silhouetted against the torch at the tavern. His trousers hung around his knees. His suit of dirty gray underwear gaped open at his crotch. Abraham might have laughed at that, except for Pell's rage:

"I said come out! I'm gonna whip your balls off one at a time—"

Blood glistened on Pell's cheek; the raking marks of Elizabeth's nails, Abraham realized suddenly. The wagoner dropped his right wrist close to the ground, intending to lash Abraham's legs under the front of the wagon. It required a tricky horizontal strike—and by the time Pell stretched his whip hand behind him, Abraham was ready.

The whip shot forward with an explosive pop. Abraham took the cut on his right forearm—raised deliberately. The tip of the snake wound round and round his sleeve like a band of fire. Clenching his teeth, he closed his left hand on the whip, then his right. He yanked.

Pell was jerked forward. He crashed head first into one of the iron-tired wheels. Bellowing, he fell to his knees and let go of the whip's butt.

Abraham still had the end wound around his right arm. He reached upward and to the side, seized the hickory spokes of the left front wheel that Pell had struck. He dug in his heels and pulled himself—and the whip—out of Pell's reach.

He crawled into the open, stumbled to his feet beside the wheel, conscious of people gathering. Elizabeth's cries had changed to low, hurt sobs.

He lurched to the front of the Conestoga, the whole left side of his face bloody. For one nauseous moment he thought he might faint. He fought it, then noticed two odd things:

Not one wagoner stepped forward to lend Pell a hand. And the bulldog, growling, didn't attack as Abraham crept up behind the groaning man.

Pell was still on his knees. Abraham wrapped the whip around Pell's neck, pulled with both hands—

Pell tried to plead. Only gagging sounds came from his throat. He struggled, clawed over his shoulder at Abraham's fingers. But the fall against the wheel had weakened him. Abraham jammed his knee into Pell's back, tightening the rawhide noose.

Let him go, a voice cried in his mind. *Don't murder him. He's beaten—*

But he could still hear Elizabeth sobbing. He pulled harder.

His hands trembled from clenching so tightly; trembled and turned white as bone—

Mercifully, he blanked out during the rest.

He felt his fingers being pried loose. He blinked, relaxed his grip, stared down. Several torches showed him Leland Pell, cheeks purplish, tongue protruding. Pell's trousers were still tangled around his calves. His underwear hung open to reveal a tiny penis as dead as the rest of him.

Abraham felt so ill he almost wept:

"Somebody cover him up, for Christ's sake! And see to my wi—"

The bones in his legs melted. He tumbled to the ground, unconscious. One hand lay across the wagoner's distended right eyeball.

vi

During the night, a man who claimed to be an apothecary cleaned Abraham's face in the tavern. He applied a stinging, sulphurous-smelling paste to the wound, then wrapped Abraham's head with an oval of rags, as though he were a toothache patient.

The man told Abraham he had already administered whiskey to Elizabeth. She was sleeping.

Abraham wanted to go to the wagon and see for himself. But he hurt too much. Exhausted, he let the groggy landlord spread a filthy blanket on one of the trestle tables, help him up, then cover him with a second blanket. In a moment, his eyes closed.

By dawn the other wagoners had disposed of Pell's body. Where, they didn't say. Nor did Abraham ask.

The landlord reported that the fiddler-boy had been

treated by the same fellow who'd doctored Abraham's face:

"The boy weren't as lucky as you. Even after the burned skin sloughs off an' his hair grows back, his face'll likely be ruined fer life."

Sickened, Abraham shoved away the fragrant cup of coffee the landlord was extending. He tottered into the frosty air where his breath plumed. He saw Elizabeth peering at him over the front of the wagon, her face as pale as marble.

He started running. But a few long strides set his head throbbing. He walked the rest of the way, trying not to be aware of the horror in her blue eyes.

Stopping next to the wagon, he reached up. She put her hand down to find his. Her fingers were stiff; cold as the dawn air.

"Elizabeth, did he—?"

"He only touched me. Just—touched me, that's all." Her voice shook.

Her fingers constricted around his suddenly:

"Abraham, let's leave. Please, please, *let's leave this place!*"

Alarmed, he chafed her icy hands until she calmed down. He promised they'd drive down to the ford and cross the stream as soon as he made some necessary inquiries about the dead man's rig.

Staring through him, she said nothing.

He walked back to a silent band of thoroughly sobered wagoners gathered outside the tavern. The smell of their sweat was rank in the crisp air.

"I know the outfit belonged to Pell," Abraham said. "Did he have any kin?"

One toothless fellow spoke: "A wife and a flock of young 'uns in Harrisburg. But the woman turned Leland out a couple of years ago."

"She still live there?"

"Think so."

"Still under the name Pell? Not remarried?"

"Not so's we've heard."

Abraham nodded in a grave, tired way. "I'll get the rig to Pittsburgh. Make deliveries of the freight as best I can, then sell the wagon and the horses. After I deduct the hundred he charged me for the trip, I'll deposit the rest at the postal office. There *is* a postal office—?"

"Yes, sir," said the toothless man.

"I'll leave the money for Pell's wife. I'll leave it in her name. One of you see it gets back to Harrisburg."

Murmurs of consent. Abraham stumbled back to the Conestoga. Elizabeth had disappeared.

The eastern sky was empty of clouds. But in the west, gray banks promised rain, or even early snow, reminding him of the lateness of the season.

He climbed up the front of the wagon, glanced into the crowded interior. Elizabeth was sprawled on her blanket pallet, hands over her face. She was crying, almost inaudibly.

He thought about going to her; decided she might respond more favorably to the feel of the wagon in motion. As if in penance, the other wagoners helped him hitch up in record time.

Abraham dragged himself into the saddle on the left wheel horse, picked up the jerkline. He didn't have Pell's whip. He wouldn't have used it if he had.

Just as he was maneuvering the rig into the water at the ford, he heard a loud bark. He leaned out to the left, looked behind, saw the bulldog, tongue lolling, wet old eyes red in the dawn.

"Come on, Chief."

With a bound and another bark, the bulldog shot to his customary place beneath the bright blue bed. Abraham smiled, but the smile was empty. It made his face hurt.

He started the six horses into the purling stream. Listened—

Inside the huge wagon there was only silence.

CHAPTER VIII

Ark to the Wilderness

THE BRIM OF Abraham's hat and the shoulders of his thick wool coat were as white as the sugared buns he remembered with longing from breakfasts in Boston. Tonight, as he climbed the unlit stairs of the Pittsburgh rooming house in sodden boots, feeling thoroughly downhearted, he thought of all the splendid meals he had quite taken for granted as he was growing up.

What a contrast between the luscious aromas memory conjured and the stenches of this old building that creaked in the winter wind. He smelled tobacco. Unwashed linen and unclean bodies. The ghastly fish stew served by the bad-tempered landlady for the evening meal—

Elizabeth hadn't eaten the wretched stew. She hadn't felt well enough to go downstairs with him. Poor health did have its blessings—!

Ah, that was a shameful thought. He should be, and was, desperately worried about his wife. Of late she'd been unusually pale and fatigued. He supposed it was the result of living cramped in a single combination bedroom-sitting room for most of the winter—and eating the landlady's swill when hunger overpowered good sense.

Even Chief, laboring up the rickety stairs behind him, looked bedraggled; moved with rheumatic slowness. The old bulldog acted as tired as he felt.

On the second floor landing, a single lamp shed a feeble light. Abraham paused, his attention captured by sounds from behind one of the closed doors. With bleak eyes he listened to the unmistakable rhythm of a bed being strained up and down. He heard a woman's strident moan—

At least one of the transient couples paying the landlady's gouging prices while waiting for winter to loosen its grip on the Ohio was managing to take comfort in each other.

The reflection was more sad than angry. Elizabeth had retired early every night for six or seven weeks. She seemed incapable of any affection save a prim, dutiful kiss now and then. How long had it been since they'd last lain in each other's arms? Centuries! he thought, though the truth was less melodramatic: early January—

He climbed on toward the third floor, Chief panting behind him.

Abraham blamed the dead wagoner for the apprehensive look in Elizabeth's blue eyes whenever he tried to touch her. She still refused to tell him exactly what Pell had done that night. But it was obvious that scars remained.

He blamed himself a little, too. He lacked the ability—the right words, the proper degree of tenderness—to cut through her moods; her aura of remoteness.

His failure in another area didn't help either. He had been totally unable to find a way for them to leave cold, crowded Pittsburgh with its heartless profiteers and its hordes of gray-faced immigrants who wore their hope like a badge. Again today he'd tramped the docks along the Monongahela; kept making inquiries and returning to the notice board even after the snow began to rage out of the northwest.

Yawning and shivering, he tapped the door of their room, murmured a few words to identify himself. He heard Elizabeth's slow, shuffling tread as she came to lift the latch.

The room was unbelievably small. They'd moved the ancient bed against the wall to make room for their trunks. Little extra space remained—and two scarred chairs, a plain table and a wash stand took up most of that.

As usual, the plank floor fairly radiated cold. Elizabeth was already robed for bed. He shut the door after Chief lurched in, flung off his snow-soaked hat and coat.

"Still no luck," he said, sinking into a chair. "Every man I approach seems to have a full load by the time I get to him."

"Nothing new on the notice board?"

"Nothing. We may have to buy another wagon and go along Zane's Trace after all."

Abraham referred to a new road cleared the preceding year. It ran from Zane's Station, on the Ohio's northeast-southwest salient, to Maysville, where the river flowed generally westward again. Traveling by land part of the way to their destination would be possible, if extremely difficult.

Abraham and Elizabeth had arrived in Pittsburgh in the late fall, just as the first snows fell. After disposing of Pell's horses and wagon and seeing to the delivery of his goods, Abraham and his wife had agreed to make the remaining portion of their trip by riverboat. It was relatively safer, for one thing. The great number of boats shuttling upstream and down had sharply reduced the danger of Indian attack.

But even after recouping the hundred dollars paid to Pell, Abraham couldn't afford to buy his own flatboat. More important, the arks that plied the Ohio required more than one man to handle them, particularly if the boat was going on past Cincinnati to the shallow but treacherous rapids at the falls of the Ohio. A shared-cost, shared-labor arrangement was the only solution.

Now it seemed no solution at all. He'd trudged the docks literally for weeks, unable to find anyone who needed an extra man come spring. Part of the problem was the fact that a partner would also have to transport Elizabeth and their baggage. Space was precious on most of the riverboats.

Abraham sat motionless in the chair, listening to the whine of the February wind. Snow ticked at the windows. His eyes seemed to be focused on Chief. The bulldog lay under the foot of the bed, sleeping. But Abraham really wasn't looking at the animal. He saw instead the comfortable house on Beacon Street—

Aware of Elizabeth standing near him, he glanced up. Pointed to his sodden coat:

"I did buy a recent paper. Just came in with a pack train from Harrisburg. In December, John Adams was elected to the presidency. But the second highest total of votes cast by the electors went to Jefferson, so he's vice president. I doubt papa's happy about that. It shows the Democratic-Republicans are gaining strength and influ—"

He broke off, startled. Elizabeth was staring at him in a most peculiar way. There was a glow in her eyes such as he hadn't seen for months.

She was *smiling!*

He shot to his feet, seized her chilly hands. He could only infer the smile was the result of some new abnormality in her physical health or her mental state:

"Elizabeth, what's wrong?"

"Nothing, darling. In fact, for the first time since we set foot in this wretched town, I'm happy."

The smile grew. At first, he couldn't believe what he suspected. But that smile gave him encouragement. Happiness surged through him like a tonic, washing away his exhaustion, his frustration—

Yet he still didn't dare to believe it. Not until she spoke:

"I've been making a count of the days and weeks. I think enough time's passed so that I can say with fair certainty we're going to have a child."

"Oh my God, that's *wonderful!*"

He whooped, wrapped her in a hug, then leaped back. He'd practically crushed her—

She laughed; really laughed. Faint spots of color showed in her cheeks.

"Yes," she said softly, "I think so too."

Abraham whooped again, did a little dance step on the cold floor. Chief's head came up. The wet, ugly eyes opened. They were already closing by the time Elizabeth added:

"I just wanted to be sure before I raised any false hopes."

Abraham started pacing:

"I know there are doctors in Pittsburgh. We must get you to one immediately. No matter how much he charges—"

He stopped, faced her:

"And I think we should stay right here until the baby's delivered."

"Not see our own land till the autumn? I won't hear of it! I want the child born where we're going to make our home."

"But traveling just this far was taxing enough. And you haven't been yourself since the first of the year—"

"Because I'm going to have a baby! It—it frightens me more than a little."

"That's why you've been so—?"

He didn't finish.

"So cool? Yes. I suspected I might be pregnant right after New Year's, but as I told you, I vowed I wouldn't speak until I was positive." Her radiant expression dimmed as she surveyed the cobwebbed corners of the mean, dingy room. "I simply won't stay here once the weather breaks. It's a prison. And a filthy one at that."

She put her hands on his shoulders, smiling again: "Besides, everyone we've talked to says river travel is much smoother than going overland in a wagon."

"Yes, I know, but—"

"We must double our efforts to find passage."

Her blue eyes narrowed. He had seen that prologue to an angry outburst many times before.

"I mean it, Abraham. I will not stay in this dreadful room, this vile town, any longer than is absolutely necessary. I'm strong enough to make the river trip—"

"I'm not sure—"

"I *am!* We *must* go!"

He doubted her claim about her strength. But he didn't doubt her determination. He knew further argument would be useless. So he gathered her into his arms while the snow of February, 1797, whined the lodging house windows, and he said:

"All right, Elizabeth. We will."

ii

The luck of the Kents seemed to change with the coming of sunshine and a late February thaw. The notice board near the docks, where new arrivals posted their partnership propositions, sent Abraham running to a wagon camp at the edge of town. There he located the Clappers, a family from the Genessee River valley in upper New York state.

The Clapper clan consisted of Daniel, the father, a barrel of a man with a gray-streaked red beard and huge, hair-matted arms; his wife, a leathery little woman named Edna, and their two youngsters. Daniel Junior was sixteen; tiny, doll-like Danetta, nine.

Yes, Daniel Clapper said, Abraham had read the notice correctly. He meant to sell his wagon—but not his horses or all the merchandise the wagon had carried—and invest in a one-way ark.

"What's your destination, Mr. Clapper? The notice didn't say."

"Destination?" Clapper combed out his beard with thick fingers. "Wherever it strikes my fancy to squat, I reckon. I'm a storekeeper, y'see—"

He led Abraham to the wagon, showed him an assortment of goods from bolts of cloth to kegs of nails.

"Had a right good location up New Hampshire way for eleven years. All of a sudden one day, I just got sick of it. We packed up our goods, toted 'em cross country and opened a new store near the falls of the Genesee. Kept that seven years—till the movin' fever come on me again. We been bogged down north of here for a whole month, waitin' for the snow to melt. I can't get out o' Pittsburgh fast enough—just *look* at all these damn people—!"

His wave encompassed fifteen to twenty cook fires glowing in the twilight among immigrant wagons of every description.

"I'm fixin' to go towards the Ohio land, where there's a tad more room," Clapper continued. "Got all I need to open me a store the day I arrive. Put up my tent, lay a board 'twixt two kegs and I'm in business. I'll sell what I brung with me till I can pick up more from the packets comin' downriver. I'll use my horses to peddle in the back country, an' there I am—set up as pert as you please!"

Abraham tried to put the conversation back on course:

"According to the sheet you posted, you need three men for your ark. One more besides you and your son—"

"I need some cash, too." From his coat pocket Clapper pulled two paper-covered pamphlets, opened the first, shut it again. "Wrong one. That's the river map with the islands an' hazards marked—I can't afford me one of them high-priced pilots—"

Tucking the pamphlet away, he handed Abraham the other one:

"This here *Compleat Guide to the Western Territories* says arks run four dollar a foot. I need one about sixty feet, I guess, to haul the wife and Daniel and Danetta and my horses and goods."

"That's about two hundred and forty dollars."

"Yessir."

"I'd be willing to put in half."

"She wouldn't all go to waste, y'know." Clapper pointed at the pamphlet. "Says in there someplace that you can recover about a quarter o' what you spend for a boat if you tear her up and sell the lumber at the other end."

"Fine with me. Do we have a deal?"

"Hold on, Mr. Kent! We ain't covered all the details."

"What details?"

"Well, f'rinstance—are you travelin' all by yourself? I never seed so blasted many bachelors in one place in my life!"

"I'm married. I have my wife to take along—a small amount of luggage—a bulldog—"

Clapper scowled. "Does he bite?"

"Don't think so."

"Good. Miz Rachel hates mean dogs. That it?"

Abraham smiled. "Yes and no."

"What the hell's that mean?"

"My wife's expecting a child in the fall."

"Why, congratulations to you!" Clapper grabbed Abraham's hand and pumped it, squeezing so hard the younger man winced.

Pale, Abraham said, "Any more details?"

Clapper pondered. "Nope. It don't take me long to make up my mind about a feller's cut, Mr. Kent. If you're agreeable, it's partners."

"Partners," Abraham said, declining to shake the hand Clapper once again extended. Anxious to tell Elizabeth about their good fortune, he started away, then stopped short. He pivoted back to the huge tree of a man who was busy pulling a few chips of wood from his chest-length beard. "Mr. Clapper, there is one very important detail we didn't settle."

"What, Mr. Kent?"

"You still don't know where my wife and I want to go."

Clapper thought again, then shrugged:

"Don't much care. You can tell me if you want to."

"I've a deed to a plot of land on the Great Miami River, above Cincinnati."

"Used to call it Losantville 'bout ten years ago—I read that in one o' them guide books. I got a whole box of guide books about the new country—"

He jerked a thumb at his wagon. Over the end-board, a red-headed young man and a little rose-cheeked girl were watching.

"Where you're goin' sounds all right to me, Mr. Kent. Maybe I'll head on west, maybe I won't. Miz Rachel won't much care. She sighs a lot when we move, but she follers wherever I've a notion to go."

"You mean it really doesn't matter to you where you end up?"

"No, sir. I always like a place for a spell while I'm there. But then the itch sets in—can't explain it any better'n that. It's the goin', not the stoppin', I enjoy the most. Suppose that sounds crazy, huh?"

It did, but Abraham was too polite to admit it:

"I understand perfectly."

"Will you have a talk with Miz Rachel sometime? She sure as hell don't."

"How about this evening? I'd like to bring my wife over to get acquainted—"

"Bring her to supper! Miz Rachel don't mind fixin' for one more."

"Shouldn't you ask her?"

"Never ask a woman anything, Mr. Kent. She might tell you what she wants. Then wouldn't you be in a fix? Listen, you get a move on! The sooner we lay our plans, the sooner we'll be shed o' these damn mobs of people!"

Abraham vanished in the blue wood smoke of the cook fires Daniel Clapper continued to eye with disgust.

iii

April came, bringing longer days, warmer air, the first warbling birds, the first shoots of green on the coal-veined hills around Pittsburgh. To Abraham and Elizabeth, it seemed that the new season marked an end to their own long night of frustration and hardship as well.

To those with enough money, obtaining one of the huge flatboats known as arks was no problem. Any of several yards along the two rivers could hammer one together in the space of about two weeks. Morning after morning, Abraham and Daniel Clapper watched theirs being constructed: a rectangular scow sixty-two feet long, twenty-two feet wide.

The ark hull was built of timbers ten inches square, carefully caulked to minimize leakage. The entire deck was enclosed with four-inch planks that rose flush with the vessel's four sides.

A door in the larboard side near the stern was large enough to admit Clapper's horses to their appointed space. Forward of this, canvas hanging from the slightly pitched plank roof created temporary walls. One large area was set aside at the bow for communal dining and socializing. The partners agreed to pay extra to have a mud-brick hearth and chimney installed. The ark was quite literally a floating house and stable in one.

A ladder from below gave access to the roof through a trap door. From the roof's stern, a great steering oar nearly as long as the ark itself trailed into the water. She was a clumsy-looking craft, Abraham thought. He already felt confined just glancing into the canvas-partitioned sleeping cubicle he and Elizabeth would share. The ark had no windows, only small loopholes through which muskets could be poked in the event of an Indian attack from shore. But that danger was minimal, everyone said, at least above the falls.

The real hazards, according to Clapper's pamphlets, were sunken obstructions. Limbs and occasionally entire trees were swept away from the banks into the current. A few of the largest planters—trees whose upper ends protruded above the surface—and sleepers—trees with their upper ends submerged—were marked on Clapper's map, along with islands and sandbars. The map also noted a few well-known sawyers, submerged logs whose upper ends rose and fell in cycles as long as twenty minutes to half an hour. These were the most dangerous obstructions of all. Unfortunately, the map located only a fraction of them.

But that didn't intimidate the Clappers or the Kents. They watched families with just as little river experience confidently board their arks and set off around the bend of the Ohio in high spirits. One or two vessels a day departed from the Pittsburgh landings.

Finally, one brilliant morning in late April, so did theirs.

Abraham and Daniel Clapper leaned on the end of the great sweep. Daniel Junior cursed down below, struggling to calm the panicky horses. Edna Clapper, Danetta and Elizabeth were at the hearth, forward, preparing breakfast.

It was a smooth and auspicious beginning.

iv

The Ohio was more beautiful than Abraham remembered it. Their journey, while requiring long, tiring hours at the sweep, was almost like a holiday in some respects. Every sundown, they anchored in midstream, as did all boats traveling up and down the river. The Kents—Elizabeth growing noticeably around the middle—shared the physical warmth of the hearth at the bow, as well as the less tangible but very real human warmth generated by the Clappers. Indeed, the younger couple already felt themselves almost part of the family.

Elizabeth was unstinting when it came to helping Mrs. Clapper with the cooking. And she did her share of the washing that hung on a line strung across the roof. All of them took pleasure in innocuous chatter about the sights of the day, or in the lusty singing of a few hymns—Daniel Clapper enjoyed hymns—after the spring sun went down. Chief grew fatter on the scraps Rachel Clapper fed him.

At night, lying close together in their cubicle while Daniel Clapper snored noisily beyond the canvas partition, Abraham usually asked Elizabeth for reassurances that she was feeling well. Her spirits seemed remarkably improved but her color didn't.

She gave him the reassurances—truthful or not, he was unable to tell. He still felt occasional stabs of guilt over not being more sensitive to his father's warnings about the hardships they'd face in the west. He now saw clearly that he'd permitted his passion for Elizabeth, as well as their shared defiance of Philip, to lure him into the false certainty that love would sustain them in the face of all difficulties. Elizabeth's extreme fatigue every evening, and her parchment-white cheeks, were constant reminders that it just wasn't so.

Despite his concerns, the unvarying routine of the days and the continual pageant of towering forests and tiny settlements slipping behind them began to lull Abraham into a sense of security he enjoyed. A week passed without a mishap of any kind. He looked forward to one or two more such idyllic weeks before they reached the little frontier settlement of Cincinnati.

On a Friday evening, just at dusk, Abraham came up from below with two mugs of coffee freshly brewed by Mrs. Clapper. Her big, red-bearded husband was seated near the chimney. His legs hung down over the bow wall. Daniel Junior was taking his turn manning the sweep.

The river here ran straight and smooth. Some two or three miles ahead, Abraham glimpsed another ark preceding them. Half a mile behind, a two-way boat was being cordelled upstream against the four-mile-an-hour current. Its crew plodded along a clear stretch on the south bank, the long tow rope strung across their shoulders.

"Thankee," Clapper said, accepting the coffee. He squinted into the sunlight falling through the cathedral-like trees and burnishing the river. "Be dark soon. Time to drop anchor." He sipped from the mug. "Your wife seems to be weathering the Ohio mighty fine."

Abraham sat down; drank some coffee. "Did you think she might not?"

"She's a lovely lass, but she *is* a mite frail." Clapper stared at the younger man with disarming directness. "Surely you had doubts of your own."

"Yes. I did."

That seemed to conclude the subject. Abraham

turned to another that had kept him curious for days:

"Have you come to any decision about your final destination?"

"No, sir, I feel the same as I did in Pittsburgh. We agreed to split up the ark an' sell off her timbers in Cincinnati. I'll decide where we're goin' after that. Told you before—it don't make a hell of a lot of difference. I know a little about plenty o' things, but not enough to be a success at any one. In a way, that's mighty fortunate—"

When he grinned, his teeth literally materialized in the midst of the red hair covering the lower part of his face.

"I can relax some. Don't have to feel the least bit ambitious."

Abraham smiled, nodded. Clapper had a way of putting an immutable period at the end of certain conversations. Though he would have liked to question the older man about the origins of his odd attitudes, he didn't. Instead, he contented himself with savoring the coffee and the sunlight scattering golden sparks on the river.

The sweep creaked in its mounting as Daniel Junior changed course slightly. Ahead, the other ark was coasting out of sight around a bend.

Clapper surprised him by saying, "What do you want out here, Mr. Kent? You don't exactly fit."

"Why not?"

"Fer one thing, it's plain you're more of an educated man than I'll ever be."

"I'm not sure about that, Mr. Clapper. There's all sorts of education—"

"You know what I mean, Miz Edna, she keeps sayin', Daniel, that young Mr. Kent's got all the marks of a real gentleman."

Abraham chuckled. "I suppose that means I'll be a bad farmer?"

Clapper sugared the truth with a smile: "Probably won't make it any easier."

"To answer your question, I first came out here with the army. I served in the campaign of '94."

"Under Mad Anthony?"

"Yes. I liked the look of the country. And when I got home to Boston, I decided I didn't care to stay in the east. Right now my wants are simple."

"F'rinstance?"

Abraham shrugged. "The obvious things. To see Elizabeth content. To raise a family. To be happy myself—"

"As a dirt farmer?"

"I'm not sure. We'll find out."

"Least you're honest."

"Mostly I guess you could say I came west because I knew what I didn't want."

"Life in a big city—"

"That's right."

He thought of Philip, but he let the reply stand without amplification. The river burbled around the ark's hull. A hawk swooped through the green gloom of the woods to starboard. Abraham took another sip of the potent coffee, said:

"I didn't give you much of an answer, did I, Mr. Clapper? Knowing what you don't want—having to search for something else you can't even name—that's a pretty poor excuse for taking up a new life. The only trouble is, in my case it's true."

"You needn't look so glum about it. You think any of the other young people pilin' down this river are any smarter 'n you in that respect? No, sir." Clapper shook his head. "All *they* know is the same thing both of us know—what they don't want. They hope to heaven there's somethin' different out here—"

He waved the mug at the bend where the ark ahead had disappeared.

"—but don't ask 'em to name it!"

"Puts them on a spot, does it?"

"Right smart! They can't answer. Not so's a feller who's been around can believe 'em, that is. Oh, you'll hear plenty of gab about how everybody's free an' equal in the western lands—free an' equal, yes, sir! The west is *demo-cratic,* ain't that what that Mr. Jefferson says? No rich nabobs to crowd a young man, or make him feel second best. Maybe a mite of that's true—"

He held index finger and thumb close together.

"'Bout this much. I'll tell you something. If a man could be happy in the east, do you imagine he'd up and leave? Lord no! They can be loads o' reasons *why* he ain't happy. Money. Women. Mebbe he's ugly as that bulldog of yours—"

"I wouldn't wish that on another human being, Mr. Clapper."

The other man still refused to smile:

"Lots of times, a man can't be happy and just plain don't know why. He might have a bit of cash put by, even some regular schooling—"

"But he leaves anyway?"

"Yes, sir, 'cause he's so blamed unhappy. Mr. Kent, believe me, that's the whole reason. A man don't *never* cut the roots if everything's right with his world—or his head. Folks can turn it other side backwards all they want. They can shout *'Free an' equal!'* till they're blue. But just like your case—it really ain't a matter of goin' *toward,* it's a matter of runnin' *from*—"

Clapper encompassed the western horizon with a sweep of the cup:

"And once you catch the urge to run away, you never lose it. You just keep movin'—miserable as ever."

Abraham shivered. "That's a grim view."

"True, though."

"Well, if all you say about people being unhappy is correct—"

"It is!"

"Then we're fortunate we have room to run, aren't we? If we had to stay bottled up back east with all the grief you describe, I suspect we'd soon go crazy. So that makes the western country a blessing. And people moving into it—that's a good, healthy thing when you consider the alternative."

"Got to think that through a minute," Clapper informed him, dubious.

"In my case it's a blessing. I had to have somewhere to escape to, and that's a fact."

"Yeh, but you can't pin down what you're huntin'—you said so."

"I know. Still, I'm hoping I'll find something good—and be smart enough to recognize it for what it is."

"Something, something," Clapper parroted. Then, a snort: "You feel that way 'cause you're young."

"You don't feel that way?"

"Not no more. You want to keep hopin', Mr. Kent, don't ask questions of folks my age."

"Why not?"

" 'Cause you'll find that a mighty lot of the settlers swarmin' out here have stopped other places before. Lookin', always lookin'—for *something*. The ones that got ten or fifteen years on you—they already found out."

"Found out what?"

"*Something* don't exist. No place."

"But surely—"

"No. It don't." Without self-pity, Clapper added, "I found out. Now you understand why it don't make any difference to me where this boat's headed, or where it stops?"

"Yes, I do."

Clapper bobbed his head once, and drained his cup.

God in heaven, Abraham hoped Clapper wasn't right. He prayed he and Elizabeth wouldn't reach their tract of land only to come face to face with the futility of their flight—

No, surely the big man was in error; embittered by personal failures barely hinted at. To believe what Clapper said was too disillusioning—

The sudden, violent impact shattered his dour reverie. With a great crunch, then a prolonged grinding, the ark wrenched broadside to the current. Clapper almost pitched into the water.

Abraham's grab saved him. He dragged Clapper back as the bow of the ark came around, then lifted sharply on the larboard side.

Both men were nearly hurled off the roof as the ark rode up on some underwater obstacle, slid off and slammed down.

Below, the terrified horses neighed and kicked against the plank walls. The kicks were loud as gunshots.

"Sweep broke clean off, pa!" Daniel Junior yelled from the stern. "We musta hit a sawyer—"

"Damn! The log was probably way down when that boat ahead of us went by. Then she bobbed up—go see how bad we're busted up, Daniel."

Abraham studied the tilt of the roof. "We're taking water. She's listing."

Daniel Junior vanished below. Clapper began, "We better—"

"Danetta!"

Clapper and Abraham exchanged terrified looks. The cry came from Edna Clapper—and she wasn't given to excesses of emotion.

All Abraham could think of was the ark's brief but

jolting rise and fall. *Where was Elizabeth when they hit—?*

He ran to the roof trap and scrambled down the ladder, hardly aware of Daniel Junior's urgent cries from the stern. Clapper came down the ladder after him. Chief was yapping. The horses kept kicking the ark walls, *bang, bang—*

Mrs. Clapper screamed for her daughter a second time.

Abraham batted canvas hangings aside, dashed forward through sloshing water and burst into the communal room at the bow.

"Elizabeth!"

Tumbled into an awkward position against the bricks at one side of the hearth, his wife didn't respond, or see him. Her eyes were nearly closed. One of her white hands constricted on the small mound of her belly.

Mrs. Clapper was kneeling beside her, partially concealing Elizabeth's legs. Abraham felt sick to his stomach as he watched Edna Clapper withdraw her hands from beneath Elizabeth's twisted skirt.

The hands were bloody.

"She fell," Mrs. Clapper said in a faint voice, as though holding great emotion in check. "When we hit, she fell against the fireplace—"

Suddenly her eyes smoldered:

"This is no place for men! *Find Danetta.*"

Anguish held Abraham rooted. He realized Clapper had come up behind him—and even the big red-bearded man seemed horrified into helplessness.

Edna Clapper turned her wrath on both of them: "In God's name, will you hurry? Mrs. Kent is losing the baby!"

Book Two

The Enemy Land

CHAPTER I

The Cabin

"ONE FOR THE crow, two for the cutworm, three to grow. One for the crow, two for the cut—"

Alarmed, young Daniel Clapper suddenly broke off the monotonous chant.

He and Abraham Kent had been marching side by side down the new checkrows plowed with the help of one of Daniel Clapper's horses. At every transverse row marking the cleared four-acre plot into yard-sized squares, man and boy dropped half a dozen kernels of seed corn. Now Daniel had stopped.

A moment later, Abraham halted too. Looked back. Young Daniel remained motionless, signaling with his eyes:

"Yonder, Mr. Kent. Injuns on the ridge."

Slowly, so as not to show his concern, Abraham Kent slipped the seed bag off his bare shoulder. He wore only buckskin trousers and soft moccasins padded with leaves for comfort. His glance traveled first to the edge of the plot, where Chief rested next to a smoldering stump. On the ground near the bulldog's paws lay Abraham's Kentucky flintlock rifle, his horn and his shot pouch. It would require a good run to reach the weapon. But it was primed and ready to fire, as always.

The wind this gray, thundery afternoon in late May, 1799, cooled the sweat on Abraham's chest in an instant. His gaze moved quickly on toward the cabin.

The windowless, twenty-by-sixteen building was half hidden by the inevitable trees that made clearing and planting even a single acre an exhausting task. Abraham had felled the smaller trees around the cabin. The larger ones showed the cuts where he'd girdled them to kill them. Several other stumps he was burning out fumed like the one at the field's edge, mingling their smoke with the reassuring column rising from the cabin chimney. The chimney's surrounding log superstructure jutted from the end of the cabin facing the river. The offset cut down the danger of fire, but not much.

Near the cabin, their once-fat milk cow nibbled at a patch of grass. In one of Elizabeth's rare moments of good humor, she'd insisted on naming the cow Henrietta Knox.

Pretending to draw several deep breaths, Abraham finally completed the covert inspection. Once again he had cause to regret the location of his property: a good four miles above the settlement at Fort Hamilton.

Finally he turned. He wiped his forehead with his forearm to conceal his interest in the western ridge-line. Just as he spotted the four tiny figures, young Daniel let out a relieved breath:

"They're movin' again. They was just standin' and watchin' when I seen 'em first."

Abraham's heart slowed down. He picked up his seed bag.

"We can finish, then."

He licked his lips, resumed walking. Young Daniel followed along the adjacent row. But he didn't continue his sower's chant.

The Indian danger kept Abraham constantly alert. It terrified his wife. Although raids in the district were infrequent—and were usually limited to cow thefts or cabin burnings—they did happen. Occasionally they were augmented by atrocities. Usually the victims had chosen to live a good distance from a fort or village.

The atrocities were by no means confined to one side, though. Abraham knew several white men in the settlement around Fort Hamilton who would automatically shoot and butcher any Indians they caught on the trails that ran parallel to the river.

Trudging and scattering corn, Abraham said in a listless voice, "I suppose they were Shawnee again."

Young Daniel nodded. "Goin' back to their towns north o' here, I reckon. Pap says General Wayne never should of 'lowed them to hunt in the treaty lands. Only makes 'em resent what the gummint took away—and crave it worse every time they travel through."

Too tired to enter into a discussion of Indian policy, Abraham kept walking. A few spatters of rain landed on his bare shoulders. Although it couldn't be later than four o'clock, the silver-gray clouds sweeping out of the west were rapidly bringing near-darkness. The wind had turned gusty. A little less than half a mile away, the surface of the Great Miami showed white riffles.

When the rain began to fall harder, Abraham swore and closed his seed bag:

"We'd better wait till morning to finish, Daniel."

"All right," the gangly boy agreed. "Be back right after sunup."

"You want to rest in the cabin till the storm's over?"

"I would, but pap's waitin' for me to unload them tools we brung up from Cincinnati."

"I really appreciate your help, Daniel."

"Oh, hell, it's nothin'."

"I couldn't get by without it and you know it. I only hope to God I can raise four good acres this year, and give your father half."

"Mr. Kent, he don't expect you to settle up right away."

"Well, I'm going to, Daniel."

Abraham was sincere in his promise to repay Clapper the only way he could. Yet repeating the pledge depressed him too.

Even if four full acres of corn matured, half of the yield would barely keep the little family over the winter, while the other half would hardly make a dent in the various debts he'd run up at the small store Daniel Clapper had established near the fort, simply by partitioning half of his large cabin and hanging out a sign.

Daniel was embarrassed by Abraham's sober expression. Without understanding its cause, he tried to dismiss it with a wave:

"Folks got to help each other, Mr. Kent. Otherwise none of us'd make it, isn't that right?"

"Yes," Abraham said in an absent way.

"See you in the morning."

Running, young Daniel disappeared into the trees west of the cabin. As Abraham watched the boy go, he noted that all the smoldering stumps were being drenched by the rain. He'd have to relight them tomorrow. Another chore—

That was the extent of life out here: chores. Seven days a week, indoors and out. The rigors of it had stripped all the fat from Abraham's body; thickened his muscles noticeably. But he felt tired every waking minute.

He put on his linsey shirt, grimacing at its wetness. He picked up his pouch, horn and flintlock, taking care to shield the lock in the crook of his arm. Burdened with those items plus the two seed sacks, he tramped toward the cabin.

Under the protection of one of the big girdled trees, he watched the clouds sailing out of the west and reflected on the understated truth of young Daniel's parting remark. Without mutual assistance, few settlers could survive the first year or so in the new land.

Abraham and Elizabeth had been fortunate in several ways. He often forgot that in his weariness and frustration—

Repairing the ark struck by the sunken log had been fairly easy, thanks to the help of some coarse-talking but genial boatmen who had come upstream, sail raised to a freshening wind, an hour after the accident. Elizabeth had indeed lost the baby, and been weak for more than a month. But the tragedy hadn't destroyed her ability to bear, thank God. The evidence of that was in the cabin.

On their arrival at Cincinnati, Daniel Clapper, that odd, cheerfully pessimistic man of small education and large wisdom had declared that he and his brood might as well open their store at Abraham and Elizabeth's destination, because it was "probably as good as anyplace else—in fact just the same as anyplace else."

So the Kents and the Clappers had ridden the thirty-odd miles north along the Miami in a hired wagon pulled by Clapper's two horses. On their property, the younger couple found the blessing of a half-faced camp, ramshackle but serviceable during the first weeks. People at the Fort Hamilton settlement said squatters had been on the Kent land the year before. But the squatters had moved on out toward the Wabash River country. No one in the settlement even remembered the squatters by name.

Leaning against the gridled tree and watching the rain fall, Abraham recalled that first hard summer and autumn. He particularly recalled his desperate rush to hoe a few holes in the ground between the trees and plant a small amount of corn to tide them over the cold months. The corn not only failed to grow, it failed to sprout.

By custom, all men in the district came to raise the

Kents' cabin in September of '97. Since that time, Abraham had taken part in six three-day cabin raisings for others.

During the winter of 1797–98, Abraham spent almost all of his remaining money for provisions to tide them through until spring. He bartered a clock Elizabeth had brought from Boston to obtain the rifle they needed for protection. A number of settings of fine china were surrendered to storekeeper Clapper for a pair of cheaper pewter plates, seed and a plow. Abraham knew Clapper was getting the bad end of the bargain. No one out here would purchase that exquisite china off Clapper's shelf.

The last of the money paid for Henrietta Knox, who delivered the milk he and Elizabeth learned to drink sour, although they abominated the taste. There was no way to keep milk sweet for long; storing it in a crock in the cold, clear spring at the back of their property only retarded the souring a few days.

The following year, '98, Abraham had laboriously cleared a two-acre plot, planted it and harvested the corn. Half the crop was ruined by a disease that blighted the ears as they were forming. But at least the family had some food for the winter. The baby, born in the fall with the help of a local midwife, took its nourishment directly from Elizabeth's breast.

Under the bellies of fast-flying clouds, Abraham saw a wedge of birds streaming north. Plump and tasty passenger pigeons. When they stopped to roost, you could practically knock them out of the lower branches with sticks. Abraham watched the birds longingly. A cooked pigeon would have been a welcome change from their diet of corn mush and sour milk.

The movement of the birds against the strangely luminous gray-and-silver sky drew Abraham's mind back to the conversation with Daniel Clapper just before the ark hit the sunken log. Abraham had changed his thinking since then. He believed Clapper was, in part if not entirely, correct. The desire to see the other side of the hill *was* rooted in discontent, whether it took the form of a yearning for wealth the east denied, a second chance to repair a wrecked life, misery generated by crowded conditions in the cities—or even plain, cussed boredom.

In his case and Elizabeth's, the goal had been escape from Philip's domineering influence. Abraham could admit that freely to himself now, without shame. He *was* ashamed of his desire to see the Boston house again. He never revealed it to his wife.

Still, it was odd, he thought as he watched the gray rain pour down on his newly planted field—odd that unhappiness was the motive force behind so many people moving west. And my God—they were moving west by the thousands!

Just this past March, he'd gone to Cincinnati with Daniel Clapper and his son, to help them transport an unusually large stock of new staples and implements back to the store. Cincinnati was no longer the tiny frontier outpost Abraham remembered. It had boomed since the Kents and Clappers passed through in the late spring of '97. Population had spurted to over five hundred, not counting the Fort Washington garrison.

What astonished Abraham most was the river traffic. With boats tied up everywhere, pushing off at all hours only to be replaced by new ones coming down the Ohio, the river town actually looked more crowded than Pittsburgh. Almost all the transients were heading further west. Americans, Abraham concluded, were the damnedest bunch of perpetual malcontents civilization had ever seen.

As he strolled the packed, noisy piers, observing families as well as young bachelors armed only with hunting rifles preparing to set out, he recalled Daniel Clapper's dour prediction that most of the travelers would never find the ideal life they sought. Yet they took pleasure in haggling over flatboat passage, and spoke glowingly in the taverns of all the freedom and promise of the bountiful land waiting out ahead—

That country just *had* to be more attractive and comfortable than the coastal belt, where a swelling populace was growing more and more alarmed over the undeclared naval war between America and her former ally, France.

From time to time a letter written by Philip or Peggy—a letter months in transit—expressed the Kents' open hostility to Philip's native country. The letters were further signs of how Philip's conservatism was hardening into unqualified pro-British sentiment.

The French Directory had been angered by Jay's treaty with England, the letters reported. And despite President Washington's specific warnings in his farewell address against all alliances with foreign nations except those alliances of the most temporary, expedient nature, Minister Pinckney had gone to Paris along with Commissioners Elbridge Gerry and John Marshall to attempt to secure a treaty guaranteeing friendship and, more important, commerce.

The commissioners were outraged by a request for an outright bribe to be paid to foreign minister Talleyrand, in return for consideration of the requested treaty. The bribe wasn't to be paid directly, of course. It was to be funneled through three intermediaries tactfully dubbed Messieurs X, Y and Z. All but the most illiterate passing along the Ohio had heard of—and by and large approved—the ringing toast that had become a catchphrase. The toast had been given Minister Pinckney after his furious refusal to pay Talleyrand, and his return to the United States:

"Millions for defense but not one cent for tribute!"

That was a sentiment Philip Kent heartily endorsed in his letters—especially as it applied to post-revolutionary France. He was pleased, he wrote, that a Navy Department had at last been created. He was delighted that *Constitution* and the other frigates had finally been completed, and launched to oppose French harassment of American shipping.

Most of the settlers Abraham talked with in Cincinnati weren't articulate about the question of war. But they were quite aware of its possibility. Thus they had an added incentive to get as far away as possible from the vulnerable seacoast.

Perhaps some would end up at a destination that satisfied them. Or perhaps they'd pretend that was the case, anyway, so as not to confront their families—or themselves—with the sad truth of their error.

A few might actually better themselves. But no gentle Edens awaited them, Abraham was positive of that. The fact had come home to him long before the Cincinnati trip. It had come home to him as he lay beside his wife during the summer and winter nights, his body hurting so badly from physical labor that he literally couldn't sleep.

Something else struck him in Cincinnati—struck with the power of a revelation:

He and Elizabeth were just as much prisoners of their surroundings as they would have been had Abraham taken a place and done Philip's bidding at Kent and Son.

Thousands were moving west but they could not. They had mortgaged their lives to twenty acres along the Miami River, and were consumed by the challenges of daily living: food, shelter, the Indian threat—

Survival.

He and Elizabeth would never see another place. At

least not easily. Clapper said it made no difference—one was identical with the next. Still, what Abraham was denied, he somehow coveted.

After the excursion to Cincinnati, he began to think of the twenty acres in a new way. No longer was the land a haven. It acquired quasi-human characteristics in his mind—especially when he tramped to Fort Hamilton for supplies and wound up accepting too much of Clapper's corn whiskey. Then the land became a true opponent. A captor whom he could and did curse aloud—

Even basic survival on the land was still in doubt. Abraham was succeeding, but only marginally; and that success would have been impossible without the cooperative spirit that tended to tie the settlers together, each helping the other.

The preceding autumn, for instance, Abraham had worked all night many a night at husking bees, since no man could husk a large corn crop alone. He had lent his time and his strength to those cabin-raisings, in return for the help he had received with his.

Yet even with human allies, he found the land a formidable foe. Many—like the vanished squatters who'd built the half-faced camp he and Elizabeth had originally inhabited—lacked the will and the wits to win against it. Abraham had done his best; given the struggle everything for nearly two years—and all he had to show was a meager four-acre plot, and no guarantee of a good crop on that.

It might be different if Elizabeth were stronger physically, he thought. *Tougher mentally—*

But as he stared into the heavying rain that hid the river and extinguished the last of his burning stumps, he admitted she was not. He'd have welcomed an occasional smile of pleasure at his small accomplishments; a word of encouragement about the tasks still to be done.

Elizabeth seemed incapable of giving either. Somehow it doubled the rigors of his work.

A noise on a nearby tree branch diverted him from the gloomy meditation. He spied a fat squirrel perched where the limb joined the trunk. He found squirrel meat in a pot pie not too unpalatable. So he raised the Kentucky rifle to his shoulder slowly, and aimed down the acid-browned octagonal barrel. The trick was to avoid hitting the squirrel and destroying the flesh. Instead, Abraham would try to bark him.

The rifle exploded. Smoke curled. Chief began to snap and run in a circle as Abraham grimaced—it couldn't be called a smile. His ball had flown true. Smacked the thick wood where the branch met the tree. The concussion had spun the squirrel to the ground, where it now lay stunned.

"Stay back, Chief."

The bulldog reluctantly obeyed as Abraham picked up a stone and ran forward. He killed the squirrel with one quick stroke that broke its head open but left the carcass undamaged.

Abraham trotted to the end of the cabin opposite that where the chimney rose. He stowed his corn sacks in the little shed he'd built and chinked carefully. He tied Henrietta Knox to the bar on the shed door, although the rain was beginning to pelt down so hard that the cabin wall would afford her little protection.

The cow lowed uncomfortably. Stamped and jangled her bell as Abraham felt her udder.

Full. Elizabeth hadn't milked her again.

Well, he'd have to do it when the rain let up.

More and more often this spring, Elizabeth seemed to be forgetting or ignoring important work. He never spoke of it, adding the burden to his other ones in the silent hope that doing so might make his wife less weary and somber. It never seemed to. Yet Abraham refused to give up the effort to lighten her load. At the same time, the lapses troubled him.

He returned to retrieve his rifle, horn, pouch—and, by the tail, the squirrel. He slopped through the mud at the front of the cabin. From several feet away, he saw the thick plank door standing slightly ajar. The thong that raised the inside latch dangled from the small hole.

He always insisted Elizabeth keep the door barred and the latchstring in, even when he was near the cabin. She refused, claiming the cabin was confining enough as it was. She shrugged off his statements that women had been murdered by stealthy Indians while their husbands worked only a short distance away.

As he reached the door, he heard one-year-old Jared Adam bawling. His scalp prickled with a belated realization:

Elizabeth should have come to the door when she heard the shot.

Fearful, he jerked the cabin door open as the blackening sky rumbled.

ii

Abraham stepped out of the downpour, held up his prize:

"I picked off a squirrel for—"

His face froze in surprise.

Not one of the three tallow candles in tin wall sconces had been lit. The cabin was dark except for the flickering logs in the hearth.

Above the logs the family stew pot hung from a pole mounted across the inside of the chimney. A burned stench drifted from the pot. Elizabeth had been cooking corn meal into mush. All the water had boiled away.

There was an oppressive stillness. It was broken only by the rattle of rain on the hand-riven roof clapboards. By the tick of Chief's unclipped nails on the puncheon floor. And by Jared Adam's fretful crying, off to Abraham's right where the firelight failed to reach.

He saw his wife clearly enough. Her back bowed, she sat on one of their two block chairs—sixteen-inch hickory logs standing on end. Her hands were fisted on the knees of her soiled dress. Her blue eyes stared into and through the fire.

Angry, Abraham flung the squirrel on the puncheon table projecting from one wall. The squirrel struck so hard, the table's pole legs quivered. The dead animal's head stained the wood. He never noticed:

"Elizabeth."

No answer.

"Elizabeth, the baby's crying. Don't you hear him?"

An eternity seemed to pass before she turned her head. Tears shone on her cheeks.

He dropped his pouch and horn, laid his rifle beside the squirrel, rushed to her as the baby howled all the louder. His rage left him in an instant, replaced by grief. He gripped Elizabeth's shoulders, felt them trembling, whispered:

"What's wrong?"

Her voice was feeble:

"I—I don't know. I sat down—I'm so tired, Abraham. I felt so miserable all at once and—I don't know," she repeated in a futile tone.

Her face had a distinct pallor. She had lost weight over the past months. The bosom of her dress looked almost flat because her breasts sagged.

"Elizabeth, you're not carrying a child again, and haven't told me—?"

She shook her head. The fair hair that once had

glowed so brilliantly was seldom washed these days; it hung dull and tangly at her shoulders. She began to rock back and forth.

"I don't know what's wrong, except I hate this place. I hate it, oh God, I *hate* it—"

Sobbing, she covered her face and turned her back on him. Unseen in the darkness, the infant still made his presence known with his damnable howling. Abraham came close to cursing him.

Struggling to keep his voice calm, he said, "I brought in a squirrel. Elizabeth, do you hear?"

She gave no sign.

"I thought a squirrel pie might be a welcome change. I'll fix it—"

"I'm not hungry."

"You've eaten next to nothing all week!"

"I don't know why," she said. "I don't know."

Terrified by her glazed eyes but not knowing exactly what to do, Abraham gripped her shoulders again, tried to lift her from the block chair:

"Let me put you in bed. I'll see to the boy—"

She offered no resistance. He guided her to the double bedstead in the angle of two walls. The bed's outer corner was supported by a pole similar to those beneath the table, but thicker. He lowered Elizabeth gently to the double deerhide spread over a thick matting of corn husks. Despite the padding, the bed was as hard as anything he'd ever slept on, the earth included.

Elizabeth started shivering. He covered her with one of their few luxuries—a hand-made Kentucky quilt in the simple yet beautiful Star of Bethlehem pattern.

In a moment or two, her shivering stopped. Abraham knelt. He suspected the chill and misery were products of her mind, not her body. He kissed her wind-roughened cheek:

"Don't fret, I'll have the baby quiet soon. Don't worry about a thing—"

She began to cry again:

"I don't know what's wrong with me, Abraham. I knew the corn meal was burning. I could smell it. I sat there and didn't care—"

"There's nothing wrong with you except lack of rest," he said. Neither of them believed it:

"No, Abraham, it's something else. I'm not strong enough for you. For this—"

"My God, don't say that! You've done so much work—"

"But I hate it, I despise it, sometimes I just don't want to go on—"

She controlled her crying; wiped her eyes; looked at him and spoke more lucidly:

"You've never heard much about my father, have you?"

"Only the talk at home. What has he to do with us?"

"He has a great deal to do with me, I think."

"What do you mean?"

"Mama told me more about him than she ever told anyone else, including your father. He was—a peculiar man. Wild and—and brave in some ways. But weak in others. He ran from whatever he disliked. Or drank to forget it. Perhaps—no, listen to me, Abraham, you must hear this—perhaps his nature was strength and weakness in one. Mama calls it the Fletcher blood."

"I've never heard her mention—"

"Fletcher blood. I have it. I know it's one reason I resented your father so, and insisted we come to this place."

"Don't forget that took courage, Elizabeth. Great courage."

The moment he said it, his mind showed him an image of Daniel Clapper. He heard Clapper speaking of why men fled toward another horizon, then another, another—

"I don't have any courage left," she said. "Two years out here and—any that I may have had—it's gone. All I feel is hate. Tiredness, and hate—"

Her hand closed on his, an iced claw:

"I know what I am—"

"Stop."

"I don't want it to hurt you—"

"Elizabeth, don't—"

"Most of all I don't want it to hurt baby Jared."

A long silence. Then:

"How could it?"

"He has the same blood, doesn't he?"

Abraham felt a terror so deep and devastating that he couldn't speak for several moments. The child's howls dinned in the confined space, ceasing only when the baby gulped a breath. He tried to ignore the squalling; tried to quell the fear Elizabeth's strange ramblings generated. He soothed her forehead with a palm, and lied:

"You're feverish. You need rest."

She stared up into the darkness where the timbers of the loft floor were barely visible. He tucked the quilt around her throat and shoulders:

"I'll pile an extra log or two on the fire—it promises to be a foul night. Maybe you'll feel like eating something in a few hours—"

She closed her eyes. Tears ran down her cheeks as if she were in great pain.

"See to the baby," she whispered. "See to the poor baby."

She rolled onto her side, away from him. He covered his eyes, wondering if what she'd rambled about was true. Did some streak of inherited temperament drive her to these despairs that grew deeper and more frequent as the weeks passed?

Or was it the land? Some weren't strong enough to win the struggle with the land. Was she one of those—?

Forcing himself to activity, he placed two smaller logs atop the others, then walked across the cabin as flames leaped up beneath the stinking pot of burned mush. Jared Adam kept shrieking.

Abraham reached down for the bundled boy, raised him to his shoulder, felt the sopping wetness of the coverlet in which Elizabeth had wrapped him.

"Papa's here," Abraham whispered. "It's all right, Jared. Papa's here."

The infant cried less stridently. Chief tick-tacked across the floor to the cradle Abraham had hollowed from half a gum log and finished with crescent rockers pegged to the ends. The bulldog sniffed the aroma of urine permeating the crib, lumbered back to the corner where he always slept. Outside, Henrietta Knox lowed loudly, her bell clanking.

Abraham started for the trunk to find clean rags for the baby. After he'd discarded the soiled ones, he wrapped Jared carefully, then went back to the trunk for a dry coverlet. As he picked Jared up again, he glanced at the bedstead. Elizabeth lay motionless under the quilt. Her eyes were shut but he didn't believe she was asleep.

All at once he couldn't tolerate the ripe smells poisoning the air in the cabin. In spite of the downpour, he jerked the latchstring, stepped into the open doorway—

My God, how dark it was! And not even nightfall yet.

Gusts of wind blew cool rain in his face. He covered Jared's head hastily.

He pondered what his wife had said about the Fletcher blood. Despite a death some called heroic, Fletcher had been a tainted man. There was certainly mounting evidence of a similar taint on Elizabeth—

Had it passed to the baby boy on his shoulder? Unconsciously, he tugged up the blanket, all but hiding the dark-fuzzed skull.

Westward, the clouds had lowered. The western ridge had disappeared in the murk. The small amount of daylight remaining showed Abraham the damaging effects of the flash storm. All his checkrows were washed away. The rain had cut new channels in the ground. He would have to start again. The plowing, the seeding—everything.

With his wife lying silent behind him and Jared fretting on his shoulder, Abraham stared at the storm-raked field and almost shook with rage.

What an accursed land! It treated a man's hopes and a man's labors and a man's loved ones with inhuman indifference—

He stood there for almost half an hour, looking at the rain but seeing his mortal enemy.

CHAPTER II

Old Ghosts and New Beginnings

ONE AUTUMN SATURDAY a year later, Abraham walked back from Clapper's store to find the farm unexpectedly quiet.

He stopped at the edge of the property, frowning as he scanned it. His eye drifted from the cabin to the small barn built in the spring with the help of neighbors. Henrietta Knox grazed near the barn. From within came the mournful bellow of the ox he'd bought using money Daniel Clapper loaned him. He was deeper in debt than ever before.

His gaze moved on to the cultivated ground—eight acres now, the corn already standing in shocks that cast long shadows in the cool amber sunlight of late afternoon. In addition to the corn, he'd put in patches of turnips, which had done well, and watermelons, which hadn't.

He quickly shook off the lethargy induced by a generous amount of Clapper's whiskey. Elizabeth had planned to make soap today. The process took hours. She boiled wood-ash lye and fat which she'd saved, producing harsh, slimy lumps of soap that seemed to remove more skin than dirt. But Abraham saw no smoke rising from the chimney into the flurry of leaves whirled across the roof by the wind.

No smoke—nor any sign of activity in or around the cabin. He didn't see Elizabeth or their two-year-old son anywhere.

He put down the jug of New Orleans molasses he'd

obtained at Clapper's. Packet boats brought the sweetening up the Mississippi and the Ohio regularly now. He'd lacked the exact change for the purchase, so the storekeeper had snipped another piece from one of his few paper dollars.

A second close scrutiny of the property produced no evidence of trespassers. But just in case, he made sure his Kentucky rifle was loaded and ready to fire.

"Elizabeth? Jared?" His voice boomed back at him in the stiff wind—*Elizabeth? Jared?*—unanswered. Henrietta Knox turned her head briefly, then resumed chewing the brown grass.

Moving slowly toward the cabin, he saw Elizabeth's splint broom lying abandoned in the dooryard. Damn! She was supposed to stay locked inside while he was gone.

Again he called her name. Again no answer. He prodded the cabin door open with the muzzle of his rifle.

He saw nothing but darkness. Not a single tallow-dip was lit against the coming dusk. The river murmured in the distance.

It was the letter, he decided. The damned, hurtful letter from his father. A pack train had delivered it to Fort Hamilton thirty days ago—

During the past twelve months the elder Kent's letters had changed noticeably. The tone grew steadily less cheerful, and items of interest concerning the east and Europe had become more and more sparse. The last bit of information Abraham could recall his father reporting with genuine enthusiasm was months old. Philip Kent's boyhood friend, Lafayette, had finally been released from prison in Austria and allowed to return to France. There, living in relative seclusion, he had resumed correspondence with his old comrade in Boston.

Of late, however, Abraham found himself relying almost totally on other settlers for news—

News of President Adams' refusal to go to war with France, for instance. Adams resisted war even though many in his political party—including Philip, presumably—favored it.

There were new developments in France. By means of a coup, a military leader had seized power. The soldier named Bonaparte was a man of vast ambition, it was said. As first consul of his country, he announced his intention to deal with the United States in an amicable way—no doubt to prevent an American alliance with France's traditional enemy, Britain.

Bonaparte's avowed friendship might end the hostilities between American and French naval forces. People in the east were suspicious of the new ruler, though. Didn't he openly express his dream of a worldwide French empire? Might he not press the Spanish to recede the vast Louisiana territory—including the port of New Orleans—in return for France's surrender of portions of Italy? The anti-French faction east of the mountains claimed such negotiations were in fact underway in secret. Ultimately, Bonaparte could endanger the use of the Ohio and Mississippi as commercial routes for the western part of the country.

Philip hardly touched on these matters. Abraham heard about them from men gathered around Clapper's cracker barrel. When the recent, extremely brief letter arrived via pack train, Abraham at last understood his father's silence on more general subjects.

Philip wrote that in late February of this year, 1800, Peggy Ashford McLean Kent had died of a wasting disease that shriveled her body and tortured her senses for six months before death gave her release. Since reading the letter, Elizabeth had lost her appetite, gone listlessly about her chores, paid little attention to Jared and less to her husband.

They still slept side by side. But Abraham hadn't touched her in a month, sensing her unspoken wish that he refrain. As a result, he often felt angry with her. His anger found an outlet in Saturday visits to the settlement. She seldom felt strong enough to walk with him. He usually came home more than a little drunk—

"Elizabeth!"

This time he shouted. The echo rolled away through the trees and died under the murmur of the wind. Invisible in the brush that screened part of the river bank, someone answered:

"Papa?"

Exhaling loudly, Abraham hurried forward:

"Jared, you stay right there—"

What in hell was the child doing outside, unattended?

Abraham clambered noisily down through the brush. He heard Chief's feeble bark. The bulldog was ancient now, barely able to walk.

Once more Abraham searched the woods and the portion of the river bank visible to him. Still no sign of Elizabeth. Fear turned to wrath again as he parted a screen of low branches and discovered his son.

Moccasins off and feet dirty, Jared was seated on the ground, alternately scooping dirt from a hole and building it into a small mound. The boy looked up with bright blue eyes—the Fletcher eyes he'd inherited from his mother. Chief, lying a few feet away, lolled his tongue but made no effort to rise and greet his master.

Jared's tawny hair hung matted over his neck. His hide shirt showed rips at the elbows—more indications of Elizabeth's neglect. Almost fearfully, the boy continued to stare up at his stocky father.

"Why did mama leave you alone, Jared?"

Although Jared was only two, Elizabeth had been

able to teach him to use rudimentary sentences. He answered with one:

"Don't know."

"Where did she go?"

The boy looked away. "Down there." A grimy hand pointed.

Abraham scowled. "The river? Whatever for?"

"Don't know. She said to play. Then she left." As if to show that he'd tried to do as he was told, he glanced down at the mound of dirt.

Abraham started to say something. A faint sound from the bushes behind Chief brought his head snapping around. His hand turned cold on the stock of his rifle.

Eyes fixed on the brush concealing the source of the rattle, he said:

"Jared, listen. Get up. Come to me."

Jared frowned. "Want to finish—"

"I said *come to me!*"

Abraham's palms were slick with sweat. He dared not look away from the brush for an instant—

Tears appeared in Jared's eyes. But he rose obediently and walked to his father—moments before the head of the snake jutted from the underbrush.

"Get behind me, Jared!"

The boy was gazing up at his father. He didn't understand the reason for the harsh command. The snake coiled out of the shadows, rattling—

The snake was sixteen or seventeen inches long. Its brown ground color was blotched with black. Its puffy head darted a few inches to the right, then a few inches to the left—

Abraham stepped around his son, jammed the rifle against his shoulder and fired.

Chief barked, struggled to stand up as Abraham's ball missed the head of the pygmy rattler, blasting up a shower of leaves and dirt. The rattler's fangs glistened as its head shot forward. Chief yelped when the rattler bit.

By then Abraham had lunged forward. He drove the rifle's brass butt plate toward the front part of the snake's body. The snake whipped its head back a moment before the rifle struck. The blow cracked the snake's skull.

Using the rifle stock as a kind of shovel, Abraham hoisted the snake and hurled it away. On his belly, Chief tried to turn his head far enough to lick at his wound. The old dog was too stiff; his tongue wouldn't reach.

Jared clutched his father's leg:

"What—what was it?"

"A snake."

"What?"

"*Snake,* Jared. Dangerous. Hurt you."

"Didn't see it—"

"I know you didn't. That's the reason you should never play out here alone. That's why mama should never leave you here alone!"

The boy pointed to the floundering bulldog. "Chief's hurt."

Abraham doubted he could do anything for the animal. The bite of a pygmy rattler was seldom fatal to a grown man. But the venom might affect a dog—or a child—differently. He seized Jared's hand, pulled him away:

"If we leave him alone he'll be all right. Come with me and we'll look for your mother."

The wrath in Abraham's weary eyes made Jared obey without complaint.

ii

"Baby? Baby, where are you—?"

Elizabeth's voice!

Running, he broke from the trees twenty feet from the river bank. When he saw her, a lump thickened in his throat.

He halted. Surveyed the area to be sure it was safe. He saw nothing to threaten the boy. He leaned his rifle against a maple, said:

"You wait here while I speak to your mother, understand? *Wait here.*"

Fidgeting, the boy nodded. Abraham turned around, grief-stricken at the sight of his wife wandering aimlessly through the reeds along the shore. The wind blew her dirty hair around her cheeks. Her plain, patched dress was soaked and mud-spattered from the knee downward.

Abraham deliberately made noise as he approached. She didn't seem to hear. Her fatigue-ringed blue eyes darted back and forth across the shallows:

"Baby? Baby, I know you're here. Don't hide from me."

"Elizabeth!"

The loudness penetrated her daze. She faced him, a peculiar half-smile curling her mouth. She hardly resembled the bright, fiery-spirited girl he'd taken into his bed in Boston. Barely into her twenties, she had become a pale, sagging old woman—

But she recognized him:

"Oh. Abraham dear. You've come back from the settlement."

He splashed toward her, his moccasins soaked in an instant. On the far bank of the Miami, the autumn-colored trees shimmered and flamed in the wind.

He gripped her arm. "Why did you leave Jared by himself? It isn't safe!"

"Please let go." She pried at his fingers with a cracked and reddened hand. "Please, Abraham. I only left him for a short time—"

"I shot a pygmy rattler up there. Right where the boy was playing!"

"Shot?" She shook her head. "I didn't hear any shot." Again that pleading smile. "But I've been busy searching for the baby."

His spine crawled. "What baby?"

"Ours, Abraham. Our baby—the first one. I don't remember the baby's name, but all at once, up in the cabin, I remembered the baby was lost on the river."

"You lost the baby on the Oh—" Sick and stunned, he couldn't continue.

"Please help me look, Abraham. I know the baby's here somewhere. Help me look before it's too dark—"

Tears started in the corners of his eyes. He fought to hold a rein on his emotions—the self-hate; the sadness. *How had this happened?*

He knew Elizabeth had been growing weaker and more distant month by month. But what had pushed her into this delusion? This retreat into a world of phantoms where the miscarried infant somehow cried out to her? Her mother's death? The hardships of the land? Both—?

Empty of anger, he curved his arm around her and tried to speak gently:

"It's growing dark. We should go back to the cabin."

"The baby's lost, Abraham!"

"I'm sure we'll find the baby tomorrow, when the sun's up. I'll help you search then if you'll come with me now."

She eyed the reeds and gleaming river. Then, with a sigh, she leaned against him:

"All right. I am tired. I would like to rest. I've been searching an hour or more."

In utter despair, he comforted her against his shoulder as they worked their way out of the shallows to solid ground. They walked up the shale slope to the tree where little Jared watched, white and wide-eyed.

The man, the woman and the boy plodded toward the cabin. Elizabeth's voice grew fainter in the shadows lengthening among the trees. She murmured sadly, absently, about the lost child that needed finding—

iii

Abraham lighted one of the wall candles and tucked Elizabeth into bed. He got the fire going in the hearth, and then he and Jared left the cabin.

They hunted for Chief. They found him dead where he'd fallen. Abraham dug a shallow trench in the loamy soil. They laid the bulldog's body in it. Crying, Jared helped cover the grave with handfuls of earth.

They finished the work in almost total darkness. Abraham sheltered the weeping boy against his side on the way back to the cabin. He could feel little sorrow about the dog. Chief was old. Elizabeth was young. And she was dying too.

He knew some of the reasons: grueling work for which she wasn't suited; loneliness; the absence of amenities with which she'd grown up. Women grew old too soon on the frontier. Abraham saw such women every time he visited the settlement. Women of twenty-five or thirty with lusterless eyes, leathery hands, browned, foul-smelling teeth. A few like Edna Clapper, were hardy enough to thrive. Those who weren't hardy, the land destroyed.

And I brought her here so she could be killed, Abraham thought as he approached the cabin. That was the moment he first admitted the land had beaten them.

He would not—*could* not—permit them to go on living as they were living now.

The unseen trees hissed in the wind, almost like laughter. He made up his mind that he'd find them a means of escape as soon as possible. He hated being defeated almost as much as he hated the land—

But accepting defeat was better than seeing his wife destroyed.

iv

The next day was the Sabbath. Abraham opened the cabin door as soon as he got up. Elizabeth woke a few minutes later. The sight of the sunshine spilling onto the cabin floor seemed to put her in good spirits immediately.

She had been restless during the night. But she greeted him normally enough, making no reference to the incident on the river.

As they ate their morning meal, Abraham read a few verses from their Bible. Elizabeth listened with a cheerful expression. Yet he remained tense. At any moment he expected her to recall his pledge to search for the lost baby.

Nearly an hour went by with no mention of it. The nervousness persisted. He went for a stroll in the sunshine, kneading his knuckles against his chin as he walked.

God, what he'd give to be able to share the excitement and optimism reflected in the Saturday talk at Clapper's store. A few months before, a whole new century had opened. The successful settlers in the district discussed it with high hopes. President Washington's death the preceding year at age sixty-seven seemed to bring one era to an end and set a new and better one in motion.

A new president would be elected before this year was out. Many around Fort Hamilton predicted that Federalist John Adams was finished; would be replaced at last by a less aristocratic candidate—one who recognized the growing importance of the west and acted accordingly. The ideal man, of course, would be Mr. Jefferson.

Already there were sixteen states in the union. More would certainly be organized and admitted as the tide of migration swept on west beyond the Ohio country. The future looked splendid indeed—

Until you brought it down to a personal level, Abraham thought as he walked back into the cabin.

Elizabeth welcomed him with a smile. She was busy tending a skillet over the coals. Preparing the johnnycake they'd eat for Sunday dinner even though they'd already eaten the same thing for breakfast. Jared sat silently in a corner, building bits of stick into a cabin. Abraham bent down to watch. The boy accepted his father's presence silently, without a smile.

Soon almost two hours had passed, with no reference to yesterday. Abraham relaxed a little. Apparently she'd forgotten—or, more correctly, the memory had somehow been locked away again in the recesses of her mind.

Still, he had been thoroughly shaken last night. He didn't intend to forget his silent vow to change their situation.

How he'd do it, he didn't know. As a first step, he'd ask advice from his friend Daniel Clapper. During next Saturday's visit to the settlement.

Having decided just that much buoyed him a little; it

was a positive step. Out of it would come an eventual answer.

Not too late, he hoped.

V

"It's your business how much you slosh down," Daniel Clapper said the following Saturday night. "But Daniel Junior's off at the camp meetin' with the girl he's courtin', an' I'm damned if I want to carry you home."

Abraham tilted the jug and poured more whiskey into a small earthenware cup.

"I'll make it fine on my own, Daniel."

Clapper looked skeptical.

Abraham had already consumed two cups of whiskey while waiting for the other man to close up the store for the night and join him behind the curtain that separated business from daily living.

In addition to the family's everyday furniture and utensils, and curtained areas for sleeping, the rear half of the large cabin was crowded with goods for which Clapper had no room up front: boxes of slates and slate pencils; small kegs of gunpowder; cartons of foolscap paper—even a fresh shipment of books. Waiting for Clapper, Abraham browsed through them. He discovered three copies of a Kent and Son edition of *Pilgrim's Progress*. The moralistic work was popular among the settlers who could read.

He held the book a few moments, staring at it, then replaced it in its box, wishing he could put memories of Boston aside as easily.

Having built his cabin within sight of the others that formed the settlement around the palisaded walls of Fort Hamilton, Daniel Clapper had allowed himself the luxury of window openings with shutters. Away from a settlement, windows were a disadvantage. They could let in marauders along with sunlight and fresh air.

Now the red-bearded storekeeper pushed open one pair of shutters next to the stone fireplace. Abraham drew a deep breath between gulps of whiskey. The blazing logs in the hearth made the room stifling.

Clapper seemed to sense something important on Abraham's mind. His forehead furrowed as he watched his guest drink. Abraham didn't say anything. Clapper gazed outside again as a squad of mounted soldiers clattered toward the fort.

In the distance the horizon glowed orange. The light came from torches around the camp meeting tent. The week-long event was being conducted by a Bible-brandishing Methodist evangelist who'd ridden up from the state of Kentucky. People had driven rigs or come on horseback from as far away as thirty or forty miles, just to attend tonight's final meeting. Abraham could hear the shouts of praise and joy as the crowd replied to the evangelist's exhortations.

Clapper's wife Rachel and his daughter Danetta, as well as Daniel Junior and his young lady, were attending the four-hour service that combined hymn singing, hellfire preaching, public confession of sin and the evangelist's promise of salvation. *Maybe I should be there,* Abraham thought, pouring one more drink—

Clapper stayed his hand:

"Listen, I been waitin' ten minutes! Speak your piece!"

"I need to ask your advice."

"Ask away."

"The reason is—I'm going to give up the farm."

With a sigh, Clapper ambled to the table. He poured a little whiskey for himself, then combed fingers through his long red beard.

"Figured it might be comin' to that. Of late you been lookin' mighty spiritless."

"It's Elizabeth I'm worried about. She—well—she's been acting strange."

"Expect you want to talk about it. Else you wouldn't bring it up, am I right?"

Slumping in his chair, Abraham nodded. He poured out the story, finishing:

"She was hunting for the baby she lost on the Ohio, not Jared."

"Yep, I caught that drift."

Abraham peered into his cup. "I don't even know whether it was a boy or a girl."

"Don't know myself. If Miz Rachel knows, she's never said—and I ain't asked. I *do* know what she'll discuss and what she won't. Women things is on the won't list."

"I don't suppose a doctor could explain what's wrong with Elizabeth. Something in her mind, maybe. Her father was supposedly half crazy."

"Never heard that before."

"It's true."

"I told you once I thought she was a mite frail—"

"I remember."

"Why'd she ever agree to come out here?"

"Oh, a lot of reasons. I went along with them. Obviously we both made a mistake."

He filled his cup again, ignoring Clapper's frown.

"The point is," he said, "I've got to remedy the mistake before things get worse."

"So you're puttin' the farm up for sale."

"I think I should be able to get rid of it, don't you?"

"Lord yes! On my last trip south, the Ohia was blamed near solid with boats."

Abraham grimaced. "We're already being passed by —I saw that for myself when I went with you to Cincinnati."

"Don't get to thinkin' it's *too* civilized around here," Clapper cautioned. "The Shawnee, they're still burnin' farms and stirrin' up trouble. I musta seen a dozen of 'em when I was out peddlin' the first of the week. They been a lot more active ever since ol' Tecumseh's brother set up his town on the Wabash. Soldiers at the fort say Tecumseh an' the Prophet are preachin' some sort of wild scheme to pull all the tribes together, from New York State clear down into the Creek Nations."

"Why?"

"To push out the white people that took Injun land, why else?"

"The tribes signed a treaty with Wayne—"

"Not that Tecumseh. 'Cording to what you told me, he never set foot in the door at Greenville."

"That's true. We're off the subject. I'm going to sell the farm, but I don't know the next step. I hate like hell to crawl back to Boston and tell my father I failed."

"This father of yours—the one what printed the Bunyan book in the box yonder—he a pretty strong-minded soul, is he?"

"A banker friend of his once said my father could make Satan look indecisive."

"Sounds like an all-right sort. You an' Elizabeth *could* go back an' see him if things really got bad, couldn't you?"

"I'd rather not. I was hoping maybe I could find a way to make a living here in the settlement. Elizabeth might be more comfortable with more people around."

Quietly, Clapper asked, "Did the two o' you ever sit yourselves down and decide what it is you want?"

Abraham shook his head. "Pointless. We don't know. I've come to believe what you told me on the ark, Daniel—that most people who chase after some vague hope are only running away from problems."

"Absolutely right! Mebbe I got one answer for you, though—"

Abraham noticed a peculiar glint in Clapper's eyes. The storekeeper fingered his beard a while before he continued:

"The urge is on me again, Abraham. I want to pick up an' head out. Injuns or no, this part o' the country's gettin' crowded. Ten years ago there wasn't more'n three or four thousand souls settled north o' the river. Now I hear there's ten times that many. People are sayin' there'll soon be enough folks in the territory to make Ohia state number seventeen. I need elbow room, Abraham! Next spring, I'm goin'!"

"Does your family know?"

"Miz Edna's been watchin' me mighty close lately. She can feel it comin'. You're the first to hear, though."

Abraham thought a minute. "Are you suggesting maybe I could take over the store?"

"Yep."

"I don't know as I'd be any better running a place like this than I am at running a farm, Daniel."

"Hell, it's easy! Everythin' practically falls off the shelves—"

"Except that china I traded to you."

"Well, that's fancy stuff. The necessary things sell themselves—an' like you say, Miz Elizabeth might be easier in her mind livin' closer to the fort. Havin' womenfolk to visit with regular—"

Abraham did see how the plan could work. With a little more animation, he said:

"If the pattern of the last couple of years holds next year too, there'll be new families arriving in the spring. I could sell the farm to one of them, buy you out and pay you every penny I owe you—"

"I'll only sell you the building an' half my goods. I'll

need some stocks to set up when I get where I'm headed."

"Got any idea where that is?"

Clapper grinned. "Nope. I'll light there same way as I lighted here. But once I take a notion to go, I want to git —fast. So I won't gouge you on the price, an' it'll be a fair deal all around."

For the first time in weeks, Abraham laughed aloud:

"By God I think I've found the answer, thanks to you."

Now it was Clapper's turn to stare into his whiskey cup. "Hope so."

"You don't think I have?"

The big storekeeper's eyes locked on Abraham's. "I don't want to discourage you, boy. You need *en*couragement—"

"But you think we won't find living here any easier than on the farm?"

"Easier, maybe. Not better. Even this far west, I see a mighty lot o' people movin' on, Abraham. Movin' on for the fifth an' sixth time—"

"I think Elizabeth can be happy here. I've got to believe that, Daniel. The only other choices are to go on west—and she's not strong enough—or to head home to Boston—and I'm not ready to give up *that* completely. The settlement will make everything right—"

"Sure," Clapper nodded. "Forget what I said."

A hymn thundered by scores of voices drifted from the camp meeting. Clapper squeezed his friend's shoulder:

"What's true for me ain't necessarily true for you. Things'll get a lot better if you move in here. Provided you don't pickle your liver in the meantime—gimme that cup!"

"No, let's have one more. To celebrate."

Abraham poured whiskey to the brim, raised the cup. "I give you Mr. Abraham Kent, merchant."

Daniel Clapper raised his own cup but for some reason wouldn't look Abraham squarely in the eye.

vi

Elizabeth greeted Abraham's plan with complete agreement and overwhelming enthusiasm. As winter approached, she began taking better care of herself. She watched Jared more attentively; Abraham was busy making frequent trips to the settlement mill. There he had his corn ground, retaining what the family would need during the cold months and selling off the rest.

There were no repetitions of the search for the lost child.

During January and February, Elizabeth kept busy cooking, mending, doing laundry—and teaching Jared how to recognize and pronounce part of the alphabet. Watching his mother print large block letters on a slate, the little boy seemed happier than ever before. He enjoyed trying to say the names of the letters correctly. Elizabeth, surprisingly patient, encouraged him. Before long he had progressed to the letter M.

At least once an evening, Elizabeth's conversation returned to the forthcoming change in their lives. Abraham was glad. She was affectionate again. Amenable to lovemaking. Several times she clasped him with an ardor that reminded him of the first night she came secretly to his room.

According to the way Abraham figured it, new families should be starting up the Great Miami about the first or April, either to squat or to settle on ground whose deed they held. At the end of February he began thinking about the wording of a notice for the settlement's public message board. He felt confident that if he could find some squatters with money, he could convince them that buying his prime bottom land was a better investment than occupying free land someone else might eventually claim. Most good river acreage in the district was already taken, and that was in his favor.

The first of April, 1801, began to loom as a magic date: the end of their hardships; the start of a new, more rewarding life. Abraham consciously avoided thinking about Clapper's dour philosophy. For Elizabeth's sake, he couldn't permit himself to believe that disillusionment always waited, no matter how far a man roamed, or where he settled.

Occasional traders working their way through the ice-bound forests brought trickles of news:

Congress had at last convened in the district christened Columbia. There, the new capital city was rising, named in honor of the country's first president.

The unwieldy electoral college system had turned January's national election into a shambles. Jefferson and Aaron Burr deadlocked in a first-place tie with seventy-three votes each. John Adams, his popularity waning ran third with sixty-five.

The tie vote threw the contest to the pro-Federalist House of Representatives. After thirty-six ballots and much behind-the-scenes maneuvering, Jefferson was named president in February, with Burr vice president. Whereupon, the traders said, certain devout Federalist ladies in New England buried their Bibles in their gardens, fearing secret agents of the "godless" chief executive would seize and burn them.

The results of the election reached the Great Miami in mid-March, just as the weather turned unusually warm and sunny. Elizabeth took to singing as she worked around the cabin. Abraham too was anticipating the day that symbolized a fresh start for the Kents.

Six days before the month ended, the Indians came.

CHAPTER III

The Burning

SHE TOUCHED HIS arm in the chilly darkness. Her fingers closed, rousing him from the fog of sleep. He felt her homespun nightdress touching his forearm; heard the murmur of the March winds. He heard other sounds he didn't recognize.

"*Abraham—*"

Her anxiety brought him upright, knuckling his eyes. "What—?"

She covered his mouth with her other hand. "Be still and listen! There's someone outside."

His mind sorted out sounds: Jared breathing on the small bedstead he had built in the opposite corner; the low of the ox; the thump of a hoof on the side of a stall —perhaps that was Henrietta Knox.

Then, alert and alarmed, he made out a human voice, barely audible.

There was a louder thump, as of someone stumbling against a wall. Two voices overlapped one another; the second was angry.

The ox bellowed. Abraham wiped his upper lip.

"They're out by the barn," he said.

"Can you hear what they're saying?"

"Not clearly. But I don't think they're white men."

Elizabeth covered her face. "Oh God help us—"

"*Sssh!*"

As quietly as possible, he crawled out of bed. He

struggled into his trousers. With the tail of his nightshirt still hanging out, he pulled on his boots. He guessed the time to be dawn. A thin line of light defined the edges of the cabin door.

His heart lubbed loudly in his inner ear. He crept toward his rifle propped against the wall, listening for the intruders. Either the men were being exceptionally quiet now or they were gone—

Another bellow from the ox told him his hope was false. His throat felt parched. He returned to Elizabeth. Knelt and whispered:

"Whatever you do, don't wake the boy. And stay inside with the door barred."

He could just discern the white oval of her face as she leaned close: "You're not going out there—?"

"Yes, I'd better. Maybe I can frighten them off."

"But I heard at least two voices!"

"Perhaps all they want is food."

"You mustn't go—you've only one charge in your rifle—"

"And this."

He groped a hand toward the puncheon table, found his long-bladed Barlow knife of English steel. He tucked the knife in his right boot.

"I'll be all right. They'll probably run as soon as I show myself—a lot of them don't own rifles or muskets."

"But some do. I've heard people at the settlement say—"

"*Don't raise your voice!* I've got to see what they're up to—suppose they take a notion to fire the cabin? I tell you I'll be all right," he finished, sounding more certain than he felt.

He patted her hand, stole toward the door. He raised the latchstring slowly to free the bar from its bracket. He inched the plank door open.

"Lock yourself in, Elizabeth."

He slipped outside.

He leaned against the cabin wall, drawing long, deep gulps of air. The leafless trees looked black and stark against the silver of the eastern horizon. A warbler trilled down by the river. The water purled over stones.

He heard the soft *chunk* of the bar being lowered back in place. Now he could move. Cautiously, he advanced to the corner of the cabin, then on around. The chimney jutting from the end of the cabin concealed the barn. He leaned toward the edge of the chimney, risked a glance—

He saw a black rectangle. Someone had opened the barn door. A moment later, a man laughed softly inside.

Questions tumbled through his mind. Were there really only two? How were they armed? He wished for his pistols, hanging on pegs inside. But they were useless, he remembered. He hadn't loaded or primed them since the last time he fired them—

So it came down to the ball in his rifle, and his long knife. Against whatever the intruders might be carrying.

He decided to wait them out. Running to the barn, a clear target, would be foolish. He leaned his forehead against the chimney logs, listening.

He heard shuffling feet. An occasional word growled in an unfamiliar language. The two animals kept stamping. Time seemed to stretch out as the warbler sang down by the shore.

The light brightened. The outline of the barn became clearer. Suddenly Abraham sucked in a sibilant breath. A man had appeared in the barn door—

An Indian, right enough. Fat and toothless and old. His huge belly stretched his filthy army coat. The coat had been stolen from some other white man, Abraham assumed.

The old Indian trailed an ancient musket from one

hand. A bedraggled wild turkey feather stuck up from the greased gray of his braided hair. He waved disgustedly for the benefit of someone still invisible in the barn.

Heart knocking faster than ever, Abraham kept one eye pressed to the chimney corner, hoping the poor light would prevent the Indian from spotting him. A second man lurched outside.

This one was younger, with a hard brown face and eyes like black stones. He wore hide trousers and shirt. His only visible weapon was a spiked war club.

From the way the younger Indian weaved on his feet, Abraham guessed the pair had stolen whiskey somewhere, and now wanted more. He presumed both were Shawnee or Miami, but he couldn't be positive. If he were lucky, they might abandon their search and slip away to try their thievery in another place—

The younger one barked words Abraham didn't understand. He lifted his spiked club, pointed it toward the cabin. The meaning was unmistakable.

The fat one seemed hesitant. He finally shook his head, growled a reply that angered his companion. The younger one started walking—straight toward the jutting chimney where Abraham crouched.

He had to scare them off. But he didn't dare expend his one rifle ball to do it. He screwed up his nerve, took another deep breath—

Stepped from concealment, the rifle aimed at the breastbone of the younger Indian.

The fat one yelped in surprise. Abraham's nerve almost crumbled away when a cold smile curved the mouth of the younger one. The Indian was still a little drunk—

Abraham had seldom seen such hateful eyes.

"*Meneluh*," the Indian said.

Abraham shook his head to show he didn't understand. The young brave's smile vanished.

"Meneluh, meneluh!" A sharp gesture with his spiked club. "Drink!"

Abraham drew in a quick breath. Though the young Indian articulated English with difficulty, at least he understood it; perhaps from encounters with itinerant traders. Certain less than scrupulous white men had discovered a new and profitable market by introducing alcohol among the tribes. Heedless of long-term consequences, such traders were frequent visitors at the Indian villages, supplying rum and whiskey in return for pelts. If the savage had learned bits of English in such meetings, at least Abraham had a chance of communicating. Trying to do that was better than launching into a fight.

Aware of how his legs trembled, he shook his head several times, then said slowly and clearly:

"No whiskey."

The young brave grinned. "Whis-key. *Meneluh!*"

Abraham shook his head again. "No. No. I do not have any whiskey." He bobbed the rifle's muzzle at the trees. "Go. Go into the woods. Get off my land." He pointed at the ground. "This is mine." He jabbed his thumb against his chest. "Mine. The Shawnee can only hunt where there are no settlers—"

The scowling Indian clearly didn't comprehend the last word.

"No white men. White—" Abraham touched his face. The Shawnee continued to scowl. Abraham wasn't certain whether the next thought would have any meaning: "The treaty says—"

"Trea-ty!" The young Shawnee spat on the ground. Then he pronounced a name Abraham couldn't decipher.

"What?"

"Panther-Passing-Across. Panther-Passing-Across curses white man's trea-ty. Curses *you!*"

"Who—who is the Panther?" Abraham asked, still stunned by the violent reaction.

"Chief. Tecumseh. Other—" A garbled, obviously derogatory word. "—smoked *calumet* with Wayne." Derisively, he pretended to puff an invisible pipe. "Not Shawanese. Not Tecumseh. This land not his—not yours—not any man's to—" A hand darted outward. "Trade. Moneto gave to *all!*"

Another angry arc of the club made Abraham start. The fat old Indian giggled, revealing stumps of teeth in wrinkled gums.

"Moneto made land for all!" the young man repeated. "Cannot be—" Again the outward gesture. "Given." He pointed his club at the breaking light in the east. "Can *kesathwa* be given?" Supple fingers pantomimed falling rain. "Can *gimewane* be given?" He shook his head. "So land cannot be given. Not by one—not by many!"

The Shawnee began walking forward, sensing Abraham's gut fear now, and playing on it. He shook his head again, angrily. Then:

"Woods people who took Wayne *calumet*—sat with Wayne—" More unintelligible phrases, savagely spoken and plainly showing what the young brave thought of those Indians who had negotiated with the general. "—did not own this." He stamped the earth. "Moneto's land. For all. If we want—stay. If we want—go." A sly smile. "Look there—" The club jabbed toward the cabin. "Whis-key."

Abraham raised the rifle to his shoulder:

"No. I'll kill you. Do you understand? I'll *kill* you."

The Shawnee understood. Abraham jerked the rifle barrel toward the fields.

"Get away! Get off this—"

He was unprepared for the sudden whipping motion

of the brave's arm. The war club tumbled end over end toward his head. He lunged out of the way, stumbled, fell on his left side as the club struck the chimney logs and bounced away.

The young Shawnee reached the club in three long strides. He raised it over his head with both hands, brought it forward and down, the spike aimed at Abraham's torso. On the ground, Abraham braced the rifle against his hip and fired.

Inside the cabin, Elizabeth screamed. The ball only slowed the downward arc of the war club. Abraham rolled to the left. The bone spike raked his shoulder—

The club dropped from the Indian's hand. He seized the chimney logs for support, slowly sank to his knees. The shot had blown away his left eye and part of his cheek.

Vomit rose in Abraham's throat. The young Shawnee's trousers darkened as he urinated uncontrollably. On his knees, he moaned and slumped forward against the chimney. As he sagged all the way to the ground, his face left gore and bits of bone on the logs—

Abraham struggled to his feet, pulling his knife in case the fat Indian attacked. Marginally aware of a second voice raised in the cabin—Jared's—he heard a sound that turned his bowels to water:

The rattle of the door latch.

"Abraham?"

Dammit, he'd warned her to stay inside! Always, always, she defied advice, did as she wished—

"Abraham?" she called again. She came running around the corner of the cabin, hair streaming at her shoulders.

"Elizabeth, stay ba—"

The fat Indian's musket roared.

Abraham was facing his wife. He saw her literally fly backwards as the ball hit.

For a moment he stood numb, his gaze swinging back and forth between Elizabeth and the Indian. His wife lay on her back, a black hole oozing blood onto her right temple. The toothless old man lowered the musket as a curl of smoke drifted from the muzzle.

Howling, Abraham ran at the Indian, knife raised. The Indian wheeled and lumbered off around the barn, his grunts of fright trailing behind him.

Abraham pursued him only a dozen steps. Then he halted. Shock set his teeth to chattering. The Barlow knife fell from his fingers. He faced about; faced the sight of Elizabeth sprawled in her nightdress, her mouth open and her eyes too—

He knelt beside her, both palms on her cheeks. He heard Jared's voice from the cabin doorway:

"What's wrong, papa? Why is mama lying there?"

"Go back inside! *Close the door!*"

Frightened by the wild look of his father's face, Jared vanished. Abraham rocked back and forth on his knees, rubbing his wife's face:

"Elizabeth. Elizabeth—"

It became sobbing:

"*Elizabeth, no. No, Elizabeth—*"

The brightening dawn only heightened her waxy pallor; accented the color of the blood that flowed down past her eye to her ear, clotting in her fair hair. She had washed her hair to shiny brilliance just last night—

Still kneeling, Abraham cradled her corpse in his arms, speaking her name over and over. The cabin door stood slightly ajar. He never noticed.

Nor did he see the huge eyes of a small boy staring at the blood on his mother's face.

ii

In the pleasant March sunlight, Abraham walked the four miles downriver with Jared. His step was slow, his expression stony. The boy kept glancing up at his father, but never spoke.

When Abraham had finally carried Elizabeth's body into the cabin, Jared had repeated his questions. Abraham answered in a dull voice, saying Elizabeth had gone away from them and would not be coming back.

Jared's face showed his confusion: When Elizabeth's still form lay before him, how was it possible for her to have left the cabin—?

Then and now, as Abraham and Jared walked, a forbidding expression on the father's face kept the son from voicing any of the fear and turmoil the morning's events had produced.

People stared at Abraham's white face and feverish eyes as he led the boy to Clapper's.

Waiting on a customer, Daniel Clapper immediately recognized that something dire had taken place. He bid the customer a quick good morning and followed Abraham into the rear of the cabin.

In a monotone, Abraham reported what had happened—producing a burst of tears from Clapper's wife. She recovered quickly. She hugged Jared to her shapeless bosom, drew the boy aside to comfort him.

Abraham said to Clapper, "I'm going back to take care of her body and to collect my things."

"Let me go with you, Abraham. You're in no state to—"

"Yes I am," Abraham said, his face animating into fury. He pushed Clapper's hand aside. "I'm going alone."

Seated on a chair with Jared on her lap, Mrs. Clapper said to her husband:

"Don't let him, Daniel."

"I'm all right!" Abraham insisted. "I'll pack what Jared and I need for traveling and be right back."

Clapper goggled. "My God, boy—your wife just got shot an' you're goin' traveling?"

Abraham's eyes burned. "What good can I do her by staying here?"

A long silence. Then Clapper asked:

"Where you goin'?"

"East. Home. Away from this accursed place. I killed her bringing her out here."

"A couple of drunken Shawnee killed—"

"I did."

"Listen, Abraham, that little boy's scairt to death—look at him!"

But Abraham wouldn't. Jared burrowed his face in Edna Clapper's shoulder, began to cry.

Clapper stepped close to Abraham, whispered, "I know it's a grievous thing, Abraham, a grievous an' terrible thing. But you're carryin' on like a crazy man. You got to take hold of—"

Clapper stopped. Abraham's face was like a death's-head.

"I'm going *alone*, Daniel. I'll be back presently for Jared. Don't chase after me or you'll get hurt."

Pivoting, he ripped the curtain aside and disappeared into the front of the store.

No one followed.

iii

There was a demon in Abraham Kent that morning; a demon whose hate lent him the strength he needed to do what had to be done.

First he dragged the young Shawnee down to the river. Keeping his eyes away from the destroyed face, he lifted the corpse and flung it in the shallows. He broke off a tree limb, waded out and prodded the body into the current. When it was floating, moving slowly in the sun-dazzled water, Abraham threw the branch away and returned to the barn where he loaded his rifle.

The barn smelled of fresh manure. Abraham sighted down the muzzle to a spot between the horns of Henrietta Knox. The cow kept chewing slowly. Abraham began to tremble. At last he gave up, unable to pull the trigger.

He led Henrietta Knox outside The ground was damp. The night's frost had melted, moistening the black earth. He rubbed the cow's back a moment, then let go of her rope and walked away. In similar fashion he brought the ox to the field and left it standing.

Inside the cabin, he spent an hour with Elizabeth.

He sat on the puncheon floor beside the bedstead, his eyes closed, his hand straying to her face occasionally. Soon her skin became so cold that touching it was unbearable. He rose, carried the newly packed knapsack out into the sunlight.

He deposited the knapsack on top of a stump that still bore the black traces of last fall's burning. He brought his rifle, shot bag and powder horn to the same stump. Back in the cabin, he used flint and steel to light tinder beneath the hearth logs.

When the fire was burning well, he broke off one of the pole legs of the table. He thrust the leg into the flames for a minute. Then he set the table afire.

As soon as it caught, he bent and kissed Elizabeth's cheek.

Coughing in the smoke, he walked outside and torched the barn. Then he picked up his gear.

He sniffed the fire as he walked toward the track

leading to the settlement. He heard the cabin walls beginning to crackle, but he wouldn't look back at the puffs of black smoke. The smell was enough to remind of how he'd erred; failed; lacked the strength and wisdom to deny Elizabeth's wish to start a new life in the west. The smell was enough to remind him of how much he hated this barbarous land that permitted only the hardiest to survive, destroying the others.

Henrietta Knox mooed at him as he hurried by the field where she stood in the glare of noonday. He wouldn't look at her either, nor could he have seen her clearly if he had. Tears blurred his eyes.

He hated the earth under his feet. God, how he hated it—!

And himself.

Blind to everything except his consuming need to escape, he stumbled on toward Fort Hamilton as the treetops around the cabin began to burn. Clouds of smoke billowed into the noon sky, shot through with fire.

iv

The unkempt strangers trudging up Beacon Street on a hot morning in early July, 1801, attracted the attention of everyone from housemaids bustling on errands to gentlemen climbing into carriages to be off for the day's business. There were whispers and stares—the pair hardly resembled Bostonians from this part of town—or any other!

One was a heavily bearded man of twenty-five or so. The other was a tow-haired boy whose face looked pinched and gray. The man carried a grubby knapsack on back straps, and a rifle in the crook of his left arm. He held the boy's hand tightly. It was hard to tell which of them wore the filthier coat and fringed trousers.

The pair caused no end of curiosity as they climbed the stoop of one of the most substantial homes on the entire street. The man let the knocker fall three times.

A mobcapped girl opened the door. Abraham didn't recognize her.

The maid took a step backward, overpowered by Abraham's stench. He smelled rank for good reason. He'd obtained a small sum of money from a hasty sale of the farm to a Fort Hamilton speculator. The money had run out two weeks ago, as they approached Philadelphia. Abraham and his son had made the rest of the journey on foot, sleeping in the open, begging or stealing food where they could, and never bathing.

The maid's reaction was automatic:

"Beggars are not allowed at the front—"

"This is my home. I am Abraham Kent."

The maid caught her breath. She recognized the name. But her face showed her doubt and bewilderment. How could this greasy, bearded person in frontier garb be Abraham Kent?

The man's brown eyes piercing into hers were so terrifying, she didn't dare speak the question aloud.

"I wish to see my father. I wish to come in—*will you stop goggling?* I *live* here!"

He thrust her aside roughly, dragging the little boy after him like a mindless dwarf. In the middle of the front hall, he put down his knapsack and rifle, wiped his nose with the back of his hand, and demanded:

"Where is my father? And my brother? Have they gone to the firm already?"

The maid stammered, "Yes, Mr. Gilbert left an hour ago—"

"Is my father about the house, then?"

"Sir—sir—"

"What the hell's wrong with you, girl?"

She'd remembered some talk she'd heard about the whereabouts of Philip Kent's son. That would explain the crude, hideous clothing. She swallowed hard.

"If—if you are Mr. Abraham Kent from the west—"

His mouth twisted. "Don't I smell like it?"

"I know Mr. Gilbert wrote you two months ago—"

"Wrote what? My boy and I have been traveling for over three months. Any letter that was sent to me two months ago, I never received."

So weary he could barely stand, and maddened beyond endurance by the maid's fluttery behavior, Abraham raised his fist to her:

"Damn you, speak out! Where is my father?"

"Dead, sir," the girl whispered. "He died in his sleep on the thirtieth of April."

CHAPTER IV

Problems of a Modernist

IN THE MATERIAL as well as the intellectual sphere, Mr. Gilbert Kent was an avowed modernist. He deemed that orientation eminently suitable to the new century, and to the rapid changes taking place in the nation. He refused to close his mind to ideas simply because they had never been tried before, or were foreign to his experience.

His Beacon Street home, for example, boasted not one but three of the innovative banjo wall clocks introduced the previous year by Mr. Willard of Roxbury. He had adopted two new and novel fashions—regular bathing and the donning of clean underwear every day. He hadn't gone so far as to embrace the Napoleonic custom of a daily bath; once every two or three days seemed sufficient in a city that considered bathing the entire body bizarre.

His apparel would have found favor in fashionable circles in Britain. At eleven o'clock on a warm morning in midsummer, 1803, he approached Kent and Son wearing clothes that could only be termed impeccable:

His coat was one of the new, longer gentleman's models, lacking the severe cutaway so popular with conservative members of the business community. His shirt was linen, custom-cut, and featured the new detachable collar. His waistcoat was cut low to show off his stock and shirt ruffles. The basic ensemble was completed by snug boots over long pantaloons—the very combination said to be preferred by the elegant George Brummel, whose sartorial preferences were religiously aped by all in England's upper classes—including Brummel's intimate friend, the prince-regent.

To top off the outfit, Gilbert wore a dark, soft hat of beaver, the brim drooping slightly at front and back but rolled on the sides. The jaunty hat bobbed up and down briskly as he made his way through the crowds this humid morning. Most of the better dressed people on the street recognized the owner of Kent and Son. Those who didn't know him personally identified him from his costume precisely the way he wanted to be identified—as a modernist.

Perhaps in reaction to his late father's Federalist bias, Gilbert Kent was that rare creature—a New Englander who was also a Jeffersonian. After much thought and study, he had concluded the president was correct in his contention that all men, while perhaps not equal in their abilities, were certainly equal in their rights. He was convinced the country should be governed not by a coterie of highly educated aristocrats—to which group he would certainly have belonged by reasons of birth, wealth and talent—but by the consent of all, high-born or otherwise. He knew by heart—and despised—Alexander Hamilton's cynical expression of the opposing Federalist philosophy:

All communities divide themselves into the few and the many. The first are rich and well-born, the other the mass of the people. The people are turbulent and changing; they seldom determine rightly. Give, therefore, to the first class a distinct, permanent share in the government. They will check the unsteadiness of the second.

It was a persuasive argument, Gilbert recognized. But in his eyes it was nothing less than evil, for if it were espoused wholeheartedly, then the principles of American liberty became a sham and a deceit.

Gilbert's view wasn't a popular one in Boston. In the growing number of states in the west, and in their swelling populations, the great merchant families saw a threat to New England's traditional control of the nation's affairs. Gilbert Kent believed that to serve, not to control, was the proper function of the government in Washington—and the duty of the private citizen of more than average means. A subtle difference but, to his way of thinking, a crucial one.

Not that Gilbert Kent had anything against being successful in the private sector. He watched the Kent ledgers closely, usually examining them at midnight or later, at home—he seldom slept more than four hours a night, to his wife's annoyance—and he seized every prudent opportunity to expand the family wealth. Indeed, he had just come from a meeting with that purpose.

The meeting had been held at the Rothman Bank. It was attended by a consortium of rich gentlemen of Boston. His father's old Revolutionary War comrade, Mr. Royal Rothman, presided. Before the meeting broke up, Gilbert pledged one hundred thousand dollars of risk capital to help finance the Blackstone Company, a new cotton-spinning firm going into competition with Slater's decade-old spinning works on the Blackstone River in Pawtucket, Rhode Island.

In a private session with Rothman after the other investors left, Gilbert informed the banker that he wanted his partnership to be a silent one. His shares were to be held by the bank so that future profits would go directly to the child his wife was now carrying, as well as to any other issue of their marriage.

Rothman naturally asked the reason for the arrangement. Gilbert gave a candid reply. He wanted his wife to have her just share of his estate when he died—

"And don't say it's too soon to think of that, Royal. I've already lived more than half the lifetime of many men."

"Go on."

"My wife has a number of good qualities, but self-denial isn't one of them. She buys whatever she wishes for herself or the house—heedless of the cost. I don't mean to sound unkind, but I don't believe she could manage and conserve a large sum successfully. I'd feel more comfortable if a part of the Kent estate was held in reserve, where she could never touch it. Indeed, I don't even want her to know about it. The profits of the printing house should be ample to sustain her should something happen to me."

"I wish I were as optimistic about the success of the Blackstone Company as you seem to be," Rothman observed with a wry expression.

"Oh, I'm very optimistic. Textiles will soon become the heart of New England's economy—along with shipping."

"The bank will naturally honor your request about the confidentiality of the shares."

"I'll visit my attorney next week and have him draw up the legal papers."

"Old Benbow senior is going blind. He should retire and turn your affairs over to his son."

"His mind's as alert as ever. He'll live to be ninety."

"Which you may not—at the pace you drive yourself."

Gilbert ignored him, using a quill to scribble *Benbow & Benbow* on a slip of paper. He tucked the slip in his waistcoat pocket and stood up, extending his hand:

"To the Blackstone Company. May it enrich my children and yours."

"It almost died a-borning," Rothman said with a thin smile. "I admire your progressive spirit, Gilbert. But I fear some of the other gentlemen found it incomprehensible—not to say dangerous."

Gilbert shrugged. "They gave in."

"Because you refused to commit Kent money otherwise."

"No, not until they agreed unconditionally to provide schooling for the children who'll be hired to operate the spinning machinery. I'd actually prefer to hire adults—"

"At least you're realistic enough to understand that's unprofitable. Children can be had for a fraction of adult wages."

"Still, it bothers my conscience."

"The other gentlemen salved it for you. Gave in to your demands for a free school—"

"Gave in grudgingly! I tell you, Royal, one day we'll have to face the question of profits at the expense of people. Children shouldn't be working twelve, fourteen, sixteen hours a day—"

"And one man should not own another?" Rothman added, having heard it all before.

"Yes, there'll be a confrontation on the slave question too, you mark me."

"I wish you wouldn't suggest we're somehow involved in slavery!"

"The next thing to it."

"Would you do away with factories, then?"

"How could I? They're being built everywhere."

"My dear boy, you're unreasonable! If a child takes a job at the Blackstone Company, that's entirely voluntary!"

"When a family is poor but much too large, and the young must be put to work at seven or eight or face starvation—you call that voluntary?"

"It's an imperfect world, Gilbert. We can either refuse to deal with it altogether, or content ourselves with altering it a little at a time. The trouble with you is, you've a strong streak of idealism *and* a sharp business sense. As the factory system grows, those two sides of your nature are becoming incompatible. Today you were lucky. You satisfied both."

Gilbert sighed. "I suppose it's the best that can be done. You will remember about the shares?"

"Certainly."

"I'll have Benbow senior call on you to settle the details—provided there's no reneging on the school!"

"Don't worry, I'll see that doesn't happen," Rothman assured him.

"I insist it doesn't."

"I know," the banker sighed. "In some ways, you are a very radical fellow."

It was true. But he was honest with himself about it. Much of what he thought and said and did sprang from a solid core of conviction. At the same time, his modernism was a mechanism, deliberately employed to show his much older peers in the business world that he was their match; perhaps even a step ahead—

Gilbert had been thrust into unexpected control of Kent and Son when his father died two years earlier. For a young man of eighteen to be in charge of his own affairs was not at all unusual. For a young man of eighteen to be solely responsible for a large and growing fortune as well as a prestigious publishing company was highly unusual. Therefore Gilbert had to demonstrate to the world—and to himself—that he was in every way capable of accepting the responsibility.

In a way it was fortunate that he had been a frail child. Of necessity, most of his time had been devoted to sedentary pursuits, chiefly reading. A year at Harvard before Philip's death only demonstrated to Gilbert that he'd already learned much more than his professors could teach him.

Close association with his father during adolescence had familiarized him with every phase of printing house operation long before Philip's sudden and sad demise. Philip had died resenting Abraham's decision to carve a new life for himself in the west. But Gilbert was there, ready and eager to take up the reins—

So, at age twenty, the modernist made his way along Boston's crowded thoroughfares until he came in sight of the familiar gold-lettered signboard with the tea-bottle design. He felt in excellent spirits until he reached the main entrance.

There, in the shadow of the swaying sign, he saw several large, dark splotches on the cobbles. His pale face lost its aura of good humor.

Tall and extremely slender—at nearly six feet he was a phenomenon in the Kent family—he ducked his head to keep his beaver hat from being knocked off by the sign and rushed through the front door to learn the cause of bloodstains at Kent and Son's doorstep.

ii

The presses for the book-publishing part of the business still occupied the main floor. But now, instead of the four wooden flatbeds Gilbert remembered from childhood, six presses with cast iron frames crowded the long room. Gilbert had imported them from London.

Perfected in 1798 by the Earl of Stanhope, the new presses were operated by the familiar screw lever. But the iron framework all but eliminated breakdowns due to main members warping and splitting. Additionally, the iron could bear a greater load, critical to the inking and printing of the woodcuts Kent and Son was starting to incorporate in some of its school primers.

Twenty men and several apprentices worked busily in the press room. Among them Gilbert noted a singular absence. His parchment-pale cheeks took on an even whiter cast. On the second floor of the main aisle he detected still more bloodstains—and, behind one press, a pile of ruined sheets.

A jowly young man in a leather apron approached, moving slowly and refusing to look Gilbert in the eye.

"Good morning, Mr. Pleasant," Gilbert said to his press room manager, the son of the deceased editor of Philip Kent's *Bay State Federalist*. "I'm afraid I see evidence of a fight."

"Aye, and a royal one," Franklin Pleasant answered.

"What was the cause?"

"I don't know, sir. I was up checking the paper stores when it broke out. The other lads pulled the two apart after a couple of minutes. Regrettably, that was long enough for Tom Naughton to suffer a broken hand and an addled head."

Pursing his lips—usually the strongest indication of displeasure he allowed himself—Gilbert asked, "And the other combatant, Mr. Pleasant?"

"Well, sir—" Pleasant's eyes still avoided those of his employer. "He walked out."

"To go where?"

"I wasn't informed, sir. The truth is, your brother was in such an ugly mood, I didn't wish to ask. The lads said he tore into Naughton in what they call the frontier style—"

Gilbert sighed. "Just as on the other occasions? Kicking? Butting? Gouging eyes?"

Pleasant gave a somber nod.

Gilbert forced himself to the hardest question:

"Was my brother drunk again?"

"The lads say he stank of it. I don't doubt he traipsed off for more after he did his damage to Naughton. I—I have no right to speak about a relative of yours, Mr. Kent—"

"You certainly do. He works for you."

Less apprehensive, Pleasant went on, "Since you gave Mr. Abraham a job last year, he's done nothing but disrupt this press room."

"And it took him twelve months to shake off his despondency and reach the point where he'd even consider a menial job."

"I realize he suffered hard blows, losing his wife the way he did, then coming home to the shock of finding Mr. Philip dead and buried. But the fact remains, he can't get along here."

"Nor anywhere, it seems, except in the taverns."

"Yes, a couple of the lads have told me he consorts with the worst drunkards and trulls on the waterfront. Of course," Pleasant added hastily, "that may be no more than vicious gossip. Repayment for some of the difficulty he's caused—"

"It's not gossip, it's fact. Abraham's frequently gone from the house two or three nights in a row. I don't doubt he's visited a score of those poor women you dignify with the name trull. However—" Gilbert waved. "—it's not the facts that are wanting, Mr. Pleasant, it's the solution to the problem, eh?"

"Yes, sir."

"See you send Naughton an extra week's pay for his injuries. And my apologies."

"Oh, sir, the president of the firm needn't apologize to—"

"Enough, Mr. Pleasant. I want it done."

Pleasant looked pleased. "Very well, it shall be."

"Tell Naughton I rose later than usual this morning —well after seven. Abraham had already left the house. Sometimes, when I catch him at the table early, I can sober him up with coffee and a threat or two."

"Most days, he still manages a rum before reporting for work."

Gilbert's eyes strayed to the stains on the floor. "That would seem to be the case. It must have been an unusually strong draught today—" He cleared his throat. "Mr. Pleasant, be assured—and pass the word—that brotherly charity is not unlimited. Six brawls in as many months are five more than I should have permitted."

He indicated the working men, a few of whom were watching him in less than friendly fashion.

"Let it be known that I'll take immediate steps to bring Abraham into line. I'd hoped a job, however lowly, might help put his sad experiences out of mind. Obviously my hope was groundless. I will take steps," he repeated firmly, moving toward the stairs to the second floor.

A couple of the workmen waved and called a greeting. On normal mornings, most all of them did. Gilbert's reply was perfunctory.

He climbed to the third floor, to the cluttered office originally occupied by his father. There, along with his usual portion of day's work, he confronted the question of what to do about his half-brother.

He sympathized with Abraham, but he could no longer tolerate Abraham's sullen, destructive behavior. Nor, for that matter, could Abraham's son Jared.

He pondered the problem a while without success. Finally he put it out of mind and turned to other things. Often when a business difficulty needed a solution, he found that the answer came spontaneously if he mulled the subject, then forgot it for a few hours.

He prayed the process would repeat itself today.

iii

Gilbert Kent's first task was to check on the forthcoming issue of the firm's expanding newspaper, the *Bay State Republican*. Immediately on taking charge of Kent and Son, he had raised the paper's price to the prevailing six cents, added the job of general editor to his duties, and ordered a new masthead designed, sans the word *Federalist*.

The alteration in name and philosophic approach made him unwelcome in certain homes in Boston. But that was offset by generally widespread, if grudging, admiration for the courageous declaration of his own principles via the new name and the increasingly favorable coverage of the Jefferson administration.

Gilbert believed it was not only right but practical to provide an alternative to the viewpoint of most other New England papers. His judgment was rewarded by a slow but steady increase in circulation. Now the *Republican* appeared twice weekly.

With his coat off, his waistcoat unbuttoned and a quill in hand, he marked some minor changes on the foolscap copy describing the background of Commodore Edward Preble, newly named commander of the naval squadron Jefferson had reluctantly dispatched to the Mediterranean in an effort to get the Barbary states to end their outrageous piracy coupled with their demands for tribute. The tribute was supposed to guarantee the safety of American shipping. In fact, it didn't.

Gilbert inked a few rousing sentences at the end of the story, predicting that Preble would soon have the bandit-like Bashaw of Tripoli wishing he had not increased the sum he hoped to extract. Should some of Preble's crack marines storm Tripoli's shores, the Bashaw would regret his greed *and* his declaration of war on the United States.

He returned the copy to one of the two men who wrote for the *Republican*:

"Very good, Mr. Morecam."

"Thank you, sir."

Gilbert watched Morecam work for a few minutes, then moved over to stand behind the other reporter. Neither appreciated his hovering presence, but neither protested. Shortly he went back to his office to see to the day's correspondence.

Much of it was inconsequential. But the pile contained two important items, the first being a lengthy letter from one of Kent and Son's best-selling authors, Mason Locke Weems.

Parson Weems as he was usually called—he was an ordained Anglican, and now a bishop—was a rare bird indeed: a theologian who doubled as a bookman—both writer and seller. Additionally, Weems had an uncanny sense of what the reading public would buy.

His *Life of Washington*, written to the popular taste in 1800, was already into several editions. Gilbert had negotiated to print a deluxe volume that was selling handsomely to the well-to-do who maintained private libraries.

Weems' letter reported on his progress in revising his text for yet another edition. The parson tiptoed around the question of "*embellishing*" the biography with some "*possibly apocryphal*" material.

Gilbert smiled. The good parson had raised the subject in his last letter too. Gilbert sensed Weems intended to invent anecdotes about the first president in order to add novelty to future printings.

His suspicion was confirmed as he read on. Weems said that "*reliable sources in Virginia*" had provided a story about young Washington hacking down a cherry tree, then manfully admitting his guilt when confronted by his father.

Gilbert sharpened another quill in preparation for a reply. He didn't allow himself the luxury of a male secretary. Even though his handwriting was small and difficult to read, he preferred to write his own letters to keep costs down.

In his reply, Gilbert tactfully suggested that George Washington's life was dramatic enough without "*apocryphal embellishments*," and that Weems might do well to refrain from including such material, since it would only befuddle future generations hunting the truth. Since Weems was important to Kent and Son, Gilbert closed with an assurance that of course he would rely on the parson's "*honesty and good judgment*"—and accept the revised text exactly as submitted. He was cynically certain said text would include the invented material.

The second letter of importance was addressed in a hand Gilbert recognized at once; its owner had written him twice before.

With anticipation, he broke the letter open. It was dated the first of July.

Dear Mr. Kent—

The President has requested me to tender his thanks to you for your eminently fair and reasoned support of the purchase of the Louisiana Lands completed May second last by Minister Monroe in Paris. Your recognition of the importance of this Acquisition, and your praise of the treaty of cession in your most excellent Newspaper, have come to the President's attention, and are deeply appreciated.

The President is particularly gratified that you share his view of the purchase, viz., that it is a transaction replete with blessings to unborn millions of men. As you might assume, contrary opinions expressed in various New England gazettes have distressed him.

Gilbert could well imagine Jefferson's ire over some of the extreme reaction. A number of northeastern editors claimed flatly that because the new land would eventually be parceled into states, the influence of New England was already destroyed—and therefore, the northeast should consider seceding from the union in order to establish itself as a separate country.

Gilbert had personally written two *Republican* editorials to prick that hysterical bubble, dismissing the notion of a "southern plot" to wrest control of the country from the easterners. The editorials hadn't increased his popularity among Boston Federalists. But then, it was his opinion that the party had seen its heyday. Incurring the wrath of its diehard supporters troubled him not at all.

He started to re-focus his attention on the letter. A sudden spasm in his throat prevented it. He coughed. Then again, harder—

Damn! He hadn't been bothered with the cough for several weeks. Now it was nearly doubling him over.

He thrust the letter to the desk, gripped the arm of his chair with his other hand. He squeezed his lids shut, still coughing. Water trickled down his cheeks from the corners of his eyes. With the cough came the familiar chest pain.

As he rocked back and forth in his chair, he heard the voice of one of his writers:

"Mr. Kent? Shall I summon the doctor?"

Through sheer will he raised his head, opened his eyes:

"No, I—I'm over the worst."

His cheeks still shone from the tears. But the strangled feeling in his chest had lessened.

The reporter hesitated in the doorway. "Perhaps you ought to keep a window raised in here, sir."

"Air won't do a bit of good," Gilbert answered, wiping his eyes. "When one of those damned spells hits me, I can't get enough air no matter how many windows I throw open. When the spell passes, so does the struggle to breathe. The doctor tells me many people are afflicted with the condition and suffer nothing more than occasional discomfort all their lives."

He was fully recovered, and affable:

"Thank you for your concern, Mr. Morecam."

With a bob of his head, the writer vanished.

Gilbert cleaned his cheeks with a kerchief. God, how the infrequent but painful seizures angered him! He detested them because they impaired his ability to function at full efficiency. It was one of the few segments of his life he was unable to control.

Breathing normally again, he resumed reading:

The President is likewise grateful for your restraint in withholding an account of his special and confidential message to the Congress of January eighteenth last, even though he is well aware that certain details of that message reached you promptly as a result of your wide acquaintance with the legislators of your state. By now you surely know that the President's request for the sum of two thousand, five hundred dollars to fund an expedition into the remote Western reaches of the continent has been approved by the Congress. The purpose of the expedition is twofold—to expand our national commerce, and to perpetuate friendly relations with the Indian tribes.

That amused Gilbert. The piqued Massachusetts conservatives from whom he'd heard about the January request complained they were being asked to indulge Jefferson's "literary pursuits"—and his desire to increase scientific knowledge of the vast land mass west of the Mississippi. Gilbert had assumed there was more to it, and still did.

Gazing at the letter, he wondered who had re-copied it for the author. Jefferson's aide was known to be a wretched speller, only able to approximate the sound of certain words. An ironical failing for one who held the title of secretary, Gilbert thought.

Now, sir, it is my privilege to report that my letter is undoubtedly the last you shall receive from me in my present post, as the President has signally honored me by naming me commandant of the aforementioned Expedition. Together with my fellow officer, Mr. Wm. Clark of Virginia, whom I chose for his courage and intelligence as well as for his remarkable skills in drawing and map making, I have plans to embark with a small party of explorers from the settlement of St. Louis in the spring of next year. Our route will take us to the headwaters of the great river Missouri, and thence to the Pacific. Hopefully, we shall complete this last stage of our journey by means of the Northwest River Passage long rumored to exist.

I shall be leaving my present duties within a very few days to seek my companions, who must be good hunters, stout, healthy, unmarried men, accustomed to the woods and capable of bearing bodily fatigue in pretty considerable degree. I will also be making divers stops at the Federal arsenal for military equipment, at Philadelphia, Pittsburgh, etcetera for good calico shirts, looking-glasses, jewelry, beads, scissors and

other items to be presented to the various tribal chieftains in the most friendly and concilatory manner.
It is no longer possible to keep a venture of this magnitude entirely secret. However, a certain prudence is still necessary in view of the Nation's recent acquisitions in the approximate geographic area to be traversed by our Corps of Discovery. Your cooperation in referring to said Corps as a purely scientific body will be most deeply appreciated.
With kindest good wishes for your continued prosperity, and humble thanks for your many editorial expressions of support for the Administration, I trust I have the honor of remaining

Your obdt. friend,
Meriwether Lewis (Capt.),
Secretary to the President

With a delicious shiver of excitement, Gilbert reread the closing passages of the letter, then smiled. The Federalist newspapers had exercised no restraint at all concerning Jefferson's secret message, growling about "frivolous and costly intellectual endeavors"—which proved they were exactly as confused as the president meant them to be. Some of Captain Meriwether Lewis' oblique phrasing, however, invested the undertaking with a significance—a purpose—Gilbert believed he understood.

He laid the letter aside, turned in his chair to regard his expensive beaver hat. Such hats were increasingly popular; here too it was the Englishman, Beau Brummel, who set the fashion. If Brummel adopted a beaver hat, every gentleman must have a beaver hat! Gentlewomen too—with suitable alterations in design, of course.

Gilbert's thoughts turned to the source of the fur

which the hatters brushed and worked into such soft, lustrous nap. Montreal and the straits of Michilimackinac were already major gateways through which fur gathered around the lakes reached the European fur markets.

Most sought after were *castor gras d'hiver*—the winter skins of the beavers. The winter pelts were premium priced because only they yielded the superlative felt for the hats such as Gilbert wore. But other, less choice furs and skins were in demand as the growing middle and lower classes developed an appetite for small touches of luxury. From elk and deer came the leather for gloves. Muskrat and raccoon and the hide of the fabled bison could be turned into modestly priced coats, coat linings and collar trim.

The British in Canada dominated the fur trade on the lakes and in the country along the Missouri. Hired Frenchmen wintered on the distant reaches of that unmapped river, trapping or trading for pelts. In the spring they took their bundles to Michilimackinac or to posts of the Hudson's Bay Company north of there. Though Michilimackinac now belonged to the United States, commercial licenses issued to the Canadians permitted them to use the island as a headquarters.

But a few of the French winterers—the men whose fathers and grandfathers had pioneered the trade years earlier—disliked all Englishmen, and journeyed down to St. Louis on the Mississippi to sell their catches to Americans trying to gain a foothold in the lucrative industry. Gilbert didn't doubt that one of the objectives of Jefferson's western expedition was the discovery of new routes to help American traders capture a larger share of the fur business. Because national rivalries were involved, a purpose like that would, of necessity, be kept secret until it was accomplished—

As would other details of the mission, simply because the president's monumental purchase—which some New Englanders called totally illegal—was sketchy on certain questions of boundaries. By exploring, Captain Lewis might help settle future disputes. Possession, as the old saying claimed, was still nine points of the law.

Establishment of territorial rights would blunt the thrust of Canadian expansion, too; balk the fur entrepreneurs already pushing their trapping parties west and south—

The Louisiana acquisition had made it all possible. It had also come as a stunning surprise to the country.

Minister Plenipotentiary Monroe had sailed to France the preceding January to investigate the possibility of buying the port of New Orleans, and perhaps some additional territory in the West Floridas, for no more than two million dollars. On arrival, Monroe was offered not merely the requested territory, but all of the Louisiana lands west of the Mississippi and north of the Gulf!

The turnabout in French policy—marking the abandonment of Bonaparte's vision of an empire in the western hemisphere—had two causes: the failure of the French military to suppress a decade-long slave revolt on the island of Haiti, and, closer to home, the threat of renewed hostilities with Britain.

More than eight hundred and thirty thousand square miles were involved in the offer. Astonishingly, Jefferson quickly accepted it—and the price of sixty million francs, or about fifteen million in dollars. The sum included the payment of some American war debts. By Gilbert's reckoning, the purchase itself amounted to something like three pennies per acre—which had to be one of the most remarkable real estate bargains of recorded history.

Gilbert had already read an edited text of the treaty

of cession. For safety's sake, three copies of the full document had been rushed to the United States by three different couriers aboard three fast packets. The Senate had yet to ratify the treaty, however. And in the inevitable debate, old positions were being turned topsy-turvy:

The president, known to favor strict interpretation of the Constitution, adopted a somewhat broader view where the purchase was concerned. He argued that constitutional power to govern territory implied the right to acquire it. The majority of New England Federalists, normally loose constructionists, had likewise reversed themselves, insisting that nowhere in the Constitution was the president authorized to buy new land. Gilbert suspected Jefferson had made a pragmatic decision, bending principle to accommodate his conviction that the purchase would enrich the country in everything from minerals and timber—and fur-bearing animals—to much-needed land for settlement and agricultural cultivation.

From reading the edited text, Gilbert was well aware that the boundaries of the ceded land were vague, especially in the north and far west, where a vast mountain chain separated the inland prairies from the Pacific coastal region which a Boston skipper had explored in 1792. Discovering a great river that poured down out of the mountains—the western end of the legendary Northwest Passage, perhaps?—the skipper had christened it with the popular name "Columbia."

Gilbert admired Jefferson's labyrinthine thinking. With one stroke—the expedition—he could solidify the nation's claim to new territory *and* aid an increasingly important sector of the economy.

Suddenly he sat upright. Snatched Lewis' letter and scanned it.

He blinked several times. A smile slowly lifted the

corners of his mouth. He just might have stumbled onto something—!

He rose quickly, tucked the letter into the pocket of his coat which lay neatly folded over another chair. He paced back and forth for a minute. Then he sat down. He tented his fingers and tilted his chair back, soothed by the faint and rhythmic *thump-thump* of the book presses churning out pages on the first floor. Despite his youth, he resembled nothing so much as a frail old man cogitating.

Gilbert knew what his critics said of him. That he had an almost driven desire to succeed—to be a good steward of the assets left by Philip Kent's passing. As a result, he sometimes behaved like a man three times his years. He never let it trouble him. Thinking without the passion of youth could be an advantage.

It proved so now, as he looked at Abraham's problems in an objective way.

He believed the problems sprang from three interrelated sources. The first was Abraham's obvious guilt about being responsible for his wife's death.

The second, perhaps as deep and fundamental as the first—although Abraham had never even mentioned it to Gilbert—was the rift between father and son when Abraham and his bride set out for the west. Philip's death during Abraham's absence had effectively prevented any healing of the wounds of either party.

The third source of the problems was Abraham himself.

Looking back to his own boyhood, Gilbert could recall very nearly worshiping his half-brother. His precipitous entry into the world of adult affairs had purified his thinking on many subjects; burned away old illusions. He could make a more accurate appraisal now: Abraham was a man of weaker character than their father.

Gilbert didn't consider it callous to form such judgments of the living and the dead. In all things, he tried to be rational. He knew it would have been difficult indeed for almost any young man, himself included, to have matched Philip Kent's mental and physical toughness.

To offset his limp, Philip had kept himself in perfect condition. He had constantly educated himself—a process made easier by his professional involvement with books and journalism. Gilbert, sickly as a child, had never faced the necessity of competing with his father on both fronts. Physically he was no match. That gave him leave to devote himself to keeping up with Philip's mind as best he could.

Abraham, sadly, had lived completely in Philip's shadow—and suffered by comparison. When Abraham married Elizabeth, stirring the so-called Fletcher temperament into the brew, no wonder explosions resulted.

Against that background, Gilbert analyzed the idea that had popped into his mind a few minutes ago. A mad idea, some would say; perhaps even Abraham himself! Yet Gilbert embraced it because he could no longer permit Abraham's behavior to go unchecked. Not only was his half-brother destroying himself with his drinking and trouble-making, he was harming his son. Perhaps irreparably.

As Gilbert sat and pondered, beams of slanting sunshine turned his cheeks to the color of warm ivory. His mind roved over tales told by fur factors who had made the difficult trip to the country's western outposts, St. Louis and Michilimackinac, there to bargain with the trappers whose wanderings had taken them into the country Lewis proposed to cross and map. The factors brought back astonishing, almost fanciful accounts of a sea of grass stretching west toward the mountain rampart. They spoke of gigantic herds of the bison like those the Kentucky settlers had slain and eaten for years.

Out there, it was said, the red tribes were different from Indians of the east. They raised and rode horses, acquiring a dangerous mobility lacked by nations such as the Shawnee.

And now Mr. Meriwether Lewis was captaining an expedition to that very land. Abraham had soldiered with Lewis under General Wayne. Yes, and with the other one—the younger brother of George Rogers Clark. By God, it was perfect!

Even though the solution carried an element of risk, Gilbert didn't shrink from it. In the two years since he'd taken charge of Kent and Son, he had proved over and over that risk-taking could pay off handsomely. The only difference now was in the nature of what was at stake. Not money, but a man's life and sanity.

The question, then, was whether to consult Abraham first or present him with an accomplished fact. Thinking a few minutes more, Gilbert decided on the latter course. Abraham must have no excuse to back out; no more latitude in which to indulge his excesses. The press room was nearing the point of mutiny.

His mind raced. Much remained to be done before he went home for the evening. And much remained after that. He'd have to speak to Abraham as soon as his half-brother returned from whatever den he'd crawled into after the fight.

Beyond that, he needed to gain his wife Harriet's consent to her role in the plan. She had disliked Abraham and Jared—but particularly Abraham—since the day the two had come home after Elizabeth's death. The fact that Harriet was now in her eighth month of her first pregnancy wouldn't make Gilbert's job any easier. It would require extra effort on his part to make sure dinner this evening was composed and cordial—an appropriate forum for him to share his plan with his spouse before broaching it to Abraham.

Yes, he had much to do—

Commencing with the draft of a letter.

iv

He found fresh paper, inked his quill and began to scribble in that small, compressed hand others found so difficult to decipher:

My dear Captain Lewis,

I am in receipt of yours of the first instant, for which my deepest thanks. I hope I do not place you under an undue burden by tendering a most urgent request which, at the same time, could well work to your benefit—

Ten minutes later, Gilbert stepped to the office door. "Mr. Morecam?"

The reporter hurried over. "Sir?"

"Can you spare an hour from your duties?" Gilbert asked rhetorically. "You've a good hand—and I have a letter that needs to be copied three times—and kept entirely confidential. I want the letter to go to Pittsburgh, Cincinnati and Louisville, so that I'm certain it reaches the recipient—just like the purchase treaty, eh?"

"I'll be happy to make the copies, Mr. Kent."

"Bring them in as soon as you're finished and I'll see about the posting."

"By the regular mails? I can do that for you."

"Speed is essential. I want to engage private couriers."

Morecam goggled, contemplating the expense of that. Gilbert wheeled back into his office—and rushed out of the building an hour later. Seldom had employees of Kent and Son seen the youthful owner depart in such haste—and so early! A full hour before closing.

Nor had they ever seen such an intense luster in his dark eyes—or such touches of emotional color in his cheeks.

If Mr. Gilbert Kent the modernist was engrossed in another venture, it had to be a very important one indeed.

CHAPTER V

The Mark

"YOU MAY SERVE the plum pudding," Harriet Kent said to the girl in the striped cotton dress and gingham apron. "No hard sauce for the boy. But refill the milk pitcher."

On the side of the dining table opposite Abraham's empty place, Jared Adam Kent made a face:

"I don't want any more milk, Aunt Harriet."

The maid hesitated. The young woman at the foot of the table glared:

"Jared, I am growing tired of your impertinence. You behave like a dock boy instead of a child reared in a Christian home."

"Harriet," Gilbert said softly, pursing his lips.

"The boy is disrespectful! To me, to the servants, to everyone! He's a willful, headstrong child—"

As if to confirm it, Jared said, "I won't drink any more even if you whip me." He was handsome for a five-year-old, with long tawny hair and brilliant blue eyes. But his face had a fatigued, pasty look.

And his retort made Harriet furious:

"You see what I mean, Gilbert? He not only looks like his mother, he acts like her!"

Jared reacted with a stunned look, then with obvious anger. In a controlled voice, Gilbert said:

"Raking over the past is futile and cruel. Especially in front of—"

"I disagree. We've tiptoed around the issue too long.

You've told me how his mother behaved. Defiant of everyone—"

"Please stop," Gilbert broke in, aware of the hurt and hostility in the boy's eyes.

Harriet opened her mouth; hesitated; then glanced sharply at the maid.

"Bring the milk, Esther."

"Papa wouldn't force me to have it," Jared said.

Harriet leaned forward awkwardly; she was approaching the end of her term. Her huge stomach couldn't be minimized; not even by the expensive, high-waisted maternity gown of lavender lawn she wore over a matching petticoat. Gilbert pushed his chair away from the table, noting unhappily that his wife's features had taken on a familiar, pinched look. It had to do with her dark eyes. When she was angry, she tended to slit them, and frown. The contraction changed the proportions of her features subtly.

"Your father is not in charge of this household," she said to the boy. "Indeed, if he were present for meals a little more often—present and sober—he'd take you in hand."

Rapping his palm on the table, Gilbert said, "That will be quite enough, Harriet."

"Why? It's true—but you're always evading that issue, too." She gestured to the vacant place. "Abraham's gone more than he's here!"

"We had a great deal of work at the firm today. I asked him to stay late to help with it."

Harriet's pale lips compressed, branding the lie for what it was. She had an oval face, dark hair, fine patrician features. But bad temper destroyed the total effect.

Gilbert glanced at Jared. The boy sat on a pillow that raised him to table height. His downcast expression showed that he too disbelieved Gilbert's statement. Jared had seen his father's place empty too many evenings; watched Abraham come stumbling in from Beacon Street, unkempt and incoherent, too many times. Sadly, Gilbert reflected that Jared might not understand the word *sober*—or its opposite. But instinct surely told him his father's behavior was abnormal, and wrong.

The maid waiting nervously for a final resolution of the milk question started to speak to Harriet. Gilbert was quicker:

"We'll not have any more milk, Esther. Nor the pudding either. You may retire."

"Yes, sir." She curtseyed and left.

"Jared, be so good as to go up to your room," Gilbert said.

The boy started to protest, then took note of Gilbert's stern expression and slipped off the pillow. Irked by her husband's intervention, Harriet stared at him, spots of color showing in her cheeks. The color deepened when Jared blurted:

"You don't like papa, do you, Aunt Harriet?"

"That is not a suitable question for a boy your age! This house is partly his—"

"But you wish it weren't, don't you?"

"Jared, go," Gilbert said, soft but firm.

Jared paid no attention: "You wish we'd both leave and never trouble you again, don't you?"

"Jared!" Gilbert rose half way out of his chair.

Eyeing his uncle, Jared looked less pugnacious all at once. Gilbert sat down again:

"You owe your Aunt Harriet the same politeness she owes you. And please remember, she's expecting a child. That makes a person—well, rather cross at times. You do understand?"

Jared's tawny hair shone in the light of the chandelier candles. His blue eyes were almost venomous as tears sprang into them and he cried:

"I understand she doesn't want papa here—or me!"

He spun, dashed to the hall and clattered away up the stairs while thunder muttered in the distance.

ii

The moment Jared had gone, Harriet vented her anger:

"I'm sick of the way you coddle that boy. You've said time and again how willful his mother was—and when he flaunts his temperament, you overlook it!"

"Harriet—"

"Must we suffer another Elizabeth Fletcher in this house? Abraham is bad enough, but—"

"The immediate concern is the father, not the son. I don't believe we should continue to discuss—"

"Why not? The boy resists the slightest imposition of authority! Absolutely refuses to behave as any respectable boy shou—"

"God's sake, Harriet!" he burst out, in such an unusually loud voice that his wife recoiled in her chair. "Is that all that ever matters to you—respectability? Did you look at that child? He's tormented with fear!"

"Of me?" she asked in an arch way.

"Of you *and* his father. Harsh discipline won't alleviate the problem. Nor will constant harping about his mother's faults. You'll only make him feel worthless—and his behavior will get worse."

"Do you deny he's headstrong?"

"Of course not. But the way to cure it is with kindness, not rancor. He hasn't lived like normal children. Have you forgotten he saw his own mother murdered?"

"And whose fault is *that?"*

Gilbert uttered a dismayed sigh. "Is it necessary to place blame? It happened, that's all."

Harriet leaned forward again, a movement that emphasized her bulk and clumsiness:

"But it would *not* have happened if Abraham hadn't subjected his wife to the hardships of the west. Had he stayed in Boston, Jared wouldn't be a spoiled only child. He'd have an older brother or sister—"

"You're now blaming Abraham for Elizabeth losing her first baby?"

"Yes, he was responsible."

"Nonsense. Utter *nonsense!*"

Harriet's dark eyes suddenly became very bright. Her voice grew cool, malicious:

"Is it? My dear, you told me a few weeks after Abraham returned that Elizabeth was the one instrumental in their departure."

"I don't see how that makes him responsi—"

"He was manipulated because he's weak! As a man—the husband—he could have refused her unreasonable requests. He could have said no. But he didn't. And he was repaid for his cowardice by the death of his first child, and then by Jared—who has inherited the worst qualities of both his parents!"

Gilbert seethed. "I wish I'd never repeated one syllable of the story! You twist it all so terribly to fit your view of Abraham—justify your dislike—"

"He *is* weak," Harriet repeated emphatically. "God judged him so, and exacted punishment. You can see that in the way Abraham behaves—and his son too!"

Almost on the point of shouting at her, Gilbert controlled his temper with difficulty. He put the palms of his slim hands on the dining table. Through the strained softness of his voice he tried to show his wife how angry she'd made him:

"May we leave metaphysics out of this? The problem is tangible, urgent—and heaven has damn little to do with a solution."

"I would appreciate your refraining from cursing in my—"

"You drive me to it!"

He drew a deep breath, leaned back in his chair, finally went on:

"Harriet, it's absolutely pointless to debate who was responsible for what happened. That there's any debate at all is my fault. I was foolish to discuss past history and Abraham's confidences—"

"But you did."

Gilbert's mild demeanor seemed to harden:

"I do ask you, as I've asked you before, never to mention any of what I told you. Don't mention it in Abraham's presence—or, from now on, in mine."

"That has the distinct sound of a threat."

"No, no," Gilbert said hastily. "A request."

Harriet gave a sniff of disbelief. Gilbert's eyes fastened on hers:

"But it's a request I expect to see honored."

Harriet averted her glance. She pretended to be hurt.

Gilbert wasn't sure he'd succeeded in making his point. In public, Harriet accepted her husband's dominance, as did most wives of her station and circumstance. But the festering dislike she felt for his half-brother was an unusual factor in a marital relationship. In the privacy of the family, she might not bow to his politely phrased intimidation.

But he hoped she would. He was sure Abraham carried quite enough guilt without the burden being increased by his sister-in-law's spite.

During the ensuing silence, the tension between Gilbert and his wife gradually diminished. Finally he felt comfortable enough to try to return the conversation to its original course:

"The problem, Harriet, is not in the past but in the present. Abraham is not himself—"

"How long are we expected to suffer because of that?"

Gilbert struck the table. *"Enough!"*

For the second time, Harriet looked genuinely alarmed. He drew his hand back, wiped the damp palm on his trousers, swallowed once and went on:

"Let the past rest. I don't excuse Abraham's behavior, but I understand what drives him to it. I see nothing to be gained by punishing him—if indeed he deserves punishment, which I doubt. I see a great deal to be gained—I should say lost—if we fail to bring his son safely through this difficult period. You know very well that whenever Abraham walks in the door, Jared can't predict whether his father will hug him or hit him. We have a duty to alleviate that situation if we can."

"A duty I don't accept."

"But it must be accepted. It *must* be!"

Harriet obviously heard the strain, the emotion in her husband's voice. She seemed unmoved:

"Trying to help Jared is useless, Gilbert. He comes of bad stock, and he'll never overcome that."

"No, not if you keep telling him so. But I repeat—my first concern is with his father. I ask you to be tolerant just a short while longer. Just until I persuade Abraham to follow this plan I have in mind. Today I received an unexpected letter from Meriwether Lewis, the president's secretary. You'll remember Abraham served with him out west—"

Rapidly, Gilbert told his wife about the forthcoming expedition, and the chance he saw for Abraham to become part of it. By the time he mentioned the three letters he'd dispatched, enthusiasm had gone out of his voice, though. Harriet's face was growing more and more sour.

The moment he finished, she said, "The very idea is idiotic."

He pursed his lips. "Indeed. That's your considered opinion? Having thought it over for all of five seconds?"

"I don't need to think it over."

"Just condemn it out of hand? It may be an unusual plan, but it's not an impossible one."

"I disagree."

"Why?"

"Because I know Abraham. He'll have nothing to do with it. He'll laugh at you. Perhaps he'll even thrash you—that would be like him. He's a beast! Drunken, uncontrollable—what's the matter?"

Gilbert started to answer, then quickly lifted a hand to cup his mouth. The spasm of coughing went on for almost a minute.

At last, recovered, he asked:

"Why are you so averse to the plan? Why do you resist my efforts to help Abraham and the boy? Why do you detest them?"

"Abraham occupies too much of your time! I want this household to put attention where it belongs—on *our* lives. *Our* child!"

Unconsciously, her hand dropped to her swollen middle. Her features softened. She looked at her husband in a pleading way:

"Even if you can get him to agree, it still means we'll have to care for that vile-tempered little boy a year or more."

"That's true. But with Abraham gone, we might find Jared more tractable. I honestly think fear of his father has a great deal to do with the way he acts—"

"He has bad blood in him! He'll never amount to anything!"

"Help me give him a chance!"

After a moment's silence, Harriet sighed and struggled up from her chair.

"Very well. Speak to Abraham. I want this intolerable situation resolved."

"I will speak to him," Gilbert nodded. "Tonight—when he returns."

She couldn't hold back a last thrust:

"*If* he returns."

She turned clumsily and waddled through the door that led to the kitchen and pantry, a sagging, somehow slovenly figure despite her elegant clothes.

Gilbert almost went after her. Instead, he forced himself to remain in the chair, one hand over his eyes. The verbal duel had drained and exhausted him.

Presently his angry feelings moderated again. His features smoothed out. He sat up straight. He brooded a good half hour before uttering a short sigh and rising.

His plans for a cordial, peaceful meal during which he would win Harriet's cooperation were in ruins. As he consulted the banjo clock and noted the lateness of the hour, he had to admit the prospects for the remainder of the evening didn't appear much better. Abraham might not come back until tomorrow—or next week!

The trouble in the household wasn't entirely Abraham's fault. Harriet exacerbated the difficulties. But much as he disliked certain facets of his wife's character, Gilbert couldn't place all the blame on her either. Jared Adam Kent *was* impertinent; rebellious; resentful of the most common and proper forms of discipline.

Though he felt he was being a traitor to his mother's memory, he again asked himself whether Harriet might be correct. Perhaps there *was* something bad in the child's bloodline. Something inherited from Elizabeth, who had in turn drawn it from that shadowy father about whom Gilbert knew so little—

Useless speculation. *Bury the past!* Hadn't he just urged that on his wife? Yet here he was, exhuming it as he desperately tried to fathom and resolve the turmoil Abraham and Jared caused.

The challenge lay in the present, not the past. With more than a little apprehension he fixed his mind on that fact. He left the table looking far older than his twenty years.

iii

The July evening with its threat of thunderstorms turned the air in the house sweltering and heavy. Gilbert loosened his stock and detached his collar as he crossed the hall to Philip's old library. Even lighting one lamp seemed to raise the room's temperature drastically.

Gilbert had converted the library into an office, with furnishings of dark wood. He slouched in the chair beside the littered desk and regarded the large oil portrait of his father hanging between the windows on the outer wall.

The portrait had been painted the year before Philip's death. Gilbert stared at the strong, almost truculent face on the canvas. Probed the painted eyes that appeared to defy the world. How would Philip have dealt with the problem of his older son—?

A boom of thunder roused him. The reverie was futile. No one could resolve the dilemma except Gilbert himself. That inescapable fact gave his eyes a remote, gloomy look as the curtains belled at the partially open windows. The lamp flickered. He heard the first spatters of rain on Beacon Street.

Gilbert loved his wife. He appreciated that pregnancy put her under a strain. Still, there *was* a sour, even cruel streak in her makeup that he wished were absent.

The coldness of her nature carried over to the marriage bed. She lacked spirit there; took no pleasure in making love. Though Gilbert had never been so indelicate as to question her on the subject, he suspected she'd been taught that sexual intercourse was basically sinful, to be indulged in only for the purpose of begetting children.

He found that disappointing though by no means unbearable. Perhaps because he'd always been less than robust, or perhaps because he was usually preoccupied with business affairs, he did not often experience a strong desire for sex. That reduced Harriet's reluctance to little more than an inconvenience. What he missed most in her was simple, straightforward affection.

For this and a number of other reasons, he had never considered their match perfect. But he'd learned at an early age that little in life was perfect, so he was reasonably content.

Harriet Lebow of New York City was one year older than Gilbert. She was the only child of a prosperous commodities dealer whose family had settled on Manhattan island four generations ago, when a majority of the residents were Dutch. The family originally spelled the name *Lebouwe*.

During his first year managing Kent and Son, Gilbert had found it necessary to float a loan for the new presses. The Rothman Bank provided the funds. With the money assured, Gilbert took a trip to New York to visit a machinery importer.

After inspecting one of the presses, Gilbert placed his order. He remained in the city a few more days, spending most of his time at the one place with which no rising American businessman dared be unfamiliar—the center of the country's expanding commerce, Wall Street. He was told an actual wall had once stood there, defense against attacks by Indians who lived in the woods at the north end of the island.

On busy Wall Street, Gilbert met Harriet's father

through a mutual friend to whom he presented Royal Rothman's letter of introduction. The friend entertained Gilbert at the Tontine Coffee House building, which housed the growing Stock Exchange. Among the gentlemen gathered on the Tontine porch was the wealthy Lebow.

Later, Gilbert's friend provided some of Lebow's background. The commodities dealer had managed to keep his Tory leanings concealed during the Revolution. After the war, he built his fortune by speculating in the government certificates issued to soldiers in lieu of pay.

By 1783 these promissory notes had declined so sharply in value that their owners, pressed for cash, were eager to sell them to speculators like Lebow for as little as twelve cents on the dollar. Lebow, in turn, was gambling that the government would eventually untangle its finances and make good on a major part of its obligations.

Under Secretary of the Treasury Hamilton, it did—though as everyone knew, Hamilton had traded the location of the new capital city, Washington, for the southern votes necessary to pass his financial legislation. Mr. Lebow, now an avowed Federalist, blessed Hamilton ever afterward. He prospered mightily as a member of what Mr. Jefferson sneeringly described as "the stock-jobbing herd."

While Gilbert was conversing with Lebow on the Tontine porch, Harriet called for her father in the family carriage. More introductions were performed. Soon Gilbert found himself making return trips to New York, first as a regular guest at the Lebow table, then as a prospective son-in-law.

Gilbert found Harriet intelligent and attractive, if overly concerned with matters of status and appearance. In the rational way his mind worked, he decided she would make an eminently suitable wife for a substantial businessman. She would also give him important connections in New York's financial community. Though her parents were both dead now, those connections remained intact.

He did love her—as much as a man of deliberately dispassionate temperament could love another person. He doubted that she loved him at all. He suspected love was alien to her experience—except as it applied to herself. Still, it wasn't a bad bargain—

Except at times like this, when Harriet's personality disrupted the entire house and created genuine ill-will among those living there.

A glare of lightning lit the office as Gilbert paced back and forth, still pondering the various approaches he might make to his half-brother. A quarter hour passed. Another. He was becoming convinced Abraham would be gone all night. He was almost relieved. Tomorrow or the next day, he'd be better rested. This evening he was edgy; prone to anger—

His relief was short-lived. At the end of a long rumble from the night sky, he heard irregular footsteps on the walk outside. Then an oath.

He didn't bother to glance out a window. He opened the double doors and waited in the dim hall, watching the front entrance.

In a moment, Abraham lurched through the doorway.

iv

Gilbert Kent was eight years younger than the shorter, stockier man who stood blinking at him in a vaguely hostile way. Yet Gilbert somehow seemed the older of the two.

Another lightning-burst lit Abraham's filthy, unshaven cheeks. His brown eyes looked addled. His ink-stained shirt, leather vest and homespun breeches bore an assortment of stains. He smelled of rum and vomit.

Gilbert said, "Come into the office please, Abraham."

Abraham slammed the door, started by, his step unsteady. "Spare me the lecture on self-discipline and deportment, will you? I've a terrible throbbing head—"

"That's not my doing." Gilbert seized Abraham's arm.

Abraham looked at his brother's hand resentfully. But Gilbert refused to let go:

"It's imperative that we speak privately. You can clean up later."

Releasing Abraham's arm, he re-entered the library, not glancing around. The sound of Abraham's shuffling footsteps signaled that he'd won the first skirmish. But he took no satisfaction. The major engagement remained to be fought.

Gilbert crossed to one window, then the other, opening them wide despite the rain that soaked the curtains. He could barely tolerate Abraham's stench.

Abraham rolled the double doors shut. He took a chair, turning it, Gilbert noticed, so that his back was toward the portrait of their father.

Gilbert glanced at the letter on the desk, then to his half-brother's sullen face.

"May I ask where you have been all day?"

"You can ask but you won't get an answer."

"Be so good as to speak to me in a civil way, Abraham! I'm your brother, not one of your tavern cronies."

Abraham covered his brow with a dirty hand. A small raw spot shone on one finger.

"I'm tired. Can't this wait?"

"No, I'm afraid not. This morning you completely disrupted operations at the printing house—for the sixth time. I don't count your innumerable verbal assaults on my employees."

"I didn't start it! That damned Naughton—"

"Whose hand you broke. A man can't set type with a broken hand."

Abraham pretended not to hear. "He made one sneering remark too many."

"About what?"

"About me not being fit to hold a job at Kent's."

"Don't sound so proud! Unfortunately, the remark appears to be correct."

"The bastard said I was only kept on because I'm your brother."

"In that, too, Mr. Naughton is regrettably accurate. I've given you repeated warnings, and you've disregarded every one. Therefore—"

Here was the delicate part; the first stroke of strategy so necessary to the working of his plan:

"—I've no choice but to discharge you."

That, at least, fully caught Abraham's attention. He raised his head. Stared in disbelief that changed to fury. A blue-white flash suffused the office, putting an eerie sheen on Philip's portrait.

"Thrown out? Is that it?"

"Yes."

"Out of the house too? That would make your wife happy!"

"I don't deny Harriet has little admiration for your gutter ways."

Abraham's jaw clenched. "I wonder how she'd feel if she saw you shot down, the bitch."

Gilbert turned scarlet. One hand closed into a fist. Abraham noticed. The harsh mask of his face seemed to crumble, revealing a man abruptly ashamed and vulnerable. Very softly, he said:

"Forgive me for that."

The scarlet faded.

"Certainly."

He walked over, laid a hand on Abraham's shoulder.

He could feel the trembling; the physical manifestation of misery. Abraham's hand hid his eyes again. Gilbert asked:

"Would you let me pour you a rum?"

"That would help. That's all that seems to help any more."

Gilbert fetched the decanter and a glass from the cabinet where he kept liquor for business visitors. "I'll only pour you a small amount, because I want you to listen to what I have to say."

The older man accepted the drink, tossed it off quickly, extended the glass. Gilbert set the decanter on the desk beside the letter.

"I told you—no more until we've talked."

Abraham peered ruefully into the empty glass. Then he stretched his legs out. His body seemed flaccid; defenseless.

"All right. Lecture away."

"No lecture. Just facts. I can no longer tolerate your presence at Kent and Son. For the sake of efficiency, of morale—"

"Efficiency. Morale!" Abraham snickered. "Good old Gilbert! An eighty-year-old clerk in a boy's body."

Gilbert pursed his lips. "Unlike you, Abraham, I didn't have the benefit of good health when I was young. I had very little to do except follow father about and—and practice being old, perhaps you could say. On the other hand, I think every family needs someone with a clerk's mind, to keep its affairs in balance. The affairs of the Kents are definitely *out* of balance right now. They—Abraham, kindly stop staring into space and give me your attention! Destroying yourself is one thing. Destroying your son is quite another."

Abraham's gaze seemed to re-focus on the reality of the room. "Jared? What about him?"

"Have you watched him closely these past months?"

A vague gesture with the glass. "I see him when I can—"

"Once or twice a week? For a moment or two? Do you seriously believe that's enough?"

"I—" Abraham shook his head. "Who knows?"

"Even when you do speak to Jared, you're seldom sober. He's mortally afraid of you! Why, he—"

Shocked and angered, Gilbert stopped. The older brother was smiling in a strange, joyless way.

"You find this amusing, Abraham?"

"No. Oh, no. I was just thinking of a picture that comes into my mind sometimes. A picture of—"

He indicated the painting.

"I see him with his hand raised to me. He's angry, though I can't hear what he's saying. Father once told me that when he came home from the Continental army, wounded and unable to walk properly—came home to Boston with my mother dead—well, he said there was a period of nearly a year when he treated me very badly. By his own admission—treated me very badly! How unlike Mr. Philip Kent to admit he had faults, eh? In any case, I was apparently terrified of him—"

A humorless laugh. Silently, Gilbert waited.

"You know, Elizabeth always worried about the Fletcher blood being in Jared—"

"We are not discussing Elizabeth's parentage."

"Oh, no reflection on your mother—I just thought of it because—" He shrugged, wearily. "—because the Kent heritage has proved damned near as damaging. I'm acting the way my father did, if what you say is true."

"Isn't it?"

A lengthy pause.

"Yes." Once more he shielded his eyes. "God, yes—"

Pressing his advantage while Abraham's defenses were weakened, Gilbert pried the glass from his half-brother's hand. The rain beat heavily against the front of the house.

"I understand what you're going through, even though I can't condone your actions. You drink because Elizabeth died and you blame yourself—"

"Sufficient reason, don't you think?"

"—you hate the western country for what it did to her—"

"You're quite astute. Shall we drink to the land of opportunity beyond the Alleghenies—?"

His eye on the decanter, he started to rise. Gilbert pushed him back. Undeterred, Abraham took the glass from Gilbert's hand, raised it in a mock toast:

"To the great and glorious west—and the thousands of others it will ruin."

"What a strange enemy for a man to have," Gilbert said. "Land. You think it took Elizabeth, so you ran from it—"

"What the hell should I have done? Stayed there? The land *destroyed* her!"

"Land is land, Abraham. It can't be good or evil. Only the men who inhabit it have those qualities."

"No philosophic quibbles, thank you," Abraham snarled. "I've heard that argument till I'm fairly sick of it! Yes, I know two Shawnee came to the farm, and one shot her. But that's still the land as far as I'm concerned—"

Abruptly, he fixed his half-brother with a penetrating stare:

"Do you remember when we visited the president's home in Virginia?"

"Monticello? Yes, I recall a little of the trip—"

"In the orchard—I remember it distinctly—Mr. Jefferson went on at great length about the nation's future lying in the west. About the bounty of the land—"

Abraham spat.

"Of course it's very easy for a gentleman to find good in something he's never seen with his own eyes."

"You don't believe he was correct?"

"How can you even ask?" Abraham wiped his perspiring forehead. "I've mentioned the Clapper family to you, haven't I?"

"A few times."

"Did I ever tell you what Clapper said about the west?"

Gilbert shook his head.

"He said people went there not to seek something but to escape something."

"What?"

"Unhappiness."

"I think that view's wrong. Wrong and warped."

"Is it? I went to Ohio to escape his influence—" A hand jabbed toward the portrait. "So did Elizabeth."

"That doesn't make the generalization valid for everyone. Nor cancel the truth of Mr. Jefferson's words."

"I disagree—even though that makes me—what was your word? Warped—?" He shrugged. "You've been saying that in one way or another ever since I came home."

Gilbert bowed his head slightly, as if to avoid the scathing bitterness. Abraham exhaled loudly. Then:

"Well—perhaps you're right." One hand lifted absently to scrub at the stubble on his dirty face. "I can't help how I feel. I admit I'll never think of the western country without prejudice—"

"When a man allows himself to be defeated by an enemy, he has difficulty living with himself. Hides from himself. Destroys himself, sometimes—unless that enemy is overcome. If you had a second chance to defeat what you hate so much, you should take it."

"*A second—?* Gilbert, what the hell are you driving at?"

"I believe you understand."

"You're not suggesting I go west again?"

"That," Gilbert said, "is exactly what I am suggesting."

Violently, Abraham turned away. "Christ on the cross! Of all the insane, ill-conceived—"

Speechless, he couldn't finish.

On the precipice now, one misstep away from failure, Gilbert spoke with extreme care:

"I don't think you fully understand everything I've said. I want you out of this house. I want you out of Boston. I will see to it that you can't find decent employment anywhere in this city—believe me, I have the connections to do that."

"I know you do." Again Abraham shook his head. "What kind of monster have you turned into?"

"Call me that if you like. I have reasons for what I'm doing. I'm absolutely convinced you'll never hold your head up again—never drag yourself out of this slough into which you've fallen—unless someone forces you to best the enemy that bested you."

For a long moment, Gilbert was afraid Abraham still didn't comprehend one syllable, or his seriousness. Then, slowly, the older man lifted his head to stare at his taller brother:

"You've something in mind. Something you haven't mentioned."

"Indeed I do. Here—"

He snatched the letter from the desk.

"Sit down and read it through. I'll pour you another drink."

As he filled Abraham's glass, ashamed of resorting to such bribery, he heard the sheets crinkle. Abraham exclaimed softly:

"Meriwether—? This is from the president's secretary."

"Yes."

"I didn't realize you and he were in touch."

"Read it from the beginning," Gilbert urged.

He held out the glass. Abraham took it but didn't drink, concentrating on the letter. He read the sheets and dropped them on the floor one at a time.

A gust of wind blew rain against the back of Gilbert's neck. A carriage went rattling by in the aftermath of a thunderclap. Finally Abraham finished. The last sheet fluttered down. He drank the rum in a gulp, said:

"I don't understand why you wanted me to read that."

"Come, of course you do! You fit the specifications for the type of man Lewis wishes to recruit. Single, strong, in good health—"

"I am not precisely single. I have a son."

"Harriet has already agreed to care for Jared."

"She doesn't like me *or* Jared. And you'll soon have your own child—"

"I'll see she fulfills the promise. I swear that as your brother."

"What—" Abraham almost chuckled. "What kind of insanity has possessed you—?"

"A fear of the insanity that's possessing you."

He knelt beside Abraham's chair; rested one hand on his half-brother's forearm:

"You've our father's blood. He could never tolerate being beaten by anyone or anything. You hate the western country because of what it did to Elizabeth—right or wrong, that's how you feel. So what I'm saying is that you'll never be whole until you *prove* you're stronger than what defeated you. If you don't do it—if you don't try to win back your self-respect—you'll end up in some Boston alley, and your son will despise your memory."

Abraham jumped to his feet. "I still say it's the maddest, most absurd—"

"It is *exactly* what you need!" Gilbert sank the last barb: "Unless, of course, you're willing to admit you're too weak and cowardly to set foot beyond the mountains a second time. *Do* you feel that way? Do you mean to say you couldn't survive?"

"I don't know, goddamn it!"

"Then find out! Look your devil in the face!"

Abraham bit his lip; gestured at the fallen sheets of the letter:

"I—I'd be gone a year. Maybe two—"

"Yes, the expedition could take all of that and more. What of it?"

"It wouldn't be good for me to be away from Jared for so long."

Gilbert had the feeling that Abraham was arguing every question except a central one—which he was being careful to avoid. Uneasy, he contented himself with countering the surface argument:

"You know damned well being close to your son in your present state is next to worthless. I tell you, Abraham, you lost more than your wife in Ohio. Without self-respect, no man can survive."

"Yes, you're right about that, anyway—"

"Gain it back! I know we can arrange it. You served with both officers in charge of the expedition—"

Abraham nodded, a strange, bemused look in his eyes. "And thought well of both, too. Brave men. Good soldiers—"

"I'm certain they'd take you on—"

He'd come to the turning point; he drew a long breath.

"—so certain that I've taken the liberty of writing Captain Lewis a letter." Disconcerted by Abraham's lack of reaction, he rushed on: "Three letters, in fact.

Each a copy of the other, and already dispatched by courier. One went to Pittsburgh, one to Cincinnati, and the third to Louisville—*blast it, why are you smirking?"*

The bemused expression grew into a smile:

"Because your grand intentions and your efficiency will come to nothing."

"Even though Lewis is on the move, I'm sure one of the letters will reach him."

"That's not the point. I didn't particularly want to burden you with my personal problems—"

He reached for the decanter and glass. Spine crawling with inexplicable fear, Gilbert didn't protest.

"—but the truth is, you've trapped yourself. You've discharged me. Ordered me out of the house—to go back on those decisions would be difficult for a man of your principles. But I know Captain Lewis won't accept me. I fail to measure up to all of his lofty specifications."

"What the hell do you mean?"

Glass and decanter held in one hand, Abraham showed Gilbert the other. The small, raw sore Gilbert had noticed before gleamed in the lamplight.

"During my various jaunts around town in search of a bit of amusement—"

Not amusement. Punishment, Gilbert thought.

"—I've spent time with certain women—" He wriggled his hand. "Surely you understand. I am not in the excellent health Captain Lewis demands. Even lying wouldn't conceal the evidence for long."

Gilbert started to turn away.

"Look at the sore, damn you!"

Slowly, Gilbert swung around again. Abraham's hand held steady a moment, then dropped to his breeches.

"I've worse ones here. I've caught the pox."

"Oh my God."

The house shook with deafening thunder. Lightning lit Abraham's face, and Philip's on the canvas.

Gilbert sank down in the desk chair. He rested his elbows on the litter of papers and held his head.

Face locking into that odd smile again, Abraham said, "You're a remarkable fellow, Gilbert. How old are you?"

"What does that matter, for Christ's sake?"

"Just answer You're twenty, aren't you?"

"That's right."

"I marvel at your understanding of people. I suppose it was a necessity, eh? When our father died, someone had to take over the business and operate it successfully, else it would fail—and you're not the sort to accept failure readily, just as he wasn't. You've learned a great deal more than I did by age twenty—everything from accounting to dealing with press room helpers with bad tempers and worse morals. Well, I'm sorry none of your skills will avail this time, but they won't. I believe I'd better go upstairs. I expect you'll be wanting me out of the house immediately. Harriet wouldn't tolerate a man carrying the pox—"

Gilbert had grown light-headed. He sat watching his half-brother between the hands pressed to his temples. Abraham continued trying to make light of the situation, showing Gilbert the decanter and glass:

"I'll take these along if you don't mind. I'll pack up quickly—I wouldn't force you to compromise yourself by having to renege on the discharge, either. I—I do thank you for your good intentions." The last few words were barely audible.

"We'll consult a physician—" Gilbert began.

"You know the pox can't be cured, only abated for a few months or a few years."

Gilbert rose abruptly. "I won't let you leave."

"You have no choice. I'm going up to get Jared."

"You're not going to take *him?"*

Abraham's smile disappeared in an instant. "Of course I am. I wouldn't under any circumstances leave him with a woman who hates him the way Harriet does. That would be worse for Jared than living with a father who has the pox, don't you agree?"

"No, I don't. I won't permit—"

"You've nothing to say about it, Gilbert."

Weaving a little, Abraham jerked the library doors open. The ringing in Gilbert's ears—his feeling of being disconnected from reality—intensified in that awful instant when Abraham swore and stepped back from the listener outside.

The glass and decanter slipped from his slack fingers, shattering. The splattering rum stained the hem of the maternity gown of lavender lawn.

"Well," Abraham said, and again, "Well. I can keep secrets from no one, it seems."

Suddenly his face grew ugly. Harriet let out a small, startled cry as he thrust the sore-marked hand toward her face:

"You've snooped and heard about it, my dear. Now you can see the evidence for yourself."

For a moment Gilbert thought Harriet would faint away into the dangerous litter of glass. She clutched her immense belly, looking very nearly as pale and stricken as Gilbert himself. He stumbled away from the desk to intercede before things worsened—

Abraham acted first, shoving Harriet aside, not gently:

"I'm going to fetch my son. You'd be wise to stay out of my way."

CHAPTER VI

Blood

ABRAHAM STARTED FOR the foot of the staircase.

Shadows clotted in the hall. The one lamp burning there had been extinguished by the gusting wind that came with the storm, slamming doors all through the house. The almost constant flickering of lightning cast a bluish tinge over furnishings and faces.

On the second floor, another door closed, loud as a pistol shot. A nimbus of yellow seemed to float across the landing. One of the maids, invisible behind the bobbing ball of light; the maid was bound for Jared's room, Gilbert suspected. Frightened of the storm, the boy cried out as Abraham climbed the first half dozen steps.

Hampered by her swollen belly, Harriet lurched after him. Hands on the railing, she dragged herself up two steps, then two more. She looked behind her:

"Gilbert—?"

"Harriet, come down!" he shouted, knowing somehow that the situation was careening toward an ugly conclusion.

Lightning glowed. Harriet's cheeks looked sweaty as she hung on the rail at the fifth riser, trying to locate her husband in the gloom of the lower hall. The wind played with distant doors, *crash* and *crash*. In Gilbert's old room, Jared's incoherent voice grew strident.

"Help me, Gilbert!" Harriet cried. "You can't let that filthy creature touch the child—"

Four steps above, Abraham spun around.

A drunken feeling overwhelmed Gilbert as he staggered around the shards of glass and the spilled rum. His pulse raced. His head buzzed. It was as if he had taken some unfamiliar drug that had coursed through his bloodstream in seconds, affecting his mind—

In the next burst of lightning, he saw Abraham's wrathful face:

"Such concern!" Abraham jumped down two steps, to tower over Harriet. "Such sudden and unexpected concern for a boy you've treated like scum. You'll pardon me if I don't believe your little turnabout."

Harriet cringed away. "You depraved, bestial—"

"You're contemptible!" Abraham roared. "You pretend to protect Jared so you can revenge yourself on me! The worst dock whore has better morals than you, woman!"

At the foot of the stairs, Gilbert clenched his hands. The wild, dizzy feeling increased. Frustration and fear edged his voice:

"I don't care for your language, Abraham. This is Harriet's house, and if she wants you to keep away from the boy—"

"The boy is my *son!*"

Abraham whirled and started upward again. Harriet let go of the railing, groped toward him, managed to catch one of his boots:

"I won't let your diseased hands touch—"

Abraham twisted, kicking out the leg Harriet clutched. Gilbert leaped forward, trying to catch her even as he realized he was in the wrong position. Harriet sagged, tumbled down the stairs, struck his legs and sprawled. She shrieked.

Then, panting, she still managed to wrench her head

around, seeking Abraham, blue-limned a few steps above:

"You—seem to have—a skill—for harming—women with unborn children—"

"God *damn* you!" Abraham howled, rushing down at her. He shoved Gilbert aside, bent and lashed her cheek with the back of his hand.

Gilbert heard the sickening thump as her head hit a riser. She arched her spine, dug fingers into the lavender fabric of her gown. She slid to the hall floor and lay there, eyes closed as she hugged her heaving belly.

Abraham's mouth dropped open, as if he himself were stunned by what he'd done. He stumbled down one step, one more. Incoherent emotion destroyed Gilbert's reason. He *knew* Abraham was going to strike her again—

He spun and ran.

In the front sitting room, lightning guided him to the mantel. He jerked the French sword from its pegs. He never recalled returning to the hall, was only peripherally aware of colliding with a woman. A face distorted by fright swam in lamplight as he passed in a rush—

Abraham crouched by Harriet, the sore-marked hand moving toward cheeks that glistened with perspiration. Harriet moaned, struggled to roll out of his reach. Gilbert raised the sword:

"Get away from her!"

"Gilbert, I'm sorry I—"

"You'd better do as I say!"

"Don't be a damned fool. Put that sword down. Give me a hand with her—"

"Don't touch her!" Gilbert cried. Lightning lit the sword as it slashed down, cutting edge foremost.

The maid with the lamp uttered a cry of alarm. Abraham tried to scramble out of the way, banged against the wall of the staircase, wrenched his head aside—

The blade hacked his left cheek, glanced off.

Abraham swore, jerking his head back and cracking it on the wall. He shot a hand out, clamped Gilbert's sword arm in a tight grip. The sword fell with a clatter.

The left side of his face streaming blood, Abraham pushed Gilbert hard. Gilbert nearly fell over the maid, who was kneeling beside Harriet.

The hall seemed to tilt as Gilbert skidded, windmilling his arms to regain his balance. His mind cried his anguish:

What has happened in this house? WHAT HAVE I DONE?

Unreasoning terror had driven him to attack—he, Gilbert Kent, who had never used a weapon in his life. The kneeling maid pressed her hand to Harriet's stomach. Ashen, she turned to search the hall's darkness:

"Mr. Gilbert? I think—I think the child is coming."

Gilbert lunged to the dining room door. "Esther? *Esther—!*"

A faint voice replied from the rear of the house:

"Yes, sir, what is it? I'm coming—"

"Run for Dr. Selkirk—*run!*"

"Yes, sir, at once—"

Someone slipped past him. The front door banged.

Gilbert wiped sweat from his eyes. Took one shaky step toward Harriet's convulsing body.

"Let's move her to the sitting room—"

"I think we'd best not move her at all," the maid said.

Slowly, Gilbert raised his head. His eyes sought his half-brother on the stairway. The maid had set her lamp on the floor. Abraham was visible at the edge of the circle of light, his bearded cheek bloody and one hand as well: he'd touched the deep cut.

That same hand left wet red marks on the wall as he braced himself then started upstairs.

Gilbert shouted his name.

Abraham turned. "I didn't mean to hurt—"

"Get out."

"Gilbert—"

"Leave this house. I've never harmed a living creature in my life, but if you don't go I'll pick up that sword and do my best to kill you."

Abraham started to answer. His dark eyes welled with a grief Gilbert perceived only dimly, and responded to not at all.

Thunder muttered. Lightning flickered. A second lamp was placed beside the first; another servant had come to help.

Gilbert couldn't bear to look at his wife more than a moment. His mind bore an image of white hands pressing against the great lump of her stomach—

Abraham's beard glistened with little drops of blood. He bobbed his head suddenly, left a red handprint on the railing as he resumed his climb to the second floor. On the landing, the ball of lamplight shone again. The unseen maid had rushed back from Jared's room.

"Leave *now!*" Gilbert demanded.

"I want my son."

He kept on, dragging himself almost as Harriet had, his reddened fingers smearing the railing. Gilbert darted for the fallen sword.

Bent over, he checked; straightened; glimpsed a pale oval at the top of the stairs; recognized Jared's face lit by the serving girl's lamp.

Abraham kept climbing toward the boy, his bloodied hand outstretched:

"Jared, come to me. We've leaving—"

Two steps below the landing, he closed his hand on the boy's gray ankle-length nightshirt. Suddenly Jared seemed to comprehend the meaning of the great red stains on the staircase wall and railing. He jerked back, cowering against the maid's skirt.

His sudden movement startled Abraham. He let go of the boy's garment. He and his son both looked down at the same time.

Jared's nightshirt was sticky with blood.

The boy flung his arms around the maid's legs, closed his eyes and screamed.

Abraham shouted at the boy—what, Gilbert couldn't hear above the thunder and Harriet's sudden wail and Jared's too. Again Abraham tried to touch his son. The boy literally flung himself away into the darkness. His shrieking rose and rose, a mindless keen—

Abraham's red-slimed hand was still stretched out toward the vanished boy. Dully, he blinked at it. A peculiar guttural noise tore out of his throat. He peered into the gloom of the landing:

"Jared—?"

In a hushed voice, the maid with the lamp said, *"For pity's sake, sir! Leave the poor child alone!"*

A last, low-pitched mutter of thunder died across the night sky. Gilbert leaned weakly against the pillar at the foot of the staircase. Abraham's hand fell to his side, staining his breeches. His shoulders slumped. He turned and came down the stairs, one slow step at a time.

Gilbert's head snapped up, his dark eyes venomous. But they found no venom in Abraham's as the latter went by; only dull horror and shame—

Gilbert pivoted slowly, his malevolent stare following his half-brother. Abraham reached the front door. Opened it, leaving a last bloodstain. He stumbled down the steps in the pouring rain, lit in bluish silhouette for a heartbeat's time—

The lightning faded and he was lost from view.

ii

Slumped in the chair beside his desk, Gilbert heard the library doors open.

On Beacon Street, the first glow of dawn reflected from wet cobblestones. He smelled his own sour sweat. Glanced up to see portly Doctor Selkirk rolling down his sleeves.

"There seems to be no injury to your wife, Mr. Kent."

Gilbert pushed up from the desk. It was an effort to speak calmly:

"Is she resting?"

"Quite comfortably. It wasn't an easy delivery, but I'm happy to say it was a successful one."

Gilbert almost wept. "The baby is—?"

"Alive. Alive and nicely swaddled by two of your household women." Selkirk, a middle-aged man with a lined face, covered a yawn. "The child is slightly underweight, as frequently happens in terms which are prematurely completed. Other than that, there are no problems. You may congratulate yourself on having fathered a splendid daughter."

Weak, Gilbert sank into the chair. "God, that's good news. Thank you, doctor."

Selkirk drew on his coat. "I'll catch a bit of sleep, then come back. Meantime, I suggest you have that gruesome mess in the hallway cleaned up. While it's none of my affair, I'm curious as to who bled so badly."

Gilbert's mouth had a dry, metallic taste. Sleepless for the entire night, he felt a hundred years old as he answered:

"I'd prefer not to discuss it."

Selkirk shrugged. "As you wish." He turned, ready to leave.

"Doctor—"

"Yes?"

"Did you look at the boy?"

"I did. He was talking—or, to be more precise, raving. About someone being hurt."

"You mean bloodied?"

"He didn't use the word. That was my inference, however."

"Did he—did he speak of his father?"

"As I indicated, *speak* is hardly the correct term. Surely you heard his outcries—?" Gilbert nodded. "I had trouble making sense out of them. Sometimes the boy seemed to be referring to a man who was hurt. At other times, unless I misheard, it was a woman. He was asking one or both to get up."

"Did he mention my wife's name?"

"No. He used the word mother once. I know his mother's dead—did the boy ever see her injured?"

Hoarsely, Gilbert said, "Yes."

"Obviously it left him disturbed. Whatever happened here tonight exacerbated the situation, I suspect. I dosed the boy with an opiate tincture. He's sleeping now. May I take the liberty of asking the whereabouts of his father?"

"I don't know his whereabouts."

"I gather he's not in the house—"

"That's correct."

"Will he be returning?"

"Not if I have any say." Concern for Abraham had disappeared in that moment when Abraham sent Harriet tumbling to the bottom of the stairs.

Outside, a produce cart clattered by. The two countrymen riding the cart were arguing about how much to charge for their cabbages at the day's market. Dr. Selkirk arranged his lacy stock, rolled his tongue inside his lower lip, then overcame his hesitancy:

"If I may make another comment, Mr. Kent—"

Gilbert looked at him.

"It is my conclusion that the boy—Jared is his name?"

"Yes, Jared."

"While I don't know all the circumstances behind his emotional condition, his behavior is far from normal. I believe he needs very careful attention. Affection. A feeling of security to overcome his fears. A new baby in the household will be taxing for you and your wife. It might be advisable to have his father look after him—"

"I'll see to Jared's care, doctor."

"But—"

"Thank you, doctor. Good day."

Looking baffled, Selkirk retired, closing the library doors. Gilbert laid his arms on the desk and rested his head for perhaps five minutes.

Then, by an act of will, he raised his head. His eyes accidentally touched the painting of Philip Kent.

Gilbert wished that he had as much courage and strength as that face suggested. Last night he had discovered a capability for blind rage and violence he had never suspected he possessed. The discovery—and the entire night—had been shattering. Abraham fled; Jared terrified and drugged to sleep; his wife delivered of the baby too soon—

He was deeply ashamed of his failure to cope with all that had happened. Ashamed too of his role in precipitating some of it—

A new thought popped into his mind. What would they call the child?

He was too weary to think about it. He slumped at

the desk while the dawn brightened the ceiling and suffused the face of his father with light.

Philip couldn't help him. He was the one who would have to deal with all the problems sure to arise from the tragic events that had taken place in the house.

But his confidence had been shaken. He wasn't sure he could.

iii

On a steamy morning in the first week of August, Gilbert Kent—more haggard of late than his employees had ever seen him—looked up from some copy he was editing. The story dealt with progress in the construction of Boston's first Roman Catholic church, due to be completed and dedicated in September.

The reporter, Phineas Morecam, stood at the open door.

"Yes, Mr. Morecam? Any news?"

"No, sir, it's the same as the last five days in a row. The boys we hired spent all night combing the docks. The whole blasted city, in fact, from Roxbury to the North End. There's no sign of Mr. Abraham."

"Damn!" Gilbert tossed his quill aside. "How difficult is it to locate one man? Especially a man clearly marked by a wound on his left cheek?"

Morecam looked gloomy. "There are plenty of fellows who carry scars, sir. I hear that complaint from the boys practically every morning."

"But how many of those men will answer to the name Kent?"

"I know, sir—it should be easy. But it's not proving so. Maybe he's not giving his proper name."

"Has anyone seen him? His friends—?"

"Not since last week. Perhaps he's left Boston."

"You said that yesterday! *And* the day before!"

"Because it's a possibility, sir. He could be in some village miles from here—"

"The boys aren't doing the job. Hire men with horses. A dozen—two dozen if you need them. Have the men check every printer in the state! Printing's the only trade Abraham knows, and he's got to make a living somehow—I want him found!"

Morecam nodded unhappily, started out. Then he turned back to ask an obligatory question:

"How is Mrs. Kent faring?"

"She's recuperating splendidly, I'm happy to say."

"And your daughter?"

"Amanda is starting to gain weight thanks to the wet nurse we engaged. I believe both she and her mother have come through unscathed."

"That's wonderful. Does—does Mr. Abraham's son know his father has vanished?"

Gilbert nodded. "His reactions are strange. He acts neither happy nor sad. It's as if he's locked his feelings deep inside—"

And he's not the only one who has done that, Gilbert thought with a profound sense of guilt.

"Plagued odd, the whole business," Morecam said. "I should imagine it's disappointing, too, since you took such an interest in Mr. Abraham's welfare. Have you had a reply from Captain Lewis?"

"It's much too soon."

"Yes, I suppose." Morecam scratched his chin. "Do you have any idea why Mr. Abraham ran off?"

"None," Gilbert lied, turning away from the reporter. Surely his face was betraying him. His soul felt heavy as stone.

"Well, I'll see to hiring some men at once."

"Thank you, Mr. Morecam."

The reporter's footsteps faded, blending into the rhythmic *crumph-crumph* of the presses down on the first floor.

Gilbert stared out the grimy window, reflecting that there was but one source of joy left in the whole world: the tiny, gnarled and wondrously red face of the gnome-child that would, with luck, grow into girlhood and womanhood someday. He looked at Amanda often when he was at home. Suckled and cooing in her blankets, she was an astonishing creature. He held her with extreme care whenever he picked her up. His feelings at such times were as close as he'd ever come to a religious experience.

He already loved the child with a devotion that managed to scatter some of its warmth on Harriet. He was solicitous about her comfort. Never angry when she asked him—scathingly—about Abraham, usually coupling her inquiry with a declaration that she hoped he stayed away forever.

Gilbert was beginning to feel Abraham might do just that. Dear God, how many scars were left from that one night in July—!

He had seen a beast let loose within himself and had still not recovered from the experience. Very likely he never would, completely. In a peculiar way, his own violent outburst had drawn him closer to his vanished half-brother. They were more alike than he had ever suspected.

As as result, his new desire to find Abraham had become a fixation—even though Gilbert had no idea what he would do if his brother suddenly turned up.

Would he welcome Abraham back to the family? Harriet would resist—and the harm to Jared might make such an action doubly unacceptable. Gilbert didn't understand exactly what Jared felt about the events of that night—he refused to discuss them—but there was no question the boy's mental state had been affected. Perhaps permanently.

Why, then, did Gilbert pursue the search for Abraham? He had admitted the answer days ago.

Guilt.

The guilt was a constant, almost unendurable burden. And he couldn't share it with another human being; certainly not with his wife.

Like his own suddenly discovered capability for violence, Gilbert's guilt added a new perspective to his understanding of Abraham's actions after his return to Boston. He was able to see his half-brother's erratic behavior in a different, more compassionate light; was able to comprehend, and not just intellectually, how Abraham must have felt when Elizabeth died—

Staring through the fly-specked windows at slate roofs and church spires, Gilbert saw Abraham's eyes as they were a moment before he rushed into the rain that fateful evening.

Accurately or not, his memory told him Abraham's eyes had been filled with tears.

"Find him," Gilbert murmured to the yellow haze in the August sky. *"Find him—!"*

iv

But every man and boy hired by Gilbert Kent ultimately failed in that assignment. By late September, he reluctantly concluded that Abraham had either left Massachusetts or—the possibility could not be escaped—done away with himself.

That only heightened Gilbert's sadness on the mellow afternoon when a special messenger brought a letter posted three weeks before, at the city by the falls of the Ohio.

From Louisville, where he had stopped with a river pilot, ten recruits and a Newfoundland dog christened Scannon, Captain Meriwether Lewis wrote to say that he and Captain William Clark would welcome former Cornet of Dragoons Abraham Kent into the Corps of Discovery that would start up the Missouri River the following spring. The letter was still in Gilbert's pocket as he walked slowly up the incline of Beacon Street in the late afternoon.

He had left Kent and Son early, unable to concentrate on his work. He'd roamed streets he couldn't remember, attempting to do the impossible—forget.

From the Common rang the cries of a band of small boys rolling hoops. Leaves streamed down from the trees under whose boughs his father had strolled while courting his first wife. The recurring cough brought Gilbert to a halt suddenly, a lace kerchief at his lips.

In a moment the spasm passed. He put the kerchief away and walked on.

The light had leached from the sky, leaving little more than a ribbon of bright amber beneath clouds lowering in the west. Gilbert drew Captain Lewis' letter from his coat. How pointless to carry it about, he thought. Harriet, occupied with baby Amanda, wouldn't be interested. A corner of the letter snapped in the autumn breeze as he remarked mentally that Abraham had certainly been right in one judgment:

Harriet's concern for Jared had only been pretense; a gambit to employ against Abraham in order to hurt him. Since Abraham's disappearance, she had barely spoken to the boy. Only from Gilbert did he ever hear a cordial word.

But it was to Jared's father that Gilbert's thoughts returned as he slowly ripped the letter into long strips, then tore each strip into smaller squares, finally letting the whole catch the wind and rise upward, blown and scattered in the fading amber light. The figures of the boys with their hoops were growing indistinct. Shadows covered the Common. Objectively, with no sense of superiority, he said to himself:

I have never been strong and never shall be. But poor Abraham—in many ways he was weaker than I. Well, all vessels have different flaws—as I have discovered.

But I am the only one left to help Jared survive.

That responsibility bore heavily on him as he resumed his slow progress up Beacon.

How different things might have been if Abraham hadn't caught some whore's pox. Perhaps the journey with Captains Lewis and Clark would have restored his faith in himself and his abilities—

Ah, but speculating on that was profitless. The chance was gone, just as the pieces of letter were gone in the clouds of dead leaves and debris whirled away by the twilight wind.

A servant girl from a house near Gilbert's went by. She carried a hamper of vegetables and a firkin of country butter. In response to her deferential greeting, Gilbert forced himself to touch the rolled brim of his beaver hat. A tall, emaciated figure in the dusk—an eighty-year-old clerk in a boy's body, wasn't that how Abraham had phrased it?—he gazed toward the lamplit windows of his own elegant home.

I must see that Jared does not merely survive, but grows into a sound, whole man—free of Abraham's legacy of failure and self-hate—

He had no illusions that it would be easy. Jared did carry the Fletcher blood. He lived in a household dominated by a woman who deemed him worthless, despised his very existence and seized every opportunity to show her feelings. As to the damage to Jared's young mind that dreadful night, who could say whether it would prove—as Gilbert often feared—irreparable?

Still, calmed by the beauty of the radiant light in the western sky, he knew he would try his best. One kind of blood—family blood; the blood of caring and compassion—must wash out the lingering traces of other, uglier blood that had marked the walls of the Kent house.

Was it possible? Though he vowed to try, it didn't seem so—

Then he thought of his father.

Gilbert stopped again, transfixed by the last golden sunshine under the darkening clouds above the Charles River. His eyes reflected the light like coins. From boyhood he recalled fragments of long conversations with Philip.

What was America if not the eternal promise of beginning again? Philip Kent had sensed that promise long before he first stepped on shore.

True, in his later years, he had rejected Jefferson's visions of an expanding nation. But to Gilbert that rejection was superficial, overridden by a deep and abiding kinship with Philip's most basic convictions. He and his father might differ on geography but they'd never had any fundamental differences about the promise of the land. They believed passionately in the enduring hope of change, renewal, rebirth that America's free air made possible—

His upturned face caught the last glimmers of the sunset. He felt a moment of almost supernatural closeness to his father. It was as if Philip stood near him in the shadows of evening, a presence at the edge of his vision, a powerful force that diminished his pain and strengthened his courage—

Unwilling to break the moment, Gilbert remained motionless, causing whispered comments from pedestrians hurrying by. Finally he roused himself, shivering in the sudden bite of the sunless wind. The aroma of wood smoke from chimneys enticed him homeward—with a quicker step now.

He would exchange trivial pleasantries with Harriet at dinner; rock and coo at baby Amanda for a few minutes afterward; and then he would speak with Jared. He would begin the long, hazardous and difficult job of raising Abraham Kent's son to manhood.

On his front stoop, Gilbert Kent paused one final time to stare into the western heavens, all clouds of ebony. His shoulders lifted, as if in anticipation of a struggle.

He turned and entered his house.

Book Three

Voices of War

CHAPTER I

Jared

IN THE GLOOM of the vast building, the boy's breath plumed as he pointed to the plank-covered pits:

"Ten blocks of your best pond ice, Mr. Dawlish. Delivered to the house by six o'clock tonight. Six o'clock sharp. The poultry's due to arrive from the country by half past."

He extended a handful of coins. The ice house owner didn't take them:

"Anyone notice you two coming in here?"

The boy bristled. "Is that important? Money's money."

"Sometimes. Kent money ain't the most popular in Boston these days."

The slim but sturdy-looking boy stuffed the coins in his pocket and seized the hand of the little girl beside him.

Though only eight years old, in her cape and bonnet of purple velvet she resembled a miniature woman—as was intended. She had her mother's pale skin, brilliant dark eyes and hair. But her mouth was more generous, her expression more cheerful—never marred by the sourness the boy associated with Uncle Gilbert's wife, the girl's mother.

"Come, Amanda," the boy said. "Someone else will sell us ice."

Dawlish snatched the boy's forearm. "I'll deliver the order! Just do me a favor. Leave by the rear door."

Disgust showed on Jared Kent's rather sharp-featured face. He slapped the coins into Dawlish's hand and ushered Amanda toward the indicated door, walking with long, swift strides. Like his cousin, he was superbly and expensively dressed: nankeen trousers; a fine linen shirt with a frothy neckerchief; a vest cut straight across the bottom. Jared's uncle didn't insist he wear a striped vest, the symbol of Democratic-Republican sympathies. Gilbert Kent frequently appeared in such a vest, though—scandalizing most of his Boston peers.

From beneath Jared's vest hung a fob, without which no gentleman, whatever his age, was well dressed. Jared lacked a watch to attach to the hidden end of the fob, but that didn't matter—only the fob's display counted.

He'd received the fob from his uncle the preceding Christmas. The obverse of the medal at the bottom of the broad green ribbon had been struck in the pattern of the tea-bottle symbol. There was also a Latin inscription:

Cape locum et fac vestigium.

The reverse bore the words Kent and Son, and the year. Jared liked wearing the fob as much as he hated wearing his tight-fitting jacket with its ridiculous short tails, a perfect duplicate of the adult male style.

As the cousins stepped into the surprisingly warm sunshine of a Saturday in early December, 1811, the varnish on the leather brim of Jared's cap glittered with highlights. He pointed suddenly:

"'Ware the cat."

Amanda hiked up her skirts and hopped over the dead animal rotting in the alley's drainage channel.

"Jared."

"Mm?"

"Why didn't that man want papa's money?"

Head tilted back, the boy was eyeing the slope of the roof at the rear of the ice house. Then he turned his attention to a pile of empty crates at the end of the building. His tawny hair, worn three inches long in the current youthful fashion, shone in the sun. His sky-blue eyes darted from the crates back to the roof. Finally he answered the question:

"Because Uncle Gilbert is about the only rich man in Boston who believes we should go to war, I guess."

Amanda covered her mouth. "Mama would take the birch rod to you if she heard what you just said."

"You're being silly. Tradespeople say 'I guess' all the time."

"But it's vulgar!"

With a grin, Jared leaned down, whispered:

"Shirt."

"Oh, don't!"

"Corset!"

"You *mustn't* say those words aloud!"

He laughed. "Going to report me to Aunt Harriet?"

The small, lovely girl shook her head in a serious way:

"No, you get enough punishment on your own. I hate it when she takes the rod to you."

"At the slightest pretext!" He started for the crates.

"It's no wonder. You're not polite to her."

"Amanda, she despises me. I'm sorry to say that about your mother, but it's true. Politeness has nothing to do with the thrashings—which I'm not going to allow much longer, I'll tell you. After all, I'm thirteen years old."

Stunned by the declaration, Amanda stood stock still. Jared strode straight on to the crates and climbed on the lowest one.

"Where are you going, Jared?"

He pointed. "Up to Mr. Dawlish's roof peak. There should be a splendid view of the harbor."

Holding her bonnet, Ananda looked upward. "It's too steep!"

Jared shrugged. "For you. Wait there."

"No! I want to come with you."

Jared glanced both ways along the alley. He heard a dray rumbling in the street that crossed one end of the narrow passage behind the ice house. But he saw no people. He crouched down on the crate, extended his hand, smiled a dazzling smile:

"All right. Take hold."

Amanda was lithe and strong. In spite of her skirt she climbed the swaying pile of crates with little difficulty. Jared pulled himself up past the gutter, flung a knee onto the roof. A moment later he helped her up. He braced himself on the shingles, let her crawl ahead of him toward the peak. He saw her as a silhouette against the clear December sky.

Up here the wind tugged and gusted. Jared's cap blew off, skittered out of sight down in the alley. He paid no attention, amused at Amanda's panted complaint:

"If I dirty this cape mama will thrash me too. *Why* do you always have to do whatever comes into your head, Jared? If you'd just stop and think first—"

"That would spoil all the fun." His smile turned faintly bitter. "I only do what your mother expects of me—"

"Don't be unkind again—!"

"I'm not. It's a fact."

Clinging to the shingles, she breathed hard. "But you know what gets you into trouble. And you go right ahead! You always have to see sights from a roof, or—or dash off to the next corner to look at what's beyond—"

"Because—" Jared strained to keep from slipping.

"—because I usually don't like where I am at the moment, and I want to see where else I might go." His eyes hardened. "I don't get caught all that often—"

"That's because—" Looking back at him from the peak, Amanda drew deep breaths. "—you're a boy. It's easy for you to go wherever you please. If I want to, I can't."

"You're on the roof, aren't you?"

"It's too high."

"No one forced you to climb up!"

"Oh yes," she countered with utter seriousness. "You did. I want to do whatever you do, Jared. But sometimes that's very hard for a girl."

"You'd be wiser not to be such a good friend of mine," he said, still working his way upward by means of his knees and his elbows.

They hung over the peak side by side, gazing at a panorama of rooftops and, beyond, the piers of the South End where ships bobbed at anchor. Seaward, the harbor islands stood out with great clarity. The islands broke a horizon line that seemed incredibly distant.

The brisk wind gave Jared's cheeks a stiff, raw feeling. Yet the cold, pure light flooding down exhilarated him; produced a sense of freedom that was all too often lacking in the crowded streets below.

Amanda's assessment of him was entirely correct. He *did* like to gaze on new sights—collect them, you could say. Maybe it was because he was always unhappy in the confinement of Uncle Gilbert's large, comfortable, but somehow unfriendly house on Beacon Street. Jared despised being at home—or in school—anywhere, in fact, that he was supposed to be. He much preferred turning unfamiliar corners, or rattling through the ship yards, or hunting for coins in the muck beneath the piers.

"Oh!"

Amanda's cry jerked him back to reality. One of her tiny gloved hands shot out helplessly. A gust of wind had blown the bonnet from her head—the ties had evidently come unfastened during her climb. He saw the bonnet sailing into the next street.

She stretched both hands toward the vanishing hat. "It's gone!"

"Amanda, don't let go—!"

His warning came too late. She began sliding.

In panic, he grabbed for her elbow, missed. She slid further down the roof.

"Grab the guttering if you go over!"

Thankfully, she did. As he negotiated his way down the shingled incline, scraping his palms and his kneecaps, she hung from the edge of the roof. Then she disappeared. He heard a clatter as she struck the crates and toppled them.

By the time he slid over the gutter, dangled, then dropped, she was picking herself up from the cobbles. Ruefully she examined her cape. Mud and a long rip were her rewards for joining her cousin's little excursion.

She stamped a foot, as if that would somehow make the damage vanish. Her dark eyes filled with tears. Jared retrieved his sodden cap and wadded it in his coat pocket. To conceal his gloom over the little adventure ending badly, he scowled:

"Here, Amanda, it's only a cape. Don't snivel so."

"Do I care a penny for the cape? I'll get the rod and so will you!"

He pulled her against him; comforted her. She was probably right.

Eyes on the ice house door in case Dawlish came charging outside, he knelt. He began to dry her tears with his cuff. He noticed a raw place on the back of his left hand, which he'd scraped sliding down.

Blood oozed, bright scarlet. And the same thing happened that always happened when he chanced to cut himself. At the sight of blood, nausea churned his stomach and welled in his throat. For a seemingly endless moment, he was totally unable to move—

At last he wrenched his hand down, thrust it under his other arm, closed his eyes and applied pressure.

Puzzled, Amanda forgot her own difficulties. "Are you all right?"

"Yes, I—I'm fine."

Slowly he withdrew his hand. Thank God the scrape was superficial The blood no longer oozed. His nausea lessened.

As usual, the reaction mystified and unsettled him. Why should the merest nick of a finger bring on that awful turmoil in his belly? That complete immobility?

Deep within himself, Jared had long ago answered the questions in a way that produced a feeling of utter hopelessness—and a secret conviction that Aunt Harriet was right in all she thought and said about him. He *did* have a quick temper; a wayward nature—and in some manner he couldn't fully comprehend or explain, he was being punished for it. Because he *deserved* punishment—

Jared could find no other way to explain the riddle of his uncontrollable sickness, always of short duration but always paralyzing.

He forced himself to glance to the ice house door. It remained closed. Evidently Mr. Dawlish had retreated to another part of the big building and hadn't heard them clatter off his roof. That was one bit of luck, anyway.

"Are you sure—?" Amanda began.

"I'm perfectly all right. Let's be off."

He closed his bigger hand firmly around hers. The bedraggled cousins started for home, and the inevitable reckoning with Gilbert Kent's wife.

ii

On the way, they passed a knife grinder singing a bit of New England doggerel:

"Our ships all in motion,
"Once whitened the ocean,
"They sailed and returned with a cargo.
"Now doomed to decay,
"They are fallen a-prey
"To Jefferson, worms and embargo—"

Though national and international politics held little interest for Jared, he had a good deal of knowledge about both subjects. His uncle discussed them often at meal time.

Thus he knew the three-year-old song was connected with the troubles currently besetting the United States; troubles that seemed to weigh more and more heavily on Gilbert Kent as one month succeeded another.

Almost alone among rich Bostonians, Uncle Gilbert had supported the former president, Mr. Jefferson of Virginia, just as he now supported Jefferson's chosen heir, President Madison. As a result, the Kent family had lost numerous friends.

Jared didn't understand all the reasons. But he did know that the bitter political feud between his uncle and men of similar position in the community went back at least to the early part of the decade; to what New Englanders termed the foul murder of the Federalist, Hamilton, by the Republican, Colonel Aaron Burr. Actually, as Jared understood it, Hamilton had not been murdered at all. He had died in a theoretically illegal but perfectly fair match with dueling pistols.

Gilbert said contemptuously that because of "fossilized adherence to Federalism," Massachusetts and its neighboring states were becoming an alien island in the republic. He claimed most upper-class Bostonians were hysterics: falsely convinced that New England was being "submerged" by a "Virginia junto" which controlled the government.

Much of the current disagreement between Federalists and Democratic-Republicans had to do with the French conqueror, Bonaparte. Bostonians called him the Antichrist. In an effort to keep America from becoming embroiled in hostilities between the so-called Antichrist and his traditional enemies, the English, Jefferson had bottled up American shipping. Imposed something called the embargo. *Dambargo* was New England's name for it.

The embargo was the only one of Jefferson's policies that Gilbert had reluctantly disavowed. It was disastrous for New England's economy. Her merchants could not trade with England, France or any other foreign country. Her ships stood idle in port, protective barrels capping their masts. The other boys at Jared's academy jeeringly referred to the barrels as "Mr. Madison's teacups"—Madison, then Secretary of State, supported and implemented the president's strategy.

Finally, the embargo was canceled—only to be replaced by the Non-intercourse Act. The Federalists considered it just as noxious as the embargo, since it still prohibited trade with Britain. That it also prohibited trade with France made no difference—France was the enemy, the Federalists shrilled, and why didn't America wake up to that fact?

Meantime, both Britain and France continued to interfere with American shipping. The British were particularly guilty. Their squadrons blockaded the American coast. Their frigates and ships-of-the-line stopped and boarded American vessels at will, supposedly searching for runaway English seamen who preferred to sail under the stars and stripes because American naval discipline was less cruel and capricious. The tensions at sea had all but nullified Jefferson's attempts at neutrality—and had produced an atmosphere in which the word *war* was mentioned more and more frequently.

New England wanted no part of a war with Britain. The rest of the country felt differently. Everywhere but in the northeast, people had cheered the preceding May when they heard the news of an encounter between a United States frigate and a British corvette.

The frigate *President* had mistaken the corvette *Little Belt* for a much larger and more infamous vessel, *Guerriere,* which had a long history of causing trouble for American ships in coastal waters. When *Little Belt* refused to answer *President*'s hail or raise identifying flags, there was a chase, then an exchange of salvos. The engagement ended with nine dead and twenty-three wounded aboard *Little Belt.*

Although the U.S. government offered to settle the resulting claims, many people said *President*'s action was completely justified, considering that three Americans had been killed, eighteen wounded and four alleged British deserters seized when H.M.S. *Leopard* stopped and searched America's *Chesapeake* in international waters in 1807. That four-year-old incident hadn't been forgotten. *President* had settled the score—and if the British wanted more of the same, they could have it! Were, in fact, begging for it. Despite diplomatic attempts to get the British to cancel their Orders in Council—the orders authorizing seizure of seamen on American vessels—the orders still stood.

So now, in 1811, practically all the nation except New England felt Britain should be called to account. Jared had heard Uncle Gilbert say that the settlers in the states and territories of the west were actually demanding war, to stop a rash of new forays by the Indian tribes supposedly taking orders from Canada.

Just a month ago, the activities of the tribes had driven the Americans to action. The prime troublemakers, the Shawnee Tecumseh and his brother the Prophet, who preached a mystical doctrine of Indian supremacy, had been fomenting a union of all the tribes; a union whose purpose was to halt the encroachment of white settlers. As Tecumseh's voice gained more and more listeners around council fires in the north as well as the south, General William Henry Harrison took to the field to stop him. In a stunning defeat, Harrison's small army routed Tecumseh's braves and razed his headquarters, the Shawnee village on Tippecanoe Creek in the Indiana Territory.

But Tecumseh was only at bay, not defeated. The Indian threat could materialize again—particularly since the British had a financial stake in driving the Americans from the fur lands around the Great Lakes and beyond the Mississippi.

Furs remained the west's prime commodity. The expedition of Captains Lewis and Clark had only heightened the fever for exploration and exploitation of the Louisiana Purchase. Near the slopes of a great north-south mountain chain in the far west, Lewis and Clark said, beaver and other fur-bearing animals teemed. Thus America was in a race for control of the territory—

One evidence being the 1808 chartering of the American Fur Company headed by John Jacob Astor.

The German was already something of a national legend. Every boy Jared's age knew his name and his story.

A butcher's son, Astor had been born in a village called Waldorf, not far from the Rhine. He crossed the ocean and landed in America in 1785. His wealth consisted of seven expensive flutes which he hoped to sell at a profit.

The music business lost its appeal, however, as young Astor became interested in the growing fur trade. He made trading trips to the forests of upstate New York, returning with small collections of pelts. That was the beginning. Now he was incredibly wealthy, controlling his fur empire and his real estate holdings from a countinghouse in New York City's Liberty Street.

The Waldorf Astors would undoubtedly have been astonished to see how far their descendant had come in his lifetime, Gilbert said—but he predicted that Astor meant to go even further.

Long a familiar figure at the Montreal fur market, and closely connected with Canadian firms such as the North West Company, Astor knew the trade intimately. Gilbert believed Astor's formation of the American Fur Company was a naked grab for control of the fur business in the Louisiana lands—where the Canadians already operated freely. Gilbert supposed that if Astor's private ambitions were not at odds with the expansion plans of the United States—and on the surface they were not—Jefferson had been wise to throw his influence behind the granting of Astor's charter.

All in all, the reasons for a debate about war were many and tangled. None was considered valid in Boston, however—except in the Kent house. Gilbert steadfastly aligned himself with the American majority, and scoffed at those wealthy men who still talked of the New England states, seceding in order to form a separate country, friendly to England.

As Jared and Amanda neared the familiar streets in the vicinity of the Common, the boy recalled the elaborate dinner being arranged for tomorrow evening. The servants hadn't been told the names of the guests—nor had the cousins. The guests were supposedly arriving by private coach, from another city.

And the meal was scheduled for the unlikely hour of seven in the evening—after dark. Normally, dining began at two in the afternoon.

Could the mysterious preparations and the unidentified visitors have anything to do with all the talk of war?

iii

On Beacon Street, Jared pushed his cousin toward the curb suddenly. A dairyman's wagon went rumbling by, much too fast. Speeding vehicles were just one of the many manifestations of change about which Jared's aunt complained.

Jared supposed he should be grateful that Uncle Gilbert's wife tolerated him as part of her household. But he couldn't find it within himself to feel even a moment's gratitude. Aunt Harriet made it obvious that she'd thoroughly disliked Abraham Kent, who had disappeared and not been seen again since the year of Amanda's birth, 1803.

His aunt also seemed to know a good deal about Jared's mother. The boy had been told she was fair-haired and blue-eyed, as he was. Her maiden name had been Fletcher. Her roots went back to a fiery-tempered Virginia family.

Jared had long since conditioned himself to avoid thinking too much about the parents he'd never known, though that was difficult. Harriet Kent constantly reminded him of their flaws, and their unhappy ends—

Her attitude made the Beacon Street house a hostile

place. But slowly, after much pain and inner turmoil, he had become resigned to that, and to his position in the house. No matter how kindly Uncle Gilbert treated him, he was an outsider; and an undesirable one.

Accordingly, he had come to realize that he would have to make his way alone, always fighting back his doubts about his ability to succeed at anything. His determination, however, only seemed to reinforce Aunt Harriet's feelings about him.

Whatever the source of his independent, even rebellious, nature, one thing was certain. He wasn't too young to indulge it—and much more completely than he had up to the present moment. Many young men ventured into the world at age twelve or thirteen. It might be time he joined their number. He was growing less and less willing to accept Aunt Harriet's criticism and discipline. The only reason he accepted them at all was Uncle Gilbert.

As he walked with Amanda, he pictured his uncle and felt a touch of sadness. Stoop-shouldered and already turning gray, Gilbert Kent was not yet thirty years old. A gentle, thoughtful man, he was burdened with too many worries. Everything from poor health and his complicated business interests to his lonely position as an opponent of men who should have been his friends—

Jared noticed a piece of paper blowing in the street. The type looked familiar. He picked up the paper and saw more evidence of his uncle's unpopularity.

The piece had been torn from the front page of the *Bay State Republican*. At the head of the central news column Jared saw a familiar black-ruled box surrounding four numbers set in a heavy face, in the style of a death notice:

6257

The number was carried on the front page of every issue. More symbolic than accurate, it represented the best available count of American seamen seized by the English navy as runaways from the King's service. The count had begun in the early 1790s, and the number had one objective—to inflame war fervor.

In the case of the person who'd bought this copy of the *Republican,* then ripped it up, it had inflamed something else. The words *Gilbert Kent Editor and Publisher* appeared in small type directly beneath the paper's masthead. Across them, another word had been crudely scrawled.

Turning around and seeing Jared stopped on the curb, Amanda skipped back.

"Is that papa's paper?" she asked, brushing at the dried mud on her cape. She craned her head over. "Someone's scribbled on it—"

"A filthy word." He balled the paper and pocketed it quickly. Amanda was bright; she might understand the meaning of *traitor.*

"You mean a word as wicked as corset or shirt?" She tried to smile. But it was evident that her fear of returning home was undermining her spirits.

"Worse," Jared said. "Forget about it. We'd better decide what we're going to tell Aunt Harriet."

"Tell her?" The girl's eyes rounded. "You mean a lie?"

"Who said anything about lying? We'll just doctor the truth a bit! Now listen carefully. The alley was a mess of mud. I slipped and fell, then you fell trying to help me up. It's partly true, you know. We both tumbled pretty hard. We just won't mention that we started from Mr. Dawlish's roof."

Amanda looked dubious. "It's still fibbing. I never fib to papa or mama."

"Well, this is one time it's necessary! Even if we get

away with the story, we'll probably take four or five whacks apiece, just for dirtying our clothes."

He gnawed his lip. But there was a sly gleam in his eyes:

"However—I won't fib unless you agree to it. So what's it to be? A fib to help me out? Or the truth—to get me in trouble?"

"That isn't fair! You mustn't make me take sides!"

A cloud hid the sun, throwing Jared's face in shadow. It was a handsome face, yet it turned ugly in the brief darkness. Something in him took pleasure in admitting that he did spite Harriet, and spite her well, by playing on the bond of affection between himself and his young cousin, whom he loved without reservation. He did it because it was one of his few means of striking back at his aunt; repaying her for the hurt she inflicted—

Abruptly, shame overwhelmed him. To use Amanda that way wasn't right, and he knew it. He squeezed her glove:

"See here. I wouldn't make you take sides for the world."

The cloud drifted away. So did the wrath on his face.

"Here's what we'll do instead. When we get home, you rush straight up to your room. Change those clothes while I handle the explanations. I'll insist what happened was completely my fault. I teased you so hard, you ran away—that's how you fell. I expect Aunt Harriet will believe it."

Amanda nodded in a grave way. "Yes, she might."

A bit startled, he smiled: "You agree very easily. You must think as little of me as your mama does."

"You know that's not so. But she—oh, I don't know how to say it right. She wants me not to like you."

His fair brows hooked together. "Does she tell you that straight out?"

"No, never. But she—I mustn't."

"Yes—" Jared's voice was flat. "Yes, you must. Go on, Amanda. What does Aunt Harriet tell you?"

"A great many bad things I know aren't true."

"That I'm disrespectful? Won't go to church? Slide through my studies at that wretched academy?"

"Things like that, yes."

Although he'd suspected as much, the confirmation hurt. It took him a moment to continue:

"And what do you say in reply?"

"Mostly I listen. I—I care for you, Jared. So I keep still and pretend I believe her." A hint of tears showed in her eyes again. "I suppose that's a kind of fibbing too. But I can't help it."

He touched her gently. "I never want to be the cause of your deceiving your mother and feeling bad—"

"I don't feel bad. Well—not too much." Her small, grave voice added years to the sound of the simple words. "It's just that—part of me belongs to her, Jared. Part belongs to you, and another part to papa—and you're both ever so much nicer than—well, I mean I try to be good with mama even when she speaks false, wicked things against you. But she makes me afraid. She says she won't love me if I stand up for you. I suppose all mothers act that way—"

He evaded the truth with a smile: "You know I can't speak from experience." A pause. "Does she talk to Uncle Gilbert about me?"

"All the time."

"Never when I'm present, of course."

"That's right, never."

"And—how does he take it?"

"Papa doesn't get mad very often, you know that. But I can tell that everything mama says makes him terribly angry because he puffs out his mouth—" She imitated

Gilbert Kent's pursed lips. "—the way he does when something goes wrong at Kent's and they come to the house to tell him."

Quietly, Jared said, "I didn't realize I'd become such a burden to him."

"You haven't! He loves you just as I do!"

"But if Aunt Harriet's constantly carping about me, that's one more load he must carry—"

The blue eyes chilled. How careless and oblivious he'd been, not to sense that his aunt would actively work against him whenever he was absent—

With a gravity that outdid his cousin's, he said:

"No, I can't have Uncle Gilbert worrying on my account. Here's one more story—and this is the one I'm definitely going to tell." Rapidly, he repeated it for her:

After leaving Dawlish's ice house, he had insisted on climbing the roof. She begged him not to, but he went ahead. He slipped and fell to the alley. When she tried to help, he grew quarrelsome. Grabbed her cape, then pushed her down—

"That's how your clothes got all dirty and torn."

"It's just as much a fib as the other two stories, Jared."

"Yes, but it's the sort of fib your mother will believe without question. No mights, no maybes—"

"Are you trying to make her dislike you all the more?"

"Perhaps I am. Things can't go on as they are. I'm getting too old to stand for Aunt Harriet's punishments without—"

He stopped.

"Without what?"

"Without doing something about them."

"What can you do?"

He was silent a moment. Then, impulsively, he said,

"Take myself away from her. Out of Boston—for good."

"Oh, no, Jared!" She clutched his arm. "I'd be so unhappy without you—you're the only true friend I have."

"But it's time I made my own way."

The thought had already solidified into a conviction. His mind raced at the new possibilities. Perhaps he could apprentice himself to a craftsman in another city. He'd need Uncle Gilbert's permission, though—

A sudden insight told him how to speed the arrival of that permission. Amanda seemed to sense what he was thinking:

"You're being so foolish! You want to take all the blame. You *want* to—!"

He patted her cheek affectionately.

"For eight years old, you're not only a beautiful child but a damned smart one."

"There you go cursing again—!"

"I'm sorry. Come along."

"Jared, you'll make me miserable if you go away—"

"And I'll stay miserable if I don't. If you really care for me, you'll let me do what I must."

Her dark hair shining as brightly as her silent tears, she hung her head and held his hand as they walked on toward the entrance to the Kent house.

iv

The cousins were hardly given a moment's notice by the servants scurrying through the downstairs, arranging furniture, dusting, polishing—preparing for the Sunday evening guests. Disappointingly, there was no sign of Harriet.

Jared and Amanda went up to the third floor, to their respective rooms. Jared's had once belonged to his father. It was small—and made even smaller by his passion for collecting. Over the years he'd turned the room into a miniature museum and library; a junk shop, Harriet preferred to say.

Stacks of glass-fronted cases displayed all sorts of natural specimens: fossils, feathers, butterflies on pins, dried leaves and pressed plants. Tottering piles of books rose halfway to the ceiling, a huge and varied assortment. There were gazetteers and atlases of the country and the world—once, on a map of Ohio, he had marked a heavy charcoal cross on the approximate spot where his mother had met her death, then gazed at it for a quarter of an hour, and finally wept.

He had accumulated works of fiction and collections of essays too, including the very first volume ever published by his grandfather, Thomas Paine's *American Crisis* papers. On the top of one stack was 1809's international literary sensation, Diedrich Knickerbocker's *History of New York*. The pseudonymous author of the tongue-in-cheek narrative of the early days of New Amsterdam was a New Yorker himself, a Mr. Washington Irving. After hearing of Mr. Irving's manuscript, Gilbert had taken his private coach non-stop to Irving's home in an attempt to secure American rights to the work. To his annoyance, he had been outbid by another publisher.

But Kent's had scored a march the following year, successfully negotiating a contract to print an American edition of a rousing adventure tale, *Scottish Chiefs*, written by a woman named Porter. The book had done extremely well, salving Gilbert's disappointment at failing to land Washington Irving as a house author. *Scottish Chiefs* lay open on the bed; Jared was reading it for the third time.

He kindled a fire in the grate. As he finished, he heard Amanda's step in the hall. He peeked out to see her going down the back stairs, probably to the jakes at the rear of the second floor. She had already changed clothes.

He flung off his muddied coat, warmed his hands at the flames, re-examining his conviction that he must leave the house, and soon. He found no flaws in the idea —except one.

Where would he go?

Unbidden, thoughts of his father came, stirring a deep anguish. He knew so very little about Abraham Kent: that he'd served in the army under Mad Anthony Wayne; that he'd spent a few years in Ohio as a farmer; that he'd brought his son back to Boston after marauding Indians killed his wife. Gilbert hinted that a quarrel with Philip Kent had driven Abraham out of the household the first time—and that a second quarrel with Gilbert himself had been responsible for Abraham's abrupt departure in 1803.

Jared's uncle refused to be explicit about details, but Harriet's invective made up for that. The boy's mental portrait of his father showed him a man who had been a failure. His image of his strong-willed mother was similar. Harriet made it clear she saw no hope for their son —and events often seemed to confirm that to Jared.

More often than not, his impulsiveness landed him in trouble. The little adventure on Dawlish's roof, for instance; Amanda could have been seriously hurt—

Perhaps he was destined to fail at everything he tried —and to be carried to that failure by his own temperament. The queer sickness he suffered at the sight of blood came to mind again. If there wasn't something wrong with him, why was he cursed with such an affliction?

Absorbed in the melancholy thoughts he was somehow unable to banish, he started at the sound of a voice:

"I was informed you had returned, Jared."

He turned. His aunt stood in the doorway, the birch rod in one hand.

"Good evening, Aunt Harriet," he said politely. "I didn't hear you come in."

"The door was not quite closed."

She proceeded to close it. His heart leaped when she spied his mud-fouled coat lying in a corner. He was let down when the coat failed to keep her attention:

"You ordered the ice?"

Jared studied his aunt a moment. In a way, she was a beauty. Stunningly dark-haired, dark-eyed. But her face lacked the wholesomeness and good humor of Amanda's. On occasion it was a pinched, mean face—and this was one of the occasions:

"I asked you a question. Did you order the ice?"

"Ten blocks, Aunt Harriet. I did exactly as you instructed."

"How unusual."

He glanced pointedly at the stained coat.

"While you were gone," she said, "Mr. Tewkes paid a call."

He almost crowed with a perverse delight. From a totally unexpected quarter, here was an issue that would serve as well or better than the roof-climbing incident. Silas Tewkes kept a young man's academy in the North End. There, for a handsome fee from every pupil, the fussy old fellow taught Latin, sums and bits of natural science, history, philosophy and theology. Only the sons of wealthy citizens were welcome as pupils at the private school.

"Mr. Tewkes!" Jared repeated, rubbing his hands together in front of the fire. "That's a surprise."

"Don't act so cool and innocent! It's not a surprise at all—you surely know the reason."

"I suspect it."

"Well, it's going to earn you the rod."

Vastly pleased, Jared said nothing.

"Jared, it will be less difficult if you admit—"

"That I didn't appear for classes Tuesday or Wednesday? Of course I admit it. There was still a little ice on the Charles. I went fishing. Tewkes is a dull old fart."

He was delighted at Aunt Harriet's horrified gasp.

"You have a filthy mouth, Jared."

"I beg your forgiveness."

"Don't mock me!"

"Aunt Harriet, I'm sorry if I—if—" He could hardly keep from chortling.

"You dare to laugh! Silas Tewkes is a respected citizen and teacher! You've tried him sorely—when you've bothered to attend classes. And you've been absent repeatedly during the past several weeks, I discovered. He is thinking of dismissing you from the academy."

With a grand shrug, Jared said, "That's a bluff. Tewkes huffs and puffs, but he'll teach me till I'm a hundred if Uncle Gilbert keeps paying."

Harriet Kent tapped the rod against her skirt. "I have yet to report the visit to my husband—"

Smiling to soften his answer, he said, "I wouldn't do it. Uncle Gilbert seems in quite a state over these unknown visitors coming tomorrow. Who are they, by the way?"

"That is none of your concern. I find your defiant attitude intolerable—though not unfamiliar. You're just like your parents."

Here was an old, familiar weapon of attack; one that angered him as no other did:

"With all due respect, Aunt Harriet—don't bring them into this."

"You won't dictate to me what I will or will not discuss!"

"In this one area, yes, I will. For years I've listened to your slurs—"

"I only tell the truth!" she burst out. "Your father was a weak man. Unwilling to accept the standards of respectable behavior. That destroyed him, you know."

Jared's eyes burned. "The damned—"

"Stop that foul-mouthed talk!"

"—barbarous west everyone prattles about so glowingly—*that* destroyed him. Life out there is too hard for some people—"

Harriet's cheeks were mottled. She controlled her anger, but with difficulty; shook her head:

"It was his weakness. His weakness made him prey to your mother's foolish, rebellious—"

Jared took a step forward:

"Don't say any more."

"He took up a life in the west because *she* demanded it. They did it against all the advices of your grandfather, and she died as a result. Your father paid with his sanity and probably his life too. The night he left this house, he was insanely drunk. Bestial. And you've inherited the worst of both—"

Jared snatched at the rod in Harriet Kent's hand. Quickly, she retreated toward the marble fireplace. The color deepened in her cheeks. A tremor in her neck gave him a clue to the enjoyment she derived from baiting him.

For a moment they faced one another, eyes locked. All at once Harriet seemed to realize how tall Jared had grown; almost as tall as she was. Showing him the birch rod, she trembled:

"Stand aside. We'll discuss your parents another time—"

"We will not discuss them any other time, ever."

Harriet's mouth curled. "What a fine, proper boy we've raised! What a decent, respectful—"

A furious wave: "Don't use that flummery on me!"

"Flummery, is it—?"

"I never once begged for your not-so-kind attention!"

Scathing: "My! You've a masterful command of the language—"

"I haven't skipped all my classes with that pompous boot-licker."

"—but your expensive education seems to have generated no humility. Just the opposite. It's given you the desire—and the means—to flout your filthy temper and your arrogant views! I have no doubt—"

"Oh, be quiet, woman!"

"*I have no doubt you'll ruin yourself the way your father did!*"

His fists clenched at his sides:

"I'd rather be ruined, as you call it, than continue to live under the same roof with a mean-spirited bitch like you. Tell your husband *that*, why don't you?"

Harriet Kent whipped up the rod, intending to strike Jared's cheek. He caught her arm with one hand, seized the rod with the other.

Stepping back, he broke the rod over his knee and threw the halves onto the flames.

V

Ashen, Harriet whispered, "You're *exactly* like him! A *monster*—"

Jared stepped forward again, so close to her that he

was overpowered by the citrus scent she wore. He fought to keep his hands at his sides:

"If you speak one more word about him—"

Harriet dodged toward the door:

"We're finished with words, Master Jared. I'll see you get your wish. *I'll have you out of this house!*"

Jared Adam Kent beamed:

"That would suit me admirably. *Admirably!*"

The door crashed shut.

He stared at it, the smile and the cocky feeling draining away all at once. He had widened the gulf, exactly as he'd planned. But it was less satisfying than he'd expected. Having given cruelty for cruelty, he felt unclean.

Sinking down on the bed, he held his head with both hands. The break had come sooner than he might have wished. But he'd been unable to control himself during the argument. That was disturbing—

Again the secret doubts swept over him. He wondered bitterly whether Harriet could be right. Was he taking the same kind of rash step his father had, at his mother's insistence? He'd heard it said that their confidence in their ability to survive in the west had been ill-founded. The results were death for Jared's mother—guilt and ruin for Abraham Kent—

Would he fail the same way? The fear of it grew consuming all at once—

And a distorted memory of his sickness when he stared at his own scraped hand seemed to turn the fear to a certainty.

Head starting to throb, he realized it was a little late for second thoughts about his decision. Fear or not, he'd have to face the consequences of the stormy scene just concluded. He must begin to think—and immediately—of a place to go. He had to be ready when Aunt Harriet spoke to Uncle Gilbert, and Uncle Gilbert spoke to him—

He needed a destination—a means of escape—*something!*

The muddy coat forgotten, he leaned on the mantel and stared into the flames.

No answer came.

CHAPTER II

A Mackerel by Moonlight

THE FOLLOWING MORNING, Jared delayed his arrival at breakfast as long as possible.

Normally, the first meal of the Sabbath would have been served early, to permit the family to attend church. This particular Sunday it was re-scheduled for the regular weekday hour—ten o'clock. Church was forgotten.

Jared felt intense relief as he entered the dining room. Uncle Gilbert was in his customary place, but Aunt Harriet was absent. He heard her out in the kitchen, shrilly warning the servants not to damage the Spode as they washed it.

So the best porcelain was to be set, eh? It was one more indication of the importance of the evening dinner party.

Uncle Gilbert sat at the head of the table, wearing a threadbare dressing gown and slippers. Harriet often complained about Gilbert's casual morning attire. Once Jared had heard his uncle reply that if a dressing gown and slippers were suitable for President Jefferson to wear while answering knocks at the door of the executive residence in Washington, he could dress the same way in his home with no loss of status. Harriet Kent used the word *status* often, with complete seriousness. When Gilbert used it, he did so jokingly.

"Good morning, Jared."

"Morning, sir."

"Sleep soundly?"

"Fine, thank you."

Gilbert's breakfast, hardly touched, was his customary slice of salt fish, piece of cornbread and glass of whiskey and water. At one side of the plate lay two piles of manuscript. The dark-haired, ascetic-looking owner of Kent and Son resumed reading. When he finished the page, he picked up his fork, absently ate a small bite of fish, glanced again over the top of his spectacles at his nephew, seated now. But he said nothing.

Gilbert looked almost as uncomfortable as Jared felt. His uncle took longer than usual arranging his fork, knife and spoons on his plate, the signal that he'd concluded his meal. He wiped his mouth and his hands on the hem of the tablecloth; utensils had made napkins unnecessary.

He coughed. Reached out; tugged the bell pull. Finally, fixing Jared with dark eyes made large by his spectacles, he brought up the subject the boy was dreading:

"You and I must have a conversation."

Jared wanted to be polite, but not overly defensive:

"I'm sorry I lost my temper with Aunt Harriet yesterday. She said unkind things about my father and mother."

Gilbert frowned. "She also said you were ready to strike her—which cannot under any circumstances be allowed or forgiven."

"Actually it was the other way around. She was going to strike me."

Expressionless, Gilbert digested that. Then:

"You've absented yourself from the academy twice this week, I hear."

"Aunt Harriet keeps you well informed, I hear."

Gilbert sighed, refusing to be baited by the bitter echo of his own words.

"She does. But even without that, your unhappiness lately has been quite evident. We must do something about it. Having said all I'm going to on the incident yesterday—specifically, that I won't tolerate a repetition —I'm prepared to sit down with you and discuss what's best for your future. I suggest we talk as soon as possible. This evening—after our guests depart."

"I'll be glad to, sir."

Jared could never stay angry at his uncle longer than a second or two. Gilbert's nature was essentially kind.

Not that he lacked strength of will. Jared knew he had that, in plenty. A weak man couldn't run a firm as large as Kent and Son successfully.

Yet Gilbert seldom raised his voice. Quiet reasonableness and a firm tone lent him just as much authority as bullying. Or more. Most people respected Gilbert's strength, no matter how they felt about his politics. And Jared knew better than to take Gilbert's mild warning about quarreling lightly.

In an effort to lighten the mood, he said, "May I ask who you're entertaining tonight, sir? From all the secrecy, I've wondered if it's someone who shouldn't be seen here." He forced a smile. "Mad old King George? Prinny?"

"The king and his dissolute son the prince-regent would be publicly welcomed in Boston," Gilbert said, returning the smile. "But they'd hardly call on us. I'm afraid I'm pledged not to reveal the names of our guests until they've left the city. You and Amanda will be served dinner upstairs, by the way."

Jared wanted to question his uncle further, but a serving girl entered, bringing his breakfast. It was the same as Gilbert's except for the beverage. Since his twelfth birthday, he'd been permitted beer in the morning instead of cider.

Gilbert returned to his reading while Jared picked at his food. A few moments later, Harriet came in from the kitchen, carrying a highly polished spittoon.

After a caustic glance at Jared, she paced around the table, searching for a place to put the gleaming brass pot.

"Really, Gilbert, you're occupying this room much too long," she said. "The girls need to begin preparing the table."

Gilbert sighed, removed his spectacles. "I'll take my manuscript to the library." He started to consolidate the two piles of paper.

"Why a respectable house must provide a place for men to spit their filthy tobacco is beyond me," Harriet complained, finally putting the spittoon beside the wall near the head of the table.

"There are spittoons all over Washington, my dear," Gilbert said. "The fad is spreading to some of the best homes in Boston."

"Not to ours, I trust! I never fancied I'd be forced to entertain one of those barbarous Kentuckians—"

Jared's hand went rigid, the fork halfway to his mouth. Hurriedly, he swallowed the bite, pretending not to see Gilbert frown slightly, and purse his lips. His glance at his wife, mild enough, still carried unmistakable warning.

Annoyed by the silent reproof, Harriet flounced out.

Jared's mind was afire with curiosity. A *Kentuckian* coming to dinner? Who could it possibly be? He determined to find out.

All at once his eye darted to a corner of the dining room. There right in front of him was the way to learn the identity of his uncle's guests—

"Finish quickly, Jared," Gilbert said as he left. "The day is going to be difficult enough, so try not to supply extra inducements for your aunt to fly into a temper."

He didn't act angry, merely resigned. Jared listened to

the slow shuffle of his uncle's slippers as he proceeded to the library.

Gilbert did, however, shut the doors with a bang.

ii

Gilbert Kent had always been a devoted student of the thinking and the habits of the former president, Mr. Jefferson. At considerable cost, he had copied one of the mechanical innovations the Virginian had installed at Monticello: a dumbwaiter.

Via a platform controlled by pulleys, the dumbwaiter lifted food from one floor to another. Carpenters had ripped out part of a dining room wall to install the shaft, which connected the downstairs with Gilbert's bedroom directly above. Jared had realized that, by means of the shaft, he might be able to hear the dinner conversation. He was so excited at the prospect, he quite forgot to be nervous about the coming discussion of his future.

Around three o'clock, he found an opportunity to slip into the dining room unobserved. In the kitchen, Aunt Harriet was yelling at the servants again. The roasting capons hadn't been properly stored in the ice delivered by Mr. Dawlish. One bird had spoiled—and she was going to take the cost out of the guilty party's wages!

Jared barely heard, busy unfastening the brass latch on the door of the dumbwaiter. He only opened the door a couple of inches. To open it more would invite discovery. He prayed no one would shut the door accidentally.

One of the servants in the kitchen commented that a Kentuckian would probably think a gamy capon very flavorful. Other servants laughed—which only made Harriet Kent launch into another tirade.

With a smile on his face, Jared stole out of the room.

iii

"Jared, what are you—?"

Angrily, he jerked his head around and put a finger to his lips.

Robed for bed, Amanda stood in the doorway. She blinked in dismay when Jared scowled. He sat on a chair pulled up to the opening of the dumbwaiter in Gilbert's bedroom. The room was plain, its furnishings wholly masculine. For as long as Jared could remember, Gilbert and his wife had occupied separate quarters.

"You scared me half to death," Jared whispered. "Why did you open that door?"

"Because it was closed."

"Don't you suppose doors are shut for a reason?"

"But papa's downstairs, Jared. He never closes this door unless he's in here by himself, read—"

"Keep your voice down! Leave or come in, as you please. But whichever it is, do it quietly! They've served the fruit and wine. Aunt Harriet will be leaving in a minute, so the gentlemen can talk."

The little girl darted a glance into the gloomy second floor hall. Then, curiosity mastering apprehension, she shut the door.

She padded across the carpet, her shadow long and distorted. Jared had turned down the single lamp always lit in the room after nightfall. Gilbert usually retired early, to work on copy for the newspaper or read one of the countless manuscripts submitted to the book department. With the bell pull at the side of his narrow bed, he summoned tea and cakes during the evening. The dumbwaiter brought them up—the same shaft that now carried hollow-sounding male voices to Jared's ears.

"Sit down. Here." He pointed to the floor near his knee. Amanda still looked a bit fearful. But she folded her legs beneath her, leaning her head against Jared's leg, her dark eyes large. She smelled pleasantly of soap.

"It's terrible to spy on grownups—" she began.

"You spy with your eyes, you ninny."

"Then what's the word for doing it with your ears?"

"Eavesdrop. Do be silent!"

"But who is down there? I saw Mr. Rothman's carriage drive up—"

"Yes, he came in the front way. The other two guests arrived in a coach that pulled into the alley. They used the rear entrance. At last I understand why," he added, with the smugness of one privy to a secret. "If your papa's guests showed their faces in Boston, they'd be mobbed—or worse."

"You still haven't said who—"

"Politicians! All the way from Washington. Very important men—hush! I hear Aunt Harriet leaving."

From below, a muddle of voices, one female, indicated the formal part of dinner was finished. Jared bent his head near the open door of the shaft, heard another door close distantly.

Glassware clinked—more wine being poured. Someone offered a compliment about the excellent capon. A loud spitting sound was followed by a *pling* as the jet hit the spittoon. Gradually, Jared began to sort out the voices.

He recognized Royal Rothman's easily. The middle-aged Jewish banker was a frequent guest at the Kent table, because he was involved with Jared's uncle in business ventures. His bank provided money whenever Kent's needed to float a loan.

The voice of the spitter was rich and deep. His accent was definitely not that of the northeast.

The third guest spoke English with a foreign accent.

"—indeed generous of you to arrange this meeting, Mr. Kent," boomed the Kentucky tobacco-chewer. "The secretary and I felt the long journey and the inconvenience of traveling incognito were justified if we could sample the sentiment of New England first-hand."

"I'm flattered you chose to do it at my table, Mr. Speaker," Gilbert said.

"Mister who?" Amanda breathed.

"That's not his name, it's his title. Mr. Clay of Kentucky is a new member of the Congress. One of the Republicans called war hawks. He was just elected Speaker of the House. I don't know anyone in Boston who doesn't hate him."

A moment later, the cousins heard the voice of Royal Rothman. Despite surface politeness, his hostility was evident:

"Shall we address the issue, gentlemen? Mr. Kent and I wish to know whether there will be a war—which I would personally consider a national disaster. Mr. Kent must speak for himself—"

"In due course," Gilbert murmured.

Rothman went on, "You gentlemen in turn want to know New England's position. I trust I made that clear during dinner. And I believe I express the attitude of the entire business community."

"I'd be careful there," Gilbert said.

"Sometimes, Gilbert, I have the impression you actually favor a war. God pity you if you're that misguided! Your pardon, gentlemen. But I believe in being frank."

The heavily accented voice drifted up the shaft:

"Your candor is appreciated, Mr. Rothman. However, the Speaker and I are seeking somewhat more specific information."

Jared bent, lips to Amanda's ear:

"That man's name is Gallatin. He's in charge of the government treasury. Money. He's foreign-born. French, Swiss, something like that—"

"If we are forced into a second war for independence —" Henry Clay began.

"May we dispense with slogans, Mr. Clay?" Rothman asked curtly. "The issue is neither independence nor the one expressed in that other overworked phrase, free trade and sailors' rights. We know perfectly well what the main issue is. You and your associates—Mr. Calhoun and Mr. Cheves and Mr. Grundy and all the rest —you want Upper Canada, don't you?"

"That is the desire in the west, yes, sir," Clay returned, a chill in his voice. "It's a matter of—"

"Avarice," Rothman cut in. "Your constituents are greedy for the land. For the furs—"

"We are not acting out of greed, sir! We are acting on one of mankind's oldest principles—self-preservation! The lives of thousands of citizens of this country are being threatened. The British are inflaming the tribes of the entire Ohio valley!"

"The British foreign minister has repeatedly denied that charge."

"And I say Castlereagh's a damned liar, sir," Clay shot back, punctuating the retort with another loud spit.

The man did have a marvelous, resonant voice, Jared thought. He was a trial lawyer and, according to popular gossip, he'd trained himself as an orator by reading heavily, then going alone to a cornfield in his native Kentucky and speaking aloud for hours, discoursing on what he'd read. Most Bostonians wished he had never left that cornfield.

Secretary of the Treasury Gallatin spoke more moderately:

"We also have evidence that the Hudson's Bay Company is pledged to a plan to monopolize the fur trade— and is arming the savages with fusees to that end. You know how the British have coddled and encouraged that devil Tecumseh and his fanatical brother—"

"All of which," Gilbert said, "Castlereagh has denied."

Furious, Clay burst out, "If you gentlemen refuse to be reasonable about a clear threat to—"

"We will be reasonable if you will be truthful," Rothman said.

"Sir, are you calling me a liar?"

"I am saying every argument you put forward is spurious. Taken together, they resemble a rotten mackerel in the moonlight. It shines beautifully from afar. Up close, it stinks."

Clay snapped, " 'So brilliant, yet so corrupt—' Those were Congressman Randolph's exact words, I believe."

"I didn't claim the simile was original," Rothman said.

"But your choice of a source is regrettable. You're quoting an effeminate fool!"

"John Randolph of Roanoke is—"

"Half a man! Can you take seriously *anything* said by a scarecrow whose proudest claim is his descent from Pocahontas? Who struts into Congress wearing silver spurs, armed with a riding whip, and trailed by a damned slavering hound? Why, Randolph can't give a speech without stopping every ten minutes while the door keeper brings him a tumbler of malt liquor! Even that doesn't make his voice manly. He squeaks and squeals like a goddamned eunuch!"

Gilbert said, "Nevertheless, Mr. Speaker, John Randolph of Roanoke argues his positions in a compelling way."

"Not to Kentuckians he doesn't!"

"Ah, but you must grant he has a wit," Gallatin chuckled. "Adore him or despise him, you must admit that. I relish the time he was accused of lacking virility, and told his opponent, 'Sir—you pride yourself upon an animal faculty, in respect to which the Negro is your equal and the jackass infinitely your superior.' "

No one but Gallatin laughed. "I doubt if any black man would find that witty," Gilbert said. Gallatin harrumphed.

Rothman said, "We've strayed from the point. It's public knowledge that your faction wants Upper Canada, Mr. Clay, so we'll save time and eliminate distasteful acrimony—"

"It's you who were acrimonious, sir, not I! You brought up the mackerel by moonlight—*and* as much as called me a liar."

"Will you accept my apology so we can proceed?"

Clay grumbled something inaudible.

"Proceed from the assumption that war is inevitable," Gallatin suggested.

"Let's hope to heaven it's not!" Rothman cried.

"American liberty is again threatened on the land and on the sea," Clay declared. "There's just one way to teach Johnny Bull a lesson. At the point of a gun! From the mouth of a cannon!"

Once again Gilbert spoke, quietly but with authority:

"Since you raise the subject of guns, Mr. Speaker, perhaps some simple mathematics are in order. My newspaper keeps track of the state of the army. We have, I believe, not quite twelve thousand men in uniform—most of those green recruits. Moreover, the forces are widely scattered. A few at Michilimackinac, a few at Fort Dearborn out on the Illinois prairie—"

"The navy is in somewhat better shape," Gallatin said.

"You're joking," Rothman said. "Six frigates and scores of those worthless Jeffersonian gunboats—the whirligigs of the sage of Monticello? That's nothing compared to six hundred British men-of-war, more than one hundred of which are ships of the line."

Clay objected: "But Britain still has her hands full on the continent."

"And that is where *our* attention should be focused. On the true enemy. Bonaparte!"

"I must raise another hard question," Gilbert said. "I don't mean to be rude. But have you gentlemen in Washington ever considered the danger to this country if Britain suddenly finds herself in a position to free large masses of men and great numbers of ships now committed to the struggle with Napoleon? We stand every chance of being crushed."

Clay quickly overcame the argument:

"War will be declared before that ever happens, Mr. Kent. We'll overwhelm the British, not vice versa."

"So you intend to have your way regardless of *any* consequences?" Rothman demanded.

There was a strained pause. Jared leaned his head against the wall, his blue eyes large, his expression awed at the thought of men discussing the fate of millions of human beings over wine and the *pling* of tobacco hitting a spittoon.

"Answer me, please, Mr. Clay."

"We will press ahead," Clay said.

"To disaster!" Rothman predicted.

"Gentlemen, please," Gallatin put in. "Once more we have drifted from the question Henry and I came here to discuss. It is no longer a matter of whether a war will be fought, but *how* it will be fought—"

"Why are you so set on this hasty, reckless course?" Rothman roared, pounding the table. "Britain has already shown some small sign of yielding eventually. Rescinding her Orders in Council. Stopping the impressment—"

"Don't forget Castlereagh is shrewd and slippery," Gallatin said. "He may be playing for time."

"I don't think so," Gilbert said. "At least not according to what I hear from sources I trust. Visitors who've just returned from England. Aboard ships lucky enough not to be chased, stopped or fired upon, I might add!"

"Now you sound like a hawk," Rothman complained.

"I'm only stating facts, Royal. But like you, I believe we can bring the British ministries around. Convince them to change their policies. *If* we have time."

"We don't," Rothman replied. "And it makes no difference to Mr. Clay anyway. The west is hungry for land—nothing but land. Last year Jemmy Madison grabbed the West Floridas—"

"Annexed," Clay corrected.

"—and at the moment he's eyeing the East Floridas. You know who to blame, Gilbert. Your blasted Monticello squire started the fever. Now it's epidemic!"

Gilbert had no immediate answer. Gallatin said:

"Since New England is so important—indeed, we might say paramount—in commerce and finance, I must ask the position of gentlemen such as yourself, Mr. Rothman, in the event hostilities do break out."

"Are you asking about loans to the government, Mr. Secretary? War loans?"

"I am."

"You'll not get a dollar from Rothman's. I venture every other banking house in New England will say the same thing."

"And you gentlemen will have a difficult time funding a war without New England money." Gilbert said.

"We will make do," Clay said in a flinty way. "We've obtained the answer we came for—"

Sounding dispirited, Gallatin said, "Indeed we have."

"I warned you what it would be, Mr. Secretary." Clay spat again.

Now that the hard truth had been brought into the open, Rothman attempted to soften it a little:

"I'm sorry, gentlemen. New England simply can't afford a war. We depend on overseas trade for marketing our goods. Jefferson nearly destroyed us with his embargo, and a war would bring complete ruin."

"That's sheer imagination—" Clay began.

"That is our position," Rothman countered, cold again.

"Thank God, it's not the position of the rest of the country. We *will* make do."

"You can't dismiss New England quite so quickly," Rothman warned.

"Why not, sir? Isn't she ready to set herself up as an independent nation?"

"Not as yet, sir. But if you and your cohorts persist—"

"I believe we have exhausted this subject, sir."

"No, we have not!" Rothman shouted. "I fought for these states in the Revolution, but I am not going to see your damned, unwashed mobocracy plunge them into a second, useless war with a people who should be our closest friends!"

"Is that patriotism speaking, sir? Or the balance sheet?"

"You damned poltroon—!"

"Royal, you forget yourself!" Gilbert exclaimed.

"To the contrary! New England is the bedrock of this nation—"

"No longer!" Clay thundered. "You are living in the past, sir! The west is the rising star!"

And may it sink to hell, Jared thought, the memory of his father breaking his concentration.

Downstairs, voices rose in a confusion of accusations and epithets until Gilbert cried, "Gentlemen, this is my house, not a tavern! Please act accordingly!"

That elicited another round of half-hearted apologies, and a degree of calm. The subject of war was dropped, in favor of perfunctory conversation about business in general, and Gilbert's newspaper in particular. Avoiding the question of whether the *Bay State Republican* would support a war, he tried to interest his visitors in some of the innovations he had in mind.

He spoke of his plan to launch a penny paper, undercutting the prevailing six-cent price in order to capture a larger share of the increasingly literate population.

He speculated about the possibility of employing boys to sell papers on the street in an organized way, not haphazardly, and of sending the same boys door to door to boost circulation even further.

When the troubles at sea cleared up, he said, he wanted to purchase a dispatch boat to sail out and meet incoming ships, so he could get the latest European news into print ahead of his competition.

By the time he started to discuss the possibility of modern invention being harnessed to improve printing equipment—"The prospect of a steam-powered press is staggering, gentlemen, and not at all out of the question."—his guests were murmuring that they must leave.

Chairs scraped. The goodbyes were stiffly polite. Jared closed the door of the dumbwaiter and caught his cousin's hand, hurrying her out of the room.

"They kept talking about war," Amanda said when they reached the stairs. "Do they mean men fighting other men?"

"Yes, that's what they mean."

"Will you have to fight?"

Startled, he realized her question raised an entirely new issue; injected a completely new factor into the uncertain future.

"I don't know whether I'd have to. But I might want to," he answered.

At the back of the house, a coach clattered away. In the lower hallway, Royal Rothman was having a final word with his host. Jared heard the banker growl something about the rotten mackerel stinking worse than ever—

He patted Amanda's rump and started her up to bed:

"Tuck yourself in and put out your lamp—"

"Won't you come do it for me?"

"No."

"Please—?"

His face oddly drawn, he shook his head.

iv

You do have a passion for satisfying your curiosity—regardless of the possible consequences."

He drank, not realizing that his nephew took the remark as an accusation. An unconscious one, perhaps; but an accusation all the same.

"You must forget everything you heard, Jared. Mr. Rothman particularly would be badly compromised if it were known he'd even been in the same room with Henry Clay."

"I'll say nothing." *And I must tell Amanda not to, either.*

"The gentlemen are staying the night in Roxbury," Gilbert went on. "Under false names, of course. They'll start back to the capital tomorrow—" He sank into a chair and peered at the rum in his goblet. "I'm glad they came. I have a better perspective, meeting one of the leading war hawks in person. I believe war will come. And while Clay's motives are far from spotless, I believe it should."

"You do? You didn't make that clear during the conversation."

"Royal was already upset. I saw no reason to add to his unhappiness. I'll tell him my feelings in due course. He suspects them already—"

Another long swallow of rum. "I don't favor war for the reasons Mr. Clay does. Royal was correct—the hawk faction can only screech 'Canada! Canada!' It's their obsession. Impressment's a side issue—while to me it's the central issue. The same sort of issue which drove your grandfather to join all the others who refused to have their liberties abridged forty years ago—"

The eyes of both were drawn to the portrait of Philip. After a moment, Gilbert set his drink aside.

"But we have a different issue to discuss."

Tense, Jared murmured, "Yes, sir."

"I know you're not happy in this house. There's no need to dwell on why—"

"I *must* get away, Uncle Gilbert. I've no patience with school any more—"

"Oh, I think you've already had quite enough to carry you through life. The trouble is, I don't know what you *do* want. Where you hope to go, in the broadest sense of those words. Is it an apprenticeship you're after? I can offer you that at Kent and Son."

"But I'd have to stay on here, and I feel I shouldn't." Jared leaned forward. "Please understand—it has nothing to do with you."

"I understand." Gilbert covered his mouth briefly, coughed.

"I'll be less of a burden if I'm gone."

"You're no burden, Jared."

"That's kind of you to say, but I know otherwise."

"I've never particularly pressed you about joining the firm—"

"I appreciate that."

"From the time you were very small, I somehow felt commerce wouldn't interest you. I think you've inherited more than a touch of your mother's restlessness."

Jared tried to smile. "That Virginia blood you talk about?"

"This country is being created out of such restlessness. Created, expanded—it's not a bad thing."

"I've no desire to go into the west the way my father did," Jared said, his voice harder. "It's a brutal place. It killed him."

"Well—in part."

Gilbert didn't amplify the remark. He looked at his nephew with disarming friendliness.

"I know it would be wrong to urge you to stay and work at the firm. You can't abide your aunt—no, don't say anything. Don't pretend. That's a truth neither of us should hide from—though it's not necessary to delve into the reasons. As you well know, Harriet doesn't harbor warm feelings for you either. Regrettably, there's blame on both sides."

Jared nodded slowly. "I—I just want out."

"I'm willing—if we can find something suitable for you to do. You look surprised."

"I didn't think you'd agree to my going."

"I want to spare you *and* your aunt further quarrels you both might regret for the rest of your lives. I've let my temper carry me away a few times in the past—the night your father left, for one—and I've cursed myself ever since."

"You've hinted about that quarrel, but never described it. Was it—?"

"Bitter," Gilbert interrupted. "Bitter, hateful, viol—oh, but that's the past." He faced away. "It's enough to say that, ever since, my conscience has driven me to launch a search for your father at least once a year. Never with any success, alas."

He paused. "I'm wondering, though—"

The library lamps put pinpricks of light into his dark pupils.

"—suddenly I'm wondering whether the answer to your dilemma might not be a leaf from your father's book."

"What do you mean, sir?"

"I think I've mentioned that your father went through a period of conflict with his father and mine—" He gestured to the portrait. "As a temporary solution, your father chose the military service."

Jared turned cold at the implications of that. His negative reaction didn't come from cowardice as much as from his basic doubt about his own ability to survive in inherently difficult circumstances. But he kept silent, letting Gilbert continue:

"I wouldn't want to see you in the army. As you overheard, it's hardly worthy of the name. Its highest commanders are dodderers, incompetents or both. But the navy, now—that's another matter. Though small, the navy's acquitted itself splendidly over the past ten years. From all I've heard, the officers by and large are first-rate—a match for any British captain afloat. And the half dozen frigates under sail must constantly replenish their crews as enlistments run out—"

"How old do you have to be to join?"

"For powder monkeys or cabin duty, they take boys from eight on up. You might have a chance at something better. A midshipman's appointment. I could perhaps direct a letter to the Secretary of the Navy—yes," Gilbert said with growing animation, "navy duty could be the answer. It would certainly suit the family tradition I've tried to keep alive."

"What tradition, sir?"

Gilbert didn't give a direct answer to the question. He walked to the portrait of Philip; gazed at it a moment, then said quietly:

"It's a pity you never knew him, Jared. A remarkable man. I loved him without reservation. When I was growing up, I was sickly—a disappointment to him, I'm sure. Yet he was unfailingly kind. The older I grew, the more I came to respect his convictions. I don't mean his conservative politics—most men become more conservative as they reach middle age. I'm talking about something deeper and much more fundamental. He used to say this country gave him hope when he had none. It gave him love when he had none—gave it twice over. Your grandmother Anne, and my mother. He said he always felt it was his duty to repay those debts—"

Jared looked at the strong face on the canvas. "I remember your telling me how brave he was."

"Brave in the most meaningful way. I'm sure he felt fear just as all normal men do—but in spite of that, he chose to fight for liberty when it would have been easier and more comfortable to remain a Tory. Beyond that, he pulled himself up in the world from nothing, and built a business. To make money, to be sure—but also because he believed the printing trade is of inestimable benefit to mankind. 'Take a stand and make a mark.' That was the sum of his life and his belief. He said those words to me shortly before he died. I've never forgotten them. I hope you won't either. That's why I had them inscribed on the fob I gave you last Christmas. In the navy, I think you could find the kind of fresh horizons you always seem to be hunting. Yet at the same time, you'd be giving as well as taking. Just as your grandfather did. Just as I try to do in my limited way. That's what I mean when I speak of carrying on the tradition he established."

In the ensuing silence, both gazed at the painting again. Then Gilbert became brisk; businesslike:

"Unless you say otherwise, tomorrow I'll draft a letter to Washington. I'll make inquiries as to the whereabouts of our frigates. And, if possible, learn whether one might be berthing in Boston soon."

Despite his earlier apprehension, Jared found himself warming to Gilbert's suggestion. Perhaps it was exactly what he needed: to test himself in hard circumstances. Perhaps that way, he could prove Harriet wrong—

Yet fear remained. What if he did say yes—only to fail?

He wouldn't! He swore that silently; fervently—

The idea of naval service wasn't all that ominous if he stopped to think about it. There were aspects that excited him. Small as it was, the navy had a certain dash. He vividly recalled the previous April when the city's own frigate, *Constitution*, Captain Hull commanding, had put in briefly to fill out her crew roster. The town had taken on a festive air—and rocked with laughter at the story of a green farm boy who had apparently swallowed too much of the recruiting officer's rum. The country boy signed on believing he was to be the captain's gardener.

When he sobered up and demanded his rake and hoe, a light touch of the cat convinced him to accept the tools of a carpenter's mate instead.

Boston had an ambivalent attitude about *Constitution.* She would sail against the British if war came—and Bostonians detested that idea. Yet the locally built warship remained a source of intense civic pride.

Alas, there seemed little chance of serving aboard the city's own vessel. In August, *Constitution* had cleared the Virginia Capes, bound for the dangerous waters along the French coast. She was carrying the new minister to France, Mr. Barlow, and his family. The *Republican* had run an item about it.

But as Gilbert said, the Boston ship was only one of six frigates now in service. Perhaps Jared could find a place on another. The thought of it—of laying Aunt Harriet's convictions to rest—put a glow in his eyes—

Abruptly, the glow faded. Gilbert noticed:

"What's wrong?"

"Do you really think they'd take me? I have no experience with ships."

"Nor do half their recruits. You'll learn, and quickly.

The life's hard. But most American captains aren't the martinets their British cousins are—and there are fewer cruel and unreasonable punishments for breaches of discipline. There *is* a real reason why English seamen desert and wind up on our ships, you see."

He scrutinized his nephew.

"Of course, in any service, one's expected to obey orders. As I've said before, you're much like your mother in some respects—"

"Aunt Harriet keeps reminding me of that."

Gilbert frowned, then shrugged off the retort. "The fact must be faced, Jared. It would be folly to consider the navy if you feel you couldn't do what's expected of you. *Without* resentment."

More moderately, Jared said, "I can follow orders, uncle." He hoped it was the truth.

Gilbert's expression softened "I'm heartened to hear you say it. Perhaps life in this house hasn't been a fair test of that."

All at once Jared felt as if fetters had dropped from him. He recalled all the times he'd lounged along the Boston piers, watching the tall ships running in through the island channels, homeward bound from faraway ports. He'd never imagined that sort of life for himself. He was astonished at his oversight.

With enthusiasm, he declared, "I think the whole idea's wonderful. Please write the letter tomor—did I say something wrong? You're smiling."

"For no sensible reason. You said nothing wrong."

Absently, Gilbert passed a pale hand across his brow. He walked to one of the windows overlooking the Common.

Jared sensed an abrupt and extreme tension in his uncle. Gilbert's slow pivot from the window suggested physical labor. His eyes were sad; remote—as if he'd looked outside and gazed on something other than the Sunday evening darkness.

The boy waited, his hair glinting bright as metal in the radiance of the library lamps He actually saw his uncle's eyes return from whatever private vision had bemused him—return and focus on Jared's face—and still with that sad air:

"I repeat, I had no reason to smile. I was struck by a thought, that's all. How everything changes and nothing changes. Some—"

His voice grew firmer as he composed himself.

"—some years ago, in this same library, I offered to write another letter for another—"

He hesitated. Jared contained his surprise at the glitter of tears Gilbert quickly dashed away with the back of one slim hand.

"—another man, in the misguided hope I could re-direct his life. I'll tell you the whole story one day. But not this evening. The—the dinner was quite tiring."

Jared accepted the falsehood in silence. Somehow he knew it was the recollection, not the argument about war, that had unsettled his uncle.

Gilbert went to his nephew. Put an arm around him:

"I trust I'll be more successful with the second attempt than I was with the first."

He removed his hand, averted his head.

"Now—"

Again the broken voice.

"It's best we retire, I think."

V

The moment Amanda heard the news at the dinner table, she wept—and refused to stop when Harriet ordered it. Harriet marched the little girl from the room and whipped her long and hard.

Yet Jared soon noticed that once he and his uncle announced their joint intention, Harriet treated him with unexpected cordiality. She was attentive, cheerful and permitted him to take as many holidays from the academy as he pleased.

He knew why. She was delighted at the idea of getting him out of the house.

Ordinarily, he might have hated her all the more. But he didn't because he was intoxicated by the winds of freedom he was scenting all at once. Strong, clean winds that blew frustration and unhappiness out of his life at last.

As the year 1812 opened, the inflammatory talk from Washington grew hotter still. Except in New England, the country seemed to be in a ferment of anticipation—

"Canada! Canada!"

"*Free trade and sailors' rights!*"

"*SHOW THE DAMN BRITISH ONCE AND FOR ALL!*"

Jared fully appreciated that in a war, men died. Yet he was young enough to accept the possibility without worrying too much about it. In return, he would escape from Beacon Street. He was getting the better end of the bargain, he felt.

If he stayed under Harriet Kent's thumb much longer, his spirit would wither and perish altogether—

Or erupt in some terrible act of rage and rebellion that could mar his life forever, as Gilbert said. By going to sea, he might escape all that. *And* answer some fundamental questions about himself.

Buoyed by a new sense of confidence, he found his fear lessening.

War was like that rotting mackerel in the moonlight, he decided. So long as you stood far enough away to miss the stench, it gleamed with considerable attraction.

CHAPTER III

The Frigate

IT WAS MID-May before Gilbert received a reply to his letter to Secretary of the Navy Paul Hamilton. The secretary apologized for his delay in answering, but as Mr. Kent could well appreciate, pressing matters occupied the department. Gilbert and Jared both understood the nature of the pressing matters.

Regrettably, Hamilton said, no appointments for midshipmen were available at the moment. Should Mr. Kent's nephew still wish to serve, he would have to do so as a ship's boy, receiving six dollars per month for an enlistment of one year. Mr. Kent would also understand that Mr. Hamilton could provide no information concerning the whereabouts of the larger United States vessels, but with luck, one of the frigates might soon put in at Boston or another New England port, and Mr. Kent's nephew could then apply.

Jared was disappointed. But the setback didn't change his plans.

On the eighteenth of June, President Madison declared war.

ii

Boston's bells tolled in mourning. New England's Federalist press raged. The declaration had only been approved in the Senate by *six* votes!

Pastors took to their pulpits to decry the step. Toasts

at conservative dinner tables condemned *The existing war—this child of prostitution—may no American acknowledge it as legitimate!*

Although the American army had to depend on the militia for immediate manpower, Governor Strong of Massachusetts, as well as the governors of Rhode Island and Connecticut, refused to permit their militias to operate outside their respective states—or obey any order of the federal government.

New England's fury mounted when packets slipped past the British vessels cruising off the coast and delivered news that seemed to confirm the declaration as a tragic mistake. On the twenty-third of June, Lord Castlereagh had suspended the Orders in Council—those hated edicts responsible for the harassment of American ships.

The news arrived too late. The army, such as it was, would soon be launching an attack on Upper Canada from its headquarters at Detroit. The commander was to be General William Hull, an outdated relic whose Revolutionary service hardly equipped him for modern frontier warfare. Few seemed worried. Hadn't Jefferson himself written that conquest of Canada was "just a matter of marching?"

In July, Bostonians could sneer at Jefferson's confidence with justification. The key United States garrison on Michilimackinac Island, gateway to the western fur country, surrendered to an enemy force.

But worse was in store.

Rumors spread that the Shawnee Tecumseh would definitely align his braves with General Isaac Brock. The Federalists shook their heads. Brock had twice the wits and ten times the courage of that old fool Hull.

A pattern of hideous blundering began to emerge. The British on the frontier had of course received word of the declaration by special couriers. But while Hull was plodding northward through Ohio to Detroit, some dunderhead in Washington chose to send him the same news *by ordinary mail.* The British commanders knew war was definite eight days before Hull did. Thus they seized an American ship on Lake Erie and captured an unexpected prize—secret orders for the American general.

When Gilbert learned the whole unbelievable story, he penned the *Republican*'s first editorial in favor of the war. He demanded the firing of the incompetents in Washington who had informed Hull too late, and insisted on replacement of the general with a younger, more competent man. But he also voiced support for President Madison's decision, and the action of Congress.

The night the editorial was published, a dozen hooligans appeared on Beacon Street and hurled rocks at windows in the Kent house. Three were broken before Gilbert dashed outside, his father's Kentucky rifle loaded and ready to fire. He had taught himself how to use the rifle several weeks earlier, anticipating just this sort of nocturnal visit.

The hooligans screamed obscene insults and lobbed a few more rocks. Gilbert raised the rifle. Instantly, the small mob disappeared in the darkness. An hour later, still white from the incident and suffering sharp pains in his chest, Gilbert was rushed up to bed.

Against the advice of Doctor Selkirk, he was up and working twenty-four hours later.

iii

On the twenty-sixth of July, sails appeared in the President Roads below Boston harbor. The sails belonged to the city's own frigate, *Constitution.*

She anchored and poured her tars into the streets soon after. They spread a story of an incredible feat of seamanship. Jared heard the particulars on the afternoon of the twenty-seventh, when he went to the recruiting office newly opened in a rooming house operated by a Mrs. Broadhurst in Fore Street.

He ran most of the way. *Constitution* hadn't filled out her crew roster before clearing Annapolis in early August.

iv

A plank table had been set up in the first floor parlor of the rooming house. After a few preliminaries, the officer behind the table asked:

"You're familiar with the ship for which we're recruiting, I take it?"

"I am."

"I mean to say, our recent exploits?"

"The town's talking of nothing else—though to be honest, nobody seems quite clear on all the details."

"I don't doubt there's considerable exaggeration in the retelling," the young officer commented. "Hardly necessary. The truth's remarkable enough." He helped himself to a drink from a jug of rum.

The young man was one of *Constitution*'s lieutenants, slender and tanned. Jared reckoned him to be twenty or twenty-one. And almost too handsome. His dark hair pinned up in a queue looked as glossy as a woman's. His brown eyes had a languid quality—maybe from rum. He had profferred the jug the moment Jared walked into the airless, musty parlor, but Jared had declined. Now he almost wished he hadn't. Somehow the officer made him self-conscious.

The young man put the jug down, his tongue creeping slowly along his pink upper lip. His eyes ranged over Jared's face. The boy grew even more uncomfortable; tried to distract the lieutenant:

"How long were you actually chased—?"

"Three days," the young man answered in a slightly slurred voice. "Three days and two nights. Almost sixty-seven hours." He didn't sound like a southerner, but neither did he speak with a New England accent. Jared decided he must be from one of the middle states.

"And you realize"—the officer punctuated the remark with a pointing finger—"not a man or boy aboard caught a wink of sleep during that entire time. You are not volunteering for a life of leisure."

"I understand that."

"Good—excellent."

The young man rose, strolled to the front window, his black pumps clicking on the scarred floor. Jared fidgeted. The room was depressing, its appointments old and shabby, in sharp contrast to the lieutenant's elegant white stockings and breeches and blue tailcoat. His huge half-moon hat lay on the table near a litter of forms. He gazed out the window a moment, then let the curtain fall.

"If you're prepared to work hard, you'll enjoy the privilege of serving under a damned fine sailor—"

"Captain Hull."

"Quite right. He's a fighter—but no fool. We came on the enemy three days out of Chesapeake Bay. Five of His Britannic Majesty's best—"

"I heard it was six."

"Exaggeration again. Five were sufficient to give Hull pause, I assure you. There were four men o' war and *Guerriere*, the frigate that's caused so much trouble recently." The lieutenant gestured in a languorous way. "Hull knew we stood no chance against those odds. Besides, the enemy had a slight breeze and we had none. But the captain vowed we wouldn't be captured." The lieutenant smiled. "Not quite the same attitude as you find in the army. There, it seems, they surrender the moment the enemy farts."

Jared shifted his weight from one foot to the other. He supposed this praise of the navy was intended to generate eagerness in new recruits, but in his case it wasn't necessary:

"I had no desire to join the army. My father was a soldier, but—"

"Was he!" the lieutenant broke in. "So was mine. Where did he serve?"

"In Ohio—when it was still the Northwest. He fought with Wayne at Fallen Timbers—"

"Remarkable! My father was there as well. Got himself killed, the poor wretch. Perhaps the two knew each other. Is your father still living?"

It was easier to simply say no than to give a complicated explanation about Abraham Kent's disappearance.

"Well," said the lieutenant, moving closer to Jared and squeezing his shoulder, "we have something in common, don't we?"

The dark, languid eyes held the boy's. Jared felt acutely uncomfortable; said quickly:

"How exactly did you escape the five ships?"

For a moment the lieutenant acted annoyed. But he released Jared's shoulder.

"First we put men in rowboats, to tow us ahead. We gained a little headway, but not enough. And as soon as their wind died, the damn Britishers used the same trick. So next morning, we began kedging. Do you know what that is, my boy?"

"I don't," Jared replied, growing irritated himself. To be called a boy by an officer barely out of his teens was demeaning.

Besides that, the lieutenant's half-lidded eyes had a disturbing way of focusing on odd places. Jared's mouth; his hands; and once, he was sure, his groin—

"You'll discover what it means if we sign you on," the lieutenant told him. "To kedge, a special anchor's fastened to the longest, stoutest hawser you can put together, using all the cordage aboard. Ours stretched half a mile—"

"I did hear someone talking about a long line," Jared nodded, anxious to conclude the business and get away. But the lieutenant was in no such hurry. Jared took it as another bad sign.

"The hawser's rowed ahead of the ship, don't you see, and dropped with the kedge anchor. Then the ship's pulled forward by men picking up the hawser and walking aft. That helped us move along in pretty fair fashion. Whenever one of the enemy got a little too close, Captain Hull ordered shots from four of our long twenty-fours. To set them up in the stern, we cut away—am I boring you?"

Jared's head jerked up at the abrupt change in tone. He had clearly angered the lieutenant—

Well, what of it? He was ready to walk out. He disliked the atmosphere in the dark, stifling room; and he disliked the officer even more—

Abruptly, he remembered his larger objective. He had no desire to fail at this early stage. So he held his temper and forced himself to shake his head:

"It's a fascinating story."

"I should hope you'd find it so," the lieutenant sniffed. "We want our recruits to be enthusiastic—satisfied—in every way." Again there was a faintly lewd undertone to the words. Or perhaps Jared's nervousness was making him imagine it—

"As I was saying, we cut away the taffrail to make room for two guns, and two more were poked right out through the windows of the great cabin—Hull's cabin."

"And you did get away at last—" Jared said, hoping to hasten the end of the interview.

"By using every trick. To lighten us up, the captain dumped most of our drinking water. Ten tons, almost. He sent the topmen aloft to wet the sails. A wet sail holds more air than a dry one—another bit of information for you to store away in that handsome head."

Feeling feverish and desperate for a breath of outside air, Jared pressed his palms against his legs and struggled to feign interest. The lieutenant uttered a low chuckle. Was his pretense so obvious? Jared wondered.

"On the second night, we ran into a squall. Hull shortened sail just as we bore into the storm. He knows the Atlantic weather back and forth, you see. He predicted the squall would be a small one—"

I must get out of here! Jared thought wildly. Then, in his imagination, he saw Harriet Kent.

How smug she'd look if he came home with excuses instead of an enlistment agreement. Though he was writhing inwardly, he stood his ground.

The lieutenant seemed to be enjoying his discomfort. Prolonging it—for sport. The young man tilted the rum jug again. Fastidiously dabbed his lips with a kerchief taken from his sleeve. Only then did he continue:

"The British, on the other hand, obviously feared a real blow. They hauled down everything. Shortly we lost sight of them—the squall hid us. Hull got busy and cracked on canvas. Sure enough, we were out of the squall soon, picked up a nice wind and showed 'em our heels. It was a hell of an effort, but every man did his part, without sleep and without complaint. And not twenty days ago, many of them were as green, as—" A pause. "—inexperienced as you." Another silence. "My boy, I'm disappointed."

"Why?"

"I expected you to be more impressed."

"But I am! I wouldn't have come here otherwise—"

"You can bet the Britishers were impressed. I'm sure

there was plenty of cursing on their part that night—especially aboard *Guerriere*. Her captain, Dacres, is an old friend of Hull's, you know. They met in England some years ago, and they've a standing bet. If they ever engage, the loser presents the winner with a first-quality hat—"

Jared tensed. The officer was walking toward him again. He almost cringed from the touch of the supple hand on his shoulder:

"I've only told you all this in order to demonstrate the sort of effort that's expected from young fellows who sail with Captain Hull." The fingers constricted slightly. "Maximum effort and obedience. Absolute obedience to every command—every wish of your officers. But you and I will have no problem there, will we? We've already discovered we have things in common—"

Unwilling to suffer the fondling any longer, Jared jerked away. The lieutenant's dark eyes widened.

"Well. I see you have a ready temper." The smile was gone. "You'll have to curb that, else it'll be curbed for you."

Just a simple nod of assent required immense effort on Jared's part. A muscle in his jaw quivered. His eagerness to join *Constitution*'s crew had all but disappeared. He wondered whether the young officer was the sort of warped person he'd heard about but never met—one of those who disliked the opposite sex and preferred their own—

Even speculating about that, he couldn't walk out. He couldn't quite bring himself to throw away his first real chance to discover whether he was capable of surviving—and succeeding—in a difficult situation. So he endured the officer's pointed stare, and reminded himself that it was hardly fair to judge a company of more than four hundred sailors and marines by the actions of one.

The lieutenant resumed his seat, picked up a form.

Jared's conclusions about the officer were abruptly shaken when a door opened down the dim hall leading back from the parlor. He saw a fleshy young woman pulling up one shoulder of a bed gown to cover a heavy, red-nippled breast.

The young woman swayed. Drunk, was she—?

Livid, the lieutenant jumped up. He stalked two steps down the hall.

"I remind you, Mrs. Broadhurst, we rented these rooms for official business. Kindly keep yourself out of sight."

The blowzy young woman ran a palm down her thigh.

"But you said—"

"Presently," the officer whispered. Some unspoken communication seemed to leap between the two. With an undertone of savage force, he repeated the word: *"Presently."*

The young woman kept rubbing her thigh. The lieutenant took one more step in her direction. She blinked, turned and lurched out of sight. The door closed.

The officer returned to the parlor. He smiled as if to dismiss the incident. But his eyes were humorless:

"You'll forget what you've just seen. As a personal favor to one of the officers with whom you'll be serving, Mr.—?"

Jared fought a shiver of fear. "Kent."

Relaxed again, the officer strolled back to the table. "Ah, that's right. You did mention your name at the start of our chat. I thought it had a certain familiarity. You did say your father fought at Fallen Timbers—?"

"Yes."

"An officer?"

"A cornet in the dragoons."

"I don't recall the name in the letters my mother's kept almost twenty years. Still, there's *something* famil—"

He snapped his fingers. "Are you perchance related to a Mr. Gilbert Kent of Boston?"

"He and my father are half-brothers."

"Then Gilbert Kent's your uncle."

"Yes. Do you know him?"

"Do you know him, *sir*? You must begin to get accustomed to showing your officers the required respect, Kent."

Jared kept silent, but the muscle in his jaw quivered again.

"I know your uncle by reputation only. Although the citizens of this city crowded the docks to applaud our escape, their enthusiasm doesn't extend to their purses. Colonel Binney, the local naval agent, has exhausted his current allotment of government funds. No bank will grant him a loan. So Captain Hull's been reduced to begging donations in order to replenish our stores—principally our water. I was told that a Mr. Gray and a Mr. Kent jointly volunteered the sum of seventeen thousand dollars to furnish what we must have before we can weigh anchor."

"I hadn't heard that," Jared said, truthfully. The officer's eyes flickered. "Sir."

The lieutenant seemed more hostile now, very likely because he sensed how Jared felt about him:

"Don't expect your uncle's generosity to earn you any special favors. Only your responsiveness to the desires of your officers will do that."

Though severe, the young man still managed to invest the words with a faintly lascivious quality. Having seen the woman, Jared was totally confused. What sort of person *was* this lieutenant?

The lieutenant set about completing the required forms. Presently he handed them across the table.

"Read, then sign your name or make your mark."

"I can sign, sir. I've had schooling."

The lieutenant drifted to the window again, lifted the curtain, stared into the August glare.

"Yes, I should have guessed that from your rather quick tongue. Aboard ship, however, we're more interested in the strength of your body."

Jared's hand jumped. He barely managed to write his name in a legible way.

The officer took the papers, signed one copy. The street door opened. A man stumbled to the parlor entrance, his voice gruff:

"This the recruitin' place? Can't see a damn thing—"

The smell of gin was overpowering. But the lieutenant instantly exuded good humor:

"Come right in, sir. Your eyes will adjust in a moment—"

He handed Jared his copy of the enlistment agreement, then leaped forward as the ragged man swayed. Only the lieutenant's hands kept the drunk from pitching on his face.

The officer maintained a façade of friendliness as he helped the man to a chair, repeating an earlier speech to Jared almost word for word:

"You've come to investigate service under Captain Hull?"

"Mebbe."

"Well, you'll be joining a proud ship, sir."

"Just one 'at pays money an' hands grog around regular is all I give a shit about." The drunk belched, nearly toppling from the chair. The lieutenant cleared his throat behind one hand:

"Understandable, perfectly understandable. I'm sure you've heard of our escape from *Guerriere* and four other British vessels, though. We were chased three days. Three days and two nights—"

Jared folded the agreement, tucked it in his breeches, started for the parlor door. The lieutenant called after him:

"Report to the end of Long Wharf at dawn tomorrow. A longboat will be waiting to take new recruits out to the ship."

"I'll be there, sir," Jared said, not looking back.

The hot, humid air of the street engulfed him. He sat down on the stoop, tugged the agreement out of his pocket and studied it without really seeing it. He had just signed away one whole year of his life. It was what he'd wanted when he walked into the recruiting office, but now he wondered whether he'd done the right thing.

The whole city—excluding the influential anti-war faction, of course—was hailing Isaac Hull as a hero; a master of naval tactics. Jared reminded himself that he was fortunate to be going to sea with a captain of Hull's caliber.

Yet serving with Hull also meant serving with that odd lieutenant—

He realized he didn't know the man's name. He looked at the signature at the bottom of the agreement.

Hamilton Stovall, 6th Lt., U.S.S. Constitution.

He made up his mind to avoid Lieutenant Hamilton Stovall insofar as that would be possible within the confines of a two-hundred-and-four-foot frigate.

V

By his own choice, Jared went to Long Wharf alone the next morning. He put everything at Beacon Street, from his Uncle Gilbert's prideful good wishes to his cousin Amanda's sobs, out of mind as he walked jauntily along, a small canvas bag dangling from one hand.

The bag contained a few personal articles, including

his fob and a surprise gift from the family: a sharply honed knife of Spanish steel in a leather sheath. Gilbert meant for him to use the knife to scrape away the young man's beard that had started sprouting recently.

Sunrise etched a thin line of light along the horizon. Gulls wheeled overhead, occasionally swooping to snatch a tiny fish from the water. The air smelled salty and clean.

Eagerly, Jared searched for the officer supposedly waiting at the end of the pier, saw him—

It wasn't Stovall, thank heaven.

Out in the harbor, Boston's frigate bobbed gently, her tall masts catching the first scarlet out of the east. The breeze raised whitecaps around her hull. Jared could glimpse figures scurrying on the main deck.

His spirits lifted even more. That sleek, beautiful vessel with her intricately carved figurehead—a truculent Hercules—was his new home.

Having been raised in Boston, he had an advantage over country boys. He knew something about ships and their nomenclature. No one would have to tell him which mast was the mizzen, explain the system of watches and bells or point out starboard and larboard. With acquaintances from Mr. Tewkes' academy, he'd sailed the harbor in small pleasure boats, sometimes in heavy weather. He was confident he'd have no trouble with seasickness.

Another recruit had already arrived at the end of the pier. The drunk Jared had encountered yesterday.

As he approached the officer, he watched the poor fool from the recruiting office nearly fall off the pier ladder. He made sure his salute was smart, his name crisply spoken and his feet sure as he descended to the longboat heaving up and down in the chop. Within ten minutes, seven other recruits arrived. The longboat put out into the harbor.

Stovall all but forgotten, Jared gazed at the almost

magical sight of the dawn-reddened masts growing taller and taller as the boat approached the frigate.

Twenty-four hours later, reality had replaced magic.

vi

Constitution carried a complement of thirty boys. They were outfitted in summer uniforms exactly like those worn by the older seamen: white canvas slops, cut wide through the legs to afford freedom of movement; wide-collared white blouses with flowing black scarves; round, flat-crowned black hats gleaming with varnish.

Most of the boys were younger than Jared. He was at first appalled, then amused, at the quantity and range of their profanity. To listen to a weather-browned ten-year-old cheerfully boast that he was already man enough to *shove the ramrod into a whore's muff* was startling, to say the least.

The boys were a rowdy, quarrelsome lot. They slept, as did the ordinary and able seamen, in canvas hammocks on the stifling berth deck. Hung up each evening from iron eyes in the beams of the gun deck above, the hammocks had to be taken down again in the morning and stored in special net racks along the ship's rails.

On his first night in the six- by three-foot hammock, Jared was cramped and uncomfortable. Barely able to breathe in the heat. The other boys kept him awake with chatter about their sexual conquests—an area of experience still foreign to him. They also exchanged opinions about the officers. Captain Hull and First Lieutenant Charles Morris were well liked. The rest were held in varying degrees of contempt; Sixth Lieutenant Stovall was mentioned as a "mean, dirty sod."

Some of the boys discussed duels of honor in which they'd taken part. Jared could hardly believe it, but apparently these near-infants occasionally settled disputes with pistols or swords. He got the impression the officers never interfered.

The routine of the frigate in port was less demanding than it would be at sea, he was told. But it was hectic enough. Four hundred and sixty-eight human beings jammed virtually every square inch of deck and gangway space. There was constant shoving and jostling and cursing as men and boys went about their duties.

In a day, Jared learned the ship's geography, from the magazine and shot locker in the depths of the orlop, up through the berth, gun and spar decks. He was assigned to the officer's wardroom, aft on the berth deck. His responsibilities included mopping the floor, maintaining the lamps, polishing the table and benches. When the officers ate, he ran food from the galley, forward on the gun deck.

He was fortunate to find a likeable companion assigned to the same job—a runtish, homely, but strongly muscled boy of twelve, Oliver Prouty. The boy came from Charleston, in the Carolinas.

On Jared's third night aboard, Prouty fought another boy barehanded for the right to hang his hammock next to Jared's. The southern boy's opponent, taller and older by a year, nevertheless succumbed quickly to Prouty's combination of punches, butts, kicks, gouges and bites.

The two fought by lantern-light on the berth deck. Just when Prouty was getting the best of it, two of his opponent's friends started to intervene. One raised a foot to stamp Prouty's spine while the other grabbed his hair. Jared snatched out the knife whose sheath he kept illegally tucked into his slops at his left hip.

He showed the knife and said, "Let them finish it alone."

The two boys fell back, eyeing the Spanish steel in Jared's hand.

Oliver Prouty finished demolishing his opponent's

nose. He wiped his bloody hands on the other boy's blouse, then cheerfully helped his victim up:

"There, now. We change places, agreed?"

The other boy limped away, snot and blood dripping from his nose as he nodded weary assent.

Prouty slung his hammock in place just before eight clangs of the ship's bell signaled the end of the night watch and the beginning of the mid-watch.

"You've come aboard with one thing in your favor, Kent," Prouty said, putting his foot on a gun carriage and hauling himself up into the hammock.

"What's that, Oliver?"

"Being as tall as you are, nobody much wants to fight you. Still—" with a lewd grin, he stretched out, hands laced under his head "—one chap I know has eyes for you in a different way."

Jared climbed into his own canvas bed. Down the row, a boy shouted, "Douse the fucking lamp!" It was doused. In a moment, Jared and Prouty heard the soft groans of a boy beginning to masturbate.

"Give 'er a thrust fer me, Davey," someone called. There was laughter.

Jared understood Prouty's last remark well enough. He'd been very conscious of eyes watching him with more than usual interest in the wardroom.

"You mean Stovall, I imagine."

"Aye, Mr. Handsome Stovall. He fancies himself a prize beauty, the shit."

"He's the one who signed me up."

"Lucky he didn't fling you down and try to bugger you. 'Course, on shore, he was probably sober—"

"Not quite. He was helping himself to the rum he was supposed to be serving to recruits."

"Well, beware of him if he's into the grog heavy. That's when he gets the urge. Thank the Lord I got an ugly phiz or I 'spose he'd be after me. You met Rudy—

fourth down the line? Stovall got him to his cabin the night after we outran the five Britishers. Damn near raped the life out of Rudy, he did."

Aghast, Jared asked, "You mean you have to go along with something like that?"

"What's the choice? Accuse Stovall, and he'll up and call you a liar. Cap'n Hull has to take the word of another officer over ours. And then Stovall can make it miserable for you afterward."

"Doesn't the captain know Stovall's—tastes?"

"Think he does. But he just can't do anything unless an officer really steps out of line—in front of witnesses."

"He'd better not lay a damn hand on me," Jared said.

"Pray he doesn't. It's either give in or suffer a lot worse for refusing."

vii

The evening of August first, Jared was on duty in the wardroom when Captain Isaac Hull said:

"Gentlemen, I've decided. We're going to sail."

Four of the five officers seated with him at the table expressed surprise. One voiced approval—the first lieutenant, Morris. Stovall raised a limp hand, a visual question mark:

"But we've yet to receive orders from Washington, sir."

"Damned if I want to receive 'em, Lieutenant," Hull replied. He was a short, pot-bellied man of thirty-eight, with ruddy cheeks. A bachelor, his genial, almost carefree manner belied his experience and toughness. Jared already knew a good deal about him:

Hull had been a sailor since age fourteen, having run away from home in Derby, Connecticut. His naval career was interrupted for a period of two years, during which he read law. He claimed he gave it up because he was a poor writer. Everyone else said it was really because he loved the sea.

He had trained on *Constitution,* as fourth lieutenant under Talbot, a famous privateersman of the Revolution. He'd been to High Barbary, where Preble's squadron had twisted the tails of the arrogant deys and bashaws of the North African coast. And he'd achieved his captaincy through talent and hard work, not connections.

Mathematics were required for command of a bridge, so Hull had learned what he needed to know by diligent private study. He could be friendly with individual British captains, but he made no secret of his hatred of their country. His enmity dated from the time of his father's mistreatment on a prison ship anchored in New York harbor during the War for Independence.

Hull pressed the tips of his stubby fingers together, leaned forward to answer Stovall's objection:

"The navy department knows where I am, though I'd prefer not to hear from 'em. I wouldn't want to be handed anything smaller than this frigate. The way they're shuffling commands these days, it could happen. The longer we stay in port, gentlemen, the greater the danger you'll be deprived of my company—"

Muted laughter. Hull's eyes grew sober:

"—and the greater the danger we'll be blockaded by the English."

First Lieutenant Morris said, "I'm anxious to start hunting those bastards on *Spartan* and *Guerriere."* The two notorious ships had been ranging the coast and, almost daily, fishing boats slipped back to Boston with word that one or the other had seized and burned yet another American vessel.

Captain Hull broke a biscuit, munched half. "You forget one of those bastards is a friend of mine, Mr. Morris."

"Jimmy Dacres?"

"Aye. He owes me a hat and I mean to collect."

"All the more reason to weigh anchor!" Morris grinned.

"I agree. We're provisioned—we leave tomorrow."

Sixth Lieutenant Stovall was quick to change tack: "I think the whole crew will be pleased. Certainly I am."

Hull said nothing, peering at his biscuit.

Stovall motioned Jared forward, indicated his cup which Jared had earlier filled with tea. Four of the others were drinking their daily ration of rum. But Jared had already heard Stovall profess—for Hull's benefit—that spirits dulled a man's mind. Hull hadn't seemed impressed. Jared thought the captain recognized Stovall for what he was—a bootlicker.

As Jared poured, Stovall contrived to brush his shoulder against the boy's hip. Without thinking, Jared jerked back. Tea jetted from the spout, staining Stovall's impeccably white breeches.

He leaped up, hand raised. "You clumsy whoreson—!"

"I'm sorry, sir," Jared blurted—only because form required it.

Hull shot out a pudgy hand, seized Stovall's arm: "If you please, Mr. Stovall. It was an accident."

Seething, Stovall sank down again.

Hull said to Jared, "What's your name, lad?"

"Jared Kent, Captain."

"Signed on here in Boston?"

"That's right, sir."

"We have a benefactor named Kent—" Hull mused.

Jared saw no point in modesty; especially not with Stovall glaring at him.

"My uncle, sir."

"Is that right! Well, we'd be thirsty as the devil without him—*and* stuck in this blasted harbor. His generosity was deeply appreciated."

Hull scratched at one rosy cheek. "Your uncle's quite a wealthy man, I understand. Publishes books?"

"And a newspaper."

"Peculiar to find such a man—a Bostonian, that is to say—supporting what some call the west's war."

"My uncle believes it's Boston's war too, sir." Conscious of Stovall watching him, he went on, "New England ships can't sail out in peace until the British stop trying to control the oceans. But that doesn't seem to occur to most New Englanders. My uncle says that's tragic."

Hull nodded. "Your uncle is perceptive. I'm delighted to have you aboard. I hope we can show you some lively action—and His Majesty's ensign being hauled down."

"I hope so too, Captain."

Still avoiding Stovall's stare, Jared cleared plates and utensils and left the wardroom. In the galley, he told Oliver Prouty what had happened.

"Oh my Lord, Jared," the homely boy sighed. "You messed up his uniform?"

"Not intentionally."

"He'll have your back under the cat for certain. I told you there's nothing Handsome Stovall fancies more than his fine appearance."

"Ollie, I have a strange feeling about him. A feeling he's not quite right in the head."

Prouty nodded. "There are plenty of odd stories afloat. That he's a bastard—I mean a real one. That he's rich as hell, and loves to gamble for high stakes. I even heard he got in his cups once and said everyone would be astonished if they knew who his father and mother were."

"Famous people?"

"Don't think he meant that. His father was a soldier out west if I recollect—"

"Yes, Stovall told me that at the recruiting office."

"His mother had another name—Free something. I guess he meant to suggest they were relations."

"Cousins?"

"Closer."

"That's not allowed."

"Christ on the mount! I know that!"

Jared grinned. "You know a lot for someone so young."

"'Round the Charleston docks you don't miss much when you're on your own. I had nobody to raise me but a grandma—half blind and no teeth, poor old woman. I went to sea when I was nine. It was either that or starve—"

For a moment the twelve-year-old looked more like a gnome ten times that age.

"If even half the tales about Stovall are true, it's no wonder he's crazy," he added. "He'll settle up with you, don't think he won't."

A memory of Stovall's eyes flickered in Jared's mind. His hand stole unconsciously to the concealed knife.

"I'll be on my guard."

viii

On August 2, 1812, *Constitution* raised sail and put Boston behind the fierce eagle that spread carved golden wings across her stern.

As Jared had anticipated, seasickness didn't trouble him. He experienced an hour of mild nausea when the frigate first reached open water, but after that, he felt perfectly fit. He quickly developed the sea legs necessary to maintaining balance on the crowded, constantly tilting decks.

Almost every man aboard was eager to come in contact with the enemy. *Constitution* was still the target of disdainful remarks from British captains—and from the admiralty in London. War or no, that kind of talk got around among the seagoing fraternity.

The frigate was a joke on more than one count. Badly designed, His Majesty's naval architects sniffed. Far too much white pine, especially in her fished masts. And live oak for hull timber? Who ever heard of that?

Jared thrilled to the first morning on the open sea. He marveled at the agility of the topmen who scrambled aloft to work the yards, only their dexterous hands and feet separating them from a fall to death in the water. They cracked out the flax canvas with astonishing speed; and there was a lot of it—forty-two thousand square feet.

As the great sails were set, the frigate seemed to leap ahead, boiling up a snow-colored wake astern, splitting the cobalt summer sea at her bow. Hercules glowered at the horizon, the painted symbol of her readiness to do battle.

Once the coast vanished, the training of the crew—especially the several dozen recruits ultimately rounded up in Boston—began in earnest.

Gun drills perfected the teamwork required to open the ports, run out the cannon, load, fire and reload in minimum time.

Though rated as a forty-four, *Constitution* actually carried much heavier armament: thirty twenty-four-pound long guns, for accurate distance firing; twenty-four thirty-two-pound carronades, of shorter range but capable of throwing a much heavier load of metal. One long eighteen-pounder brought the total to fifty-five guns.

The enemy Hull hoped to find was *Guerriere*. Her name meant "female warrior," and she was rated at thirty-eight. What interested the American sailors more was a recent report that she was only shipping sixteen carronades, reducing her close-range firepower.

Such comparisons were dismissed by the British.

Their traditional skill and daring would always carry the day. They considered the American navy insignificant, and American captains upstarts—except on land, where friendships such as Hull's and Dacres' were both common and completely permissible.

All in all, the officers and men of *Constitution* had good reason to yearn for an encounter with *Guerriere* or a ship of similar rate.

The frigate stood eastward for two days, raising no enemy sail. Hull changed course, bearing northwest toward the Bay of Fundy. On the tenth, *Constitution* intercepted a lightly armed British brig outward bound from Newfoundland to Halifax. A second brig was overtaken and captured the following day. Both vessels were burned, and their crews set adrift in longboats. The brigs were of too little value to be sailed back to American waters by prize crews.

A few more equally minor encounters put Captain Hull in a bad temper, and finally caused him to set a course for the Bermudas, where he hoped to find bigger prey.

On the eighteenth, off Cape Race, Newfoundland, *Constitution* overhauled a good-sized brig. She proved to be *Decatur,* a fourteen-gun American privateer. When her captain came aboard, he said he had assumed Hull's ship to be an enemy frigate. As was customary, *Constitution* had showed no colors until the other vessel was identified.

The American captain told Hull he had eluded a real British frigate only the day before. Within an hour, the news spread through the ship. Oliver Prouty repeated it to Jared:

"The captain thinks he's on to Jimmy Dacres. *Decatur* outran a frigate slower than we are. A big one, too—it must be *Guerriere!*"

Excitement gripped the ship all through the night.

Next day, at three bells into the afternoon watch, *Constitution* was plowing through a heavy sea. Men aloft searched for signs of a sail—

But Jared, below, had forgotten all about the pursuit. He had just been dispatched from the galley, carrying a lunch of salt beef, suet, biscuits and hot black coffee.

The lunch was for Sixth Lieutenant Stovall, who had stood the watch till dawn, and was now indisposed in his cabin.

CHAPTER IV

The Devil's Companion

JARED'S HAND TURNED sweaty as he knocked. He glanced along the dim starboard gangway. Overhead, he heard men moving. But the gangway was empty and still; the officers' sector of the berth deck totally deserted.

The sea boomed against the hull. He started to knock again; hesitated. Perhaps Lieutenant Stovall had fallen asleep. Perhaps he wouldn't have to face—

"Come in."

Jared stood unmoving, his left hand white on the handle of the wicker basket. The second time, the voice was less languid:

"I said come in."

Reluctantly, he did.

It took his eyes a moment to adjust to the feeble light of Stovall's single lantern. Tobacco smoke coiled slowly in the tiny cabin, fanned to motion by the opening and closing of the door. Through the haze Jared saw the young lieutenant lounging in his bunk, his throat stock undone, a long-stemmed pipe clenched between his perfect teeth. He didn't look a bit ill.

Stovall set aside the wooden lap desk on which he'd been playing some form of patience with an oversized deck of hand-colored cards: crimson diamonds, purplish-red hearts, blue spades, green clubs. As he swung his legs out of the bunk, two of the court cards slipped to the floor.

He leaned down gracefully; picked up the cards. One was a heart king with the face of President Washington, the other a queen in the form of a classical goddess. He replaced the cards in the deck.

With a straight face, he said, "I trust you won't put me on report, having discovered me with this—" He waggled the deck. "New England divines call it the devil's picture book, don't they? Alas, I'm more comfortable as a companion of devils than of divines."

Jared kept his head down, knowing he was being mocked. He set the basket on the small bolted-down table.

"There is your meal, Lieutenant Stovall."

"Thank you, Mr. Kent. I wasn't up to the wardroom. Caught a touch of grippe in the damp night air, I think."

Jared took a step backward.

"If that will be all—"

"Not quite."

Stovall's manner was cordial enough. But his dark eyes had a bright, cold gleam. Walking slowly toward the boy, he talked with his pipe clenched in his teeth:

"I had no idea you would be on duty, Mr. Kent—"

Jared believed that was probably a lie, but said nothing.

"I thought they might send the lunch with that coarse Prouty fellow. However, since you're here—improperly dressed, I might add—"

Before the boy could stop him, the lieutenant tucked the bottom of Jared's blouse into his slops. For a moment he felt warm fingers probing past the waist of his pants—

Stovall withdrew his hand, sat in the chair beside the table, examined his pipe. It had gone out. He knocked dottle into his palm, carelessly discarded it on the floor.

"—since you are here, I say, we should perhaps discuss your clumsiness in the wardroom. Tea, as you know, leaves an abominable stain. You quite ruined my best breeches."

The dark eyes slid to Jared again. The boy felt a strangling tightness in his throat; a sense of being utterly cut off from the world. He spoke with difficulty:

"As the captain said, it was an accident—"

Stovall sat up straight. "An accident, *sir.*"

Jared's cheeks reddened. His hands shook a little. But he gave Stovall what he wanted:

"An accident—sir."

Stovall licked his lips, his eyes moving again. To Jared's throat; his arms; his chest.

"I am prepared to be forgiving—"

"Captain Hull seemed to think the matter settled. Sir."

"What Captain Hull thinks and what I think are not the same thing. You will sit down, Mr. Kent—"

Stovall vacated the chair.

"—while we consider whether reparations are in order, and if so, what kind."

"Begging the lieutenant's pardon, the steward and the cook instructed me to come straight back to the galley after—"

"I take orders neither from the steward, who is a syphilitic sot, nor the cook, whose swill would win this war instantly if it were served to the enemy three days in a row. That a human being should be expected to eat suet —Christ! What barbarity!"

Then he smiled. "You will sit down."

Jared slipped into the chair. Stovall strolled to the door, leaned against it, his handsome face a pale oval in the smoky gloom. The single hooded lantern swayed gently from one of the beams supporting the gun deck. Jared knew with a dismal certainty that it wasn't going to be easy to get through that door again.

Hamilton Stovall returned to the bunk. He picked up

his cards, began to shuffle them as he perched on the bunk's edge.

"You don't seem to be adjusting to naval discipline too well, Mr.—*turn and look at me, please!*"

Jared swung his legs from one side of the chair to the other.

"Every time you're given an order, I notice a certain —shall we say—hostility? Perhaps you don't even realize you're reacting that way. But as I advised you once before, you won't do well in the service until you curb your rebellious temperament. Of course—"

A slow, limp gesture.

"—in other, more informal circumstances, your lively nature might have a certain charm."

Stovall's hands, somehow seeming quite independent of the rest of him, resumed the shuffling of the deck, pulling cards from the center and bringing them to the front. The rustling sound began to torture Jared's nerves.

He worked up the courage to speak again:

"May I ask the lieutenant the purpose of this—?"

"Damn your impertinence! I told you the purpose. We are discussing the damage done to my breeches. You will sit there and listen until I dismiss you!"

The cards moved again, whispering in counterpoint to the crash of the sea against *Constitution*'s hull. Abruptly, Stovall smiled:

"I want us to settle our difference amicably. You already know I consider us to be kindred spirits. Like you, I am not all that fond of the fuss and protocol of the navy. I accepted a commission out of necessity, frankly. A suitable position in my family's iron finery in Baltimore won't be available until my grandfather passes, bless his soul."

There wasn't a shred of feeling in the last remark.

Jared knew Stovall was toying with him. Short of outright insubordination, he didn't know how to put an end to it.

"I don't intend to get myself killed in this war, I promise you that. I believe I mentioned that my father died in the army almost twenty years ago—of carelessness, I presume. That's the only reason a clever man comes to harm in a war. I am not careless. On the other hand, navy life can broaden a young man's perspectives on the world. It can be salutary in developing—oh, how shall I say it? Manly traits—?"

The soft rippling of the cards stopped. Stovall tossed the deck down, stood and rummaged beneath the bunk bolster. With his back turned, he said:

"Mr. Kent, have you ever had a woman?"

Jared's spine crawled. He couldn't answer.

Stovall swung around, a metallic object gleaming on a chain in his right hand.

"Damme, you're a rude lout!" he exclaimed softly. "You will answer any and all questions put to you by officers of this ship!"

He took two long strides forward, planting his boots wide apart. Jared's mouth turned dry at the sight of the bulge beneath Stovall's tight trousers.

"I repeat—have you ever had a woman?"

"N—no, sir, I haven't."

"Don't you think about it? Many young men your age are fathers."

"I think about it, yes—"

"Do you think it would be pleasant?"

"I—I imagine so."

"Louder, Mr. Kent. You're whispering."

"I said—I imagine so."

Stovall flicked a catch on the oval locket. One side fell away to reveal the most astonishing miniature Jared had ever seen: a reclining nude; a voluptuous woman. Her fingers hid only part of the dark triangle between her legs.

"Lovely creature, isn't she? Her name is Mrs. Free-mantle."

He leaned down toward the seated boy, his breath ripe with the smell of the tobacco he'd been smoking.

"Does the sight of a naked woman excite you, Mr. Kent? Make you imagine those pleasures and sensations you've never experienced before?"

Jared jerked his head up, so that he didn't have to stare at that obscene picture cupped in Stovall's hand. He said in a hoarse voice:

"Not really, sir."

Stovall's right brow hooked up. "Indeed? Why not?"

"I expect it would be better to—to wait for the real thing."

"You're a clever one," Stovall chuckled. "Practical, too, since we've no women on board." He snapped the locket shut, tucked it into the pocket of his breeches. "Still, Lord Cock can be a most impatient master. Surely at night, you sometimes feel his yearnings. His strainings—"

Stovall's hand dropped toward Jared's knee; touched it lightly.

"Surely you understand there are ways in which discreet gentlemen—pledged as friends—can relieve—"

"Take your hand away."

"What's this? *You* giving orders to *me?*" The fingers caressed his leg.

"I'm just telling you—take your hand away, or—" Jared swallowed.

"Or what, Mr. Kent?"

"Or I'll kill you."

Stovall's eyes widened. Jared braced for a blow of the lieutenant's fist. Instead, the young man guffawed:

"Kill me, will you? How, in heaven's name?"

"With—with my fists or any way I can," Jared said, having decided at the last second not to reveal his one small advantage.

Stovall let go of his leg, slapped him on the shoulder. Jared wrenched away.

"By God, Mr. Kent, those blue eyes tell the truth. You've spirit. Style! Imagine!—telling an officer you're going to kill him. That's incredible brass! But I admire it—"

He picked up the cards from the bunk.

"—I admire it because it's so atypical. The deeds—the lives of most men are so pathetically small and ordinary. Scruples hamper them—scruples being another name for fear. I never permit myself to be cowed that way. When I gamble, it's for thousands, not pennies. I don't shrink from the pleasures cowardly little men call vices—I seek them out!"

He gestured flamboyantly with the oversized cards. Jared's earlier suspicion had become a conviction. Although the lieutenant might put on a respectable face for his superiors, he was dangerously deranged. The boy pressed his palms against his knees to keep the lieutenant from seeing how badly he was shaking.

"That's why I do admire that chap Bonaparte," Stovall went on. "Everyone else damns him, but I appreciate the scope of his ambition. His willingness to abandon himself utterly to a grand vision. For the same reason, I rather admire our highly moral captain, surprising as that may sound. His escape from those five Britishers was magnificent! No mundane fellow could have accomplished it—or would have tried. We gambled everything—risked everything for a single puff of wind, a quarter mile of distance—we staked our lives and damn near broke our backs, *but we won—!*"

Abruptly, Stovall drew a deep breath and riffled

through the deck. Jared watched with mingled fascination and horror as he plucked out a blue-tinted spade—a knave represented by a scowling Indian chief with upraised tomahawk. Stovall twirled the card back and forth between thumb and index finger:

"I'm telling you all this, dear boy, to show you that we are much alike—"

Flick, the knave's face was hidden.

"We should be, we *will* be intimate friends—commencing now."

Flick, the savage popped back into sight.

"I have a certain desire that you can satisfy, and it will be to your advantage to do so. As the special friend of an officer aboard this ship, you would be able to obtain certain favors. Preferred duties. Further, anyone who affronts you would have to deal with me. Do you understand what I'm saying?"

"Yes, but—I won't have any of it."

"I'm afraid you've no choice." Stovall released the knave. It fluttered to his feet. "You are expected to obey orders."

He took hold of Jared's shoulder again. "Come, now. No more sparring. Pull off your trousers and climb into that bunk."

Jared shot from the chair, throwing Stovall off balance. He jerked his right knee up, striking the bulge at Stovall's crotch.

The lieutenant staggered backwards; let out an almost feminine scream:

"You filthy little bastard! I'll have fifty laid on you with the cat!"

"You know twelve's the limit, you damned—"

"Oh yes? You'll take a hundred!"

Jared backed swiftly around the table, spun and ran to the door.

"*Come here!*"

In the distance, Jared heard another man yelling. On the gun deck above, feet thudded suddenly. He had the door halfway open when Stovall's fist struck the back of his head.

His forehead slammed into the edge of the door. He gasped as Stovall pushed him aside, booted the door shut, whirled him around by the shoulders—then back-handed him across the face three times.

Strong as he was, Jared couldn't match the lieutenant's height and weight. He tried the tactic of a knee to the midsection a second time. Stovall jerked backwards at the waist, avoiding the knee. His fist pounded Jared's temple. The boy staggered, fell.

Stovall kicked Jared's belly, doubling him in pain. Then Stovall crouched, hands reaching for his throat. The clamor of voices grew louder overhead. *Constitution*'s gangways echoed with a hammer of running feet.

Jared's arms were crossed over his aching belly. Stovall seized his neck. Jared slid the fingers of his right hand beneath his left forearm and down to his waist. He tugged the Spanish knife from its sheath, jerked it into the light where Stovall could see it shine.

The lieutenant dropped his hands to his sides, macabre amusement twisting his mouth:

"Damme, the pup has teeth!"

Jared's right hand trembled. It took will to steady it. He held the knife between himself and Stovall. In a moment, staring at the steel glitter, the lieutenant ceased smiling.

Jared twisted the point of the knife in a small circle. He was too frightened to speak, but Stovall understood quite well. He rose slowly, retreated a step; another—

"You touch me again and I'll cut your face," Jared whispered. "Whatever else happens, I'll cut your face to pieces."

Stovall turned pale, began to curse; monotonous, obscene oaths that gave Jared an odd sort of hope. He'd struck a vulnerable spot—Stovall's vanity.

Jared dragged himself to his knees, then stood, back against the outer wall of the cabin. He had perhaps three feet to travel to the closed door. He moved his right foot, eyes never leaving the lieutenant. At any moment he expected another attack.

He dragged his left foot after his right, inching down the wall. The beam lantern swayed, flinging Stovall's shadow back and forth. The lieutenant's cheeks glistened with sweat.

Another step to the right. One more and he'd break for it—

Stovall's body tensed slightly, telling Jared the attack was coming. He raised his right hand higher, at the same time elevating the point of the knife. The blade's angle was about forty-five degrees.

Stovall's eyes flicked to the steel. He recognized the risk. One misstep, or a fall, and Jared could impale his face—

Rage overcame reason. Stovall whipped up his right fist. Too late, Jared saw the strategy: knock down the hanging lantern; force him to maneuver in darkness. He whirled toward the cabin door—

Stovall's smash was stopped in midair as someone knocked.

"Lieutenant Stovall? Captain requests all officers to the wheel at once. We've sighted—"

Jared jerked the door open and bowled past the goggling master's mate.

As if demons were after him, he plunged forward to the ladderway amidships, sheathing the knife as he ran. He streaked up to the gun deck and burst into the light at the waist. In the heavy sea, spray broke across *Constitution*'s rail. He'd never felt anything so welcome as that chilly salt water showering him while he scuttled up the steps to the fo'c'sle.

The Atlantic showed whitecaps with deep troughs between. Towering white clouds hid the sun, yet some of its light leaked through, putting a glare on the slopes of the swelling waves. Everywhere, men were shouting; running; going hand over hand up the ratlines.

Still blinking, Jared stumbled ahead through the press of seamen and marines. A glance over his shoulder revealed Captain Hull near the wheel. Some of the men on deck looked half dressed, but Hull's uniform was, as usual, impeccable: black silk stock; straight-cut jacket; tight white breeches over his bulging paunch.

The captain paced back and forth, fiddling with his fob. Finally he demanded the glass from the sailing master. One long look, and he began shouting orders.

Jared hurried around the foremast. He had trouble with his footing on the spray-slicked deck. He stumbled into a topman hurrying to the shrouds. Took a cuff on the cheek from the angry man, and almost fell.

The man rushed on. Jared searched for someone he knew; spied Oliver Prouty and a half dozen other boys just beyond a group of marines with rifles. Gathered between the fo'c'sle carronades, men and boys were watching a sail that jutted above the horizon off the larboard rail.

Once more Jared risked a look back; saw Sixth Lieutenant Stovall, now in full uniform, climb up from below.

Stovall spotted Jared. His expression made it plain the boy would be punished. Jared guessed the lieutenant would charge him with a long list of infractions, so he could be given the maximum penalty for each.

As if to confirm it, Stovall touched fingertips to the forward edge of his braided half-moon hat, a mock salute. Then he pivoted and walked smartly toward Captain Hull, the center of a growing crowd of excited men aft of the mizzen.

ii

Still limp from what had happened in Stovall's cabin, Jared joined the other boys. Oliver Prouty elbowed a place for him, then leaned out over the rail. He pointed at the scrap of sail:

"Caught sight of her at two sharp. I've already laid six bets that she's a Britisher."

The ship hidden below the horizon appeared to be bearing east-southeast. If that were true, her course would take her across *Constitution*'s bow. Jared stared at the sail in a vacant way.

The Charleston boy noticed; brushed windblown hair out of his eyes; took hold of his friend's arm:

"You're white. What the hell's wrong?"

"I—" Jared wiped his mouth. "I had to pay a visit to Stovall's quarters."

Oliver Prouty blinked, searched the aft part of the spar deck. "I see him near the wheel."

"Looks mad as the devil, too," one of the other boys said.

The sea blinded Jared with its glare as he swung around. Positioned between the sailing master and First Lieutenant Morris, Stovall was attempting to get Hull's attention. Jared knew what the Sixth Lieutenant wanted to say.

Hull wasn't interested. Eyes shielded with one hand, he watched the setting of canvas in preparation for pursuit of the other vessel. There were scores of men aloft. But all the masthead flags had been hauled down.

Once more Stovall spoke to Hull. The captain's

dumpling face reddened. He said something sharp to the lieutenant. Jared thought he could make out two words: *Not now.*

Stovall withdrew, scarlet. Oliver Prouty bent his head close:

"What happened in his cabin?"

"What do you think?"

"You mean he—?"

"He tried."

"And you hollered?"

"Worse than that. I had my knife out, ready to cut him up."

"Jesus! You're in for it."

Jared nodded. "At this point, I'd probably be better off jumping in the ocean. He'll have the cat on my back as soon as he can."

"Well," Prouty said, "that ship's bought you a little time. Hull won't put his mind to anything else until we've learned whether she's friend or foe. If they beat to quarters—"

"*When* they beat to quarters," said another boy. "From the size of that sail, she's got to be a big ship—and you've already wagered she's British."

Prouty nodded. "So little Isaac will fight. Look at him! He's so excited, he can't stand still!"

Prouty's expression grew sly. "Suppose we do engage. You can always hope some metal from the enemy's cannon puts Lieutenant Handsome out of commission. Or that *something* happens to him—"

Jared looked at his friend, comprehension slow in coming. Prouty's eyes were unblinkingly cruel.

"I never thought of that. Lieutenant Stovall could be one of those killed, couldn't he?"

"With things confused—cannon going off—marines

sniping from the tops—any man can be killed—" Prouty snapped his fingers. "That quick."

Slowly, Jared moved his gaze to another of the young, tanned faces around him.

Then to a second.

A third.

A fourth—

What he saw in those faces was chilling. He recognized an unspoken promise. The boys would protect him with their silence.

He ran a hand over his forehead. That Hamilton Stovall was both unbalanced and vengeful, he didn't doubt for a moment. And it would be so easy. During gun drills, he'd seen how much smoke just a few of the cannon produced. Imagine the smoke from an entire broadside; clouds of it, to make faces indistinct; conceal one quick stroke of the Spanish knife—

God, he was tempted.

Prouty sensed his hesitancy:

"If you don't do something, I can tell you what'll happen. Stovall will have you punished so hard, you'll be lucky not to be crippled for life. Even if you take the cat and pull through, you'll be looking over your shoulder the rest of the voyage, wondering when he's going to come at you—"

Prouty's hand closed on Jared's forearm.

"Do it, Jared. *Do it.*"

Jared started to say yes. An image of his uncle flashed into his mind. His shoulders slumped.

"I can't, Ollie. I want to, but I can't."

Scowling, Prouty studied his crestfallen friend. After a moment, he gave a resigned shrug:

"All right. It's your skin. You know you're being a fool."

"I know. I'll just have to take my chances."

Waves thundered against *Constitution*'s hull. All sails set, she bore off on a course to intercept the stranger. As Jared watched the horizon, he could almost feel Hamilton Stovall's eyes on his back.

CHAPTER V

"Her Sides are Made of Iron!"

BY HALF-PAST three, no doubt remained. The sails of the ship *Constitution* was chasing identified her as a member of the frigate class.

By four, her hull was in sight. Jared could make out small figures scurrying on her deck. From the wheel, word was passed that the captain had definitely identified the stranger as *Guerriere.*

The American frigate drew closer, running in front of the stiff northwest breeze. Her bow rose and plunged in the heavy swells. The deck tilted at increasingly extreme angles.

About half past four, Hull ordered tampions removed from the muzzles of all cannon.

At a quarter of five, he began rattling a stream of orders. The topgallants, staysails and the flying jib were hauled in, the topsails reefed a second time, the royal yards sent down and the courses sent up. A final order started the drummers beating to quarters. All over the spar deck, men and boys joined in three loud cheers.

Everyone scrambled to battle stations. Jared kicked off his shoes just as the others did; bare skin held a bloody deck more firmly than leather. He stripped off his shirt; lint festering in a wound could bring on gangrene—and amputation. As he took his position on the fo'c'sle, he almost forgot about the ominous presence of Lieutenant Hamilton Stovall, aft.

About half the boys were assigned to running back

and forth between the orlop and the upper decks, bringing shot and leather buckets of powder to the guns. Jared, Prouty and three other boys formed a chain on the fo'c'sle to pass the powder and shot to the forward gun crews.

Constitution plowed ahead under shortened sail. Topmen came scrambling down as the last of the drumrolls died away under the steady crash of the waves. The gunners were busy checking the breeching ropes of the fo'c'sle carronades. The ropes, secured to the rail timbers through eyebolts, prevented the cannon from recoiling too far.

Working next to Jared, Oliver Prouty seemed in high spirits:

"Just heard they're double-shotting the twenty-fours down on the gun deck. Round and grape'll bloody the fucking British quick enough!"

Jared shivered. He had never seen grapeshot used. But he'd heard about the effects of the small iron balls wrapped in canvas around a wooden dowel, then secured to a wood disc that slid into the cannon's muzzle; the whole split and flew apart when fired, filling the air with murderous fragments of metal.

Guerriere showed every intention of fighting. She'd already backed her main topsail, and was no longer making headway. Captain Hull bounced up and down on the balls of his feet, alternately observing the enemy through his glass and snapping orders.

Constitution bore down on the other ship, approaching with her bowsprit pointed at *Guerriere*'s starboard bow. Jared heard one of the fo'c'sle gunners complain that Hull was playing a dangerous game. From her current position, the American would only be able to fire a couple of the twenty-fours mounted in the bow. *Guerriere*, on the other hand, would be able to rake with a full starboard broadside.

The clang of the ship's bell told Jared it was five o'clock. A moment later, men began to point and curse. A familiar and despised scarlet ensign was being run up each of *Guerriere*'s three masts.

Slow matches wrapped around iron linstocks curled acrid smoke into the air beside each gun. Jared judged the frigates to be less than two miles apart. The Britisher was rolling violently in the white-capped swells.

All around him, he smelled sweat. Saw hands raised to rub watering eyes. Marines in groups of seven—one to fire, six others to reload the rifles for the marksman—were climbing quietly to the fighting tops.

Amidships, Lieutenant Morris called out, "Shall we give her a shot to catch her attention, sir?"

Hull's voice carried all the way forward:

"Mr. Morris, I will tell you when and where to fire. Stand ready—and see not a single shot is thrown away."

The frigates drew closer together.

Closer—

Jared saw a single puff of smoke erupt from *Guerriere.* A second later, he heard the slam of the explosion.

Almost at once, the enemy's entire starboard side poured out smoke and thunder. Men aboard *Constitution* jerked their heads up—the Britisher's shot would hit high if it hit at all.

Not a single round found a target. The accuracy of the guns depended on the precise moment of firing, Jared knew. Someone aboard the enemy had miscalculated—given the order to fire just as the starboard side rose on the up-swell of a wave.

He whirled around, saw and heard the British cannon balls raise huge, noisy geysers of water—every round having traveled all the way over *Constitution*'s masts.

Guerriere immediately began to wear around to bring

her larboard batteries to bear. Hull shouted so everyone on deck could hear:

"Men, do your duty now! Your officers can't command you every minute. You must each do everything in your power for your country—!"

Then he called for flags.

Wild cheering broke out as the three jacks traveled up their lines to snap in the wind at the three mastheads. On the mizzen, a huge seventeen-star ensign unfurled. New eighteen-star flags, recognizing the addition of Louisiana to the union in April, had yet to be supplied to the navy.

On Hull's next command, the forward gun crews swung into action. Smoldering linstocks dipped. The bow chasers boomed. But the shots dropped into the sea well short of the enemy.

Jared was fascinated by the agility of the gunners. When fired, the twenty-fours recoiled like juggernauts, their carriages slamming backwards from the open ports and jerking the breeching ropes so taut Jared fancied he could hear the thick lines whine. The moment the recoil spent itself, a member of the gun crew shoved the rammer into the muzzle. Once all sparks were swabbed out, reloading could safely begin.

Because *Constitution*'s first shots had missed, the bow chaser crews grumbled about their error as they worked. They'd mistimed their fire by a second or so, and profanely swore it wouldn't happen again.

Guerriere had come about. Her larboard batteries began to spout smoke and orange fire. Some shot plopped into the water midway between the two vessels. But a few rounds struck quite close to the American, raining water on Jared and the men nearby. Jared heard a peculiar thudding amidships, pivoted to see a gunner leaning over the high rail, pointing down at the hull.

"That one hit us! But the ball bounced right off."

Grinning, he whirled back to the disbelievers in his crew:

"I swear to God it bounced, lads. With that live oak, it's like her sides are made of iron!"

For almost an hour, the battle continued without much result. *Guerriere* kept wearing in order to rake with her starboard guns, then with those on the opposite side. But Hull was quick to respond, tacking and half-tacking so that most of the salvos fell short, or hit the sea where *Constitution* had been only moments before. Occasionally Hull ordered one or two shots. But no more.

As the inconclusive chase wore on, Jared grew increasingly nervous. So did the men at the fo'c'sle guns. They were openly impatient with Hull's tactics. *Constitution* was making slow headway, using the interval between the enemy's broadsides to bore in closer and closer. But the captain still refused to commit the frigate's full firepower.

The light was beginning to fade from the towering clouds. Getting on toward twilight, Jared thought. Perhaps there'd be no decisive end to the engagement—

A strange quiet descended. *Guerriere*'s guns were silent. She seemed to be standing completely still. Hull called for the main topgallants to be set. As men clambered aloft, he bawled another order:

"Sailing master—*lay her alongside!*"

Jared's throat tightened. At last, Hull was taking the offensive. In moments, he felt the frigate surge forward—on a course that would carry her directly past the enemy's larboard side—and larboard cannon.

Bells clanged six o'clock. Steadily, *Constitution* drew up nearer the stern of *Guerriere*. Evidently some of the American fire had done damage; Jared saw hands aloft at the enemy's mizzen, furiously re-rigging lines.

Out across *Constitution*'s starboard rail, he watched

the frigate come abreast of *Guerriere*'s stern and pass it. Perhaps the distance of a pistol shot separated the vessels. He could pick out the braid-decorated uniform of the lean captain, Dacres, on the enemy's quarterdeck.

Guerriere's larboard cannon began firing, stern batteries first. The sea echoed with the rolling thunder; fiery bursts at the muzzles brightened the darkening day.

Geysers shot skyward between the ships. The American's hull thumped several times as more enemy shot caromed off. Then a round struck amidships and penetrated with a tremendous crashing of timbers. Men screamed in pain.

Shot ripped several of *Constitution*'s sails. Hull sent more men up to repair the damage. Impatience edged the voice of Lieutenant Morris:

"Sir, we have men badly hit on the gun deck. When can we fire?"

"Not yet, not yet!" Hull shouted back, clambering up on an arms chest in order to see the enemy more easily.

The fo'c'sle gun crews tried to encourage one another during the enforced inaction:

"They got blind men firing them guns. Can't hit a thing."

"Must be 'cos they got no sights on their pieces the way we do."

"I seen three more rounds bounce off our sides, just as pretty as you please—"

Slowly, inexorably, *Constitution* drew abreast of the British frigate, whose gun and spar deck cannon continued to boom intermittently. Overhead, the frigate's canvas whined and cracked in the wind.

Gunners standing to the right of their pieces blew on the smoldering lengths of cord to raise sparks, then lowered their hands as close to the priming pans as they dared. Jared stood motionless not far from one of the carronades, the powder and shot relay having suspended activity because of the lack of American fire.

One of the carronade gunners gave his quoin a kick, making sure the elevating wedge was firmly in place. On *Guerriere,* Jared now saw faces clearly; he could even judge the relative ages of the men. My God, how close the frigates were running! Why didn't Hull—?

"On the next one, sir?" Morris shouted.

"On the next one!" Hull replied, still balanced atop the arms chest, watching the slow rise of the rail in relation to the enemy's hull.

Suddenly he flung up his arms:

"Now, sir—*pour in the whole broadside!*"

Jared had never heard such noise. The deck shook beneath his feet as the forward gun deck batteries fired, then the midships batteries. The carronades on the fo'c'sle roared, and recoiled, billowing smoke from the depths of scorching-hot barrels. Starting at the bow, *Constitution* threw everything on her starboard side.

Almost immediately, jubilant shouts rang from the tops. The marines aloft were the first to see the damage double-shotting had done to *Guerriere*'s masts and rigging. Jared saw it for himself when some of the thick smoke cleared.

He saw another kind of damage, too. Aboard the enemy, men writhed on the deck and tumbled out of the rigging. A new sound blended with the last of the American cannon fire—cries of agony from the wounded and dying aboard *Guerriere.*

Bouncing up and down on the arms chest, Captain Hull yelled even louder:

"By heaven, that ship is ours!"

The captain seemed oblivious to the fact that, in his excitement, he had split his trousers from crotch to knee.

Men laughed. But not for long. In less than a minute, *Constitution*'s batteries reloaded and fired a second broadside.

Hurriedly passing shot and powder buckets again, Jared coughed and gritted his teeth against the acutely painful roar of the fo'c'sle pieces. The carronades recoiled wildly on their wheeled carriages, checked only by the humming ropes. His world shrank to a small piece of deck, smoke-choked, filled with deafening crashes, lit by bursts of orange that glared, then quickly dimmed. In the hellish light, Oliver Prouty's dirty, grinning face resembled some imp's.

Through rifts in the smoke, Jared saw men fallen on the deck. He saw blood, and felt the old, puzzling nausea begin to build in his belly. He fought it, but it grew stronger moment by moment, almost paralyzing him. His only relief came from avoiding a direct look at the wounded.

For the next fifteen minutes, *Constitution* ran alongside *Guerriere,* suffering few hits from the enemy guns but doing devastating damage with her own.

ii

Shortly after six, *Constitution*'s broadsides broke *Guerriere*'s mizzen several feet above the deck. The Americans cheered as the huge mast began to topple, cordage and all.

Jared watched screaming men plummet from the yards and rigging. Some fell in the sea. Others landed on the deck, the luckier ones dead or unconscious, the rest broken and twitching.

Near the wheel, Captain Hull continued to bob up and down, his linen underdrawers showing through the tear in his trousers. As *Guerriere*'s mast crashed across her rail, Hull waved a fist:

"Huzzah, boys! We've made a brig of her! Next time we'll make her a sloop!"

iii

The British gunners still seemed unable to inflict much damage on *Constitution,* but the American fire was highly effective. As he passed shot and powder forward, the procedure almost automatic by now, Jared tried to figure out why.

When the smoke blew away enough to permit it, he studied *Guerriere*'s badly ripped hull, noting the exact moment at which her cannons went off. At last he saw the difference:

She tended to fire as she rolled upward on cresting waves. Hence the principal damage she did occurred aloft. *Constitution*'s gunners, on the other hand, usually fired on the down-roll, taking their toll on the enemy's deck, and hulling her in the bargain.

A few more men aboard the American frigate had been wounded. Jared still avoided looking at them; the nausea, barely manageable, was with him every moment.

Except for the humiliating sickness—and a growing ache in his arms and shoulders—he did his job as if he'd been at it for years. The first few broadsides had terrified him. Now he hardly glanced up as the batteries roared.

Constitution changed course again. She swept across *Guerriere*'s bow, then put her helm hard to larboard. Orders were barked—stand by for another broadside!

The frigate began to veer back before the wind. Her larboard gun crews readied their slow matches. Oliver

Prouty swiped his face with his wrist, peering into the gray billows around the tops:

"We got some of our braces shot away. She's not falling off fast enough—"

The significance of that escaped Jared until a few moments later, when he heard alarmed cries aft. He whirled, squinted through the smoke—and saw a sight that froze him:

Like the prow of a phantom ship materializing, *Guerriere*'s jib boom and bowsprit appeared in the smoke.

Prouty yelled, "She's going to hit us—!"

The enemy's bowsprit thrust against the American's larboard stern quarter with a prolonged grinding noise. The impact splintered the taffrail and crushed the stern longboat.

Almost instantly, the British frigate dropped into *Constitution*'s wake—or tried. A man pointed:

"She's fouled on the mizzen rigging!"

A moment later, sheets of fire seemed to leap from *Constitution*'s fighting tops. The marines aloft raked the enemy's deck with their rifles.

Tangled, the two ships bobbed on the swells, their rails not six feet apart. A voice screamed from the foretop:

"They're preparing to board!"

Someone near *Constitution*'s wheel—Jared couldn't see who—took quick action:

"Boarders away!"

"Come on, Jared!" Prouty exclaimed, pulling his friend aft.

They scrambled along the gangway amidships, men running behind and ahead of them; all except the few hands responsible for the sails had left their stations and headed for the cutlass racks.

The rifle fire from the tops thickened the smoke even

more. Above the din, Jared heard men shriek aboard *Guerriere* as the marines hit their targets.

But the enemy, too, had sharpshooters aloft. A man just in front of Jared took a ball in the shoulder and pitched against the rail. Jared made the mistake of glancing at him. Blood stained the man's blouse; big, bright patches of blood—

"Keep moving or you'll be trampled!" Prouty screamed behind him, shoving. Jared dashed on.

They seized cutlasses from their assigned racks. A few yards aft near the larboard rail, Lieutenant Morris doubled over suddenly, gut-shot by a ball from a British pistol half a dozen feet away. A lieutenant of marines clambered up on *Guerriere*'s fouled bowsprit, searching the blowing smoke for his commanding officer:

"Captain Hull? Shall we boar—?"

A ball hit his forehead, drove him to the deck. Jared swallowed the bile in his mouth, closed his fingers tight around the cutlass hilt. At the enemy's rail, he could see the British sailors milling. One side or the other would seize the advantage at any moment, and cross the bowsprit—

He watched Captain Hull bend over the fallen Morris. The first lieutenant grimaced, took Hull's hand, struggled to his feet. The front of Morris' coat was a red ruin. Bone-pale, he pressed his hands against his wound. Slimy red coils showed between his fingers—

Jared gagged. Morris' stomach had been torn open. Yet he was up and moving, literally holding his own entrails.

Hull spun away, sword drawn, as if he intended to lead the boarders personally. Morris reached for the captain's shoulder with one gory hand. Hull whirled, in a fury until he saw who had taken hold of him.

Morris ripped one epaulette from Hull's uniform, then the other.

"Now—" he gasped. "Now you won't make such a prize target—"

Hull understood, clapped a hand on his lieutenant's arm. Both men disappeared as heavy clouds of smoke rolled across the stern.

The din of rifle and pistol fire had become continuous. Jared and Prouty pushed and shoved, but a crowd of men, uncertain as to their orders, prevented forward movement. Jared's left foot slipped. He didn't dare look down. The deck was slick with blood. Men lay everywhere, wounded or dead—

Jared's ears began to ring. All the blood started him trembling violently.

Prouty pushed him:

"What the hell's the matter with you? Go to the left! Around the wheel! These simpletons may want to stand here, but I want to get aboard *Guerriere!*"

Jared swayed; let Prouty circle away from him, past the wheel on the starboard side. The crowd was beginning to break up, move toward the stern. Jared stumbled after his friend—and came to a halt again a few steps aft of the wheel.

A dead seaman lay at his feet, blouse pierced by three balls. Jared was so mesmerized by the sight of the man's bloodied torso, he completely forgot his own danger—until another British ball chewed the deck a yard to the right.

Flying splinters stung his cheeks and throat, jolting him back to reality. The tumult of confused voices and small arms fire—suddenly blending with another long, crunching noise—made his head throb.

Aboard *Guerriere,* the wails and groans of the wounded were unbelievably loud; a chorus of condemmed men howling in hell. Jared's eyes stung; the smoke was thick again. He could hardly see anyone.

To larboard, the smoke parted slightly. Jared lurched

in that direction, saw another sailor spin around and fall. The grinding noise grew louder—the sound of the two frigates tearing apart, driven off from each other by the heavy waves.

Rigging broke. Wood snapped. Jared stumbled into lines tumbling from overhead. *Guerriere* separated just as the Americans were massing at her bowsprit, finally organized to board.

Watching from a good twenty feet away, Jared spied Oliver Prouty at the fringe of the boarding party. The Charleston boy was scowling and flourishing his cutlass. He dropped to his knees with a stunned look as a chance shot from one of *Guerriere*'s two remaining tops blew away the back of his head.

"Ollie!" Jared screamed, slipping and sliding aft and to larboard at the same time. In a second, more smoke hid the boarders.

A hand from the smoke caught his arm.

"*Let go, goddamn y—*"

The yell died in his throat. Standing beside one of the aft guns, Sixth Lieutenant Stovall glared at him. In his other hand Stovall held a navy pistol.

Writhing, Jared tried to free himself from the lieutenant's grip. He saw the round, black eye of the barrel pointed at his forehead. And behind it, Stovall's crazed smile:

"Everyone will think it was a British ball, won't they, Mr. Kent?"

He shoved Jared backwards, away from the rail.

"Won't they?"

Jared swung his cutlass as Stovall cocked the pistol. The lieutenant dodged the downward sweep of the blade. It struck something that vibrated. Jared heard the creak of carriage wheels—

Its right breeching rope severed by Jared's cut, the cannon by which Stovall had been standing swung away from the rail. The left breeching rope snapped; the cannon was loose—

Stovall saw it coming, rolling slowly as the left side of the frigate lifted. Stovall released Jared's arm. Both leaped back—but not before Jared swung his cutlass a second time.

The tip barely nicked Stovall's jaw. Then the runaway cannon rumbled between them, the wheels narrowly missing Jared's bare feet.

Stovall slapped a hand against his nicked chin as the deck tilted even more sharply. He stumbled to starboard, lost his footing, dropped his pistol, flailed wildly with both hands, seeking something to check his fall.

His hands closed on the muzzle of the cannon. He screamed.

A foul odor mingled with the reek of powder. The rest happened incredibly fast.

Already on his knees, Stovall pitched forward. As his hands slipped off the metal, the right side of his face slammed against the breech below the firing pan. His second, piercing shriek testified to the searing heat. The cannon slid out from under him and rolled on to come to a jolting stop against the far rail.

In the smoke, men were still swarming aft on both sides of Jared. Several had leaped clear of the runaway cannon, but not a one paid any attention to the fallen lieutenant midway between the two rails; he was just another floundering casualty.

Screaming again, Stovall writhed on his back, both hands clutching his right cheek. All at once a stain spread at his crotch.

He fainted. His hands fell to his sides. Jared saw reddened facial tissue. The odor of burned flesh was overpowering—

Guerriere's batteries roared. *Constitution* shivered as

round shot burst the rear wall of Captain Hull's great cabin. In a moment, flames licked upward over the stern. A fire crew assembled, disappeared in the gray billows—

The two frigates had separated completely. Jared snatched up Stovall's pistol, discharged it at the barely visible bow of the other ship. As far as he could see, he hit nothing. No wonder. His hand was trembling.

In despair, he threw the pistol away. He turned toward the bow, walking as best he could on the treacherous deck. *I should go back,* he thought. *Go back and make certain Stovall's dead—*

He couldn't. He was too weak from the shock of what had just happened. Too overcome with sickness from the sight of bleeding men. He let the cutlass drop from his other hand. He fell against the rail as the opposite side of the ship rose. He seized the rail, thrust his head over, violently sick—

When he raised his head, he saw *Guerriere* astern—and blinked in disbelief. Not one of her three masts remained.

Her deck was a litter of broken wood, ripped sail, tangled cordage. On the quarterdeck, her captain was being supported by two of his officers. Even at this distance, Jared clearly saw the large, dark stain on the back of the captain's uniform.

"She's done, by heaven!"

Hearing Hull shout somewhere in the smoke, men all over the ship began to cheer. But not Jared. He remembered Stovall. And Oliver Prouty—

Ollie was dead. *Dead.* How could that be?

Tears came to his eyes.

They were gone a few moments later when he stumbled back to the spot where Stovall had fallen.

The ship's sixth lieutenant was nowhere to be seen.

iv

In the lowering light, the two frigates continued to roll in the heavy sea, guns silent. *Constitution* was damaged but *Guerriere* was totally out of action. As the smoke gradually cleared, a tatter of white became visible on the enemy quarterdeck.

An officer strode to Isaac Hull's side. The little captain was grimy now. During the engagement his other trouser leg had split.

The officer called Hull's attention to the wigwagging white square. "I believe she's asking quarter, captain."

"Well she might. There's not a stick left standing for showing a flag—white or any other kind. What the devil is that man waving, Lieutenant Read?"

"As nearly as I can make out, sir, a tablecloth."

Isaac Hull's face looked as merry as Jared had ever seen it:

"Take a boat. Find out whether she has actually struck."

"I'm sure she has, sir. But I'll go at once—"

Hull caught him as he left: "Read—"

"Sir?"

"See to Jimmy Dacres. I watched him take a ball in the back when she fouled us."

The captain was no longer smiling.

v

Shortly after seven o'clock, a returning boat brought *Guerriere*'s captain alongside. Hull himself went to the ladder as men assisted Dacres up to the victor's deck.

Near the top of the ladder, Dacres paled visibly; Jared saw it from his place at the rail. He was crowded among men and boys eager for the sight of a British captain surrendering to one of the Americans his admiralty scorned. But all Jared could think of was Stovall; and the way he'd botched his one chance to put an end to the threat Stovall represented—

Captain Hull put on his half-moon hat, stepped to the head of the ladder:

"Dacres, give me your hand. I know you're hurt."

James Dacres replied with an oath. Hull backed away, waiting until the wounded skipper negotiated the rail.

Dacres approached Hull with an unsteady step. Blood stained his coat front and back. He looked ready to faint. Yet he managed to give his opponent a salute:

"My compliments, Captain Hull." He groped downward, grudging admiration and bitterness mingling in his voice: "You've earned my sword—"

Suddenly Dacres' head jerked up. Hull had stayed the hand struggling to unfasten the blade:

"No, Jimmy. I won't take a sword from one who knows how to use it so well. I will, however, trouble you for your hat."

Dacres almost smiled. But the cries of anguish still drifting across the chop from the foundering *Guerriere* prevented that. Dacres took off his half-moon hat, handed it to Hull. The American captain slipped the hat beneath one arm.

"Come to my cabin, Jimmy. I'm told they've put out the fire. We'll get our surgeon to dig out that ball you took."

"Not until my wounded are looked after."

"Of course. I'll see they're brought aboard at once." He took Dacres' elbow.

"Isaac, let me ask you a question. What have you got for men in the tops?"

"My marines? Only a parcel of green bushwackers."

"Backwoodsmen?"

"According to your admirals."

Dacres caught the irony, shook his head. "You outsailed me. You outgunned me. Why the hell you weren't hulled as I was—"

"Live oak," Hull interrupted. "Your architects hold it in contempt, remember?"

Dacres flushed. "Be that as it may, one battle isn't the war."

As Hull led him to a ladderway, the British captain suddenly glanced back at his ship:

"You can't put a prize crew aboard her, can you, Isaac?"

"I doubt it. She's too badly riddled." Hull pointed. "With the sea so heavy, she's shipping water through her gun ports. I'll have to blow her up tomorrow."

Captain Dacres looked as grieved as if he'd lost a relative, Jared thought.

"One favor, then."

"It's yours."

"In my cabin there's a Bible. Given me years ago by my mother. I've carried it ever since I first went to sea."

"I'll see it's recovered and restored to you," Hull said, handing Dacres into the care of two seamen who helped him down the ladder.

Before Hull followed, he moved briefly among the men standing nearest to him. He shook a hand here, murmured a word of praise there. He never reached Jared. A shout summoned him to the surgeon's quarters, where Lieutenant Morris was being attended. Hull waddled to the ladderway and vanished, torn pants first, stained coat sans epaulettes next, round face last of all.

God, Jared admired the man's skill and courage. As innocent-looking as a rustic, Hull had been masterful during the engagement. If there were a few more captains like him, the outlook for America might not be as gloomy as many of her citizens believed—

By this time Jared had regained a measure of calm. He started asking questions, and discovered Sixth Lieutenant Stovall had been taken to the surgery. The news reinforced his sense of having failed at the critical moment, and kept him from sharing the festive mood that accompanied the process of cleaning up the frigate. He didn't drink the extra ration of grog ordered for all hands. And he slept poorly.

No one hung up a hammock in the place Ollie Prouty had occupied only twenty-four hours ago.

vi

On August thirtieth, *Constitution* dropped anchor a mile and a half southeast of the Boston light.

A few hours later, she moved to Nantasket Roads. She sent a boat ashore with news of her stunning success—and with a request that facilities be readied for the prisoners and wounded from *Guerriere,* whose ruined hull had been torched and sunk at sea.

The party returning from shore brought a curious report. Despite New England's hatred of the war, most of the city had paradoxically gone wild with joy at word of the victory.

Constitution's triumph offset discouraging news from the west: in mid-August, General William Hull had surrendered Detroit to General Isaac Brock without firing so much as one shot. The officer in charge of the landing party said people were already clamoring for General Hull's court-martial. Captain Hull made no mention of the fact that the general was his uncle. Jared had to learn it from a seaman.

In the ten days since the engagement, everyone had taken to calling the frigate by a new nickname—Old Ironsides. A new pride had kept the crew working cheerfully at their duties. The atmosphere had somewhat restored Jared's spirits, too. He slowly forgot the grim sea burial of the dead from both sides—fourteen Americans and seventy-nine British.

He took added encouragement from what he learned from boys who worked for the surgeon's mates. Yes, Lieutenant Stovall was alive. But the pain of his injury kept him unconscious most of the time. He had suffered severe facial burns in an accidental fall against a hot cannon.

"You have anything to do with that?" asked one of the boys with whom Jared talked.

"Would I tell you if I did?"

The boy studied Jared with foxy eyes. "Not if you was smart."

"What's to become of Stovall, Harry?"

"He'll be transferred to a hospital in Boston, then sent home when he's well enough."

Jared relaxed a little. That ended the immediate threat. He assumed Stovall would still be recuperating when *Constitution*'s crew went ashore for the huge civic welcome being planned.

Jared intended to be part of that welcome—though in truth, he was less than satisfied with his performance during the battle.

Yes, he'd stood in the thick of the fighting and carried out his duties well enough. But he'd failed miserably when confronted with the opportunity—at the time, the necessity—to get rid of Stovall. Blind chance had done it for him; he could take no comfort.

And the troubling sickness had recurred. At the critical moment with Stovall, it had undone him. That seemed an ominous sign.

So on balance, he was disappointed. Rather than resolving basic questions, the events of the past days merely continued and even sharpened them—and brought back the feeling that he might never escape the bent for failure that seemed to be his inheritance from his mother and father. The gloomy feelings persisted all through the flurry of preparations for going ashore.

He was on deck when *Constitution* warped into Long Wharf and began unloading prisoners and wounded. The fresh air improved his spirits a little. If there had been no fundamental alteration in his doubts about himself, at least he could be proud of outward changes that had accelerated during the past month. He stood more erect now, shoulders back, blue eyes shining in the sun. If he was not yet physically a man, he felt as if he were—even though his fourteenth birthday wouldn't come until October.

While the wounded were carried off, he and the other boys told each other how bold they'd been in combat. They bragged of the feminine conquests they planned to make in the city. Jared's boasts were even emptier than those of his shipmates. And all at once, he was silenced by the sight of Stovall being carried down the gangplank on a litter.

A bandage swathed most of the lieutenant's skull and the right side of his face. Jared swallowed. Even lying helpless, the young officer had the power to stir terror—

He told himself his fear was foolish. He'd repaid the lieutenant in kind, and they were even and quits. He'd probably never see Stovall again—he should focus on that, not on his failure to take the officer's life.

The last of the prisoners filed off. Crowds began to stream up Long Wharf to welcome the sailors. Soon the entire dock was jammed with people.

Jared set off among them with his chin up and his eyes a bit harder, a bit colder than they'd been on that morning he first boarded his ship—

A hundred years ago, it seemed. Could it really be only a month—?

In that time he had done and seen much. But dizzying

change was the way of the world these days, Uncle Gilbert said. Finally, in the noisy throng on Long Wharf, he allowed himself a touch of pride. Perhaps some things hadn't changed. But others had—

The boy was dead. Long live the man.

CHAPTER VI

Heritage

JARED STRUGGLED UP Long Wharf against the human tide rolling toward the *Constitution.* Because he wore a uniform—newly laundered slops, blouse and scarf, varnished black hat—he was automatically a candidate for congratulations, boisterous backslaps, squeezes, pokes, pinches and pats. In the face of such enthusiasm, the going became difficult. He curled his left arm around the small canvas bag containing souvenirs for the family, lowered his head and kept shoving his way to the head of the pier.

People around *Constitution*'s gangplank rushed aboard. Some of the women ran to the sailors still on the ship and grasped them in ardent embraces. Hanging onto his hat and looking back, Jared wondered enviously whether he could find some attractive young woman to favor him with a kiss. Or something more—

As if the wish had conjured bad luck, he found himself approaching a woman, but hardly a desirable one. He was out of the heaviest press now, and had room to maneuver. He sidestepped to avoid a direct confrontation. The woman's dress and cap were filthy. Most of her teeth were gone, even though she didn't appear to be thirty. A whore, he was certain.

The woman changed course to intercept him:

"Here's one of the lads from the frigate!"

Her remark was directed to a short, wide-shouldered man lurching along behind her. Jared paid no attention to the fellow; he was too busy avoiding the whore's outstretched hands.

Rum fumes barely masked the stench of the woman's body. But she wasn't so drunk that she couldn't move quickly. Darting in front of Jared, she seized his shoulders and gave him a wet buss on the cheek.

Jared tolerated it, but with difficulty. The woman's incredibly dirty fingers and rouged, pox-pitted face turned his stomach. The woman's companion laughed—a wheezy, consumptive sound—and tapped her shoulder. His voice was slurred by drink:

"Back off, Nell. The lad's not old enough to buy what you're selling."

"Oh, he looks plenty old enough to me." The whore simpered, showing her discolored gums. "Want to come up the street a ways? I'll pleasure you for half the usual price. It's a special rate for any of the brave lads from Boston's frigate—"

"Let go of me, please," Jared said, concerned that the encounter might turn ugly. The whore reached for his groin. Her man restrained her:

"Nell, he said no. Leave him be."

"Thank you, sir, I'm obliged," Jared said while the whore grumbled.

For the first time he got a clear look at her companion; the woman's pimp, obviously. He was about forty; stocky, with untrimmed hair, whiskers and beard shot through with gray. He smelled even worse than the whore.

Because of the man's position and the angle of the sunlight, only the right side of the man's face was visible beneath his hat brim. But that was quite enough to make Jared queasy. The man's skin was covered with seeping sores. His right eye had gone milky with blindness—altogether, a ghastly specimen. But not unusual around the docks.

The pimp gave him a muzzy grin. Extended his right hand:

"Privilege to meet any of the lads who—"

Abruptly, the pimp stopped. Withdrew his scabby hand. He stared at the boy in an intense way, saying nothing.

The whore was anxious to rush on and find another customer. The pimp lingered.

"Boy—?"

Jared would have left instantly but he didn't want to provoke the drunken man. He held a hand over his brow to cut the sun's glare. Even so, he still couldn't see much of the man's face.

"Yes?" Jared said.

"Would you tell me your name?"

"Why?"

"Because you resemble someone—I mean to say—someone I once—"

"It's Prouty, Oliver Prouty," Jared said. It was the first name that popped into his head.

"Oh." The pimp nodded slowly. "Mistake, then—"

"Yes, sir. Good day."

Shivering, Jared turned and left.

The pimp tugged off his hat and fanned himself, staring after the tawny-haired boy. The pox sores glistened in the sunlight. The disease-blinded right eye shone like a white marble.

"He lied to me—" the pimp murmured, sounding more sorrowful than angry.

The whore rushed back to him. "For Christ's sake, let's get to the ship!"

"But the boy didn't give me his right name."

"What difference does that make?"

Collecting himself, the pimp brushed a hand against his watering left eye. "None," he said softly. "None."

He put his stained hat on his head. The shadow of the

brim blotted his face again, hiding the badly healed ridge of scar tissue on his left cheek.

He pulled a bottle from his coat pocket, swigged and followed the whore down Long Wharf.

ii

Jared had hoped Uncle Gilbert and Amanda might bring a carriage to meet him. When he searched the street at the head of the pier and failed to find them, he was disappointed.

He could understand Aunt Harriet not coming; she wouldn't care whether he was alive or not. But Uncle Gilbert wasn't that way. Jared told himself his uncle must not have known the exact time of *Constitution*'s docking.

He knew the excuse wasn't valid—especially for a newspaperman. But he needed some kind of balm for his let-down feeling. His step was much less jaunty as he set off along a narrow street.

He'd gone no more than a few blocks when a voice challenged him:

"Hello. Are you off the Boston ship?"

Jumping across the refuse channel to the dark doorway, Jared peered at the person who had spoken; a girl, lounging in the shadows with her forearms crossed over small breasts barely concealed by a thin blouse.

Unlike the whore on the wharf, this one was reasonably attractive. Brown-haired, with a clear complexion and clean skin.

And she had most of her teeth.

"Yes, I am," he told her. "I'm headed for my home."

Wondering if this might be a deadfall, he glanced along the mean, littered street. No one else was in sight. Half a block away, a tavern showed closed shutters, as if the patrons had all departed. To welcome the frigate, perhaps—?

He felt reassured when the young woman smiled at him:

"Are you in a terrible rush? I could make you happy to be on land again."

Lazily, she dropped her arms and let him see her breasts covered by the thin blouse. The dark circles of her nipples showed clearly. Temptation set off peculiar sensations within Jared. Excitement and shame mingled as he felt the unconscious response of his body to the girl's.

"I have no money," he said truthfully. "We've yet to be paid."

"Surely there's something in that little bag to take a girl's fancy."

"Nothing of value. Two bracelets of tarred cordage, plus a four-inch splinter from our ship's mast."

"Would you show me one of the rope bracelets?"

She said it so gently, he couldn't refuse. He opened the canvas bag.

The brown-haired girl turned the crude bracelet in her fingers, then smiled again.

"If you swear this comes from the Boston frigate, it would be acceptable payment. I mean, today's a special day, isn't it? Everything about it should be special. For you. For me too."

He eyed the souvenir he'd tied and tarred himself. If he gave one away, there would only be one left—and that one must go to Amanda. Much as he despised Aunt Harriet, to neglect her would only provoke trouble.

Nervously, Jared hooked a finger in the collar of his blouse. He was perspiring. Partly from excitement, partly out of fear.

Why couldn't he present the souvenirs privately?

Aunt Harriet didn't need to know she'd been shorted—

"All right," he said in an unsteady voice.

"The bracelet's mine?"

"Aye."

She seemed genuinely pleased, and bent to kiss his cheek lightly as he passed from the blue shadow of the street to the deeper shadow and mystery of the shabby ground-floor room.

iii

When he emerged an hour later, a greater mystery had been solved—pleasantly if a little clumsily this first time.

The young whore had never even told him her name, leading him straight to her narrow bed and helping him undress. The moment she drew off his underclothes, he confronted her with an enormous erection—and a deep red face. But she laughed with delight, wriggling free of her own garments.

She lay back, one hand closing gently until he tingled with a tension altogether foreign to him before.

"Come, lie down with me," she said. "You'll find it nice, I think."

As he slipped down beside her, she pressed his erection against her tuft and left it straining there, stroking his cheeks with her palms, then opening her lips against his. Her tongue caressed the inside of his mouth, arousing him all the more.

Her breasts touched his chest. He started breathing heavily. He'd watched dogs coupling in the street a few times, but he'd never imagined a similar act between humans could produce such marvelous sensations—

Kissing, fondling, she guided him between her thighs, then began to slide up and down beneath him. He clasped his arms under her back, awkward in his movements until he found the proper angle. Soon she was breathing as loudly as he. She began to moan against his throat—

The explosion of his loins was matched by her own violent wrenchings; up and down; side to side. After that came a delicious lassitude. They lay close together, he feeling sad, somehow. He put his lips against her warm ear and whispered that he loved her very much. She laughed again, touching his nose and saying she loved him too.

Leaving her, he whistled as he walked. The odd sadness had passed.

Perhaps he'd experienced it because he knew their lovemaking was an exchange of pleasure for a price, nothing more. Yet the act seemed far too beautiful and moving to be of such fleeting significance. For a moment he wished he could see the girl again. He wished their declarations of love had been real ones, not lies born in the heat of the moment—

What foolishness!

Even so, her face lingered in his thoughts. He suspected it always would.

He whistled louder. Why feel bad? Hadn't he learned one of the things a man must know?

At an intersection, he paused and looked back. The brown-haired girl was waving goodbye from her doorway. The little bracelet of tarred cordage jiggled on her wrist.

He waved in return, then hurried on.

iv

At Beacon Street, Amanda came to answer the door. When she saw Jared, she squealed with delight.

He dropped the canvas bag, caught her around the waist and whirled her above the stoop, nearly causing the driver of a dray to run his team onto the sidewalk.

Amanda was as pert and lovely as ever. He hugged her fiercely. The touch of her soft skin against his cheek made him feel he was truly home.

"Dear Jared!" she gasped when he released her. "How fine you look in that uniform!"

"Not fine enough for anyone to come greet me at the pier. Other families were there. But not mine. That demands an explanation, by God!"

"Oo, do all sailors swear that way?"

"I know a hundred other words—all worse!" he teased, making a terrible face. Amanda covered her mouth and giggled.

Jared feigned anger:

"See here!—I meant what I said. Why didn't anyone meet me? I might have had an arm blown off—even been killed! Didn't anyone care?"

"Of course we care, Jared. But we already knew you were all right."

That caught him short: "You did?"

"Papa sent one of his reporters to the pier when some sailors from your boat—"

"Ship."

"What's the difference?"

"You're too little to understand."

"I am not, I am *not!*"

"Amanda!" he said sternly. "Go on!"

She huffed, then said, "Well—these men came to town a day or two ago—"

"The first shore party."

"—and papa's reporter gave one of them money for a list of the dead and wounded." She pronounced the last word to rhyme with "sounded."

"The word is "wounded."

"I don't think it's the same word I saw in the paper."

"Yes it is." He spelled it.

She looked dismayed. "Mercy, it is the same word."

"Wounded," he repeated. "As in moon, loon—you're not quite as grown up as you think, Miss Amanda!"

Perfectly serious, she asked, "Will I ever be?"

"I doubt it."

He said it too dourly. She started to weep.

"Amanda, for God's—for heaven's sake, stop that! I was only teasing!"

She bawled all the louder.

"Oh, God," Jared groaned. They were attracting stares from pedestrians. He grabbed her arms. "Amanda, you're grown up. You're *very* grown up. There!—I said it. Now stop. You seem to forget I'm the one who's supposed to be upset!"

Instantly, the tears vanished. "I was trying ever so hard to make you forget that."

"By crying? Typical woman's trick!" He pinched her chin with gentle affection. "Well, it worked. Let's go inside."

As he caught his cousin's hand, she said:

"Papa even made the reporter bring the list here, Jared. He's been in bed for the last four days."

"In bed?" Frowning, Jared closed the front door. Harriet Kent's voice drifted from the back of the house; she was hectoring one of the servants. "He's ill?"

"From too much work, the doctor says."

She led Jared into the front sitting room. Outside, he hadn't noticed the boards nailed across two of the windows.

"We've had visitors," Amanda told him. "Twice! The last time, they broke the glass with stones. I was so scared—!"

"Why were the windows broken? Because of Uncle Gilbert's position on the war?"

"I think so. Papa's hired watchmen at the printing house—"

She glanced toward the hall, where footsteps rapped.

"Amanda, were you the one squealing and shrieking outside—?"

Her back to the hall, Amanda stiffened at the sound of Harriet's voice. Jared did too. Amanda's small fingers knotted in her skirt.

Dressed in mauve and looking paler than usual, Harriet Kent darted a hand to her bosom:

"Jared!"

"Good morning, Aunt Harriet."

"We had no idea when to expect you—"

He set his canvas bag on a highly polished table. Harriet didn't allow her best furniture to be used so casually—the exact reason he deposited the bag where he did.

Her eyes flicked to the table. Her lips compressed. That delighted him. On the surface, however, he was polite:

"It all depends on when the pilot comes aboard to steer us in. He came aboard first thing this morning. Where's Uncle Gilbert?"

"At the printing house."

"But Amanda said he's ill—"

"When did that ever stop him from doing exactly as he wished?"

Jared indicated the boarded windows. "You've had unexpected callers."

Harriet sank into a chair. "Every time Gilbert writes one of his editorials, he's pilloried in the opposition press, abused on the street—or we're visited by vandals. The strain is getting to be more than I can bear."

Jared concealed his disgust. "Evidently the strain's been worse on Uncle Gilbert."

"It's his fault, not mine, if he chooses to endanger his health by working long hours for an unpopular cause!"

Jared was aghast at her lack of feeling for her husband. He was angry, too. Not only because of the callous way she spoke of Gilbert; but also because she didn't even trouble to ask one question about how he'd gotten along on the frigate.

Instead, she stood up, marched straight to the polished table, removed his canvas bag and set it on the floor.

"Your uncle and I have parted company on political matters, Jared. I now attend Federal Street Church, where I find Mr. Channing's sermons more to my taste."

"I see."

Jared knew of the church, naturally. Its pastor, the Reverend William Ellery Channing, was Boston's most popular preacher. He'd taken a pacifist stand on the war. Jared wasn't surprised that Harriet Kent would show her vindictiveness by refusing to attend the Kent family's church, and by displaying herself publicly, alone, in a place of worship whose pastor was more attuned to the thinking of those whose admiration she coveted. Christ, he didn't know how Gilbert stood the woman!

In a few moments, the joy of homecoming was wholly gone; destroyed by the sight of those ugly planks hammered over the empty window frames, and by Harriet's hauteur.

His black mood drove him to pick up the canvas bag: "Here, Amanda, I brought you something."

"What is it, what?" she exclaimed, dancing up and down.

"A bracelet of rope from *Constitution.*" He slipped it easily onto her small wrist. "I made it myself."

He swung around.

"I'm sorry I have nothing for you, Aunt Harriet."

Her eyes showed her hostility. "I wouldn't expect it of you, Jared. You are your mother's child, not mine."

She whirled, her skirts belling, and vanished into the hall.

Scarlet-cheeked, Jared kicked the canvas bag. Amanda hugged him again and thanked him for the present, oblivious to the hatred that had crackled between the boy and the woman only a moment earlier.

V

The skies grayed in the early afternoon. A chilly rain began to fall, hinting of autumn. Gilbert returned a few minutes after six, to be greeted by a complaint from Harriet: some of the kitchen help were unhappy about preparing and serving large meals in the evening. In most other wealthy homes, by nightfall the kitchens were quiet, the day's work largely done. Why couldn't Gilbert try to change his habits? Learn to dine in the early afternoon, as respectable people did—?

Gilbert was wan; thinner than a month ago. But Jared's presence put him in high spirits. He refused to let Harriet's harangue bother him:

"My dear, you and the servants will wait in vain for that kind of change in me. We are Kents first and foremost. Respectability, if any, is incidental."

Harriet wasn't amused. "So I've discovered."

"Jared, come along to the table! I want to hear all about Hull's victory—"

Gilbert wrapped his arm around his nephew's shoulder, walking him past Harriet's vindictive eyes. "By God, I've never seen the old town in such an uproar. Do you know they're going to give you a parade down State Street? And a dinner at Faneuil Hall?"

"Not me, surely," Jared laughed.

"You're part of the crew, aren't you?"

"When is the dinner?"

"September fifth. In the evening," Gilbert added, for Harriet's benefit. "Even Royal's planning to attend, much as he loathes the war. The curious dualism of Boston continues! Bursts of patriotic fervor on one hand—widespread refusal to help the government on the other—"

Gilbert coughed as he slipped into his chair at the head of the dining room table. Amanda took her place opposite Jared, elbows on the tablecloth. That earned her a smack on the wrist from her mother. Jared wondered whether Harriet's choice of wrists was accidental. She slapped the one on which Amanda wore the bracelet.

Harriet sat down at her end of the table. Her husband virtually ignored her:

"Before you begin, Jared, what news do you want to hear?"

"About the war? I only know General Hull surrendered Fort Detroit—"

"Without shooting at the enemy once! Something much worse happened about the same time—the middle of August—but the reports took weeks to reach the eastern seaboard. Immediately the fort at Michilimackinac fell, Hull ordered Fort Dearborn evacuated—that's at the foot of the lake in the Illinois country. Sixty-six men, women and children dutifully obeyed Hull's stupid order, and left the fort. They were promptly massacred by Indians lying in wait."

Jared shook his head. "That's horrible. I suppose the Indians were equipped by the British?"

"Undoubtedly. If it weren't for *Constitution*'s splendid performance, morale in the country would be nonexistent."

"Did you know Captain Hull's going on leave?"

"I did not."

"His brother died suddenly."

"Will Hull resume command when he returns?"

"No, *Constitution*'s going to put to sea before that. I don't know this for certain, but I heard Hull's already been reassigned to the Boston Navy Yard, and Captain Bainbridge will command our ship."

"I want to hear about the fight!" Amanda said.

Harriet leaned forward. "Such an interest on the part of a young girl is not suitable or—"

"Oh for God's sake, Harriet!" Gilbert said. "We all want to hear Jared describe the battle."

"You needn't include me," his wife retorted. "You'll forgive me if I retire. I'm not feeling well."

Lips pursed, Gilbert stared after her as she left the room. They listened to her rush upstairs. Amanda seemed relieved that her mother was gone. She fairly bounced on her chair:

"The battle, Jared—!"

"Wait, dear," Gilbert said. "I want to ask one question." He looked at Jared. "Are you planning to sail out with Bainbridge?"

"Certainly, sir. My enlistment runs for a year."

"Then you and I must have a chat after dinner."

It was said lightly enough. But from the forthrightness of Gilbert's eyes—their dark color heightened by the unhealthy hue of his skin—Jared knew something serious was afoot.

Amanda responded to the exchange by pouting:

"And I'm to be sent to my room, I suppose?"

Gilbert pondered. "Not necessarily. I believe it might be well if you joined us." He showed more animation as the maid brought in their plates. "Now, Jared—every detail. From the moment you first sighted the enemy."

Jared obliged his uncle, omitting only his trouble with Stovall and his strange sickness. While the problem of the sixth lieutenant could have been described in a reasonably rational way, the other could not.

And since Jared was positive his uncle couldn't explain the ominous flaw, he saw no reason to bring it up.

vi

Because the rain had chilled the house, a fire had been lit in the sitting room hearth. Gilbert pulled a heavy chair up near it. Amanda snuggled at his feet, fondling her bracelet and yawning.

Gilbert's right hand moved gently, caressingly over her shining hair. In his other hand he held a goblet of port. But he drank very little of it.

Jared reveled in his uncle's recognition of his maturity: Gilbert had poured wine for his nephew without any reference to his age. He finished the first glass quickly, helped himself to another and resumed his seat, crossing his legs. His polished boots reflected the firelight. He had changed to civilian clothes for dinner. His fob hung below his trim purple jacket.

"I appreciate your thoughtfulness in bringing me that bit of wood from your ship," Gilbert said. "I'll treasure it."

"It's really of no value, uncle—"

"On the contrary. And the fact that you chose that sort of gift says something interesting about you."

Amanda yawned again. The goblet sparkled with fiery highlights as Gilbert raised it toward the mantel where the French sword hung above the Kentucky rifle. The green glass tea bottle shimmered directly below the gun.

"You are—instinctively, it seems—a Kent. A collector of mementos. That's good. But in other ways, you've changed remarkably in a very short time—"

Though Gilbert spoke matter-of-factly, Jared was disturbed. He had a strange feeling the conversation was about to take a gloomy turn. The rain ticked against the planks nailed over the windows. By the light of the fire, Gilbert looked weary and withered—

Jared tried to fend his uncle's comment with a smile:

"It's mainly because my voice has gotten deeper, I think."

"No, it's more than that. The way you carry yourself, for instance. I've been told danger can gray a man overnight. If that's true, I see no reason why it can't pull a boy from childhood to manhood in a month."

Gilbert set the goblet on a table beside his chair. Amanda had closed her eyes. Careful not to disturb her, he rose and approached the mantel.

"I am not a man of particularly morbid temperament, Jared. But all of us are mortal, and in my case, the time granted me on this earth may be shorter than that granted to others. *May* be," he repeated, a hand raised to silence his nephew's automatic protest.

"I say that only because my physician has said it to me. I don't like to borrow trouble. I've always believed, however, that those who are blind to future possibilities are certain to be punished by them."

"Amanda told me you were ill again," Jared said. "Do you mean to say it—it's more serious than we know?"

"I've no idea whether it is or not. I just have—oh, call it a premonition."

That was the moment Jared knew his uncle was concealing something:

"Uncle Gilbert, please tell me the truth. What has your doctor said?"

Gilbert waved. "The usual nonsense about too much work. The strain of trying to convert others to my viewpoint—a lot of twaddle. I'll probably live to be an old horse."

Jared stared into his uncle's eyes and didn't believe it. Neither did Gilbert, he realized with a jolt.

"But since you *are* old enough to discuss such matters, it's wise for us to at least recognize the possibility that

I could be removed from the affairs of this family at any time."

With a glance, Jared tried to warn his uncle that Amanda had awakened. She was listening, her head leaning against the chair, her eyes large. Gilbert appeared not to notice that, or Jared's warning:

"In that event, what would be your attitude about a career with the firm?"

"I'll have to answer you honestly—"

"I'd have it no other way."

"I don't know if I'm the sort to run a printing house."

"Very well. Should anything happen to me, you must then rely on my general manager, Franklin Pleasant. He would be a good steward of the Kent interests until such time as you might decide to throw your lot with the firm—or, barring that, sell it. Naturally I'd hate to see it sold. But I won't force you into a mold of my own devising. Your father was almost—never mind, that's extraneous. Do you understand what I'm saying?"

Jared nodded slowly. He hesitated to speak what was in his thoughts. But his uncle's frankness and the fire-shot darkness conspired to make his mood as somber as Gilbert's:

"I think you're saying decisions should not be trusted to Aunt Harriet."

"Yes, God forgive me."

"I still think it's premature to imagine something will hap—"

"Perhaps, perhaps," Gilbert interrupted. "But indulge me a little while longer, if you please. It's often struck me that a man's life is something like one of those gambling games the clerics abhor. In cards, for instance, the outcome depends partly on what you're dealt and what you draw by chance. At the same time, you have the opportunity to make choices—to show skill or lack of it; boldness or cowardice—in your disposition of the hand.

A man also has certain things given to him. His capacity for learning. Sometimes his health—but those factors needn't control him completely. They needn't defeat him if they capriciously take charge for a while. That happens in this world, despite our best efforts to order our own lives—"

Jared remembered Stovall; remembered Ollie Prouty's death.

"I know."

"I want to share some thoughts about your life, Jared. How you might control and guide it in the years to come. As I said before, I'd never tell you exactly what to do, for reasons we won't go into. But whatever you do and wherever you go, I do want and expect you to remember one thing. You are a Kent. A member of a family not content to simply prosper without concern for this country which makes prosperity possible for all. Everything we are—you are—is summed up in our odd penchant for collecting little souvenirs of the times in which we've lived. I've noticed the books and scientific samples in your room, for instance. During your absence, your aunt wanted to store them away. I said no. Those things are signs that you're a Kent—as is that splinter of wood you brought home."

He returned to the mantel. "As a Kent, I want you to share the reverence I have for these objects—"

A hand encompassed the sword, the rifle, the bottle.

"—because they are the sum and symbol of the way your grandfather pledged his life to what he believed. Many men—and women—pledge themselves to nothing but their own self-interest. That's not the Kent way. Not my way, and I hope not yours. If Kent and Son must vanish one day because you choose another course, don't let these objects vanish—or what they represent. Guard them as you would your own life. Humor me in this, Jared—promise me you will revere and protect what you see before you."

In a whisper, Jared said, "I will."

And the voice of his doubt whispered in turn, *If I am strong enough. If I am not what my father was—*

He was conscious of Amanda's upturned face, evidently still unnoticed by Gilbert. With an almost mystical fascination, she stared at the bottle and the fire-lit weapons.

"See that you live up to the words on that fob as well."

"I'll try."

"Finally—take care of your cousin. I fear you are the only one who can do that adequately."

Jared opened his mouth, ready to tell his uncle Amanda was listening. Young as she was, she apparently sensed the reason Gilbert spoke as he did; she understood his references to poor health and the possibility of death. Nestled against the chair, she had tears in her eyes.

Jared said, "I'll take care of her, sir."

Gilbert walked to the front windows, stared at the rainy darkness beyond the one remaining glass.

"If we survive and win this war—as we must—there will be great challenges for a man who is willing to look for them without fear. We are gaining new territory all the time. The pace of invention and technical progress is astounding. The United States can expand, and prosper. Despite greed and faulty thinking and all the cruelties and aberrations of the human condition, this nation can become something unlike any other state or kingdom in the world's history. Your grandfather recognized that, I have tried to, and I want you to do the same. I hope you will not be drawn into selfish byways, but will stay on the high road—the road of cause and contribution and commitment. In the Kent family, that's a kind of religion. Those are its altarpieces—"

Jared's gaze followed the slender hand back to the mantel.

"—and you are called to be one of its priests. Strong men of conviction will be needed, Jared. They are always needed, but they will be needed more and more urgently in the years ahead."

He began to pace. "The country's still in its infancy—growing, experimenting. Like a child, it could fall and flounder—and be abandoned by the march of history. Many questions over and above the immediate ones of this war remain to be resolved. The nation's survival depends on their resolution. One is the matter of the franchise. I have thought long and hard on it, and I've concluded that although the men who founded this country had great wisdom and courage, in some respects they were narrow traditionalists. Influenced by an English heritage—a heritage of aristocracy. It was natural that American aristocrats should lead the drive for independence. It's easier to find leaders among the rich simply because the rich can concern themselves with issues larger than making a living. But we've gone past that stage. If the principles of freedom Mr. Jefferson expressed so well are to have any validity, all men must have the basic right to control their government through their elected officials. *All* men, not merely those who meet their state's voting requirements—so much money, so much property, so much education. Such requirements must be abolished or the democratic ideal is a sham."

"Did President Jefferson really believe in freedom, uncle? He still keeps slaves down in Virginia, doesn't he?"

"Yes, he does. Like all human beings, he's a study in

contradictions. I doubt he'd ever favor granting the vote to a black man."

"How do you feel about that?"

"I'd be horsewhipped for saying it, but I feel it must come. First, however, the whole slavery question must be addressed—and God knows where that confrontation will lead."

"Would you even let women vote?"

"Oh, no, I draw the line there! Men are temperamentally suited to the tasks of the world. By their very nature, women are domestic creatures."

Unseen by her father, Amanda scowled. Gilbert went on:

"Another problem is this dreadful business of the northeast seceding—or talking about it. Some of my acquaintances claim that since the Constitution grants only certain powers to the central government, it therefore implies that the states retain all others—including the privilege of deciding whether to remain in the union or withdraw. However, that same document begins with the words, 'We the people.' It does not say, 'We of the several states.' Once founded by the consent of all, the union can't be sundered at the whim of a few. Any other interpretation could tear this country apart. Men must recognize that danger. Be prepared to counter it—"

Again he pointed to the fob Jared was wearing.

"No matter where you are, or what you are, I expect you to be one of those men."

Stunned into silence by everything his uncle had said, Jared simply stared into the dark, sunken eyes. At last, Gilbert smiled:

"I think that's quite enough for one evening. Shall we have another glass of port?"

"You didn't finish the first one, sir."

"So I didn't! My mind wanders lately. Damned annoying—"

He passed a palm over his forehead. With a start, Jared saw that his uncle's brow was wet with sweat. He was breathing in a raspy way. He groaned softly as he lowered himself into his chair, tousling his daughter's hair.

Jared said, "She's been listening too, uncle."

Gilbert looked at him. "Yes, I was aware."

"You were? I thought—"

"I wanted her to hear. She's just as much a Kent as you are, Jared."

He bent and kissed his daughter's cheek. The rain rattled on the planks. Jared helped himself to more wine, wondering whether he could ever live up to all his uncle expected of him.

vii

Accompanied by a harpsichord moved in for the occasion, the baritone sang every verse of the song Jared now knew by heart:

"The first broadside we poured
Swept their mainmast overboard,
Which made this lofty frigate look
Abandoned-O—
Then Dacres he did sigh,
And to his officers did cry,
'I did not think these Yankees were
So handy-O!' "

Jared reflected dully that the songwriter had gotten things a bit mixed up; *Guerriere*'s mizzen, not her mainmast, had gone down under the first salvos.

Two more verses, he thought. *Then the toasts begin. We're going to broil here half the night.*

But most of the several hundred men gathered in Faneuil Hall were enjoying the performance, tapping or stamping the beat of the drinking song to which new words had been set. Copies of the lyrics were available all over Boston in a fast-selling broadside.

With appropriate fervor, the baritone launched into the final verse:

> *"Now fill your glasses full,*
> *Let's drink a toast to Captain Hull,*
> *So merrily we'll push around*
> *The brandy-O—*
> *For John Bull may drink his fill,*
> *And the world say what it will,*
> *The Yankee tars for fighting are*
> *The dandy-O!"*

Loud applause greeted the end of the song, and earned the baritone several bows. Jared sat back in his chair, folded his arms and closed his eyes. The hall was an inferno, and the dinner had made him sleepy. He ached for a breath of outside air, hot as it was. But since he couldn't make a spectacle by walking out, a surreptitious nap was the next best thing.

A voice droned from the dais. Another was still droning when he woke up to discover nothing had changed, except for the temperature, which seemed more hellish than ever, and the quantity of pipe and cigar smoke, which had reached asphyxiating proportions.

In his place of honor, Captain Hull still looked quite alert and attentive, however. His cheeks gleamed like polished apples and his dress uniform was resplendent. At his right hand lay a velvet box containing a commemorative medal struck in gold at the order of the Congress. Silver medals had been struck for the officers.

All of them were present on the dais except for Morris and Stovall, who were still under medical care.

"Won't they ever stop?" one of the boys at the table whispered as yet another well-dressed gentleman rose to offer a toast.

"That's only sixteen so far," a second boy said.

"Fourteen," said the first.

"It damn well seems like a hundred and fourteen!"

A gentleman at the next table shushed them. The speaker raised his glass:

"Our infant navy! We must nurture the young Hercules in his cradle, if we mean to profit by the labors of his manhood!"

Every man in the hall stood up, and drank. Many stamped or shouted, "Hear!" The boys were required to stand but not to drink. Only the hardiest topers among them kept pace with the toasts, and that group didn't include Jared.

The guests resumed their seats. Waiters brought more wine to each table. Jared perked up slightly when Gilbert, seated at the extreme left end of the dais, stood up with glass in hand. Jared noticed a few sour expressions when his uncle rose.

"Christ, he's white as chalk," a boy whispered as Gilbert cleared his throat. Jared sat forward, wide awake and alarmed. The boy was right.

Gilbert held his glass aloft.

"To unconditional victory! We have suffered the injuries and insults of despotism with patience, but its friendship is more than we can bear—"

A groundswell of grumbling greeted the extreme anti-British sentiment. But it hushed the instant the glass fell and broke.

Gilbert swayed, his eyes rolling up in his head. His fisted left hand jammed against the center of his chest. In the silence, his gasps could be heard in every corner of the hall.

Jared jumped up. Gilbert toppled, smashing china and dragging the tablecloth after him as he slid to the floor.

viii

In the sharp air of late October, *Constitution* put to sea. Jared Kent was aboard. So was a new sixth lieutenant.

After the frigate passed Boston light, Jared looked back at the blur of the channel islands. Uncle Gilbert had suffered a seizure from which he had not yet recovered. His heart rhythm remained irregular. He'd been unconscious when Jared slipped in to kneel at his bedside and bid him a silent goodbye.

As the familiar coastline receded and the noisy routine of shipboard began in earnest, Jared remembered the responsibility with which Gilbert had charged him on the night of his homecoming. Gilbert had spoken of a premonition, too. Although the doctor continued to refuse comment, Jared still had the feeling his uncle had known much more about his own failing health than anyone in the household realized.

In a way, Jared was thankful Bainbridge had put to sea in company with *Hornet,* a twenty-gun sloop of war. Shipboard gossip said they were to rendezvous with Captain David Porter's *Essex,* thirty-six guns, then proceed south to search for enemy convoys bound around Cape Horn on their way to the Far East. Dangerous duty—but preferable to remaining behind while Aunt Harriet raved and wept over the injustice of her husband being struck down at age twenty-nine.

Constitution swept out into the Atlantic. But distance couldn't relieve Jared of worries about his uncle—

Or about his own ability to cope with the future, if he came home from the cruise to find himself the surviving male of the Kent family.

Book Four

Cards of Fate

CHAPTER I

Mr. Piggott

IN THE DRESSING room adjoining her bedroom on the second floor, Harriet took off the bandeau that held her breasts in place when she was dressed. She added the bit of lingerie to the pile of petticoats and the long-waisted, lightly boned corset lying on the floor.

Harriet's upstairs maid had been ready to assist her in undressing, of course. The lascivious girl undoubtedly wanted to see what sort of nightgown her mistress had chosen—so she could gossip about it with the other servants. Harriet refused the help. Her bed apparel this evening in mid-July, 1813, was solely her affair.

A moth circled the chimney of the lamp on her dressing table. She studied the beating beige wings. She felt exactly like that poor creature—frantic—though only her quick breathing and her racing heart betrayed her state.

With the greatest of effort, she'd endured the ceremony performed by the Reverend Channing in the front sitting room. She'd feigned composure during the modest reception afterward, chatting with guests and concealing her inner turmoil. But she wasn't at all sure she could stay calm now. She faced the rest of the night with disgust, even outright fear.

Outside, the hooves of a carriage horse clopped rapidly. Beacon Street was becoming a raceway for commercial vehicles and young bloods on horseback. The hoofbeats set off a wistful yearning for the safe, quiet days of her childhood in New York. Being a woman certainly had its undesirable aspects—

Undesirable? Why not be truthful? The word was loathsome.

She had often expressed her loathing during the initial year of her marriage to Gilbert. By the time she became pregnant with Amanda, it was unmistakably clear to him that physical intimacy repelled her. After the child was born, he left her alone.

But her current situation reminded her all too vividly of her first wedding trip. Reminded her of the revulsion; the anguish—

Like a prisoner, she was sentenced to that again tonight.

Well, it was the price she had to pay for marital respectability. But she refused to gaze at the mirror and confront the reality of her own body; especially the breasts her opaque cotton chemise concealed from sight but revealed in contour.

Her lips compressed angrily. She snatched at the moth, crushed it between her fingertips and flung it aside.

Seating herself, she began to comb out her long, dark hair.

Something else stunned and angered her suddenly. She leaned forward, touched the top of her head. In the mirror, she saw gray hair.

She'd never noticed it before. She counted only six or seven strands. But they upset her horribly.

Gilbert was responsible for that gray hair! He'd wrenched her whole life awry last December when he died. He had been bedridden ever since his collapse at the Faneuil Hall dinner in early September. On Christmas Eve, his heart had simply stopped beating while he slept.

The household was in a turmoil for days. Immediately, Harriet found herself coping with problems normally the purview of men: funeral preparations; arrangements for burial of the body at the family plot in Watertown —there had been no end to the aggravations. She recalled one of the worst—the necessity of sending servants all over Boston just to find a fashionable mourning costume for Amanda: a black cashmere dress with white frills; a white mull cap; gray stockings.

The whole period was a dreadful ordeal. But she got through it—only to be plunged into another. At the end of February, that wretched Jared had come home.

He'd been discharged from service along with most of his crew because *Constitution* was to be laid up in the Navy Yard indefinitely, for repairs. Having taken part in a second major engagement—the capture and sinking of the British frigate *Java* off the coast of Brazil—the boy was decidedly changed. Harriet had noticed a difference in him when he returned with Captain Hull. But at the second homecoming, the change was even more marked.

Physical maturation was part of it, of course. Abraham's son had grown taller. The relatively soft flesh of childhood had turned to muscle. But the change went deeper than mere passage through normal adolescent development.

Jared carried himself differently. With confidence; even a certain air of authority. Harriet could recall years gone by when she had deliberately intimidated him—and taken secret pleasure in the way it visibly withered his spirit; lent his eyes a nervous, unhappy quality—

Now her sharpest admonishments produced little response—other than a cool, almost hostile stare. It was harder than it had once been to make him lose his temper. She found the boy's new self-assurance infuriating. She regretted that she'd lost her power to make him feel terrified and demeaned.

Mercifully, Jared wasn't underfoot too long after his

return. At his own request, he went to work at the firm under the supervision of Mr. Franklin Pleasant, a jowly, phlegmatic man who seemed to understand the ins and outs of the coarse, controversial trade in which her husband had been involved. Mr. Pleasant had taken over operation of the company pending a decision from Harriet as to whether she wished to put Kent and Son up for sale. On several occasions he begged her not to sell. His pleas carried little weight. He was a tradesman and always would be; why, the fellow didn't even have a diploma from one of the lesser colleges!

Although Pleasant gave her a weekly report, Harriet paid scant attention to the business. She was aware that the list of titles to be published in the fall had been reduced. And she knew circulation of the *Republican* was off sharply. No one could match Gilbert's way with words, Pleasant said. Even those details failed to interest her.

Gilbert's demise had brought one benefit, however. It had put an end to those horrid visitations by anti-war hooligans who threw stones. To make doubly sure, she had given Mr. Pleasant definite orders that there were to be no more articles or editorials stating or even implying support of the war.

That action helped her in another sphere as well. She was once more accepted and treated cordially by members of Boston's better families.

Except for minor naval victories of the sort Jared talked about with quiet pride, the war was proving a disaster. The New England Federalists took smug satisfaction in having foreseen that—

To punish the upstart nation, Britain had clamped a blockade on Chesapeake and Delaware Bays the preceding December. The blockade had been extended to the mouth of the Mississippi and the ports of New York, Charleston and Savannah in May. Though New England's harbors were still open, the northeast felt the effects of the blockade in shortages of everyday goods, and in rising prices.

In consequence, the outcries from press and pulpit grew louder. They culminated in gloomy predictions of American defeat. As if to confirm the predictions, news reached the city that the much-touted Captain James Lawrence had lost the frigate *Chesapeake* to the British just thirty miles from the Boston waterfront.

Through most of the month of June, Harriet was forced to endure Jared's defense of the defeat: Lawrence might have lost his frigate, but not his fighting spirit! Dying, he had exclaimed, "Don't give up the ship!"

In vain, Harriet tried to convince the misguided boy that such sloganeering was foolish. It certainly hadn't helped save Lawrence's life—and it gave the country a false confidence. President Madison was steering the ship of state straight onto the rocks of military and economic disaster—all Harriet's friends and their husbands said so. The sooner America pleaded for terms, the better!

During one such argument, Harriet almost succeeded in goading Jared into a rage. But he controlled his temper and replied, "You—and your friends—are entitled to your opinion, Aunt Harriet." She seethed over the little exhibition of self-control.

The war made daily living difficult. Even a family as well off as Harriet's had trouble buying the necessities—and if they were available, prices were cruel. Managing household affairs by herself was a strain. Perhaps that was part of the reason she'd succumbed relatively quickly to the marriage proposal of a man she had only met in March, at Reverend Channing's church.

What she had liked immediately about Mr. Andrew Piggott was his gentility. He wore the proper clothes. Cultivated the proper people. Disavowed and damned the war. He was educated—a graduate of Yale down in New Haven. That wasn't Harvard; but one couldn't have everything.

More important, Mr. Piggott didn't misuse his education by wandering into philosophical byways and espousing radical causes, as Gilbert had.

Piggott told her he had become a man of independent means when an uncle in Albany left him an inheritance. Harriet made a few inquiries around town and found no evidence to contradict Piggott's claim that the uncle was a prosperous fur factor associated with Mr. Astor. She had to admit the inquiries were superficial; in her eagerness to end the lonely struggle that was widowhood, she accepted Piggott's credentials almost at face value. He was urbane; polite; and appeared to be welcome in the best circles.

She wasn't totally imprudent, though. Mr. Piggott first proposed in June. She put him off. She needed to satisfy herself that he wasn't marrying her in order to take possession of the assets of Kent and Son. She questioned him about it several times. Repeatedly, Mr. Piggott assured her that he wished to live a gentleman's life, not soil his hands in business. He would be perfectly content to let Franklin Pleasant operate the company until Harriet decided about its disposition.

He also disarmed her by confessing to two vices. He liked liquor, he said. And he enjoyed card-playing. In fact, when he wasn't squiring her to salons, dinner parties, or the Federal Street Church, he spent most of his time at the Exchange Coffee House, hunting up other affluent and respectable gentlemen he could engage in a marathon game of solo. At other times, the game was shemmy—the one French invention whose origins Mr. Piggott, a good Federalist, overlooked.

The games were always played in private rooms rented for the occasion, he said. His fondness for cards would never cause a scandal. Everything was conducted with the utmost discretion.

Another small investigation seemed in order. Harriet called on Franklin Pleasant, and he in turn sent out one of the *Republican*'s writers. She got back a report that yes, Mr. Piggott did involve himself in card games organized at the Exchange; games in which the stakes were rumored to be quite high. But he seemed to have the income to support his passion.

Finally, then, Harriet accepted the proposal, telling herself she could wean Mr. Piggott from his not-quite-respectable pastime after they were man and wife.

She had yet to learn the extent of Mr. Piggott's interest in sexual matters. It was a topic one didn't discuss prior to marriage. Tonight would surely shed some light on that repellent subject, however—

As she finished brushing her hair and walked to the wardrobe to select a gown in which to greet her new husband, she resolved that in the boudoir, too, she would rule. She had accepted Mr. Piggott because he seemed a decent, pliant man of good social connections; a man who would understand her wishes and accede to them. She meant to make sure he did—

A noise in the outer room startled her. The latch!

She darted back to the dressing table so he wouldn't see her in her chemise.

"Andrew? Is that you?"

"Indeed it is." He had a deep, mellow voice. A little too mellow right now, she decided. He had imibibed somewhat heavily at the reception.

"I won't be ready to receive you for at least a quarter of an hour."

He laughed. "Don't trouble yourself with bed clothes, my dear—"

Andrew Piggott appeared in the dressing room entrance, gazing at his wife with alarming directness.

He was about Harriet's age, with good features and a ruddy complexion. His eyes tended to be squinty, and he carried a fair amount of flesh on his frame: some might even describe him as portly. But that mellow voice charmed everyone, compensating for the small signs of self-indulgence: a florid nose; the beginning of a paunch.

Harriet caught her breath as he studied her. Mr. Piggott had already discarded his dark green clawhammer tail coat with its elegant black velvet collar. She saw it on the bedroom floor behind him. He stood before her in his pea-green waistcoat, fluffy stock, fawn trousers and gaitered pumps. His eyes moved slowly from her throat to her breasts.

Undone by the sudden interruption and his candid stare, Harriet crossed her arms over her bosom.

"The clothes will come off soon enough anyway," Piggott said with a genial smile. The dreaded moment had come—too quickly.

Harriet Lebow Kent Piggott was terrified.

ii

"I wish you would retire and permit me—" she began.

"Nonsense." Piggott waved. "We're married now. Very enjoyable affair, too."

"I noticed you dipping into the punch quite often."

Piggott's eyes grew a bit less cordial. "That's my business, I think. By the way—your nephew refused to say more than a couple of words to me."

Turning her back, Harriet hurried to the wardrobe. "You can be sure Jared will hear about that." She was less than confident that a reprimand would do any good, though.

"Not necessary," Piggott said. "If he persists in his

rudeness, I'll speak to him. We will come to an understanding, I promise."

Piggott's tone made Harriet glance around. His smile remained fixed. But his eyes were humorless.

"I mean to say, if he doesn't show proper respect for his new father, I'll take him aside and thrash him."

"Jared has grown to be a very strong boy—"

"Headstrong is more like it. Sea duty quite inflated his hat size, I think."

"He's like his mother now. She was an arrogant creature—"

"Well, I can deal with him. Gentleman at Yale don't spend all their hours musing over the classics! They've been known to fight free-for-all—"

Piggott rubbed the fingers of his right hand against his palm, as if in anticipation. Then he walked toward her.

"Time enough for that in the weeks to come. At the moment our concern is pleasure."

Harriet was afraid she might swoon. She noticed a disgusting lump under Piggott's trousers. She groped behind her for a gown—

Piggott seized her around the waist, pulled her to him, sounding a shade annoyed:

"Let's not concern ourselves with false propriety, my dear. I trust you *are* happy to be Mrs. Piggott—?"

"Of—of course."

His dark eyes focused behind her, on a shelf of the wardrobe.

"Not sufficiently happy to wear one of my wedding gifts."

His clasping fingers hurt her waist. She writhed away, spun to the shelf, plucked down the pair of white linen tubes decorated with bright red ribbons:

"I have certain standards, Andrew—"

"Pantalets are coming into fashion."

"But false pantalets are worn only by dancers and harlots."

He nodded, his face enigmatically empty of emotion:

"I'll forgive your reluctance. If you're less reluctant in bed—"

He took hold of her waist again. She realized that he might be drunk. She smelled the ginned punch on him, blending with the odor of his cologne. As he dragged her against him, she felt something stiff press her flesh through the chemise.

Her mouth went dry. Her eyes blurred. She gasped.

Visibly annoyed, Piggott stood back.

"What's this? You *are* reluctant."

"No. No, it's—a vaporish dizziness. Just give me a moment—"

She moved quickly to the dressing table, sank down, eyed Piggott in the glass. His features had hardened—exactly as his flesh had hardened beneath his trousers. He stared at her in an accusing way; he wasn't deceived by her lie.

He took two steps, came up behind her, deliberately thrust that bulge against her back while his hands slipped under her arms. He started fondling her breasts. She blurted the first thought that came into her head:

"Has Amanda retired?"

Piggott jerked his hands away. He laughed, a harsh sound.

"Amanda, Jared—who else shall we discuss, Mrs. Piggott?"

"I only wanted to know—"

"Is that what you propose to do this evening? Talk? It's not what I propose to do!"

"I thought—I thought you respected my wishes—"

"Yes! But I remind you that we're married. I have rights."

In a faint voice, she said, "And I'll permit you to exercise them—"

"Well! That's generous of you! My dear, there's no *permitting* about it."

Seeing her shocked expression, he forced another smile. But the way he raked a hand through his thick black hair revealed his anger:

"To answer your blasted question—yes, Amanda has gone to her room." Piggott ran his tongue over his lower lip. "Quite a fetching little creature now that she's started to fill out. She's begun to bleed, I assume—?"

"Andrew—!"

"It's a fact of life, isn't it? And she has, hasn't she?"

Harriet swallowed. Not even Gilbert had ever posed such a frank question. It was all she could do to answer:

"In—in April. Prematurely."

"Thought so from the way those breasts are popping out. Your daughter's going to be a beauty. I've noticed the way she glances at men. Teases them with her eyes—"

Harriet could hardly believe what she was hearing; Piggott sounded almost lustful.

"—I venture she'll be tumbled before she's twelve. And enjoy it!"

"That's *vile!*" Harriet cried. "Such talk isn't suitable even between husband and wife."

"Then shall we try something that is suitable between husband and wife? You've jabbered enough!"

He dragged her up, wrapped one arm around her waist and drove his tongue between her lips.

iii

What had begun as a day of nerves and worry ended as an utter nightmare.

Mr. Piggott wouldn't be denied. He carried her bodily into the bedroom, refusing her even the decencies of drawing the curtains or dimming the lamps. The harder she struggled, the rougher he became.

He flung her on the turned-down bed and sprawled beside her, nuzzling her throat, her temple, her eyelids—

Thick-fingered hands rubbed and pinched her nipples. He pulled up her chemise, forced one hand between her legs.

"By God you're a prime one," he groaned as he fingered her. "But I'll have you craving more before we're finished, Mrs. Piggott—"

He seized the bodice of her chemise, tore it. She lay exposed on the bed, her nipples wrinkled as prunes. She was incapable of speech. She rolled her head from side to side, making small, incoherent sounds.

Piggott shed his clothing. He had soft white skin. He pulled her legs apart and flung himself over her body.

Harriet's dry flesh hurt when he assaulted her. Piggott could feel that. But he kept thrusting in spite of it. His fingers found her bosom again. Harriet moaned under the hard caress of his thumbs—

Piggott moaned too, jerking back and forth as the rhythm quickened. Harriet felt a muscle jump in her awkwardly bent left leg. Piggott's whole midsection seemed to pummel her. And there was not even darkness to conceal his noisy rutting—

He jammed his hands beneath her buttocks and squeezed:

"Ah—*ah*—"

When he withdrew and rolled on his side, she dragged herself toward the opposite edge of the bed. He shot out a hand, seized her hair:

"Where are you going, Mrs. Piggott?"

"To find—clothes. I trust you'll—allow that. You've satisfied yourself—"

"Not by half, my dear!"

He told her what he wanted next.

"Dear God, you must be mad!"

"Mad for a taste, Mrs. Piggott," he laughed.

She had no strength to fight him. The buzzing in her ears became a roar. She tried to pretend he wasn't doing what she felt him doing: a filthy, unnatural act—

There was no rest for her until well after two in the morning. Piggott assaulted her twice more. The last time seemed endless. He'd worn himself out, yet he wouldn't halt the pounding that tortured her body and numbed her mind. After the first time, he'd blown out the lamps. But that no longer mattered.

Finally, he convulsed; groaned; withdrew. He crawled under the covers, chuckling:

"For a wife, Mrs. Piggott, your behavior is exceedingly odd."

"Yours—" She could barely speak. She lay on her side, her spine toward him. She clutched her stomach, the stickiness of him an abomination between her legs. "—yours is an animal's."

That generated a deep laugh. *How had she misjudged him so badly?*

Until today, his caresses had been discreet, almost hesitant. Seldom had he done more than peck her cheek. His frantic desire for—*copulation* was the only word she allowed herself to think—gave him a bestial quality. And he was laughing about it!

The mellow voice boomed in the darkness:

"I am always a gentleman in public, Mrs. Piggott. But in the bedroom, I have my appetites—yes, I do. D'you honestly believe they've never heard of fucking at Yale College?"

"Oh, your vile mouth. Your vile, vile—"

"Be quiet, woman! You make me sick."

"I—I will never again permit—"

"Oh yes you will. This is one area of our marriage in which I mean to call the tune. I've quite a few more novelties to show you."

"Novelties? *Indecencies!*"

"Call 'em what you will, Mrs. Piggott. We shall indulge, never fear. Good night."

After a noisy plumping of his pillow and a few moments of heavy breathing, he began to snore.

Harriet Lebow Kent Piggott lay rigid in the warm air of the bedroom. She listened to the wheels of another carriage speeding along Beacon and wondered how she could have been so deceived. So misguided as to have married the kind of debased man who slept beside her now in perfect contentment.

What a ghastly mistake she'd made. What a ghastly—and irrevocable—mistake.

iv

News of some encouraging developments in the west reached Boston in the autumn of 1813.

An officer of talent had at last replaced the bunglers who had led the western army. William Henry Harrison, the same man who had routed the Shawnee at Tippecanoe, was commissioned a major general of militia by the alarmed Kentucky settlers, then given a national command by Secretary of War Eustis in September. With the rank of brigadier general and a force of some ten thousand soldiers, he was ordered to retake Detroit.

But it remained for a twenty-eight-year-old naval officer, Captain Oliver Perry, to make that possible. Perry handed a crushing defeat to the British blockade squadron at Put-in-Bay on Lake Erie. The dispatches said the flagship of Perry's small flotilla flew a pennant inscribed with Lawrence's dying words aboard *Chesa-*

peake. But the dispatches also carried an even more positive slogan that was soon on the lips of every literate citizen. At the end of his bloody three-and-a-half-hour battle, Perry had sent a message from his heavily damaged ship to General Harrison somewhere on the Sandusky River. In it he wrote, "We have met the enemy and they are ours."

Sweeping the British from Lake Erie permitted Harrison to advance on Detroit. He found the enemy had evacuated it and slipped across the river to Upper Canada. Harrison followed. A battle at Moravian Town on the north bank of the Thames River caused only a few deaths on either side. But one of those deaths brought great relief to the western settlers. Never again would the Shawnee Tecumseh terrorize the frontier.

Harrison and Perry helped end the threat of an Indian confederation manipulated by the British. They cleared the enemy from the northwest. The redcoats withdrew all the way to the Niagara frontier.

Harriet Piggott read the news items in the Kent paper from time to time. But they had no power to excite or even interest her. A much more personal battle was being waged in her own household.

On a Tuesday in late October, Franklin Pleasant called. The face of the graying general manager was unhappy:

"Mrs. Ken—forgive me. I meant to say Mrs. Piggott—"

Wan, Harriet lifted a hand to wave aside Pleasant's embarrassment:

"I wish it were Mrs. Kent again, Franklin. I don't doubt the whole town's laughing about the way a foolish widow was victimized."

"I pay no attention to that kind of nasty gossip," Pleasant declared. "However, a problem has arisen at the company, and I thought you should know. Actually there are two problems. Let me take the more serious one first."

Harriet's dull-eyed silence showed she expected the worst.

"This morning," Pleasant said, "I was served with papers. One of our six book presses is to be removed. It seems your husband—"

"Who has not been in this house for three days."

"Yes? Well, I believe I might have some grasp of the reason. Evidently he's been engaged in another of his gaming sessions."

"Cards?"

"Aye. At the end of a losing streak, he—"

Pleasant swallowed.

"—he refused to retire gracefully. It's not my place to say it, but Mr. Piggott's fondness for alcohol evidently leads to rash decisions. He insisted on continuing in the game. To finance his play, he signed a chit wagering the press I mentioned."

"Wagering the press?" Harriet whispered. "Is that legal?"

"The claimant sent a lawyer to Kent and Son this morning, and I asked the same question. I'm afraid it is quite legal. I verified that by consulting Mr. Benbow before I came to see you."

"Who is this claimant?"

"I've since discovered that too. His name means nothing, but he's known for loitering in the coffee houses—striking up friendships with prosperous-looking people—and drawing them into games for high stakes."

"Which he wins by cheating?"

"There is that suspicion—but no evidence has ever been brought forward. Very likely his victims are too humiliated—"

"And our lawyer can't block this—act of robbery?"

"He cannot. Had Mr. Piggott won his game, there'd be no problem. But he continued to lose. The press will be taken from the premises, and sold."

Harriet covered her eyes. "Oh dear God, Franklin. It's all my fault—"

Pleasant touched her hand. "Don't score yourself. We all make errors in judging other people. You were—you'll forgive me—not at all yourself during those weeks in which you kept company with your present husband. Mr. Gilbert was dead. It's only natural you'd want someone to fill his place. But what's done is done. We can make do without the press. I'd urge you to speak to Mr. Piggott, however. Insist that he refrain from similar wagers." Pleasant's smile was feeble. "Else he's liable to strip us to the walls."

After a moment Harriet said, "I'll speak to him."

"Good."

"But I have no legal means of compelling him to do anything."

"You mean—there was no agreement signed before marriage to limit his access to your property?"

Sadly, she shook her head. "I believed his lies about wanting no part of the business. Kent and Son is as much his as it is mine."

"Then—if I might suggest—"

He stopped, red-faced.

"Yes?" Harriet prompted.

"I *am* correct in assuming you're not entirely happy with your husband's character, am I not?"

Harriet almost burst out crying. She cried often these days. Piggott had dropped his mask of gentility. He treated her as a chattel. He was absent from the house more than he was present. But almost every time he returned, he demanded his rights in bed. Of late she'd taken to retiring to her room by five o'clock, and locking the door.

"That hardly covers it, Franklin," she said. "I have been duped. I was a willing, even eager accomplice, but the fact remains—I have been duped. And I don't seem to have any legal recourse."

Pleasant's eyes turned shrewd:

"Perhaps we can establish one."

"What do you mean?"

"Only that I'd like your permission to have one of our reporters do another bit of probing into Mr. Piggott's background and behavior. A little more thoroughly this time. It may yield nothing. But if there's evidence of immorality at these card games, for instance—women present—"

He shrugged, his cheek still deep pink.

Harriet said, "You have my permission."

"I'm happy to hear you say that. Now we come to the second matter. The day before yesterday, Mr. Piggott called on me in person—"

"Whatever for?"

"To inform me ahead of time that the press would be attached, and that I should not cause any difficulties. I'm afraid he and your nephew got into quite a heated argument. They do dislike one another—"

Harriet pressed her shaking hands into her lap:

"Intensely. Tell me exactly what happened."

"Mr. Piggott had been imbibing. To be honest, I didn't believe what he said about the press. I thought it was a drunkard's joke—else I'd have consulted Mr. Benbow before today, I guarantee you. In any case, Jared was working close by. There were—remarks exchanged. At one point, Master Jared completely lost his temper. I thought he was going to attack your husband. I prevented an actual fight, though—"

In the midst of her misery, Harriet felt a brief twinge of pleasure hearing about Jared. But the pleasure faded quickly:

"What did my husband say?"

"First he maligned Master Jared's character—unjustly. The boy has worked hard and done well in the press room—" The statement displeased Harriet, but she said nothing. "I told Piggott as much, too. He then made one utterly indecent reference to your daughter. About her—physical appearance. I hesitate to say more—"

Dread closed over Harriet then. On several occasions she had noticed Piggott watching Amanda closely. Amanda was a beautiful child. Much too beautiful for her own good.

Pleasant was waiting for a reply. She composed herself:

"You needn't say any more, Franklin. I understand."

"That was the remark which sent Master Jared into a fury. Mr. Piggott had to flee for his own safety. I—"

Pleasant started. Harriet had buried her face in her hands, weeping uncontrollably.

"—I agreed with Jared to say nothing about it. But when the disposal of the press proved to be anything but a joke, I changed my mind—"

His voice trailed off. Harriet gave no indication that she'd heard.

"Good afternoon, Mrs. Piggott," he whispered, picking up his hat and stealing out.

V

"Be damned to you, woman!" Andrew Piggott exclaimed.

"But you have no right to wager—"

"I said be damned to you!" Piggott shouted, raising his hand to her.

Harriett dodged away. She had asked her husband to come to the library when he returned to the house two days after Pleasant's visit. She hoped privacy would allow them to have an amicable discussion. The hope was misplaced from the beginning. Piggott had proceeded to grumble about needing a change of linen. He barely listened to her pleas. Now, at the end of the confrontation, he got control of himself and lowered his fist, saying:

"We share tenancy of all the assets of this family, Mrs. Piggott."

"I'm sure you made certain of that before the wedding," she said in a bitter voice.

He smiled. "I did. And I couldn't afford to be embarrassed during the game in question. I had to find some way to recoup—"

"So you gambled something which wasn't yours, and lost that too!"

He fussed with his stock. "Your shrillness is annoying. I'm going upstairs and then I'm leaving. I'm overdue at the Exchange Coffee House. Met a couple of Maryland gentlemen there only this morning. They're in metal refining. Pig iron into wrought—think that's what they said. A new version of something called a puddling furnace has been perfected on the Continent but they can't secure any information about it because of the blockade. They're hoping to put an inquiry agent aboard one of the neutral ships calling at Boston. Most agreeable chaps—"

"What's the point of all this?" Harriet demanded.

"Why—just that we're playing this evening, Mrs. Piggott."

"With *your* money!"

At the library door, he gave her a murderous look.

"With ours, if I choose. And there's not a damned thing you can do about it, my dear."

He raised his beaver hat to his forehead, tipped it and walked out.

CHAPTER II

Act of Vengeance

AMANDA KENT COULDN'T keep her mind on the book she was supposed to read by Monday, as part of her study of what the mistress of the dame school termed "fine literature." The book was a handsomely bound edition of a long poem that had something to do with a lady and a lake. The story took place in Scotland, but Amanda only succeeded in reading part of the first canto. The poem was as dreary as the weather!

She wandered to the library window. Watched dead leaves blowing across the Common. Noticed a few snowflakes in the air. Pedestrians passing the house looked chilly and uncomfortable.

Despite the darkness of the day, no lamps had been lit as yet. It was a Saturday afternoon in early November, and no one was home. No one, that is, except the servants. But they were virtually invisible. Very faintly, back in the kitchen, Amanda could hear cook singing to herself. The rest of the house was silent.

Amanda picked up an unfamiliar newspaper. Mr. Franklin Pleasant had brought it to the house only the day before. Of late, Mr. Pleasant called on Amanda's mother quite often. Amanda had asked why, but Harriet refused to answer, saying only that Mr. Pleasant's visits would soon change their lives for the better.

What could that mean? she wondered, idly scanning the front page of the paper which mama said had been started up in competition to Kent and Son's *Republican.*

Amanda found the family newspaper totally boring, packed as it was with paragraph after paragraph about the war. This new one, the *Boston Daily Advertiser*, seemed a little more lively. One story had to do with Indians in the Mississippi Territory; that was down south, wasn't it?

The Indians were called Creeks. Amanda hadn't heard the name before. It struck her as funny. But there was nothing amusing about the paper's vivid description of a massacre of white settlers at a place called Fort Mims. Near the end of August, a fanatical Creek faction, the Red Sticks, had slaughtered at least two hundred and fifty men, women and children.

Amanda wasn't familiar with the word "fanatical." After reading of the grisly activities of the Red Sticks, however, she thought she understood its meaning. The paper declared the Red Sticks would rue their brutality. A man named Jackson, a major general of the Tennessee militia, had raised two thousand volunteers to fight the Indians. The *Advertiser* stated that the former congressman and judge whose nickname was Old Hickory would punish the bestial savages in fitting fashion.

Amanda enjoyed several delicious shivers while reading the article—and another giggle over that nickname. Imagine a soldier being described as an old tree. Americans had such a passion for funny names!

Another item on the front page diverted her for a few moments. It described the death of a well-known New England witch, Moll Pitcher, who lived out in Lynn. The story said Moll had been famous for her ability to predict the future, locate lost articles and brew love potions.

With a sigh, Amanda put the paper down. How she wished she had a potion! Several, in fact. One to correct each of the unhappy circumstances that were making day-to-day existence so miserable. Glumly, she walked back to the window, planting her elbows on the sill and twisting the bracelet of tarred rope.

Amanda had grown taller in the first half of 1813. Mama said she'd soon have to wear a bandeau with her chemise, to contain those fleshy bumps that had appeared shortly after that hateful flow began—

If she'd had access to magic potions, she'd certainly have used one to stop the strange and alarming changes taking place in her body. Though mama assured her the flow was perfectly natural, it made her head hurt whenever she got it. And it was an untidy nuisance besides.

Another magic potion to restore her flat chest would have been welcome, too.

Then one more—to bring papa back. If only he were here, he'd set things right in the house. In its vast and almost imcomprehensible finality, her father's death had left an empty place in her existence. No one, not even her cousin Jared whom she worshipped, could fill it.

But if no potion were available to restore her father to life, she'd certainly wish for one to put her mother in better spirits. Amanda often felt guilty because she loved her mother out of a sense of duty, rather than spontaneously and with joyful abandon, as she'd loved Gilbert. Still, she hated to see Harriet unhappy, because that unhappiness affected the entire household. And mama had been miserable ever since her marriage during the summer.

Well, it was no wonder! How could she be happy as the wife of that Mr. Piggott with his syrup voice? His squinty eyes—?

And his hands. Amanda despised his hands most of all. They strayed in a too familiar way over her arms and shoulders whenever she was unlucky enough to be alone with him. He pretended he was touching her because he was affectionate; because he wanted to be a second father to her.

She didn't believe him. She was sure papa would never have touched her breasts and then claimed it was an accident.

Yes, a potion to forever banish Mr. Piggott from the house was perhaps the most desirable potion of all, provided she could have her real father back at the same time. What a pity the witch had died! If she hadn't, Amanda fancied she might very well have gone all the way to Lynn to consult her.

She did count it a blessing that Mr. Piggott played cards. That pursuit, which all preachers condemned, took him away from Beacon Street for long periods. In fact he hadn't been home during the past week and a half except for brief visits to change his clothes.

Late in the evening two days ago, Jared had revealed a piece of shocking news about Mr. Piggott. The family —except for Piggott, of course—was gathered in the front sitting room just before Amanda went to bed. All red in the face, Jared told his cousin that Mr. Piggott had gambled away one of the company's printing presses.

It was the first time in a long while that Amanda had seen her cousin genuinely angry. Since coming back from the navy, Jared didn't act like his old self. He spent most of every day and often part of the night at the printing house, and when he was home, he said very little. He no longer proposed deliciously dangerous adventures, such as climbing the roof of an ice house. He was obviously trying to behave properly, but he frightened Amanda a little because he looked so severe. He seemed to be keeping all his feelings locked up inside himself—

He didn't keep them locked up while describing what Mr. Piggott had done, however. He growled that Piggott had better not do anything like that again. In a way,

Amanda was glad to see her cousin angry. He was more like the Jared she remembered—

The rest of the evening was puzzling, though. Instead of expressing anger toward Mr. Piggott, mama grew upset and argued with Jared. He had no right to reveal such matters to Amanda, she said. And besides, the loss of the press was a good thing. It had opened her eyes to the need for drastic steps. Ever since then, Amanda had been trying to form a mental picture of someone hurrying along the street taking drastic steps. But she still couldn't imagine what such steps looked like.

The same evening Jared blurted the news about the press and incurred Harriet's wrath, he stole into Amanda's bedroom after she was tucked in. Like a conspirator, he led her to his own cluttered room and latched the door. From under his pillow, he took something that both frightened and fascinated her.

A pistol.

He'd bought it with his wages, he said. He meant to keep it down at Kent and Son, in case Piggott dared to gamble away any more of the firm's equipment. He looked quite angry and determined, and when Amanda reminded him that mama said Mr. Piggott had the legal right to gamble a printing press, Jared turned red a second time, flew into a fury and called her stupid.

She was hurt. Yet, oddly, she was comforted too—just as she had been earlier. Jared was Jared again—

He told her courts and lawyers were useless in dealing with rascals such as Piggott—only he used a much more wicked word than *rascals*. He said courts and lawyers actually helped men like Piggott steal what wasn't theirs—but no one was going to steal from the Kent family.

Mr. Piggott might have a *legal* right to bet a Kent press in a gambling game. But the next lawyer who showed his face at the firm with such a claim would answer to a higher law. The law of possession—

When he said that, he raised the pistol.

It was all rather mystifying to Amanda. So many large words and complicated concepts. But Jared's feelings certainly weren't secret any longer. She begged him not to do anything that would land him in trouble. The red faded from his face and he promised he wouldn't. But she knew he was fibbing. She had never seen his blue eyes so unpleasant.

Amanda hoped there would be no trouble. No more terrifying shouts and thumps from behind the closed doors of the library as mama and Piggott screamed at one another.

She hoped there wouldn't be any more gambling of the kind that provoked Jared, either. But that hope was probably foolish. Just yesterday, mama had let slip the admission that Mr. Piggott was again involved in a card game somewhere in the city. This particular game had been in progress for more than a week, and mama was worried. Amanda had suspected the reason for Piggott's prolonged absence, naturally. She prayed the man was wagering money and not printing presses—

Oh, it was such a dreadful muddle! And to top it off, she just couldn't work up enough interest to finish Scott's tedious poem by Monday. That would earn her a bad mark—

Life had been so good until papa died! Why couldn't he come back? Tears appeared in the corners of her dark eyes. Leaning on the sill, she twisted the cordage bracelet one way, then another—

With a little cry of fright, she straightened up. She saw a familiar figure lurching toward the stoop. It was Mr. Piggott, red in the cheeks and clutching his hat against the wind!

Amanda bolted out of the library, raced across the dim hall, started up the stairs. Piggott opened the front door before she'd climbed half a dozen steps. He called her name.

She felt a blast of cold air on her neck. Letting go of the heavy rail of the stair, she turned. Saw her stepfather silhouetted against the gray light of outdoors.

He closed the door. Its click echoed loudly in the still house.

"Amanda dear? Come here a moment."

He stood in the deep shadow by the closed door; she could barely see him. But his voice was quite loud; harsh. It started her heart beating fast under her frock of yellow percale. She climbed another step. Her high-topped cloth shoes seemed to weigh pounds apiece.

"Do you hear me, child? *I said come here.*"

Piggott shuffled out of the shadows, looming in the cross-light from the library. Digging her nails into her palms, Amanda descended the stairs.

Where were the servants? Why had she been caught by herself like this—? Oh, if only she were a witch from Lynn! She'd cast a spell and strike him dead—

At the foot of the stairs, she stopped. He approached, bent down, laid a hand on her forearm. She was certain she was going to faint dead away.

ii

Piggott dropped his hat as he squatted beside her. She wriggled but he wouldn't release her. He acted quite agitated:

"Where is Mrs. Piggott, Amanda?"

"Mama's gone out."

He looked relieved. "Do you know where?"

She hesitated before answering:

"She didn't say."

"You're lying to me, child." His fingers tightened. "I

want you to tell me where Mrs. Piggott has gone, and how long she'll be away."

"I don't know how long—"

"Ah!" He smiled in a sly way. "But you do know where?"

"No, I—"

"No lies! I am your father, remember."

"You're not!" Amanda cried. "You're not and you never will be! Mama went to Mr. Benbow. About *you!*"

Shrieking the last word, she wrenched free and leaped toward the stairs. Piggott caught her, ripping her silk sash as he dragged her back.

Amanda stumbled, sprawled across the lowest stair. Piggott crouched, clasped both arms around her, pulling her against him. She smelled the bad odor from his mouth; and his cologne; and rum.

"She went to the attorney's? Why—? *Put your hand down! If you dare strike me—*"

"Mr. Piggott?"

Pinned on the stairs, Amanda saw him go rigid. He released her, leaped up and whirled toward the dim spill of light from the dining room. Amanda recognized Florence, the downstairs maid.

"I heard someone cry out," Florence said. "Was it you, Miss Amanda?"

"Yes, he—"

"She fell," Piggott interrupted. "Leave us alone."

The maid looked uncertain: "But if Miss Amanda's hurt—"

"I'll see to the child. Get out of here!"

Florence fled. The door to the kitchen crashed shut, sealing off the light.

Piggott breathed loudly. He leaned toward the ten-year-old girl, cupped a hand beneath the small swell of her right breast:

"In other circumstances I'd strip you naked and give you a hiding you wouldn't forget, my girl—yes, and something else, too."

Amanda tried to cringe away from him. Away from that wicked, fondling hand. But Piggott was too big. And she was trapped on the stairs, pinned between the man on her left and the wall on her right.

All at once he drew his hand back.

"But I've no time. I'm going upstairs for a valise—"

Amanda thought the front door had opened. Piggott apparently failed to hear; his voice was very loud:

"—and if you call the servants or interfere in any way, I'll punish you as you've never been pun—"

"Punish her for what, Andrew?"

He straightened up as if he'd been whipped.

Amanda scrambled past his legs, hurled herself at the dim figure near the front door:

"Mama—*mama*!"

Sobbing, she wrapped her arms around Harriet's skirt. She felt her mother's hands on her hair. Those hands trembled almost as badly as her own.

"What was he doing, Amanda?" Harriet asked.

Controlling her tears, Amanda gasped, "Making me tell—where you'd gone."

"You have some special need to know that, Andrew?"

"None of your damn business, Mrs. Piggott."

"He said he's going to pack, mama—"

"Is that right?"

Harriet approached the foot of the stairs. Piggott had moved up to the fourth riser, an indistinct hulk in the chilly darkness. Some of Amanda's terror passed, driven out by the strange, almost happy tone of her mother's voice:

"You're leaving, Andrew? Good. You'll save me considerable trouble."

"Trouble? What the hell are you talking about?"

"Legal proceedings."

"Yes, I heard you'd gone to see that old bastard Benbow—"

"Amanda told you?"

"He forced me, mama."

"That's all right, dear—don't worry. It's typical of Mr. Piggott to threaten a child. But we won't be bothered with him any longer—"

Hugging the wall near the front door, Amanda watched Piggott jump down two steps, whip up his fist. Harriet darted out of range. Piggott called her a filthy name.

"Curse all you want, Andrew. That won't change anything. I have indeed been to the offices of Benbow and Benbow. I've passed certain information about you into their hands—"

"What information?" For the first time, he sounded shaken.

"How you lied to me before our marriage. You're not from a well-connected family. You never attended any college. You're a tanner's boy from South Boston—"

"You set spies on me?"

"Yes, and it was long overdue. This card game that's occupied you all week—"

"What about it?"

"That too has been observed from the street outside. Women have been seen going in and out of those rented rooms. Women of bad character. I won't be more specific in Amanda's presence. But I have ample grounds for a bill of divorcement. Mr. Benbow senior will undertake the suit on my behalf. I have been victimized, Mr. Piggott. Deceived and victimized—"

"It's no less than you deserve, you harpy!" Piggott roared, darting down the last two steps. Harriet lunged aside as Piggott lashed the air with his fist.

"Get out!" Harriet breathed. "Take your personal belongings and get out of my house. If you try to claim any of my property, Mr. Benbow will have a warrant drawn for your arrest."

Piggott laughed then; loudly.

"You've developed a surprising amount of courage, Mrs. Piggott—"

"Henceforward, my name is Mrs. Kent!"

"Well, that's all you'll have *henceforward*—your name. After our—our chat last week, I had a feeling you might go to your lawyer. So I haven't worried too much about the size of my wagers with the gentlemen from Maryland."

"The card-players—?"

"We started with cards. Then we changed games. We tried a new one just introduced in New Orleans by a young sport named de Mandeville."

"What has this to do with—?"

"Hear me out, Mrs. Piggott. I want you to hear every detail before I go. The game is played with dice—do you know what dice are, Mrs. Piggott?"

"Of course I do. You will stop calling me—"

"The gentlemen told me the game's a variation of hazards—very popular in English coffee houses, where Mr. de Marigny de Mandeville picked it up. The New Orleans gentry call it crapaud, after Johnny Crapaud, which I gather is a scornful name for Creoles. Wouldn't you like to know how I fared at crapaud, Mrs. Piggott?"

"Damn you, *get out!*" Harriet cried, raising her own hand.

Piggott rushed at her, struck her forearm with his fist. Harriet let out a low cry. Piggott seized and shook her:

"You'll damn me ten times over before this day's done, woman!" He let go, stood back, his smile vicious. "My luck ran against me. I kept losing. Heavily. But the gentlemen were quite pleasant about it. They accepted my note wagering the assets of Kent's. They suggested the idea, actually. It didn't pain me greatly when I lost the final rolls. As I say, ever since our chat, I suspected you were going to act against me—"

In a whisper, Harriet said, "Wait, sir."

"—I suspected some ploy like this bill of divorce. I'm sorry to inform you, madam—"

"Wait. You said the assets of Kent's—"

"—because of my losses, you no longer own—"

"What assets of Kent's?" she screamed. Amanda covered her ears, buried her face against the wall.

The kitchen door banged open again. Amanda heard a scurry of feet as several servants rushed to discover the cause of the new commotion. She wouldn't uncover her eyes, though. She was too frightened.

Piggott boomed all the louder:

"The printing house, woman. The whole goddamned printing house!"

Silence.

Four of the servants watched from the dining room doorway, not daring to speak. Piggott chuckled:

"Need I point out that I was still your husband when I signed my note? Your interview with your blasted Mr. Benbow is a mite tardy."

"You—you lost—?"

"Everything."

"God in heaven," Harriet said softly. "Oh dear God in heaven—" Suddenly her head came up. She stalked him. "You did it to spite me. You did it because you knew—"

"Suspected," Piggott broke in. "Suspected, my dear. Same thing, though, I suppose. There was precious little disappointment in losing what I didn't own in the first place. But there was a great deal of pleasure, I don't mind telling you. Of course, if the final rolls had gone the other way, I'd have taken the gentlemen's money and left here with it. Whichever way the game came out, I'd already decided to leave. I can do so now with immense satisfaction. You'll have to sell this house. Dismiss these cattle who fawn and wait on you—"

One of the servants, the young gardener, took a step forward. Florence held him back. Harriet began crying:

"It isn't true—"

"It is, and it's what you deserve."

"No. It can't be legal—"

"As legal as the first wager. Entirely legal. If you don't believe me, go down to Kent and Son this minute. My friends should be there with the same attorney who was engaged after I lost the press playing shemmy. They're taking possession this very afternoon."

"You're lying. *Lying to me—!*"

Piggott could no longer contain his rage. He ran at Harriet again. Through fingers pressed over her eyes, Amanda saw the man lift his right arm to his left shoulder, then slash outward with his fist. He struck Harriet's cheek, a loud, pulping blow.

She fell. Amanda screamed, "Mama—!" and rushed toward her as Piggott roared:

"If you don't believe you've nothing left, go down there and see, you fucking bitch!"

The family's young gardener slipped from the group of servants, flung off Florence's restraining hand, wiped his fingers on his leather apron:

"You'd better take your things out of here quick, Piggott—"

"Put a hand on me and I'll break your spine," Piggott said.

The young gardener blinked, hesitated. In that moment, Andrew Piggott spun and ran up the stairs two at a time. His laughter floated behind him, heavy, rich, triumphant.

iii

Amanda pushed past Florence, knelt at her mother's side. Cheeks wet from crying, she chafed Harriet's hands:

"Mama, get up. Please get up."

"We'd best help her into the sitting room, Miss Amanda."

"Yes," Harriet breathed. "Help me up, Florence—"

Her bonnet fell off as she tried to rise. She clutched the maid's hand, pulled herself to her feet. Amanda gave her the bonnet. Her eyes widened in surprise as Harriet put the bonnet on, struggled to fasten the ties beneath her chin.

"Come rest, mama—" Amanda begged.

"I must go to Kent's. Now. This instant."

"No, mama, wait—!"

"This instant!" Harriet repeated, turning and moving unsteadily toward the front door.

She jerked the door open, spilling gray light over the stricken servants and the almost hysterical child. Her step remained unsteady as she descended the front steps and disappeared. A moment later, Amanda heard a heavy rumbling, the snap of a whip, the rattle and ring of shod hoofs on the cobbles—

A shout:

"Watch out, woman!"

The unseen horses neighed wildly. Then, through the open door, Amanda saw them plunge past, pulling a dray loaded with big barrels. The frantic driver was hauling on the reins and jamming a boot against the brake lever—

The wagon shot out of sight, sparks spurting from the rear tires. Dazed, Amanda didn't immediately understand why the servants gasped and rushed outside. But when the young gardener's voice drifted from the street —"Christ save us!"—she realized something terrible had happened.

iv

Amanda slipped through the doorway, blinked and shuddered in the bitter wind sweeping along Beacon Street.

The servants had all left the stoop. She saw them down on the walk, to the left, huddling over someone fallen half into the gutter.

To the right, the dray was stopping; the driver had gotten his frightened team under control. He leaped down, raced back, his leather cap flying off, his boots clattering.

He checked at the edge of the crowd as people appeared from nowhere to surround the servants, hide Amanda's view of the fallen body—

Her mother. Harriet's bonnet lay on the sidewalk, stained red.

The dray driver shrank from the hostile eyes of the servants.

"She—she come along the curbstone," he stammered. "All of a sudden, she—fell right in front of the horses. I couldn't stop in time—"

Standing abruptly, Florence said, "We must carry her inside."

"I don't know," the young gardener said. "It might hurt her worse to move her—"

Florence cried, "We can't leave her lying in the cold —on the street—all these people staring—!"

Sounding reluctant, the gardener said, "All right."

"Is she breathing?" the dray driver asked him.

"Just barely."

V

The servants lifted Harriet gently and bore her up the steps into the house. On the stoop, Amanda got a clear view of her mother's head. It seemed to loll at an odd angle. Her cheeks were bruised and bloodied. Still numb from watching the awful scene with Piggott, Amanda couldn't quite believe what she saw.

The servants put Harriet in the front sitting room, on blankets spread on the floor. One maid rushed out of the house to fetch a doctor. Then the gardener dashed past Amanda who was watching from the hall, afraid to go in.

The gardener ran upstairs. In a minute or so, he came back swearing. He informed the others that Andrew Piggott had vanished. Out the back way, most likely.

"Why isn't mama getting up?" Amanda said in a hushed voice.

The gardener began, "Her neck is—" Florence silenced him with a sharp look.

Then the maid said to Amanda, "She can't get up, child. She's hurt. You'd best go to your—"

She broke off as one of the other girls motioned.

Florence knelt down. Put her ear close to Harriet's mouth. When she rose, tears tracked her cheeks.

She came toward Amanda, hands extended as if to gather the child to herself and comfort her. Gazing past her, Amanda saw the gardener pick up another blanket and cover Harriet's face.

"Amanda—" Florence could barely contain her misery. "—come with me to your room. You mustn't stay and look—"

Amanda knew then. She knew the second blanket meant permanence—

She tried to rush to Harriet's body. Florence barred her way:

"No, child!"

Amanda's grief burst out in a wild cry:

"Jared? *Jared, come help me—!*"

She fell against Florence's skirt, wailing hysterically.

CHAPTER III

Act of Murder

"JARED? WE GOT a visitor. It's that damn lawyer."

Jared barely heard the first words. But the last one struck him like an icy shower. He almost dropped the stack of untrimmed sheets as he deposited them on the pallet behind one of the thumping flatbed presses.

He straightened up, the sound of his own breathing loud in his inner ear. His heartbeat quickened as he turned toward the open front door. Snow swirled there. He'd been too busy to notice when it had started falling from the dull Saturday sky.

He scowled, recognizing the short, portly man just closing the door. In one hand the man carried a valise Jared had seen before.

"You'd better fetch Mr. Pleasant," he whispered to the pressman who had spoken to him.

The pressman reached for a rag to wipe his inky hands. Jared grabbed the rag, flung it aside:

"Right now!"

The pressman didn't protest being ordered around by a fifteen-year-old boy. He knew there was trouble looming. The presence of the well-dressed gentleman surveying the first floor work area charged the atmosphere with tension.

Jared felt that tension with mounting intensity. His temper had flared when he spoke to the pressman. That mustn't happen again. He had to stay calm until he learned the reason for the lawyer's call—

Instantly, his resolve was threatened. He could feel anger starting to simmer. A dull ache spread across his forehead as he studied the lawyer's expression. Smug. Disdainful—

One by one, the four other presses stopped. Two apprentices who had been cuffing each other quit suddenly. The pressman raced for the stairs.

The portly gentleman continued to scrutinize the room. Lanterns hung from the ceiling beams stretched Jared's silhouette across the floor as he walked toward the front. He recalled with bitter clarity the last time the man—and his infernal valise—had been on the premises. A large, empty section of floor space was a constant reminder of that visit.

"Good afternoon," the portly man said. His gaze jumped past Jared's shoulder, a deliberate affront. The boy reddened.

"What do you want?" Jared demanded.

The portly man condescended to look at him again. "I'll communicate that to the manager, if you don't mind."

"You'll tell me first! My aunt's the owner."

The portly man was amused:

"Not any longer, I'm afraid."

A knot twisted in Jared's midsection. Surely he hadn't heard correctly—

The man brushed by and strolled down the aisle between the presses. Jared almost grabbed him; then literally fought his hand back down as the man passed. The lawyer seemed unperturbed by the hostile stares of the men and boys on both sides of the room. Jared thought of the pistol he'd gotten in case something like this happened again—

No. Forget the pistol.

Only hours after buying the second-hand weapon, he'd decided the purchase was rash. He'd gone to the gunsmith's when the first press was taken; gone there with an almost drunken feeling of fury. But then, with the gun in his possession, he'd realized his mistake—

For weeks, up until the lawyer called the first time, Jared had consciously struggled to keep a check on his temper. To disprove, through new patterns of behavior, his old fears about himself. He hadn't succeeded completely. But he had made large strides, and he took pride in the fact. Then the lawyer arrived—and afterward, he bought the gun, and stored it in a niche up in the second-floor warehouse section.

That's where it must stay, he said to himself now. *Don't even think about it—*

Footsteps hammered on the stairs. No one moved save the portly gentleman, who propped his valise on one of the rails separating the central aisle from the work areas. The man opened the valise, fished out papers.

Franklin Pleasant appeared on the stairs, his waistcoat unbuttoned, his cravat undone. The pressman who'd gone to find him was right behind.

Wary, Pleasant approached the portly man:

"I trust you're not here to attach more of our equipment, Mr. Elphinstone."

"I'm flattered you remember my name, Mr. Pleasant."

"As I'd remember any thief's."

Elphinstone met Pleasant's glare with a smug smile:

"I deplore your animosity, sir. I am only an attorney, hired by my clients to conduct business on their behalf. I have no interest in removing another press—"

Franklin Pleasant looked relieved. Having lulled him, Elphinstone closed the trap:

"I have come to inform you that new owners are taking over this establishment."

Pleasant gripped the rail, his knuckles white. The ache in Jared's head worsened instantly.

"You must be insane," Pleasant said.

"Is that right? Be so good as to scan this document. Particularly the attached note. Signed by Mr. Andrew Piggott in the presence of my clients, and duly witnessed by two residents of the rooming house where Mr. Piggott and my clients were gaming. The document—and the note—will stand up in any court of law in this state. They're just as legal as the note Mr. Piggott signed in connection with the press."

Outside, Jared heard wheels grind to a halt. A restless horse stamped and blew. Laughing voices blended with the slam of a coach door. Footsteps approached the front entrance.

Jared didn't look around. He was watching Pleasant's face.

The manager leafed through the legal sheets. Fingered a slip of paper waxed to the last one. Pale, he let his hand fall to his side.

Elphinstone snatched the legal-size sheets and began to fold them. Pleasant looked at Jared, but his words were addressed to everyone:

"Elphinstone's right. This time Piggott's lost the whole place."

Despite the effort of will that had held him white-lipped and silent, Jared felt his anger loosed like a flood within him. In a tick of time, his mind swirled with distorted images of Uncle Gilbert. His throbbing head rang with remembered words: the promises he'd made about protecting the Kent interests. A faint inner voice of warning faded as he lunged forward with a shout:

"I don't believe it!" He seized the lawyer's collar. "You're a damned, deceitful liar—!"

Elphinstone squealed as Jared shoved him against the rail:

"Take your hands off me or I'll have you clapped in jail!"

"You'd better do as he says, Jared," Pleasant warned.

"But that paper can't be legal—!"

Pleasant shook his head. "The last one was."

Beyond Elphinstone, Jared saw an apprentice's head whip toward the front door. The sound of the door opening had barely registered in Jared's mind. Now he noted a startled look on the apprentice's face—

And heard a voice that numbed him:

"It's legal, Mr. Kent. You are now working for me."

Two men, elegantly dressed, stood at the front entrance, framed against the background of a carriage and swirling snow. Jared's blue eyes locked onto the man nearest to him; the other fellow, older, was a blur.

All Jared could see of the first man was half a face. A glowing brown eye. The young visitor wore a white silk bandana tied around his forehead. The edge of the bandana made an oblique line that ran from the left side of his forehead across his nose and right cheek to the curve of his jaw.

Perfectly relaxed, the visitor used a lacquered stick to knock snow from the brim of a beaver hat in his other hand.

"Mr. Kent and I are old acquaintances," the young man announced to the goggling employees. "Permit me to introduce my companion—Mr. Walpole, general manager of the Chesapeake Iron Finery, Baltimore. My name is Hamilton Stovall. My family owns the refinery—and now, it seems, a Boston printing house."

ii

"Jared—"

Pleasant's voice sounded remote. The boy's ears were filled with a roaring again, as of a huge wind unleashed.

He could have sworn the earth shook—then realized it was only the frantic, heavy rhythm inside his own chest. The scope of the monstrous duplicity began to register —and with it came an overwhelming sense of failure—

I should have killed him. I didn't, and because I didn't, this has happened—

"—who is this person?"

Stovall said, "Why, I'm the fellow who became acquainted with Mr. Kent's uncle by marriage. Played cards and dice with him—"

"Not by accident," Jared breathed.

"Oh no, dear boy," Stovall smiled, tapping his lacquered stick against his flawlessly cut mauve trouser leg. "Ever since my untimely separation from the naval service—"

His free hand touched the bandana hiding half his face.

"—I've laid plans for a return to New England. We are trying to secure information on the new modification of the Cort furnace being used in Europe. And it's impossible to get an inquiry agent aboard an outbound ship down in our part of the country. I could as easily have visited Providence to make arrangements, but I chose Boston for a special reason—which Mr. Kent of course understands."

Again Pleasant whispered:

"What's he talking about?"

"I—"

Jared licked his lips, trying to still the shaking of his hands at his sides.

The pistol. Remember the pistol—

Without thinking, he glanced at the stairway. Stovall noticed. Jared forced his eyes back to the young man with the stick; saw him for a moment as a blurred image. He had to leave the pistol where it was. *Had* to, or he'd only compound the damage he'd already done—

But reason's voice was faint, its promptings overwhelmed by humiliation and guilt. Jared watched lawyer Elphinstone sidle along the rail, out of his reach. He clenched his fists so tightly they ached.

Pleasant was waiting for an answer. Jared finally finished the sentence:

"—I served with Mr. Stovall aboard *Constitution.* He was sixth lieutenant."

"Tell them what happened," Stovall said affably. But there was hate in his glaring eye. "Tell them how you caused me to fall against a cannon that broke loose during the action with *Guerriere.* How my face came in contact with the heated barrel. My face and my hands—"

Tucking his stick under one arm, he showed his palms. Jared and the others saw the ruin of puckered scar tissue.

"Even having recovered, I'm no longer welcome where I was welcome before. Hostesses—young ladies—decline to invite me to their levees—" Despite an effort to control his voice, it grew louder. "Thanks to you, Mr. Kent, I'm disgusting to look at. Do you wonder I planned to return to Boston from the first moment I awoke in the hospital?"

"You can also tell them why we had trouble," Jared said.

"That's not neces—"

"He talks about young ladies but he fancies men and boys."

The older man, Walpole, spoke at last:

"Take your stick to the young liar, Hamilton!"

Stovall rapped the lacquered wood against a scarred palm; a heavy sound.

"It's a shotted stick, Mr. Kent. It could ruin you for life—as you've ruined me. However, since my family now controls this company, I have a duty to behave as befits an owner. To put a curb on my temper, no matter how filthy and false your accusations. I'll defer physical punishment in favor of what's already been exacted—"

He started forward, a slow, languid walk that held every eye in the room.

"I readily admit I thought of hiring men to waylay you, Mr. Kent—I can't be imprisoned for a thought, can I? I decided that was entirely too coarse. Too quick. I wanted something more lasting. It struck me nothing could be more suitable than destroying you by destroying your family. I entertained various means. But a few inquiries in the local coffee houses showed me one that was ideal. The stupid sham gentleman who married your aunt is rather notorious. More to the point, so is his passion for gaming."

"So you made his acquaintance—"

"Actually," Stovall cut in, "a sharp we hired made his acquaintance first. The sharp—shall we say—tested Mr. Piggott's skill at cards? The sharp was the chap who won the press. When he reported Mr. Piggott to be the soul of gullibility—especially after a few rounds of rum—Mr. Walpole and I contrived a seemingly accidental meeting at the Exchange—"

"Contrived to cheat him too, I don't doubt!"

Hamilton Stovall smiled. "That, my dear boy, you'll never know."

"Of course Piggott was cheated," Pleasant fumed. "Marked cards. Weighted dice—"

Stovall waved. "Immaterial. The games are over. What remains is—this—"

The stick shimmered as Stovall tapped the legal papers in Elphinstone's hand.

"Our proof of ownership. It was quite easy to tempt Piggott into his last, excessive wager. Plenty of that strong drink I mentioned—a few apparently spontaneous suggestions during the heat of the betting—"

Slap went the stick against the paper.

"—and Kent and Son belongs to the Stovalls."

From behind Jared, Pleasant burst out, "We'll fight you, by God! Our attorney Benbow—"

"He'll be able to do nothing." Elphinstone waved the document. "Nothing!"

The pressman who'd run upstairs stalked to the rail: "Damned if we need any lawyers to settle this—"

Stovall spun and rammed the ferrule of his stick against the pressman's throat.

The pressman gasped, his right hand flashing up to the stick as other employees started forward, fists ready.

"You had better restrain yourself, my friend—"

Again Stovall jabbed with the stick. The pressman turned scarlet, grabbed the stick at the mid-point.

"—else you'll rot in jail for assault."

"It's not an idle threat!" Elphinstone exclaimed. "I'll see to it!"

"Let go of the stick, Joe," Franklin Pleasant said. "These—gentlemen and I will retire to the office upstairs and discuss—"

"There's nothing to discuss!" Jared shouted. "Stovall and his cronies, they're—"

"Jared, be silent! For the sake of every employee of this company, don't say another word. Joe—let go of the stick."

The pressman scowled. But he obeyed the manager. Stovall examined the finish on the stick as Jared wiped his sweating upper lip. He glared at Pleasant:

"I won't let you just surrender—"

"Be silent!" Pleasant directed the warning not only to the boy but to all the confused and angry men and apprentices. "I am still manager here—"

"In the employ of *the Kents!*"

"My dear boy, you forget—that's all changed," Stovall said, strolling past Jared and pushing through the gate in the rail. A huge, tow-haired pressman blocked his path. The young Marylander raised his stick. Sweating, Franklin Pleasant shook his head. The pressman retreated.

Stovall gave a short, brittle laugh and walked on, tucking the stick under his arm again:

"The firm of Kent and Son is now irrevocably part of the assets of the Stovall family—to do with as we please. We may wish to change the politics of your paper—"

He rapped knuckles against the screw lever of a press.

"—suspend publication of your books and your gazette altogether—"

He approached a type font, grasped the top of the case, pulled. The case crashed to the floor, scattering hundreds of bits of metal.

"—or raze it to the ground."

Trembling, Jared cried, "You goddamned, conniving—"

Pleasant grabbed his shoulder: "I demand that you hold your temper! Nothing will be gained—"

Jared flung off Pleasant's hand and sprinted for the stairs.

iii

The rage in Jared Kent was out of control. He knew Hamilton Stovall wouldn't be making boasts if he lacked the legal means to back them up. Let Pleasant quibble and delay. He wouldn't.

As he reached the second floor, he heard contentious voices erupt below. Pleasant was shouting. Some of the pressmen too. And the lawyer—

The voices faded as Jared raced between the towers of books in the warehouse area. At the wall niche in the back, he stood on tiptoe, groped, pulled down the pistol. The English box-lock piece was a good fifteen years old. Six stubby barrels clustered around a seventh, central one. A plate above the trigger guard on the right side carried the maker's mark, and his name, Nock.

Jared had loaded and primed the pistol before storing it in the niche. He pulled the lock back to cock position; the first shot would discharge the central barrel and one adjoining. He hid the pistol under his shirt, then sped for the stairs again. Stovall would never take the place. *Never!*

On the third floor, one of the *Republican*'s reporters glanced up from his copy.

"What's all the row downstairs, Jared? Pleasant fairly tore out of the office—"

Jared didn't bother to answer. He dashed into the cluttered office once used by his grandfather, then by his uncle. Mr. Pleasant had installed a convenience lacking until his occupancy—a small Franklin stove that heated the room to oven temperature.

Breathing hard, Jared jerked open the doors of the free-standing stove. His reflection in the smoke-stained windows looked like a goblin's. He snatched sheets of newspaper copy from the desk, tossed them onto the fire.

Then invoices. More foolscap copy. A book. Another—

He moved with incredible speed. He pitched everything on Pleasant's desk into the stove. Finally the grate could hold no more. Flames shot from the stove's front as the fire grew—

Let Pleasant prattle about lawyers! Let him *discuss!* Jared knew it was too late for any of that to help. He knew Stovall.

"For Christ's sake, Jared, what are you doing? *Catch those things—!*"

The reporter lunged into the office, jerked back as Jared pulled the seven-barrel flintlock from his trousers.

"I don't want to shoot you, Tommy—"

"Have you gone mad?" The reporter pointed. Two

smoldering books and a pile of blazing sheets had fallen out of the overflowing grate. Smoke was curling from the ancient flooring. "You'll burn the place down!"

"That's just what I intend."

The reporter's sweaty face glistened as the fire brightened. Smoke hazed the office now. The tawny-haired boy—taller than the reporter—crouched with the seven-barrel pistol in his right hand, and something akin to lunacy in his bright blue eyes.

The reporter whirled and fled down the front stairs: "Fire! *We've a fire up here!*"

Jared darted behind the Franklin stove. He touched the top gingerly, gave it a shove. The stove tipped forward, crashed, spilling the contents of the grate. Jared's face broke into a ghastly smile as the flames spread to the desk, one wall—

The heat was intense. Coughing, Jared backed out of the office. Ran to the head of the stairs—

Men were coming up. He recognized the loudest voices. Stovall and his companion—

He waited, the back of his neck hot from the flames. The blaze wasn't yet bright enough to illuminate the lightless stairs. He barely made out dim figures appearing on the landing halfway between the two floors.

But someone down there saw him clearly:

"*He's got a gun—!*"

Jared thought he saw a patch of white on the landing; the silk bandana. He aimed the seven-barrel, pulled the trigger. The central barrel and another went off simultaneously, a second after Hamilton Stovall wrenched someone in front of him.

The other man—Walpole—shrieked. Flung his arms wide and fell back to the landing, blood darkening his coat where one or both of the balls had struck. Jared felt the old, devastating nausea sweep up from his belly—

"Murder!" Stovall cried in the confusion below. "The boy's done murder!"

Jared revolved the barrels on the spindle, readying another shot. His hands shook. The nausea was almost overpowering—

Fire shot from the office door, burning the wall on either side. Stovall had cheated him again.

"Murder! He's done murder! THE PLACE IS BURNING—"

Stovall's shout thundered as Jared ran for the rear stairs.

He emerged in the alley behind the building. Fat, wet snowflakes struck his hands and face. Their coldness sobered him a little.

But in his imagination, he still saw Walpole falling, his coat bloodied—

Jared careened across the alley to a fence. He dropped the pistol, shot out his hands. He could find no purchase on the fence planks. He fell to his knees, his palms raking over the wood. Splinters stabbed his skin as the shuddering shook him, spasm after spasm—

Once the trembling passed, he scrabbled in the snow until he located the pistol. He stuffed it into his trousers, stumbled for the end of the alley.

There he stopped. He glanced right, to the intersection of the narrow cross-street and the one that ran in front of Kent's. At the intersection, he saw men racing by, heading for the printing house in response to voices crying fire.

He turned and gazed up through the pelting snow to a rear window on the top floor. The window glowed orange. The fire had spread all the way to the back—

Jared's mouth twisted into a peculiar smile. His ears buzzed. His belly ached. But the trembling was over, and he still felt the intoxication of the rage that had seized him just before he bolted upstairs.

I did what had to be done, he thought. *Better that Kent and Son burn than fall into the hands of someone like Stovall—*

He wasn't entirely oblivious to the consequences of his actions, though. He'd shot Stovall's accomplice. For that, they could hang him—

Like some pursued animal, he spun and ran to the left, slitting his eyes against the snow. The darkness of the narrow street soon hid him.

iv

Observed surreptitiously from the blackness of the Common, the house on Beacon Street seemed quiet enough. The snow was falling harder now.

Jared hurried along Beacon to the end of the block. Cutting left, then left again, he approached the house through the small backyard.

His teeth were chattering and his soaked shirt stuck to his skin as he crept from the darkness into the stairwell behind the pantry. Beyond a door to the kitchen, he heard voices. Two or three servants, talking softly. He started up the stairs, testing each riser so it wouldn't creak.

Fortunately the servants had lit a fire in his room on the third floor. With the door shut, he pulled off his sodden shirt and warmed himself a moment.

On hands and knees, he groped under his bed. He dragged out the small canvas bag he'd brought home from sea duty. Backing up, he knocked over a stack of books.

The books thudded on the carpet. Jared tensed, listening—

A half minute passed.

A minute.

He stood up, carefully opened his wardrobe, found a fresh shirt, a few underthings—

His hand went slack. The clothing spilled to the floor. Blinking, he knelt to pick it up. In that moment, the dizzying anger that had possessed him for the past hour faded—replaced by a full realization of what he'd done.

He had destroyed Kent's.

Destroyed it!

Part of the blame was Stovall's. But only a small part. He, Jared Kent, was the truly guilty one. Surrendering to rage and unreason and the stunning shock of seeing Stovall again, he had behaved as he always did: At the moment when coolness counted most—the moment of crisis—he had been unable to deal with the situation except in one, destructive way. He had failed again.

And the new Jared he'd worked so carefully to create—the Jared who could be proud of his self-control—proud of finally giving the lie to everything Aunt Harriet said about him—he had destroyed that Jared Kent along with the printing house.

What a fool I was, he thought, still kneeling but seeing nothing around him. *A fool to think I could change—that I had the strength to change.* He remembered the terrible nausea moments after the pistol discharged. The punishing sickness was proof once again that all his old feelings about his worthlessness were correct; and that for the past months, he had only been deceiving himself—

An almost animal cry burst from his lips then. He buried his head in both hands.

After another minute or so, he lifted his head; drew a long breath.

All right. It's done. You are what you are. Now you have to save yourself as best you can—

He fumbled with the clothing, stood up unsteadily,

trying to assess the situation calmly. That Stovall, his intended victim, had let someone else die in his place only compounded his problem. No magistrate would put much importance on Jared's contention that he meant to shoot the man who had cheated his family. Murder was murder. He'd be sought and arrested if he didn't run—

Despairing, he gazed down at something he'd pulled from a drawer in the wardrobe without being aware of it. The medal and the broad green ribbon—

His feeling of having betrayed Gilbert's trust was sharp and hurtful. He touched the tea bottle on the medal's obverse. Rubbed his thumb slowly back and forth over the raised Latin legend.

Take a stand and make a mark.

Well, I've made a mark, he thought. *But it's not one to be proud of—even if it is the only kind I'm capable of making.*

And because of it, what kind of life is left for me—?

The door opened suddenly. Jared's hand constricted on the medal as he whirled:

"Amanda!"

It took him a few seconds to realize that her face looked raw; her eyes puffy.

"Come in and close the door!"

With a peculiar, lethargic slowness, his dark-haired cousin shuffled into the room. He shoved the fob into his bag, then added the sheathed Spanish knife and a few more items of clothing.

"You mustn't tell anyone you've seen me here, Amanda."

She didn't respond. But she recognized the contour of the pistol butt showing beneath his shirt:

"Is that your gun, Jared?"

"Yes."

"Why are you putting things in the bag?"

"Because I'm leaving, and you mustn't tell Aunt Harriet you saw me."

"Leaving? Where are you going?"

"Away from Boston. As far as possible as fast as possible."

He jerked the drawstring tight on his bag. Then, seeing that his curt tone had alarmed her, he dropped to his knees beside her, touched her face.

"I don't want to leave. I must. I'll be all right. Promise me you won't tell your mama—"

Amanda whispered, "Mama's dead."

"Dead?"

His hand fell away from her cheek. His mouth hung open. He understood why her face was tear-reddened. Yet he somehow couldn't believe what she'd told him:

"I hope you're not making up a story. Death is a very serious—"

"She's lying in the sitting room this minute! Florence said I mustn't look at her. She said I had to stay in my room until someone takes mama away. But I heard a noise in here—"

"Where's Mr. Piggott?"

"I don't know. I was alone when he came home this afternoon. Then mama came home, and there was a terrible fuss. Shouting and cursing and crying—Mr. Piggott hit her. Then mama ran out into Beacon Street. A wagon was coming along, very fast. She fell in front of it—"

"Oh my God."

"Mr. Piggott ran away just like you're doing."

The boy was speechless. Amanda flung her arms around his neck.

"Please don't go away and leave me, Jared. I'm frightened of Mr. Piggott. What if he should come back?"

Jared guessed the reason for Piggott's abrupt flight.

And for the quarrel. Harriet must have found out about her husband's last, disastrous wager.

"Jared—?"

"I doubt he'll come back."

"Why won't he?"

"Never mind!"

Her eyes brimmed with tears. "Don't talk to me that way, Jared. *Don't be cross*—"

He patted her arm clumsily. "I'm sorry. I'm—upset, that's all." He stood. "I must go—"

Yet he couldn't move. His eye traveled from his cousin's face to the cheerful hearth, then to his display cases. On one of the glass fronts, the fire twisted his image into an ugly distortion.

Murderer—

By his own hand, all the underpinnings of his world had been cut away—

But Amanda was no better off. He looked at her, small and lovely, watching him with fear and uncertainty—

How would she survive?

In the answer to that, he saw both a heavy responsibility that had fallen to him, and one slim opportunity to redeem himself a little. He put gentle hands on her shoulders.

"Amanda, you must listen carefully—"

"I will."

"There's been trouble at the printing house. I think I killed a man." Her eyes grew huge. "That's the reason I must go away. I'll be arrested and sent to prison if I don't. I think you'd better come with me."

She was slow to grasp the idea:

"You mean—away from here—?"

"Yes. Tonight. I'll take care of you. That is—" Bitterness showed in his eyes. "—I'll try. I *am* old enough—"

"But I don't understand why—"

"Your mama isn't here to protect you, and I promised Uncle Gilbert I would."

And if I don't keep that promise somehow, I'm finished.

Seeing her reluctance, he added, "Mr. Piggott might come back—"

"That's not what you said a minute ago."

He struggled to keep his voice quiet and firm: "I was wrong." He hated to lie. But he knew of no better means to persuade her to accept his protection than invoking Piggott's spectre.

He sensed her wavering:

"I looked outside, Jared. It's snowing—"

"Goddamn it, I know it's snowing!"

"Oh, don't lose your temper! Don't swear at me—"

"I apologize. Please, Amanda—no more tears. Let's go to your room. Find some clothing. A warm coat—"

She held up her hand. For the first time, he noticed the cordage bracelet.

"Will you let me take this?"

"Yes, yes—but hurry!"

She fought as he tugged her hand:

"What's happened to you, Jared? Your face is funny. You don't look like yourself—"

And what do I look like? What I am?

MURDERER—

"Stop talking and come along!"

He said it with such ferocity that she obeyed without another question. As they passed the head of the stairs, he glanced down. He saw no one on the second floor; heard nothing. The house seemed an enormous well of silence. Silence that mourned the passing of the dead, and the destruction of the living.

V

Twenty minutes later, two figures emerged from the darkness around the Beacon Street stoop.

Jared had decided to risk stealing out the front way in order to satisfy himself about Aunt Harriet. He'd crept to the door of the lamp-lit sitting room; seen the body beneath the blanket.

Leaving Amanda shivering in the dark hall, he stole in, his eye turned warily toward the passage leading to the kitchen where voices still murmured.

He lifted the blanket. Stared. Let the blanket fall. There was no satisfaction in seeing her dead.

"I'm cold, Jared," Amanda said as they slipped across the street to the Common. He'd insisted she put on her heaviest coat and fur-lined bonnet. But already her teeth were chattering almost as badly as his. He tried to make light of it:

"Oh, you won't be cold for long. I know a cozy stable in the South End. We'll stay there tonight, very snugly. In the morning we'll slip across the Neck to Roxbury. We'll have a wonderful adventure—"

What a pathetic sham! But Amanda was young enough to believe him—almost. She sniffled, clutching his hand tightly.

From the Common, Jared looked back at the Kent house, its windows shedding warm light into the moving pattern of snowflakes. The sight engulfed him in a pessimism blacker than any he'd experienced before. Hope was futile. He could never be anything more than what he was: the inheritor of weakness and unbridled emotion; a creature possessed by the past, and carrying its curse forever into the future—

He turned away. Lowering his head against the wind, he guided Amanda into the dark.

vi

Hamilton Stovall stood across the street from the printing house, watching it burn.

In the distance, a clanging bell and the clatter of hoofs signaled the approach of a fire wagon. The snow continued to fall, but Stovall, bareheaded, seemed perfectly comfortable as he gazed at the flame-filled windows.

Close by, lawyer Elphinstone looked as if he were freezing. A man ran up to him, spoke briefly. Elphinstone bobbed his head, approached his employer:

"Hamilton?"

"What is it?"

"The doctor that boy fetched just looked at Walpole. He's going to pull through."

"I suspected he would. I examined the wound myself."

"Is that why you were so slow to send for the authorities?"

Stovall said nothing.

"How did he get in the line of fire, Hamilton?"

"He stumbled."

"Oh. I understand only one of the balls struck him—"

"Yes."

"Well above the heart, luckily."

Stovall's uncovered eye glistened with reflections of the blaze now threatening the adjoining buildings. Noisy men milled in the street. The fire bell clanged louder. Stovall seemed oblivious to everything but the flames gutting Kent and Son.

"Going to be a total loss," Elphinstone muttered.

"I imagine it's well insured."

"Will you keep the money, or rebuild?"

"I haven't decided." After a moment, he added, "Has anyone seen the Kent boy?"

"No. I expect he's fleeing for his life. He heard you shout murder. He undoubtedly thinks Walpole's dead."

Hamilton Stovall's mouth curved up at the corners. His brown eye glared as the fire shimmered on the white silk of the bandana.

"Let him," he said.

CHAPTER IV

Ordeal

THE ROAD LED on toward a town whose lights gleamed faintly in the darkening day.

Jared wished they could push on to that settlement. There, they might find a public house like the one in Philadelphia where he'd worked part of a week, scrubbing floors and washing ceilings. The labor had left him stiff and sore every night, but it had given them a temporary haven in the stable attached to the public house —plus a quantity of biscuits and meal for the next stage of their journey.

Now the biscuits were eaten, and the meal too. They had to stop again. But going on to the town was impossible. He was too tired and weak. And Amanda was beginning to make small, fretful sounds that indicated her own exhaustion.

She was nearly as disreputable looking as Jared himself. Her cheeks were pale. Her dark hair hung tangled around her shoulders, picking up snow-crystals beginning to blow out of the northwest.

The draw-cord of the canvas bag was slipping from his shoulder. He tugged the cord up close to his collar as he surveyed the first of two farmhouses ahead. The houses and outbuildings were set about a quarter mile apart, and windows in both dwellings were lighted.

"Might as well try the first one," he said.

Amanda didn't respond. She acted dazed. Her hand moved aimlessly, brushing snow from her sleeve, then fingering a rent in the front of the coat that had once been clean and fashionable but now, in December, bore the marks of hard use.

"Come on, Amanda."

She murmured something that might have been an argument or a complaint. Jared took hold of her elbow, guided her around the worst of the ruts in the road to the first farmyard. An almost sensual joy possessed him when he thought of resting behind solid walls.

They'd taken no more than a couple of steps toward the house when a huge brindle animal shot around the corner. Amanda screamed. The shepherd charged them, barking. The sound seemed loud enough to reach to the end of creation—

"Run!" Jared yelled, turning and starting away. An instant later, he heard his cousin's second outcry, whirled back and saw her on the ground, floundering.

The shepherd came on, teeth bared. The dog made straight for Amanda.

Jared lunged, caught the girl's arm, literally dragged her to him. The watchdog jumped at his legs. Jared kicked, struggling to pick his cousin up at the same time. Somehow he avoided the snapping jaws and reached the road.

The dog stopped at the edge of the property, but kept barking. Jared cradled his cousin in his arms and staggered down the road, unnerved by the yapping of the animal, by the thought of the harm Amanda could have suffered—and by disappointment.

"There, he didn't hurt you," he panted. Amanda kept moaning softly against his neck. "Amanda, stop that! You're all right."

"Yes. Yes, but the dog scared me—"

"He scared me too." The barking stopped abruptly.

Jared glanced back. He could barely see the huge animal as it padded toward the house. He set his cousin on the ground.

"We'll try the next place. There are lamps in the back —see?" He pointed. "Let's go around that way—"

She stumbled as they started into the second yard. Jared caught her and held her up. Night was coming fast. The wind was stiffening, driving the snow harder. The ground was already covered with a white crust.

A memory of the warmth of the Boston house tormented Jared for a moment. He put it ruthlessly aside. He could allow himself no weakness; no regrets. They had come a good distance, but they had to go even further, surviving day by day and hour by hour—

He led his cousin down the side of the shingled house. They must keep on; never falter; never stay in one place too long. This was still civilization. He was still a murderer—

He'd considered it an accomplishment just to reach Philadelphia before the worst weather began. But he'd been nervous working at the crowded public house. Even with the war going on, Philadelphia attracted a great many visitors. What if someone from Boston recognized him—?

So they'd taken to the road again, putting more miles between themselves and the threat that Boston represented. As yet, Jared had no clear destination in mind. He knew he'd have to choose one eventually. Eventually, but not tonight—

The snow was growing steadily thicker. It reminded him that it wouldn't be as easy to steal food in deepest wintertime as it had been on the long trip down to the Quaker City. He hoped they wouldn't have to resort to thievery tonight. He hoped begging would serve instead—

The rear porch creaked under his feet. Amanda refused to climb up with him. She stood in the yard and stared at him with a slack expression. Her thin fingers kept plucking at the tear in the coat. God, how despicable he was to subject her to this—!

His stiff hand rapped on the door. Inside, he heard a man's guttural voice. Then a woman's, a little lighter, not so foreign-sounding. A small boy asked a question and the woman shushed him. Boots clumped.

The door opened to reveal a man in his late twenties, plainly dressed, with curly blond hair and blue eyes. An old flintlock glinted in his hands. The young man peered at Jared, then glanced beyond him, wary.

"Ja?"

"Good—good evening," Jared stammered. "My—sister and I—" He stood aside so the farmer could get a clear look at Amanda down in the whitened yard. With fair glibness, he slid into the tale that had served them before: "We're on our way to Pittsburgh—"

"Alone? No von else?"

"Just the two of us. We're from Rhode Island—" He didn't intend to tell anyone they came from Boston. Who could say how far Massachusetts law might reach? "Our parents died in a fire, so we're going to Pittsburgh to live with our uncle."

The young man's eyes remained suspicious. His wife appeared behind him. Despite her youth, she was rough-skinned and stooped. Jared was almost dizzy inhaling the aroma of fresh bread that suffused her kitchen.

"Children, Karl?" the woman asked.

"Ja. Dey say dey're going to Pittsburgh—"

"Look, I'm not armed in any way—" Jared raised his hands. He'd concealed the Spanish knife and the London-made pistol in the canvas bag on his shoulder. "There's nothing to fear. We'd only like permission to sleep in your barn."

The woman's face softened. "The barn will be frigid in a storm like this. We could let them come in, Karl—"

Jared was quick to capitalize on her sympathy:

"If there's any way I could work for you for a day or so, I'd be glad to, in exchange for a little food to take with us—"

"De roads are very bad dis time of year," the farmer advised him.

"I know, but we need to get to Pittsburgh as soon as we can."

The young man set the butt of his flintlock on the floor. Jared felt relieved.

"Might find one of de wagon men in town who'd take you," the farmer said.

"Town?" Jared repeated.

The young man gestured in the direction of the lights glimpsed on the road. "Langaster. But I cannot gif you charity, dis is a poor household—"

"I told you I'd work! Please, can't we come in? My cous—my sister's nearly frozen."

For a moment he thought the farmer would say no. Had something hinted to the young man that the visitors weren't brother and sister? Jared's light eyes and Amanda's dark ones, perhaps? Just as the farmer was about to speak, his wife touched his arm.

The man glanced at her, shrugged and stepped aside. "*Ja,* all right. But you sleep in de barn."

"Karl—"

"No, dey go to de barn."

"That's fine," Jared assured him.

"If you can help me split wood, I maybe gif you some corn—"

"Amanda, come on!" Jared cried, darting down the steps into the blowing snow. His excitement at having found them a sanctuary disappeared as he gazed at the dim oval of her face. Her eyes were tear-filled.

"I want to sleep, Jared," she said, teeth still chattering.

"We will! These people are going to let us stay in the barn. But first we can go inside."

"You better carry her," the woman said. "She don't look so well."

Wearily, Jared picked his cousin up and bore her to the porch and into the lamp-lit kitchen where the smell of fresh bread drifted, indescribably rich and sweet. *One more step taken,* he said to himself as the farmer closed the door against the wind's whine. *Don't worry about tomorrow or about the day after—be glad you've found a place away from the storm—*

But as he set Amanda on her feet and started brushing snowflakes off her brows and eyelashes, he thought again of the immense distance still ahead of them; thought of all the cheerless roads yet to be walked; of all the strange doors that might or might not open when he knocked—

It seemed too great an effort to ask of any human being, let alone two who were not even adults.

But Jared was able to banish that kind of pessimism very quickly. All he had to do was remind himself of what lay waiting for him back in Boston. Hungry and tired as he was, he showed firmness in guiding Amanda to the chair the farmer's wife pulled out from the table. Her son, a blond copy of his father, was awestruck by the visitors.

Jared spoke because he knew he must:

"I'd like to thank you for doing this. We've come a long way today."

The farmer stood his flintlock in a corner, saying nothing. His wife broke the tension with a smile:

"That is very clear. Please—sit down and eat."

ii

Jared and Amanda stayed four days with the German couple. Jared split eighteen cords of wood for the farmer, whose name was Konigsberg. The young man never quite lost his suspicion of the visitors. But his wife, whom he called Hilde, accepted their stories at face value, and treated them generously. By the time the cousins set out with Konigsberg on his weekly trip to Lancaster for supplies, the woman had persuaded her husband to give them not only a good-sized ration of corn, but some bread and a thin blanket as well:

"That will keep you a little warmer on the way to Pittsburgh, *ja?*"

iii

The wagon creaked and swayed. From the head end, Jared heard the teamster cursing. His whip popped like a gunshot.

The driver, Francis Quilling, had agreed to take them to Pittsburgh on this, perhaps the last trip he could make before the roads became impassable; he had agreed because Jared would provide the extra strength needed to free the wheels from deep, muddy ruts.

Quilling was a garrulous man, and a braggart. No one made shrewder investments than he did. His house was one of the largest and finest in Lancaster, envied by everyone. His seven children were all supremely intelligent; paragons of Christian virtue. And during good weather, he wouldn't lower himself to take help along on one of his runs; he could do it all, no assistance required.

But he did admit that in early winter, particularly after the sun shone for a while, boggy places presented a problem. If the wagon mired, Jared's job was to jam pieces of plank beneath the iron tires, then help Quilling push the wheels while the straining horses pulled the wagon forward over the boards.

It was just before sunset. Amanda sat staring at her cousin in the wagon's dim interior. Quilling had allowed Jared to take a short rest because the ground hereabouts was frozen hard.

As Jared yawned, Amanda touched his hand:

"Where are we going, Jared?"

"Why, you know very well. Pittsburgh. Be there in a couple of days, Mr. Quilling said."

"And after that?"

"I don't know."

"Can't we stop in Pittsburgh?"

"We'll have to, until the river opens up again."

She shook her head. "I mean for longer than that."

"No, we've got to keep going."

"Where?"

"I don't know yet, Amanda!"

"But I'm tired!"

"Then sleep. Put your head down."

"I mean I'm tired of walking and being dirty and hungry—"

"We'll find a place to stop," he said, sounding confident.

"I don't believe you. I don't think you know where we're going. You're just pretending. Telling me lies. Aren't you? *Aren't you?"*

He didn't reply. She rolled away from him, covering herself with the blanket given them by the Konigsbergs. He stared at her filthy hair, accused by her silence but unable to admit his guilt aloud.

iv

An old poster preserved on the wall of an emporium in Pittsburgh provided the first hint of an answer.

Even in winter, the boat yards at the head of the Ohio didn't shut down. Work was done indoors, in sheds that protected the river craft under construction. Jared found a job as a boy-of-all-work in the noisy Suck's Run yard at Boyd's Bluff, across the Monongahela from the busy town. All during January and into February, he ran nails and lumber to the laborers sawing and hammering on flatboats and keelboats that would take to the water when good weather came.

At the end of his fourteen-hour day, Jared rode the ferry raft back to Pittsburgh. The ferrymen worked in pairs, using long poles to push away floating chunks of ice. The trip was always tedious because Jared was always exhausted. All he wanted to do was clean the sawdust and shavings from his hair and his body, then go to bed and sleep.

With his wages, he and Amanda had been able to take a room in a shabby boarding house whose owners, an elderly couple, obviously weren't too scrupulous about their guests. Jared was never questioned about why he and a small girl were traveling together.

Jared's pay was low, so the room was tiny. He slept on a blanket on the floor while Amanda occupied the bed. The landlady set a fair table, though. And Amanda had a place to stay during the day, safe from the none-too-savory men who drifted in and out of the downstairs parlor.

Occasionally Jared spent a little of his money to bring his cousin a newspaper. Apart from that, entertainment for Amanda was non-existent. Confined in the room, she grew even more sallow and unhappy. Only Jared's return in the evening revived her spirits.

Two or three times a week she questioned him about their destination. He always gave the same answer:

"I still don't know."

Then they saw the poster.

Jared worked six days a week. One Saturday evening, he took Amanda to a store to buy her some penny candy. As the cousins walked in, the storekeeper was conversing with a couple of rough-looking types lounging in chairs by the cracker barrel.

The storekeeper came to wait on them. Amanda's eyes glowed as she surveyed the candy spread out in small wooden trays. But Jared's attention had been captured by the poster tacked to the wall:

March 17, 1811
Premier Voyage
Down the Ohio and Mississippi!
The Unique and Remarkable
STEAM-BOAT
"New Orleans"
constructed by
Mr. NICHOLAS J. ROOSEVELT
Associate of the Celebrated
Steam Pioneer
Mr. ROBERT FULTON
Captain A. Sack, Pilot

Busy counting out licorice pieces, the storekeeper didn't pay much heed to Jared. The boy continued to gaze at the name of the vessel. Certain things that he'd read and been told about the south came back to mind. How warm it was there. How gentle and easy a life—

True, the Indians had been active in that part of the country. But the military was moving against them. The name of the steamboat suddenly seemed to provide exactly the sense of direction he needed.

The storekeeper accepted Amanda's coin and turned to her cousin:

"That was quite a day."

Startled, Jared said, "What?"

"The day they launched *Orleans*. Never saw such crowds in this town." He scratched a white eyebrow. "But you sound like you come from back east—"

"We do."

"They got steamboats on the New York rivers, don't they?"

"Yes, but I've never seen one."

"Well, old *Orleans* was mighty handsome. Had a great big wheel in her stern. We sent her off with a hurrah you could hear for miles. She was supposed to make trips between here and the mouth of the Mississippi. Turned out she wasn't built quite right. She didn't have the power to get through the falls of the Ohio very easy—and once she did, she never could come back upstream past Natchez. She's hauling cotton down there, they say. There's a lot of talk about putting bigger steam boats on the Ohio soon. Then you'll see goods being carried like you never saw before—"

The storekeeper broke off; swung around. One of the men from the cracker barrel, burly and thick-lipped, had walked to the counter. Pretending to examine a tin of tobacco, he was actually staring at Amanda in an oblique way.

"You want to buy that, Rafe?" the storekeeper asked. "If you don't, then don't shake it. Ruins the tobacco."

"I might want to buy it," the man answered, nibbling at his lower lip. All at once Jared comprehended why Amanda was being scrutinized.

Though still only ten years old, she was maturing rapidly. Her face promised beauty in adulthood. And her breasts, already grown large for one so young, showed clearly beneath her dirty coat.

Jared tugged his cousin's hand. From Amanda's expression, he knew she was aware of the man's interest. It obviously upset her. Jared doubted that she understood the reason for the attention, though. As he led her past the burly fellow, he heard the tobacco tin rattle back on the counter. Fingers closed on his arm:

"Ain't seen you two in this store before, have I?"

Jared wrenched loose. "Does it make any difference?"

"Leave them be, Rafe," the storekeeper warned. His tone made clear that Rafe wasn't exactly his favorite customer.

The burly man grinned, his eyes lazy-looking in the lamplight. "Hell, I was just bein' cordial—"

"You can be cordial with folks your own age."

"Now Morris, don't carry on so. If I got a mind to greet somebody—"

"Let me put your candy away," Jared said, seizing Amanda's wrist. The chunks of licorice dropped into his other hand. He opened his coat. The butt of the London-made pistol and the sheathed Spanish knife were clearly visible at his belt—as he intended.

He tucked the candy into his pocket. As far as he could tell, the older man wasn't armed. At the sight of Jared's weapons, the man's interest cooled rapidly:

"Shit, you're makin' a fuss for nothin', Morris—" He ambled back to his crony.

Outside, Jared realized just how upset Amanda was:

"Why did that man stare at me like that?"

"Because—" He didn't hesitate long. It was time she understood. "—because you're very pretty."

"No I'm not. I'm all dirty."

"Makes no difference. You're a handsome girl, and you look older than you really are. That's why I insist you keep the door locked while I'm over at the yard. And why I never want you to speak to men when I'm not around."

As they tramped toward the boarding house in the winter darkness, Amanda seemed to brighten:

"You're not teasing me?"

"No."

"We're so raggedy—I never thought anyone would look twice at us."

"Not me, Amanda. You."

"Did he really think I was pretty?"

"You saw how he gawked."

She nodded, actually smiling a little. Then she shivered. "Mercy. Imagine!" A moment later: "You're *sure* you're not teasing?"

"Believe me, Amanda—some men lose their heads over pretty girls, and you're going to be one of the prettiest. That'll be nice for you, but it'll also be a problem."

In the light from the front of a hotel, he saw her lips still curved in that thoughtful smile.

But it vanished quickly enough:

"I want my licorice."

"Here. Want to know something?"

"What?"

"I know where we're going."

"You mean we can't stay in Pittsburgh?"

"Don't start that again. I've already said no."

"Why can't we?"

"Just because."

"Oh, I'm sick to death of hearing that, Jared!"

"But you'll like where we're going."

"Tell me and see if I will."

"We're going down south. A city called New Orleans."

"Is it far?"

"Not very," he lied. "We should be there by late spring or early summer."

"Is it warm?"

"Yes, it is."

"Did you just think this up, Jared?"

"Why, no," he said, trying to summon a smile himself. "I've had it in my head several days now."

"Liar."

He laughed and rumpled her hair.

New Orleans. The more he turned it over in his thoughts, the more certain he was that the poster had provided an invaluable inspiration. He'd decided long ago that they'd never go into the west—into the country where his mother had died and his father had failed. But the south—that was different. It was a mellow, gentle land. He'd heard that New Orleans was a splendid old city, full of wealthy folk who spoke Spanish and French and lived in a grand style. From the storekeeper's remarks about river commerce, and from what he knew personally about the frantic pace of boat construction, Jared suspected that New Orleans was also a thriving commercial center. If Mr. Fulton's steamboats made their appearance on southern rivers as they had in the east, travel and shipping time would be cut drastically. More and more cargo would be moving up and down the Mississippi. Someone who was industrious should be able to find work easily at a major port—

So, for the first time in weeks, each of the cousins had something to be happy about. Amanda had her licorice. And Jared had his destination.

v

In late February, he quit his job at the Suck's Run yard. It hadn't been profitable employment. His small salary barely met expenses. Thus he was immediately forced to look for a means of financing the next stage of their journey. After several days of combing the docks, he managed to sign onto a keelboat making a run to Louisville, at the falls of the Ohio.

But the captain was parsimonious. Jared would be allowed rations and sleeping space for one, not two. He didn't quarrel. By now he was used to sharing everything with his cousin.

Soon after the boat got under way, he realized again that Amanda had ripened to the point where she was bound to attract the stares of older men. Despite her disreputable appearance and her pale skin, the luminous beauty of her eyes and the curves of her swelling figure drew many a sly glance. Jared kept his pistol and knife visible at all times.

Amanda seemed conscious of the attention. Once Jared caught her returning a man's rough greeting with a coquettish smile. That evening he lectured her severely. She was too young to experiment with her newly discovered ability to interest the opposite sex!

Amanda retorted that she'd only thought it might be fun to see how bad-smelling, bearded men reacted to a little friendliness—

"Besides, I was only teasing."

"They don't know that. You tease them too much and they'll want to try—"

Uncomfortable silence.

"Try what, Jared?"

"Never mind."

"Are you trying to say they'll want to do what men and women do together?"

Jared actually blushed. "Do you know about—?"

"Of course I do."

"How?"

Now it was her turn:

"Never mind."

"Damn you for an impudent little minx—!"

"Don't you dare curse me, Jared Kent!"

"All right, I'm sorry. But you pay attention to what I'm telling you about—"

"Pooh! If any man starts to—to hurt me or something, I'll just tell him he mustn't. If he thinks I'm pretty, he'll do what I say."

He would have guffawed except for the fact that she was serious. He replied the same way:

"You may be able to twine men around your finger when you're twenty, Amanda, but it won't work when you're only ten. You mind what I say. Don't lead them on."

She made a disappointed face. "Oh, very well."

But her eyes were still merry. She was entranced with her new-found power. God help me, Jared sighed silently, I've forced her to learn too many hard lessons too early. His familiar sense of guilt put him in a bitter and depressed mood the rest of the evening.

vi

The keelboat glided on down the Ohio, and Jared found himself studying the terrain with a peculiarly intense fascination.

In the misty meadows and towering trees that moved slowly astern on both sides of the river, he saw primitive beauty. At the same time, the vistas of silent forest and shining river filled him with loathing.

Occasionally, on clear days, he glimpsed game on shore. Great prong-horned deer. Fat pheasants. Wild hogs. He began to understand why people would seek this new country, content to huddle together in small settlements of the kind the keelboat passed from time to time. The boat's coming was always announced by a blast of an old bugle owned by a member of the crew.

When the bugle pealed, men and women in the settlement ran down to the shore and held their children up to see the vessel. Jared felt sorry for the children—and the parents. The older people usually waved with great animation. But they had a lonely, haggard look about them. Perhaps that was why they waved.

There was a strange duality in Jared's interest; a duality that didn't escape him. The great forest did impress him with its stark splendor. He could tell the land would be beautiful the moment the weather warmed. He could visualize the greening boughs; the bursts of wildflower color—

Yet he hated all he saw.

He tried to find a rational explanation for that feeling. On the surface, it seemed simple. The land had lured his mother and father with false promises of ease and abundance. They had found reality far different. The land had subjected them to the same hardships it worked on anyone who came to challenge its dominance. They had not been strong enough to endure, and they had been destroyed.

Jared loved the memory of his parents to the extent that it was possible for him to do so, knowing so little of them. But what had happened to them had happened in the past. It seemed insufficient to explain the loathing and unease that gripped him in the present.

One morning, unable to sleep, he went out on deck just as the light was breaking. He yawned and rubbed his eyes in the red dawn—and blinked suddenly at movement in the brush on the left-hand shore.

An animal stood there, its hindquarters concealed by a spray of ferns. Its great shoulders and head were fully visible. It resembled some huge, sleek, tan-colored cat. Its eyes caught the rising sun for an instant, burning like pieces of iridescent crystal—

Jared shuddered.

In its jaws, the cat held the remains of a smaller, darker animal.

A raccoon? A possum?

No way of telling. The prey was dead; crushed; nothing more than mangled meat and brown, blood-stained fur. Jared put the back of his hand against his lips, feeling the sickness rise—

With immense grace and power, the cat turned and loped away from the shore, and then Jared understood.

The land was like the cat. He and all the others who came to it were prey. Some survived. Some could not.

He was one of the latter. Bone-deep, he knew that.

Times beyond counting, Aunt Harriet had told him that he was what his parents had been: flawed. He had seen countless evidences of his own. Wasn't the tremor in his belly, stirred by the sight of the bloody carcass in the cat's mouth, just one more?

He was the child of Abraham and Elizabeth, knowing with a certainty that he bore their weaknesses. Sometimes he tried to tell himself the conviction was irrational. Yet he believed.

If he challenged the land, it would destroy him. That was why he and Amanda had to flee to New Orleans; to civilized comforts. It wasn't merely a matter of being far from Boston. He probably could lose himself anywhere out here. But he would not—

He understood, on that scarlet morning, the real reason he hated the land.

He hated it because it made him afraid of himself.

vii

Louisville impressed Jared as a prosperous, if faintly pestilential, place. A profusion of ponds dotted the forests of oak, hackberry and buckeye that surrounded the town. But Louisville proper was as lively as Pittsburgh, and the warehouses and docks testified to its importance in commerce. Kegs and barrels containing everything from whiskey and flour to corn and lard were piled high on the wharves. Chickens and turkeys squawked in great tiers of wooden cages. The river men who carried and handled the goods kept the taverns and bordellos noisy all through the night.

Jared found temporary work unloading and uncrating newly arrived shipments at a general store. The store's signboard read *Audubon & Rozier, Merchants.* Mr. Ferdinand Rozier was the only partner in evidence. During the week and a half that Jared worked for Rozier, he learned that the man's former associate perferred fine art to business. Audubon and his wife had moved down the river to Henderson a few years earlier. There, Rozier said, Mr. Audubon had no doubt abandoned storekeeping entirely, in order to make sketches and paintings of what interested him most—wildlife; birds, chiefly. Rozier laughed at that. There was no market for portraits of birds! He was convinced his former partner was destined for failure.

Rozier agreed to pay some of Jared's wages in trade. Provisioned again, he and Amanda set off along the Cumberland Trail during a warm spell in early March. In forty-eight hours, the weather changed. Sleet began to slant down from the sky.

The cousins were struggling along a heavily wooded stretch of road at twilight. Great tree limbs soughed in the wind. Within minutes, the sleet completely soaked their clothing.

They hunted for a farm that might offer shelter, but found none. They were forced to spend the night in the open.

The storm continued until the following morning. When the light broke, Jared's head was hot and his eyes had a glazed look. Though not ill, Amanda was almost as miserable.

"We—we've got to hole up a while," Jared gasped as he and his cousin started out. The whole world seemed gray, wet and forlorn. "Anyplace—I'm not feeling good—"

The sunny visions of New Orleans were gone. Instead, he saw only his cousin's drawn face—or feverish imaginings:

Hamilton Stovall strutting through the main floor of Kent's—

Stovall's general manager dying in a welter of blood—

The printing house afire—

"Take my hand," Amanda said, sniffling. Jared was terrified by the sickly whiteness of her skin. What if she caught a chill and died just because he'd dragged her all this way—?

They managed to negotiate another half-mile of road, passing a bogged and abandoned freight wagon. Jared's eyes watered and blurred. The world seemed to consist of gargoyle trees against a sodden sky—

Suddenly Amanda exclaimed, "There's a creek ahead!"

"I don't see—"

"And a cabin!"

"I can't make it out—"

"Here, hang onto me. I'll lead you—"

It was the longest distance Jared had ever walked. Or so it felt. His head ached. One moment he burned; the next, he froze. After an interminable time, they reached the creek and crossed.

The water soaking his feet felt warm—another indication of how sick he was. As they stumbled across the dooryard of the cabin, a damp rooster scolded them from a small shed nearby.

Jared's voice had a wheezy sound:

"Knock on the door, Amanda—"

She did, loudly. In a moment the door was opened. Swaying, Jared heard a young girl speak:

"What do you want?"

He tried to focus his eyes; saw only shifting gray shapes.

"Who is it, Sarah?" a woman called.

Before the girl could answer, Jared lunged forward. Not intentionally; his legs simply gave out. He fell toward the door, his hands scraped by the rough logs on either side. The last thing he heard was the girl's shriek of fright.

Adding her wail to the commotion, Amanda threw herself on top of her cousin. Sobbing, she begged him to get up. But he lay motionless, his head and chest resting on the cabin's puncheon floor, his legs extending into the yard where the sleet beat down.

CHAPTER V

Reverend Blackthorn

"JARED?"

On the other side of the small fire he'd built at sundown, the boy rolled onto his belly.

"What?"

"Are you feeling all right?"

Jared peered through the flames at his cousin, who was even more wan and pinch-faced than she'd been just a few weeks ago. He tried to make his lie convincing:

"Yes."

"You look funny."

"I'm fine."

She regarded him in stoic silence. He tried to recall when he'd last seen a smile on her face. It was in Kentucky, he decided. At the cabin on Knob Creek, below Louisville, where he'd collapsed from sickness and exhaustion in early March.

The cabin belonged to a farmer and his family. Jared and Amanda stayed with them almost two weeks. The famer's wife put cooling poultices on his sweating skin, and brought him slowly out of his lethargy with generous helpings of food and attention. At the end of his recuperation, Jared was convinced he'd beaten the disease.

But now it was mid-May, and since leaving the cabin on Knob Creek, he'd suffered a similar illness twice more. It had shaken him with fever and chills; watered his bowels, left him limp—and forced them to stop for a day or so each time.

From the way he felt at the moment—weak and shivery—he might be in for still another attack. Apparently Amanda saw it coming too.

Across the fire, she locked her frail arms around her knees. Her shoes were splitting apart at the soles. The hem of her muddied skirt was ragged, and so was her fine coat. She stared dully into the darkness of the Tennessee woodlands beyond the perimeter of light.

She was the same young girl who had left Boston with him, yet she had changed. Almost without his being aware of it. It was more than a matter of growing an inch or so; more than the pronounced development of her figure. She no longer protested about the hardships they were undergoing. She shared the work of building evening fires. Sometimes lately, he gazed at her and thought he was looking at a grown woman. Her strength seemed to be increasing while illness drained his away—

Trees newly leafed rustled in the night wind. The cry of an owl drifted through the clearing. Unseen nearby, a small river purled over stones.

"I'm so tired tonight," Amanda said at last. Not complaining; stating a fact. "I'll be thankful when we get to New Orleans."

Bracing on one elbow, Jared shoved his long and dirty yellow hair off his forehead. As he did, he felt the clamminess of his skin. He tried to sound encouraging: "I'll bet we make it before the end of June."

"Those men with the wagons—the ones who came over on the ferry with us—"

"What about them?"

"They said there was a town near here."

He nodded. "Nashville."

"I think you should see if someone will put me to work while we're there."

"*You*—?" He laughed; a kind of croaking sound. She jumped up, tearing a burr out of her dark hair: "Don't make fun of me, Jared Kent!"

"I'm not—" He forced a straight face. "But I'm the one who works."

"I can wash floors and carry water just as well as you can! Besides, you're sick."

"I am not."

Stamping her foot, Amanda showed some of the animation he remembered from another time—another world:

"You're fibbing. I can always tell when you're fibbing—" She circled the fire to kneel beside him. "Do you know what I'd really like? To stop for good—so you don't keep getting sick—"

"Amanda, the answer is no."

"I've heard that till I can't stand it any more!"

Jared sat up, trying to keep his temper. He held out his hands to warm them at the fire. His nails were cracked and grimy. His hair hung nearly to his shoulders. His cheeks were sunken, his good looks all but destroyed by paleness and the fever-glint in his eyes.

With a sigh, he said, "You know I won't stop anywhere around here. This is the kind of country where mama died."

"Yes, I've heard that too. Over and over! I still don't understand—"

"Because you're too young. Let's not argue. We're going where life doesn't demand so much of people. It's warm in the south. New Orleans has soft air—balmy winters. I didn't stop in Louisville for the same reason I won't stop more than a couple of days in Nashville. I despise this country, and you'll just have to accept that."

Unsatisfied, she flounced back to her original place. "Oh, I don't understand you, Jared. Why does it make any difference where your mama and papa lived?"

"It does, that's all! You don't know what this country did to them. I do. We're going to find a better place."

She shook her head. "You don't make sense."

"I'm tired—so let's drop it!"

His anger produced another unhappy look from the girl. She started to reply, but didn't. She sat down, arms crossed on her knees, her face stony.

Jared's ears rang as he stumbled around the fire, feeling ashamed all at once. He dropped down beside his cousin, tried to cradle her against his shoulder. At first she resisted. But the loneliness and the chill of the spring night proved stronger than anger. She huddled close.

"Take my word, it's better that we go on to New Orleans," he said. "The worst part's over. The warm weather's coming. And the wagon men said General Jackson whipped the Red Sticks for good a month or so ago. The trace from Nashville should be safe to travel—"

"We *could* stop," she said quietly. "We could if you didn't hate everything so much—"

"We're going on." His tone carried a note of finality, warning her to say no more.

She sighed again. "All right. I know better than to talk to you when you're sick."

"Dammit, I'm not—"

"Jared, be quiet and cover up."

She pulled up the thin blanket given them by the Konigsbergs in Pennsylvania. Then she changed her position so that he could lean against her shoulder. She started to stroke his forehead. Spent and dizzy, he didn't protest—

Unquestionably, the fever was back, brought on by continued exposure to the elements, and poor food. Their diet lately had consisted of creek water, wild berries, and occasional corn filched from the cribs of isolated homesteads.

Her hand moved slowly, comfortingly across his damp skin. "You know what I'm thinking about now?" she asked in a drowsy voice.

The fire seemed to afford very little warmth. His bones felt locked in ice, and his teeth clicked as he answered:

"No."

"Knob Creek. I could have stayed there the rest of my life. It was such a nice, warm cabin—"

"But too small for permanent boarders. We were lucky the Lincolns took us in as long as they did."

Lost in her memory of bright lamps and kindness, she mused on, sounding almost happy:

"I could have gone to blab school with Sarah—it would have been such fun, being in a schoolroom where everyone reads their lessons out loud at the same time. I could have taught her little brother, too. Taught him his letters—Abraham was fascinated with letters. Always trying to draw them on his slate with charcoal, or in the mud with a stick. He'll be smart when he grows up, I think. For five years old, he was very quick—"

"He was," Jared nodded, shuddering. The owl hooted again.

"He liked me. He kept asking me to write words for him. We could have stayed somehow—"

"No. I heard Lincoln and his wife talking about moving to Illinois or Indiana, where the soil's better for crops."

He did remember Tom Lincoln and his wife Nancy with fondness, though. They had been much more open and generous than the German farmer in Pennsylvania. For a moment he almost wished Amanda's dream could have come true—

"I only hope New Orleans is as nice as you say, Jared."

"It will be," he murmured, not at all certain.

"I never want to be cold again. I never want to be hungry again. I've had enough."

"Well, we finally agree on something. I have too. Now go to sleep."

ii

When Amanda closed her eyes and began to breathe regularly, Jared eased away from her. He didn't want to move, but the fire needed more wood.

He covered her with the blanket. Circled the embers, stumbling once—the fever was rapidly growing worse. He was sweating heavily.

He shuffled into the darkness at the edge of the clearing. It seemed to take an eternity to gather a small quantity of loose brush. As he worked, he glanced occasionally at the stars visible through the treetops.

He hadn't learned the geography of the heavens well enough to use it to judge direction with complete accuracy. He tried to recall the conversation of the teamsters coming across the ferry further up the Cumberland. The men said the north-south stream near which they'd camped was a small river known as Stone's. It emptied into the Cumberland. A few miles west of the point where the rivers met should be the town of Nashville. There, Jared hoped to find a place where they could rest out of the weather for a day or two.

He'd also have to find some chores to do again. He almost smiled, thinking of Amanda's insistence that she hire herself out. Lord, how she'd changed in only a couple of months!

Once supplied with food, they'd head south along the trace, the Chickasaw Road, that would take them nearer New Orleans. And by summertime, there might be an end to the weariness and hunger and pain—

He dumped a last armload of green sticks on the fire and coughed as smoke clouded up. God, how he ached! His face was wet with perspiration—

He mustn't weaken now. They had survived the winter, and he was thin and hard because of it. He didn't know how many miles they'd traveled since leaving Boston, but it must be an incredible number. What seemed ironic was the possibility that something entirely uncontrollable might defeat them. Not the danger of animal predators. Not unscrupulous humans, either; but sickness. The sickness that had gripped him intermittently since late February, and threatened to reduce him to helplessness again—

He stumbled a second time as he returned to his cousin. He lay down beside her and tugged part of the blanket over his legs. The back of his head rested on the hard ground. He stared at the stars. They blurred and changed position too quickly as the fever mounted—

iii

He opened his eyes. Felt the brush of the May wind on his face. Saw, as if through gauze, the high, budded limbs of trees against the rosy sky.

Dawn.

He heard the soft rush of Stone's River. And another sound, totally unexpected—

The stamp of a horse.

He lay still, trying to clear his throbbing head. Where was his pistol—?

In his canvas bag. But his knife—

He felt its reassuring hardness at his belt.

Only then did he lift the blanket so as not to disturb Amanda. He rolled on his side, scrambled up—

A lean man hunkered beyond what was left of the fire: a few red coals glowing amidst white ash. The man wore a filthy beaver hat with a hole in it. Behind him, a swaybacked gray horse fretted, tied to a low branch.

"Morning, boy. Trust you don't mind sharing your fire with another traveler—?"

At the sound of the voice, Amanda stirred, sat up. Jared put his hand behind him, moved it back and forth, a wave of warning. He heard her quick intake of breath. She understood. She got to her feet, hid behind his back.

"Who are you?" Jared asked. "Where'd you come from?"

The man chuckled. "Why, I might ask both questions of you."

He rose, dusted off his hands—big, hard-looking and bruised. As he turned slightly, faint eastern light pinked his face beneath the brim of his beaver hat.

Tufts of gray hair showed around the man's ears. His linen and stock had a yellow cast—like the teeth he displayed in a smile that struck Jared as false. The man's fingers hung nearly to his knees. His abnormally long arms looked powerful.

He extended his right hand in greeting. Jared didn't offer to shake:

"I want to know where you came from."

Frowning, the man lowered his hand. His arm brushed the flap of a coat pocket aside. A small black-bound book stuck out of the pocket. A testament—?

The man jerked a thumb over his shoulder. "Came up Stone's from Nashville. I'm headed for a little place I own a few miles east of here. Left Nashville late, and without supper. So when I saw the fire—"

He shrugged. "I stopped to get warm, that's all."

The glow of dawn set small fires in the pupils of the man's sunken eyes. Jared had grown through the winter. He was approaching six feet; but the stranger was taller. The man's slumping shoulders tended to minimize his height but not his aura of strength.

"Hardly expected to find two youngsters camped in these woods," the man said. "You realize we're all trespassing—"

Jared said, "I didn't see any signs posted."

The man swept his hand in a wide arc. "Belongs to the judge all the same. Oh, but I doubt he or any of his niggers will be out this far this early. We can eat breakfast in peace and go our respective ways."

Just then Jared noticed two other odd things about the stranger. Bruises showed not only on his hands but on his throat. And part of his right earlobe was missing; a half-moon of tissue had somehow been torn away.

The man swept off his disreputable beaver. "My name is Blackthorn, Reverend William Blackthorn. Who do I have the pleasure—?"

"Never mind. Amanda, let's get our things together."

"You mean you're not going to eat?" Blackthorn's heavy brows hooked together. He gestured to the bags hanging on his saddled horse. "I'd be happy to split some of my biscuits and wild honey—"

"No thanks, we're going on to Nashville."

Jared got busy folding up the blanket while Amanda peered at the stranger, her dark eyes sleepily curious. The man acted polite enough. But for no reason he could pin down, Jared didn't like him.

The Reverend Blackthorn sniffed. "Traveling on an empty belly certainly isn't good stewardship of the health the Almighty granted you, boy. Strikes me that you and your ladyfriend—"

"My sister," Jared snapped, angered by the lingering emphasis the Reverend put on the last word.

"Is that a fact?" Blackthorn ran a palm down the side of his patched trousers. "You're fair and she's dark—and you're shoots off the same tree? Wondrous are the ways of God. Eh, boy?"

The sunken eyes—greenish, Jared noticed—seemed

to stray past him again. He stepped to Amanda's side. He wondered whether the Reverend actually deserved his title. The bruises, that bitten place on his earlobe—those hardly seemed appropriate for a man of the gospel.

Blackthorn scratched his groin. "How old are you, girl? Fourteen?"

"You're way off," Jared said, stuffing the blanket into the canvas bag. He had trouble speaking; the fever thickened his tongue and made his teeth click.

"Am I, now? Remarkable! I'd have sworn she was a young woman—"

Blackthorn's eyes flicked back to Jared. "It's strange indeed to find two persons your age abroad in the Tennessee wilderness. Run away from home, did you? Or maybe you're indentured people? Give the slip to your masters?"

"None of your affair, Reverend."

"Here, now!" Blackthorn's voice roughened as he approached. "That's no way to speak to a pilgrim who only seeks to share your fire—"

"We're leaving. The fire's yours."

"You don't look well, boy. Don't sound it, either. Your teeth are knocking so loudly, I'm surprised it doesn't wake the judge in his bed. Are you sick too, girl—?"

Blackthorn reached around Jared, brushed his fingers across Amanda's forehead. She retreated quickly:

"Don't you touch me!"

Jared's hand dropped to the hilt of the Spanish knife. He made sure the man saw the move.

"Come!" Blackthorn exclaimed. "I meant no disrespect to your—ah—sister. I only intended to see to her health—in the manner of the man of Samaria."

His eyes fastened on Jared's, hostile despite the yellow smile. "I'd hardly say your behavior's Christian, boy—"

"And you don't act much like a preacher."

Blackthorn rubbed his chin with one bruised hand. "I am. At the same time, I claim to be the best free-for-all fighter in half a dozen counties. I've had some setbacks in Nashville. Circumstances make it necessary for me to move on after a stop at my cabin for a few belongings. Traveling takes money if a man wants to sleep under a roof and partake of decent food. No doubt you have a little money—"

Dropping his pretense of cordiality, he extended his hand.

"Give me that canvas bag."

Dizzy with fear and fever, Jared jerked out the knife. He was totally unprepared for the astounding speed with which Blackthorn moved.

The man grabbed Jared's arm with both hands, twisted. Jared's fingers opened. The knife fell into the coals. Bobbing down, Blackthorn closed his big yellow teeth on the back of Jared's hand.

Jared yelped. Blackthorn let go, stepped back, wiping his lips.

"All's fair in free-for-all, boy. Now may I examine that bag?"

Jared launched himself with fists up. Blackthorn sidestepped, brought his knee up savagely. Pain erupted in Jared's groin.

He tumbled into the ashes and embers, yelped again, rolled away. Amanda's cry of terror sounded above the chatter of birds and the burble of the river.

On his back, Jared started to get up. Blackthorn dropped on Jared's belly with both knees. The tall man's face twisted with glee as he jabbed his thumbs into the outer corners of Jared's eyes:

"I can pop 'em neat as grapes," he breathed. "There's several in Nashville who can testify to that—"

The thumbs dug deeper. Jared kicked, to no avail. Tried to tear at the massive wrists against his jaw. Futile—

The edge of a thumbnail scraped Jared's left eyeball. Wildly, he hammered at the tall man's forearms. He couldn't dislodge the huge hands.

"Shame to blind someone so young," Blackthorn panted. "Shame to rob you of the sights of God's bountiful creation. But you're not Christian—"

He wrenched his left knee over, drove it into Jared's crotch a second time. Jared screamed.

Amanda leaped on Blackthorn, trying to claw his face.

"Goddamn you for a spiteful child!" Blackthorn roared, battering her with one fist. Amanda sprawled, the wind knocked out of her.

Jared jerked his head to escape the darting thumbs. Blackthorn pounded his nose twice. Already dazed, the boy watched the tall man and the rustling trees blur and distort—

Gasping, Blackthorn lurched to his feet. One huge boot lifted; Jared saw the hobnails on the bottom. Blackthorn stomped his stomach, leaving him retching and half conscious.

"Now I'll have that peek in your bag."

Amanda crawled toward her cousin, repeating his name. Jared locked his hands over his middle, thrashing from side to side. He *had* to get up—

He heard Blackthorn open the canvas bag, dump its meager contents: the pistol; the fob; the blanket; items of dirty clothing—

"Nothing!"

He flung the bag on the ground.

"You've not been Christian, either of you. I think I'll repay that in kind before I ride on—"

He pointed down at Jared. The bruised hand seemed huge, the fingertip even bigger:

"I'm glad I didn't take your sight. I want you to watch what happens next. William Blackthorn's fought boys and made 'em grow up right while they bled. Done the same thing for girls in a different way—"

The gray-haired man tossed his hat on the ground and unfastened the buckle of his belt.

Frantic, Jared drove his right hand toward the knife lying in the ashes. Blackthorn paused in unbuttoning his trousers, raised one leg and brought his boot down on Jared's fingers.

Again Jared cried out. His limp hand flopped into the coals. He smelled burning hair, pulled his hand back as pain seared it—

"Amanda—*run!*"

She tried. But the stranger was faster. He caught her around the waist, laughing. Her shrieks stilled the birds in the nearby thickets. Blackthorn's horse stamped and blew noisily.

Still laughing, the Reverend tumbled to the ground, the girl trapped in his arms. Jared dragged himself to hands and knees. He tried to move fast but he couldn't. Blackthorn flung Amanda on her back, fastened hands at the throat of her dress and ripped.

Jared kept crawling toward the big man as he straddled Amanda's thighs. Blackthorn plucked aside her gray chemise, fondled the small nubbed mounds of her breasts. He bent down, nuzzling her cheek:

"Thy lips, o my spouse—drop as the honeycomb—honey and milk—are under thy tongue—"

Jared realized the crazed preacher was quoting scripture. He careened to his feet, took one faltering step and fell.

Wailing, Amanda pounded fists against Blackthorn's ribs. But he overpowered her by sheer size and weight, ripping and tearing until her body was bared below the waist.

"—the smell of thy garments is like—"

Jared saw a bruised hand draw out a huge, stiffened penis; press it down on the tiny mound where a few dark hairs had sprouted to signal the start of womanhood.

"—is like the smell of Lebanon—"

Blackthorn wedged a knee between Amanda's thighs, forced them open.

"A garden—enclosed—is my sister," he grunted. *"My—spouse—a spring shut up—a fountain—sealed—"*

Blackthorn jerked his hips forward. Amanda cried out and arched her back.

Jared started crawling again, around the fire toward the interlocked bodies. Amanda struggled feebly now that Blackthorn had penetrated her. The girl's eyes were closed. Her palms pressed against the ground. The tall man's trousers and drawers hung around his calves. His coat tails flapped over his humping buttocks.

Jared heard the shrill, hurt screams of his cousin; tried to shout:

"You—filthy bastard—I'll kill—"

Pain weakened his braced arms. The ground lifted toward his eyes with a strange, terrifying slowness—then slammed his face.

Time went by. How much, he didn't know. Once more he fought upward, catching a glimpse of Amanda. Her dark hair was fouled with dirt. She bit her lips and flailed her head back and forth and beat the ground, the cordage bracelet bouncing, *bouncing*—

Blackthorn convulsed. Groaned. Withdrew his dripping, bloodied organ and panted for air.

He pinched Amanda's chin between his fingers. His

green eyes glowed in the sunrise. His yellow teeth bared in a grin:

"Now," he breathed, "now you're worth something. Many a man won't pay to pleasure himself with a virgin your age. But once a girl's torn, that's another story. You'll finance my travels nicely—"

The words whined and echoed in Jared's mind as he pitched onto his side, blacking out. When he awoke sometime later, the gray horse, its owner and his cousin were gone.

iv

Bedraggled and heartsick, Jared ranged the clearing, trying to discover some sign of the trail Blackthorn had taken. On the clearing's east side he found a few low branches broken off. He knelt over them, gulping air and fighting off tears of rage.

He still could hardly believe the inhuman act he'd witnessed. But there was no denying Amanda had been abducted. By a lecher—a maniac—who called himself a man of God—

Guilt overwhelmed him for a moment. When Amanda had needed him most, he'd failed her. Just as he always failed. He couldn't excuse the failure on the grounds that he was ill—or that Blackthorn was too strong for him. He was supposed to take care of her—and he'd let her be kidnapped.

Well, now he had another responsibility. To *find* her—

The boy stumbled on through the brush for several hundred yards. He lost the trail. There were too many broken branches; too much brush disarranged by animals.

He shouted Amanda's name, heard it boom through the stillness of the woods. On the way back to the clearing, he had to sit down once. The physical punishment he'd taken at the hands of the self-styled preacher had left him almost without strength. He sat very still, cursing himself silently—oath after damning oath.

In the clearing, he collected the few belongings spilled from the canvas bag. The stranger had found nothing worthy of theft except Amanda. He'd left Jared his knife, his pistol, his clothing—

Stuffing them into the bag, he almost missed the fob partially buried in the ashes of the dead fire. He flung the fob on top of the other things and jumped up—too fast. He swayed, sickeningly dizzy.

When the spell passed, he dragged the bag to the trees along the river. There he sat down again, trying to order his thoughts.

What Blackthorn wanted with Amanda, he couldn't imagine. Surely the man wasn't so vile and deranged that he'd do what he said—use her; sell her as a whore to pay for what he called his travels—

Travels, Jared said to himself. *Start there—travels.*

The man had left Nashville. There was a strong intimation of trouble connected with the departure. Blackthorn also had a cabin in the vicinity—

Where?

He needed to find someone who could tell him that —without delay.

Another of Blaekthorn's remarks surfaced in his mind. A reference to someone named the judge, living nearby—

He glanced back toward the clearing, trying to guess where the judge's house might be. Toward the south or in the other direction?

He decided to go the latter way, to the winding Cumberland River. If he found no house, he'd work southward again.

Groaning, he stood up. He stumbled to the edge of Stone's River and checked the position of the sun. He set off as fast as his bruised, aching body permitted, trying to shut from his mind the images of Amanda's rape. She wouldn't be eleven until the summer—and Blackthorn had savaged her—

Better that he'd slain her outright!

No, don't think of that.

Find the house of the judge.

Someone—*anyone*—to tell you where Blackthorn might have gone.

v

The trees grew thickly here, screening the source of the sound Jared was too dull-witted to identify. He was weak; damnably weak. The fever and Blackthorn's pounding made him stagger like a drunken man. Branches stung his face as he stumbled toward brighter light that indicated an end to the dim woods—

He emerged on open grass. He took a few more steps, blinded by the sunlight. He scuffed a boot in dirt. He was standing on some sort of smooth track—

Only then did he recognize the thundering sound on his left. A horse—

In a whirl of dust, a big bay stallion with a black-skinned rider pounded along the track. Jared had walked directly into the rider's path. The frightened black saw him, frantically reined in—

"Whoa, Truxton! Hol' up—!"

Jared hurled himself toward the far side of the track. Halfway there, he stumbled and went down.

Sharp front hoofs dark against the sky, the bay stood on hind legs, neighing wildly—

The last thing Jared saw were those hoofs slashing down toward his head.

CHAPTER VI

Judge Jackson

A SWEET SMELL drifted through the dark of Jared's waking mind. He didn't know the origin of the pleasant odor then, and it wasn't until later that he learned it came from the blossoms on scores of apple trees surrounding the two blockhouses.

A passage connected the main blockhouse and a similar one for guests. It was in this last that he opened his eyes, resting on unbelievably clean linen.

He discovered his battered ribs and hand were bandaged. He blinked, saw a slender, sinewy black woman drift into his line of sight and bend over him. Her cheeks glowed. So did the whole room. May sunlight fell through one large window whose shutters had been opened all the way.

From Jared's right, beyond his range of vision, fragrant blue smoke drifted. The black woman felt his forehead.

"Well, his eyes are open, Miz Rachel. Fever's gone, too."

Jared twisted his head to see the source of the smoke: a plainly dressed woman running to stoutness. At one time she might have been quite pretty, but sagging flesh, and strain suggested by her melancholy eyes, had left little more than a hint of beauty. She pulled a corncob pipe from between her teeth and laid it on a small table.

"I'm not so sure the young man will be thankful to be awake when the judge comes home," the woman said.

To Jared: "Truxton is the prize horse in my husband's stable. You nearly lamed him by dashing out of the trees onto the race course."

Jared tried to sit up. The effort hurt. He tugged the wool nightshirt from under one arm. It itched ferociously.

"I didn't mean to startle the horse," he said. "I'm sorry it happened. Is the animal all right?"

"Yes."

"I was pretty worked up. Not thinking clearly—"

"Sick, too," said the black woman.

Jared nodded. "I was trying to find help because my cousin was kidnapped—"

The white woman and the Negress exchanged quick glances.

"Where 'bouts?" asked the latter.

"We were stopped at a clearing on your property. Near the river, south of your race track. How did I get here?"

"Grooms brung you in. You were mutterin' something fierce," the black woman said.

"Early yesterday," said the white woman.

"Yesterday—!" Jared started to struggle upright again. The white woman pressed him back. She had strong hands.

"Last evening, the judge fetched the doctor from Nashville to look you over. The doctor said you weren't to get out of bed for three days."

"I can't lie here!" he exclaimed. "I've got to find my cousin!"

"What's your name, boy?" the Negress asked.

"Jared Kent. My cousin Amanda—"

"A girl?" the white woman interrupted.

He nodded. "She's not yet eleven. She and I met a man in a clearing—"

The black woman raised a hand. "Hold on, you're

sashayin' way too fast. You and this cousin—you're not from these parts?"

The white woman picked up her pipe. She tapped cold dottle into her palm, walked to the window and let the dottle blow away in the pouring golden sunlight. "I should think that's obvious from his speech, Clara. Where do you come from, Master Kent?"

"New England."

He said it carefully. He didn't know the identities of these people. Yet there was something about the white woman's name that struck a responsive note in his mind. What was it?

They were watching him. He finished his thought: "We have no relatives left back there, so we were heading for New Orleans—"

"You've relatives in New Orleans, then?"

"No, not a one."

A growling in Jared's belly told him it was empty. But food didn't matter—nothing mattered except the horror of what had befallen Amanda. And he'd been sleeping a day and a half! Who could say where Blackthorn might have gotten to by now?

"I just can't do what that doctor said," he told the white woman. "I don't mean to act ungrateful, but I can't, Mrs.—"

"Jackson. Rachel Jackson."

Jared was startled. Of course that was it. The judge whom Blackthorn had mentioned was Judge Andrew Jackson, the Tennessee soldier. He should have guessed that was who Blackthorn was talking about. He remembered an account in the *Republican* that stated Jackson's home was near Nashville. It was the name Rachel that had almost brought the memory to the surface. From pressroom gossip, Jared knew a few things about this woman who was Jackson's wife.

"Mrs. Jackson," he went on, "I have to go after the man who—attacked my cousin."

Clara frowned, glanced sharply at her mistress. Mrs. Jackson asked:

"How was your cousin attacked?"

"She was raped."

The woman turned pale at the forbidden word. "And, as you said, she was then carried off—?"

"Yes, ma'am."

"By whom?"

"A man who claimed he lived in a cabin near here. A man with part of his right ear torn out. He pretended to be a minister. Acted friendly. That was a trick, so he could catch us off guard and steal our belongings—"

Quickly, Jared searched the puncheon-floored bedroom. He spotted the canvas bag sitting in a corner. The Negress noticed his concern:

"Everything's there. We took your clothes out, though. Boiled 'em good 'cause they were crawlin'."

"Tell me the name of the man," Rachel Jackson said.

"He called himself Reverend Blackthorn."

"Exactly what I suspected," Mrs. Jackson whispered. "That trash—!"

"You know him?"

"Sure we do," Clara said. "William Blackthorn isn't any more of a preacher than I'm a brood mare in the judge's stable. Only way Blackthorn got the title reverend was by givin' it to himself."

Jared looked puzzled. "Why would he do that?"

Rachel Jackson said, "Visiting evangelists who hold camp meetings are popular up in Kentucky and Ohio. Blackthorn has a certain talent for eloquence, and if he rides into a hamlet a hundred miles from here and identifies himself as a preacher, it's doubtful anyone asks to see his credentials from a divinity school. I'm afraid he found that masquerading as a minister could pay handsomely. The evangelist keeps the offering money after expenses are met, you see. Blackthorn leaves several times a year and comes home with enough cash for three or four months. The Nashville clergy have sent out circulars to the larger towns, but it isn't possible to warn every settlement in two states. I pity the poor people who've been taken in by his sham piety."

"Around here, nobody's fooled," Clara said. "Why, just this past year, Blackthorn's been in the stocks for fightin' and raisin' hel—the devil. Like Miz Jackson says—trash."

"If he was bound for his cabin, he won't be there long," the judge's wife added.

"How do you know, ma'am?"

"Because three days ago, a number of gentlemen in Nashville arranged to have him run out of town."

"Yes, he hinted about that. I didn't know whether to believe him."

"It's true. William Blackthorn is a vicious, illiterate brute. Half crazy, I think. He's gouged out more eyes and bitten off more fingers than anyone can count."

Jared showed his wrapped hand. "He tried that with me. He hit me enough so that I couldn't stop him. He talked about taking Amanda with him, on what he called his travels. I didn't understand then—"

"Now you do," said Clara in a grim voice.

Jared nodded. "He carried on about selling Amanda. Selling her like a who—a prostitute," he amended. "I couldn't believe any man would do a thing like that."

"William Blackthorn would," Rachel Jackson said. "I pity you, but I pity your little cousin more. Ten years old. Imagine—!"

"She's well developed for her age. Blackthorn mistook her for older."

"When the judge be back, Miz Rachel?" Clara asked.

"Nightfall or later." She turned to the boy. "My husband is major general of the state militia—"

"Yes, ma'am, I know. Some teamsters I met at the ferry on the Cumberland said that he and the militia had beaten Weatherford's Creek Indians—"

"At the Horse Shoe Bend. There's talk the judge may be given a major generalship in the regular army and put in command of the Seventh Military District. The war with the British is going badly in the north and east. Now there's fear of an attack by sea, somewhere down on the Gulf. Mobile Bay, New Orleans—those may need to be defended. The judge is settling some affairs in Nashville, in case he receives orders from Washington."

"The judge ought to be receivin' orders to rest for a year!" the black woman declared.

Rachel Jackson smiled sadly. "You know he'd tear any order of that kind to pieces."

"But he shouldn't be so active in his condition! It's bad enough that he's got a ball in his lung from duelin' Mr. Dickinson—"

"I can't score him too severely for that, Clara. He published his card in the paper because of me. Because of what Dickinson said—"

"Any man shot once would rest a while! But he's carryin' a double dose of lead!" The black woman explained to Jared, "One of the Benton brothers shot the judge in the left arm last November. Another duel. Then he drank bad water while he was chasin' the Indians, and he says it's fluxed his bowels for life."

All of that confirmed what Jared had read about the Tennessee lawyer and soldier. Judge Jackson, as he preferred to be called, was a gamester; a brawler; a man who settled affairs of honor by dueling, illegal though that might be. Jared wasn't overly interested in the judge's health, however. Amanda was all that counted. If he had to hobble, he was going to hunt for her. He announced that intention—

And Rachel Jackson again shook her head:

"No, young man. You'll obey doctor's orders—and speak to the judge when he returns."

"Ma'am, I can't wait for—"

"Indeed you can. If William Blackthorn actually went to his cabin, he's probably left again. Didn't you hear me say he was ordered to leave the vicinity of Nashville? He was given twenty-four hours—I suspect he's already taken your cousin out of the area. Still, if it will put your mind at ease, I'll have Culley, one of our nigras, ride over to Blackthorn's cabin immediately. He'll be back before the judge is, I expect. When the judge gets home, you can discuss your plans with him. I'm sure he'll take a personal interest—"

She smiled, somehow emphasizing the melancholy of her eyes:

"My husband doesn't mind flouting the law and putting a pistol ball through a man's head. But free-style fighting—Blackthorn's forte—is intolerable to him. The judge was one of those responsible for getting Blackthorn out of Nashville."

The black woman patted Jared's hand.

"You rest. I'll bring you up some food."

The two women left the room. Presently he heard a mule clatter by beneath the window of the log house.

He obeyed the women's orders because they made sense. He realized he was still too weak to travel any distance with speed.

Yet inactivity tortured him. In his mind, he re-lived every moment of the rape for which he blamed himself. Over and over, he promised himself he'd kill Blackthorn when he saw him.

And see him he would. Somewhere. Somehow.

ii

When he woke again, around dusk, he discovered a mug of molasses and a dish of berries in honey on the table beside the bed.

He spooned out some of the fruit and honey mixture, relishing its flavor. The molasses he found thick and unpalatable.

As he ate, he tried to recall what he knew about the judge's wife. Some scandal having to do with her marriage, wasn't it? A scandal twenty years old or better—

Slowly it came back. She had been married to another man. He had divorced her. Jackson, a rising Tennessee lawyer who had suggested the name for his own state, promptly married the young woman, only to discover that her husband hadn't obtained a divorce decree at all. He'd merely petitioned for, and received the grant of, an enabling act that would *permit* divorce if he could show reason why the marriage should be dissolved.

The first husband—Robards, Roberds, something like that—had churlishly waited two years before seeking the actual divorce. His grounds became his former wife's illegal and adulterous marriage to the young Jackson.

If Jared recalled the story right, the charge was technically true. The story was frequently circulated in Boston, because Jackson had served in the national legislature, and because the tale illustrated, for easterners anyway, the crudity of western mores.

The double humiliation of his wife being divorced *and* branded an adulteress supposedly weighed on Jackson's mind. Though he and Rachel had been remarried in legal fashion after the divorce, a stigma remained. Insulting remarks about living with a fallen woman were one of the main reasons Jackson was prone to calling out so many men. Jared wondered whether it might also be a reason for Rachel Jackson's strained look—

In any case, Jackson's propensity for shedding blood—his own as well as that of his opponents—was well known in the east. And mocked.

As Jared was finishing the berries, the black woman brought in a lamp to light the room.

"Is the judge back?" he asked.

Clara frowned. "No. Culley is, though."

"Did he find—?"

She shook her head. "Just like we figured—he's gone. The place is stripped bare. Culley said the tracks of Blackthorn's horse were 'bout a day old."

"Surely someone knows where the man was headed!"

"I don't," Clara answered. "Mebbe the judge will."

The door closed with a soft click. Jared pressed both hands over his eyes.

iii

A rapping noise wakened Jared sometime later. He started up in bed, seeing a long, grotesque shadow on the wall.

The figure at the foot of the bed was hardly less grotesque. Jared had never seen a man quite so spindly, with such narrow, almost feminine shoulders and long, high-waisted legs. The man leaned on a cane. Even glanced at, he was a veritable exhibit of afflictions: a left arm held stiffly at his side; a hunched posture—perhaps the ball lodged in his lung pained him? Pox marks pitted his face. One cheek bore a white, badly healed sword scar.

Yet for all his ungainliness and his general air of physical ruin, the judge—for surely this must be he—had a strangely commanding aura as he stood tapping his cane and studying his uninvited guest. A crest of thick white hair rose above his forehead. His unblinking eyes were a glacial blue. When he spoke, his voice was rather high; almost shrill. But Jared had absolutely no urge to laugh.

"I've heard your story from Mrs. Jackson, Kent. If you'd lamed Truxton—one of my best studs—one of my main sources of income in his racing days—I'd pitch you out of that window yonder."

"I apologized to your wife for frightening the horse—"

"She told me."

"You're Judge Jackson?"

"I suspect," the other said in a dry way, hooking a chair with his boot and pulling it to the bedside. "Surely no one else could be such a catch-all of ills and aches and old bullets."

He settled into the chair, leaning forward with palms resting on the cane head. The blue eyes pinned Jared.

"I understand you ran afoul of Blackthorn—whom we should have caned till he couldn't walk."

"Yes, sir. He raped my cousin—"

"A young girl, I'm informed."

"Ten."

Jackson sniffed. "She isn't the first."

"Your wife sent a black man to the reverend's cabin—"

"Don't call him reverend! Satan has more right to the title than he does! The only place William Blackthorn's fit to preach is hell, and it's a shame he's taking so long to reach his destination. Yes, the girl's gone. Blackthorn too."

"They thought you might know where."

"I do not, because if I did, I wouldn't be here. I'd be on a horse going after him. I'd see he never maimed a man or molested a child again."

Jackson laid a bony hand on Jared's arm. "I appreciate your anxiety. We'll do our best to locate the blackguard. I presume you'll go after him—?"

"Wherever he is, Judge."

Jackson ruminated a moment, scratching the tough white skin of the sword scar.

"I believe you. I'm not overly fond of easterners, which I understand you are. But you've got a certain look about you—determined. It could fool many into thinking you're a Tennessean. That's a compliment, in case you missed it."

Jared couldn't even articulate a thank-you. The judge made him more than a little nervous.

Jackson's stare remained fixed and hard. "How old are you, Kent?"

"Sixteen this coming October."

"And you trudged all the way here from the east?"

"That's right."

"Did you have any money?"

"Only what I made working along the way."

Jackson thumped his cane on the floor. "By God, at your age that's quite an accomplishment! You must have had a mighty good reason to undertake such a trip."

Worried that he might face this kind of questioning, Jared had barely heard the judge's praise. He kept his voice as level as possible:

"Yes. Our kin—my cousin's and mine—are no longer living. We were making our way to New Orleans."

Jackson scrutinized him a moment.

"What are you running from?" he asked abruptly.

In confusion, Jared answered, "Is it that obvious—?"

"No youngster would travel as far as you have without a compelling reason. You said your kinfolk are dead—"

"That's the truth."

"Are you a runaway apprentice?"

"No, Judge."

"In trouble with the law?"

Jared knew he couldn't lie successfully for long. He nodded. "The Massachusetts law."

"Serious trouble?"

"I shot a man."

Silence. Then:

"In good cause?"

"Yes, sir."

Another pause, even longer. At last Jackson shrugged:

"Well, I've done the same. We won't pursue it unless you want to—"

"I'd rather not, sir."

"All right. I like your cut so we'll leave the matter closed. However, I'd advise you to steer shy of the Gulf Coast for a while."

Relieved, Jared said, "Your wife did mention possible military action there—"

"I have a feeling the British will attack somewhere on the Gulf. The numbskulls in the department of the army have thus far botched all engagements with the enemy, and I reckon it's going to be up to the west to do the work right. It'd be just like Johnny Bull to sneak around the back way, thinking we're napping out here. If I get command of the Seventh District, we won't be napping."

Again he stabbed Jared with those glacial eyes:

"Were you ever in the military?"

What in the world did that have to do with Amanda? the boy thought, resentful. But the judge's intimidating stare, plus Jared's feeling that he owed the man politeness, made him answer the question:

"The navy, for two cruises, under Captains Hull and Bainbridge on *Constitution.*"

"Well, our seamen have acquitted themselves better than the fools and charlatans in charge of the army. By the Eternal, if they just give me a chance, I'll show those redcoats how Americans can fight!"

The emaciated man—nearly fifty, or at least looking it—screwed up his features into a caricature of menace. Only Jared guessed Jackson was serious:

"I despise Englishmen damned near as much as I do the butchering Cherokees and that lot." He touched the old scar. "I got this in the Revolution—"

Abruptly, Jackson compressed his lips and shook his head.

"You'll forgive me. I've been thinking about nothing except the Red Sticks for months, and now that we've cleaned up that business, the other enemy's on my mind."

Still trying to be courteous, Jared said, "I understand. My grandfather was in the Revolution too, as a matter of fact."

"Was he!"

"At Monmouth Court House, a British ball gave him a limp for the rest of his life."

"I acquired this charming mark when I was fifteen, riding dispatch in the Waxhaw district of South Carolina. Some of Tarleton's dragoons caught me. One of his snotty subalterns sabered me because I wasn't properly deferential. My brother Hugh died of wounds in the war, and my brother Robert of illness. My mother went aboard one of those British prison hulks to nurse the American captives and contracted ship fever and *she* died—"

"I'd say you have plenty of reason for wanting to do the British damage."

"I hate every goddamned one of them!" Then he smiled, wryly. "I do tend to get carried away on the subject. However, I realize another subject is of more importance to you. So if you'll forgive my preoccupation with my enemy, we'll see what we can discover about yours—"

He stood, leaning on his cane and coughing, his head

averted toward the open window. The mellow darkness billowed the scent of apple blossoms into the room. Distantly Jared heard soft, slurred voices singing an unfamiliar melody.

Cane tapping, Jackson hobbled toward the door.

"I'll do all I can to find out whether our bogus reverend gave any indication of his destination, following the expression of our communal will that he remove himself—"

Jackson turned, whipped the cane across in front of his chest in such a swift arc that Jared jerked back even though the cane's tip was several feet from his nose. "Remove himself or be shot down like the dog he is!" Jackson exclaimed. "Too bad we gave him a choice!"

He yanked the door open.

"I'll order several of my best niggers to make inquiry in Nashville tomorrow. In the meantime—"

He pointed the cane at Jared.

"—you don't give my wife any cause for worry. Take what you're fed and stay abed as you're instructed and we'll all get along splendidly."

iv

Jared chafed under the enforced delay that resulted from Judge Jackson's absolute domination of the estate he called the Hermitage. The property, six hundred and forty rolling acres with a slave population of twenty, was centered around the crude but somehow comfortable two-story blockhouse attached to the other, similar one in which Jared recuperated.

He was invited to the main house as soon as the doctor removed a few of the bandages and pronounced him well enough to get up. The Hermitage proper consisted of one huge room on ground level. The room had a mammoth hearth, a puncheon floor and massive smoke-blackened joists overhead.

Upstairs, Judge and Mrs. Jackson and their miscellany of children—three or four, Jared was never precisely sure—had their quarters. One of the small boys was named Andrew Jackson, Junior. Jared couldn't keep the names of the others straight, since they were usually all mixed up with the slave children with whom they played. He did learn from Clara, who controlled the kitchen attached to the back of the house, that all the children were adopted. To add to the burden of being publicly called an adulteress—a burden already turning her into a recluse—Rachel Jackson had proved barren. Clara said scandalmongers called it Divine punishment. But never within the judge's hearing.

Various men in military uniform came and went on horseback at all hours of the day and night. Jared soon decided the judge seldom slept. At the end of Jared's fifth day at the Hermitage, Mrs. Jackson informed him that the judge had indeed been named to a generalship in the regular army as a result of his spectacular rout of the Creeks. Plans were being made for his early departure to the south, where he still anticipated a British thrust.

Several times Jared wandered into the main house, searching for the judge and failing to find him. He began to fear Jackson had forgotten his promise about gathering information on Blackthorn's possible destination. Then, one noon, he was abruptly told that a huge banquet was being prepared for evening. "Last meal the judge figures to eat here for a spell. You too, I guess," Clara smiled.

Jared stuffed himself sampling everything set out on the thick plank table in the lower room: slabs of bear and venison; tender meat from ducks and wild turkeys;

heaping bowls of vegetables and fresh, mealy cornbread; maple sugar lumps tied on a string for a confection—and the strongest coffee he'd ever tasted. The judge spent most of the meal railing against the British.

Afterward, he cleared the lower room of blacks, the assorted small boys and his wife. But he instructed Jared to remain.

Jackson produced a stoneware jug, pointed to a chair.

"Pull that up here close to me, Kent."

Looking like a long-legged bird, he folded himself into his own chair with a groan. He tilted the jug over his forearm, swigged, then wiped the neck and handed the jug to Jared:

"Treat it with respect. That's the sweetest sipping since God made Eden. Tennessee whiskey. I reckon you're old enough. Go on! Take a good slug—"

Jared tilted the jug over his arm, hopefully showing the grace Jackson displayed. But he slopped liquor on his sleeve as the judge added:

"—because I have glum news."

Some of the whiskey scalded down Jared's throat. With unsteady hands, he held onto the jug. The judge's expression was unsmiling.

"Yes, sir?" Jared prompted.

"One of my niggers finally caught a whiff of Blackthorn's trail."

Jared waited.

"Before he left town, Blackthorn visited the bar of the City Hotel. He boasted that he'd be glad to leave. Said a man could do better where there's less law. He mentioned the sort of place he meant. St. Louis."

Jared wiped his mouth, feeling the whiskey burn his belly. He set the jug on the puncheons near the ferrule of Jackson's cane. The tall man looked wasted and weary. Clara had told Jared that while the judge was off commanding the militia against the Creeks, his body had pained him so greatly, he could neither sit down nor rest in bed. So he'd ordered a sapling spiked to a pair of posts in his tent, and spent hour after hour standing, one arm and then the other hanging over the sapling for support.

"St. Louis—" Jared repeated. "That's a long way off."

Jackson's eyes showed more animation:

"Northwest, all the way to the Mississippi. But if you've the gumption to go there, maybe you can catch the bastard."

Jared nodded, his face unhappy. "I'll go."

"I thought you would." Jackson picked up the jug, drank. "St. Louis is the capital of the new Missouri Territory. Your best source of information would be the governor."

"I'll remember that."

Jackson pointed a skeletal finger.

"Don't get your hopes too high, though. If Blackthorn's gone any further, you're pretty near done. By yourself, you'd have as much chance of locating him west of St. Louis as you would of finding the Ouragon."

Jared frowned. "The what?"

"Oh, that's what they call the damn river that's supposed to cut from the Missouri to the Columbia but doesn't. A myth—the Ouragon. You'd better make a speedy departure, Kent. Get to St. Louis before Blackthorn fades away just like the dreams of finding the Ouragon did, once the beaver men started heading up the Missouri to see what the country was really like—" He sniffed. "You do realize Blackthorn could have been throwing out a false scent, too?"

"And not be there, but someplace else? I do."

Jackson whacked the ferrule of his cane on the floor. "All right, then. You know there's a chance it's a blind trail. But don't look so damn grieved! It might not be.

You've got a scent to follow—which you didn't have before. That'd be plenty for a Tennessean!"

"Well, I'm not a Tennessean!" Jared shot back.

"That's very plain, Kent, very plain. I changed my estimate of you since that first night we talked. It's no less complimentary, mind—just different." Jackson didn't speak with malice; only bluntly. "I've glimpsed you around the property once or twice. Your whole manner fairly yells your dislike of these parts. You're not one of those goddamned, ass-kissing Federalists, are you?"

Jared tried to give as stern a stare as he was receiving:

"No, sir! The opposite. I just never wanted to wind up in the west. My—"

He hesitated, then poured it out, relieved somehow, yet pained:

"—my father homesteaded in Ohio for a couple of years. I was born there. My father failed as a farmer. After Indians killed my mother, he went back east. He never got over the failure, either. He turned into a drunkard, disappeared—I never saw him again."

Jackson's craggy features seemed to soften. "And then you had to come back out here to escape the law. I can appreciate why you don't think much of the west—and less of your present situation."

Jared was thankful he didn't have to amplify his answer; didn't have to explain that what really tormented him was not his parents' failure but his fear that he was doomed to repeat it in a land that invited failure. He'd certainly made a good start, losing Amanda as he had—

After a moment, he said, "Regardless of how I feel, Judge, I'm going to try to find my cousin."

He thought he saw a flicker of approval in the judge's eyes. "You know," Jackson said in a surprisingly gentle voice, "you're nothing special in these parts, Kent."

"What do you mean?"

"I mean, it must seem to you that the whole world has its eye turned on you. Because of the trouble back east—"

Jared nodded at the uncomfortable truth.

"That's not so. Out here, what a man is counts for more than what he was—"

And what I am is my parents' child.

"—and for good reason. If you checked the history of people who settled in Tennessee, for instance, you'd find plenty of cases just like yours. Some came here for land. Some came because they had a yearning to see new country, and when they got tired or the yearning wore itself out, they stopped. But quite a few came here because they had to—and that's where you fit. You're a westerner, like it or not."

Then I'm condemned.

But all he said aloud was, "I guess I am."

"Hell, boy, it's not that grim! This is a bountiful land—"

"Oh, yes, I've heard that—often."

"Don't sound so sour! It's the truth! I love the land out here—and the people. They may lack manners, but that lack's more than made up in fortitude. I've had some dealings with your part of the country, you know. I was in the Congress and the Senate a while, until I got my belly full and came back here to spend six of the happiest years of my life, on the bench of the state supreme court. I hated the capital about as much as you hate the idea of going to St. Louis. When I used to walk into a room crowded with all those rich, educated politicians cozying up to each other, trading favor for favor, vote for vote like they belonged to some private club, I could feel them looking down their noses at me. Backwoodsman! they were thinking. Not fit to help run a country! Back east, some of our *gentlemen* don't put much stock in common people. Got to keep those poor, dumb backwoodsmen in line! They don't know what's good for themselves, so the members of the private club will have to show 'em. In Tennessee, it's different. We *believe* in the kind of government Mr. Jefferson professed to admire but somehow never managed to put into practice. I'd like to see a western man in the presidency one day. A man who understood what the freedom of this country's all about—by the Eternal, I would! Salt of the earth, westerners—"

Jackson sounded almost sad. He shook his head:

"The only blood relations I have in all the world."

After a moment, he went on, "You know I'm exaggerating. Blackthorn's a western man—the worst kind. I think the east has a bigger quota of Blackthorns, though. Only difference is, they do their killing and maiming with words and money—"

Not wanting to launch into an argument, Jared said, "I'll agree with you from the standpoint of kindness, Judge. I've been wonderfully treated at the Hermitage—"

Jackson shrugged, brushed a bony fingertip across one eye. "Nothing special about your welcome here. Rachel takes to lost boys. You've seen the pack we're bringing up. Pity she couldn't bear her own," he sighed. "She's a wonderful woman—as I'm constantly forced to remind the sons of bitches who defame her. Well—"

He braced both hands on the top of his cane and stood, wincing in pain.

"Are you sufficiently well to ride, Kent?"

"I think so. Most of my aches are gone—"

"Nothing broken, thank God. You were lucky Blackthorn's thoughts were on your cousin. Else you couldn't go after him. He'd have crippled you."

"I'll give him plenty of his own if I find him," Jared promised.

Jackson smiled. "By the Eternal, I think you will." He laid a lean hand on the boy's shoulder. "Culley will have a horse for you at sunrise."

"Oh, Judge, I can't pay for—"

"Who said pay? I'm making an investment!" He flourished the cane. "An investment in the punishment of the good reverend. I'm investing a horse and food and some sturdy frontier clothing and five dollars in gold Culley will wrap in a kerchief. I'll be off for Nashville before daylight myself. We're mustering men—" His eyes actually looked merry a moment. "The Tennessee regulars could use you, Jared Kent."

"You know I've got other fighting to do, Judge."

With myself.

With my fear—

"Yes," Andrew Jackson said. "Bend down and pick up that jug and let's drink to it, what do you say?"

V

At dawn, Clara filled him with a hearty breakfast. Culley gave him the kerchief containing five gold pieces, then brought the horse to the front of the Hermitage.

Rachel Jackson handed Jared an unexpected gift—a black-bound Bible with a ribbon marker in it.

"The judge has left for Nashville—" she began.

"Yes, he told me he was going early."

She smiled in a melancholy way. "He's not the most religious man who ever walked the earth. At least not so you would notice in public. He might think you need a jug of whiskey more than you need that book. But perhaps it'll sustain you better than whiskey in the weeks ahead."

A bit uncomfortable, Jared ran a hand over the pebbled cover of the Bible.

"Mrs. Jackson, I thank you very much. For everything."

"I pray you'll find your cousin in St. Louis."

He tucked the Bible into his canvas bag. "I will."

Their expressions said neither of them fully believed it.

Jared swung up into the saddle. "Goodbye, Mrs. Jackson."

"Goodbye, Jared. God guide you in your search."

CHAPTER VII

Pursuit to St. Louis

ON THE TWENTIETH of July, 1814, Jared Kent approached St. Louis from the south, riding Jackson's sorrel mare along the west bank of the wide, sun-glaring river. He'd followed the river shore since ferrying across two days earlier.

Necessity had turned him into a passable rider. The sorrel was a gentle animal. Even so, he'd been thrown three times during his first two days on the road. Having thus demonstrated her mastery, the horse settled down and Jared traveled the rest of the distance without mishap—if you discounted the brutal aches at the end of each day. By early July his body was more limber; accustomed to the up-and-down rhythm of riding.

He reined into a grove of cottonwoods on a slight rise overlooking the Mississippi. From there he surveyed the town ahead. St. Louis shimmered in the intense heat.

Sweat slicked Jared's body under the heavy shirt and trousers the Judge's wife had appropriated from one of the slaves at the Hermitage. His untrimmed hair was tied at the nape of his neck with a thong. His hands and face had turned a dark brown from exposure to the elements, and the skin was marked with dozens of insect bites that itched ferociously. He looked tall and fit sitting there. But he didn't feel fit. The insides of his legs were still raw from long hours in the saddle. And during every one of those hours, guilt and the sense of his own inadequacy had been his constant companions.

He dismounted. As he scratched at a puffy bite on the back of his left hand, he gazed at the canvas bag hanging over the sorrel's flank. The Bible that Rachel Jackson had given him had gone unread across all the miles of forest and prairie. Although he'd sat in the family's box pew at Christ Church often enough in his boyhood, he'd never been especially religious, nor particularly attuned to the meaning of the Scriptures, the prayers and the preaching. He doubted there was much God could do to help him in the present situation. The outcome had probably been decided way back in Tennessee, when his blundering cost Amanda her freedom. Very likely his long journey had been for nothing—

Or almost for nothing. It absolved him of a little of his guilt. But only a very little.

Caught in the pessimistic mood, he gazed westward to gentle hills blurred by the midsummer haze. For miles on end, long prairie grass whispered in the wind. A lifeless landscape. Lifeless as his own hope, perhaps—

He tethered the mare and clambered down to the bank. He knelt and cupped river water in his mouth. It was warm; cloudy with silt. But it refreshed him.

He poured several handfuls over his head, shook off the excess, then went back up the slope to the mare, still a little surprised at the size of the town less than a mile away.

He'd expected a frontier hamlet. Instead, he saw two-story houses, church steeples and sizable commercial buildings. How large was St. Louis? Several thousand at least, he guessed.

Mounting up, he continued along the river bank. Insects buzzed loudly and constantly. The mare kept flicking her tail to drive away fat green flies.

Presently horse and rider reached the low limestone flat that provided a natural setting for the buildings overlooking the river. Along the St. Louis waterfront,

Jared counted more than forty river craft tied up: long keelboats, flatboats, broadhorns, some of their muscular crewmen loitering in the blistering sun. Black men in tattered clothing unloaded cargo into wagons and carts. Here and there, elegant gentlemen in frock coats and beaver hats opened snuff boxes or puffed long cigars while overseeing the arrival of goods.

In mid-river, a ferry scow carrying six horsemen and a small wagon floated toward the docks. Over on the Illinois side, another wagon was waiting, this one big and canvas-topped. Near it, half a dozen miniature figures—a man, a woman, four bonneted little girls—watched the ferry's progress.

Anxious to cross the river, Jared thought somberly. *Can't wait to enter the promised land—the fools.*

On the trip from Nashville, he'd passed other families like the one on the ferry. The people carried their worldly possessions in rickety wagons or packed in bags on a string of horses. They usually greeted him with enthusiasm. He was going in their direction. The best direction; the *only* direction—

West.

Leaning to the left, Jared spat in the dirt.

Then he gave a gentle tug to the mare's rein and turned up into the town proper, following a procession of three high-wheeled oxcarts.

Coughing in the dust that clouded up behind them, he listened to the French and English curses of the sweating drivers. He smiled at the monotonous profanity. Unlike that family waiting over in Illinois, the cart drivers had been around St. Louis a while. They knew the realities. For them there was no dream here, only a laborious job of coaxing and whipping dumb oxen one more block—

He passed a large limestone warehouse displaying a signboard that said *Manuel Lisa.* The business of the warehouse was apparent from the bales stacked in rows outside. Jared wrinkled his nose at the gamy stench of the furs.

He spent an hour jogging around the frontier town. He had to admit he'd seldom seen a place so sharp in contrasts, or so bursting with rowdy life.

Even the houses contrasted. There were old French residences, identifiable by the logs being set vertically, rather than horizontally, American style. There were newer buildings of Spanish stucco; even a few homes so squarely built and neatly bricked, he would have sworn he was back in Boston.

Many of the people in the busy streets appeared quite well-to-do. Others had the scruffy look of riffraff. And he was surprised to see quite a few Indians in blankets, beaded shirts and quilled trousers of animal skin. Many of them congregated at an open-air market. Bartering for the various items of trade goods on display, they offered birchbark sacks and skins that held commodities unknown to the boy on horseback.

Near the market, he passed a small jeweler's shop. The proprietor blocked the doorway as if reluctant to permit his three Indian customers to enter. The jeweler held a tray of glass eyes. The Indians were examining them with great interest.

A few moments later, Jared was forced to the side of the street by a half dozen whooping red men on horseback. They thundered by brandishing tomahawks and shooting arrows at a couple of mongrel dogs racing ahead of them. Jared thought it a cruel and disgusting exhibition—until he watched a couple of the arrows bounce off the flank of one of the dogs. He realized the arrows were blunt.

Though scowling, the whites on the street made no move to interfere. Jared suspected the reasons. The Indians came to trade with the local merchants, so they contributed to the town's economy. They also came armed. He hadn't seen one savage without a tomahawk.

Having retraced his route to the part of town nearest the river, he rode by a crowded café, a billiard parlor in which someone shot off a pistol, then a ramshackle building. From a second-floor gallery, a young woman in a gaily patterned wrapper beckoned to him. She opened the wrapper to show him her small breasts, smiled and ran her fingers down below her waist. She held up two fingers, questioningly.

Jared shook his head. She closed the wrapper and cursed him—whether in French or Spanish, he couldn't be certain.

Everywhere he rode, he searched faces. But his pessimism was deepening. What if Blackthorn had only been making idle conversation in Nashville? He could have ridden hundreds of miles for nothing.

He consoled himself with one thought. If Blackthorn had said nothing at all, he'd have been completely balked —with nowhere to search; no way to temper his stinging guilt.

A decent-looking tavern called the Green Tree offered him a room and a stable for the sorrel. A small black boy promised to rub her well and feed her amply. In the crowded taproom, Jared ate a platter of unfamiliar but tasty fried catfish washed down with strong beer.

To pay for everything, he handed the landlord his last dollar. The man placed the coin on a wood block. With expert strokes of a cleaver, he proceeded to chop the dollar into eight wedges. Bits, the westerners called them. He took six and returned two.

Jared ordered a second glass of beer and walked back to his table. The taproom was jammed with all sorts of people. Near him, several well-dressed gentlemen rose while one introduced two new arrivals: a beak-nosed older man identified as a Mr. Moses Austin. The younger man with him was his son Stephen. The group fell to discussing the current state of lead mining. Jared assumed the mines must be located somewhere in the vicinity.

The olive-skinned tap boy brought his beer. After a careful glance behind him, the boy leaned over and whispered in broken English:

"M'sieu Fink is presenting another show at eight tonight, Boston."

Jared's blue eyes widened. "How do you know where I'm from?"

"You come across the river, didn't you?"

"Yes."

"It's plain you're a Yankee—"

"And my home's Boston."

"Oh! Now I see. In St. Louis, the Spanish and my kind of people—"

"French?"

"Yes. To us, any American is a Boston. Until now I never met one who really was from that place. Listen, m'sieu—Fink's performance is at Lester's barn. Anyone can tell you how to find it. Cost you two bits for the wildest show you have ever seen."

"I don't know this man you're talking about."

"You don' know Mike Fink? Only the meanest damn fellow on the river. And the best shot! He puts on a splendid exhibition—" The boy's voice dropped. "For the climax, his woman, Mira Hodkins, she takes off every last stitch and places a can between her legs, so—" A quick gesture; a lewd smile. "Then Fink, he shoots it out. Unbelievable—!"

"I'll pass," Jared said. "I've got business to look after."

The boy shrugged, "Up to you, Boston. Not my fault if you don' know what's good." He walked off. Jared smiled and shook his head and gulped beer.

On his journey he'd acquired a fondness for strong drink. It helped ease worries about Amanda, not to mention the assorted aches and pains at the end of a day's riding. Though he wouldn't be sixteen until the fall, he felt twice that old.

The events of the past year had worked a great change. It showed in the way Jared carried himself; in the strength of his sunburned, insect-bitten hand curled around the beer glass; in the wary alertness of his blue eyes as he surveyed the patrons of the tavern and listened to the polyglot conversations he couldn't understand.

The beer made him sleepy. He went for a walk, still sweltering. He found a general store that sold newspapers, returned to his steaming room on the second floor of the tavern and latched the shutters to minimize the glare of the sun.

Using rags and the tepid water from an ewer on a stand, he washed. Then he flopped on the bed and scanned the front page of the *Missouri Gazette*.

His pressroom training made him critical of the typographical errors he found. He was contemptuous of the generally uneven inking. And much of the paper's content was local material, not of interest. Only a few items dealt with the war.

One article announced peace negotiations due to open in early August in Ghent, Belgium. Among the American delegates were Clay of Kentucky—Jared could almost hear the ring of the spittoon the night he'd crouched beside the dumbwaiter shaft—and John Quincy Adams, son of the former president. Whether the peace commissioners would be able to come to terms with Castlereagh's representatives was a moot question, the article said.

With a sigh, Jared folded the paper, laid it on his belly and closed his eyes. The war seemed far away, hardly touching this town on the edge of civilization. And he had other things to think about; all of them tainted by his guilt at having failed Uncle Gilbert in so many ways.

He slept for an hour. Then he tugged on his shirt and checked the powder and ball in his pistol. In the stable he asked the small black boy where he might find the governor. He was given directions to a farm a short way out of town:

"Gubnor Clark, he spend mos' of his time there in the summer."

Jared's brow hooked up. "Clark? What's his first name?"

"William. You know—the captain what went all the way to the ocean—?"

Surprised, Jared thanked the boy and went to saddle the mare.

ii

Tall and slightly stooped, General William Clark, governor of the Missouri Territory, welcomed Jared in the sitting room of the small but pleasant farmhouse.

Jared's horse had been taken away by a slave who tied the animal in a walnut grove at the rear of the property. The large open windows of the sitting room brought a banquet of aromas: the warm fragrance of summer grass; the sweet odors of flowers blooming all around the cottage. Sounds drifted in as well: slave children laughing at play; the buzz of bees in a hive near the house; the rustle of catalpa trees in the late afternoon wind.

The sitting room was plainly furnished, yet comfortable. Several things indicated the character of the man who made it his home. A russet-colored hound slept under a window. A rifle and game bag stood in one corner. An Indian calumet hung over the hearth. The windows opened onto the west where hills and sky blended into a hazy line below the disc of the sun.

"I knew a man named Kent many years ago," William Clark said. His voice still carried gentle Virginia accents. "At Fallen Timbers. He was from the east just as you are—"

"My father served at Fallen Timbers, General. Abraham Kent."

"You're Abraham's son?"

"Yes."

Clark's face broke into a grin. "By heaven, this makes an occasion!"

He fetched cups and a whiskey decanter from the mantel.

"How is your father? I've not heard of him since we soldiered together—wait, I did see one letter. Addressed to Merry Lewis—"

Clark's voice grew a little more somber when he mentioned the other man. Preceding Clark as governor at St. Louis, Meriwether Lewis had died on the Natchez Trace under mysterious circumstances some years earlier. There had been rumors of suicide brought on by mental depression.

Clark poured liquor. "As I recall, your father proposed to go with us to the Pacific. Merry and I welcomed the idea. But we heard nothing more."

Jared fidgeted on the Philadelphia settee, an elegant import perhaps added by Clark's wife. "My father died unexpectedly," he lied.

"I'm exceedingly sorry to hear that, Mr. Kent."

The general passed Jared his whiskey. He had removed his blue officer's coatee with its horizontal herringbones of braid. He lounged at a window in his shirtsleeves, sipping his drink.

"I must say you don't resemble Abraham very much."

"I'm told I take after my mother's side."

"Ah." Clark wiped the back of his hand across his sweating forehead. "You're a long way from home. Your family's business was printing and publishing, wasn't it?"

"Correct."

"You didn't find that to your taste?"

"The firm changed hands."

"Financial problems?"

"Something like that."

"Is it still operating as Kent's—wasn't that the name?"

"Kent and Son. Perhaps, I don't really know. I left Boston before the matter was settled. My cousin and I—a young girl—started for New Orleans—"

Clark looked startled. "By yourselves?"

"Yes."

"New Orleans is a long, long way from New England. Many people twice your age wouldn't even think about hazarding such a journey. Are there members of the family down south, may I ask?"

Jared had learned to avoid the trap the question posed:

"Distant relatives. We got as far as Nashville when we ran into trouble—"

In guarded language, he told the story of Amanda's kidnapping. He omitted the rape, finishing:

"The man responsible called himself Reverend Blackthorn. When they ran him out of Nashville, he mentioned coming to St. Louis. I assume he would have brought my cousin along—"

"He could have sold her as a bound girl anywhere along the route—"

"I realize. Still, I had to come looking for her. Judge Jackson said I should ask you whether you know Blackthorn, or have heard of him."

Clark pondered. "Blackthorn. We've no preacher in the city by that name."

Jared felt his worst fears confirmed. A few words from Clark and his journey was reduced to a futile exercise.

Clark saw his pain, said quickly, "He might have taken another name. A lot of men do that on the frontier. Describe this Blackthorn for me."

Jared had no trouble recalling the greenish eyes; the yellow teeth; the damaged earlobe. "—and he's a tall man. Exceptionally tall. With big hands, and a fondness for what they call free-for-all fighting."

"Of which we have more than enough," Clark smiled. "I wonder if it could be the fellow who went by the name Wilford Black."

Jared's blue eyes glinted as he sat forward. "Does the description fit?"

"Perfectly. We had this Black in jail a few months ago. He maimed an Osage brave who'd come in to trade some wild honey. There were witnesses to the fight, but afterward the Osage couldn't be found. Between the time of the attack and Black's arrest, there was a gap of several hours. The judge handling the case speculated that Black had killed the Osage in that interval and done away with the body. But without evidence, the most the court could do was throw Black in jail a short time for disturbing the peace. I don't honestly know whether he's still in St. Louis—"

Jared was on his feet. "You didn't hear anything about a young girl with him, did you?"

"Nothing."

"Do you have any idea where he was staying when he was arrested?"

Clark thought again, his profile sharp against the sunlight falling through the western window.

"A place called Mrs. Cato's. Down near the river."

"A boarding house?"

Clark compressed his lips. "Not exactly. A brothel."

Jared set the whiskey aside unfinished. "I'd best ride back to town and inquire. I thank you for your help, General."

Clark waved. "Black may well have left us by now—no loss. We have too much scum in St. Louis. A town on the edge of civilization—and a river town at that—just normally attracts a bad element—"

Including murderers, Jared thought. What would Clark do if he knew he were talking to one?

As he turned to go, Clark put a hand on his arm: "Mr. Kent—"

"Yes?"

"May I ask your plans if you fail to locate Wilford Black?"

"I have no plans," Jared confessed.

"Will you stay in St. Louis?"

"I doubt it."

"There are a good many fur traders looking for *engagés.* Hired men to go up the Missouri during the winter—"

"That's the last thing I'd do, General."

"You dislike this part of the country?"

"Intensely."

"Well—" Clark shrugged. "It's your affair. However, I must pass along one caution. Should you be lucky enough to find your man, remember that we have courts. Don't take justice into your own hands."

"General, I'll be honest with you. I couldn't make any promise about that. Blackthorn's mean and unpredictable—"

"So was Wilford Black, if they're one and the same. Still—"

"I'm sorry, General. I'll have to deal with him my own way."

"And we'll have to deal with you if it's the wrong way."

"Understood, sir."

Clark's eyes were unsmiling. "I hope so."

Jared wheeled and left.

iii

Mrs. Cato's establishment stood on a dark, grubby street a block from the Mississippi. With his seven-shot tucked into his belt, Jared approached the dilapidated building shortly after the sun set around eight o'clock.

The street sloped down toward the lights of moored river boats. From a passage on his right, Jared heard sounds of struggle. He glanced around, perceiving two dim figures. One was a man on his knees; the other was battering him with both fists. Jared had no intention of interfering. His interest was centered on two lanterns above a high stoop. The sign of Mrs. Cato's, a man at the Green Tree had told him.

His heartbeat quickened as he approached the rickety steps. He climbed to the door, raised one hand to knock. Suddenly there was a ferocious crash inside. A woman screamed.

Jared tried the door. Unlocked. He stepped into a lightless foyer.

The racket grew louder. Men were shouting, laughing, cursing; women were shrieking; furniture broke and glass shattered. No one was in the foyer to question his presence.

He slipped forward until he was opposite a large doorway on the right, the source of the noise. In a lamp-lit parlor, half a dozen men in fringed buckskin and several women in gaudy gowns surrounded an immense, greasy-haired man who seemed bent on destroying the place. Jared gaped at the brawl from the darkness.

One of the women, older, was struggling to get hold of the big fellow doing all the damage. As he weaved on his feet, he battered away anyone who tried to grab him. Only the older woman, a dumpy harridan with dyed red hair, seemed serious about it. Some of the others were actually handing the man chairs or bottles which he proceeded to hurl against the walls, producing more squeals and laughter from the onlookers. As the big man lurched back and forth like a ship tossing in a sea of hands and heads, another man brandished a rifle and whooped encouragement.

The wrecker bellowed at the top of his lungs:

"—no damn snot-nosed French bastard calls me a *Kaintuck!*"

The dumpy woman managed to seize his shoulder. He knocked her hand away. The woman screeched, "Elijah Weatherby, I'll have the military on you!"

Thoroughly drunk, the big man in buckskin laughed louder than anyone else:

"Go ahead, Mrs. Cato, get 'em! I'll toss 'em all in the river! I'm from Tennessee—" He let out a wild cry, half crow, half bark. "—and calling me a *Kaintuck* is the worst insult I ever—*leggo my leg, you bitch!*" He lifted his knee to shake off a whore who was hugging his calf like a tree-trunk. She fell to the floor, giggling.

The big man accepted a small table from one of the other men. He began to break off the table's legs:

"Yessir, I'm from Tennessee! That means I'm half horse—half alligator—"

Crack.

"—an' part snapping turtle—"

Mrs. Cato seized the leg he'd dropped. She bashed him over the head. The Tennessean hardly blinked.

"—the original yella blossom of the forest! A ring-tailed roarer, by God! Men see me comin'—"

Snap went another leg. Mrs. Cato howled obscenities.

"—they step outa the way! They know I can crow like a rooster, neigh like a stallion—an' jump ten feet in the air and bust their heads with my heels!"

Snap, snap—that was the end of the table. Men scrambled for the pieces, holding them up as souvenirs. The whores fought to take them away as the Tennessean kept bellowing:

"—I can stand three bolts of lightning without a blink! Look a panther to death! Put a rifle ball into the moon pretty as you please—!"

Jared ducked as someone in the melee flung another whiskey bottle. It sailed over his head and shattered in the dark behind him. On the floor of the parlor, he glimpsed the unconscious form of a slight, well-dressed man with a goatee. The Frenchman who'd set the big man on his rampage—?

Jared's eyes had adjusted to the poor light in the foyer. At the rear, a staircase led upward. On the second floor, voices complained about the noise. Jared looked speculatively at the stairs as the Tennessean, overwhelmed by two of the whores trying to kiss him, tumbled over backwards. He fell on top of the Frenchman, still whooping with laughter.

Mrs. Cato extricated herself from the crowd, rushing straight toward Jared in the dark foyer:

"Abel? Abel, fetch the soldiers before Weatherby puts me out of busin—"

She saw Jared and clutched her throat.

"Jesus and Mary, you scared me to death! I thought you were my nigger boy—" Breathing hard, she looked around. *"Abel, where the hell are you?"*

"Mrs. Cato—"

"Leave me be, damn you! That fool's demolishing my parlor. I should be whipped for ever letting a Kaintuck in the front door—"

Jared grabbed her arm as she swept by. "I want to speak to you!"

Mrs. Cato started to curse again. She saw his face in the light from the parlor. Something in the starkness of his expression made her catch her breath.

"You had a man staying here a while ago. Went by the name of Wilford Black—"

"He's still here. Second door on the right, upstairs."

Then she was gone into the gloom: "Abel, I'll switch your black ass if you don't answer me—"

Jared ignored the sounds of carnage in the parlor, wiped his lips with the back of his hand and drew his seven-barrel English pistol from his belt. He climbed the stairs two at a time, thinking one uneasy thought:

If there was ever a time you needed a cool head, it's now.

iv

The upper hallway smelled vinegarish. At the far end, a dim candle in a tin wall sconce provided the only illumination. Behind a doorway on his left, he heard the steady thumping of a man and woman making love.

As he tiptoed along, a door opened further down. A bearded face poked out:

"Who the hell's makin' all the racket downst—?"

The man saw Jared, who had stopped in the center of the hallway, the seven-barrel in plain sight.

Jared raised his free hand to signal silence. The bearded fellow eyed Jared's face, the pistol—and disappeared.

Jared stole up to the second door on his right. He

leaned his head against the wood, his breathing thin and reedy. He heard irregular snoring.

Good.

He crouched, examined the crack at the bottom of the door. He detected light inside. That was good too. He wouldn't be operating in total darkness.

He wondered why the occupant of the room had gone to sleep with the lamp lit. And the door—it was unlocked.

He inched it open slowly; saw the answer to both puzzles. The tiny room had a sour odor compounded of whiskey and sweat. Its occupant, dressed in a filthy nightshirt, sprawled on the bed. A jug lay on the floor near the man's dangling right hand. He had evidently fallen asleep in a befuddled state; left the latch off and the lamp burning—

Jared's jaw clenched. He could feel anger starting to seethe within him. He fought it; swallowed once; slipped through the door. At the bedside, he bent over, lowering the seven muzzles of the loaded pistol to within an inch of the head of Reverend William Blackthorn.

Then he pulled back the cock—a loud sound against the background of shouts, oaths, shattering furniture downstairs.

"Wake up."

V

He repeated it, louder. The ungainly man on the bed mumbled; fluttered his eyelids—

The lids lifted. Jared stared into black dots at the center of greenish pupils.

The man stiffened, hands pressing the filthy sheet. Jared leaned one knee on the edge of the bed. Next to the head of the bed, he glimpsed his own blurred image in a smoke-stained pane of glass that showed a vista of rooming-house roofs.

"Oh God in heaven—"

Blackthorn could only get that much out before Jared pressed the seven barrels against his forehead.

"You recognize me."

"Let me get up—"

"No. Where's my cousin?"

Blackthorn's right hand closed into a fist.

"You better not do that. Where's Amanda?"

"She—she's not here," Blackthorn gulped.

"God damn you, I can see that! Answer my question straight or I'll blow your goddamned head onto that pillow."

"Do that," Blackthorn breathed, "you won't ever find out."

"You bastard—!" Jared exclaimed, grabbing and twisting Blackthorn's patched, rancid nightshirt.

The hand's constriction shifted Jared's weight ever so slightly as he knelt. Blackthorn felt the change. His green eyes opened wider.

Realizing his mistake, Jared started to straighten up. In that instant, Blackthorn jammed his right fist upward and out. The fist struck Jared's gun wrist, knocking his hand aside. His trigger finger jerked. Two charges thundered at once, the balls ripping the pillow where Blackthorn had been lying a moment before.

Breathing loudly, Blackthorn seized Jared's head, twisted his own head sideways and sank his teeth into Jared's throat.

The pain was hideous and stunning. Blackthorn let go, drove a knee into the boy's groin. Jared staggered back from the bed, coughing. Blackthorn's bare foot whipped up, kicked the pistol out of his hand.

Then Blackthorn pounded him in the belly. Jared crashed against the wall.

Blackthorn lunged again, teeth and lips bloodied from biting Jared's throat. Jared saw the blood; choked—

Blackthorn picked him up bodily and hurled him across the room.

Jared shot his hands out, smacked his palms against the wall on either side of the windowpane. His head crashed through, his shoulders—

His hands stayed his forward motion. He pushed off from the wall as he fell. The shards of glass in the frame barely missed his eyes. He knocked his head on the sill and hit the floor. A fragment of glass cut his left cheek.

He snatched at the sill, hauled himself upright. Without thinking, he rubbed the left side of his face.

A door closed. Bare feet thumped, receding.

Jared stared at the bright red smears on his palm and fingertips. The old, overpowering nausea churned his belly—

He bit down on his lower lip, lurched forward, dizzy. He fell across the bed, fighting the sickness that turned his bones watery.

Stand up! he screamed at himself. *Stand up—Blackthorn's running—!*

He pushed up from the bed, sourness in his throat as he saw the red handprint on the gray sheet. He wanted to bury his head, hide from that harrowing redness—

On hands and knees on the bloody bedding, he spoke Amanda's name aloud. He started to shake; he screamed it:

"*Amanda—*"

No physical pain, no mental anguish had ever been worse than the next few seconds. Jared Kent literally drove himself to a standing position again; blundered around the room until he found the pistol; palmed it in a trembling hand—his right. Not bloody, thank God. He couldn't bear the sight of his left hand. He kept it by his side as he stumbled down the hall toward the staircase.

He shoved past a man and a girl, both naked. How much time had passed? Half a minute? More—?

From the head of the stairs, he saw Blackthorn making for the front entrance. Only Mrs. Cato and her slave boy stood between the man in the nightshirt and escape.

"Stop him!" Jared shouted.

The smash of another bottle testified to a situation still out of control in the parlor. Almost faster than Jared could comprehend, men and women appeared at the parlor entrance. One was the man Jared had seen brandishing the rifle.

The black boy was in Blackthorn's path. The running man seized the boy's shoulders, flung him aside—and lost his balance when the boy screeched and hung onto his arm.

Jared was halfway down the stairs. Blackthorn glanced wildly over his shoulder. regained his balance, shot out both hands and ripped the rifle away from the astonished onlooker.

Blackthorn whirled and pointed the rifle at Jared on the stairway.

Already twisting the multiple barrel to its next position, Jared locked it in place in the seconds Blackthorn's finger squeezed the trigger. Jared's pistol exploded first.

William Blackthorn shrieked and slapped a hand to his stomach. A black hole marked his nightshirt just above his waist.

He dropped the rifle, tottered forward and slammed on his face, his nightshirt tangled around his buttocks. Mrs. Cato took one look at him and fled for the front door. As Jared stumbled the rest of the way down the stairs, he heard her yelling on the stoop:

"Get the soldiers! A man's been shot—"

If I've killed him—Jared thought. *Oh, God, if I've killed him—*

vi

Both hands were bloodied now; how. he didn't know. He knelt over Blackthorn; rolled him onto his spine. The man's lips flecked with spittle. He had difficulty focusing his eyes on Jared's face.

The noise in the parlor had stopped. Even the Tennessean's voice was stilled as all the people from the parlor crowded the doorway.

"What did you do with Amanda?" Jared said to the dying man.

Blackthorn pressed his hands against his bleeding belly; grimaced.

"Sold her, you son of a bitch."

"*Sold her!* To who?"

Blackthorn's tongue licked at the corner of his mouth.

"Trappers heading—up the Missouri. Told them she was—my indentured girl—"

Hearing that, Jared almost wept.

"—made—a sweet profit, too—" The green eyes were vicious with hate and pain. "—enough to keep me half a year, until you—"

Blackthorn arched his back, shutting his eyes.

"Oh Jesus, you hurt me. I think you killed me—" The eyes opened again, deranged:

"They'll fuck her bloody till they trade her. The better she's used, the better the savages will like her. Up in —Sioux country—plenty of young bucks and old chiefs take to—a white girl. She'll bring plenty of pelts—"

Jared seized Blackthorn's cheeks, marking them with blood:

"Tell me the name of the men who bought her!"

Blackthorn's eyes streamed tears as he arched his back again. When the spasm passed, he worked his lips—

And spat in Jared's face.

The warm, sticky stuff trickled down the boy's chin. Blackthorn said through clenched teeth:

"You find out who—bought her—"

Like a madman, Jared struck Blackthorn's jaw, smearing the blood already there.

"Oh God, it hurts me!" Blackthorn cried, rolling from side to side, lifting one shoulder, then the other in an effort to lessen his pain. The tears coursed down his cheeks, mingling with the blood, a pink wetness. "It hurts me, it hurts me something awful—"

Yellow hair hanging over his forehead, Jared watched Blackthorn die. A squad of mounted men clattered up in front of the bordello in response to Mrs. Cato's alarms. The tall Tennessean who had destroyed the parlor belched and draped an arm over one of the wide-eyed whores.

"Dunno who that boy is," the man said in a thick voice. "But bless his heart for takin' the heat off me. Mrs. Cato won't worry so much about her furniture if there's a man lyin' murdered in her hallway—"

Jared was numb. Numb and beaten. On his knees beside Blackthorn's corpse, he pressed his bloody palms against his thighs and stared at the rifles of the soldiers rushing through the front door.

CHAPTER VIII

The Windigo

GENERAL WILLIAM CLARK personally took Jared's deposition next morning. The boy repeated the story of Amanda's abduction, and what Blackthorn had told him about selling her to white traders heading for the country of the Sioux tribes. In the afternoon, he was summoned to the governor's presence again.

"I can find no witnesses to corroborate the alleged sale of your cousin," Clark told him.

Jared simply looked at the general across the latter's desk.

Clark seemed disturbed by the young man's lackluster stare:

"See here, Kent! I should think you'd show some interest in this inquiry—"

"I heard what you said, General," Jared answered in a dull voice.

Still ruffled, Clark said, "I'm trying to establish the facts in the case. You did shoot a man dead."

"He was going to shoot me. And he deserved it."

"That doesn't condone it. I remind you, the rifle Black or Blackthorn aimed was empty."

"I had no way of knowing that. I'm just sorry he died before he told me the names of the men who bought Amanda."

"If anyone really did. I've had investigators at the fur houses of Manuel Lisa and the Chouteaus all morning. Those gentlemen know virtually everything that happens in the local trade. They've heard nothing about a girl, or a transaction, such as you describe. However—"

"I doubt if Blackthorn would have advertised the transaction, General."

"That's true. You didn't permit me to finish."

"I'm sorry," Jared said, without feeling.

"I was about to say I do have evidence that a girl resembling your cousin was in St. Louis."

Jared's head lifted abruptly. "What evidence?"

"The statement of Mrs. Cato. She said Black had a girl with him for a short time after his arrival. A quite well developed and handsome young girl. She was poorly dressed, and showed signs of having been injured or abused—bruises, that sort of thing. She seemed to obey the dead man without question. Mrs. Cato got the impression she was mortally afraid of him."

"Did you find out whether the girl was wearing a cordage bracelet?"

"She was. Mrs. Cato noticed it because tarred rope is hardly what any woman would consider fashionable."

"Didn't Mrs. Cato wonder about Blackthorn having a young girl with him?"

"In her—ah—profession, the lady is not greatly concerned about the history or the morals of her guests. She accepted the man's story that the girl was a relative, and she thought no more about it when the girl disappeared in a few days. So Mrs. Cato's deposition does give credence to yours—"

Again Jared said nothing. He stared at his hands. So much had been destroyed so quickly—

The firm in Boston belonged to the Stovalls—if they'd kept it. Perhaps Kent and Son already had another name; another owner. The objects from the mantel—the tea bottle, the French sword, the Kentucky rifle—had probably been sold for junk. He thanked God his Uncle

Gilbert was in his grave, and couldn't see the straits into which the family had fallen—

Because of me.

The destruction he'd brought down on the Kents only confirmed the feelings about himself that he'd had for so many years. Aunt Harriet always said he was made of the same flawed clay as his mother and father. He believed it today more than he ever had before.

He'd come into the west just as his father had, and the land had defeated him—and that, too, held no surprise.

Now there was the news about Amanda. It should have cheered him. It didn't. He suspected she was dead. Either at someone else's hand, or by her own.

He could hardly bear to think of her alive in the circumstances Blackthorn had described. He wished she were with him, if only for a moment, so he could tell her how sorry he was for what he had done to her—

"Kent?"

He glanced up. "Forgive me, General. My mind wanders. You were saying—?"

"I was saying that Black is no loss to the community. But if the law takes that posture, there's no reason to have law. Nor can I permit you to go scot free, regardless of how much provocation you had in attacking the man you killed."

In a tired voice, Jared began, "It was self defense—"

"The magistrate who hears your case will certainly take that into account. After you've served your sentence for disturbing the peace, I'll grant you an extra ten days' grace. In that time, you're to remove yourself from St. Louis. Don't come back."

"How long will I be in prison?"

"A minimum of ninety days—you find something amusing, Mr. Kent?"

Jared's mouth lost its bitter curl. "No, sir. I was just thinking it might as well be ninety years."

Clark was thrown off guard; moderated his tone: "Come, you act as if your life's over—"

"Yes, sir. That's exactly how it feels."

ii

The stifling summer dragged on. Jared grew to hate the small, gloomy cell in which he was confined. The jailer allowed him the Bible Mrs. Jackson had given him, but he never opened it. His only reading matter was an occasional copy of the *Missouri Gazette,* which usually contained dismal news from the east.

A United States naval victory on Lake Champlain and the resulting British retreat into Canada were more than offset by the devastating success of another enemy probe into the Potomac district. In late August, the British marched on Washington virtually unopposed. The president and his cabinet had already fled when the enemy arrived, but the capitol was torched. So were the new White House and all of the departmental buildings save the patent office. Several private homes went up in flames along with the Navy Yard, which was deliberately destroyed to prevent it from falling into British hands.

A violent storm and the mustering of fresh American troops combined to push the enemy out of the city by the first of September. But the secretary of war was forced to resign because of the debacle. He was replaced by Monroe, who also held the post of secretary of state.

In mid-September, a British thrust at Baltimore was repulsed. Fort McHenry withstood an all-night pounding by the cannons of an enemy flotilla. Witnessing the bombardment from one of the British vessels on which he was being held prisoner, a young lawyer and sometime poet, a Mr. Key, had been moved by the sight of fire in the heavens: the British employed the spectacular but relatively harmless Congreve rockets during the bombardment. Key wrote a patriotic poem about the successful resistance by the Americans in the fort. Jared read the poem's opening lines—*"O say can you see, by the dawn's early light—"* with the same interest he'd have had if he'd been perusing a description of events on another planet.

The conflict was dragging on too long for both sides. Britain was occupied with a renewed Napoleonic threat in Europe. The Americans were realizing that the war had perhaps been ill-advised in the first place. Even western papers such as the *Missouri Gazette* were expressing hope that the commissioners at Ghent might reach a peace accord by year's end.

It didn't matter; nothing mattered. Jared was consumed by his sense of failure—

Failure to deal with Stovall.

Failure to protect Amanda.

Failure to make Blackthorn reveal the names of the men to whom he'd sold the girl.

Worst of all—the cause, the wellspring of all the other failures—was his own seeming failure to be something other than what his father had been; to find the strength to overcome the taint he carried.

For one brief moment at Mrs. Cato's, he thought he might have mastered some of his own weakness. When he'd slashed his cheek on the broken window, and seen blood, and felt the familiar sickness, he'd still been able to function. He had *willed* himself to function.

Hardly conscious of that small victory at the time, he had thought of it occasionally since. But he found it laughably, pathetically insignificant in the light of everything else that had happened.

Night after night, he lay awake on the pallet in his cell, condemning himself and praying to a God with whom he wasn't on very familiar terms. A conviction that his cousin was dead never left him—because he saw no way that she could survive. But if by some perverse chance he was wrong, and she had indeed been bartered to an Indian, he prayed she'd find a means for suicide. She had already suffered more than many women did in a lifetime.

He thought about suicide for himself, too. Somehow he lacked the courage. Count that one more failure.

Other than the Bible, the only personal belonging he kept with him in his cell was the worn green ribbon and medal; the fob given him by Uncle Gilbert. He often stared at the Latin inscription and the tea-bottle design, alternately cursing himself for the way he'd besmirched the statement of his grandfather's purpose, and pondering whether the medal might unlock some answer about what he must do next. It didn't.

Toward the end of his term, his jailer announced a visitor.

Jared glanced toward the wooden door and his mouth dropped open. Huge and formidable-looking in buckskin leggings and a fringed blouse decorated with beads and quillwork, there stood the Tennessean who had all but destroyed Mrs. Cato's parlor. A long white feather stuck up from the back of the man's head.

From outside the cell, he said, "Mr. Kent, ain't it?" He sounded far less truculent than when Jared had first seen him.

Jared laid the fob on his pallet, stood up. "Yes."

"I'll trouble you for the musket," the jailer said.

"Christ, you think I'm gonna shoot him?" the Tennessean grumbled.

"Hand it over or stay out."

Reluctantly the man surrendered his short-barreled gun. It was decorated with a curious piece of metalwork: a fork-tongued sea serpent with curling tail, all done in bronze and screwed to the wood just beneath the lock. The big man shook a cautionary finger:

"That's a genuine North West trade musket. I've had it nine years. Handle it real gingerly or I'll handle you so's you won't get over it."

The Tennessean ducked his head and entered the cell. The jailer, noticeably pale, closed the door.

Jared guessed his visitor to be thirty-five or forty years old. He had high cheekbones; tanned skin heavily marked with lines; eyes whose dark color and deep sockets lent him an air of melancholy now that he was sober.

He acted ill-at-ease. When he spoke again, his tone was surprisingly gentle:

"I come to pay some overdue thanks, Mr. Kent. I owe you a hell of a lot."

Jared shrugged. "I don't recall you owe me a thing."

"Oh yes I do. The night you shot that man, I was crazy drunk. I didn't mean to harm nobody, mind you—I was just havin' a frolic—but Mrs. Cato, that old whore —she'd have hauled me up before the law for certain if you hadn't been around. You kind of took her mind off me. Not completely, o' course. To cover the damage I done, she made me pay half my profit from winterin' last year. That put me way behind in makin' up my assortment."

"Your what?"

"Assortment."

"You've lost me, Mr.—"

"Weatherby. Elijah Weatherby."

Unconsciously, he stroked his shoulder-length gray hair before extending his hand. The hair glistened with some kind of grease. Jared shook reluctantly. Weatherby's palm was slick. But his grip was strong.

"An assortment's what you take to trade when you're spendin' the winter amongst the Injuns." Weatherby perched on the stool Jared had vacated, all but hiding it with his huge frame. "Red men'll trade prime pelts for the damnedest trifles. Don't sound sensible, but it's so. They don't have any trifles, y'see, but they can get hold of a heap of furs. Supply 'n demand is what the Chouteaus call it. I used to work for them, but now I'm a free trader—got my license from the governor an' all—and I still sell my bales to the Chouteaus every spring—" He massaged his jawbone, leaving a greasy residue. "I'm puttin' my assortment together right now. Spendin' every last penny I got, too. Only thing I won't take along is the trade whiskey they make up special at the distilleries here in town."

Jared started to insert a question about why he was being told all this, but Weatherby simply kept talking, perhaps out of nervousness:

"I ain't a man of outstandin' morals, Mr. Kent. But I don't hold with poisoning people. Trade whiskey's nothin' more than river water with some plugs of tobacco and pieces of soap thrown in. Oh, and some red pepper an' dead leaves to darken it up proper. A whole barrel of that slop gets cut with just two gallons of alcohol an' two gallons of strychnine—"

"Strychnine's a poison!"

"That's what I said, ain't it? The strychnine makes up for the scant amount of alcohol. The braves want to get drunk on *somethin'*. Also, they don't consider it good whiskey 'less they have a healthy puke after drinkin' some. The tobacco takes care of the puke."

Weatherby noticed Jared's puzzled stare. He grinned in a shamefaced way. "I guess I'm ramblin'—"

"It's pleasant to have a visitor after being cooped up alone for a couple of months, Mr. Weatherby. But I can't see that what you're saying has anything to do with me."

"Well, yes it does. How much longer you gonna be in here?"

"Another couple of weeks. Why?"

"Mm. That'd work out just fine."

"What are you talking about?"

Weatherby reached to the back of his head, plucked the white bird feather from his hair and began to twirl it in his fingers. Jared thought the feather was an affectation, like the man's flamboyantly beaded shirt. He learned later it was the fur trade's universal symbol of wintering. Less hardy men only ventured into the Indian lands from the spring to the autumn. The feather thus became a badge of stamina and status.

"Roundabout," Weatherby resumed, "I heard the story of what that man called Black done with your little cousin—"

"Sold her to some trappers going up to the Sioux tribes, he said. I almost don't believe it."

"I believe it. There's nothin' a Mandan chief prizes so much as a woman with white skin. Same goes for the dog soldiers out amongst the Tetons."

"What in God's name are dog soldiers?"

"A special bunch of young braves picked to take charge of a buffla hunt. They're mean as sin—an' when you consider that the Teton Sioux are already about the wickedest of all the Dakota Injuns, you got a fair idea of what a dog soldier's like. Compared to one o' them, a Mandan Sioux's an old woman."

"So you're telling me there's a ready market for my cousin."

"Afraid so. That ain't what fetched me here, though. I—well, what I wondered—y'see, it's like this," he said with an explosion of breath. "I lost my last partner this past February. A Frenchman, Marcel was his name. He got all messed up with a buffla dance. That's where a whole lot of Injuns and mebbe some real important visitors sit in a circle in a lodge. The old men make big drum medicine. Then their young wives come up behind the circle bare-ass naked except for a buffla robe. Each wife picks a man—not her own, y'understand—and goes outside with him, an' right there in the snow they make the two-backed beast—with everybody's one hunnerd percent approval."

"That's incredible."

"The truth! I been in the snow myself. Seen a dozen, two dozen couples humpin' away not six feet apart. It's part of the religion. 'Sposed to attract the herds in winter time. Get 'em to come close enough to the village so the braves can ride out an' lay in some meat. Well, the point is, my partner Marcel, he took a fancy to the squaw that picked him out. So he's livin' with the Mandans now, sort of a second husband to this young woman. I ain't found anybody but rum-sots to replace him—"

Weatherby raised a hand quickly. "Don't get me wrong. I drink some myself."

Jared almost smiled. "I know."

"But I only do it when I'm in town and havin' a frolic. To get right to it—"

Jared fervently wished he would.

"—I need a partner for *this* winter. I'm goin' back up toward the Sioux villages. You look like a sober, steady sort, and you ain't yella, that's plain from what happened at Mrs. Cato's. If you was of a mind to go with me, mebbe we could hunt for your cousin—"

He left the last words hanging, his tone punctuating them as a question.

"I expect my cousin's dead."

Weatherby frowned. "Well, by God. You mean you give up on her?"

"Don't you think I should?"

"I dunno about should. I didn't 'spect you *would.*"

He rubbed his chin. The melancholy cast of his expression started resentment simmering in Jared.

Weatherby clucked his tongue. "Yeh, I had you pegged for a different sort. I mean, you stepped up to the mark pretty smart at Mrs. Cato's. Plugged that bastard cool an' clean right while he was aimin' square at you." The trapper slitted his eyes. "How old are you, boy?"

"Sixteen."

"Plenty old enough for me to teach you the trade. Where you hail from?"

"Boston. Look, Mr. Weatherby—"

"Boston! Ain't that way up by the Atlantic Ocean someplace?"

"Yes, it is. I—"

"An' you come all the way out here with that little girl?"

"Actually she was stolen in Tennessee. We were heading south."

"Godamighty! You musta rode a thousand miles or more."

"I guess. We walked a good part of it."

"I sure wouldn't have any doubts about takin' on a youngster who could do that," Weatherby declared.

"Thanks, but I'm not interested."

"I sort o' got that idea. Appears I made a mistake—" The big man rose, jamming the feather in his hair. "You goin' back east when you get out?"

"I can't go back east."

"Why not?"

"Because—because the law wants me."

"Thievin'?"

"Something else."

"Murder?"

Jared didn't answer.

Weatherby's reaction was unexpected and puzzling. First he shrugged. Then, with a remote look, he said:

"Hell, I done a lot worse than that."

"I didn't say I'd—"

"Yes you did—by not sayin' anything."

"And you've done worse?"

"I sure have."

"For instance?"

"Well, for one thing, I left a woman and four young 'uns in Tennessee. I come out here eleven years ago. I couldn't stand farmin' fifty acres month in, month out. Got so bad I couldn't sleep nights, thinkin' how I had to escape. It was like hands on my neck, stranglin' hands, that feeling. I was locked up on fifty acres and I'd see the same sights all my days—well, I begged my wife to come along. She said no. So one night I—just left. I ain't proud of it. But I had to do it or I would have died."

Strangely moved by the hoarseness of Weatherby's voice, Jared found his own softening:

"That's still not as bad as killing a man. And I've botched up a whole lot of other—"

"I ain't finished." Weatherby stared at him. "You know what a windigo is, boy?"

"No."

"Big medicine with the Injuns. Scares hell out of 'em. I'm carryin' that name now."

Some remembered agony shone in his eyes. Suddenly he glanced away.

"What I'm sayin' to you is, the country west of here forgives just about anything a man wants or needs to have forgiven. I heard a preacher say once that God forgives His wayward children, so maybe God's part of the prairies an' rivers, because a man can sure find a mighty lot of forgiveness—"

"Mr. Weatherby, I'm leaving St. Louis—"

"I know that! It's no secret Clark ordered you to hightail."

"I expect to head south, where I was going when Blackthorn stole my cousin. New Orleans—"

"Down where it's soft an' easy, huh?"

"Listen, I'm not asking advice from you or anyone!" He was angered by the Tennessean's contemptuous stare. "My mother was butchered by Indians in Ohio. My father failed when he farmed there—"

Weatherby shrugged:

"So?"

"What the hell do you mean—*so?*"

"So what's your point, is what I'd like to know."

Jared flushed. "If it's any of your business."

Weatherby blinked, then said in the mildest of voices, "Well, fuck you for a snotty pup," and started out.

Ashamed, Jared exclaimed, "Weatherby—"

The tall trapper turned back.

"Yeh?"

"Look, I—I'm sorry for that remark. I do appreciate your asking me to throw in with you. But there are—quite a few reasons why I can't."

Weatherby studied the boy. Crooked an index finger and scratched his upper lip. Finally said quietly:

"You want to talk about any of 'em?"

Jared was stunned. "Why should you be interested?"

"Oh, I dunno—" The man's deep-hued cheeks actually turned darker, the equivalent of a blush. "Mebbe because I never quite got used to bein' without sons an' daughters. I don't feel natural 'less I'm worryin' about young 'uns. Told you I had four in Tennessee—an' I must have sired me three times that many off all the squaws I hung out with over the years. Seems to me like we're kind of a pair, Kent. You got nobody real close an' neither have I—"

He searched Jared's eyes a moment. Then:

"I ain't so good with fancy phrases, but I got a feelin' soon after I come in here that you're hurtin' pretty bad over somethin'. It's a lot better to speak it out than to drown it with whiskey like I'm in the habit of doin'."

Oddly touched, Jared said, "You read me pretty well, Mr. Weatherby." He lifted a hand toward the stool. "I'd be pleased if you kept me company a while longer."

iii

The trapper bobbed his head and resumed his seat: "All righty, get it off your chest."

Jared looked at the wall as he started to talk:

"The plain truth is, I'm scared of this country."

"Scared! Why on earth—?"

"I told you. My father tried farming, Indians killed my mother—the west destroyed both of them. I—"

He turned and gazed straight at the older man, pent-up tension draining away. It was a relief just to be able to share the torment with someone:

"—I've made a lot of the mistakes my parents did. My father and mother weren't tough enough to beat this country, and I don't think I am either."

Weatherby digested that for a moment. Then he inclined his head very slightly to one side and puckered his lips to express his doubt.

"I'd say you're crazy."

"What?"

"You heard. Crazy. I don't know what your pa was like, but I know this. There ain't one man in fifty in St. Louis—no, nor west of here, neither—that could travel a thousand miles haulin' a little girl like you done an' live to tell of it. 'Specially at sixteen. Most of 'em would have quit 'fore they got halfway."

Perplexed, Jared shook his head. "I didn't think it was anything special. We had to do it—"

"You just take my word, boy. Unless your pa was a hell of a lot bigger an' better man than it sounds like, you got him beat a mile."

Jared scrutinized Weatherby, trying to decide whether the trapper was flattering him. He saw nothing in the man's demeanor to indicate that was the case. Yet he couldn't quite believe what Weatherby said—

The older man sensed the boy's doubt:

"You think I'm funnin' you. Tell you what. When you get out, you haul yourself down to Manuel Lisa's warehouse, or the one the Chouteaus run. You tell any trapper you bump into that you walked all the way from the Atlantic to St. Lou' by way of Tennessee. Tell 'em you tracked the man who stole your cousin, an' killed him instead o' lettin' him kill you. You'll see how fast you get work. Why, you'll have so many offers, your head'll whirl!"

"But it wasn't that big a thing—"

"You ain't got much pride in yourself, have you, boy?"

Jared glanced up suddenly. Started to speak; hesitated; then said:

"No, I guess I don't."

"Well, it's time to start havin' some! I'd be proud to call you my partner."

That was when Jared recalled something Judge Jackson had said. Something about the accomplishment of reaching Nashville on his own. At the time, he hadn't paid much attention. But he remembered it vividly now.

He remembered Governor Clark expressing astonishment over the journey, too. He began to feel a little heartened—

Do you suppose we never know we've fought some battles until they're over? he asked himself. *Maybe I do have some reason to hold my head up—*

The thought pleased him. True or not, it lent him a touch of courage he'd lacked for a long time.

Weatherby said, "Tell me something."

"Sure."

"Your cousin—did she make the whole trip, like you say?"

"To Tennessee? Yes. Then she obviously came this far with Blackthorn—"

"How'd she get along?"

"When she was with me, not too well—at first. By the time we left Louisville, though, she'd toughened up a lot. She—"

He stopped, sensing the trapper's intent. Weatherby said:

"What you're saying is, she's got the stuff too. That oughta give you some hope that she's still alive. Hell, I bet you taught her plenty about how to get along—and did it without even knowin' it."

Jared would have liked to believe that, too. But skepticism brought a bitter laugh:

"You're just softening me up so I'll throw in with you. I haven't got a cent."

"The money was to be my part. I was only askin' for a strong back an' a strong belly. I think you got both of 'em—only somebody or something has whipped you so bad, you talked yourself into believin' the belly part ain't there. You think it over. I mean really think about what it took to get all the way out here. Think about that little girl, too. Whether you really want to act like she's dead when there's a chance she ain't. If you change your mind, I'll probably still be roomin' at Ungerleider's Hotel when they let you out."

"Do you honestly think we could find her, Mr. Weatherby?"

"I know we could have a damn good shot at it."

Jared stared down at the fob on the pallet, confused, his emotions churning—

Weatherby put a hand on his arm.

"Listen here. I can hire me a dozen no-goods. But I don't come across ones like old Marcel—or you—very often. I ain't never kissed any man's boots to make him feel good. When I say somethin', I mean it. Life's too goddamn short to have it any other way."

Weatherby turned and hammered on the cell door. When the jailer let him out, he snatched back his trade musket and disappeared, calling over his shoulder:

"That's Ungerleider's Hotel. Anybody can tell you how to find it."

iv

Jared Kent sat cross-legged on his pallet a long while afterward, running his finger across the surface of the fob medallion and scrutinizing the Latin inscription. The ball of his thumb began to work back and forth over the raised letters.

He *did* want to believe what Weatherby had told him. He wanted to believe that he had passed through a testing fire without even being aware of it. Making mistakes, yes; dreadful ones—

But surviving.

And what had the trapper said about the country where he traded? That it forgave almost anything a man wanted or needed to have forgiven—? Perhaps that was one reason why people sought the land by the hundreds and the thousands—

Jared's thumb stopped, resting on the tea bottle again. Was it possible Amanda could be alive? His thoughts raced; back to Tennessee just before Blackthorn's appearance. He recalled the night beside the fire when he'd been struck by the new strength in her.

But God above, she'd been raped! And who knew how many times since then Blackthorn—and others—had abused her?

Still, he had to admit in the privacy of his conscience that he *was* guilty of inventing reasons for going south and abandoning the search—which was another way of saying he was guilty of giving in to his fear.

Maybe he didn't need to give in any longer. Maybe on the long, arduous journey from Boston, step by step and mile by mile, he'd trampled an enemy underfoot *and never known it*—

If he didn't quite believe it yet, he had the desire to believe, and the desire lifted his spirits in a way that had been foreign to him for months.

He stared at the medal.

Assuming Amanda was dead—or that he couldn't find her, which was just as likely—he was the only Kent left. What was he to do with his life?

Weatherby offered him a chance to learn the fur trade. He'd find no similar opportunity ready-made in New Orleans. If he could go with the trapper and not be afraid of the land—not be afraid because he had already won one battle against it—

Then wouldn't he be a fool not to accept Weatherby's offer of a new start? He could provide for himself. Perhaps even prosper—

His thumb began moving on the medal again.

He was the last of the Kents.

Not Abraham Kent.

Jared.

Not a poor creature tormented to failure, but one who had walked a thousand miles—

Before he was sixteen years old.

He had always believed everything Harriet Kent said about him. But he knew she had hated him. Perhaps some of the things she'd said were born of her hate; not altogether true—

Desperately, he sought for proofs of the possibility in the past. Once more he thought of his father.

After Abraham Kent had failed, he had gone home. To despair. To ruin and, presumably, death.

But he, Jared, failing in Tennessee, had kept on—

Perhaps he wasn't doomed to repeat the past. Perhaps he needn't be its lifelong prisoner. As Weatherby said, that was one of the promises of the western land: it forgave, and let a man begin again—

He was not Abraham.

He was *Jared*—

Unless he ran away.

He looked at the medal.

Take a stand and make a mark.

Who was right? Weatherby? Or Harriet—and the voice of self-doubt that had been his companion for as long as he could remember—?

Was there a possibility Amanda was alive?

And had he made too many terrible mistakes, and put himself beyond all chance of self-forgiveness? Weatherby claimed he had sinned great sins. How could they possibly be worse than Jared's own—?

Alternating between bursting hope and cynical despair, he paced and fretted for nearly an hour. He still did not know clearly what he should do—or whether he was capable of anything except helpless retreat.

Evening deepened outside the bars of the cell. From the riverfront he heard the sounds of the town's lusty life: horses drumming; men singing; a gun going off—

Weary of self-examination, he sought diversion. The only thing that offered it was a newspaper. He shouted through the small grille in the cell door—

No answer. The jailer had gone off to supper.

Frustrated, he ran a hand through his yellow hair. His eye fell on Rachel Jackson's Bible.

He picked it up. Turned pages aimlessly. Came at last to the ribbon that marked a place in the Old Testament. He supposed the marker had been inserted randomly, and he was just about to flip to the next page when something caught his attention.

Someone—the judge's wife, evidently—had inked brackets around a passage in—

He tilted the Bible so he could make out the page heading in the dying light of sunset. Ezekiel. The thirty-fourth book.

The brackets marked the sixteenth verse. He read it and realized the position of the ribbon marker was no accident. He read the verse a second time:

I will seek that which was lost, and bring again that which was driven away, and will bind up that which was broken, and will strengthen that which was sick—

With a shiver, he sat down on the stool and began reading at the head of the chapter.

When he reached the sixteenth verse, he closed the Bible and held it on his knees. Jackson's wife must have suspected he would falter, hesitate and question along the way. And so she had carefully marked those few words. In the Lord's promise to His people, Jared saw, at last, a clear sign of what he himself must do.

I will seek that which was lost—

Bring again that which was driven away—

Failure to carry out that command would forever break the vow he'd given Uncle Gilbert. Failure would make the precious medal a mockery—

Only one question remained, then. But it was of such magnitude that it wracked him all through the sleepless night:

Could he do what must be done?

Was he strong enough?

Was he Jared Kent—?

Or Abraham's helpless, doomed son-and-twin?

Even in the ruddy light of a new morning, there was no sure answer.

V

When Jared was released, he reclaimed his few belongings and put the Bible and the fob with them in his small canvas bag. In a deserted street near the jail, he squatted down in the shadows. He drew a long breath, then did something which two Indians wandering by watched with amazement.

Using the Spanish knife, Jared pricked the ball of his left thumb.

He sheathed the knife and squeezed his thumb until the blood ran freely, bright red—

The nausea churned up from his belly, horribly sour in his throat. He gripped his left wrist with his right hand and forced himself to stare at the small wound—at the blood—his teeth locked together, his forehead sweaty, for some five minutes.

During that time, he felt faint. Felt the urge to hide his hand behind his back; shut out the sight of that awful redness—

But he watched the tiny wound until his trembling stopped and the nausea receded.

The prick in his thumb clotted. He stood up, pale but satisfied on one score.

This strange, debilitating enemy might be with him to the end of his days. But at least he saw the affliction in a truer perspective. Not so much a curse—punishment for unworthiness, real or imagined—as a burden whose origins, though they might be rational, would be forever hidden.

That, he could endure.

Walking with long, swift strides, he started for the fur warehouse of Manuel Lisa.

vi

The clerk checking through the bales outside the warehouse looked at Jared as if he were a lunatic. With an annoyed shake of his head, the clerk turned his attention back to his ledger:

"I haven't got time to answer fool questions about Indian fairy stories—"

Jared stepped around in front of the clerk. The clerk's head lifted. He met Jared's blue eyes and almost dropped the ledger.

"You'll tell me where I can get an answer, then," Jared said.

Nervous, the clerk glanced past the boy, pointed his quill:

"Maybe—maybe old Jeanette. See her over there?"

Jared followed the direction of the pen; saw what he hadn't before: beyond two gaudily quilled and beaded trappers cutting the bindings on bales of summer pelts, a figure hunched against the warehouse wall, seated in the shadows and almost lost within them.

"She's half Osage, half French. She speaks pretty fair English. But she's—"

The clerk tapped his temple with the quill.

"She's waiting for her husband. A free trader." The clerk went *"Huh!"* softly, either in pity or derision. "He disappeared up the Mizou ten years ago and never came back."

Nodding, Jared pivoted away.

He walked by the trappers to the deep shadow along the wall. Though it was full daylight, and the October sun was warm, a chill settled over him as he inspected the old woman sitting cross-legged, her clothing layered on her frail body in filthy pieces, no two of which matched.

The old woman's face was like a finely detailed map, crosshatched with dozens of delicate lines. Her hair was almost pure white. The hands resting in her lap were emaciated. She smelled of dirt and human waste and tobacco.

Jared crouched down in front of her. The old woman's eyes were closed. But in her lap, one hand moved; fumbled with the flap of a worn pouch; reached in for a small, moist gob of tobacco.

Without opening her eyes, the woman slipped the tobacco between her lips and up against one of her diseased, toothless gums.

He said softly, "Jeanette?"

The ancient, leathery jaws began to work the tobacco. Her closed eyelids seemed lifeless.

He repeated her name.

She looked at him. Jared caught his breath.

The old woman's eyes were brown and clear. He saw no hint of madness in them, but neither did they hold any emotion. They seemed like natural objects—great stones; a river; the earth itself—that had no need of human feeling.

"Jeanette," he said a third time, "my name is Kent. The clerk said you might tell me something I need to know."

Slowly, so slowly, the lined jaws worked the tobacco and the old eyes remained fixed on his, unblinking.

The wrinkled lips opened, no more than a slit:

"Ask."

"I met a man. He used a word—he said it meant something very bad—"

Her voice was thin, a thread of sound, and raspy:

"What word?"
"Windigo."
She uttered a strange, chant-like syllable, and swayed from side to side. Her eyes seemed a little more animated.
"The devil. The great devil who walks in the dark. Accursed. A monster. Not fit to look upon."
"Not a real person?"
"Some men—a few—whom the Father-spirit chooses to hate—they become like the great windigo."
"But what is it that makes them so terrible? Do they kill—?"
"The great windigo kills. He kills out of pain and anger that the Father-spirit has made him what he is."
"Have you ever seen him?"
She was silent almost half a minute, the brown eyes opaque again; unreadable.
"The great windigo? No. I have seen two men in my life—maybe three—who became as he is. Accursed."
"Why are they accursed?" Jared persisted, feeling he was drawing close to something he might be better off avoiding. The old woman was undoubtedly senile. Yet somehow, he feared her—
"Because they have done what the great windigo does," she said. "They have eaten the flesh of a human being."

vii

Jared's throat felt thick. He fought for a breath of air in the foul-smelling shadows. The old half-breed woman looked at him, and he thought that she saw him for the first time:
"The Father-spirit in heaven made the windigo so man would be humble and thankful. When the great windigo walks, higher than a house, with fire burning here

—" One hand touched an eyelid. "—so bright it lights the night, an ordinary man knows the Father-spirit has showered him with love. An ordinary man is humble and thankful even if he is weak and evil, because no matter how terrible a man's lot, he will bless it forever if he meets the windigo."

In a whisper, Jared said, "Thank you."

Her right hand lifted from her lap, her palm a crosswork of lines.

"Do you have a little snuff for me?"

"I don't, I'm sorry. I wish I did."

She became agitated:

"Have you seen Langlois?"

"Lang—?"

Jared stopped. Did she mean her husband?

"He will be back by sunset, they say. I told him I would be waiting here."

Jared stood up. Grasped her open hand and pressed it gently:

"Yes, I heard he was coming back."

She relaxed, and seemed to smile.

"You have heard that? I am glad. That means he is truly coming. I will go on waiting."

Jared turned away, shaken and full of pity for the old Osage woman. But he understood why Weatherby had revealed his shameful secret.

viii

Jared stayed at the Lisa warehouse the better part of an hour, speaking to several men. Then he asked directions to Ungerleider's Hotel. He set off at a run, hoping he was not too late.

CHAPTER IX

"I Will Seek That Which Was Lost"

ON THE FIRST of November, 1814, Elijah Weatherby and Jared Adam Kent boarded a keelboat that would take them several hundred miles up the Missouri River with Weatherby's assortment.

In the assortment were the standard twenty-five-yard bolts of coarse woolen cloth called strouding. The Indians fashioned it into clothing. There were several bolts each of calico, melton and cotton cloth; two dozen three-point Mackinac blankets, prized by the Indians for their warmth; and a collection of carefully packed kettles, needles, threads, axes, awls, hand mirrors, animal traps, shot and powder.

The assortment also included less utilitarian items which the Indians favored for personal adornment: cheap combs; a rainbow of ribbons; falconry bells; and white, red, gray, black and purple shells polished and strung to make wampum.

Weatherby had used the last of his funds to buy three dozen silver trinkets. There were gorgets and half-moons, some bracelets, and fifteen pairs of enormous silver earrings, which Weatherby said the vainer braves wore with great pride. Weatherby had also bought two horses and enough food for three months.

ii

The keelboat pushed up the Missouri under a favoring wind. Jared stood at the bow on the twelfth day of November, 1814. His new buckskins were stiff; sweat and exertion had yet to lend them the desired pliability.

The early evening was warm; unusually warm and dry for this far north and this late in the season, Elijah Weatherby said. But the sun was darkening rapidly, Jared noticed. Huge black clouds spilled out of the northwest. In the clouds, lightning flickered.

He gazed at the fast-flowing, muddy Missouri for several minutes. He was struck by the way his own fate and his father's had been so closely linked with rivers.

A river had taken the older brother or sister he'd never known.

Another had flowed by the place where he was born, and where his mother died.

A third had meandered past the dreadful patch of ground where he and Amanda met Blackthorn.

He'd followed a fourth to St. Louis.

And still one more was bearing him toward an unguessable future.

The west was growing chiefly because of the rivers. The seekers of escape and the seekers of dreams poured forth from the east, and the rivers in their silent, eternal power carried them; changing the nation; changing the lives of its people, including the Kents—

He lifted his gaze from the river to the land. He was spellbound by the vista. The prairie seemed to stretch away endlessly on both sides of the Missouri, broken only here and there by small groves of trees. On the starboard side, he saw bison—for the first time—two or three thousand, a great mass of hide and hair and horn moving slowly along the bank.

The majestic motion of the herd, the wind-lashed water and prairie grass, the turbulent, white-lit clouds folding in upon themselves as the storm advanced made him feel as he had long ago, times when he'd clambered to a Boston roof or dashed to the end of a pier and beheld sea and sky together, immense and breathtaking—

My God, he thought. *How beautiful it is.*

The wind blew harder now, flattening his hair against the top and sides of his head. He strained to keep the distant horizon in focus, no longer despairing, but thrilled; expectant—

In searching for Amanda, maybe he could find a place where he belonged—

A place where I can be happy.

I see what Weatherby meant. Out here, there is *room for hope to begin again—*

His fear of the land had begun to wane when he had ceased to fear himself so much. He no longer felt contempt for the family he'd glimpsed at the ferry on the Illinois side of the Mississippi. He no longer pitied the men and women and tiny children huddled in wagons or riding on mules or horses—or walking—he'd passed on the trails up from Nashville. He understood them.

He was one of them.

The clouds had darkened the sky overhead. The keelboatmen hauled down the sail and pitched the anchor overside, preparing to ride out the storm.

Thunder blasted. Lightning hit the river about a mile ahead. Open-mouthed, Jared watched as the forked whiteness licked down a second time, striking the earth in front of the plodding buffalo. In moments, fire ignited.

It spread quickly, fanned by the wind until a monumental wall of scarlet rose toward the heavens. Even on the keelboat, Jared felt the heat.

The silhouettes of the frightened buffalo passed before the scarlet wall, stampeding. The earth shook. The sky turned black and so did the surrounding land. Only that towering rampart of flame lit the stygian gloom—

Marveling at the sight, Jared was unprepared for the slash of the rain. With a yelp, he headed below. He was soaked by the time he got there.

The rain lasted a quarter of an hour, then slacked off abruptly. In five more minutes it was over. He returned to the deck, the wind cool against his cheeks.

The clouds cleared. A gold sunset burnished the river and the wet prairie. To starboard, billows of smoke marked the site of the drenched fire. The distant reverberation of the stampeding buffalo blew along the wind.

He felt a presence at his elbow.

"What you lookin' at?" Weatherby asked.

In a hushed voice, Jared answered, "Everything."

"Makes a man feel right clean again, don't it?"

Weatherby had that sad, remote look in his eyes, Jared noticed. It brought something to mind; something that had needed saying for a couple of weeks.

"Elijah—"

"Uh?"

"You know one of the reasons I decided to come with you?"

Weatherby shook his head.

"I talked to some other fur men before we left St. Louis."

"Did you tell 'em where you come from?"

Jared smiled. "I did. I said I'd come on foot and on horseback and by wagon and keelboat all the way from Boston. I had three solid offers to hire on."

"Knew you would."

No longer smiling, Jared went on, "I also asked about the windigo."

The words seemed to crush Weatherby like a blow.

But after a moment, he straightened up and faced his younger companion:

"So you know the story I spun about my Frenchie partner was a lie."

"I found out you had a partner who was French—"

"But he didn't disappear because of no buffla dance. We was in the mountains last winter—"

"You don't have to tell me."

"I want to. It was snowin' to beat hell. We lost the pack horses with all the food. Then my partner, old Marcel, he—"

For a moment it seemed as if Weatherby couldn't continue.

"—well, there was a rock fall, and Marcel, he was broke up pretty bad under it. There was no way he could live, an' no way I could carry him out. It was all I could do to keep myself alive. I had to make the filthiest, meanest choice a man could be asked to make. I'll say this. Old Marcel, he helped me make it. I was ready to die with him but he wouldn't have no part of that. He —finished himself with his own gun. Then I was able to walk out of those mountains seventeen days later. Alive because I had flesh to eat."

iii

Even now, Jared experienced the horror that had gripped him outside Lisa's warehouse.

Presently the trapper said, "There ain't much worse a man can carry on his soul, Jared."

"I'd guess not."

"Sometimes I can't carry it all, so I frolic, like I did at Mrs. Cato's. Now you see why I told you what I did? That any mistakes you made ain't nothin' compared to mine? But I swear—there *is* somethin' of God in this land. I know it, dumb as I am. I can't read nor write, but I know that much. A man's born like a cracked jar, and livin' don't improve the condition. There's never a way to repair the jar so it's perfect. But somehow, it's so clean and blessed beautiful out here, you're—"

"Forgiven."

"Yes. Maybe it's because there ain't many souls in these parts yet to see the crack in the jar. Maybe it's because you're so busy keepin' alive, the crack ain't very important. Even after last winter, I can stand up and start over."

"You showed me how I could do that, Elijah."

Weatherby managed a smile. "Then I'm good for somethin', I reckon."

"Listen, I'm counting on you to show me a lot more. I intend to make some money in this fur business."

"Fair enough. I don't guarantee it, but we'll give 'er a Tennessee try. I do promise you one thing, though. A year or so out here, and there'll be a fire in your soul like you never felt before. A fire to make that burnin' prairie look like sparks in brushwood."

Jared smiled back. "You've a poetic turn of mind, you know that?"

"Wouldn't go quite that far. But a fur man spends a lot o' hours inside his own head. Most times, there's nobody else for company—"

"And what kind of fire is it that's going to burn me up?"

"Why, the one that made me commit a great sin an' leave my woman and my youngsters. You keep hankerin' to see past the next hill, then the next, and one day it gets so bad, you can't stay in the same place more'n a week without goin' crazy."

"I had a curiosity about new things once upon a time. Somewhere along the way, I lost it."

"Well, you wait. The fire'll stoke up hot and you

won't be satisfied till you've set eyes on the mountains —then the ocean—"

"You've seen the Pacific?"

" 'Course I have. I've et and smoked with the Haidas on the very shore of it. I've been a while in the earth lodges of the Pawnee and I've worked trap lines in the country of the horse tribes, too—the Cheyenne, the Blackfeet, the Crow. You'll see wondrous sights out where we're goin', Jared—"

There was silence broken by the whisper of the wind and the lap of the Missouri against the hull.

"Y'know," Weatherby continued, "I really did mean what I said in jail. I think you got the stuff."

"Kind of soon to tell, isn't it?"

"Oh, no. I've had three partners and I reckoned their good points and bad points mighty quick. Old Marcel, he was the best of the lot, God keep him. But I'd be proud to call you my kin."

Moved, Jared couldn't reply immediately. Finally, very softly, he said:

"The feeling's mutual, Elijah."

Weatherby clapped his hands. "By damn, I think we *will* make some money! You may even find an Injun girl you fancy. A lot of 'em are right pleasing."

And start the Kents growing again? It was an unexpected idea, but a warming one.

Rain-washed hills gleamed amber as the last clouds passed. A single shimmering star lit the pale blue far overhead. In his mind, he saw the passage from Ezekiel.

I will seek that which was lost, and bring again that which was driven away, and will bind up that which was broken—

He had it in his power to begin the family anew. He must do it as best he could. Whether a hope of locating Amanda was justified was another matter—

Once again Weatherby exhibited his uncanny faculty

for sensing what was in Jared's mind; perhaps because Jared's eyes were focused on the remotest point on the river.

"I think we'll find her, Jared."

"Sometimes I think so too. Other times, I wonder."

"From all you told me about her, I'd say she's got too much life in her just to lie down an' die. I got a powerful feelin' she's still alive somewhere out yonder."

"I've almost come to believe that myself."

"Even if we don't find her, you got to remember it's the tryin' that counts most. It's the tryin' that makes a man worthy of the name."

Jared nodded slowly. His hand moved to his belt and touched the fob tied there by the raveling ribbon.

But his eye remained fixed on the horizon.

Epilogue

In the Tepee of the Dog Soldier

AMANDA KENT OPENED her eyes.

In the first seconds of wakefulness, she noted details of her surroundings without recognizing their significance. She floated in a pleasant state of lassitude, fascinated by the colorful geometric designs daubed on the skin lining of the tepee. The lining stretched from the ground to perhaps a height of five feet.

Amanda was lying on one of three beds arranged around the tepee wall. Hers was positioned to one side of the oval entrance, which was closed. The entrance faced east, away from the prevailing winds.

On the other side of the entrance were the two beds for the tepee's regular occupants. The head of one abutted the foot of the other. All three beds were similar in most respects: two poles had been staked parallel on the ground, and the space between filled with dried prairie grass, then covered with hides. But only one of the beds had an angled backrest of closely spaced willow sticks. The top of the backrest's frame was connected by a thong to a tripod directly behind it.

Perhaps twenty poles, most of them toward the rear, formed the skeleton of the tepee, which was reasonably large, and filled with a delicious warmth that prolonged Amanda's sense of euphoria. Three very long poles, again in a tripod arrangement, shaped the tepee's basic structure. Additional poles spaced around the perimeter, plus a cluster at the back, stretched and braced the hide covering. Outside thongs staked into the ground helped keep the tepee standing in high winds.

Slightly behind the center of the dirt floor, a small fire burned—buffalo dung, though Amanda did not know that. She was only conscious of a peculiar aroma she had never smelled before. From the various poles hung items that obviously belonged to the tepee's owner:

A large, ornately painted parfleche. A shield of bull buffalo skin decorated with a crude representation of a bird with a great curving beak and immense wings. A willow bow reinforced with sinew. A quiver of arrows. A medicine bag.

A long thong hanging from the smoke hole suspended a bundle of saplings above the fire. The smoke, rising straight upward, cured the saplings that would become iron-headed arrows—

Awareness was returning slowly. Amanda recalled that it was fall, and the evening was chilly. Hence the fire. Overhead, she saw that the smoke wings had been opened about halfway to permit air to circulate. Where the smoke drifted into the darkness, she glimpsed a few faint stars. She heard, then recognized, sounds—

Heavy thumping, as of hide drums beaten.

Stamping; rhythmic clapping; the chant of many voices.

Occasionally a man or woman shouted something in an unfamiliar language. Or a child squalled. Or one of the dozens of dogs she had seen in the encampment barked—

Encampment—

She remembered where she was, and why.

With a low cry, she lunged upward to a sitting position, all at once feeling the thongs that bound her dirty wrists and ankles. As her angle of vision changed, she saw an object previously hidden by the willow backrest.

A huge horned skull, the bone yellowed, the eye sockets black and terrifying—

She almost screamed aloud as it all came back.

The traders had brought her here. On a keelboat much like the one she remembered from another, almost unreal period in her life.

After the boat, the traders used horses. There were four of the white men, led by an immense, reddish-bearded fellow with a veined nose. His name was Maas. She had slept at the foot of his bed on the boat, and whenever he had wanted her beside him, he had dragged her up by the hair.

The scream gathered in her dry throat. She fought it. She was sickened by the filthy feel of her skin. Something crawled beneath her arm on her left side, under the greasy buckskin dress that had replaced her other clothing.

She ached from the days of traveling across the empty grassland, sometimes permitted to ride behind Maas when he was in a good mood, but most of the time walking, connected to his saddle by a halter looped around her neck. Gazing down at her unwashed feet, she saw half a dozen healed cuts.

When the traders had finally reached the encampment earlier in the day, they had met with the Indians in the open. Amanda was relegated to a position some yards from the large group surrounding the whites, and from there watched Maas communicate with the ferocious-looking brown men in a combination of their tongue and hand-signs. There was much display of, and haggling over, the contents of the bales the white men had brought with them.

One moment was unforgettable: when the crowd parted abruptly, and she saw a tall, well-built but cruel-looking Indian gazing at her.

The Indian, in his twenties, made more hand-signs at Maas. The final sign was a finger jabbed in her direction.

Maas grinned, nodded—and she knew without being told that she now belonged to the Indian, who wore a bonnet of eagle feathers.

The bonnet was a kind of cap with thongs hanging down. Some of the feathers projected from the back of the cap. Others were attached to the thongs. Each feather had an ornamental tip of white weasel fur. What struck her was the absence of such bonnets on most of the other young men.

She saw several bonnets on older Indians. Some of those bonnets had trains of feathers that reached all the way to the ground. Instinct told her the Indian who had pointed to her was very powerful and much respected—thus the honor of the bonnet—but because he was younger, his bonnet was not yet as impressive as those worn by his elders.

Tonight there was a celebration in progress outside the tepee. At dusk, Amanda had seen chunks of the carcass of some kind of animal being dragged toward blazing cook fires. She remembered an Indian carrying a hairy hump, its underside gory. Another proudly displayed what appeared to be a tongue.

Then Maas had come to her, and officially informed her that she had been sold to the young man in return for buffalo hides gathered in the hunt two days ago. The young man was the son of one of the tribal elders, Maas said. He had counted coup many more times than any other young man of the tribe. The number of feathers in his bonnet attested to that. At birth, the young man's father had christened him with a name that anticipated this prowess—

Here Maas reeled off guttural syllables, then gave them an approximate English translation: Plenty Coups.

The trader said Plenty Coups was further distinguished by belonging to the dog soldiers, the elite group that controlled and directed the all-important buffalo hunts.

In cynical fashion, Maas wished her well with her new owner.

Amanda was not permitted to take part in the feasting and celebration. She was led away by several young women, one of whom carried a sapling, and struck her in the face several times before supervising the tying of the thongs in the tepee. Amanda was deposited on the hide-covered bed. Miserable and exhausted, she fell asleep—

Now she was awake. *Remembering*—

Very little spare flesh remained on her rapidly maturing body. She had trouble recalling her last solid meal.

But that was of trifling importance. What mattered was the man who had bought her. He would surely come to her before the night was over. No doubt he'd do what she dreaded: strip her dress away, lower his body on top of hers, and heave back and forth until he had satisfied himself.

A sharp memory of the first time it had happened set her to shivering. She remembered faces—one of them fondly. She remembered blue eyes, tawny hair, kind and gentle hands that had helped her when she faltered—

Tears came to her eyes at the thought of her cousin Jared. Where was he now? New Orleans, she hoped.

She gazed at the bracelet of tarred rope, partially hidden by the thongs around her wrists. The bracelet was her last tangible link with the past—and Jared. As she looked at the blackened cordage, she knew she'd never see him again. But she'd keep the bracelet until she died.

She blinked the tears away as her mind conjured the other face. The man who called himself a preacher. The man who had inflicted the horrifying, unexpected hurt on her body ages ago, in Tennessee—

The day Blackthorn carried her off to his cabin, she wanted to die. She wanted to close her eyes and never wake again—especially after he raped her a second time, on the floor of his squalid shanty. She'd screamed; tried to flee from him. But he was too big and quick, even with his trousers fallen around his ankles. She remembered the bite of splinters against her bare buttocks, and the immense, ravaging feel of him jamming up inside her, filling her with a hateful, slimy wetness—

When they left the cabin, she was tied hand and foot. She lay on her belly behind his saddle, praying for death.

For days, jolted and bruised as Blackthorn rode toward St. Louis, that was her only wish: to die. To end the shame and pain that had become her lot. Virtually every evening on the long, nightmarish trek, he had undressed her and thrust into her. She fought him each time, shrieking and scratching and crying out to God to let her die and escape the torture. The harder she resisted Blackthorn, the harder he ravaged her—and he usually beat her afterward as well.

Then one night, in the stuffy little boarding-house room in St. Louis, she was feeling so ill and so hurt that she vowed she'd throw herself out the window if Blackthorn touched her again. But she didn't, because a peculiar insight came to her.

What triggered the insight was another memory: the memory of a man's sly eyes in a Pittsburgh store. And words her cousin had spoken. Words about how men fancied her prettiness. The memory was tangled with the comforting feel of her cousin's hand, and the taste of licorice—

Thus when she saw the preacher's eyes looming over

her, she recognized a gleam in them that reminded her of the eyes of the man in Pittsburgh—

That night, she didn't struggle so much. She let Blackthorn have his way without quarrel. Though he was startled and suspicious, he seemed to enjoy himself a bit more.

From that hour, she didn't even protest when the bogus preacher fondled her growing breasts, or spread her legs with his huge hands and lowered himself between. She pretended submissiveness—total fear of him—which wasn't hard to do. As a result, he beat her less often.

When Blackthorn sold her to Maas, she began to realize the real value of her new insight. She never resisted when Maas wanted her in his bed. And if he wasn't kind to her, neither did he abuse her excessively.

Slowly, a little of her confidence came back. Even if she *was* relatively helpless, trapped among strangers, she had a weapon; a way to mitigate her suffering—

Now another man had bought her. A man totally unlike the preacher or the trader. This one was young, arrogant. His fierce eyes frightened her. And she couldn't even speak his language—

She heard a sound. Rolled her head sideways, alarmed.

The oval door-cover of the tepee, located about a foot above the ground and hinged by a thong at the top, had been lifted aside. She glimpsed figures against the firelight. Then a silhouette blotted the glow—

It was not Plenty Coups who stepped through the three-foot opening. It was the young woman who had struck Amanda with the sapling.

The young woman let the oval door-cover fall back into place. Outside, the hide drums pounded, and rattles kept the rhythm. Men yipped and barked, stamping in some ritual dance to celebrate the successful buffalo hunt. She heard one of the trappers bawl a few lines of a song in English, then discharge a gun—

The young Indian woman gazed at Amanda with unconcealed hatred. Though on the plump side, she wasn't unattractive. Her plaited black hair was clean and glossy. She wore moccasins and leggings beneath a dress of elkskin that reached below her knees. Across her shoulders and bosom, a separate yoke with long fringe gleamed and winked as she approached the younger girl. The yoke was decorated with tiny glass and porcelain beads worked into an intricate pattern. Maas had brought a bale that contained several large packages of such beads—

On the grass and hide bed, Amanda watched the Indian woman bend down beside her. The woman took Amanda's chin between her fingers. Then, with a syllable of contempt, she reached for Amanda's breasts and felt them one by one. It hurt. The woman meant that it should.

Next the woman explored Amanda's legs and genitals, as a white woman might handle a purchase of doubtful worth. Somehow, Amanda understood what the woman was thinking about her:

That she was little more than a child.

That it was humiliating for Plenty Coups to want her —and barter for her.

Amanda knew instinctively that the Indian woman belonged to the young man in the bonnet.

The girl's fear sharpened as the other woman rose and shuffled to the fire. There she reached up, pulled down one of the saplings from the drying bundle. It was relatively thick. She tested it against her palm; it was stiff.

She lowered the end into the fire. Looking over her shoulder, she smiled.

White-lipped, Amanda watched the Indian woman

heat the end of the stick until it shot off wisps of smoke and turned a cherry color. Flame spurted from the stick's end. Hastily, the woman pulled it from the fire. The flame died but the cherry color remained.

The woman walked back to the bed and thrust the stick at Amanda's right eye.

She screamed, twisted her head away, felt the heat of the stick as it plunged into her tangled hair. She smelled her hair burning.

The Indian woman seized her jaw again. Forced her head around. Amanda kept her eyes closed, writhing and struggling. The Indian woman knelt on her stomach. Heat bathed her face as the woman jabbed the stick toward her right eyelid—

Abruptly, the weight was gone. She heard scuffling. A series of heavy oaths, then the crack of a palm against flesh. The Indian woman cried out. Amanda opened her eyes—

She saw Plenty Coups, half-crouched and furious. The woman lay at his feet, the print of his hand still vivid on her cheek.

The young man drew back one of his moccasined feet, kicked the woman in the stomach. She wailed and seized her middle. Then she raised one hand and, to Amanda's astonishment, showed no anger—she wept, and pleaded.

Plenty Coups kicked her again.

And again.

With swift, fluid motions, he signed her toward the oval door-cover. The shamed, sobbing woman crawled to it and dragged herself through. The door-cover fell back in place. Plenty Coups uttered a grunt of satisfaction.

He walked to within a pace of Amanda and stood gazing down, faint amusement leavening the harshness of his mouth. But he was still an imposing figure, and a forbidding one, clad only in his moccasins, his ceremonial bonnet and a peculiar clout decorated with an ornate feather bustle. Amanda had seen similar bustles worn by a few of the hardiest-looking young men in the encampment, and had assumed the bustles were symbols of some position of honor.

Plenty Coups' body was coated with sweat, as if he had been dancing with the other celebrants. He unfastened the knot that held the bustle in place. After a lingering glance at Amanda's body, he circled the fire and hung the bustle on the pole next to the one bearing his decorated shield.

From the opposite side of the tepee, Amanda stared at the bright, hard musculature of the Indian's body; at the shining black strands of his shoulder-length hair revealed when he removed the bonnet and carefully suspended it by a thong on another pole.

Then Plenty Coups unfastened his clout. He turned back toward her. She saw his maleness standing out in a clump of black hair. His prideful smile grew, just as he was growing—

Deep within herself, she felt the old urge to close her eyes and escape this endlessly repeated nightmare. But just as quickly as the desire seized her, she resisted. Life was precious. That was what she had come to realize in the dreadful days after the preacher had stolen her. Life was precious, and she would not give it up easily, no matter what else she might be forced to surrender—

Yet the panic and terror persisted.

To fight it, she summoned another memory as Plenty Coups walked slowly back to the grass bed. Dimly, she perceived a glittering length of metal jutting from his hand. A knife—with which he slashed the thongs binding her wrists and ankles. The point of the knife just missed the cordage bracelet.

But she saw that through a haze overlaid with a picture of a comfortable, shadowed room where a fire burned in a hearth, and a sword hung above a mantelpiece; a sword and a long gun like Maas and the trappers carried. On the mantel proper stood a small green bottle. Just in front of it and slightly to one side, a gaunt man—her father—spoke with great seriousness.

She didn't know what he was saying, except for one sentence—

You are a Kent.

It was said to Jared, who hovered wraith-like at the periphery of the vision. But she knew it applied to her as well. She was not a lump of clay, nor a person without a name or identity—

You are a Kent.

She clung to those words, and to the compelling impression she had of the objects on the mantel. They were important to her father; immensely important. Therefore they were important to her—

She knew their location. Boston. Where papa had died. And mama—

Boston was the city from which she'd fled with her cousin Jared, beginning the long journey that had ended in such totally unexpected fashion here, in the middle of a vast prairie, far from the sheltered and comfortable existence that had once been hers—

You are a Kent.

She must never forget that. When she wanted to die, she must remember—

As she did now.

The blind panic lessened a little.

Plenty Coups knelt beside her, slipping his knife out of sight beneath the hides on the bed. She kept concentrating on the images in her mind. She knew, without quite knowing how or why, that the precious objects glimpsed in her imagination were the tangible symbols of the reality of her earlier life, and must be sought one day, and reclaimed, if it were possible—

How would it be possible? she thought, despairing again. She was a prisoner. Bedraggled; hungry; not even certain of her exact age any longer—

Even as the young Indian reached for her, the image of her father seemed to burn within her mind.

You are a Kent.

She *must* live; *must* struggle against the hopelessness, the—

Plenty Coups seized her arm. He was scowling as he dragged her upright, pressed his other hand to her buckskin dress and began fondling her breast roughly.

She bent over his forearm and bit him.

Astonished, he yelped. She shoved. He toppled over backwards, almost singeing his hair in the fire. He came scrambling up, dark eyes murderous. His right hand shot under the hides, seeking the knife.

Amanda clambered to her knees, watching the sharp blade swing upward, then down toward her shoulder—

She shot up her left hand, caught the powerful wrist—

That in itself would never have stopped him from cutting her. What stopped him was the way her expression changed. Though she still felt terror, she willed herself to smile.

Baffled, he wrenched free of her grip. He shook the knife at her several times, plainly unfamiliar with this sort of behavior from a member of the female sex.

She grasped his left hand, placed it carefully on her breast.

Then, still holding his hand, she moved it back and forth. Gently.

And smiled.

She thought she saw comprehension in his eyes. Comprehension—and outrage that stunned him to inaction.

To capitalize on the momentary advantage she sensed, she let go of him, seized her left arm with her right hand, shook her arm—then scowled and shook her head. The young Indian looked thunderstruck.

Once again she guided his left hand to her breast, letting it rest easily.

There was a moment in which she thought she'd failed; thought that the gap between his world and hers was too wide, and he could not understand what Maas and the preacher had come to understand—and that even if he could, he would refuse to accept her terms.

But slowly, the mouth of Plenty Coups lifted at the corners. His eyes filled with hard, grudging admiration.

He laughed loudly.

So did she.

He was handsome when he laughed, she thought. She was capable of admiring him even though her heart was beating fast and her breathing was strident.

The young Indian's eyes moved to her mouth, then down her throat to her breasts. He laughed again, this time in almost childlike pleasure. He recognized her willingness to fight—something his mate probably never did. It delighted him. She experienced a moment of joy as she realized again that, young as she was, she could protect herself with her wits, and her body—

The Indian's erection, shriveled during the byplay with the knife, quickly reasserted itself. He picked Amanda up in his arms. His face was quite close to hers, his eyes mirthful. But the cruelty she had seen in them before was gone.

He bore her to the bed with the willow backrest, putting her down with great care. Then he touched her buckskin dress.

She nodded, and reached for the hem.

The drumming outside grew louder, the laughter and the chanting more shrill. Naked, she reclined on the hides with her shoulders braced against the backrest. Plenty Coups slipped his arms around her waist and kissed her breasts one by one. Though she was still frightened and a little repelled by what was about to happen, it no longer held the terror it once had. She was able to stroke the side of the young Indian's face.

He crouched above her for a moment, then lowered his hips toward hers. As he pushed himself against her, firmly, yet not so hard as to hurt her, she closed her eyes.

She blanked her mind as he penetrated her, thinking two connected thoughts—

Thoughts which gave her hope for a certainty that, one day, she would escape from the snare in which fate had trapped her:

I will live.
I have found a way.
I will live.

The house of Kent lies pillaged by the Stovalls. To recapture and rebuild it, only two remain: a man of God and a woman of the gutter. Civil war looms to destroy them, their dream and the Union in

The Furies

Volume IV

of

The American Bicentennial Series

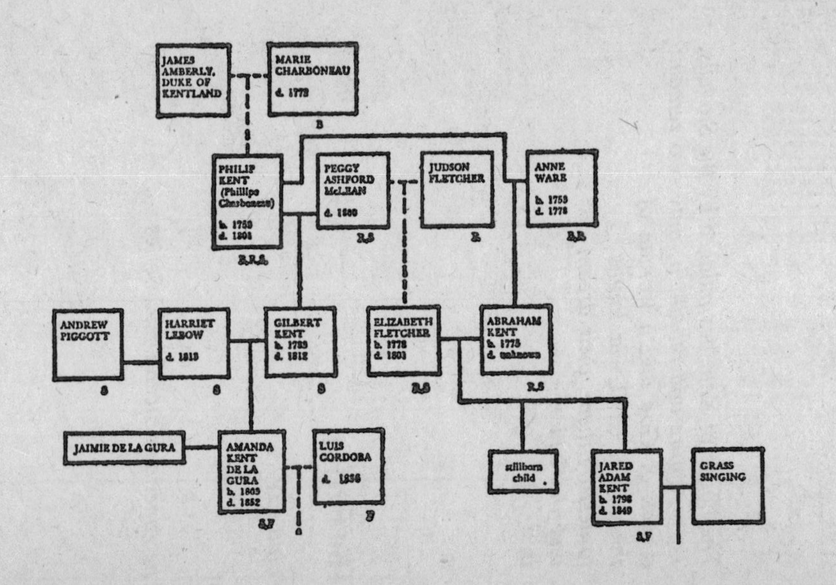
JAMES AMBERLY, DUKE OF KENTLAND
MARIE CHARBONEAU d. 1772
B
PHILIP KENT (Phillipe Charboneau) b. 1759 d. 1801
B,R,S.
PEGGY ASHFORD McLEAN d. 1800
R,S
JUDSON FLETCHER
R
ANNE WARE b. 1753 d. 1778
B,R
ANDREW PIGGOTT
S
HARRIET LEBOW d. 1813
S
GILBERT KENT b. 1789 d. 1812
S
ELIZABETH FLETCHER b. 1778 d. 1803
R,S
ABRAHAM KENT b. 1775 d. unknown
R,S
JAIMIE DE LA GURA
AMANDA KENT DE LA GURA b. 1805 d. 1852
S,F
LUIS CORDOBA d. 1836
F
stillborn child
JARED ADAM KENT b. 1798 d. 1849
S,F
GRASS SINGING

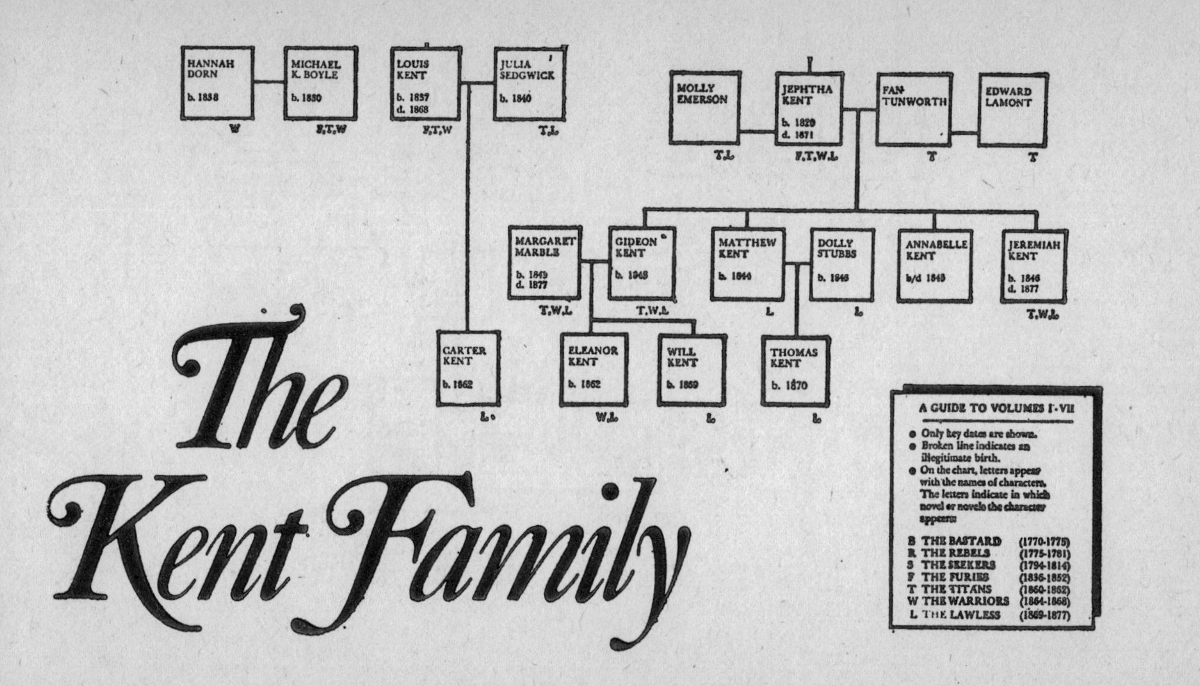

The Kent Family
HANNAH DORN
b. 1838
W
MICHAEL K. BOYLE
b. 1830
F,T,W
LOUIS KENT
b. 1837
d. 1868
F,T,W
JULIA SEDGWICK
b. 1840
T,L
MOLLY EMERSON
T,L
JEPHTHA KENT
b. 1820
d. 1871
F,T,W,L
FAN TUNWORTH
T
EDWARD LAMONT
T
MARGARET MARBLE
b. 1849
d. 1877
T,W,L
GIDEON KENT
b. 1848
T,W,L
MATTHEW KENT
b. 1844
L
DOLLY STUBBS
b. 1846
L
ANNABELLE KENT
b/d 1848
JEREMIAH KENT
b. 1846
d. 1877
T,W,L
CARTER KENT
b. 1862
L
ELEANOR KENT
b. 1862
W,L
WILL KENT
b. 1869
L
THOMAS KENT
b. 1870
L
A GUIDE TO VOLUMES I-VII
Only key dates are shown.
Broken line indicates an illegitimate birth.
On the chart, letters appear with the names of characters. The letters indicate in which novel or novels the character appears:
B THE BASTARD (1770-1775)
R THE REBELS (1775-1781)
S THE SEEKERS (1794-1814)
F THE FURIES (1836-1852)
T THE TITANS (1860-1862)
W THE WARRIORS (1864-1868)
L THE LAWLESS (1869-1877)

Afterword

Old-fashioned kindness and courtesy sometimes seem sadly absent from our world. Yet I discovered those qualities in abundance among a group of people often accused of lacking them.

I speak of the ladies and gentlemen of the broadcast media with whom I came in contact on a promotion tour to launch the American Bicentennial Series. I would like to thank all of them for their interest in the series, and for making the author feel very much at home in front of their respective mikes and cameras:

In Philadelphia, Edie Huggins and Stu Crowner; Abbott Barkley; Bill Jones; Connie Roussin and Bob McLean; Bob Perkins; and Ralph Collier.

In Cleveland, Eric Braun; Alan De Petro and John Slowey; Marcia Corsaro; and Merle Pollis.

In Detroit, Vic Caputo and Beverly Payne; Jan Gorham; Jerry Whitman; and J. P. McCarthy.

In Minneapolis and St. Paul, Jere Smith; Glen Olson; Nancy Nelson and Warren Miller; Jerry Wasley and Marcia Fleur; and Bill Carlson and Dave Higgins.

In Chicago, Bob Hale and Joe Turner; Jorie Lueloff and Phil Walters; Bob and Betty Sanders; Ralph Howard; Chicago Ed Schwartz; Karen Agrest; Mike Edwards; and Jim Conway and Steve Stein.

In Dayton, Ted Ryan and Toula Stamm; Gil Whitney; and my good friend Ken Hardin.

Special thanks go to Priscilla Russo of Pyramid Publications and Randie Levine of Accent on Broadcasting, the two charming ladies whose hard work and careful planning made it possible for me to meet all the good people mentioned above.

JOHN JAKES

About the Author

JOHN JAKES was born in Chicago. He is a graduate of DePauw University, and took his M.A. in literature at Ohio State. He sold his first short story during his second year of college, and his first book twelve months later. Since then he has published more than 200 short stories and over 50 books—chiefly suspense, nonfiction for young people and, most recently, science fiction. With the publication of *The Furies,* volume four of the Kent Family Chronicles, he became the first author in history to land three novels on the best-seller lists within a single year. The author is married, the father of four children, and lists among his organizations the Authors Guild, the Dramatists Guild, and Science Fiction Writers of America. In both 1976 and 1977 he was awarded honorary doctorates for his contribution to the Bicentennial observance. He says the most satisfying aspect of the phenomenal success of the Kent family novels is "the mail which reports that a reader has been motivated to seek out some good nonfiction in order to read about American history in greater detail. That kind of direct response is what writing is all about—and it makes all the hard work worthwhile."